PROVERBS
for the
PEOPLE

PROVERBS

⚜ for the ⚜

PEOPLE

Foreword by Jewell Parker Rhodes

Edited by Tracy Price-Thompson
and TaRessa Stovall

KENSINGTON PUBLISHING CORP.
http://www.kensingtonbooks.com

DAFINA BOOKS are published by

Kensington Publishing Corp.
850 Third Avenue
New York, NY 10022

Copyright © 2003 by Tracy Price-Thompson and TaRessa Stovall, editors

Library of Congress Card Catalogue Number: 2002116611
ISBN 0-7582-0286-5

First Printing: June 2003
10 9 8 7 6 5 4 3 2 1

Printed in the United States of America

*This book is dedicated to
the Ancestors,
both individual and collective
to whom we owe our history and our existence,
and from whom the riches of guidance,
blessings and wisdom always flow.*

CONTENTS

FOREWORD

Proverbs are potent truths embodied in a grain of sand. Fiction is an ocean full of lies ebbing with characterization and conflict. Combine the two and you have an inspired anthology that entertains, inspires, cajoles, and reflects the wisdom of the diaspora.

TaRessa Stovall and Tracy Price-Thompson have created a priceless book that satisfies the heart, mind, and soul.

Each one of us has heard a parent, a grandparent, or elder speak wisdom:

"Devil tempt, but he no force;"
"Walking in two is medicine;"
"Nothing beats a failure but a try;"

But what *Proverbs for the People* teaches us is that oft-told sayings still have resonance and power. Like guideposts, they encourage us to acknowledge how cultural wisdom has sustained and nurtured us down through the generations. Africans and descendants of Africans could always wrap pain in humor, speak universal truths in a handful of words, and shout out sayings that could lift your spirit high. Each proverb becomes a moment of revelation, a meditative moment for readers to consider their heritage and the health of their spirit. At times, I felt transported by memories: my Grandmother used to murmur, *"Every goodbye ain't gone."* As a child I'd roll my eyes but, deep inside, I knew my Grandmother was telling me that life was filled with surprises and that doors closed, often opened.

But the power of *Proverbs for the People* is not just about the power to evoke memories; it is also about the power of talented and creative writers reinterpreting proverbs in new and unexpected ways.

Donna Hill's "Rendezvous with Destiny" weaves a tale of a grand-daughter fulfilling an ancient prophecy to relive the life of a slave ancestor who was forced to abandon her husband during an escape to freedom. Through mystical dreaming, the granddaughter rescues the husband and in doing so, rescues the spirits of her Father, Mother, and Grandfather. *"Every goodbye ain't gone"* becomes a literal truth. The granddaughter heals the past and in doing so, heals the loss and heartache of the women in her family and reclaims, for all time, a healthy and united black family that transcends slavery's horrors.

Proverbs for the People has tremendous range in terms of sayings, fictional styles, and thematic approaches. Robert Fleming's story, "A Crisis of Faith," will make your heart ache for the young man imprisoned unjustly for fifteen years because of the words of an "unstable . . . white woman." Fleming's tale will make you *feel* the proverb *"We do not struggle in despair but in hope, not from doubt but from faith, not from hate but out of love for ourselves and our humanity"* in an inspired and humane way. Price-Thompson's "Miss Mary Mack" is a joyous, first person narrative that celebrates the glories of black womanhood and reminds us all that *"The compassion of a people is cultivated at a grandmother's knee."* Stovall's "The Fire This Time," limns the complexities of inter- and intra-racial prejudice and with unflinching honesty explores the African-Ashanti proverb *"The world is a mirror: show yourself in it and it will reflect your image."* Maxine Thompson's "Valley of the Shadow" reconfigures the sassy and sensual proverb "The blacker the berry, the sweeter the juice," into a testimonial of self-love and acceptance.

Many of the stories in *Proverbs for the People* stopped me cold, left me breathless, uplifted, and unsettled me. This anthology demands your full attention. My suggestion is to savor each proverb, each story, and to think about the wonderful interconnections between the two. The ocean shapes the shoreline. Or is it the other way around? The sandy shore shapes the sea?

In this big, open-hearted anthology, proverbs and stories link inextricably, gloriously embodying the spirit of our people and heralding the talents of a rainbow crew of black writers. Nancy Padron, Zaron W. Burnett, Jr., Denise Turney, Trevy McDonald, and many, many others are shouting and whispering their tales, signifying and celebrating, chastising and encouraging all of us to be better people.

Proverbs preach wisdom, but fictional lies explore emotional truths. Stovall and Price-Thompson have proven that it isn't enough to know the proverbs; rather, we need to experience them through fiction. *We need to relive the magic of our ancestors.*

Stovall and Price-Thompson have done us all proud. Each contributor should feel delighted to be part of this *"do good, say good, feel good"* book. *Proverbs for the People* is making history, awakening our hearts and imagination.

Enjoy!

Gaining wisdom has never been more fun, more entertaining, or more heartfelt.

Jewell Parker Rhodes

ACKNOWLEDGMENTS

A few years ago when TaRessa and I decided to form TnT Explosions, our collaborative literary partnership, who knew what boundless energy our creativity and exponential brainpower would generate. Inspired by the recent boom in African-American fiction, mainstream as well as self-published, we perused the shelves for collaborative works and determined that not since Terry McMillan's *Breaking Ice* had there been a major collection of short fiction that showcased the best and the brightest of today's established as well as emerging African-American contemporary authors.

We decided that the new millennium would be ripe for such a project, and that a themed anthology containing original stories would be exciting and unique. Well, you know what can happen when two creative, motivated, high-energy sisters get together and decree that something should be. *Voilà!* It becomes! Since the time of *Proverbs'* conception, there have been other collaborative collections published, but most contain a mixture of commercial and literary works of new and previously published fiction, and none have been themed anthologies that endeavored to showcase a wide range of self-published and previously unpublished talent.

Assembling our cast of authors for *Proverbs* was an amazing endeavor. We give thanks to those who answered our call and agreed to participate, not out of any financial motivation, but because they believed in the need for this collection. From Omar Tyree ("The Urban Griot") who was the consummate timely professional, and who agreed to our requests without the slightest hesitation, to my fourteen-year-old son, Kharel, who had to be prodded (okay, whupped) in order to get his submission in on time, working with our cast of authors was truly a rewarding and valuable experience. We received at least three times more submissions than we could possibly publish in one volume, and sorting and editing the stories was a "some days" type of thing: Some days it required patience, some days it took chocolate, some days we were on our hands and knees begging for ice-cream, but on most days it was a joy and an indulgence to read works from a potpourri of multi-talented authors, all of whom had selected either an African, African-American, or Biblical proverb, and used their unique storytelling skills to bring their proverb to life.

TaRessa and I are extremely pleased with the final result of our efforts and proud of the craft and energy that our authors poured into their works. While we are grateful for the contributions of many, I'd like to take this opportunity to personally thank God, my Creator and Master of the Day of Judgment, for blessing me in abundance and helping me to journey along paths of peace and balance.

To my husband, Greg, for being a solid presence in my life and for taking his colored girl out for ice-cream when the manuscripts were enuf. To our children, Kharim, Erica, Greg Jr., Kharel, Kharyse, and Khaliyah. My sister, Michelle Carr, for *everything!* My nieces, nephews, and godchildren, Toi, Damon, Eddie, Mel, CJ, Traci, LB, Jerel, Courtney Rae, Courtney Mae, Janise, Ciarra, Angelle, and Darius. My business partner, TaRessa Stovall, for her humor, wisdom, and legendary editing skills! Rip out those seams, snatch out that interfacing! Make a new dress, honey! Our agent, Djana Pearson Morris, for her constant support and advocacy. Our editor, Karen Thomas, for believing in this project and making the publishing process virtually painless. The *Proverbs'* contributors and their families, the booksellers, librarians, and general readership at large. Thank you for providing a forum for us to showcase our literary flair. TaRessa and I would love to hear your thoughts regarding the collection. We can be reached at: *tntexplosions@ aol.com.*

Peace and balance,
Tracy Price-Thompson

First, foremost, and always, I would like to thank Father/Mother God, Oludamare, for life, love, creativity, opportunity, and an abundant stream of what Patti LaBelle calls blessons. Thanks be to Ancestors, individual and collective, for giving us pathways to follow and shoulders to stand upon. And thanks to each and all of my amazing guardian Angels who truly have a sistah's back 24/7/365.

To my amazing creative partner in TnT Explosions, Tracy Price-Thompson, for her awesome talent and revved-up drive. Working with you is truly an invigorating joy. To literary agent Djana Pearson Morris for the enthusiastic support and saleswomanship that were the first critical steps in turning a concept into reality, *muchas gracias*.

To our marvelous editor, Karen Thomas, who believed in this baby and brought so much sweetness and skill to the birthing process, we not only couldn't have done it without you, but it wouldn't have been nearly as much fun! And to all of the "behind-the-scenes" folk at Kensington Publishing, thanks for your diligence, hard work, and creative prowess.

To Jewell Parker Rhodes for taking time from promoting her own fresh-off-the-press book to grace ours with a foreword that sets the tone and ties it all together, many, many thanks for this and all that you do through your writing, your teaching, and your stellar example of literary excellence.

To each and all of the authors who entrusted us with the fruits of their intellect, talent, and creative gifts, we are deeply honored and humbly grateful. Please know that without your unique "square" this literary "quilt" would not be complete. Thank you so much for answering our call and telling our stories with such style!

To the elders from whom all wisdom flows, we thank you especially for the words you've woven into proverbs to teach, inspire, and guide us through these stories and through life. We hope we've done you proud.

To Rosalyn Stone who has always nurtured my writing and taken this career seriously since I began at age seven, thanks, Mom! I love you.

To my children, Calvin II and Mariah, you are the rhyme and the reason. Thank you for choosing me to be your mother and for ensuring that I will keep learning and growing forever.

To my incomparable friends Susan Newman, Tamara Nash, Michele N-K Collison, Sherry Bennett, Niki Mitchell, Doreen Mitchum, Leasa Farrar-Fortune, Valrine Daley-Meleschi, Jo Moore Stewart, Sheila Brooks, Charlotte Roy, Victoria Pendragon, and Sherekaa Osorio; to my "co-mothers" Marya Hewins, Leslie Smith, and Joretta Cryer; and to my Spelman daughters Lori Sasai Robinson, Tracey Lewis, and Tayari Jones: I am so thankful for the many ways in which you uplift my spirit and enrich my life. And a special bow to Clark Gayton who in-spires me with his unwavering commitment to artistic purity and truth.

Finally, to our readers: We are delighted and grateful that you have chosen to spend some time with this rich collection of talent. Please re-member that *you* are the reason we write in the first place, and we strive always for the privilege of touching your heart, your mind, and your soul.

Ashe

TaRessa Stovall

Women Here Drive Buses

Amanda Ngozi Adichie

"If a youth washes his hands well, he will be invited to the feast of the elders." —African, Igbo

Every morning Ken kicks the rusty metal heater in his studio apartment. Sometimes he kicks and kicks until blood trickles from under his toenail, muttering to himself about how the people next door never stop cooking nauseating-smelling food, how the weather back home in Nigeria was never this bad, how his boss at work never seems to clean his shirt, because of the permanent brown line on his collar.

When he is done kicking, he takes a bath, cleans his teeth, and gets dressed. He doesn't eat breakfast anymore, since realizing that an early lunch saves breakfast money. Before he leaves to catch the bus on Forty-fourth and Lancaster, he glares at the heater one last time. Sometimes he says things to it under his breath, things he would not say in the presence of a child.

The heater is central, the landlord told him when he moved in some months ago. And now, after the first snow, he realizes that *central* means he cannot control it from his room. Sometimes he wakes up shivering with cold, bumps as hard as uncooked rice all over his body. Other times, he wakes up sweating because the heater is turned up too high. Or he wakes up startled by the sounds the heater makes as it heats up, clanging sounds like the groans of a sick person.

"What the hell do you want me to do?" the landlord asked when Ken complained about it. *I don't care*, Ken had wanted to say, *just do something*. But he didn't. He was scared he wouldn't stop once he started talking; he would have to yell in the landlord's face and hope his spit would land upon the man's hooked nose. He would have to tell him how the cracks in his kitchen cabinets were choked with tiny cockroaches, how the spaces between the strips of wood on the floor were wide enough for his foot to slip into. How none of this was like the America he'd imagined. But then the landlord would tell him he could leave, and he would never find an apartment for $250 a month anywhere else in Philadelphia.

Ken knows he will have to stay in the apartment for a while. At least until he can get enough money together to enroll in the computer course. Or until his mother gets better.

He sends almost everything he makes back home.

His mother's letters come every other week in her big, sloping handwriting, telling him how happy she is, how the medicine she bought with the money he sent makes her feel better, how his brothers and sisters are doing so well in the new school that he paid for. *You should see the big English words they can pronounce now*, his mother writes. *You should see the big math problems they can solve.*

He reads the letters often—smells them, too, because they smell like the kerosene fumes from his mother's stove, and if laughter has a smell, they smell like his mother's laughter. Sometimes he places them one atop the other, forming a paper pillow, and lays his head down on them to sleep.

The bus is never late, but it is today, and Ken stands at the bus stop, listening to the woman behind him talking to her child as she looks up Lancaster Avenue for the bus.

"I won't broke it, Mummy," the child says in a tiny voice, shrill like a bell.

"It's *break*, baby. Say *break*."

"Break," the child repeats.

Ken closes his eyes because the tears are in them again. Little things make him tear up now—little things like a child talking to a mother, like two people holding hands walking along the street. He feels helpless and unmanly when this happens, but he can't help it.

He started to feel this way after his first week in America, when he walked past a young girl on the street and stared in surprise when she did not greet him. He realized then that strangers greeting him on the streets would now be the exception, not the norm. When he was job hunting, he'd get the city paper and sit on one of the white plastic chairs in front of the UPenn quad to watch the people walk by.

They walked so fast. Once, he stopped a young girl wearing a Kente-print vest and asked, "How are you?" and she glared at him and said, "He's such a weirdo" to her friend.

There are some things Ken never mentions in his letters home. He keeps his letters brief, mentioning his job at the Water Department, how important it is, monitoring chlorine levels of water at the treatment plant. He doesn't tell his mother how his boss sneers and asks him questions like, "You Africans drink water straight from muddy rivers, don't you?" And he doesn't tell her that, even when he was in the Market Street mall, surrounded by people, some so close that his shoulder brushed theirs, he felt alone.

"Sir? The bus is here."

Ken opens his eyes, turns, and asks the woman and her child to go in before him. The woman says thank you; her daughter is looking at him curiously; her cornrows run down the length of her head and have bright blue beads strung through them. It reminds him of his mother plaiting his little sister's hair, his little sister sitting on the floor with her head cradled between his mother's legs.

Ken swipes his card, says "Good morning" to the bus driver, who mutters something in return. Ken stares at the elderly driver, whose blue SEPTA hat hardly hides the white sprinkled throughout his hair, and realizes that it could have been anything that the bus driver had just said. It could have been "Shut up," or "Go to hell," just as it could have been "Good morning." Ken shrugs. He can't blame the man for not bothering to open his mouth to talk. People have problems.

The next morning, the bus is late again. And Ken is glad that the woman with the daughter is not here today. He sees the bus turn onto Lancaster and start to make its way down, hears the screech of its brakes as it stops before him. The door swings open, and Ken bounds up the stairs and is just about to swipe his card, when he realizes it's not the old man at the wheel.

Ken stares at the woman at the wheel, his mouth hanging slightly open. The small SEPTA hat she is wearing barely covers the long braids that are held together in a ponytail at the back. Her skin is the even shade of the back of a fresh African yam. Ken has never seen a woman driving a bus.

"Good morning! You forgot something?" the woman asks, startling Ken.

"No, no, sorry," Ken mutters and swipes his card.

"I'll be doing Mr. Easter's route for a couple of weeks. He's out sick," the woman says and smiles, her chalk-colored teeth brightening her face.

"Oh," Ken says.

"You need a transfer?"

"No. I don't need one."

"You have an accent. You from Africa or Jamaica?"

"Africa. Nigeria."

"I have a Nigerian friend. Yemi."

"Oh," he says again. She is looking right at him, into his eyes. He has never seen such sincerity as this since getting off the plane at JFK more than a year ago.

The seat just behind the driver's is empty and he sits there, although he often sits at the back. And as she maneuvers the bus throughout the city of Philadelphia, he watches her braided hair bounce on her neck.

The bus is on time the next morning. As Ken watches it crawl down Lancaster, he practices what he will say to the driver. Something smart and warm, like her. Not the dumb "oh" he'd muttered yesterday. The bus stops, the door swings open, and Ken forgets all the smart things he has thought up. She is wearing a puffy coat, the high collar swallowing her neck.

"Good morning to you," she says, smiling. "Sorry the heater is broken this morning."

"Oh," Ken says and then adds hastily, "my heater was not working this morning, too." There, something not so dumb-sounding, at last.

She laughs. "What's your name?"

"Ken."

"Ken? That an African name?"

"Yes. It's short for Kenechi." He wants to ask her what her name is, too, because she does not wear a name tag, but there is somebody shuffling into the bus behind him, and her eyes are on that person.

After work a few days later, Ken stops at the Perfume Palace on Market Street and buys himself a bottle of cologne on sale. It is a little more expensive than the other one on sale, but he buys it because the salesperson tells him, "this has a real sexy smell."

He dabs it behind his ears the next morning and as he gets on the bus, he wonders if she can smell it. She doesn't say anything about the cologne, but she seems to smile more widely as she says, "Good morning to you, Mr. Ken!"

She remembers the names of all the regulars on the bus. "Good morning to you, Miss Wilson," she'll say. Or, "Little Dennis, how you doing this cold morning?"

Sometimes he finds himself wishing that she would remember only his name, but then he chides himself and thinks of the smiles on the faces of the kids she talks to.

Every morning, Ken plans to ask what her name is, but whenever he gets on the bus and sees that wide smile, those open brown eyes, those braids, he loses it. And he ends up saying something to her about the weather, or his heater, or his landlord. The only personal thing he knows about her is that she has a Nigerian friend called Yemi. He wants to ask if she has a boyfriend, a husband, children. Where she lives. What she likes to eat.

One day, after about a month, he hears one of the regular women, the portly Miss White, who often offers potato chips to everyone on the bus, ask her, "How much longer you got with us? I hear Mister Easter is coming back soon."

Ken is sure she responds, but he doesn't hear. His ears are filled with a fierce burning liquid. He has the sensation of missing something that is still there; he imagines he is a sock that misses the feel of a foot even as the foot is still in it.

He will ask her name the next day, he resolves. He will tell her something smart, something that will make her laugh in a more personal, more intimate way. Not that one-size-fits-all laugh.

The next morning, there is a snowstorm, and the mayor announces on the radio that all city offices are closed except for essential services. Ken looks out of the window, wishing, unreasonably, that he worked in the water emergency section. The apartment building next to his is so close he imagines he can reach out and touch the old scarred brick walls if he tried. He watches the falling snow, white flakes as thick as the outer part of a boiled egg.

The heater makes a loud sound as it heats up, and he realizes he has not kicked it in a while.

The snowstorm lasts two days. The second day, a Friday, Ken calls SEPTA to ask if buses are running, but he keeps getting the recorded voice saying, "All of our customer service representatives are currently busy; please hold," until he loses his patience and hangs up.

The whole weekend he lies in bed and tries to write a letter to his mother, but he keeps tearing it up and starting over. Finally, he gives up and throws the papers into the garbage can.

On Monday, he plows his way through mounds of snow that still sit on the sidewalk as he walks to Lancaster Avenue. He can look down and see the thump-thump movements on his chest—his pounding heart. Perhaps she is gone; perhaps old Mister Easter is back. Perhaps she might have wanted to say good-bye but couldn't because of the two days of the snowstorm. Ken sees the bus turn onto Lancaster, and he wants to push at the man in front of him so he can see better. He strains his eyes. The head in the driver's side looks like a man's, but then, he can't be sure. He closes his eyes; it is freezing; his nose is numb, but he feels sweat on his forehead. He opens his eyes after counting to five, and the bus is slowing to a stop. He stares at the driver's seat and smiles.

Her hair is different. The braids no longer graze the back of her neck; instead they are shorter, with golden highlights, and they curve and stop barely under her ears. They cover too much of her skin, too much of her radiant face.

"Good morning to you, Mister Ken!" She says.

"Your hair is different today," he says.

"Got it done Saturday. An African place, too, on South Street. The ladies are from Senegal."

"It doesn't suit you," Ken blurts out. "The old braids were better."

There is silence, but Ken hears a loud buzzing in his ears. She is staring at him, her eyes narrowed, and he wonders if he has gone too far, if she will tell him off and then stop acknowledging him every morning. He does not know what he will do, how he will live with that.

Her eyes are still on him, still narrowed, and then suddenly she bursts out laughing, and Ken feels so relieved he wants to pee.

"Is that so, Mr. Ken? Well, thanks for telling me. I will keep that in mind."

She is still laughing as she starts the bus.

That evening, after work, he sits on his bed and starts to write his mother.

Dear Mama,

I hope you and Chika and Chinedu and Amaka are well. What about Uncle Emeka and Aunty Ifesi? You did not mention them in your last letter. Greet them.

He stops writing and stares at the heater. Perhaps it might not look so bad if he polishes it with wax. He picks up his pen and resumes writing.

America is very different from what we think at home. Everybody does not have a car, there are cockroaches in houses here, too. But there are some very wonderful things about America. For example, women here drive buses.

He reads what he has written and smiles. He has never written a letter like this to his mother.

The next morning, he stands waiting for the bus, his chest puffed out. When the door swings open, even before he swipes his card, he asks, "What's your name?"

"My name?" she asks with that smile he has started to imagine on his boss's annoying face when he is having a bad day at work. "It's Carol."

"Have you ever had African food, Miss Carol?"

She laughs. "My mom is back in Alabama. There was something she used to say all the time: 'I thought you'd never ask.'"

Ken feels warm, and he doesn't know if the heater is working or not.

Life Is Short

Vicki L. Andrews

"There is no life without life." —African, Mali

Life is short, so they say. I cannot tell you how many times I've heard that phrase over and over in my lifetime, never quite grasping the full impact of its meaning until now. I understand it now. Yessiree. I understand it way too well now.

I sink deeply into my bathtub with the whirlpool twirling and massive amounts of lavender-scented bubbles, contemplating that saying again and again inside my head. I am drowning in emotions right now. Too much, too soon, and . . . life is indeed short.

I sip the champagne that has been chilling in my refrigerator for damn near six months. It was one of my Christmas presents that I actually requested from one of my girlfriends. I had every intention of popping the cork on New Year's Eve, but that holiday came and went without a bang, not even a whimper from me. I had been sitting alone on my sofa, fully clothed, waiting for the new year to arrive. I obviously wasn't really in the mood to celebrate, 'cause I was fast asleep long before midnight. And the champagne—well, the champagne stayed in the refrigerator, waiting for me to find something to celebrate.

I'm not really celebrating anything now, but it somehow seems appropriate. I'm even using one of my Waterford crystal flutes. Jeez, those had been in my cupboard collecting dust since I bought them. I remember how I had just wanted to splurge on something I'd always wanted. Crystal—real crystal—with an expensive label reflecting real class. I brought the flutes home, admired them for all of five minutes, then returned them to their expensive-looking box and put them in the cabinet, the one that's up real high above the refrigerator, the cabinet that no one uses, 'cause it's just too damn hard to get to. Yeah, I put them in there and promptly forgot them. Until today. Upon receipt of my news.

The sigh that escapes me is long and shaky; so powerful is the air that I expel that the bubbles surrounding me sort of divide like the Red Sea probably parted when Moses held his staff above it. My breasts peek out and one lone tear slips down my cheek. *How could you betray me?* I ask.

Breast cancer, they had said, words that at first were as incomprehensible as Chinese. Me? Breast cancer? But it can't be . . . I have a sore throat and my voice is hoarse and I'm just tired, that's all. What do you mean I've got breast cancer? A mass. What the hell is a mass? It was all crazy, surreal, like watching myself in a movie, the star receiving the devastating news.

This simply could not be happening to *me.*

I tried to reason with the doctor, tell him he'd made a mistake—a big, colossal, huge mistake and I'd have his ass for scaring me this damn bad for nothing.

But there was no mistake, he assured me sadly. The tests were mine and they were positive. I saw his mouth moving but I didn't hear him. My ability to decipher, to hear, to understand simply fled me after he uttered those two devastating words. Amazing. How quickly a fog settled over me and all I heard inside my head was, *Life is short, life is short, life is short, lifeisshort, lifeisshort, LIFE IS SHORT!!!*

I've overcome a lot of things in my lifetime, but this one—well, this one might just take me out. It was a demon I could not easily destroy. But I would try. I would do what they said I should to preserve my life. After all, I still had a child to see to womanhood, and Paris, London, Rome, and Venice to visit. Oh, and add Africa to that list. Always wanted to step foot on the Motherland. I've got a lot of things I want to do, and now . . . well, I've just got to speed up the process. No more lagging for me on my dreams. The time to act was now before . . . well, it's just time to do something truly wonderful for myself.

I close my eyes and visions of Eric dance behind my lids. Eric, my husband for about thirty years, until I got some sense in my head and got rid of his scary behind. Why I ever married him and *stayed* married to him is still beyond my ability to understand. When I think about all the time I've wasted . . .

He never was a good husband, but in the beginning he was fun and funny and a decent provider. Problem was, he never knew how to love. What he thought was love was anything but. And Lord have mercy, don't let that man start to drinking. He'd become a complete jerk then. First he'd start philosophizing, thinking his blabber made sense when it didn't. Then when he was good and drunk, he'd get physical, hitting and kicking me, throwing things and cussing me out like I was some damn body on the street rather than his wife, someone he shared a bed, a life, and a family with.

I took Eric's punches and his abuse for way too long. Worse, I allowed my daughter, Marissa, to see him abuse me. He was good to her, always good to his baby girl, but the way he treated me was another matter.

Sometimes he just looked at me and got real pissed off, as if the very sight of me was so revolting it sent him into a blind rage. He'd call me vile names and accuse me of truly foul acts. I tried to ignore him, rush to get out of his way, but he'd follow me, shrieking and cursing that I had no right to ignore him.

The scented bubbly water chills as I continue to remember.

I was a good wife—a very good wife, in fact—but that was rarely appreciated or acknowledged, 'cause as soon as his friends Jack Daniels, MGD, or Johnnie Walker Red came calling, I was in big trouble. Not always, but most of the time.

I flinch remembering the time he went ballistic 'cause I needed the car and he didn't want me to have it. It was the only time in our marriage that we had only one vehicle. I needed it to take care of some business. Besides, he wasn't going anywhere, just laying on the couch with his hand stuck down his pants massaging his balls and watching football. When I told him I had to run a quick errand and asked him to watch Marissa, I had no idea he'd been drinking until he turned his red, glassy eyes on me and roared, "You're not going any damn where. Not in *my* car, you ain't."

Then I saw the empty bottle with its remaining contents dripping a dark-brown pool on the cream carpet. I was not in the mood for his nonsense, so I turned and walked out the door. My heart was pounding in my chest, and in my head I chanted over and over, *Just let me get to the car; just let me get to the car.*

Well, I got to the car, and stupidly thought I was home free. Then my peripheral vision picked up movement. There he was, lips moving and spittle flying onto the window. I watched with a sick sort of fascination as he ordered me to get out of the car.

Instead, I tried to start it. He took a step back, then kicked the car window with such force that the glass exploded onto the side of my face. He returned his foot to the ground and grabbed my hair, pulling me out of the car. Then he jumped into the driver's seat and screeched off, my keys and purse still in the car.

I lay on the hot asphalt, stunned, as the blue Honda disappeared. There's no telling how long I would have been there had it not been for the sweet voice of my baby girl calling "Mommy, Mommy!" But the tone of her voice wasn't sweet that time; it was tinged with terror and tears.

I knew that day that the marriage should end, but I couldn't find the strength to leave. Not yet.

They say payback is a bitch, and indeed it is. One of our neighbors heard the commotion and called the police. Just as I was finally coming to myself, the black-and-white cruiser pulled up and two police officers helped me to my feet. *"My baby,"* was all I could say as they helped me to the house. I cradled Marissa in my lap as we both cried. Between the tears, I gave the officers a description of the car, my husband's name, and assured them that I was more stunned than hurt.

It didn't take long for them to catch Eric and slap his silly ass in jail for the weekend for assault and driving under the influence. And they impounded his car. But he came home and the shit just kept happening.

We'd had a wonderful vacation in the Colorado mountains. Marissa had the best time making little snow angels and tiny snowballs. Eric was fine until he started drinking hot toddies. By the time we left, he was roaring drunk and refused to let me drive the rental car. I was too frightened to argue.

I'm having trouble breathing now, remembering that terrifying ride down the zigzagging, slippery mountains. "Slow down, honey," I pleaded. "You're going too fast for the road conditions."

"Just shut up and let me drive!" he shouted. "I know what I'm doing."

I glanced fearfully at five-year-old Marissa, strapped into her safety seat in the back.

"Why you keep looking at her?" he screamed. "She's fine. Just sit back and shut the hell up."

"I won't stop looking at my child, Eric. You're scaring me. Please slow down, honey. Please!"

He turned completely around to face me, took his hands from the wheel and his eyes off the road. As he screamed at me to "Shut up!" the car slid off the road and down an embankment, headed straight for a tree. I grabbed the wheel and we avoided a collision by inches.

The car smashed into the tree on the driver's side. I jumped out of the car, slipping and sliding down the steep embankment. As I got my footing, Eric rushed at me, arms flailing. All I could think of was Marissa—she had to be saved!

I had just grabbed the door handle when he smacked my face so hard that my glasses flew off. Blinded, I tasted the metallic iron of blood trickling into my mouth.

That was it! I punched and kicked and yelled at the top of my lungs. I was enraged enough to kill the motherfucker. I grabbed the lapels of his ski jacket and flung his ass down the hill. He was so drunk he half stumbled and half fell. I didn't even bother to see where he had landed. I dragged a screaming Marissa from the car and struggled to the top of the hill.

Hundreds of cars sped by, not even slowing to assist a black woman holding a small child. Finally a tow truck appeared to return all of us to the hotel.

I stayed in that marriage for many reasons, most of them stupid. I worried about being considered a failure, and about raising a child alone, worried what people would say—especially my mother and father, who had been married forever. Mainly, though, I stayed because I loved Eric and I feared that if I left him, I might follow through on my feelings—the secret desires I had for women.

So many fears, but not one that would equate to what I was going through now. Never had I thought that my own body would be the one thing I feared the most.

I drain the chilled water and run a new bath, refill my champagne flute, and try to stop thinking about my dead marriage. I never should have married, anyway. It was all wrong from the start. I knew deep within myself that I was different, that my desires were forbidden in my world. Desires that no one in my family would accept or understand. So I suppressed them, hoping they'd dry up from neglect and just go away.

They had started in junior high school. I wasn't very athletic, but as part of the curriculum everybody had to take P.E. And I hated it, especially when I realized that we had to undress and put on gym clothes every day. I didn't want anyone to see my puny body with no curves. And forget about breasts. Shit, back then I had zero titties. I'd try to wait until everyone had left before I changed clothes. I acted like I was slow, touched, retarded—I didn't care as long as I could go unnoticed. I'd sit on that hard wooden bench and watch the other girls, not openly but with stolen glances when they weren't looking. I was fascinated by the beauty of the female form, loved the various shades of brown in my all-black school. Appreciated the different body types—some were short with thick, stocky legs and fat thighs, while others were slender with flat bellies and long, lanky legs. But what fascinated me the most was the triangle between their legs. Some were hairy, others just beginning to show signs of puberty. And breasts—I loved looking at their breasts. It made me tingle inside to watch them hurriedly change from street clothes to gym clothes. And when they showered, I was in heaven.

Still, I knew I was a terrible pervert, and tried hard to squelch my feelings and make the visions I saw whenever I was alone in my bedroom go away. But more often than not I would find myself thinking about Leslie, Mary, or Julie, wishing I could touch them, just to see if they felt as soft as they looked. Of course I never did, 'cause I knew it would mean a behind-kicking for sure. But the longings never went away.

But now I know I am not a pervert. I am a fifty-one-year-old lesbian.

I wasted thirty years of my life married to a complete asshole who didn't deserve or appreciate me. And now, only two years after I finally broke away from him, I'm told that my life is probably going to be cut short 'cause I've got cancer prancing through my genes.

So here I am, disgusted and scared and angry and mad as hell, sitting in my lemon-colored bathroom, sipping champagne that tickles my nose, and contemplating my next move.

I can't tell Marissa about the diagnosis. She's home for the summer break, and soon she'll return to Atlanta for her senior year at Spelman. I hope I can keep it together—keep my cancer a secret—until she is gone. It will be hard though, because in so many ways my daughter is my best friend. With all the drama her father put us through, we formed a strong bond, an unbreakable bond, and I don't want anything—not even cancer—to harm or tarnish our relationship. She means the world to me.

Reluctantly, I leave the tub, drying myself with the biggest, thickest terry cloth bath sheet I can find. Wrapping my body in the damp bath sheet, I am careful not to look at myself. The mirror must be avoided. I don't want to see my breasts. They have betrayed me.

My bedroom walls are dominated by the massive posters of my various book covers. I've written six novels and was working simultaneously on two more when this whole thing came up, taking all my strength and concentration. I sit wearily on the bed, relaxed enough from the warm bath and champagne to feel sleepy. Rest, the doctor had said; I need plenty of rest. And . . . chemotherapy. A tear slides down my cheek, and I wonder why only one of my eyes is crying, when my entire soul is in agony.

Lying back on the bed, I look at my beautifully framed book cover posters and remember how blessed I am—at least financially, although it took forever to actually make a living from my writing. When my first book sold, I was amazed at how thrilled people were to meet an actual writer. I'm just me, I'd think, but they wanted to make me a celebrity. I'd play the part as best I could, wishing they knew how long it took to sell enough books to earn back the advance that had long since been spent. It was years before I made enough money to quit my day job and concentrate on the stories that my readers seemed to hunger for.

I sit up, grab my journal, and scribble down all of the fear and anger I'm feeling—all of it. I script the jumbled maze of my thoughts and emotions, freed by the knowledge that these words didn't have to be magic, because nobody would ever read them except me.

The horror of my situation hits me, and my face is bathed in tears. Loud sobs are wrenched from my body as I fight not to sink under waves of regret. So much wasted time spent in a life of virtual hell, and now that I have finally decided to give myself permission to be exactly who I am—without shame—cancer has to come along and screw everything up. Damn!

But life isn't fair, I remind myself. My eyes are closed and I am lamenting my life when I hear a slight shuffling noise and the distinctive squeak of the door. Marissa.

"Hey Mom, what's the matter with you? You've been acting strange all day."

"Oh baby," I sniffle, using my hand for a tissue. "I'm okay. Just . . . tired I guess."

"That's not it," she argues. "I've seen you absolutely exhausted before but never in *tears*. Tell me, please."

I bow my head, and more tears blot the pages of journal. Snot drips but I don't care.

"I'm . . . I'm sick, baby. Real sick."

"What do you mean?" she says, her voice unnaturally high-pitched and shaky. "What's wrong with you? Is it serious? Are you going to be okay?"

For the longest time I can't bring myself to say the words aloud. Up to this point I haven't. Not even in the doctor's office did I utter those horrible words. But now . . . I take several deep breaths like I did when she was being born, cleansing breaths from Lamaze training. My shoulders move up and down as I try to compose myself. "It's cancer, baby. Breast cancer."

She is absolutely silent and stock-still. Her eyes stay on my face. She tries to work her mouth to speak, but nothing comes out. I hold out my arms. As she falls into them, I am so grateful for her comfort, her warmth. Her tears, warm and tender, race down my arms and down my back. We cry for a very long time.

"You know how much I love you, don't you, Marissa?" She nods. "Sometimes I worry that you don't *really* know, 'cause I don't hug you enough, or touch you enough, or say the words enough. But I do. I'm so very proud of you. Now, please don't worry about me. I will do whatever the doctors say." I have to assure her because I can be bullheaded sometimes, especially after deciding not to take any more abuse from her father. It was then that I turned a new leaf and, from that point on, never allowed anyone to walk over me.

She finally sits up and out of my arms. She, too, uses her hand as a tissue, but she seems to rub her eyes way too hard with the back of her hand, leaving a rising welt below her left eye.

"Do they have to remove your breasts?"

I sigh long and hard. I am so sleepy right now. But I must answer her. "I don't know yet. Chemotherapy for sure. Aggressive treatment, they said."

Her tears start again. She reaches out her hand and fondles my hair. "You're going to lose your hair, huh, Mom?"

That thought makes me shudder, because I absolutely love my hair, always have. It's so thick and full with streaks of gray running through it. After all these years, I still have beautiful hair. "Probably," I finally respond. Then: "I don't want to think about that right now, and I don't want to talk about it, okay, baby?"

She nods her head in weary agreement. She kisses my forehead, whispers "I love you," and goes to bed.

That night I dream in colors—vivid colors—of stark blue skies and fat, fluffy cumulus clouds, the greenest grass, and then I see the ocean in a violet blue. When I awaken I know exactly what it is I want to do today. I am not going to sit at my computer and write. No, not today. I am going to head straight for the beach. I want to walk along the Pacific Ocean and watch the waves crash into the shore. I want to see the sea pummel the rocks and leave a frothy foam. And as I walk, I will continuously remind myself that life is good, that life is precious and, for me now . . . maybe . . . pretty damn short. No more wasting time on trivial matters or trivial people. I'm a survivor. So after my long walk, I tell myself that when I get home I am going to call that woman who has been trying to hook up with me. Maybe, just maybe, I have enough time left for some love and happiness in this life.

Love Can Move Mountains

Elizabeth Atkins

"Mountain, get out of my way!" —African American

My baby's face is gray as he lies down there, cradled in that rocky crack in the earth. He is as still as death.

"Andrew!" The terror shooting up from my soul echoes off the sheer rock around us. Lord, make his chest keep rising with breath and a heartbeat under that red T-shirt. Make his legs walk again in those khaki shorts and his favorite blue Michael Jordan gym shoes.

"Andrew, baby boy!"

My cry into the canyon blends with the memory of his scream, just minutes earlier.

"Ma'am," the guide pleads from behind me, his hot, plump hands gripping the back of my upper arms, "we can't risk you falling, too. Please, step back."

I'm not really aware that I'm kneeling on a boulder, some hundred feet above my baby. One minute he's hiking along with Trevor, as comfortable as if they'd been doing this all their lives.

The next minute, Andrew is free-falling.

"Momma!" Giant brown eyes staring up at me. A soft *whoosh* as he struck that cluster of rocks. Lord, if he hit his head. Or broke his back. Or just plain died. I might as well jump right after him.

"Momma." Two little brown hands grip the back of my neck. "Be careful, Momma."

I turn back; two huge cinnamon-hued eyes mirror my terror. Trevor has his daddy's eyes. Hazel, sparkling like somebody sprinkled gold dust around the pupils. Oh, his daddy's eyes . . .

"Please, Marcus . . ." I cry up at the cloudless blue sky, way beyond the canopy of dark green leaves and gnarled branches, ". . . if you're up there, ask God! Ask God to save our baby!"

"Momma!" Trevor cries. "Get up!"

The hot, dusty rock cuts into the heels of my hands.

I spin around, ignoring the quicksilver thought of just how hard the rock feels beneath my knees. How hard it must be underneath my first-born's perfect spine and his little man-muscles that ripple over his shoulders when he dribbles the basketball back home in the driveway.

"Oh, baby," I cry into Trevor's ten-year-old shoulders. "Your big brother!" The crackle of the guide's walkie-talkie lights up my nerves.

"What's taking them so long?!" I scream.

"The chopper is coming from the Donner Lake station," the guide, Bart, says, his boyish round face now chalk white compared to the sun-tanned glow when we first started off. "It'll just be a few minutes."

I stare at him, wondering why I put my family's fate in his hands, out here an hour from nowhere. My voice quakes: "Can't you climb down there?"

"The crew that's coming," he says, "they're the best."

"How can I get down there," I demand, "until they get here?"

"We can't risk that." Bart's flat, beige hat moves as he shakes his bald head. He's a big, bulky guy, with a deep tan on his plump, rounded shoulders. He's got an Army green backpack with bug spray, a water bottle, and sunscreen dangling over his khaki shirt and shorts. Red bites dot his thick legs.

"I don't have the equipment to scale rock like that," Bart says. The guide, he's half my age, born and raised out here in the upper Sierra Nevada ridge in northern California. "Makes me feel so small," I'd said an hour ago. "Like God is putting me in my place."

All this time we've been talking about how damn beautiful it is up here: that little stream trickling over the trail a ways back, those tiny yellow butterflies fluttering all over the purple flowers, the smell of all these big pine trees. The hugeness, the breathtaking beauty of it all.

"I hear ya," Bart had said. "If you didn't believe in the Almighty before you saw this . . ."

"I don't need any more proof than I've already got," I'd said with a tender glance at my boys just ahead. "Y'all stop skippin' on this trail," I'd warned. "That's lunch you got in those backpacks, not parachutes."

We had just passed a woman with three little girls, no more than eight, who were striding down the stone-and-dirt path through these rugged woods as if they'd learn to walk right here.

"This trail is a piece of cake," Bart had said. "Nothing to worry about."

Oh, Lord, what had I been thinking? Never should've listened to my crazy sister Sharlotte and her nature-boy husband, Johnny. Moving way out here from the Motor City, always calling us to tell us about their latest white-water rafting expedition. Or rock climbing. Or camping in the middle of the damn desert!

"Don't come all the way out here for your conference," Sharlotte had said, "without giving those city boys a good dose of nature."

So here we are, waiting to see if my baby is dead or alive on this damn mountain. And all I can do is wait.

"I don't hear a chopper," I say accusingly to Bart. The half-dozen pairs of eyes behind him—all full of sympathy—barely register in my mind. I can almost hear the other hikers thinking, *thank God that's not my child down there.*

One woman, with two white-blond braids and a Hard Rock Cafe baseball cap, puts her skinny arm around me, then takes Trevor's hand. "Dear Lord," she whispers, closing her eyes and almost pressing her cheek to mine, "we beg of you to bring this child back into his mother's arms, safe and sound." Her Southern drawl cushions my nerves as she continues: "We pray, dear Lord, that we can join this precious woman tomorrow, looking back on this to thank you for reminding us to cherish every second with those we love—" I gasp. A hot well of emotion shoots through me, spilling down my cheeks in hot streams. "Thank you," I whisper through trembling lips. Through the blur of tears, Andrew's face is softer. This is a dream; he will get up. . . .

"Come back to me, baby," I cry down to my firstborn. Just as I had screamed that morning when the state troopers came up to the door. I'd been running around like crazy, curlers in my hair, trying to iron my blouse and change my snagged pantyhose and get the boys out the door to school all at once . . .

"Ma'am, are you Mrs. Marcus Dickerson?" the officer had asked as he peeked through the screen door. I turned off the morning news—always had to have the weather report to know if the boys needed coats yet with their navy-blue-and-white uniforms.

"Yes," I had said, cupping a hand around each boy's ear, pulling their little heads close to my rib cage. Those men, they told me my Marcus was gone. Left early that morning for a meeting, in his favorite suit and the red tie with the little black-checked pattern that I'd given him after the promotion. He was carrying that silver coffee mug that fit in the holder on his dashboard, briefcase . . . I'd slipped his vitamin in his pocket. . . . Gone. In the split second it took that asleep-at-the-wheel truck driver to veer head-on into the only man God had ever made for me.

Then, and now, that same numbing swirl of emotion—it starts in your lips, makes your throat get tight; your heart feels like a pulsing football pushing through your ribs, and your legs give out . . .

"Andrew!" I shout. "Andrew, wake up, baby!"

The girl in the baseball cap pulls back, toward the wall of dusty rock behind this ledge, and keeps praying out loud.

"Ma'am, I'm hoping your son fell on the brush," Bart says, his cheeks red and shiny now, like waxed apples. "It's a cushion. His backpack, too. The leaves and moss, they fill up the crevices. . . ."

I stare down. "Oh, Lord," I cry. His little face. His red shirt and khaki shorts. His favorite blue Michael Jordan gym shoes. He looks too peaceful lying there. I do not want to pull my gaze away from him, as if the power of a mother's love radiating down from my eyes can keep his heart beating, his lungs pumping—but I cannot tell if his chest is rising and falling.

I spin toward Bart, claw at the black walkie-talkie in his hand. "Let me call them! They need to hurry!" Bart steps back toward the wall of rock, about five feet away at the inner edge of this brown, needle-strewn path. Rationally, I know I'm acting like a fool.

But I'm a mother. And my baby is at the bottom of a mountain.

I turn back toward Andrew. I feel detached from my body, from that hammering heart, the sweat-drenched skin, the face all twisted with terror . . .

Mountain, get out of my way!

Grand Memaw's voice, still as deep and honey-smooth as Lena Horne's, fills my ears. I hear her again: *Mountain, get out of my way!* Her power, her strength, back in a day when a black woman needed superhuman endurance just to raise and feed a family, to stay sane in an insane world—I could feel her power radiating through me, spiraling down toward her great-great-grandson lying there like he's dead.

Baby girl, it's gon' be all right, her voice says. *We gon' get this mountain out of your way. God tol' me so . . .*

That phrase, it's something Grand Memaw used to exclaim when faced with an impossible situation. Like when my sister Claudette disappeared in the woods outside Grand Memaw's house in Georgia during our summer visit. Thirteen and beautiful, Claudette had turned more than a few white boys' and men's heads when we'd gone into town the day before. Then, no sooner had she gone outside to pick some daisies in the field . . .

Poof! Gone for three hours.

There was always a story about a girl comin' up missing in the woods, never found, or bobbing up in the river a week later. Or suddenly dazed and pregnant with a little half-white baby.

But Grand Memaw had said nothing. Her deeply etched eyes had simply focused on the willow trees all around the property; then she had stood where Claudette's footsteps ended in the sand. She held out her caramel hands, palms up, stared into the sky, and said slowly, steadily:

"Mountain, get out of my way!"

Sure 'nough, a few minutes later, Claudette comes running out of the woods by the brook, crying about how she'd taken a walk down by the old barn and gotten turned around . . . And now, Grand Memaw's voice was like a record on repeat. Over and over, that phrase filled my head.

"Mountain get out of my way!"

But Andrew remained as still as one of his GI Joe figures, tossed and left in the yard.

"Momma!" Trevor cried. "You said after Daddy died, we'd be okay. But . . ."

My heart skipped three beats. It would damn near kill us both to lose Andrew just a year after the funeral. "God is in charge right now," I whisper, squeezing Trevor's hand without looking away from Andrew's little face.

"You said that in the hospital," Trevor said sadly. "If God was in charge, why did he let Daddy die?"

"God is always in charge, Trevor," I say, choking back my own tears as I watch his drip down those still-plump brown cheeks. "We don't have to like what happens, but God is in charge, and we have to accept that." I think I'm trying to convince myself of that, too.

I press my hot palm to his wet cheek, rest his head on my shoulder. We both stare at Andrew.

I never should've listened to Sharlotte. Never should've taken this promotion that has me traveling all over the country. Too much time away from the boys. They do fine with Ma, but they still like me to tell

them a story at bedtime, a story about how me and their daddy met in
a strawberry field, then frolicked all over Guam and Germany and Hawaii
when he was a brave soldier in the Army, before we settled down to
have the two of them.

Two precious gifts from above. Miracles, considering that one doctor had told me my fibroids had tangled up my womb so badly, no baby
could grow there.

Now, just let me defy the odds once more. Please . . .

What have I been thinking? In the name of providing the best for
my boys as a single mother, sacrificing time and love with them, for all
this travel. The pay is good. And I do get to bring them along a lot of
the time—Disney World one month, the Smithsonian another, the
Cubs game and deep-dish pizza.

Now this.

"Mountain, get out of my way."

I freeze. It's not Grand Memaw's voice.

It's my own. And I'm speaking aloud.

I'm repeating her words in a whisper. Into the dusty, pine-scented
air. Into the fuzzy top of Trevor's face.

"Mountain, get out of my way."

Does that mean I should scale rock that even the guide wouldn't
dare do? No, I can't risk leaving Trevor alone. Losing a father, a brother,
a mother . . . No. A deep hum draws my eyes to the sky. A chopper. A
figure in orange, descending on a thick yellow rope. A silver mesh basket, long enough to hold Andrew's four feet, ten inches of almost-new
life, is strapped to his back. The helicopter is blue, hovering in the
clearing, its wind causing a silvery rustle on all the trees around us.

Bart's walkie-talkie is crackling as he explains what happened,
again, to someone on the other end.

"The trauma center at Washoe is waiting," a woman says.

"Mountain get out of my way," I whisper into Trevor's head. His little shoulders are trembling under the soft flesh of my arms.

"This is like me and Andrew used to play 'rescue heroes' in the back
yard," Trevor says with a tone of disbelief. "But this isn't fun. . . ."

I stroke his cold arms, even though the air, they'd told us back at
the start of the path, is a dry eighty-five. The rescue guy in orange is
hovering over Andrew. He pushes off the rock wall, then holds it as
he's lowered right onto that ledge.

Then, another person—Is that a woman? A sister, no less—in orange, descending from another rope from the helicopter.

Carefully, they slide a board under Andrew, then secure him in the metal gurney. He does not move. But the spot where he'd fallen—it's green.

And his backpack is there. Lord, any protection those green grapes and the chicken salad sandwich could've offered—and the wad of paper towels my clean-freak child had stuffed in there, bless him—I'll take it.

"There's hope," Bart says over my shoulder. "Cushion. I know a guy; he fell twice this distance—not a single broken bone. Thanks to a bush."

The rescuers, they strap all kinds of seat belts over Andrew.

He still does not move. His face—still as gray as ash. And he looks so tiny. So helpless down there. I wish the rescuers would give us a sign, or even look up at us. But they're using hooks and ropes to secure the gurney, and slowly, slowly it rises, the woman holding on to one rope, steadying him with the other. Both rising.

He's level with us, as if I could reach out twenty feet and touch him.

His lips are red. Blood. Lord, please don't let him have internal bleeding.

"Andrew!" I cry. "Andrew, baby! It's me. . . ."

He continues to rise.

I hate the symbolism of his body rising up to the sky. Just as I had described to the boys when their daddy died, that God was lifting him up to heaven to wait for us when our lives here on earth ended.

But no, please, God, not my baby. Not this soon.

The gray mesh of the orange-padded gurney reminds me of the checker game we'd played this morning at Sharlotte's house that sits too high above that lake. All she ever does when she calls is talk about how beautiful Donner Lake is, how relaxing the rugged terrain out here is, how she never gets migraines anymore.

Finally, the woman rescuer and two others inside the chopper hoist the gurney inside. She gives a double thumbs-up, then drops the ropes for the guy still waiting on the ground.

"Now what?" I ask Bart.

"We have to climb down," he says. "I'll drive you to the hospital."

My feet couldn't move fast enough down that trail. Lord knows I almost twisted both ankles into oblivion on all those rocks and sticks. And Trevor, my little trooper, hurrying right alongside me, not saying a word about the cuts and scrapes on his calves.

But we made it.

Two hours after the rescue, I am touching my baby's face. His big brown eyes are open, and he's staring up at me. "I'm sorry, Momma," Andrew whispers. "You told me to slow down. But—"

I press a fingertip to his lip. "Ssshhh. We're all right."

Trevor stands on the other side of the bed, holding Andrew's hand, staring up with wide eyes as if he were looking at Jesus himself.

"Andrew you shoulda seen the helicopter!" Trevor whispers. "They said we can go out and look at it when you get better."

"Cool," Andrew says with a weak smile. He turns to me.

"Momma," Andrew says, "I could hear him. . . ."

I draw my brows together, studying his eyes. No, Lord, don't let him have hallucinations or—

"Daddy, I think," Andrew whispers. "I could hear him telling me . . ."

I lean closer.

" 'Be strong, son,' " Andrew whispers. His eyes sparkle, but there's a faraway look. . . .

My heart hammers against my ribs. I hold my breath.

"Be strong for your momma,'" my baby says softly, " 'Now and always. Be strong, son.' It was him, Momma. It was his voice, like he was standing over me."

His face, a mini version of his daddy's face, blurs under the sting of my tears. My Marcus was speaking to me, here, now, through this mini-man symbol of our love. The living, breathing product of *us*.

All I can do is press my trembling lips to Andrew's still-dusty cheek. I clasp my hands around his head. "My baby," I whisper, "I love you, big boy."

"And Momma," he whispers over the beeping monitors, "I know this is crazy. But it was like, somebody hummin' in the background. . . ."

Memaw. He had never met her in the flesh, but I'm sure she'd had a hand in blessing me with two baby boys.

"I couldn't make out the song," he says, yawning. His head makes a deeper indentation in the crisp white pillow. "Momma, I'm sleepy. . . ."

The doctor, a thirty-something Asian American with gold-rimmed glasses, strides in with a red-haired nurse.

"Good news," the doctor says, "The X rays and CT scan are coming up negative. So besides some pretty nasty bruises on his backside, this tough guy is gonna be all right."

"What about the blood in his mouth?" I ask.

"A good old-fashioned busted lip," the doctor says, breaking into a grin to show a mouthful of silver braces. "I'd say this young man's guardian angels were working overtime this afternoon."

I stare up at the white square tiles of the ceiling, past the beeping monitors and doctors' faces and Trevor and Sharlotte and her husband. "Thank you, God," I whisper, "And thank you, Marcus, and Grand Memaw, for moving that mountain out of our way."

Go Back

Nicole Bailey-Williams

"She who learns, teaches." —African, Ethiopia

My father is the living dead.

Seeing him these days is so hard, and every time I leave him I feel a little chip of my heart break off, plunging into the abyss of nothingness where the rest of my emotions have disappeared. I want to fall apart and have him hold me again, remembering that I'm his little girl, but that can't happen. Now he's the little one and I have to be strong. And I am, for the most part. Until I'm on my way out the door of his apartment at the assisted-living facility, and he says to me, "Come back," as if I could ever forget him.

Every now and then he breaks out of the fog and he's pretty lucid. He sits up in bed looking like a satisfied prince as I file his strong, healthy nails. His hands are the only things that have remained the same. Everything else has withered away, only present in my memory. I hate seeing his body, the body I had known to be strong and powerful, now so weak and thin. His silver, curly hair hovers around his head like an angry storm cloud. His face drawn, his eyes vacant, he brings to mind three simple words: *The living dead.*

Like Abraham, we had been the pride of his old age, my sister and I. Twins. At fifty-one years old! Who would have imagined? Twins don't even run in our family. At least, I don't think they do. Family history is not something that we really ever talked about. Now, with him ailing so, I wish that we had. Then I would have more than his fading image and my empty present to cling to.

Taking a deep breath, I buckle my seat belt, put on my shades, and pull out of the nursing home parking lot, making my way to Center

City for my appointment at the salon. Lunchtime traffic in Philadelphia creeps along, but I'm not bothered by the slow pace. People-watching distracts me from my grim thoughts.

After balancing my Mercedes perfectly in the middle of two parking spaces, I trot down Walnut Street, conscious of the stares I attract from men and women alike. They are impressed, and I know it. I've spent years building a facade of perfection, and with mask in place I become everything they think I am. Sophisticated. Glamorous. Charming. Delightful. That's what *City* magazine called me in last month's issue, when I was profiled as a Philadelphian to watch.

> *At thirty-one years old, restaurateur Corrine Coleman is taking a bite out of the city. Recently divorced, Coleman says she has no time to sit and pout. "Life goes on. When you are served a bad apple, just cut off the bad part, and sprinkle cinnamon, sugar and lots of brandy on it. What you're left with will be scrumptious."*

In print, the brandy part didn't go over so well. It made me sound like a lush. I certainly don't want John to think that I've taken to the bottle over him. Truth be told, he's probably the one who has something to drink about, after living with me. I know that I drove him away. I'd just hoped that he would stay, that he would love me enough to put up with my bullshit. Instead, he showed that he loved himself more. I don't blame him. Self-sacrifice isn't something that I'd wish for anyone. I'd just hoped that he would love me enough to stay.

Sitting in Lionel's chair at the Center City salon, I sip my wine and listen to the idle chatter around me. It's the same old thing. Ava is blabbering on about her summer in Martha's Vineyard. Mimi is yapping about one of her committees. Lila is telling about her shopping spree at Short Hills.

"Corrine, do you think that four hundred fifty dollars is too much to pay for a Swarovski elephant? It's about three inches high and four inches long, but it was too adorable to pass up. I've never seen anything like it before. Richard would flip if he knew how much I paid for it, so I just wrote a check for part of it and paid for the rest in cash."

"Lila, honey, style knows no price," I lie. Really, I'm thinking that she's got to be out of her mind, but I can't say that. It wouldn't be polite. And that, too, is part of my image.

Truth be told, I'm sick of the image thing. Sometimes I get the urge to just stand up and shout, "Fuck you!" at all the pretenders who inhabit my life. I want to tell them that I am the same one they overlooked all those years ago, the same one they barred from their stupid little clubs because I wasn't good enough. Now, they toast me as the flavor of the month. Fuck them. And fuck me, too, for allowing them to buy me despite my bitterness.

Lionel runs his fingers through my hair, searching my scalp for the new growth cropping up around my tracks. "Darling, you're still okay. It's only been four weeks. All you need is a wash and a hard blow-dry."

I slowly blink my doelike eyes at him and then widen them innocently. "Sugar, Mother Nature is pulling me back to the Motherland. I truly think it's time."

He sighs before leaving his station to get the relaxer from the storeroom.

What the hell does he know? I think, taking a larger-than-ladylike swig from my glass. He wouldn't know the first thing about my roots.

Roots.

I think of my father again, sitting up in the assisted-living facility, always waiting for me. Only me. My sister Sharon hasn't been in to see him since he moved in three months ago. "I can't believe that you put my father in a nursing home," she had said.

I'd ignored her display of sole ownership of our dad and said, "Sharon, he can't stay alone. You don't have any room for him at your place, what with all of those people in and out of there all the damn time. And I'm working most of the day. Who would take care of him? Besides, I'm paying for it, so what's your beef?"

"You just don't care, do you, *Karen?*" she had asked.

"It's Corrine."

"Oh, that's right. It's Corrine now. Well, whoever the hell you are, you're lucky I don't have power of attorney."

I'd just walked away from her without another word. I wished she did have power of attorney. Then maybe she would grow up and learn to take some responsibility instead of just playing grown.

"Corrine, who's playing tonight at the restaurant?" Lionel breaks into my thoughts.

"Brian Roberts and his trio. Are you going to swing through?"

"Yeah, and I'm bringing my new friend," he says, smiling devilishly.

"Uh-oh. Tell me the delicious details," I inquire absently.

"Well, he's . . ."

* * *

I sit on the bench in Rittenhouse Square, facing the restaurant, taking a breather before making my entrance. I know that as soon as I enter, my day will be consumed with the details of running a business, and I can't handle those just yet. I'm intrigued by the quick movements of a bird flapping around in a puddle of dirt. After he flutters for awhile, he emerges from the dirt cool and refreshed, taking flight to catch up with the other birds in the air. None of them know where he's been. He just moves among them looking unflappable. That bird is like me, and as I watch him join the flock of other birds, I remember where I've been.

Sharon and I were identical in every way. Equally smart. Equally attractive. Only our ambitions were unparallel. We had already tasted the privileged life together, and it was divine. We had seen them in our school, Girls' High. The "Sandys" we called them. They were the girls who had two parents at home, not one. Two college-educated parents who held professional jobs, not like Daddy's catering gig. The Sandys belonged to exclusive teen clubs and summered in exotic-sounding places that we'd only read about. Their clothes were always stylish though not trendy. Ours were clean, but nothing distinguished one outfit from the rest. They wore the latest hairstyles, adorned with funky little touches. My attempts at the same styles made me look like a wild woman.

I learned what I needed to do in order to evolve into a Sandy: study hard and get a scholarship to a good college. Either a good black college, like Hampton, Howard, or Spelman, or one of the top-tier white colleges. A generic white college would never do, even though they recruited me heavily. I decided on Georgetown, and in the summer of 1987, I was off to D.C.

While Sharon still had her sights set on becoming a Sandy, she'd decided that acquisition through association was the way to go. Only things didn't go her way at all. She was four months pregnant when we graduated from Girls' High, and it broke Daddy's heart.

He had driven to D.C. to drop me off at Georgetown. Sharon had stayed home. I knew that she was embarrassed, ashamed, and sad, but there was nothing I could do about it. I waved good-bye to her from the car as Daddy pulled out from in front of our Mount Airy row house.

The whole ride there he talked about my responsibilities. "You've got the chance that I never had. I had to drop out of school to support my family. Besides, only one of us could go, so they chose my sister. I wasn't mad then, and I'm not mad now. I just wish she had done something with her education," he said, his face curling in disgust.

He didn't offer any more about his sister, so I didn't ask. Like in so many black families, some stories were left untold. I just didn't know how important this one would turn out to be.

In D.C., he insisted on taking me to the most expensive restaurant he could find. With his dress hat and church clothes on, he was dignity personified. He beamed across the table at me. "You'll be the first one to do something big in this family. I can feel it."

After we finished eating, he excused himself from the table, leaving me to look around. An older, white man in a suit approached me.

"He's lucky to have you on his arm. Are you sure he can afford you?"

Baffled, I smiled politely and said, "Yes."

"If he can't, give me a call." He offered me his card.

"Okay," I said, glancing at the card before shoving it into my purse. He nodded and walked away.

A few minutes later, Daddy returned to the table, holding an envelope. "Karen," he started, "I've been building this since you and Sharon were little girls." He looked at his hands, and my eyes followed.

He continued, "I planned on splitting this in half between the two of you and dividing it over your four years of college, but since you're the only one going and you earned a full scholarship, it's all yours. You'll get the same amount each year. Use some to buy your schoolbooks, and put the rest aside for good use. You'll be a business major. I want you to learn how to turn this money over four times before you graduate," he laughed.

I sat crying in my dorm room that night, with ten thousand dollars cash spread all around me on the bed. It might not have seemed like a lot to a Sandy, but to me it was a really big deal. Guilt ate away at me as I thought about how I'd compared him to other dads. I'd been ashamed of the meals he used to sneak home from his catering jobs. I'd cringed because he hadn't always worn the right thing when he showed up at our school events. He'd driven a plain old car with no bells or whistles. His job hadn't afforded him the status that the Sandys' fathers enjoyed. But he was my father and he'd sacrificed for us, for me. I had to do right by him.

I don't know what made me call the white man from the restaurant. I just did, listening as he tried to talk me into joining his group of "ladies." "Prostitution is played out," I told him, not really insulted but quick to let him know that I wasn't some dumb little black girl.

"Who said anything about prostitution?" he replied. "I just said that plenty of men would pay money to have you on their arm for an evening."

"Would I be the primary beneficiary of such an arrangement?"

He laughed. "Sweetheart, a nice split would be made between you and me."

"Oh, do you accompany me on the dates as well?"

He laughed again. "You're so cute."

"And I'm smart, too. No thanks," I said, hanging up quickly.

With that idea in place, I set out to find attractive Georgetown University students who were hungry. I didn't have to look far, and by mid-September I had six refined, intelligent, attractive young women eager to serve as escorts for extra money. While readying them for their various events, I built my network of men in need of company and began setting dates.

"Yes, Mr. Moran. I do have someone who can accompany you to the political fund-raiser. She's a twenty-year-old political science major from New York. Her name is Candace, and she'll be ready at seven. Watch out. She's spicy."

Chu ching. Five hundred dollars.

"Of course, Dr. Giordani. Kelly can attend the American Medical Association convention with you next weekend. She's pre-med, so this should be a mutually beneficial arrangement."

Cha-ching. Twenty-five hundred dollars.

"Your New York associates will be jealous when you arrive at the premier with Carla, Mr. Simmons. Her model looks will keep you in the photographers' lenses."

Cha-ching. Fifteen hundred dollars.

The girls were enthralled by the experiences and tickled by the trinkets they collected. The twenty percent that I gave them was the icing on the cake. I felt no guilt. I was simply following the basic law of business: the law of supply and demand. I simply filled a need that existed, and everyone was happy. Besides, many of them were Sandys, and I got a perverse sense of joy by "pimping" them, even though they weren't required to do anything they weren't comfortable doing.

My service grew, and so did my bank account. For a brief second, I considered dropping out of school, but then I remembered my father and his sister, and I knew that he was counting on me, so I continued my hustle on the side. By the time I graduated and returned to Philadelphia, I had become Corrine and I was rich.

I met John when he came to my restaurant one evening with friends. Initially I found him intriguing because he spoke plainly, and his smile was magnificent. Thinking that the simplicity of his speech was a front for something more mysterious, and that the smile masked something more secretive, I dove in. We were married within a year because I had no idea that I needed to wait.

I asked for the world, and he gave me his piece of it. But I wanted more: daily massages, weekly facials, and monthly seaweed wraps. I wanted Tiffany, Lagos, Mikimoto, Manolo Blahnik, Gucci, and Prada. John wanted love. I wanted to fill the hole inside. Love was the one thing I couldn't deliver, so he left me.

Alone.

After my hair appointment, I stop by to see my father. I knock on the door to his room at the nursing home, then gently push it open. He is propped up on his pillows with his eyes closed. He's been in bed a lot lately, says there's no reason to get up. "I just want to sit and think about my Lord." Today when I come in, he's humming old spirituals. I pull up a chair next to his bed and sing with him. He smiles when he hears my voice, then opens his eyes.

"Daddy, why aren't you wearing your teeth?"

"I don't figure I look any better with them than without them."

I'm worried that he's losing his will to live. Before I can say anything else, he's humming again.

I read the Word to him before I leave, and I kiss his strong hands. As I'm walking out the door, he says, "Come back," and I nod, clamping my throat shut around the ball that's rising up to my dry mouth.

After leaving the assisted-living facility, I do something strange. I pull into a space at the end of my sister Sharon's street, desperate to see her. Sitting there, I see her oldest daughter leave the house wearing a dirty T-shirt, tight cutoffs, and a rag tied around her head. I laugh at how much she looks like Sharon. I stop, remembering that she looks like me, too.

I pick up my cell phone and dial.

"Sugarene's Restaurant," my manager, Lindsey, says.

"Hi, Linds. How's everything?"

"Everything's cool here. The new linens were just delivered, and we're all set for lunch. Are you on your way?"

"Not yet."

"Oh, let me guess what you're having done. Hands? Feet? Face? Hair?"

I'm sad, because despite my being a top-notch businesswoman owning and operating one of the city's top eating establishments, she thinks I'm shallow. I know I've given her every reason to think that I only care about surface things, though.

"I'll be in by two."

"See you then, boss."

I hang up and dial my sister. She answers on the third ring.

"Hello."

I don't say anything.

"Hello," she repeats, sounding annoyed.

I hang up and weep silently, wishing that the ocean between us would disappear.

The next day, Daddy calls me to tell me to come see him. When I get there, he's fully dressed in slacks, a shirt, and tie.

"My word," I say.

He's beaming as he sits by the window, fingering the petals on the roses that I brought him two days ago.

"What's happening, cutie pie?" I ask.

He smiles at the nickname I've given him. "Nothing much. What do you know good?"

"A little of this and a little of that. I'm glad to see you're dressed. I was starting to worry about you."

"You never have to worry about me. I'm okay, and I'll always be okay. I want to make sure that you'll be okay."

"Daddy, I'm fine."

"Are you?"

"Of course."

"Well, why don't you speak to your sister?"

"I do speak to her," I lie.

He looks at me knowingly. "I know what I'm talking about, young'un."

"Daddy, I don't know what you want me to say."

"Nothin'. Now I just want you to listen. Sometimes decisions people make can seem like the biggest mistakes in the world. We can't understand why they would want to do something so stupid when they seem to have every opportunity in the world to do right and live right. But we've got to realize that at the end of the day, all we have left is love, and love is the most powerful balm for any hurt. Do you understand me?"

I shake my head, feeling like he's talking more about himself than about Sharon and me.

The next two hours are filled with talk about politics, and we wage a civil battle over the state of current affairs. I'm happy to see him lucid, and he seems happy to be living in the present.

"Daddy, let me get to the restaurant. Do you need me to bring anything on my next visit?"

"Naw, babe. I'm okay."

"All right," I say, leaning down to kiss him on the forehead and his hands.

"Go back," he says as I'm walking out the door.

This time, no ball forms in my throat.

I get the call as I'm closing up the restaurant. Before the nursing home attendant says anything, I know that my father is gone. Her voice is only confirmation of what my heart feels.

"Sharon," I say when I hear her voice, groggy with sleep.

"Hey," she says, clearing her throat.

"I'm on my way to your house, so be up to answer the door."

"What's wrong?" she asks.

"I'll talk to you when I get there."

"No, Karen, tell me now. What's wrong?"

"I'll be there in ten minutes," I say, ending the call. I don't want to tell her over the phone. Speaking the words aloud will kill me right now. I have to compose myself to deliver the news without breaking down.

She's standing on the steps smoking when I arrive. Her nightgown is tucked into her sweatpants, and tears are already racing down her cheeks. I can't speak when I look at my sister, my reflection.

"I can't believe I was too stubborn to go see him," she wails, falling into my arms. "I can't believe I let him die alone. He never knew how much I loved him. He never knew. . . ."

I try to shush her, but she won't be quieted. I take her in the house to grieve in dignified solitude.

"Mom, what's the matter?" her oldest daughter asks, descending the stairs.

Her eyes lock with mine, and I see a flash of anger pass through them. I want to address her by name, then realize that I can't remember it. In my head I've always thought of her as my sister's bastard child. It is only then that I begin to weep, crying for myself, my father, my sister, and my anonymous niece.

Cleaning out my father's apartment is more difficult than I had imagined it would be. I finger everything carefully, hoping to recapture a part of him that I didn't know. I find two envelopes in the top drawer of his nightstand. One is addressed to my sister, and the other is addressed to me. The familiar ball returns to my throat as I regard the envelope addressed to me. It reads, *Carin*. He had tried to step into my world, and his steps were unsure, but he tried for me.

I open the envelope.

Carin,

I know I probably didn't spell it right, but I wanted to address you as you like to be called.

I've had a good life. You and your sister have been a large part of that joy. Your strife has been a large part of my pain. It's like you didn't learn anything from my mistake. Even as I write this, I know how silly it is. You didn't learn anything from my mistake because I never told you about my mistake. I have a sister. You know that part. She's my twin. You don't know that.

She's the smart one. In fact, she was so smart the family sent her to college so she could come back and teach the rest of us. You know the saying, "Teach a woman, teach a nation." Well, that's what my parents hoped to do with her. But she went away, and she didn't do what we thought she was supposed to do. Now, not being college-educated, we didn't know what exactly she was supposed to do, but farming was not what we had planned for her. She was supposed to be a teacher or a doctor or a lawyer. She didn't need an education to farm.

When you came back and told me about your plans to open your restaurant, I held my tongue. I didn't want to say anything to discourage you, but my heart hurt. Over time, I came to know that the restaurant would just be your base. The connections you've made have been good, and I know that you'll use them for big things.

Now, my last request of you is to go back down south to the family farm in South Carolina. You'll find my sister there, and if you're lucky, and she's forgiven me for being such a fool to her, she'll teach you a thing or two.

Always know that I love you, Carin.

Sincerely,
Cutie Pie

As I pull my car into the front yard, I see the woman, my daddy's sister, my aunt, emerging from the side of the house. She carries a bundle of sticks woven into a broom in one hand, and a straw hat in the other hand. She wears overalls and walks barefoot, standing remarkably straight for a woman in her eighties. Her face lights up when she sees me, then falls as she drops the hat and broom.

"If you're here, that means that he's gone," she says.

"He is, Auntie," I say, walking toward her.

"Well, that's that." She breathes deeply, wiping her eyes with the back of her hand. "Let's go in," she says, linking her arm through mine.

"You're prettier in real life than in those pictures your daddy sent me," she says, pulling two glasses out of the cupboard.

"Thank you, ma'am. I was under the impression you two weren't in touch," I respond.

"We weren't. Just every now and then I would get something in the mail. A Christmas card, a birthday card, and a few pictures. They weren't ever signed, but I knew who they were from, so I knew that he was thinking of me. That was enough."

Her kitchen feels like home, and I settle back into the chair, sipping the lemonade she hands me. As she examines me, I feel as if I'm looking at myself fifty-one years in the future.

"We look alike," she says, laughing.

"I know," I respond, taking her hand. "Tell me about him and you and here."

She clears her throat, and as she begins to tell me the family history, I hear my father's voice distinctly. She speaks of my great-great-grandparents, and how, after emancipation, they acquired the 200 acres that became the family farm. She tells of people who forgave the land for absorbing the blood and tears of their ancestors. She recounts tales of strength over savagery, pride over power, and faith over fists. She walks me through decades of history with her words, and I embrace them all.

I spend the next month with her, living and learning. I am at ease in her presence, and I don't feel the need to fill the air with the useless chatter that occupies so much space in my Philadelphia world. I laugh and cry loudly, without regard for decorum or dignity. The suits I packed for the trip stay in garment bags in the closet, while I move about the farm in a pair of her old overalls. My skin has grown brown under the Southern sun, and I feel my new growth coming in. Without a moment's hesitation, I pick up scissors and sit on the back porch, where I cut the weave out of my hair. With un-manicured hands, I twirl my short natural hair around my fingers, and I smile thinking of my father's last words to me. "*Go back.*"

"Auntie," I say regretfully, "I'm going to need to head back to the city tomorrow."

"I know."

"I want you to know that I have appreciated every second of our time together."

"I have, too. Before you leave, though, I want to remind you that every generation needs a griot or an historian," she says. "You know that you've got to be the griot of your generation."

"I know."

"So take what I've given you, and go back home to teach."

"Yes, ma'am." I smile.

I don't even stop at my house when I return to Philadelphia. I head straight to my sister's house. Her oldest daughter answers the door.

"Sugar, I have to apologize before I even say this because it's a shame, and I know it. I don't know your name, and I'm really embarrassed to say that to my niece."

"My mother named me after you," she says without expression. Then her beautiful face opens into a smile. I embrace her and together we walk into Sharon's house and sit in the kitchen, where I make lemonade from scratch, following the family recipe. I begin to tell her the story of people who forgave the land for absorbing the blood and tears of their ancestors. She leans her chin on her palm and listens to the lesson with love and interest dancing in her eyes.

Something Special

Venise Berry

"Every week has its Friday." —Cape Verde Islands

Kefron smiled, a broad flash of a smile, as she checked the simulated-wood-grained clock with rotating dancing angels that sat on her large, mahogany desk. She shook her head. Only five minutes had passed since she'd last looked. She shuffled several piles of paper, straightening and sifting until they seemed more organized, then closed her eyes and sat very still, enjoying the gentle tingle that ran down her spine with the memory of D. J.'s heated touch.

It was the buzz of the intercom that finally made Kefron return to her tedious but necessary tasks.

"Ms. Beyer, Mr. Troy Jons is on line one."

At the same time that Kefron picked up the shiny black telephone receiver with her left hand, she pulled off the gold clip earring with her right.

"Troy," Kefron purred softly, "I'm so sorry I missed you yesterday. By the time I got back to the gallery you were gone, but I saw your new work, and it's fantastic!"

"Thank you, Kefron. You know death is the only thing that could come between us," Troy teased, then pulled the phone away from his mouth to smother a series of strained coughs.

Kefron nervously fingered her turquoise-and-amber necklace, willing the semiprecious stones to calm her deepened fear and anxiety. "How are you?" she asked sincerely.

"I'm okay. *HIV-positive* only means that AIDS is coming. It's not here yet. Maybe they'll find a cure in time."

"I hope so. I keep thinking how hard it would be to start a new love affair right now with the threat of AIDS out there."

Troy hesitated, then spoke softly. "Yes, but without love, life is basically worthless, like wrapping an empty box for Christmas."

Kefron reflected for a moment. "Maybe, but I don't know. I think love is what you make it, and that empty box could represent something even better on the way." An awkward pause lingered between them. "How's your partner? I was sorry to hear that you had to move him to the hospice on Fifty-seventh Street."

"It's a wonderful place with wonderful people, but you know, he's in the final stages now, so the best they can do is keep him comfortable."

Kefron pulled a blue file folder off the top of the pile in front of her and opened it. "Well, Troy, I called because I have good news. MacMillan's wants to buy two pieces of your work for their new downtown restaurant."

"That's great news!"

"Yes, it is. Less my forty-percent commission, you'll receive a check for sixty-nine hundred dollars within the next thirty days." Kefron sat quiet for a moment to allow Troy to express himself with his usual whistle. There it was, loud and shrill. She smiled, then continued. "I'll be at the gallery until five. I would love to have you come in and approve the pieces I want to send."

"Of course; I'll see you around four o'clock. And Kefron, thanks again for everything you've done for my career. I never imagined I could make a real living through my art."

"It's okay, Troy; I have enough imagination for both of us. See you at four."

Kefron pressed the receiver back into its cradle. Then she jotted down a couple of notes about Troy's next contract and slipped them in the folder just as an incessant pecking began at her office door.

"Yes?" she called, looking up to see the door fly open and her new assistant, Vikki, scurry in with a huge bouquet of yellow roses.

"These came with a card from Richard Johnson while you were on the phone." The assistant grinned.

Kefron motioned for her to put the flowers in the usual spot on the Scandinavian bookcase.

Vikki removed the old bouquet of wilting day lilies from last week and carefully sat the glass vase down. "That man of yours is really something special, Ms. Beyer," she squealed excitedly. "If you don't mind me asking, how come he sends flowers every week, and each week a different kind?"

Kefron flashed back to the trail of delicate red rose petals leading into her bedroom, where D. J. had waited last week. "Because I love flowers and D. J. loves me," she answered matter-of-factly.

"Does he have any brothers? Because I sure could use a good man in my life right now," Vikki whined.

Kefron stood up and strolled over to inhale the soft, yellow sunshine. She took a deep breath, filling her lungs and heart with the sweet, sensual fragrance. "Sorry," she finally replied through a grateful grin. "He's the only one." Kefron noticed the sad look that suddenly swept Vikki's face, and added, "Don't worry. It took a long time to find what I needed. You just have to be patient and keep an open mind. What you're looking for will eventually come."

Opening the small white card, Kefron grinned under her breath. *Tonight you're mine, D. J.* She moaned gloriously. Every Friday night was a marvelous sexual adventure because she always spent Fridays with D. J. She had chosen to limit their lovemaking to once a week because of the raw intensity. D. J. didn't believe in moderation. He gave her everything he had, every time. She also had to admit that part of the attraction was the pure sacrifice of waiting and longing and remembering all week long. In this way, she never got tired or bored when it came to their lovemaking, which often happens with too much of a good thing. Kefron couldn't believe how happy D. J. still made her after almost five beautiful years together.

"Could you call Lana and ask her to stop by my office before she leaves, please?" Kefron asked Vikki, then ambled back to her seat.

Vikki nodded her head but stopped in front of the door. "Do you need anything else, Ms. Beyer?"

Kefron settled into her black, padded chair, rested her chin in her hand, and stared at the exhilarating rays of colorful light bouncing from the flower arrangement. "No, thanks," she whispered. "Everything's perfect."

By the time Lana arrived, Kefron had finished editing the proposal for Mission Hills Insurance Company. They were interested in purchasing several pieces of artwork for their newly renovated lobby, and she wanted to add one of Troy's fabulous new collages to the estimate.

"Hey, you wanted to see me?" Lana asked as she stuck her head in the door.

Kefron waved her best friend forward. "Yeah, come on in."

Lana waddled into the room, with a huge rounded stomach leading the way. "I've finished packing the Sadler series for shipment to Montreal. Do you need to check on anything before I send it off?"

"No, I'm sure you've got it under control," Kefron replied. "What I wanted was to give you this for you and Forest and the baby." Kefron held back her smile as she handed Lana a long, thin box wrapped in shiny silver-and-gold-striped paper.

Lana spoke gingerly, trying to contain her overemotional hormones and keep the omnipresent tears at bay. "Oh, thank you, Kefron, but you didn't have to," she whimpered.

"Please. It's nothing, girl. Sit down and open it."

Lana eased her wide backside into the gray leather chair and carefully tore the wrapping from the box. When she opened it, she "awwwed," pulling three sterling silver baby angels with gold-plated wings from the white tissue paper. "They're gorgeous!" Lana said. "You and your angels. We will cherish these."

Kefron sat thinking of her own angelic boundaries. It was love that had inspired her obsession with angels. She had dreamed of D. J. the night before she found him, and in that dream there were angels, messengers from God, protective spirits who vowed to guard her heart from further emotional trauma. They had assured her that D. J. was the answer, and he had brought with him a peace and fulfillment like no other before.

Lana suddenly noticed a piece of paper that was folded inside the bottom of the box. When she pulled it out and read it, her red-painted lips parted until her mouth dropped open. "This is way too much, Kefron," she protested.

"Nonsense. You and Forest have enough to think about with your upcoming wedding. The least I can do is take the burden of a honeymoon off your mind. Once the baby is born, you know Forest's mom will be happy to watch her for a couple of weeks. Then you guys can use the tickets and my condo on Antigua Beach to relax and sip planter's punch under the three-hundred-year-old banyan tree."

Lana heavily lifted herself up from the chair as the tears fought to escape. "You're going to make a great godmother," she said, moving over to Kefron, leaning down and hugging her tightly. "And you'll be a fabulous wife and mother yourself, someday," she added.

"Not me," Kefron snorted, shaking her head vigorously. "I don't want to be nobody's wife, and I'm definitely not interested in doing the pregnancy-and-pain thing. I can handle godmother; that's enough for me."

Lana smirked, throwing her arms around Kefron one more time. "We'll see," she said, then left hurriedly to hide the streaming tears.

Kefron noticed her earring on the desk and clipped it back on. She informed Vikki that she was leaving her office for a while, then headed toward the gallery. Out of habit, she twisted the short brown locks that hung loosely, elegantly shaping her smooth oval face. Whenever Kefron surveyed the gallery, her accomplishment, her success, the overwhelming pride clung to her heart like lianas to a trellis.

It had always been Kefron's dream to support the arts in some way, and the gallery had made it happen. The early years were difficult as she and Lana identified, promoted, and established a recognizable talent base. They searched out the most beautiful, thoughtful, and energetic work they could find: watercolor, charcoal, oil paints, and sculptures. Now, ten years later, they were nationally known for their savvy good taste.

Kefron stood mesmerized beneath the beige, brown, black, red, and orange streaks that twisted themselves into sensual, exotic forms on an immense forty-by-sixty-inch piece at the center of the main wall in the gallery. She felt breathless as Troy's collage effortlessly presented a tangle of arms, hips, thighs, and legs; dancing, swaying, and loving forcefully, amatively. The sharp, colorful images made Kefron's own body grow hot with anticipation of the night to come. She couldn't wait to feel the resplendent sensations of D. J.'s intense, penetrating rhythm. She stood rocking back and forth with that suggestive hunger when Troy arrived.

"I hate to interrupt you," he whispered from behind her.

"I can hear the music in this piece," she whispered back, not wanting to speak too loudly and ruin the moment.

"The music you hear is from your own soul. Everybody's song is different."

The air hung heavy between them for a while. "That's why I love your work. It's so powerful, so unique, so sexy."

Kefron pointed at another, slightly smaller piece on the adjacent wall. "I've chosen the piece over there and this one, because they both have an amorous but tasteful style that will work nicely for Mac-Millan's romantic setting."

"You have an exquisite eye, Kefron," Troy agreed, and lightly placed his large, brown hand against the small of her back.

Kefron jumped nervously. "Thank you, Troy," she replied, silencing the ache that spread from his unexpected touch. She made an excuse and rushed back to her office. It was time to get home and prepare.

The thirty-minute drive seemed longer than usual, but Kefron really didn't mind. Tonight was her night. She purposefully found ways to prolong the yearning desire and looked forward to the thrusting and throbbing that she knew would ultimately bring precious joy.

She drove slowly into the gravel driveway and parked, letting the kiss of laughter touch her full lips. This ritual of hers had become all-consuming. She allowed nothing to interfere with Friday night. Over the years, her family, friends, and colleagues had learned not to call or drop by. A couple of stubborn Jehovah's Witnesses once found themselves talking to the doorknob about God's love and Satan's power.

When Kefron entered her three-bedroom condo on the second floor, the first thing she did was turn on a mellow jazz CD by Kirk Whalum. She listened to the sultry saxophone solo while removing the hand-woven Samathi vest and matching Bagroo skirt she had bought on an excursion to India last year. Wearing only a black silk teddy that clung to her medium, chestnut frame, Kefron carefully lit scented candles of all shapes and sizes: blue jasmine to bring peace and relaxation, lavender for a warm, emotional balance, red cinnamon to draw out passion, and her favorite: angelic root for the rejuvenation of her soul. She lit seven candles in the bedroom, seven in the living room, and seven in the bathroom, representing the six days of work and one day of rest that God used to create the blessed earth.

In the kitchen, Kefron pulled out an ice bucket and filled it. She popped the cork on a $179 bottle of Cristal champagne, pushing it down into the cold sphere until it was equally surrounded on all sides. Gazing for a minute at the flickering brilliance of the night stars through the kitchen window, she imagined each star a guardian angel in flight. She stole a moment to silently thank her own guardian angel for loving, protecting, and fulfilling her.

Only hot water ran into the large Jacuzzi tub while Kefron sprinkled in aphrodisiacal bath oils: eucalyptus, neroli, chamomile, and ylang-ylang. She sipped champagne and thought of D. J. as her body embraced the soothing, luxurious mixture. How different D. J. was from all the others who had bulldozed their way into her life, leaving carnage and destruction. He was always focused on her happiness, her satiation. He knew instinctively when to slow down or when to speed up. He could always titillate the right spots with just the right amount of pressure to bring her to climax over and over again. He was the first ever to completely satisfy her.

Kefron glanced at the three jubilant angel statues on her wicker bath shelf, recalling a faithful Zulu proverb, "Love is like a fertile seed.

It does not choose the ground on which it falls." She suddenly couldn't wait any longer. She needed D. J. She wanted him. Quickly patting her taut body dry with a soft Egyptian towel, Kefron enjoyed the lustful desire that captured her.

She floated into the bedroom, pulled a large wooden box from her closet, opened it, and lifted the royal purple velvet cloth from inside. Kefron glowed as she lovingly unwrapped her wonderful Friday-night gift. There he was: D. J., her delicious Dickey Johnson, waiting patiently, confidently, humbly; ready to please her in every way. The ten inches of soft, warm, vibrating pleasure was a lasting kiss, a tender sunrise, a potent rain, and a permanent rainbow all wrapped up into one mighty zenith.

D. J. hummed with an invigorating enthusiasm as Kefron lay gently across her king-sized bed. She tenderly stroked the bronze nipple on her pulsating breast while D. J. tickled and caressed and massaged fragile parts of her firm, eager body. He was the perfect lover. He knew exactly what she wanted, when she wanted it, and how she wanted it. He offered no diseases, no pregnancies, and no false hopes. He made her scream; he made her tremble; he made her cry perfect, exalted tears.

As the fourth orgasm rippled intensely through her satisfied soul, Kefron's body stiffened and shook, then collapsed from pure exhaustion. Taking several deep, cleansing breaths with her eyes closed and her heart full, Kefron quickly fell into a serene and restful sleep, dreaming of next Friday.

Ain't Nobody's Business If I Do

Parry "EbonySatin" Brown

"Know this to be the truth and that I tell no lie: If an older woman is to be the death of me, then Lord knows I'm just going to have to die!" —African American

Paul smiled with approval at the store display as he picked up the bouquet of Janet's favorite flowers. The scent of gardenias and white orchids intoxicated him as he checked his reflection in the sparkling-clear glass window. He'd meticulously planned every detail of the evening's events. The thought of Janet quickened his already accelerated pulse as minute beads of perspiration formed between his brows.

Paul turned quickly at the sound of his brother's voice in his head. *Man, are you nuts? She's eighteen years older than you!* David, who considered himself Paul's savior, had talked fast and furiously to try to sway him. But with a smile and a firm pat on the back, Paul had assured him, "I got this!"

Janet embodied beauty with a style and class admired by men of all ages and envied by women of all cultures. Her intelligence, wit, humor, sensitivity, independence, and skills in domino playing all added to her charm. The thought of her softness caused a stirring deep within. He straightened his posture and adjusted the Kente-patterned bow tie, which added a cultural flair to the Armani tuxedo. The custom-tailored garment cuddled every chiseled muscle on his six-foot-five-inch, two-hundred-forty-pound frame.

Fate had brought Paul and Janet together nearly five years earlier. While he perused books in the financial-planning section of a mall bookstore, her scent had tantalized his olfactory senses as only his grandmama's peach cobbler had in the past. He stepped into the aisle, hoping for a glimpse of this mystical creature.

There she stood, in black stretch pants accenting full, rounded hips that were more perfect than he could have dreamed of, a black T-shirt tucked into the pants, with lettering distorted by her ample bosom, and a fashion belt. Her baseball cap matched the lettering on the T-shirt and the belt. This woman had brought a sexiness to the casual ensemble unlike any he'd ever witnessed before. Paul's adoration of women of size had never been a secret, or popular, among his *boys*. However, with maturity had also come a freedom of expression and a growing unwillingness to succumb to peer pressure.

The woman moved with the grace of a dancer over to another section of the store. The sight of her scanning the inside flap of a hardcover release sent shock waves of desire through his body. He *had* to speak to her. He wanted to see her face, look into her eyes. Under the pretense of searching for a book that he knew wouldn't be in the mystery section, he asked casually, "Hi, have you seen the new Eric Jerome Dickey release?"

"Oh, he has a new release?" She flashed a gorgeous smile. "I think you'd find Dickey in African-American *fiction*." As she spoke, Paul was unable to concentrate. Her voice sounded so sensual, he felt as though someone were pouring warm oil down the center of his back. Struggling for words, he managed to say, "I'll check there. Thank you."

Turning to walk away, he took a deep whiff of her exhilarating fragrance. A voice deep within his soul said, "If you walk away now, you may never, ever see her again."

Paul turned slowly and blurted, "Excuse me, but would you join me at the gourmet coffee shop just down the way here in the mall?"

Janet looked amused, then flashed that iceberg-melting smile. "I'd love to, but I have to do a lot of other shopping."

Paul faltered, then asked, "May I join you for a while, then?" He cringed at how pathetic the words sounded.

A puzzled look found its way to her flawless face as she tilted her head to the side and asked, "What?"

"I'm sorry. It may sound ridiculous, but I'm just in awe of you and I'd like to get to know you better. I'm afraid if I let you walk out of this store I'll never see you again. I'm not some weirdo, I promise you."

Janet searched his eyes and saw a hint of genuine adoration. "Well, mister, what did you say your name is?"

He quickly extended his hand "Paul, Paul Baxter. And you are . . . ?"

"Janet Parker," she smiled, shaking his hand then letting it go. "It's nice to meet you, Paul Baxter. But honestly, I'm a buyer, not a shop-per. My expeditions aren't for the faint at heart."

"Being an amateur athlete I'm pretty strong in the heart depart-ment," Paul replied. "I just want to spend a little time getting to know the woman behind that gorgeous smile. I'll make you a deal. Give me one hour. If either of us is bored, we'll part company, never to bother the other again. Deal?" He extended his hand once more.

Janet hesitated, then took his hand to cement the arrangement.

Oh, Lord, what have I gotten myself into this time? He is so tall and handsome. Why is he interested in me? "Well, let's do this thing! Do you want to pick up Eric's book and we can head for the checkout counter?"

"What? Oh, yes, yes. Let me grab the book. Don't you dare move an eyelash. I'll be right back." Paul quickly moved to the African-American fiction section of Barnes & Noble, shaking his head. He'd almost blown it. He'd totally forgotten he had asked her about the popular author.

Janet used the time to evaluate what had just happened. Although she wasn't positive, she thought he looked at least fifteen years younger than she. She'd taken great care of her five-foot-nine-inch, two-hundred-thirty-five-pound frame. She defied anyone to sport 44-34-54 with more panache, but she was still labeled a "big girl," and Paul's type had never shown the slightest interest in her before. But he seemed nice enough, and they were in a mall with a million or so other people. At the very least he could carry her packages, she reasoned, throwing caution to the wind.

That fateful day five years earlier had been the start of the most wonderful years of both their lives. Paul adored Janet, from her short brown hair to her brightly painted red toes. They were compatible in every way—talking for hours, crying at the same movies, and sharing a passion for life that was hard to match. Even vacationing together was magical. At the end of their first road trip, a five-hour drive from Los Angeles to Pismo Beach, Janet had announced that she'd travel with him to the ends of the earth. "If you can be locked up in a car for five hours with someone and still emerge smiling, you're compatible for life," she reasoned. Laughter graced her lips as quiet fear gripped her heart. Was this man really her soul mate?

The years had proved her fears unfounded. As the doorbell rang, Janet was taking a final look in the hallway mirror. She never kept Paul waiting. He'd requested that she wear the black dress that showed off her hips—his favorite. She knew she was looking *foine!* Opening the door, she was surprised to see a uniformed chauffeur holding an envelope. Recognizing the handwriting, she opened it to read: *Your chariot awaits.* She grabbed her purse and pulled the door closed.

Standing beside the longest automobile she had ever seen was the man she loved, holding an enormous floral arrangement. His smile made her feel warm all over. He took her hand and helped her into the automobile that seemed larger than her first apartment. He slid in beside her as the driver closed the door. A familiar and phenomenal feeling flowed through her as she imagined that they were the only two people left on earth.

The music of her favorite saxophone player filled the air as the driver closed the partition, giving them privacy. The three-hour magic carpet ride began.

Paul filled the Waterford flutes with Dom Perignon. He toasted their love and gave thanks for yet another opportunity to share a very special time together. They chatted for a short while, and Janet settled in, laying her head on his shoulder.

She recalled the day they'd met. There before her was a man who could easily grace the cover of any male fashion magazine. The otherwise intelligent, articulate orator had stood before her, fumbling for the right words to say. He stuttered and his voice trailed off as he made a most unusual request. Janet had been too amused to take him seriously.

The first day they'd spent together had been wonderful. He hadn't missed a beat as they shopped for everything from CDs to silk blouses. By the end of the acquisition adventure, he was comfortable enough to offer his honest opinion about a not-so-wise fashion choice. They laughed a lot and were as giddy as teenagers as evening approached. As Paul escorted her to her money-green BMW, Janet was sad to see the day come to a close. She couldn't remember the last time she'd had so much fun shopping.

As he prepared to say good-bye, Paul had blurted out the words she'd hoped to hear all afternoon: "Please, may I buy you dinner?"

Janet's eyes sparkled like black diamonds as she answered, "Only if we have sushi. Let me give you my number; perhaps we can get together early next week?"

A slight frown wrinkled Paul's almost perfect face. "No, I meant now. I've never had such an enjoyable afternoon, and I just don't want it to end here in this parking lot."

Janet smiled shyly, saying nothing.

Paul put his palm to his forehead and said, "Oh, how silly of me. This is Saturday; I'm sure you have other plans. Please forgive me for putting you on the spot."

In an embarrassed whisper, Janet said, "My plans include starting the book I bought today when we first met. I'm sure my murder mystery can wait until after church tomorrow. I'd love to have dinner with you, but not dressed like this. . . ."

Paul could no longer contain his glee. "You're absolutely perfect in every way. I know a casual sushi restaurant at the beach. I'll get my car. Don't move!"

Janet watched as he darted to the other side of the parking lot, and she knew she was in trouble. This young man could steal her heart so quickly, she would never even know it was gone. Should she just get in her car and be gone when he returned? Should she take a chance on getting hurt yet again? Take a chance on lying awake night after night with her only companion a tear-soaked pillow? She wanted to run, but her feet felt like part of the blacktop. Her heart raced as she saw Paul pull his black Firebird convertible just a few feet beyond her, and she knew she should definitely flee in the opposite direction.

What had compelled her to wait for the handsome stranger named Paul Baxter? She had no idea, but she couldn't leave. Why was she so comfortable with him, like he was an old friend? That was a question they would both ask many times over the years. Neither believed in reincarnation, but they were convinced that this was not their first encounter. A light kiss on Janet's forehead returned her mind to the present.

"A penny for your thoughts," Paul whispered.

"I was thinking how wonderful it always is to be with you."

The chauffer took them from Los Angeles to Goleta Beach via Highway One. The full moon shone brightly on the Pacific Ocean, illuminating the beautiful scenery as though Paul had custom ordered the rare, crystal-clear evening.

The car came to rest in a secluded picnic area. The chauffer opened Janet's door, extending his hand to assist her out of the car. She stopped abruptly as she saw blankets surrounded by lit hurricane lamps. A champagne bucket and picnic basket sat in the midst of the romantic setting.

Words escaped the woman who made her living by her verbal skills. "All for you, my queen." Paul helped her from the car.

The night was warm. He took her by the hand and led her to the picnic area. Their favorite song filled the night.

"How did you do all of this?"

"I'm a man of many talents, my sweet."

Janet smiled up at him as he extended his strong hand.

"May I have this dance?" he whispered in the low, sexy voice that always made her knees weak.

"There's only one thing better than dancing with you," Janet said, placing her hand in his.

"Oh, really, now. And what might that be?" Paul grinned.

"Beating you at dominos!" she teased.

With one smooth spin, Janet was in Paul's arms, and they began gliding slowly and in perfect, synchronized rhythm toward the sand.

As the music changed to another of their favorite songs, they stood at the water's edge. Janet removed her sand-filled shoes and laid her head on Paul's chest. The cool saltwater air kissed her face.

"Paul," Janet began in a barely audible voice, "I love you. I couldn't have fantasized anything so wonderful. Thank you."

"I'm really glad you feel that way Ms. Parker, because you *are* the light of my life," Paul said, dropping to one knee and looking deeply into the eyes that had captured him the first moment they'd met. . . . "Janet Parker, will you marry me?"

Tears began to flow, and without the slightest hesitation Janet simply nodded her head.

Suddenly Janet saw fireworks. She wasn't sure if they were real or just a product of her elated heart.

"Are you sure you want to do this?" she asked tearfully.

"Of course I'm sure! You've brought happiness into my life I didn't know was possible. And I want it to last forever."

"But what will people say about you marrying someone so much older than you are?"

"Baby, let them say what they want, 'cause it ain't nobody's business if I do!"

Making Your Eight

Zaron W. Burnett, Jr.

"The only thing more certain than each day's date
Is the simple fact that, each and every day, You've got to get up
off of your ass, go out and make your eight."
—The Proverb of the Universal Worker

In February of 1971 I was in the twenty-first year of my exultant American Negritudinous life. And I was angry. The perfect focus of hindsight makes it pretty clear that in 1971 I was always angry, along with what seemed like an entire generation of my sistren and brethren. I thought—we thought—that anger was part of our style, part of what we presented to let the world know that we knew the deal, and it was not going to be so easy pulling the wool of racist oppression and degradation over our angry eyes. Why, the absence of palpable, nondirected anger was, on the part of a Black man my age, proof positive that that particular brother was most definitely not in the vanguard—the vanguard of anger, that is.

By the time I was in my twenty-first year, I had been angry for more than fourteen years, having read Richard Wright's *Native Son* in my seventh year. I had been certifiably angry ever since. And by angry I don't mean to suggest that we didn't laugh, party, and have all kinds of fun. Some of the best parties I ever attended were thrown by the angriest among us, the real revolutionaries. These were the people who had houses filled with the Black Panther Party newspaper, *Muhammad Speaks, The Socialist Worker, The Daily World, The Quotations of Chairman Mao, The Quotable Maulana Ron Karenga, The Autobiography of Malcolm X*, posters of Angela Davis, Che Guevera, Muhammad Ali, and Lenin, and fliers from every demonstration in an 800-mile radius. There were usually some expensive cameras hanging on doorknobs and coat hooks. At these houses, the excitement was so real and the danger so constantly hinted at by the constantly-looking-out-of-the-window lookouts that the novices claimed it made them feel that maybe even *they* were under surveillance now, just for having come to this particular party.

It was hard not to have fun in the extreme in the presence of such exuberant, insistent, death-defying anger. And believe me when I tell you we made certain everyone knew that we were defying death on behalf of our People, so great was our individual anger at our historical mistreatment.

On May 4, 1970, in my capacity as the angry leader of the Mercer County College student organization the Black Leadership Action Council Klan (BLACK), I was leading a demonstration at the Trenton Armory to protest the Cambodian activities of the Nixon Administration, when two equally significant things happened to me. First, I received on that same day, May 4, 1970, a letter from Richard M. Nixon ordering me to report for induction into the United States Army on June 18, 1970, at Newark, New Jersey. And second, the United States Army Reserves/Ohio National Guard fired on student demonstrators at Kent State University who were protesting the same thing at Kent State that we were protesting in Trenton.

I didn't get angry because, as I said, I was already angry. I was angry because the fact that the induction order arrived at all meant that all of my attempts thus far had failed to extricate me from the clutches of the Army, if not the entire selective service system. And when I say all of my attempts, I mean I tried everything I could live with. I tried to fail the preinduction physical by drinking no fewer than three-fifths of Red Ripple wine and smoking two nickel bags of reefer every day for the month and a half leading up to the physical. I tried to flunk the unflunkable intelligence test, and I exaggerated my verbal disfluencies until my speech was less understandable than an Aztec warrior in the middle of Lowndes County, Mississippi. During the hearing test, I made motions of acknowledgment anytime I wanted to, with no regard to stimulus, and my skin was unhealthy-looking due to a subsistence diet of cannoli for over seven weeks.

When I reported to the preinduction physical in Newark, I was as nasty as I could stand to be and still be around myself. And, in the end, 1-A and number ninety-six in the draft lottery. I was as good as gone. Now I really had something to be angry about.

I calmed my anger long enough to appeal to my father for assistance. Pop had served in the Navy in World War II, but he had taken no position on the draft decision of any one of his four sons. I asked him to call our congressman and solicit his aid in identifying a solution to my dilemma. I was certain that the fact that Pop was one of the directors of the Trenton Neighborhood Family Health Center, a big federally funded project, along with the fact that I was also an executive in a federally funded Model Cities demonstration summer employment project, would at least compel Congressman Thompson to take a look at my case, especially since 1970 was an election year.

I wasn't aware that Pop was already known to the congressman until he picked up his phone and dialed the office without consulting his directory. After Pop passed the phone to me, the congressman assured me that I would hear from him or his office. And I did.

The call came the night before I was scheduled to report for induction, which I was most certainly not going to do. The congressman's call cancelled my plan to escape to Hamilton, Ontario, where I would become a steelworker or a construction worker, eventually steal someone else's identity, and return to the States. That sort of thing was done all of the time in New Jersey, for a wide variety of reasons. This was just one more.

"I'm sorry it took so long for me to get back to you. Are you still looking for a solution to your situation with the draft board?"

Was I ever.

"I've looked into your case in detail and I think I have come up with a partial solution, but it's one that can work out if you can come at it right. When you registered for the draft, you requested a conscientious objector's form, but you never filled it out. Why was that?"

"I didn't need the deferment, because I automatically qualified for a student deferment, because I was already enrolled at Hampton (Institute) when I turned eighteen. I lost it when I was asked not to return, and I fell a semester behind my entering class. That's when I was thrown into the lottery. Then they made me 1-A."

"So, are your convictions still the same?"

Even more than before.

"I have a partial solution for you, as I said. I got you a ninety-day postponement so you can complete and submit your application for a CO deferment. I'm sorry I can't do more, but I think you can take it from here. Good luck to you; let me know how it comes out, and be sure to tell your dad that I send my warmest regards."

One hundred and twenty days and a lot of reading and writing at Princeton University's Firestone Library later, I was the proud pos-

sessor of one of the only three or four conscientious-objector defer-
ments that Local 30 of the selective service system has ever given out,
excusing me from direct participation in the military end-of-the-war effort. The catch was that I had to perform twenty-four months of alter-
native service in the nation's health, safety, or interest. And as far as
the Local Board Number 30 was concerned, the best contribution I
could make to the national health, safety, or interest would be at
Greystone Park State Psychiatric Hospital, in the beautiful mountains
of North Jersey. And that is exactly where I found my now gloriously
angry self in February of 1971.

Greystone Park State Hospital was a twentieth-century plantation
nestled in the mountains of North Jersey, far from the casual observer.
The administrators were all Anglo-Saxons; the medical personnel were
international transplants who were delinquent with the cash or credit
necessary to equip and run a practice; the nursing personnel were
white women and homosexual men; and the nonprofessional workers
were products of unfortunate towns and families come north seeking a
better life.

And there were about twelve or thirteen conscientious objectors,
who were sent there in legal compliance and as punishment for having
had the audacity to exercise the constitutionally protected personal
choice of refusing to engage in organized military violence of any type.

Physically, the place was a bucolic setting to the naked eye. The air
was fresh and clean, the greenery plush and abundant, all manner of
wildlife filled the thick forests with rich soundtracks of their songs and
calls day and night, and the seasons of nature took turns showing off. It
looked for all the world like a college campus out of a Mickey Rooney–
Andy Hardy movie, except, of course, for the 2,000 mental patients and
2,000 workers who lived, ate, worked, played, and courted on this plantation. They were scattered among the seven employee residences, including a huge gender-segregated dormitory and several clusters of
three- and four-story houses that had been subdivided into efficiencies
without kitchen facilities. No fewer than 70 percent of the workers
stayed glued to the grounds except for a commercial foray or perhaps
an evening of entertainment and socializing in Morristown, Newark, or
the Oranges.

I didn't know all of this right away, my anger clouding my receptors
the way it was, but I would learn all of this in short order. I was assigned to work in the employees' cafeteria, where I was introduced as

"the college boy who was thrown out of a couple of schools before the draft got him, and now he's going to be here for twenty-four months to serve his time." Needless to say, the other workers were less than enthusiastic in greeting my arrival, an act on their part that justified my already very obvious anger and displeasure with my fate.

A commercial kitchen is an absolute environment. The food must be served at the appointed hour, in the appointed amount, in the agreed-upon number of servings, and featuring the agreed-upon dishes. Anything that hinders this process is forbidden in a commercial kitchen.

I didn't know that right away, although I would learn that, too, in short order. At the time of my introduction into the life of the Greystone Park kitchen, all I knew was that I was going to spend twenty-four months there and I was as angry as I could be. I had been angry before, but now I was at a whole new level of anger. I didn't make any attempt to be the least bit civil with anyone at any time.

When the head cook, Cotton, assigned my angry ass to operate the room-sized dishwasher, he could not have cared less that my face was a mask of rage. He was focused on getting the peach cobbler cut and dished up for the 1,000 diners due to arrive in less than an hour, as well as the 22 meatloaves that were cooking for the evening meals for the same 1,000 diners. James Jackson, the dishwasher I was replacing and who was being promoted to food service worker II, didn't care if I was angry either. He was headed to a better work station, and all he wanted to do was finish training me so he could put his wet dish towel down for the last time.

By the end of the second day on the job, I still hadn't deemed it necessary to get to know anyone beyond the absolute necessity of on-the-job communication. At the end of the shift, I returned to my room, which was about the size of those hotel rooms in the gangster movies that the killers always shoot their targets from. I showered that thick kitchen smell off of me, shaved my skull with shaving powder, thereby stinking up the men's shower room, then settled down to read from one of the 250 books that shared my room with me.

I could hear the voices of people from every corner of the American South who had come here as strangers, just like me, and who now comprised a bustling community contained in one giant building. The voice of the building supervisor, who we called Houseman, was unfamiliar to me at that time, but it filled the halls. Messages were shouted from pay phones down halls through closed doors, followed by curses that were never more than a word or two at the end of any discourse. I was certain that I had died and gone to Negro workers' hell.

I was drinking my sixth or seventh Ballantine ale of the evening and watching the broadcast of *The St. Valentine's Day Massacre*, starring Jason Robards as Al Capone. The ruckus in the hall was at its usual din when my door was suddenly subjected to a violent pummeling. I stuck my pistol in the back of my waistband and opened the door. My across-the-hall neighbor, a man who would become one of my best friends ever, stood there holding a six-pack of Budweiser beer and smoking a cigarette.

"Can I help you?" I challenged more than asked.

"Naw, nigger. You can't help me. But I can sure help you. What's your name, nigger? Where your ass from?"

I answered reluctantly. "Zeke Burnett. From Trenton. Why? Who the hell are you?"

"They call me Hollywood. Clifton Earl Brown Junior is my name, but almost none of these niggers here know that shit. Too much information fucks niggers up, you understand. Little Washington, North Carolina. That's where I'm from. They say you doing time here. For what?"

"I'm not doing time. I've got to be here twenty-four months, you know, instead of going to Vietnam."

"And why ain't that doing time, nigger? You can't leave, can you? You didn't decide to come here, did you? It sounds like time to me. . . . Shit, everybody here's doing time. Doing time is doing time no matter whose idea it is. You want a cold Anheuser?"

"Come on in, man. Let's not stand in the doorway and talk. I got some cold ones, too."

"Wait a minute," Hollywood said. "Let me get my man Mod Squad. He's right across the hall next door to my crib. HEY SQUAD! GET YOUR COUNTRY ASS OUT HERE, NIGGER!"

The door next to Hollywood's and almost directly across from mine opened, and Mod Squad emerged. It was immediately obvious why he was so named. He had a perfect Afro exactly like the big crown worn by Clarence Williams III in his role as Linc on the television series *Mod Squad*.

The three of us drank the rest of my ale and the rest of Hollywood's six-pack and smoked several joints. By the end of the evening, I was awash in shame. We got along like we had gone to the same high school. They were both high school graduates with no plans for college or post-high-school training. But they had both left their low-ceiling hometowns in North and South Carolina, respectively, and were now on their own and making a living. By living on the grounds they maximized their meager incomes, affording themselves the ability to send a few dollars home each month, proof positive they had gone North and made something out of themselves.

We all had early reporting times the next morning, so our socializing ended at a reasonable hour. For the first time since I arrived at Greystone Park, I didn't feel like I was from one planet and everybody else was from another.

The fact of my new acquaintances did nothing to temper my anger on the job, however. By the end of my third week on the job, I had become legendary for not liking one single thing about the job that now consumed eight and a half of my workday hours, ten out of every fourteen days, and would do so for yet another twenty-three months and one week. I didn't like emptying the teeming garbage. I didn't like scraping the garbage off of the plates. I loathed the cigarette butts that always seemed to be stumped out in the leftover mashed potatoes. I really hated cleaning the grease traps and putting out all of that rat and mouse poison. And not one thing my boss ever said made any sense to me, let alone complied with the standard rules of grammar.

I was miserable daily until I got off work and got back to the employees' residence, where Hollywood, Mod Squad, Houseman, Slim, Badfoot Tommy, Cotton, Lenny Crazy Horse, and I would drink, smoke, and talk our way through yet another evening. We even declined to join the young men and young ladies who went to the gymnasium on the grounds on Mondays and Fridays to play basketball, because by the time the game was starting, we were way too drunk to even dribble in a straight line.

The thing about a commercial kitchen that takes some getting used to is the fact that nobody keeps up with anyone else's job. Everyone is consumed by the necessity of completing only that part of the kitchen operation with which he or she has been entrusted. The only time anyone is concerned about the assignment of anyone else is when something has not been accomplished by the time it was supposed to be completed, therefore making it impossible for the next step or action to occur. That's when everyone in the kitchen knows exactly whose job it was that was not done, and then there is always hell to pay. So you learn over time which cooks have the capacity to forgive and which ones do not. You have to work with them all, of course, but it's important to be able to tell one from the other.

As far as I was concerned, Terry was the optimal cook for me to assist. Terry, who hailed from a West Virginia coal-mining family, was what we in the American Negro community used to call raw-boned and robust. He was cigar brown, about six feet, two inches tall, with a high Negro behind that he made no attempt to minimize. He smoked cigarettes and a pipe, but neither anywhere near his pots, and he was reputed to be the best sauce and desserts cook anyone had ever seen.

It was Terry who, when two raccoons returned with the Dumpster from the landfill, decided that a couple of roasted coons was just what the kitchen staff needed for a culinary change of pace. And, as surprised as I was, that roasted 'coon was more than a little all right.

The dishwashers had little to do between meals, so we were assigned to assist the cooks with their preparations. I always liked working with Terry, because he didn't give me any shit about the draft and my refusal to fight like the older cooks did, and he worked nonstop. He was always so busy, he never looked for me unless there was something else for me to do. And when he found me, he would give me my task and then keep on doing what he was doing. As far as I was concerned, this was about as good as it could get. I was still quite angry, but not at anything new.

I was assigned to Terry the afternoon that my uncle drove up to Greystone Park from Princeton to present me with two ringside tickets to the Temptations' show at the Latin Casino in South Jersey. It seemed that a couple of gangsters associated with the DeCalvacante Crime Family of Central Jersey were business associates of my uncle in some sort of auto deal, and they were rewarding him for helping them make some assets disappear before they could become part of a nasty, expensive divorce settlement. I had worked with my uncle in many of his enterprises over the years, and he knew that I was one of the two or three most dedicated Temptations fans in the entire world. My anger receded into the far reaches of my mind as I imagined myself at ringside, doing all of the Temptations' steps and singing all of the Temptations' songs. Hell, they would probably have to invite me up on the stage, so perfectly would I be doing their routines right along with them.

I introduced Terry to my uncle, who agreed to wait for Cotton to return so I could be excused officially. Terry assured me he could handle everything in my absence. When I made my request to Cotton, he denied it without even looking up from the menu he was always working on. I didn't move one step, anger flaring up within me like a jet after-burner. I repeated my request, and he finally looked my way.

"Look, I know you've got something better to do than to stand there and huff and puff all over my desk. Now, get the hell out of my face. I've got shit to do. So do you. And if you don't, I can find something for you."

I couldn't believe it. I was angrier than I had ever been at anything in my entire life. I could not believe that that son of a bitch sat right there and, without as much as giving my request a single thought, just turned me down. I complained loudly to everybody who would listen or who had the misfortune to be within earshot of me, a distance of roughly fifty yards.

"It's just slavery," I bellowed. "It's just because I am against the damn war. That's all. That black son of a bitch! It's just a lowdown way for that shit to get back at me. That black bastard knows he's wrong, too. He's just an Uncle Tom nigger who can't stand the sight of me, a righteous warrior for the People. He can't stand to be around me because when he is, his shit is always shown to be short."

I ranted, raved, and raged, making sure Cotton and everybody else could hear me. Through it all, Cotton never once reacted to one single thing I said. It was as if he was totally deaf. This drove me insane. I hurled metal utensils into the scrub sinks so hard they left dents in the stainless steel bottoms and sides. I bent huge cooking spoons and pounded whisks into useless meshes of steel. Finally, when none of those shenanigans worked, I went out back onto the loading dock and chain-smoked cigarettes, just like they always do in the movies when someone is trying to get someone else to give them a chance to vent their pure, unbridled rage.

Several of my coworkers came by during the completion of their rounds and inquired as to my state, counseling me to "cool it" or "let it go." I didn't have any idea how to do either. I didn't want to do either. As angry as I was, there was nothing to do but be angry. And that is all I wanted to do.

I was still standing on the loading dock, smoking cigarettes with steam coming from my hot head, when Terry came outside for a cigarette break of his own. He turned a milk crate on its side, placed a folded apron on it to soften the seat, and lowered himself easily onto the makeshift stool. He lit his cigarette and extended the pack to me. I accepted, even though I had a pack of my own in my shirt pocket.

We sat there smoking, Terry on his crate, and me on the fifty-five-gallon drum of dish detergent that had not been rolled inside to storage yet. After Terry smoked one whole cigarette and lit another, he looked in my direction and started chuckling loud enough for me to hear it. I looked directly at him—a silent demand for an explanation. He kept laughing.

"Zeke, man, you're a goddamn trip. You know that shit? A goddamn trip. I have been cooking for seventeen years and I swear to God you are the maddest dishwasher I have ever seen."

"Maybe that's the problem," I said. "I ain't nobody's damn dishwasher."

"Really? My mistake, man. What are you, since you ain't nobody's dishwasher? I want to get this shit right."

"I'm a Black man. I'm a free Black man. I'm a Black nationalist. I'm a warrior."

"What the hell are you doing here, then? There aren't any positions like that here. What are you here?"

"Here, I'm a dishwasher."

"That's what I said in the first place," Terry said, laughing again.

"Why are you fucking with me?" I asked with more hurt feelings than I really wanted to show. "What have I done to you?"

"First of all, I'm not fucking with you. *You're* fucking with you. You're going to bust a gut just because you don't know how to make your eight."

"What is that supposed to mean?"

He looked at me as he threw his cigarette into the open-topped Dumpster.

"Let me give you a piece of advice, young nigger, because you're going to die long before you live, at the rate you're going. I've seen people on the chain gang that aren't as mad as your ass."

"What advice, Terry?"

He said it like people recite their favorite Bible verse.

"'The only thing more certain than each day's date is the simple fact that each and every day you're going to have to get up off your ass, go out and make your eight.' And unless you're one of them goddamn Rockefellers, that's just what you've got to do. And right now you don't have any idea how to make your eight. I can tell. I've been watching you. You think the whole world's pissing on your head, and you don't think it's right. And you want everybody to know that you have been pissed on, and that you don't deserve to be here. That you are only going to be here for twenty-four months. Is that a fair description of your head right now?" He lit another cigarette while he let me go through a mental denial and then a mental concession.

"That's close," I lied.

"Close?"

"Okay. That's how I feel. Yeah. That's all true."

"You know what, though? Who gives a fuck? Who cares about any of that shit but you? Do you know anything about Mr. Earvin's crippled twins, or Mrs. Ledbetter's son who just came back from the same war you didn't go to? I mean who was just shipped back from that war, you dig?

"What I'm saying to you is this: nothing matters really except for the fact that a grown man has to take care of his business. There's certain things a grown man just has to do to be a grown man. You got to pay for your own shelter, your own food, your own liquor, your own cigarettes, your own women, your own everything. And it's nobody else's business and nobody else's problem. And unless you're rich or got a rich family somewhere, you're going to have to make your eight hours each day to be able to pay for all that shit. That's all there is to it. You have to make your own eight, and you have to figure out a way to make it not be hell for you and all of the people who work with your ass.

"How you think people feel when you start all that complaining shit? You've already been further in school than almost everybody else here, and when your ass finishes you're probably going to go right back and pick up where you left off. Not like the rest of these niggers here, and you don't hear anybody else bellyaching all damn day like you do. You know why? Because it doesn't matter and it damn sure doesn't help.

"Now, take me. I love to cook. I hate to take instructions about how to do my job. So I make it a game between me and old goddamn Cotton. I try to go through an entire day without him having to tell me shit. Then I try to go through a week, then a month. That way, whenever he does tell me something, the thing I'm looking at was how long it has been since the last one, and I'm not even listening to what he's talking about, because I'm going to do it my own way any damn way.

"Believe me, man, it'll make all the difference in the world when you can figure out a way that you can make your eight without it being eight hours of misery every day. You're gonna kill somebody, or somebody's gonna kill you. I know—just give it some thought. You're mad, but you're not a damn fool. And you're not the first mad nigger in the world. You could be the maddest, but you ain't the first by a long shot. Think about your dad. I bet he knows how to make his eight."

He was right. At the time, my father had an advanced degree from the University of Michigan School of Public Health, following his undergraduate degree from Shaw University, in Raleigh, North Carolina. I had known Pop to have as many as three jobs at the same time, one of which was chief of Urban and Rural Health Planning for the State of New Jersey Department of Health. I knew of the times when he worked weekends cleaning homes while the owners of the homes watched his half-hour public service broadcast discussing the new polio vaccine program. On the weekends he worked as a second cook and bottle washer, and for the life of me, I can't remember one time when he expressed the palpable rage at circumstances that I routinely spewed. He kept making his eight and making our lives better.

Mom, too. Armed with a college degree and ten years of teaching experience, she worked the cafeteria line at Armstrong Cork Company while concealing her education for fear of not being hired. After the necessity of that job was past, Mom returned to her chosen work as a social worker without ever uttering any complaints about the unworthiness of her interim employment. She went about her business, made her eight, and made our lives better.

Terry finished smoking his third cigarette, stood slowly from his milk-crate stool, and stretched himself to his full six-foot-two-inch height. He could see that I was as deep in thought as I was surprised by what he had just laid on me. He patted me on the shoulder as he turned to go back inside.

"Think about what I told you, now. I'm just trying to give you another way to come at the thing, is all. Just take some time and think it out. You're almost as smart as you are mad. So you can figure it out if you really figure on it a while. Just be open to the people who want to be your friends. Man, you'll be surprised when you see exactly what is and what ain't important."

That evening, I didn't go out with Hollywood, Mod Squad, and the rest of our regular drinking crew. Instead, I stayed in my unlit room and thought about the things Terry had told me that afternoon on the loading dock. I thought about how my obsession with my feelings of mistreatment represented the very height of privileged Negritudinous self-indulgence. I listened to the muffled movements in the hallway with focused curiosity. I realized that for every voice I now had a face to go with it. For every face I now knew a job title, a home state, a style of dress, a favorite song, or a brand of cigarette. I knew they were getting ready to go back to work the next time their shifts began, and I knew they were all looking forward to living a better life the next day than they were living right then, and they were hard at work on that task.

My circle of friends and acquaintances expanded geometrically as soon as I stopped bellyaching and started learning how to make my eight. I began playing basketball on Mondays and Fridays and was soon invited to join the fast-pitch and slow-pitch softball teams as well. One of my softball teammates recruited me for his semiprofessional football team based in Boonton, and I bought a 1956 Buick Special as my official staff car. I soon even had a nickname, Magilla, because of the pith helmet I wore when I drove around the grounds in my fifteen-year-old Buick, along with a hard-earned reputation for being the fastest and cleanest dishwasher anyone had ever seen.

The other kitchen workers, many of whom had given me a wide berth, even began to let me in on the pilferage of choice foodstuffs that stretched so many of the meager paychecks at the end of each pay period.

I left that accidental meeting on the loading dock in firm possession of a major lesson that has shaped my adult life from that point until now. I know that, come what may, there is one thing I am going to have to do each and every day. And each and every day I am prepared to do just that. I am prepared to make my eight. Each day I gladly get up off my ass, go out, and make my eight. And in the process I have made my life a better life.

Eventually, Cotton and I became almost friends, and I now count my time at Greystone Park as one of the most influential periods of my formative adult years. Most important, I learned how to make my eight each and every day. It took a little longer, but I was also eventually able to purge myself of that crippling random anger and, in the process, eliminate the expressions of pointless, random rage that have no purpose and are so destructive to human interaction, even on those occasions when anger is justified.

Perhaps of equal significance, I have lived from then until now with the knowledge and shame of my unjustified feelings of superiority and privilege that were shattered on a daily basis by the very people on whose behalf I was supposed to be fighting my righteous crusade, when I was mightily fighting them in me with every fiber of my own misguided being.

And I always, always make my eight.

Always.

In the Time Before the Men Came: The Past as Prologue

Pearl Cleage

"A woman without her sisters is like a bird without wings."
—African American

I n the time before the men came, we could do everything. We were
fearless, brave, trustworthy, clean, mentally awake, and morally
straight.

In the time before the men came, back when we could still fly and
have babies by the power of Positive Groupthink, we were Amazon
women. We planned and built cities. We wrote great books and thought
new thoughts and argued about ideas and aesthetics until the sun set
and the moon rose and bathed us all in silver.

In the time before the men came, we were fearless, counting among
our number warriors, strategists, generals, and magicians who could
read the tide for signs. We plotted with impunity and precision and defended our borders with a shining combination of physical strength,
mental superiority, and absolute courage. We had integrity, scorning
the petty and the vicious, avoiding the obvious, sidestepping the curse
of sloppy thinking and obsessive, possessive love that shrinks and
strains and trains the ear for bickering and mediocrity as if they were
the music of the spheres. We knew how to call a spade a spade.

In the time before the men came, we were bold. Explorers and wan-
derers, dreamers and schemers, we lived in harmony with each other
and in constant search for the truth of this world and the next one. We
were responsible, caring for our own and each other with a bone-deep
understanding of what it really means to be a part of a whole, a sister
among your sisters.

In the time before the men came, we were loving, treating each other and those we trusted with a sensuality and sweetness unmatched before or since.

In the time before the men came, we could still fly. Do you remember that shit? Flying? I mean, flying as in step-to-the-edge-of-the mountain, bare your breasts to the North wind, rub each moon-bathed nipple three times counterclockwise, and reach out far enough and with confidence enough that from under each breast would emerge gigantic black wings with smooth blue-black feathers and a span of six feet on either side. And they spread out from underneath so that we didn't fly with that difficult, upper-body-strength-dependent motion so beloved of Icarus and the boys. We just kind of laid out on our wings and soared. The only motion necessary was a kind of rippling thing that looked the way a fish looks when it isn't in a hurry and the water is the perfect, reptilian, subnormal degree of coolness.

And we could fly for hours without even breathing hard. In fact, we developed an entire art form based on flying. Sort of like water ballet with twelve-foot wings and a touch of bop to it. That and the art of bald-head painting were both lost after the men came. Two art forms that just didn't survive the Loss of Concentration . . .

Mythology aside, I personally was quite sorry to see bald-head painting go the way of moon worshipers and winged ballet. The intricate designs and decorations, which emerged once the sisters agreed that hair was too distracting and all shaved their heads regularly, were breathtaking, and since the bald-head paintings were temporary, disappearing at the first serious bath or sudden rainstorm, they were all the more precious.

And even though the real radicals said they didn't see the difference between spending six hours working on cornrows and six hours working on bald-head painting, most sisters were so taken with the beauty and the sensuality of the whole idea from start to finish that the movement to outlaw it quickly died and was never raised again.

But that was in the time before the men came.

See, the problem wasn't so much in their coming, but in what their coming meant to us as Amazon women. Our magic was completely dependent on the strength of our collective concentration. Our ability to sit within the magic circle, join hands, and collectively focus our minds on one thing and then achieve it. But it took the complete concentration of the entire group, and so we worked hard to maintain that concentration, that focus, that power, which is one of the reasons why their lives—why our lives—were so peaceful.

Superfluous activity is distracting. It weakens you.

So they met twice a day in the completeness of their circle, and they thought about each other, and they thought about themselves, and they thought about their strength and their wisdom and their loving kindness, and they thought about their power. And then they would focus intently on the pertinent question, which on any particular day might be a problem of the mind or of the heart. Reinforcement of their gifts and powers. Defense. Healing. Flying. Birth. Birth is a good example of how it worked.

In the time before the men came, we had our babies without them. What we would do when an Amazon expressed a desire to have a child, was gather in the sacred circle, in the birth configuration, say the charms for fertility and conception, and then concentrate really hard. And if the time was right and the concentration was total, a girl child would begin to grow inside her mother. Only girl children could be conjured in this way. It was, in any case, an all-female society, so the question of male children was pretty much moot.

But if the time was not right, or if the sister was not really ready, or if someone was not concentrating really hard, it didn't work and the girl baby was not conceived. In this way, the society had a kind of extrasensory method of birth control, and the life of the group, its future, was dependent on the ability of those already on the scene to concentrate and take themselves seriously. Sisterhood was, in a very real sense, survival.

It was the same with flying. It only worked as a collective vision. If they all believed they could fly, they all could fly. But if one hesitated before stepping off into the freedom of, into the beauty of, the void, they were all in danger of the crash. It was necessary that close attention be paid at a serious life-and-death level, 24-7-365. And it was, but that was in the time before the men came.

And then one day, a young sister was hurrying back to join the midday sacred circle, and she saw a man sitting outside the gates of the Amazon city. Now, this was no big thing. Men lived in gender-integrated towns and villages all around the Amazons, and they often had male lovers, although usually not for long. Most men grew uncomfortable trying to love a free woman over the long haul.

Amazon women didn't put much energy into the discomfort of their men friends. Discomfort was distracting. When it got to be a real problem, they simply cut their lovers loose. Their society recognized no intrinsic value in heterosexual unions and held no censure for any kind of sexual coupling that took place between consenting adults. Men, however, were not allowed to sleep within the gates of the Amazon city. Even on conjugal visits, dreaming women were considered too vulnerable to the power of the men, and so at first moon, they were escorted outside the gates and wished good evening.

But somehow, this man seemed different from the others she had known. It was almost as if he had a glow around his head or something. And he was holding all the things you like to see a man holding, depending on your personal preferences, style of courting, and private fantasies. It could have been a dozen red roses. It could have been a first edition of Langston Hughes. It could have been a ripe watermelon or a perfect mango. It could have been a love poem. It could have been new music. It could have been his heart.

The only thing it could not have been are in the category of Mercedes-Benzes and Rolex watches and secure retirement plans. It has to be something that touches your soul, like it touched her soul, like it always touches mine. The real stuff. The scary stuff. The love-to-the-grave-and-beyond stuff. That's the stuff he was holding when she saw him, and it startled her, and she looked into his eyes, and he smiled and touched her cheek and spoke to her in a rich, chocolate brown voice full of love and sex and responsible fatherhood, and he said, "I think you are so fine and I want to make love to you so why don't you stop doing whatever it is you're doing and come sit down here and let me rub your head and you can listen to me talk about myself for awhile and maybe you could tell me some things I hadn't thought of on my own and maybe these things would bring peace and health and prosperity to my life, and you would feel good too, when I got around to it, and hey, I think I love you!"

And she was amazed to feel her knees get weak and her cheek flush crimson, and, alas, she trembled and she wanted to touch him and have him touch her, and she checked her watch and said to herself, "The meeting isn't for fifteen minutes yet. It won't hurt to stop for just a second and see what this brother is into. Besides, I can't see myself being swayed by a self-centered rap like that, I don't care what he's holding."

And she smiled and said, "That is the lamest rap I've heard in ages. We got cities to build, and poems to write, and gold mines to discover, and babies to create, and passion to bring into full flower. Why should I want to spend my every waking hour looking at you?"

And he said, "I don't know. Because I want you to?"

And she wanted to say, "Nigga, pleez!" but she couldn't speak. She found herself paralyzed by the glow around him. She watched herself reaching up, turning her face to his, opening her lips and her arms and her softness to him, and she was distracted and late and AWOL for no good reason that I can think of; can you? And her sisters sat quietly in the circle waiting for her, couldn't start without her, powerless without her, looking at the space her presence was supposed to fill, but she didn't come and she didn't come and she didn't come, but somewhere just outside the gates of the Amazon city, she arched her back and offered her neck and came for him/to him/with him, and her sister who was ready to begin her baby cried out and turned away, and when they tried to fly away to find and save their sister, they stumbled and jumped about like crippled birds—too old or too lame or too silly to take off—and it was over, broken, finished, finito, incognito. It was once burned, twice shy and too little, too late, and they staggered, powerless and broken, to the gates of the city and threw them open and saw their sister asleep and smiling, curled up on the chest of this glowing man and already forgetting the wonder of her wings, the miracle of her magic, the power of her armies.

And the man smiled when he saw them running toward their fallen sister, and tightened his arms around her, and she purred in her sleep like a cream-fed cat, and that was when the men came.

And the Amazons became their slaves.

And had their babies.

And cooked their dinners.

And listened to their stories.

And dreamed their dreams.

And darned their fucking socks.

And our slavery, and our powerlessness, and our fear, and our longing for the campfires where we once held hands and sang with our sisters, drove us to acts of madness and self-destruction and amnesia until we arrive at the first quarter of the twenty-first century, weakened by oppression and self-hate, degraded and distracted by all the things that don't have anything to do with being a woman. An Amazon woman.

Until we arrive at the first quarter of the twenty-first century, straining to hear the voice of the goddess and keening in the darkness for the clarity, the serenity, the strength, and the sisterhood of the time before/the time before/the time before the men came.

Wham, Bam, Thank You, Ma'am (What That Old Saying Truly Means)

Evelyn Coleman

"When God sends a woman." —African American

If you come with apology for who you are on your breath like cheap wine, don't stop here. This here ain't no story for you whining women who think God's gift to mankind come here with three legs, one front and center, as a no-good-excuse-for-a-man. Or, for you men who think women sit on pedestals and should never be knocked off. And it sho' ain't no story for them folks thinking women been cursed by God and ain't got nothing better to do than bear children. Even though I swears, this here story be 'bout my own mama.

Read no further if you suspect a knight could battle harder for you than you could fight for your own self, when he the very one done started it. Naw. This story ain't for you.

'Cause this story I'm about to tell is way before its time, about a woman sweet as honeysuckle in summer, warm as buns in an oven on a Sunday afternoon, and cold as the river frozen in wintertime—but only when she need to be.

This story is about what happens when God sends a woman.

From the moment she pops out her mama with her fists balled up ready for what the world got to offer and her mouth open wide breathing in opportunity, she swore she was gone live her a holy life.

She was never the one to decide whether the whipping needed to go to a man or a woman, colored or white, just whoever was pulling a bluff. She wore men's shirts and a woman's heart, close, close to the backbone and her chest. Rita Mae Storm was all woman, plus the sum of the wishes of her people, and the direction of Almighty God. She was a colored woman and she wasn't apologizing for God giving her the spring in her step and the spit-black shine of her skin. She was the woman God sent for, and those who didn't like it could just . . . well, it ain't right for a holy woman to speak that kind of talk.

From the day Bull Fuller seen her climbing up into a tree when they was less than the weight of ten chickens, he knew she was going to be his wife someday. That be my daddy now. By the time they were thirteen, she'd told him that she'd marry him—but only when she was good and ready, which turned out to be twenty more years in the making. Until that time, though, she looked every man she met straight in the eye and gambled that she was here to stay.

And she was right. God had sent her wrapped in the blackness of night to warn those who would transgress against him. So the first man ended up as quiet as the noise of a breeze on a hot North Carolina night. And there would be many men and women after him, all going in different ways but leaving just the same. Leastways, until her wedding/retirement day.

Her last great nemesis before her wedding/retirement day come to town on a wagon. This was way before the time of the two World Wars, but a time after the Civil War—that son-against-son war that done come and pass, bringing change so slow molasses speed on by it. But he come just the same, dust flying, his boots sinking deep in the earth with his steps, treading holy hell on every woman he met. Stopping off at her Hickory, North Carolina, sawmill town, where pulpwood liable to come out of somebody's nose instead of snot. And ain't a soul in town breathe a word after he knocked out Bertha Simms's teeth, excepting to say, "Howdy, Mr. John Bonner."

He set up in church big as day, front row, waiting for to make a speech on that same Sunday, when he done almost beat Liddy Johnson to death the night before in her own bed. When her brothers come to see 'bout her, she so weak with pain and wonder, all she scratch on the bedpost is two words: *Lord help.*

Things done in the dark by evil men and women, they fear not the light, because they think it's gone be dark like their hearts forever. Ain't nothing wrong with hoping you gone get away with something. It just ain't always gone happen, that's all.

Mr. Bonner waited patiently until announcement time in the church. He'd done been seated in a guest place of privilege, his chicken-plucked white-looking skin making contrast in a sea of multicolored Negroes. He finally stood up, towering over the heads of those despised by him, and spoke in a clear, elegant voice, in a county where pig-calling was a regular contest.

"Dear friends, I have a wonderful proposition for you. Land. I come all this way to tell you about a new government program. You can get fifty acres of land for almost nothing, right here on the outskirts of this here county. Owned by your own government. That's a heap more than they done promised us. Ha, ha," he chuckled. "And, if you make your down payments before the end of the month, Lord, I'll even throw in a mule. Hee, hee."

Great gasping Lords-of-astonishments flew through the air like angels. Ain't nobody slowed down to think why the government send this-here man to represent. Everybody just grinning and figuring on how they going to count up them pennies to come up with the ten-dollar deposit they gonna need to get their hands on a parcel of land they should have already owned. Rightly so it was theirs for all the free labor they done, 'cept maybe for the part them Indians had before the white man done stole it from them.

The preacher, Reverend Shiloh Abraham Walker, was more excited than anybody else in the whole church. He was already planning where his pot of gold was coming from as he spied the offering plate passing along from person to person.

Ain't nobody even noticed Sister Storm, all the way in the back, hunched down in an old man's overcoat humming *Rock of ages cleft for me. Let me hide myself in thee*. Nobody, not even the Reverend Walker, even cared, because folks was getting ready to strike it rich, praise the Lord!

So what you think happen when all them days pass like waterfalls and the people gather up their money and drop it by the Seed and Feed Hotel for Mr. Bonner to take back and put down on their land? Seven days it take the Lord to make the world, and it take Mr. Bonner less than six minutes to convince a whole town of colored folks to part with money that was bled straight out from their pricked fingers and worn-down souls.

Bonner laid back and laughed when he counted out all his money on the chenille bedspread of egg white and sky blue that made the money appear quiet and soft—even the change—as he plopped it down. He gathered it all up, paper and coin, and pushed it down in his already crammed-with-money satchel. This is his fifth town this year. He chuckles softly, so only the mouse peeping out from the corner hears; then he packs up. He puts on his boots. He's on his way out of town. He done got the stable boy to get his horse ready. The family-riding wagon he done already sold. He's heading farther south. Mississippi got a lot of churches—lots of good colored folk.

"Hey sir, can I sees you?" Bonner hears the soft, lusting voice calling to him as he nears the stable.

He tenses his fist, balling it up and releasing it. Maybe he can have some fun before he leaves. He squints into the darkness, making out a pretty woman who looks like a feast of brown tobacco staring at him. Her eyes dark as wells with the moonlight glinting from the corners.

"What can I do for you tonight, ma'am?"

"I'se been watching you, and I was hoping you might spend a visit with me. Not long, just enough to have a sip of tea. If'n you will? I make the sweetest cornpone this side of the Mississippi."

Mr. Bonner was not a bright man, or he'd have wondered how the tall woman wearing the low-cut laced-up blouse, with breasts full and ripe as a nursing mother, just happened to name the very place he was headed.

He rubbed his stubby palms together. "Where you live, miss?"

"Over yonder, in that old shed. It ain't far. See down there," she pointed so he could see the shack at the edge of the colored section. "I done been watching you and I got a might powerful *crush* for you, Mr. Bonner."

"My, my. You don't say?" he said, following behind her, feeling a surge of power because every colored woman in town was honoring his name. The man at the stable could wait. Dang if he wasn't a lucky dog! She was a young thing, too. Bonner felt the bulge inching like a fat earthworm in his pants as he got close enough to smell the jasmine wavering off her body with each flowering step she made. He speeded up so's not to lose the scent, and to see if he couldn't get a feel of her bottom by the time they reached her place.

She opened the door. "Come on in, Mr. Bonner. I got somethin' real special for ya."

He sucked in a breath. The place was dark excepting a glowing from the center of the room. Darkness out of his control made him pull on his shirt collar. He was an educated man. Been to school to the tenth grade, up north. His eyes was slow to adjust to the light from the one candle. "Do you have an oil lamp? I can't see," he said, figuring at the same moment, if he reached out would he be grabbing her breast?

Then he sensed her, like a blind man who knows he has come to a wall. She was there, close, her breath warming his skin like the touch of fingers. He grabbed for her softness, wanting to squeeze her so bad, his breath came out short.

Nothing. Air. She had moved away, quickly. He sniffed, a dog searching for food. "You want to play, do you?" He unbuckled his pants with both hands. He'd whip her good for making him stand in this dark stinking hole of a house without answering. "Where you at, girl?"

Whop! The sound, loud and fierce, was inside his own head. He had never been hit before, leastways, not upside the head. He went down on one knee. Felt the heat of blood gushing down his face, a river of pain. He dropped the belt. Flashes of lightning before his eyes that be squeezed shut.

"Dear Lord," she said, "Please give me strength, O God!"

Bonner's ears soaked in the sound of her praying.

Whop! He was on the floor now, his face down on the straw. Straw?

She was still prayerful when she spoke again: "You ain't gone never hit another woman again. Ya hear?" *Whop!*

He remembered his mama whipping him for doing wrong when he was a boy. It ain't feel this bad, though, or maybe he would'a never done another wrong again.

A second entreaty to God: "You ain't gonna steal no more money from your own kind. You hear?" *Wham! Bam!*

How did she know he won't no *white man*? Then his thought: he'd hit his mother once, too, but not this hard, though. Lord knows he would never hit another woman again!

"And, you ain't gonna make it to Mississippi. You hear?"

His last rites resounded in his ear like slow ripples of water at night.

She leaned close over his body and heard the voice from on high whisper gently in her inner ear, "Wham. Bam. Thank you, Ma'am."

She closed the door, slinging the heavy baggage over her back like it was a sack of air. Rita Mae Storm whispered, "Yes Lord, I am your faithful servant. You welcome, Jesus."

"*Psst* . . . Sister Storm," Bertha called.

"You wanting me?" Rita Mae said, turning around slowly.

"Did you hear 'bout what happened? Lord, somebody done beat that Mr. Bonner to death in that old shed yonder at the bottom. Quiet as it's kept, he won't no nice man," Bertha said, the open space where her teeth had been bearing witness.

"The reverend said that since Mr. Bonner's death he done uncovered that he been cheating other churches. The reverend said somebody from one of them places more'n likely caught up with him. Whoever it was, they done returned all our money back to the church. And somebody musta' done figured out Mr. Bonner won't no *white man*, 'cause otherwise the law would'a come round talkin' 'bout somebody swinging. The reverend said the Lord ain't gonna let man get away with hurting his own people no more, no matter who it is. The Lord gone put a stop to it."

"You tell the reverend he sho' know what he talking about," Rita Mae said, then watched Bertha hobble away.

Rita Mae Storm walked home making footprints in the earth with every step she took. "Lord, I am your faithful servant," she said aloud. "Sho', you right. Thank you, Jesus."

Now, me, I ain't picked up in the footsteps of my mama yet. But I'd think twice if I was you when trying to trick somebody out of what they got . . . 'cause I done vowed to live a holy life myself and be the Lord's faithful servant. My mama done taught me what that old saying "Wham, Bam, Thank you, Ma'am" truly means. It's the Lord thanking us holy women for standing up for ourselves and for all our folks, men and women alike. Sure, you right. So, live right, ya hear? And don't make me have to say, "You welcome, Jesus," on your behind.

My Wrong Is Right

Tracy Scott DesVignes

"The mouth of an elderly man is without teeth, but never with-out words of wisdom." —African, Swahili

Tuesday morning, 10:12 A.M.

"Good morning, Chief. How are you today? The sun is shining and the world is a wonderful place to live . . . wouldn't you say so?"

"Mo'nin', Misr' B-b-b-b-black."

"Chief, I don't mind you hanging around the store, but your green jacket is starting to smell like sour milk. You need to go down to the Salvation Army and find yourself another jacket—or take a bath once in a while, at least. You should fix yourself up and try getting a job. Do something productive with yourself. Stop looking like the rest of these niggahs around here."

Look at ol' Mr. Black talkin' to Chief—or listenin' to himself talk to Chief. Every mornin' he opens his store in the Valley—late as usual. I'm Mr. Givey, and I been livin' in Bedford Valley for over forty-two years. I opened my newsstand after I got outta the Army. I been runnin' it for twenty-five years. I have to say, the military ain't the best place for a black man, but it damn sho' beat runnin' the streets and hus-tlin' like these young boys do nowadays. Shoot, if ya gonna carry a gun to kill somebody, then do it on the government's dime. But these young fools don't know no better, or at least they try to act like they don't know no better. But who's to say what's right or wrong? How a person gets by is up to them. Anyway, here comes Mr. Black now.

"Good morning, Mr. Givey. How are you?"

"Doin' fine, Mr. Black. What about—"

"Well, I gotta go. Have a good day, Mr. Givey."

* * *

Me and Mr. Black never have no decent conversation. When we do talk, it's short and brief—hi-and-bye kinda' thang. If you ask me, I think Mr. Black don't like talkin' when he ain't the only one speakin'. But that's because he spends most of his time judgin' and hatin' the folk 'round here. He don't never have time to talk to the folk, or try to get to know them past what he sees. It'll catch up wit' him one day, 'cause he gonna see folk 'round here ain't as dumb and lazy as he think. Every now and then I get a good laugh out of watchin' him "give back to the community," which is the only time he really speaks to me. But that's all right. I'll jus' continue to watch Mr. Black preach to Chief. One day he'll find out which one of them is the wise one. Now, in a few minutes I'm gonna see the "troops" run from the back wit' they arms full of stuff as Mr. Black opens the front door. I still can't understand how come he can't figure out what's going on. Sometimes, though, I think he deserves it. Other times I think it's plain wrong.

10:44 A.M.

"Well, Chief, I'm opening up, so make sure you don't block the entrance. In three years I'll be able to sell this store and run my store on the Hilltop until I retire. I can't wait, because coming down here ruins my day. Oh, my God! They got in again!"

"911, this is Mr. Bryant Percy Black. I need to report a break-in! I'm at 350 Thurgood Marshall Avenue, down in the Valley, at the Good Valley grocery store!"

"Sir, repeat your address."

"I'm at the Good Valley grocery store at 350 Thurgood Marshall Avenue!"

"Sir, slow down and say that again."

"350 Thurgood Marshall Avenue . . . HURRY!"

"Okay. I'll dispatch a car to your location."

"I'm so sick of this! Chief! Did you see anything unusual last night or this morning? Did you hear anybody in my store last night? Get away from the door! The police will be here any minute."

"Mr. Givey! Mr. Givey!"

Uh-huh. Here comes Mr. Black, shoutin' my name. He musta' got robbed again.

"Mr. Givey. They broke in again. Did you see anyone around here this morning?"

"No, Mr. Black, and I got here at seven. Can I help you with—"

"No. I gotta go wait for the police."

"Mista', you got a dollar?"

"No! Get the hell away from my store, you damned bum!"

Uh-oh. Here comes Switch, the captain of the troops. Switch is a good guy. He comes from a good family. I've known him for eighteen years. He used to run newspapers to some of the elderly folk in the Valley for me when he was twelve. But his eyes got big when he saw how much money he could make runnin' drugs for these bastard dealers 'round here. He's like a lot of people in the Valley, he got caught up in doin' wrong and jus' lost hope in himself.

"Mornin', Mr. Givey. You want somethin' to eat?"

"Switch, did you get that stuff from yo' *usual* place?"

"Sho' nuff!"

"Y'all gonna get caught one day."

"No, we ain't. Ol' Black think we too stupid."

"That don't matter. Y'all jus' make things worse for folk 'round here when you mess wit' the man. Anyway, ain't you on parole?"

"Yeah, but that's for messin' wit' car alarms. Shoot, a brotha' gotta eat. Come on, Mr. Givey. Black can afford it. Besides, we be helpin' folk out 'round here, not just ourselves."

"Whatever you say, Switch."

"I gotta go, Mr. Givey."

Well, it looks like Mr. Black done "gave back to the community" again. And as always, he done gave to the same folk. It's a shame we gotta fight one another. Mr. Black fightin' the folk 'round here wit' his attitude, and them "give to the poor, steal from the rich" fools fightin' Mr. Black. But it's hard to blame them, though. A lot of folk got they nose pressed to the glass, pointin' to what they want but never able to get it. Some may call it lazy, but I call it frustratin'.

Good Valley Grocery Store, 11:58 A.M.

"Are you Mr. Bryant Percy Black?"

"Yes I am, officers. Please come in. I checked the back door, and it looks like they came in through the storage room again. I can't understand why this expensive security system didn't go off. The switch was still in the *On* mode when I came in. This is the fourth time this has happened. I purchased the security system after the second break-in and—"

"Sir, what time did you open up and notice that items had been taken?"

"I got here around ten this morning. I usually come in around ... um ... six or so, but today I had to come in a little late. My kids ... they were running late for school. ... You know how that can be."

"Right. Did they steal any cash, weapons ... ?"

"No, no. I keep all the money in a safe behind the cash register, and the only weapon I have is locked in a drawer in the front office."

"Well, it doesn't look like the back door was damaged. Are you sure this is how they got in?"

"I'm positive! The front door was locked when I came in, and the alarm went off when I opened the door. I had to punch in my security code, so I assume it was on."

"Mr. Black, we'll go ahead and file this report. Someone should be in touch with you this week. Since no one was hurt and no cash or weapons were taken, there's not much else we can do. It looks like all they took was food. You should count yourself lucky."

I guess the cops gonna rip up that report like they do the rest. Ain't nothin' like watchin' Mr. Black make a fuss over those break-ins. I don't know why he gets all huffed and puffed up, since most of the stuff he sells in that store is either day-ol', week-ol', or expired. He been doin' that ever since he opened that sto'. But he don't do that wit' his Hilltop sto'. His Hilltop sto' is one of them fancy grocery sto's that smells like those expensive coffees, and the checkout lanes are nice and wide and the cashiers don't look at ya' like they wanna beat ya down 'cause you came to they register. He got fresh flowers outside, a gourmet food section, a bakery, and a huge produce section where you can't find one rotten piece of fruit. Yeah, Hilltop is the area people call the land of the IPO buppies. But I call it the land of the first-generation-out-of-the-projects niggahs. It's the perfect place for Mr. Black to live. Like Mr. Black, a lot of them people up there give to the *right* black organizations, and their kids are members of "Bob and Buffy." You know, that organization where bourgie black folk try to make sure they kids only hang with other bourgie-black-folk kids. But not a one of them would ever step foot down here in the Valley or let their kids come down here—knowingly, anyway.

Today must be my lucky day. Ol' Black comin' to talk again . . . ha, ha, ha.

"Mr. Givey, has your stand ever been broken into?"

"No."

"What type of security system do you have?"

"None, because I rely on the people in this neighborhood for my security. I been livin' here so long that most of them know me and I know them. Shoot, I remember when half them young boys out there couldn't walk or ride a bike straight and—"

"Yeah, well, I'm not doing anything any differently than you. I open every day—a little late, but that's because most people around here don't have jobs anyway, and the ones who do don't work a regular nine-to-five."

"Uh-huh."

"I keep the store stocked with plenty of beer and liquor, the kind *they* like around here—you know, Old E, Bull, Mad Dog 20/20. And I keep the cigarette racks full."

"Uh-huh."

"Mr. Givey, people in the Valley don't want much. Look at how nasty the streets are and how poorly the people carry themselves. That's why I don't worry about fixing up this store down here too much. Heck, why should my store look like it's worth more than this whole neighborhood? There's no need to waste money on the overhead. Anyway, let me go clean this place up. I'm not restocking anything that was stolen, because them niggahs will probably come back and do the same thing. Most of the food from my Hilltop store should be ready to ship down here in another week, anyway, and I'll make the money back by raising the price on the cigarettes and beer. Have a good day, Mr. Givey."

"Yeah, you too, Mr. Black."

Wednesday morning, 9:38 A.M.

"Good morning, Chief. What are you taking out of your mouth?"

"M-m-m-m! Nuthin'. Hey, hey, hey!"

"Chief, I see you're still wearing that smelly green jacket. You ever consider getting a job and doing something with yourself? I tell you, when I was younger I made it up in my mind that I wasn't going to end up like my father. He was a *worthless* something. He didn't start out like that, but he ended up that way. He was in the Army and went to fight in the Korean War in 1951. My mother was proud of him for going, although she knew she might never see him again—*I* wish we hadn't. When he got out of the war he wasn't the same. He used to come home late and drunk and would fight my mother. It was like he was mad at us for letting him go to the war. But it wasn't us he was mad at—it was the 'System.'

According to my dad, this country and the 'System' that runs it had done him and the other Black men who served in the war a disservice by not preparing them for life after the Army. He said they put them on the front line during the war but put them at the back of the employment line when they came home. I never gave into that thinking, however, because it always seemed like an excuse for my dad not to work and support his family. That's why I can't stand to see these niggahs around here begging and full of excuses about the 'System.' I say, if you serve your country and you do what's right in society, you'll be treated right. But if you sit around and beg for handouts all your life, you'll end up with nothing."

"M-m-m-m . . . sum' time, Misr' B-b-b-bl-black—"

"Chief, you ever *had* a job? What did you do when you were my age? How old are you anyway?"

"Sev-en-tee-tee-nine. M-m-m-m . . . I was in da—"

"Oh, forget it. I don't have time to listen to you mumble today. I'm telling you, if you would get some teeth in your mouth I *might* be able to understand you better."

Newsstand, 9:43 A.M.

"Whas' up, Mr. Givey?"

"Switch, when y'all gonna leave Mr. Black alone?"

"Why? He can afford it. Besides, he got better stuff in his store than the shelter got."

"Man, you gonna electrocute yo'self one day messin' wit' dem wires. And when you do, don't come hollerin' over here to my newsstand, 'cause I ain't helpin' ya."

"Come on, Givey—"

"Boy! It's Mr. Givey. . . . Don't play wit' me!"

"Sorry."

"And tell Chief Mr. Black is right—that jacket *stinks!* I can smell him down here on my corner."

"Mr. Givey, you know that's what he gotta' do so Ol' Black go along. See, Black *think* he know more than Chief 'cause he see him sittin' in front of his store all the time mumblin' to him 'cause he ain't got his teeth in his mouth. Funny thing is, Black's teeth always in his mouth, but he's the fool. Look, Mr. Black ain't hurtin' for nothin'. Most of his money come from the store down here anyway, cause he charge so much. Whoever heard of chargin' somebody $10.69 for a quart of Enfamil or chargin' $5.28 for a gallon of milk that's gonna expire in two or three days? By that time, the milk should be marked down!"

"Well, if y'all would stop stealin' from the man, he might lower his prices. Every time y'all go and take somethin' all he do is tack the price on to somethin' everybody wants."

"Mr. Givey, you know you like watchin' him run down here all pent up and mad after he done 'gave back to the community.'"

"Yeah, it's a trip watchin' him run down here in that plaid shirt and those tight pants, callin' my name . . . Mr. Givey! Mr. Givey!—'cause he done got robbed again . . . ha, ha, ha. But Chief could pull back on that smell a little bit. I swear he smell like chitlins."

"Yeah, the smell can get to you. See ya later, Mr. Givey."

"All right, Switch."

Thursday morning, 6:05 A.M.

"Switch, you and the rest of the troops need to hurry up. You know the MPs drive around at 0620 and you guys only have two bags of rations. Mr. Owens still needs bread, Mrs. Williams needs orange juice, Ms. Nelson needs cranberry juice, and Teresa needs Enfamil for the twins. And don't forget Mr. Buttner's Preparation H."

"Yo' Switch!"

"Shhhhhhh! Quentin, I'm tired of tellin' you, you gotta lower yo' voice, man. You ain't outside."

"Sorry. Why Chief always talkin' like he in the military? And what's an MP?"

" 'Cause, he still think he's a chief of staff in the Army. Don't pay it no attention, though; he know what he's doin'. And MP stands for military police—*you know, 5-0."*

"Make sure you guys only take what you need. We aren't here to be greedy."

"Ain't nothin' wrong with a five-finger discount now and then, Chief. Black steal from us every day."

"There's nothing wrong with it, Quentin, but there's also nothing right with it, either. Stealin' is wrong. But taking advantage of people in desperate situations is wrong, too. So, since we're helping people out, it's okay—to a point. Hell, I know how unfair this country can be, and I'm not about to live on this earth and see people continue to be taken advantage of. We're still in a war, but we're fightin' ourselves now."

"Switch, don't forget to rewire the alarm."

"Got it, Chief. Let's roll."

"Hey! Chief, what are you doing here so early?"

"Mr. Black! Let me explain—"

"Chief! You have teeth!? What the hell?"

"Retreat! The enemy is about to attack!"

Junior Ain't

Frank E. Dobson, Jr.

"A united family eats from the same plate." —African, Zulu

I took 'em from under the tree and brought 'em into my room 'cause I'm tired of Skipper and Jody coming over and breaking 'em. Every Christmas, it's the same old thing: my cousins come over to our house, play with my toys, and break one of 'em. It's like Jody does it on purpose. I hate having 'em visit on Christmas. Yeah, I know, we go over to their house later on in the day. Like Mom says, "It's the family Christmas ritual. It's the way we stay close, Junior."

Well, I started my own ritual. First I was surprised Mom didn't say much when I took my toys upstairs. "Cynthia, I guess maybe your baby brother's growing up. Look at him, picking up all the wrapping paper and carrying his toys to his room."

"Yeah, right, Mom." Cynthia kept right on spying out the front room window, focusing her new telescope.

"Honey, don't you want your cousins to see your new toys?" Mom asked me.

"Mommy, they can see 'em," I said, runnin' up the stairs with my trucks and remote control 'Vette in my arms. Inside my room, I put my plan into action.

I spit on 'em, my new toys. Let my funky cousins play with 'em now. You can't even see the spit, I brushed it on so good. Been workin' on my plan since last week, after Uncle Deon came over and dropped off some food. That's what I don't understand: here they got more money than us and a big house 'n all, and two, no, three cars—well, a truck and two cars—and my cousins gotta come over here and break my toys? Not this year.

So I started spittin' in my jar right after Uncle Deon left; really, right after I finished chompin' down the Kentucky Fried he left for us. The thing is to spread it on nice and thin, so it makes 'em really shiny, makes 'em look newer. When my stupid ole cousins come, I'm gon' say, "Y'all, my toys is put up already."

But I know Jody—she ain't gon' take no for an answer; she's nosey like that, like Aunt Patty and Uncle De, too. Half the time coming over just to see what we doin', or, like Mom say, how we doin', like we need they help. We don't, and I'm gon' show 'em we don't.

"So, Junior, you get any more toys for Christmas?"

"Naw," I say, 'cause I really don't wanna do it, 'cause I hid my best toy, my remote control 'Vette, next to my spit jar in the closet so they can't even see it. I don't wanna do it, not even to nosey ol' Jody. "Besides," I say, "my name ain't Junior. It's William."

"It's whatever I say it is, Junior," Jody sneers, just wheeling my dump truck back and forth, back and forth, 'cross the rug. "You're right, your name can't be Junior, anyway, 'less you got a senior." Skipper's playin' on my Nintendo, and he not saying nothin', 'cause he don't like to pick sides, and he knows how me and Jody always go at it. Sometimes, when we alone, he says it's 'cause she really likes me, think I'm her best baby cousin, but I don't believe him. I don't like her at all.

"It's whatever I say it is, boy," Jody says again. "I think I'ma start calling you Willie, 'cause you ain't no Junior anyway—can't be, without a . . ." Then, she just stops, like she know I know where she goin', so she don't even need to go there. "Willie, mind if I take a nap on your bed? I'm getting bored, with only these few toys. When are you-all coming over to our house? We got a new Sega Genesis, and a whole lotta games, and . . . oops, I'm sorry; I didn't mean to say I don't like your toys and all. It's just that Nintendo is whack," she says, laying back on my bed.

"I got another toy."

"You do?"

"Yeah, I almost forgot."

"How can you forget a toy you just got today? Boy, you fibbin'. You just didn't want me playin' with your toys."

"Naw, that ain't it. Tell her, Skip," I say to Skipper, who's into my old NBA Live game like he's Scotty Pippen. He always plays it when he comes over—thinks he can hoop.

"My name is Bennett, and I ain't in it," Skip says, refusing to look at Jody or me. He's kickin' the game's butt, as usual.

"Okay, Jody, you got me," I say, lookin' at myself in the mirror above the dresser. I'm gettin' kinda tall; gon' be big, like my daddy, Mom's always sayin. "I'ma go get my other toy, the one I been savin' for you. You just stay right there and rest; I'll put it together real quick, okay?"

"Okay," she say. She got her eyes closed, like she gon' take a nap on my bed and ain't nothin' I can do 'bout it.

I'm pouring my spit on my 'Vette, like it's somebody being baptized in church. I'm spreading it all over, so it's nice and wet and sticky. Then I spit some more on my car, 'cause there ain't enough on there already. I'm cryin' and wipin' my tears and gettin' spit on my face and tears on my 'Vette as I spread the spit some more.

I'm standin up in this dark closet, gettin ready to go out. Gotta do this, 'cause I *do* have a daddy. 'Cause I'm tired of Jody and everybody tellin' me I don't. Tellin' us we poor. So I'ma show her, show her good. My face is wet, but I don't care. Holding my 'Vette close so it don't fall, I open the door. My TV and Nintendo's on, but ain't nobody playin'. Bulls and Lakers just standin' still, like the game's over. Dump truck on the bed where Jody left it. She's gone. Skipper, too.

"Junior, come down here for family prayer and supper. We've been waiting on you!" Uncle Deon hollers.

"On my way, Uncle De," I start to holler back, but stop and sit down on my bed, in front of the TV. Naw, I ain't answering none of 'em. Uncle De, Jody, none of 'em. Cause "Junior" ain't my name no more, and all of them, they ain't family.

Holding Hands

Crystal Irene Drake

"Memories of de bad times keep on livin. . . . They can live a long time, like a ol' dog, long as we feed dem in dey cages."
—Ex-slave

Manford decided that today would be the day he confronted his wife about her indiscretions. Today he'd get right to the point, so he called her cousin. Even in his nervous rage, or because of it, Manford remembered some of the lovely poems she'd written and had framed when they bought this house. In his fretting, he wanted to forgive, but being angry was an easier, fuller feeling. First, the details: the dirt from Ru.

His broad, knobby shoulders swayed, the left higher than the right, as his six feet, five inches stretched even longer into an angry shadow on the floor. The silver morning light spearing through the blinds was enough to use for getting dressed. He didn't want to wake his swan, Rory, his wife.

Manford paced the floor and rubbed his hands against his tight chest muscles, watched the curly hair untangle in his fingers. The swan stirred. Time to go. No more lingering. She looked like she was sleeping on a cloud, her body wrapped around the lucky body pillow, her long legs vining around what he knew must be the lover in her mind. The satin sheets had been her choosing, along with the rest of the room decor in shades of mauve and ecru. The wood floor was the only manly thing left in the room. Manford had insisted on it. Like the house of the grandparents who raised him. A wood floor gives you a solid base to start your day from, Pop-Pop had said. Manford knew that Pop-Pop wouldn't have had any cheating out of Gran, that in his angry days he'd nearly choked her to death for lesser transgressions.

It was Saturday, so he knew Rory wouldn't wake up until at least eleven. At 7:39 Manford had more than enough time to get to Ru, get it out of her, get it over with.

Manford looked at Rory's sinuous, shiny legs and pretty toes. He wanted to jump in between the pillow and his wife, and rage inside her. But he left. Snatched his baseball cap down onto fuzzy, sandy curls and slipped on his Birkenstocks. He'd have to cut his hair back down soon, returning to the uniform after his week off.

He noticed that the house was cold as he jumped down the first two stairs. Manford was proud of this house, it made him feel like a grown man. The drive into downtown was a hassle, but they loved the serenity of their country house. One of his clients at the bank had suggested the area to him. Rory said yes, this was the one, right away, but worried that their brown children would find no mirrors in the faces of their playmates, whenever that time came. He thumped up the thermostat. If she got cold, she'd wake up. Manford walked through the laundry room to the garage, both tidier than most people's garages and laundry rooms would ever be. Ever. Rory loved to keep house. Manford got in his car, opened the garage door, and let the car roll out and down the driveway a bit. The engine's rumble might wake Rory. Once near the street, he turned the ignition and sat there for a moment, feeling mighty powerful.

"Ru, this is Manford." He nearly ran over the garbage can as he sped out of the driveway, holding the tiny phone in his shoulder.

"What's up?" a sleepy tongue responded.

"I need to drop in. Are you dressed?"

"No, but I can be. Is Rory with you?"

"No, I need to talk to you, alone."

"Unh, okay. I guess you'll explain when you get here."

Runella got up, rubbing her fat face with her fat fingers. She knew something was up and that although she was always glad to see the pretty man her cousin had married, early morning pop calls usually meant death or other trouble. Her hair was a wild, wiry mess, awaiting taming by the braid "technician" who was coming later in the morning to put in new horsehair extensions. Runella had been instructed to block off at least five hours for her ten o'clock appointment.

Tall and black-brown like Coca-Cola, she rose from her flat little bed and let her pajamas fall away. Runella was nearly as tall as Manford, and thicker; yet, for all her stature, not mannish at all. Everything was just astonishingly ample. Her face was wide and beautiful. Runella was hard-core, had raised herself and, in so many ways, Rory, too.

By the time Runella pushed her legs into her jeans, the doorbell was gonging. As he walked in, Manford admired the Hornets sweatshirt he'd given her.

"Well?" she asked without ceremony.

"Runella, Runella, the human Rubella, always quick to dispense with the formalities, huh?" he said. "Good morning, Ms. Davis, I'm fine. And you?"

"What have you done to my little cousin?"

"Nothing, Old Scratch," he said, slapping her hair around. The two traded air punches.

"Where is she?"

"She's at home, still sleeping. There was a performance last night. And we were up kind of late. You know how that knocks her out."

"You or the performance?" Ru laughed at her wordplay but found no smiles in the lips Manford was biting.

"No chuckles? Why are you interrupting my beauty sleep?" she asked him.

"From the looks of that head, you could sleep until Christmas and still have work to do," he said, glad to be laughing, snatching in courage with each hiccup of breath.

"Can we get on with it?" she said in mock disgust as she reached into her bedroom to grab a bandanna from her nightstand.

"I will just spit it out, and I want the truth from you, okay?"

He sat with Runella in the valley of her sofa.

"Okay," she said. "What?"

"Rory and you go all the way back, so I know you know where her head is."

"Yeah, they said I was the bad influence. But she has always known I'm real. Now, if you don't get on with it—"

"I think Rory is creepin' on me, Ru."

Runella stared him straight in the face, leaning in for emphasis. She curled an eyebrow into a scary angle.

Manford would choose death before stirring Ru's ire. When he met her, he had just met Rory. He was stuck in a beginning ballet class, the only class available to meet his PE requirement for graduation. He had already outgrown college, already been promised a job at Carolina National. Rory was a senior and the instructor's proxy during an ankle injury. He put a noise in her head. She put a bulge in his tights. One day after class, he approached her and asked her out.

"I have to take my cousin to the doctor this afternoon, and then stay with her afterwards. Maybe we can do it some other time. Thanks for the offer," she said, gesturing too much with her hands. Rory was intrigued by the tall, impatient man who came to class in tights and sweats, carrying a briefcase.

Thoroughly rejected, he persisted. Every day for more than two weeks. But Runella's strange illness, though improving, lingered on. Finally, he played a wild card.

"I'll tell you what. You've been so consumed with your nursing duties, I'll bet you and your cousin could stand some fresh air in the evenings. What say I take the both of you out?"

Rory's game was blown, and although she was glad, she needed to get the story together. She called Runella, informing her of her fading malady, asking and telling her to come over by seven o'clock. When Manford arrived, he later told her, he felt the rawest urge he'd ever experienced. When Rory came to the door, it seemed as if she were coming out to sit down for a long talk they'd been meaning to have for quite some time. Like she could listen forever. He had never felt so at ease. Her coarse black hair was plaited into a single braid that swept her back. Her beautiful head sat atop a neck that looked too thin to hold it. It found anchor in her broad, muscular shoulders. His eyes crept down with sorrow that her blouse didn't expose the crease of her luscious, round breasts like her leotards did. And then there was Runella. She looked rough. Like she'd kill him for breathing loud.

Runella wouldn't laugh at his jokes. Rory couldn't stop. Runella had almost missed her bus to get Rory's, and by the end of the night, Manford wished she had.

"By creepin' do you mean having sex with another man, *wanting* to have sex with another man, or *flirting* with another man or men? There are degrees of creepin', you know," she said flatly.

Manford was jarred by the raw candor for which he had come.

"Specifically, I think she is having or is planning to have sex with Chris," he announced, rising from the lumpy, funky sofa in the house she kept spotless, despite the housing authority's demonstrated disregard for it or any of its neighbors.

"Do you know what you are accusing her of?"

"Damn it, of course I do. Stop playing around, Ru. Do you know anything about this?"

"About what? What are you accusing her of? I want to help, but where is this coming from? And why pick Chris out the hat? Is this some kind of get-you-before-you-get-me stuff?"

"What? I have never cheated on Rory. I haven't been with another woman since we got married four hundred and fifteen days ago," he said. He raised his eyebrows, impressed with being able to throw that in. How many men would know that number? He could always calculate which day they were on, how many days it had been. He'd read some of her books and knew that "naming and claiming" things related to him was important to her. Some of the stuff in those books made his head hurt, but this he could do.

"And I haven't wanted to. She's the last I will have until I lay down and die."

"Good," Ru said flatly.

No pat on the back. No, not from Ru. Growing restless, his grandfather's hand possessed him as it rose up to strike Runella, and his voice rose up and out.

"Ru, what . . . do . . . you . . . *know?*"

"I know you better kill that hollerin' in my house and put your hands down before I beat your ass." She drew in the scolding and went on.

"Look, I know that Rory's mind is so full of all the mess that happened that sometimes it pours out into her real world, in her poems, in her dance . . ." she said, looking his hand down to his side.

". . . In you. She dances and she dreams to stay sane. I know she thinks she has loved you since the day she was born but only met you in the flesh two years ago. She's there with her love," Runella said, pressing her fingers to her temples, marking where "there" was. *"That's what I know."*

"Yes, well, thank you for the pretty words. Glad to see she's rubbed off on your dirty mouth, but what about Chris?"

"You need to ask her; I don't answer for her every move, and me telling you that I know she wouldn't cheat on you isn't going to help you now. Obviously."

"Come on, Ru. You know what a predicament I'd be in going to her with this when it may not be true. You know how she gets. All that crying and dancing all night."

"Well, hell, what do you want from me? This is the one day I have off all week from the hospital, and I'm spending it goin' 'round and 'round with you! You come draggin' in here accusing Rory of . . . First of all, I should call her right now and get all this mess on the table."

R-r-r-r-r-ring!

He jumped at the sound of the phone sitting in front of them on the floor.

She answered it and looked wide-eyed at him, telling him who it was.

"Good God!" Manford whispered into hands he cupped to catch his face. "Nothing, just trying to get my scalp oiled before I get my braids put in." Manford looked up at her, noticing how quickly she quelled what he realized had been crescendo, not anger. Drama, a family trait, he thought.

"Oh, yeah? I'm sure he's just out for a second."

She looked at Manford, shaking her head. He snatched up and walked into the kitchen.

"Yeah, I'll be ready at about five. We can go then . . . I'll holler at you later. . . . Bye."

"Your wife wants to go to the mall. I can tell it's comfort shopping, as she calls it. How was her performance last night?"

"I don't know," Manford said as he looked for a snack.

"Hey, get out of my stuff!"

"Shut up," he said more under his breath than to her. "I didn't go last night. That's how I know about this Chris thing. I might as well get all of this out."

"Oh, Lord."

Manford came back, digging into a box of Crunch N' Munch.

"I read a few pages of her diary last night."

"I don't want to hear this! That is off-limits stuff, Manford," she said and kept saying in one way or another until all Manford could see was lips moving. Finally, she lodged her meaty fists into her hips. "Well? What did it say?"

"I thought you didn't want—"

Her pursed lips told him to him to forego the rhetoric and the stalling. She rearranged the nail polish lined up across the top of her television set as he went on.

"I was cleaning up the house and getting dinner ready. I was downstairs for a while in the studio, getting her towels and leotards to wash. I stumbled over a box of lamb's wool and, in catching myself, knocked over one of her duffel bags," he said. "And her diary fell out."

"When you could have just put it back in the bag and kept cleaning. Right, Hazel?"

"It fell open to a page that had been warped by water. She was talking about some man who has been talking to her a lot. It was always 'he.' He has pet names for her and tries to hold her! I . . . was . . . furious!

I thought it might be one of the dancers, but none of her dancer friends are straight."

"Well, you know what they say about a pipe in the dark."

"This isn't funny, Runella. And Rory knows the difference. I handle my business."

"This I have heard," she conceded.

"Anyway, 'he' has been to the house when I am not there, been down in the studio."

"What? Somebody cracked Fort Knox?"

"Look, I act concerned about her whereabouts because I *am* concerned. And she likes it, too, you know that."

"Yeah, I do know. What's that song by Barbra Striesand she likes?" Ru said, launching into song. "'To hold me and to hide me . . . That's all I ask of you,' or some mess like that."

"So, to make a long story short . . ."

"You couldn't possibly."

"Whoever this is has been coming over to watch her dance, watch her body, and she likes it. She described his large head and beard and New York accent. It's gotta be Chris. And you know he is a bartender, so he could be over there in the daytime!"

"But where did you get the cheating from, Manford? Maybe she just needed some more attention than you could give at the time. Did she write, 'And then we rolled around the studio floor and it was the best sex I ever had. Manford can't even touch it'?"

"Well, no."

Runella looked at him in a way that was her sweet way.

"Man, go home to your wife. Go to the mall with her. Or, if not, give me some money so I can go."

"Ru, you know she hasn't been with many men . . ."

"And she knew when she got married that she wouldn't be with any more. Period. She was glad. You and I both know she thinks you are the man who was sent to her to give back to her some of what her father took. She wants you to be everything he wasn't, and I know that's tough—"

"No, what's tough is knowing that if she will allow whoever the hell this is to hold her while she dances, that she's excited, that she's intrigued by this guy," he said.

"You need to talk to Rory, and I know you're in a hurry about this, but for God's sake, don't go over there jumping in her face with all this," Runella said.

"She makes it hard, " he said. "But if she is cheating on me, I am going to fucking do something crazy," he said.

"Please," Runella said. "You're just scared. You've got to talk to her about it. You'd better get on with it," she said, knowing that aftermath sometimes falls out forever, in diaries and dances and decisions.

Manford and Runella sat silent for a moment, looking at the floor. He thanked his friend for her time. He gave her twenty dollars, as he did every time he came. He loved her because he loved Rory. Simple. She rubbed his soft hair and saw him to the door. The screen was falling down and he made promises to come back to fix it, as he did every time. A smile and then he was gone.

Runella thought about making a call but remembered that sometimes the best way to handle something is to take your hands off it. She found her spot in the bed concaved to know her body.

Manford drove straight back to the suburbs. He took the surface streets to add time for the tears, time to meditate before he saw his beautiful blackbird. He couldn't think straight. This threat was unacceptable. What else came before or after those pages? Come to think of it, he had noticed her writing in her diary an awful lot lately. Or was that just because he was home this week, there to notice? Maybe it wasn't what it seemed. But how could he tell her that he had read her diary? That wouldn't work. Or maybe it would. Why was Runella so calm? But why was he seeking counsel from anyone but Rory?

He remembered when they had first started seeing each other. How she had helped him learn how to cry, taught him that it was more than okay; it was necessary. She was the one who had arrived at his door, rushing, panicked, not knowing why, moments before he got the call that his grandmother had had a stroke and died. But most of his thoughts weren't about her tears. They were about the Rory who was smart and who laughed loud. She taught him about forgiving people and sending thank-you notes. He thought about the kids she used to teach for free because they couldn't afford her lessons. Then she demanded a payment, one stellar performance by them before the city arts council as part of her application for funding. Now she and others from the company taught a class once a week downtown at the Lovett Ballroom.

Rory told him later that the first day she saw him she thought maybe he was the one. The one she could tell about her father, a jazz musician who visited occasionally, sometimes for months at a time. She could tell him how she paid a man to beat her father into a cripple the day after the night he raped her for the last time. Her mother just assumed he'd left without words and reasons, like always. She wondered for weeks if her husband was really gone for good this time. In her version of the tale (and, of course, tales were the stuff of image), Rory's mother told people that after a knock-down-drag-out, the final one, she had tossed him out on his ass. Secretly, she figured he had finally decided to stay with one of the many others down in Atlanta or maybe the one in Jacksonville.

"For a few hundred more, we could have put that piece of shit in the ground," Runella kept telling Rory. But all Rory had wanted was for him to stop, to leave. Runella had found the thug for Rory and given him the money. Anything to help Rory hold her hands under cleansing water. Manford was remembering everything now.

His options were ferris-wheeling in his head, and he felt light-headed. He was riding an old lady's bumper, almost home. The one thing—the only thing—he could settle on was that Rory would never risk losing him like this. She'd been to therapy, read all the books, developed her hobbies, made some new friends, mentored other girls, but she still cried sometimes when they made love, and made him promise never to leave her. And if she felt some need to find someone else, he thought, she would just leave. Make a clean break and not dabble in some tawdry affair. She loathed dirty things and dirty behavior and wouldn't do it again. He knew that. Even her fondness of the fantastic would never make her risk their life. Would it?

His thoughts were blurring like sounds gleaned from straining to hear a conversation through a wall. Just as one word comes through clearly, the others are muted and swollen and too far away. The kitchen lights were on. He parked and closed the door quietly.

The sight of Rory captured his breath. She had approached without a sound, standing in the doorway in boxer shorts and a sleeveless undershirt, pulling a robe up around her shoulders. He saw her erect nipples through the shirt's waffle knit. The muscles in her stomach rippled at the fill and empty of her breath. She was holding the diary.

"Good morning, honey. You didn't leave a note," she said with an open face. "Where've you been?"

Several pages of the leather-bound book were curled from the pressure of her aggressive penmanship.

"I went to see Runella," he was barely able to say. Had she just made an entry? What about, him again? Did she know it had been disturbed? Did she know he'd read it? His anger re-encouraged him. "I needed some advice."

She walked out to him, her toes curling upward at the touch of the cold concrete. He liked her toenails—a copper red glaze, each nail like a brand new penny—and that she kept them polished and the calluses on her dancer's feet shaved down.

"Advice?" She put the book on the roof of his car, cupped her hands around his neck, and plaited her fingers. "You don't look happy. What kind of advice did you need?"

"I love you, Rory," he said almost as if reminding himself out loud.

"As I do you, lover," she said plainly and truly.

He was stalling, angry, titillated by the smell of her. She couldn't be cheating on him. He so desperately wanted to buttress his faith in that.

"If there is something I am not doing, Rory, something I am not saying, you will let me know, won't you?" he asked her. "You can tell me, you know that?" he said, half looking at the diary. These questions weren't the right ones, but he couldn't hear through the wall of his panic.

"I will try."

"I want you to try *hard.*" He leaned in a little.

"Manford, what do you need?" she said.

"This isn't about my needs right now," he lied. "This is about us telling the truth."

He was clamping her shoulders in a way that must have been hurting her, and he stopped when he realized it. He was afraid. Afraid of hands that had become anger's sucker and ego's whore. Not me, he said to himself. Never like Pop-Pop. Not with her. His eyes were turning a rusty, furious green.

"Manny?" she said, rubbing her cheek against the whitened knuckles on her shoulder.

Thoughts about Chris were beginning to make no sense at all, and he thanked God that she knew better than to react to his hysteria. Rory and Manford had worked out a cool science where they each got to be hysterical, one at a time.

She clapped her hands together, then rested her square chin on her fingertips. It was a gesture that was an asking.

"I'm just working all the time. This is the first time off I've had in a long time, and I feel like maybe I've been missing something. Just give me a little hint; I'll get it."

He tried to smile. *Damn it*, he thought. *Why'd you dodge this chance to nail her?*

He felt embarrassed that he was looking for signs: an averted glance, lips bitten, words stumbling down her tongue. He thought he heard himself whimper. He couldn't find any more words. *I don't want to nail her*, he said in his head.

He pulled her to him and then it was done. They went inside and he changed the subject and the day moved itself along and the night came at its usual time. When Rory got back from the mall with Runella, she had packages and stories but seemingly no hints of earlier, so Manford continued manning his battle station in private.

During his nightly rounds to lock up the house, he went back out to the garage and saw the diary still sitting on the roof of his car. He took it to her and she put it away in its usual place.

The next morning, light came breaking through clouds, and the house was still and solid. Manford's mind felt more still and solid as he turned his head to look at her. Noticing new acne on her face, he touched her hair and envied her for sleep that was always more restful than his.

They ate breakfast and talked about things, and then she left for errands. Even as he considered that she might be a liar who was having an affair, he missed her when she left. Even when she was losing him on a tangent about some flower she saw that was a color she'd never seen, a color she wished she could dance, he missed her mouth when it was silent. He missed the poems she would tuck in his briefcase when he opened the briefcase to find no poem there. He stalked through the house hunting his courage, turning up the stereo so loud it made the wooden blinds hum. He looked for CDs that made him sad, then for ones that made him happy, then for ones that she liked, then for ones that he had bought her, then for ones that reminded him of other women he'd fucked, then ones that reminded him of the fact that Rory's limber body was not for fucking. He began to laugh out loud when he began to feel ridiculous.

So he got up from the floor, out of his pile of CDs and old things, and went to their bed. The cool sheets smelled like her. A tear broke down and away onto his cheek so fast that it startled him. Manford sat up quickly. He pushed his hand into a nightstand drawer that opened just enough. He didn't even look, because he was ashamed but not more ashamed than he was convinced that the voice in his head was giving him permission. It was that same kind of easy permission his grandfather used to take. The diary looked small and sacred in his hands, just like Rory did.

He came today for hours and kept telling me that damned thing. That men don't stay for good, they never will. I worry that Manford has begun to tire of me and the tears and the poems and the needs. I guess I want to believe my father was right about something, that he did one good thing by telling me one true thing. So maybe Manford is ready to leave. My legs looked good tonight; the muscle tone is getting back to normal. Later.

Manford read on.

Runella asked me to go with her to Reynold's and I lied to get out of it. I wish she could meet somebody to love her and put up with her in the way that doesn't show. Manford is good at that. He has never lorded that over me. Luckily, I give him something that makes it worth it to him, I think a sense of beauty in his life (other than this outside stuff) that he never really had. Anyway, I hope one day Runella will find someone. Talking to her about it is really pointless, though, because, of course, after a point there's nothing I can say that won't sound prissy and privileged. Funny thing is, it was Ru who helped me to hold on to some of that. Even as her life would never be soft and gentle and pink-flowered. He told me again today that Manford will not stay.

Manford closed the pages together. Such a good writer, he thought. So sweet. For some reason that passage reminded him of a day he was in a counseling session with her and a thought popped into his head with such a jolt, he almost slapped his forehead to keep it from bleeding through. *I can understand why her father lusted after her,* he'd thought. The months of psychiatric undressing had left him wondering if he was some kind of social miscreant. All kinds of thoughts had pushed their way into the sight of his mind's eye, parading themselves around as if to make him feel like he, too, had been raped. But this thought was just too much. If he could think that, did it mean he would one day lust after his own daughter? Or only if she looked and acted just like Rory? Because it was Rory, the accommodating smile, the gentle pressure in her touch, the eager eyes that would listen and listen and listen no matter what, the body taut and definite, the gaze just as direct and concentrated, the movement so fluid, the near-desperation with which she gave herself away, it was all of that that must have always put a rock in men's pants, even her father's.

Manford read on. His rage swelled.

I was angry at him tonight, telling him to hold me the right way. He would hold me too tightly to give my knee room during the turn. He just kept talking instead of letting me dance. Manford's mother called while I was dancing and I shouldn't have answered. Thought maybe it might be the guy calling about my car. She said I sounded funny. I hope she won't tell Manford.

Manford read on.

Manford came home today asking me about something and not asking all at once. I knew better than to press and seemed strong and unworried I'm sure but really I was standing so still because I was stuck in the ice of my fear and shame. It was old shame, old dirt. Anyway, I can't say I was surprised. My father told me it was coming, didn't he? That's why he's been so available to show up for rehearsals these last few weeks. And I can't dance fast enough to make him go away because he's delivering a message from God (do I believe he went to heaven?). Even this wonderful, magical thing I have with Manford won't last. That is such a shame and I will fall apart for sure. Or maybe not. God showed me a tender mercy to give me someone to get me to the next stage. And now God will take Manford because—OK, I can't finish that sentence. Why would God take him? It starts to unravel.

Quietly, in the chaos of his silent panic, Manford's eyes rose back up to the words: My father told me . . . His rage rested. The silence was broken by the sounds of Rory coming home. His eyes jumped from the clock to the nightstand to the floor to the diary and then backward in similar order as he deposited the diary back in its usual place.

He helped with packages and kissed her lips. Her cheeks were cold. He peeled gloves off her hands.

It was time, he thought, and he didn't know that she, too, had been out scouring her mind for the courage to come home and prove her father right.

"Rory, I love you," he said. It wasn't what he meant to say. His lips had planned, in the three minutes that had passed since he closed the nightstand drawer and nearly thrown himself off the landing to get to the kitchen in time to appear calm and uninterested at the kitchen table when she came in, an entire soliloquy about his devotion and his desire, an ode to their quirky union of souls, a sermon that summed up her need for a hero and his need to be one.

He let out a broken sound. She looked down and let her eyes creep up. It was that coquettish glance he hated to see her give other men, because there was something in the back of her eyeballs that drew them in like magnets. Maybe she did it for sport, but he hated it all the same. Of course, now he was drawn in like a magnet, hanging on her every word.

"Honey, I've been thinking about something today, thinking a hole into it—you know me—and I want to tell you about it."

She hardly stopped for a breath and kept looking straight at him even as the mucus rose in her throat. "When I dance, sometimes I am dancing for the pleasure, for the beauty of it, I admire my body and feel strong. And I think you know this, but sometimes I am also dancing with my demons and mostly, I guess, with my biggest demon, my father."

Manford wondered if he was looking surprised enough. The guilt was sitting square-bottomed on his brow, and the pressure soon pushed down warm tears.

"I tell him, 'Look at me! Hold my arm and let me spin. Hold me like you should have!' And then I try to dance, to dance him away. I've been telling him a lot lately. But I really want to tell him good-bye, Manford, and—"

"Then let's tell him," Manford said.

He scooped his swan into his arms and put his face to her breast. He suckled it until they reached their bed, made love to her until she cried, then suckled her until he slept. The sun was so bright that day.

Rory kept writing to her father, but mostly just on rainy days when she could not stop her mind from letting him in. There was more therapy and books and all, but, more on the rainy days, Manford would come to watch, too. He sat on her floor, arms folded across his chest, looking around in his mind, daring the man to show. Oh, how she danced and danced. Up and down, lunge and stroke, plié, arabesque, glissade assemblé. Leap! Leap! She drank the wine of sweat and tears as it poured into the open cup of her lips. Her arms ribboned in the air, in triumph, in love with her beautiful self. She danced so that he of her brightest nightmare could admire her body the right way, could know the lovely woman she had become in spite of his transgressions against nature. She would dance herself into exhaustion as Manford sat vigilantly.

She had been inviting her father to see her since they got married, feeling cocky enough to show off her new life to him. But the time had passed for showing off. Manford and Rory talked about it and she danced about it and they kept working on it. Years went by before she mentioned the one detail Manford had never reconciled from his reckoning with the secret pages. The one thing that cleared up the whole issue of that quirky glottal stop. Her father had grown up on Long Island. The New York accent.

Flimsy *and* Raggedy

Phill Duck

"Walking in two is medicine." —African, Mozambique

I'm usually not violent.

I couldn't get a clear read on Tamika's face. I let her nail scissors fall from my hands, shocked at myself for the damage I'd done. A precious drop of silence passed before she moaned with pain. It was that brief pause that kept me from harming myself with those same scissors. I looked from her to my hands, then back to her again. I wanted to reach for her, offer her comfort, but my arms held rigid to my sides like they were restricted in a straitjacket. She plopped down on the couch, almost missing it entirely, and fell back against the cushions.

"Never imagined you losing it like this," she gasped, fingering the wound from my outburst. Rubbing her manicured nails over the gaping hole in her new leather couch, foam cushion bleeding from its backside. "I guess even the seemingly most balanced souls fall off course from time to time," she mused.

Her words penetrated me. It had taken so much for me to confront this issue, to deal with the feelings that bubbled over inside me, and here she was talking about balance. Basically, it was a preamble to the fact that I couldn't have what I deeply desired.

"I need someone to walk *with* me, pick *me* up," she continued. "I've had about enough of holding the brothas up and the brothas pulling me down. I remember my Grans always loved this African proverb she got off one of those calendars that had a quaint little thought for each day of the year. *Walking in two is medicine.* That's what she and Pop-Pop had. They were each other's medicine."

"I can be that for you," I said. I spoke from the heart, wishing I were the type to fall on bended knee, a smoother operator.

"No, no, you can't," Tamika said, shaking her head. She looked at the scissors resting snugly in the clutches of her thick carpet. "You've proven it just now. And besides, I'm not a scandalous bitch. I have a daughter who looks to me as an example. I don't care what you think about your brother and me. As of this moment, he's still my man. You coming in here as Cavalier Kev doesn't change that."

"He's good for you?" I asked.

"Not for me, or to me, but that's my boat to row."

I was getting desperate, grasping for a corner of hope on a circular planet. "Remember last Valentine's Day?" I asked. "You'd just passed the cosmetology boards; you were so excited. That should have been a happy and *romantic* day for you. Trevor blew you off. I'm the one who took you to dinner."

"Don't do this, Kev. Don't make this hard."

"Remember when you got the flu last winter and I came by every day and prepared your herbal remedies? You got better and then I got sick, and you came by my place every day and did the same for me. I hated the taste of the stuff, but you kept telling me it would cleanse my system."

I felt the memories turning her resistance to mush.

"I know we've shared a lot, Kev, but I just can't do it."

I shook my head, snuck a seat beside her. For once in my pitiful life, I refused to let resistance push me back. Hope coursed through my veins when she didn't flinch or widen the divide between us with a scoot to the side. I hadn't wanted to come packing heat, but I figured since I still had one bullet in the chamber, I might as well cock back and squeeze. What did I have to lose except everything?

"You said Ericka is looking to you for guidance, Tamika," I said. "You think you're giving it to her?"

Tamika jammed a few fingers into the hole in her couch, stuffed as much of the foam back in as possible, and then smoothed it over. Seeing the anger on her lips, I braced myself. She got up, made a move to leave the living room, then pivoted to face me.

"Kev, so help me God, if you ever bring up my daughter like that again . . . civility is out the window. I don't need you judging me. It's not my fault that Trevor always finishes ahead of you. Don't blame me because you always fall woefully short."

I felt like the couch at that moment. In fact, I looked to make sure she hadn't picked up the scissors and shanked me. A quick inspection found them on the carpet, and my skin, if not my heart, free of any punctures. All that needed to be said, all that we'd been struggling with for the past two hours, had been summed up in a few hateful seconds.

It's not my fault that Trevor always finishes ahead of you. Don't blame me because you always fall woefully short.

She watched me from the middle of the floor, a frown on her face. Her features softened as I began my slow rise from the couch. Normally, I would have taken pride in the fact that I could get a heartfelt look of sympathy from her—that she could feel anything even closely related to love for me—but at this moment all I wanted was to make it outside so I could puke on the curb in peace.

"Look, Kev," she said, her voice teasing me with its melody, "I didn't mean that. I'm just . . . frazzled. You've got to let me figure all of this out without pressuring me so much."

"Yeah, Tamika," I answered, trying real hard not to be dramatic. "No more pressure from me. I've seen what pressure can do." I paused like a Southern preacher giving his congregation a chance to swallow the word before he pelted them with pebbles of fire and brimstone. "It breaks shit."

I circled her coffee table, bumped my shin on one of the sharp corners, and limped my way out of her living room. She called after me, but I knew it was just because she felt sorry. I wasn't about to be anybody's charity case, no matter how much my arms ached to hold her and my fingers needed to caress her.

Heading for my car, I imagined Tamika on her balcony watching me, then rushing from her apartment, without closing or locking her door, to catch me before I drove off. I pictured her inside the apartment, peering at me through her floor-length venetian blinds, doing some kind of voodoo-whispering chant that would send me back to her. She had to realize we were meant to be. We'd gotten to this point, with my wanting to wrap my lips around this forbidden fruit because Trevor didn't give her his time or faithfulness. So I ended up attempting to fill in the spaces like a good little brother. I'd filled in her open holes. Why wouldn't she fill in mine?

I pressed my car's keyless entry button, looking up to see if she was indeed watching as the *brp-brp* sound emanated from my vehicle. She wasn't there. I had used up precious personal miles on my company car and wasted a vacation day for this woman, all for naught. My heart squeezed itself into numbness. I'd lost her before ever having her.

It's not my fault that Trevor always finishes ahead of you. Don't blame me because you always fall woefully short.

I pulled away from the curb and headed around the twists and turns of her cul-de-sac. It's pitiful to admit, but I kept checking my rearview mirror. Just making sure the cars behind me kept the correct following distance. Who was I fooling? No matter how I tried to shade this thing, blue was blue, black was black, and a love jones was a love jones. Tamika had a tight hold on me, without even using her arms. I'd felt it as long as I'd known her. Why else would I have put myself out there like this today? Why else would I open myself to scorn? Why else would I find myself driving home alone, salty raindrops filling my eyes and washing my cheeks?

Thoughts of her fueled my mind as I returned to my lonely apartment and the discomfort of my empty bedroom. Before I drifted to sleep, I prayed that I'd have a sensual moment with her, wake up pleasured, my sheets mucked with life seed. Countless days I'd fallen into her arms, alone in my bedroom, controlling the harmony of Tamika's breaths. My fingers rubbing up and down the small of her back, making her gasp in slow paces. My lips on the crook of her neck, quickening her breaths. Each encounter teaching me something about her body, her likes and dislikes. I could feel her here, so real. When I sucked an earlobe, her breaths stopped altogether, and she pulled back from me. I heard her speaking to me.

"What the hell makes you think chomping on my ear is erotic? That's like me . . . uh . . . sucking on your eyelids."

"Sucking on my eyelids?"

"Yeah." She touched my eyelid with her finger, pinching it slightly. I jumped back. "You get the picture?"

"Stay off your ears," I answered.

"And on my neck." Then her eyes brightened like a fresh candle. "Or if you really want to blow me away, you can go down to . . ."

"I'll stick to your neck," I cut in.

"Selfish ass."

Then I returned to her upper region and planted soft clues on her erogenous points with my lips. Clues as to what would happen once nature got her ready. As for me, I was ready as ready can be, harder than a roll of quarters, a double major in nuclear physics and mathematics, *and* a Toni Morrison novel wrapped into one. I had just reached the point when my libido would be satisfied, when a hand touched my shoulder and shook me off course.

"Yo, get up man." It was my brother, the real keeper of Tamika's heart, destroyer of mine. He wouldn't even let me have her in my dreams.

I needed to change the locks to my apartment. One day Trevor was gonna barge in and find me up to my elbows in Vaseline.

Trevor and I appeared similar enough, but we didn't have the same pull when it came to women. In fact, I had none. Jordan has more championship rings than the number of sexual partners I've had. Damn, Lance Armstrong has won more Tours de France in the past four years than the number of women I've bedded during that same period. Not that I'm just looking for a good lay. I could get that off a side street in Asbury. Nah, I want that *"Walking in two is medicine"* jazz that Tamika's grandparents had. I want to be Tamika's Tylenol, and she could be my Advil.

"Dawg, you hear me?" My brother repeated. "Wake up, Kev. You gotta do me a solid."

I could tell from my brother's grin that this mission would entail helping him dog out Tamika. It excited and sickened me at the same time. The earlier episode with her, and my recent erotic dream, had made me dislike and love her all the more.

I sat up on my bed and scanned him over as he waited for me to ask what the favor was. We had the same build—slightly chunky but muscular six-footers. Same skin tone, almond joy all the way. Same features. I'm quite positive he's had women down through the years remark about how nice his eyes were, and how they wished they had his thick eyelashes, because even I've heard those comments more than once. So why did he always get the girl?

"What do you need, Trevor?" I asked him.

"I need a big, bruising, trustworthy nigga to run interference on my lady while I lounge in some—"

"Spare me the details." I didn't need to be hearing about how much sack time he got, especially since I hadn't moved anybody's planet out of orbit anytime recently. My love life was like a Halley's Comet sighting.

"You got me, right?" he asked.

"I didn't say I'd do anything. Besides, you think Tamika's stupid or something? Half the time you two are supposed to kick it, I end up hanging with her instead."

Trevor thought about that nugget for a minute. "The life of a promoter is hectic," he said. "Don't matter anyway; she puts up with my shit. It ain't like I'm not out in the open with her. I just like it when you go hang out with her. It makes her less crabby by the time I get back around." He whispered to me like we weren't alone. "Hittin' it at three, four in the morning—after I spent the night with some other bitch— just ain't as fun when Tamika's crabby. Nahmean?"

"Your shit is raggedy," I said.

"Flimsy *and* raggedy," he replied. "I just don't really vibe off of hanging with Tamika and her daughter. I prefer kickin' it with her during the weekends what's-his-face takes the little brat."

"Ericka's a beautiful little girl," I said. "Well-mannered, too."

"That may be all true, brah," Trevor said. "But I can't deal with the stress of it, man. I always picture Ericka coming up in the bedroom while I got her mama in some Trevorlicious position and screaming, 'Mama, come down from there, pleeeeaaassse!'" He shuddered like he was outside in the cold. "Traumatic shit, brah."

"Where did she want to go tonight?" I asked him.

"To the Olive Garden and to see *Rush Hour 2*. She's got a baby-sitter, so the dinner-and-movie thing wouldn't be too bad. But I can't see myself going through all that trouble to get back at her place and find out Ericka has a tummy-ache or some shit and can't sleep. You can kick it with her for me, then check and make sure afterwards that Ericka is sleeping sound. If she is, I'll come over and handle business from there." He flashed me a smile. "That's if this freak Kenya doesn't squeeze all the juice out of me."

"Who's this girl Kenya?"

"Thick-ass chick, brah. She dances over at the Pussycat Lounge. I told her I'd hook her up with tickets for the next concert I set up. I sweartoGod, dawg, these chicks can't get enough of me. I feel for 'em, really. Trashing themselves off for tickets to a rap show. And I don't even give 'em good seats most of the time."

I thought about my options. I had never turned Trevor down before, and if I did today he'd ask me a ton of questions, possibly enough to find out what had gone down earlier with Tamika and me. Comparable size or not, I just wasn't ready to go toe to toe with Trevor. Besides, I owed him. He'd been my father when Dad died, and then my everything when Mom passed. I mean, he wasn't perfect—he left me alone in the house plenty of times, called me a pussy when I cried about the dark, made me leave and walk the neighborhood when he brought girls over. But he was all I had.

"Okay," I said. "I got you this one last time."

"Cool." He gave me a pound. "Hook up with her around seven. Now, go back to sleep, nigga. By the look on your face when I came in, you were having a real nice dream."

"Back so soon? I knew it would be you," Tamika said, opening her apartment door, allowing me to enter. "Trevor's never on time."

I glanced at my watch: the long hand was groping twelve; the short hand was reaching for seven, not quite touching her hemline. Poetic that the short hand on the clock had done me in. Obviously, women didn't hand out cool points for punctuality. Trevor could strut in at eight and she'd be moist before he crossed her threshold. I come on time and she's giving me the TLC "I Don't Want No Scrubs" vibe. I stepped into the apartment anyway.

"Who is she this time?" Tamika asked, closing the door.

"Some girl named Kenya," I replied. If I didn't build up enough of my own points, the only way to win was to take some of the enemy's.

"He tell you what our plans were?"

"Olive Garden, *Rush Hour Two*, then some late-night boning," I said. "I'm prepared to fulfill all those duties as stand-in."

"Sixty-seven," Tamika answered.

"Sixty-seven?"

"Roughly two-thirds," she said. "You got two out of the three sewn up. Can't help you with that last one." She always had some abstract way of looking at things. Here I wanted her to apologize for the hurtful words she'd said earlier today, and she was giving me math lessons. I guess since Trevor had forced her to develop a thick skin, she felt everyone should follow suit.

"If I get you a large drink and some Goobers at the movie, you think I can get down with that other thirty-three? I mean, that roughly one-third is the most important part, right?"

Tamika smiled. A good sign.

"Only time will tell." She winked at me and sashayed to the living room.

We'd always flirted with each other to an extent, but tonight the usually covert act was actually more out in the open, less of a subliminal thing. I'd like to think that my putting all my cards on the table had opened her heart to different possibilities. But chances were, she was just playacting her way through another night of disappointment. My brother was her drug, much as she was mine, and no matter how much I disliked the fact, Tamika kept him in the warm parts of her soul that his cold fingers didn't deserve to touch. Not that I deserved to, either—

I looked at the injured leather couch, where she'd strategically placed a multicolored throw over the hole.

"Where's Ericka?" I asked.

"Her father just picked her up for the weekend."

Even the less smoothed-out brothers like myself understood the implications of such an opportunity. By mixing up his weekend dates, Trevor had left the door wide open for me. Tamika and I had an empty apartment all to ourselves. Two emotionally fractured souls looking for the right dosage of medicine. Eff it, I decided. Time to move in for the kill.

"Tamika."

She'd had her back turned to me, gathering a few things off the counter that separated her living room area from the hallway. She turned in response to the sound of her name, and I planted a soft kiss on her glossed lips. They tasted like chocolate; her lipstick must have been the edible kind. I felt her body give, and mine took. Her eyes were closed, her lids fluttering just as I had pictured them so many times in my dreams. Then she pushed back and eyed me.

"What's wrong with you, Kev?" she asked.

"You." I couldn't deny her pull.

"This isn't right. What about Trevor?"

"Fuck him." I was ready to say more, prepared to present my case with a more eloquent choice of words, but was stopped by a deep voice from behind.

"*Fuck me?* Nah, nigga, fuck you."

I spun around. Trevor stood less than ten feet away, face full of rage. He'd come from the kitchen. I looked back for Tamika, who was cowering in the corner by the hallway. She wouldn't give me the benefit of eye contact. Trevor moved in on me like a shadow. Our equal height suddenly didn't feel equal anymore. I felt dwarfed.

"Trevor, let me explain," I managed to say.

"You ain't got shit to explain, brah," he said. "I heard it all myself, loud and clear. Tamika said I wouldn't believe it, and I can't. *Your shit is raggedy.*"

"Flimsy *and* raggedy," I agreed, struggling to get back our connection.

"Bounce, man," he said, shaking his head. "Before I decide to go in your mouth."

"Trev, man, hear me out," my voice trembled. I thought about the day, some fourteen years earlier, when Mom had died. I was just

eleven, asking my seventeen-year-old brother what was for dinner. "I don't want to fight over this, man. I was dead wrong."

"Bounce," he repeated.

So this was it. This was how it all pieced together. I'd played my hand and folded terribly. I looked at them both before I made my lonely sojourn from the apartment. Tamika kept her head bowed. Trevor's glowering eyes walked me to the door and on my merry way. I stumbled down the steps, taking more than one at a time. A twisted, or better yet, broken ankle wouldn't have mattered to me at this point.

Nearing my vehicle, I pressed the keyless entry button on my keychain. As it *brp-brp*ed, I couldn't help but look up at Tamika's apartment. Force of habit, I guess. Damn! She was watching me through the blinds.

I was cruising down Broad Street in downtown Red Bank when I spotted her walking into the Bon Ton clothing store. It had been over a month since the confrontation in her apartment, but my flame still flickered for Tamika. Seeing her just poured oil on that baby and made it burn hotter. I looked in my rearview to see if I could swing a U-ie. Some type of delivery truck was barreling down my bumper's ass, so I decided to hang a right at the next street and double back to the store. If this was one of Tamika's normal shopping jaunts, I didn't have to worry about losing her. I'd been out shopping with her before, and it was an all-day affair, with whole blocks of hours spent in each store.

My pulse had traveled from my wrist to my fingers by the time I reached the Bon Ton store parking lot. I could still turn back, ride up the block with *Jay-Z* pumping loudly enough from my speakers to drown out any thoughts I had of revisiting the painful past. Trevor had won, as usual, and there was no real reason for me to push the knife blade deeper into my solar plexus. Tamika didn't want me. Her betrayal had proved it.

Still, I shook off all the negative energy and exited my vehicle. I'd just go in, pick me out a couple of those nice short-sleeved shirts with the alligator on the pocket, and go about my business. If I just so happened to bump into a certain caramel delight in the perfume section, by women's shoes, or in the petites department, we could just chalk it up as small-town coincidence.

There was no one in the perfume section except a saleswoman dressed in a white lab coat. I asked her what time surgery started, and either she didn't get my joke or, like the countless other women I've encountered through life, she wasn't trying to hear me. Women's shoes produced the same result. Petites, nada. I went for the stairs, headed to the men's department to pick up those new shirts for a big meeting with the company's bigwigs from Houston next week.

Climbing the stairs, my mood continued to sour. I'd come in here with hope and wandered around to find that hope didn't live in Bon Ton any more than it lived in my heart.

I reached the top and made a sharp turn toward men's. I couldn't believe my eyes. Standing in the men's department, unfolding shirts and holding them up to get a better view, was my Tamika. Or Trevor's Tamika—whatever. Titles suck, anyway.

I headed right over to her. Tamika was the only person I'd ever known who made me move before thinking.

"Kev," Tamika said, surprise covering her face like a rash. My name seemed stuck in her throat.

"Tamika, how's it going?"

"Good," she said, maintaining eye contact. "How about you?"

"Oh, I've had better times," I said.

She nodded in understanding. I don't know if it was the lighting or what, but her entire face glowed. I thought about something they'd said on one of those women's programs on cable the other day—about pregnant women and skin. I looked at Tamika's belly. It would kill me to have a niece or nephew germinating in there.

"So how's Trevor?" I asked her.

She actually had the nerve to smile when I asked. I was ready to leave at that moment. I couldn't take all of this glee at my expense. I'd moved my body into a position to hightail it out of there, when Tamika said, "Trevor and I aren't seeing each other anymore."

That caught my attention. "Since when?"

"Oh, I don't know, fifteen minutes or so after you left that night. We got into a huge fight, he pressed me, and I ended up telling him a lot of things. Including how I felt about you. He said a chick that would even consider you over him wasn't up to par. Anyway, we broke up and I couldn't be happier."

I was glad to be at least *considered*. That and a token would get me on the subway. But still I hadn't broken through the barriers. I looked at the two shirts she had in her hand, and wondered who the lucky dude was.

"Nice shirts," I said, acknowledging her choices with an upraised chin.

She pulled them down from my view, embarrassed. Cherry blossoms actually dotted her cheeks. "You weren't supposed to see these," she said.

"Your secret's safe with me, Tamika. I'm not a snitch or a rat."

She sighed. I saw the controls working, gears shifting in her head as she considered a response to my dig. "I just wanted him out of my life, Kev. I didn't trust myself to do it, so I used you as a means to an end."

Oh, yeah, that made me feel an awful lot better. She'd used me to break up with my brother. Destroyed the relationship Trevor and I shared, though most days it was grossly one-sided, the scale leaning more favorably to his side. And I'd gotten absolutely nothing out of the deal.

"You have to believe me; I never intended to hurt you," she said, reading my expression.

"Intent and outcome sure as hell ain't related," I answered.

"We both needed him gone. You had as many issues, or more, than I did."

"What do you mean?"

"Trevor controlled me, my emotions, how I truly felt about things in life. The feelings I had for him totally manipulated my real feelings, deep inside—the feelings that count for more. Believe it or not, Kev, but I've always loved *you*."

My mouth must have fallen open, because Tamika smiled, took my chin in her fingers, and guided it closed.

"Did you say . . . ?"

"That I love you? Yes, I did," she cut me off. "It felt good that day when you told me how you felt. I was too frightened to confront it, though. When you took those scissors from me, stopped me from doing your manicure—when we both know how much you love my manicures—and stabbed my sofa, I knew something had to give." The memory of me with the scissors made us both laugh.

Tamika continued, "I say you had issues, too, because you've done the same things as me. You let Trevor manipulate how you felt about yourself. Let him dictate what you did. Geez, you even dogged *me* out, covering for him, and you claim all this love for me."

"I admit I did at first. I ran interference, as he puts it. But I couldn't take it, Tamika. That's why I started telling you what he was really up to."

My hand rested on the clothes rack; she covered it with her hand. "I know," she said. "And I thank you for that. That's why I love you. I can see a sincere caring in you. That's why I had to use you to make us both better. Trevor was killing us both, softly, loudly—I don't know. I just know we were dying."

"This is crazy; I hope you aren't bullshitting me."

She leaned up and kissed me. Inexperienced as I was, I still knew a real kiss, the emotion and power that the real thing had. She wasn't bullshitting me.

"Now what?" I asked.

"Walk me down and we'll figure this out as we go along."

We twined our fingers and walked toward the escalators. We had made it a few steps when I remembered the shirts.

"What about those shirts?" I asked her.

"Oh, those," she said. "Now that you've seen them, I'll have to get you something else."

"Huh?"

"Your birthday *is* still next week, isn't it?"

I hadn't thought about matters so trivial in quite a while. "I guess it is," I said.

And off we walked, in two.

Chasing Horizons

Jamellah Ellis

"No matter how far a person can go, the horizon is still way beyond you." —Zora Neale Hurston, *Their Eyes Were Watching God*

From the cradle they called it.

Saw it in her eyes each time she awoke, as if she hadn't really been asleep to begin with. Saw it in her reach—for the breast, then the bottle, then the Barbie; the baton, the books, and the boys. It was there in her spirit from her first breath, and it meant to be the mastermind. Her mama, her daddy, all the grands and great-grands, the aunties and the uncles: all called it; and even the little ones who couldn't name it knew enough to sense it.

It was the reason she didn't get her name until she turned fifteen months. She frowned, jerked her infant body, and hollered to heaven every time her mama and daddy tossed around a prospect. "Cecile," they offered with confidence at first, intending to honor a beloved great-aunt, and that baby nearly jumped out of her mama's arms in protest. "Anna?" her daddy proposed softly, his eyes wide and puzzled, thinking maybe they should keep it simple. Her face turned beet red until the family swore she was trying to take herself out right then and there.

"Well, good Lordie!" Grandma Dot exclaimed, half annoyed and half frightened, "what's wrong with that child?"

"I ain't *never*," Uncle Lou muttered out the side of his mouth to Uncle Freeman, putting Stetson to bald head and slipping out of the room.

She was sister to the stars and daughter to the moon, and once they realized it, they figured they should just let loose. Figured, being the small-town, hourly-wage-earning mart shoppers they were, they should just follow her. Which was the first mistake.

In the spring of '63, her Easter dress was red velvet with a black-and-white polka-dot sash she'd cut from beautiful Aunt Suzy's chiffon roll. By then, at eight, she was Sasha, the second replacement name she'd chosen for herself on a humid Saturday morning over hoecakes and bacon, five years earlier. She'd known nothing but A's throughout school, so at the Shayside High School commencement exercise the family cared less about her speech and more about the personal statement she might choose to make of herself that June afternoon. The orange wool scarf wrapped twice around her neck wasn't so bad. What they couldn't get past was the Tootsie Roll she'd moistened and molded around her upper teeth to prove to her parents, as she'd proclaimed at dinner the night before, that "the American's thirst for knowledge is readily quenched by chosen ignorance." The aunts had raised their eyebrows at each other, and the uncles had cleared their throats, picked up their bid whist hands, and resumed their game over in the corner.

"Elevator ain't never gone up, you know, all the way up," Uncle Lou whispered over the fake brown leather tabletop that had been torn in two places, exposing the cotton underneath. "It work," he added, sweeping up the four, six, and seven of hearts with a much-anticipated deuce, "but it don't work like ours do, you see."

But it didn't matter. In fact, she'd already been told it was a good thing, a great thing, a thing to celebrate, the thing that would make her life different. It was why she had forfeited the prom, the cool cliques, and the quarterback. "Don't none of that mess matter in life," Mama had said religiously every Friday night of her teenaged life, laying the foundation for the second mistake. "None of it. You got something they ain't got. I ain't got it, your daddy sho' ain't got it, and Lord above knows I don't know where you got it from, but fact remains, you got it. Now you need to use it. And I don't care what it cost—you use it and you do whatever you gotta do to get where you going. You hear? *Whatever* you gotta do. Just get there. For me. Hear?"

Well, that was easy. For Sasha already knew where she was going; she had known it, as a matter of fact, from the time she'd watched death creep into the eyes of her beautiful aunt Suzy and claim her body in a matter of weeks. Cancer. Aunt Suzy had been thirty-two years old, and not one single doctor could give her a slice of hope to cling to. Thus far, Sasha had kicked the dirt off mountains in her path until the whole thing fell into a neat pile upon which she could stand and survey. Well, this particular mountain, which held her beautiful aunt Suzy, wasn't budging. Sasha was not used to that. But she didn't fret. No need. She just dusted off her shoes and sat down and planned. She was Sasha. The mountain would fall.

Four years of medical school, three years of interning, and five years of specialized research later, Sasha woke up one morning with the dawning thought that she might not find the cure for cancer as quickly as she had planned. No matter, though. This wasn't a failure, and it certainly was not a concession on her part. It was simply a rational decision to redirect her efforts toward a smaller goal that would energize her for the larger one. That same morning, gulping her cup of coffee in a matter of seconds, Sasha determined she'd develop a concoction to obliterate labor pain. Something completely natural, derived from God's green earth, that would make this monumental ordeal a little less burdensome. No longer would Eve's punishment involuntarily descend upon womankind.

And wouldn't you know that she did it? Some strange mix of silverweed, hops, cinnamon, and blackberry leaves that became hotter than Demerol. This was big. In the eyes of women worldwide, there was God, and then, with all due respect, there was Sasha New. For the *Time* magazine Woman of the Year cover, she wore silver lipstick on her upper lip only, and when women began to boycott the cosmetic industry until it uniformly dropped the price of lipstick and lengthened the sticks by fifty percent, it seemed as if the New movement had officially taken hold.

For weeks, Sasha was thrilled. She was genuinely pleased with herself. Her mother, who was ailing and had lost most of her capacity for speech, would sit in her recliner and smile her crooked smile, wiping drool from the side of her mouth and tears from the sides of her face. "She still ain't normal," Uncle Lou would use most of his day's allotment of breath to mutter, using the rubber tip of his walking cane to propel his rocking chair backward an eighth of an inch.

And then, just like that, it was no longer good enough. No longer gratifying. Sasha's medical discovery might have been historic and pivotal in the world's eyes, but in her own eyes it had failed to be the plateau, the meeting place that would enable her to take a seat in the high chair and smile. The sudden, unexpected end to her joy had her restless for nights, and often she would jump out of bed, sit on the windowsill in her New York apartment, and try to count each light that shone from a building's window. "Too many to count," she'd say quietly to herself. Too many roads. Too many possibilities. Too many options. Life was famous for throwing a whole bunch of stuff your way and watching you muck about. It didn't have to be this difficult. Sasha prided herself on never having given over a single brain cell to the usual liquid or herbal suspects, so she trusted her mind when it told her that there was indeed one road, which indeed led to one place, which indeed would provide her that high chair with that view of the meeting place she yearned to see. With all her talent and with all her capability, with all her promise and all her pride, it was all she ever really yearned for.

So, after five years, she returned Dooley's call. Dooley from elementary school, junior high school, and even high school; Dooley, who, as early as age six, had no problem showing her he was amazed by her, but who never did—not even as a pubescent teen—make the mistake of suggesting that his manhood depended upon her. Dooley, who had always stood apart, had always pulled his weight, had always been a loner because, to get where he was going, he saw no other way. How *was* Dooley doing? she wondered. She genuinely did wonder, and so she picked up the phone and returned his call.

And he said, "Hi, Sasha," as if he'd been expecting her call; as if they'd just talked the night before; as if the call were the well-timed, logical next step for them both. The next day they met for coffee in Philadelphia (he was a surgeon in D.C. and she insisted they meet "halfway"; his driving to New York was "ridiculous" and she wouldn't hear of it, not to mention that the mere suggestion made her feel "cornered and slightly claustrophobic"), and she found, to her surprise, that the meeting was worthwhile. For the next four months they met for coffee in Philadelphia every Sunday evening. They'd read the *Times* together, argue about comparative foreign policy in Haiti and Bosnia, bet on the month's hottest pharmaceutical stock, and otherwise enjoy each other's space, relieved at not having to explain its intricacies. Some time around the fifth month, Sasha began to hear her mother's voice—just above a whisper at first, then louder and louder, sometimes so loud that Sasha would lean forward suddenly in a cab and try to figure out whether the cabbie had heard the voice, too. Her mother had passed two months before she had returned Dooley's 1993 telephone call, and ever since, Sasha had nagged herself with the genuine belief that her mother was dissatisfied. And that was the third mistake.

The following Sunday, Sasha and Dooley were married at the coffeehouse in Philadelphia. The barrista was the best man, the cashier the maid of honor, the consumers the invited guests. Sasha was a real social butterfly that day, handing out complimentary biscotti and croissants to the guests and chatting away about whatever their hearts desired. They told her she looked "amazing" in the emerald sarong she had worn as a chest wrap and the leggings with the yellow pom-pom balls circling the hems. She beamed, Dooley nodded with pride, and for another moment and even for variable moments here and there over the next month or two, Sasha could almost feel the smooth but slightly textured surface of that high chair at the meeting place.

But the first time Sunday evening was no longer sacred—when Dooley didn't have time to read the *Times* with her and didn't have time to pick up his scrubs from Wednesday, Thursday, Friday, and Saturday that were crowding out the available floor space in the tiny bedroom in the overpriced apartment, because he could no longer ignore his pager and the calls from the hospital—the feeling of *ordinary* returned, and Sasha could not sit still. Not even to see if the creeping in of *ordinary* meant that the meeting place was being crowded out. It didn't occur to her to watch for that, so instead she began to chart her cycle, and like clockwork, on day eleven, she and Dooley conceived twins. Born nine months later without incident, Ruth and Rachel brought the first tears to Sasha's adult eyes. Never in life had Sasha known what *precious* felt like, and here she was holding it, nursing it, making it even more unbelievably so each day. Sasha had never quite known what to make of her unbridled self, but with these babies she had new and certain knowledge. She took them to church and had them blessed; she even took them back again a few months later just to visit and hear the preacher recite a psalm. She put a lot of money in the offering plate that Sunday, and then she grabbed Ruth and Rachel up under her arms and exited quickly out the side door.

She was crying a lot those days, so when Ruth and Rachel threw their oatmeal in her face for the very first time, she figured it was nothing more than extended postpartum depression that pushed her out the apartment door and forced her to ignore Dooley's concerned calls from the hallway. Her brisk walk turned into a steady sprint down the sidewalk, and minutes later she found herself in Central Park. She was running by now, and she barely noticed the haggard man standing in her path with a smile and a held-out hand. "I don't have anything," she mumbled quickly, trying to conserve her breath while she ran.

"Don't want nothing," the man said, trotting behind her. He laughed. "And you ain't gon' *get* nothing, either. Ha ha! Girl, don't you realize that no matter how fast you run, you ain't never, ever gonna get there? Ha ha! Arrival's a *lie*."

She was stopped, and not for many years did she bother to think about what it was that had stopped her that day—the shortness of her breath, her burning thigh muscles, or the gravity of her mistake that could be reduced in simplest terms to the life she had lived. The fourth mistake. Who was to blame?

Well, she could blame her mother for what her mother didn't know about the prospective future of a product like Sasha. She could blame the uncles and the aunts for their sneers and snide comments that fueled her difference. Really, she could blame everybody, for no one had bothered to tell her that the pot of gold at the end of the rainbow had been emptied, its contents spread along and embedded in the journey. No one had bothered to tell her the truth about the horizon, that meeting and greeting place of the earth and the sky. Her brilliance hadn't even afforded her the luxury of the truth. The horizon was where you chose it to be; and yet, it would always elude you. It was where Sasha chose it to be whenever impossible and probable merged; Sasha had been there and done that and didn't know it. And yet, it would always elude her because any sister to the stars and daughter to the moon is a child of God, and the horizon is His footstool.

Not Tonight

Tonya Marie Evans

"If there is no enemy within, the enemy outside can do us no harm." —African, Mozambique

It was hard for Dana to stand naked in front of the mirror, but she had to face herself. Sadness overtook her when she forced herself to see the permanent scars left behind by her man, physical reminders of the beatings. "I gotta get outta here," she affirmed, hastily wrapping the oversized lavender towel around her body.

The beatings seemed to come more frequently in the past few months, and they were more violent. Brian was out of work (again), out of hope, and out of control. Dana tried to reassure him that it would all work out and that she'd take care of everything until he got himself together. So she held down two jobs, both of which she hated. She had an abortion at Brian's insistence so that they wouldn't be burdened with another mouth to feed, even though she longed to have a child. Dana even explained away Brian's countless sexual indiscretions, because, as he rationalized, it was just sex, and he really *loved* her. And as repayment for all of her compromises, blind loyalty, and peacekeeping, she was rewarded with constant brutality at the hands of the man she loved, the man who claimed to love her.

Brian had come home one night last week around two A.M. after drinking, smoking, and only God knows what else. Predictably and, for Dana, regrettably, he demanded sex. When she refused, Brian beat her into submission, blackening her left eye and busting her lip. As she lay there in a semiconscious haze, blood trickling from the corner of her mouth, Brian huffed and grunted like a rabid animal, did his business, and then passed out on top of her.

His weight threatened to crush Dana, but she didn't move, fearing she would awaken him. Her doelike eyes were wide open as she searched the darkness for any sign of the promised bright light that angels are supposed to see when they cross over into the afterlife. No such luck, although in her mind, she traveled miles away from that bed. Her thoughts turned away from the atrocity and toward her plan to escape.

When morning came, Brian was nowhere to be found. He usually disappeared after nights like that. Brian was a coward, unable to face the dire consequences of his horrific actions in the light of day. Dana welcomed the solitude because it gave her time to think, to plan. Although she didn't know the exact day that she would leave or how she would do it, Dana knew for sure that Brian would never lay a hand on her again. And if he did, one of them would die. She hoped for the strength to do what was necessary to free herself from her own private hell-on-earth, and she vowed to get herself together and finally summon enough courage to leave.

As Dana lay in the fetal position, she tried to remember when things started to go bad, when her inner spirit died. She could not remember an exact date, a precise event. It was a slow, painful death, resulting from a series of daily, weekly, and monthly spirit injuries as Brian's wishes and wants became paramount and Dana's desires and dreams became all but inconsequential. Unconsciously, Dana's mind conspired against her soul, convincing her that she could change somebody who didn't want to change. But somehow, Dana was the only one who changed, and it was not for the better.

Dana inflated Brian's good qualities and tolerated the not-so-good in the name of love.

"He's good with his hands," she thought.

"If only he'd apply himself," she prayed.

"He's got so much potential," she mused.

"Once he gets another job and gets on his feet, he'll be able to help me with the rent and the groceries and the bills. . . . Once he finds his niche, he won't be so angry and he won't drink so much . . . and he won't hit on me. Then, we'll get married, buy a house, and raise a family. . . . Then, I'll be able to finish school and get a better job and we'll live happily ever after."

Dana sat up in the bed, shaking her head vigorously from side to side in an attempt to shake loose the fairytales. This wishful stream of consciousness had to come to an end, because Dana could no longer lie to herself. The reality was that Dana's apartment was a battle zone, her self-esteem a prisoner of war. She would escape or she would die. She saw no other way out.

Feeling hopeless, Dana fell to her knees and sobbed uncontrollably. She clasped her hands together and attempted to pray, only she couldn't quite remember how to call upon her Creator. In fact, the only prayer she could recall was the one she used to say before supper when she was a child. Finding "God is Great" to be inadequate to properly praise her Father, Dana begged the Lord to help her find a way out of no way.

Dana's grandmother, God rest her soul, had been an intensely devout woman who believed that the answers to all of life's questions could be found in the Bible. In desperate need of answers, Dana went to retrieve her Bible from the nightstand drawer, although her faith had long since been shaken. Pulling open the drawer, she spied the Bible's smooth black cover and gold lettering. Opening it, she saw a piece of paper that appeared to be marking a page. She removed the paper and read the words aloud: *"If there is no enemy within, the enemy outside can do us no harm."* She repeated it again and again and remembered the first time she heard her grandmother say those words. Her mother had left her with her grandmother in the middle of the night after escaping her own boyfriend's wrath. With Dana safe in her grandmother's house, Dana's mother returned home to smooth things over. Dana never saw her mother alive again.

The light in the room illuminated a curious object that was resting just underneath. Dana pushed the Bible aside to reveal the ornate handle of what she believed was the answer to her prayers. A gun. Dana traced the contours of the gun with her index finger and wondered whether Brian had put it there for their protection or her destruction. Dana closed the drawer, leaving the Bible, the quote, and the gun where she had discovered them. All were out of sight; none were out of mind.

Curled up on the sofa, Dana paged through the community college course outline. She was going back to school to get the twelve credits she needed to complete her degree. Brian, who had returned to the apartment, saw her intensely scrutinizing the pages and inquired, "What's that you readin'?"

"It's a listing of college courses," she snapped.

"What you reading that shit for?" he shouted, snatching the catalogue from her hands. "You ain't never gonna finish your degree, so ain't no use spendin' time and money on this!"

"I'm trying to better myself," she retorted, "which is more than I can say for *you!*" Dana was on thin ice with that comment, but she had grown tired of his insults. And she had finally found the courage she needed to stick up for herself, in the nightstand drawer.

"All I know is you betta not waste our money on some ridiculous dreams when you already got two good jobs. How you gonna work two jobs *and* go to school, huh? Your stupid ass didn't think about that, did ya?"

Brian walked into the kitchenette for a can of beer. He popped open the top, and the sound echoed in Dana's mind like a starter pistol. *And they're off!* After his first sip, Dana could tell that this was going to be one of those nights. Still, she pressed her point.

"I can do both, Brian. I can do anything I set my mind to. You should be happy for me and support me instead of being so damned negative. Don't you want more outta life than *this?*" She spread her arms wide and looked around the room. Her nonverbal cues suggested that she was not satisfied with a cramped one-bedroom apartment with chipped paint, the more-than-occasional roach, leaky faucets, windows that were painted shut, and radiators that hissed and creaked in the winter. Brian, needless to say, could not see her point and was growing tired of the positive-Black-woman thing that she must have learned from watching Oprah.

"Oh, what's that supposed to mean? What you tryin' to say? I ain't supportive?" Brian took a long swig of beer from the can and strode toward her. Fight and flight struggled for control within her. Dana was not sure whether she should stand her ground or back down. Brian was getting more and more agitated.

"You know I'm going through a rough time, and you gonna use that against me and make me feel like I ain't shit and you all that 'cause you wanna go back to school!" He was screaming now, and Dana realized that the point of no return was in sight. The lights in the room seemed to be getting brighter.

"Brian, there's no reason to yell. I'm just saying that it would be nice if you could support my decision to better myself. You can't get a decent job without a college degree, you know."

"Well, I ain't got no degree and I'ma do just fine. Believe that!"

"Brian, if you went to school with me, we could do it together. Then, we'd both be able to get good jobs and do better for ourselves. I thought that's what you wanted."

Brian drained his beer and crushed the can in his hand. "Well, you thought wrong, woman, and this is what you get for thinkin'." He hurled the empty can at Dana, and she batted it away, giving him the look of death. He hated her defiance. Dana looked different to him for some reason. Fearless. He puffed out his chest and charged toward her.

"Who you lookin' at like that, woman?" He snarled the words. "Don't forget who you are and who I am, and we won't have no problems tonight. All I'm sayin' is you wastin' your time."

Brian burped a loud, obnoxious burp right into Dana's face. She did not flinch. He moved forward with pursed lips to kiss her. She held up her hands to protect her newly drawn personal boundary. Confused and angry, he furrowed his brow, pushed Dana up against the wall, and hissed, "Don't get it twisted, Dana. I'm runnin' things here. If I say you don't go wasting money on school, then that's it, and that's what I'm sayin'. You always busy tryin' to make me think I ain't shit. But guess what? You the one. *You* ain't shit. Remember that!" With that final declaration, he pulled her to him and forced his tongue into her mouth. The taste of beer and the smell of stale sweat assaulted her senses. Unmoved, Dana stood firm until he backed away.

"I'm outta here. I don't need this! I just know that you'd better be awake when I get home, 'cause you know what I want." He stared at Dana as he backed away toward the door. She watched him open it, turn his back to her, and close the door behind him. Momentary relief. Private enemy number one had left the building, but he would return sooner or later. Tonight would be the night, for sure.

Dana's mind returned quickly to the nightstand drawer where her trinity was safeguarded—the gun, the Bible, and the quote. Each in its own way represented the way, the truth, and the light. Still, the quote vied for her attention. *If there's no enemy within, the enemy outside can do us no harm.* As a ten-year-old girl who'd been left with her grandmother when her mom needed to get away and deal with her own domestic drama, the saying had made little sense. Now, the words rang so true that the mere thought gave Dana chills. She spent so much time focused outward, and understandably so, but what inside her made her stay in a chaotic, destructive situation that could result in her own death? What enemy inside her allowed her to rationalize brutality as love? How much self-hate must live inside Dana for her to believe that she didn't deserve more than Brian would or could give? Who was the real enemy?

Dana had no time to grapple with the issues and come to a conclusion. She heard the familiar sound of music blasting, then silence, then the slamming of a car door. Footsteps. Laughter. The main apartment building door creaked, acting as an alarm. Brian had returned earlier than expected.

Dana went into high-alert mode. She turned off all the lights, retreated to the bedroom, and closed the door. She crouched down on the side of the bed, next to the nightstand, and waited.

Brian's keys jingled; then the lock turned and yielded, and he entered the apartment. As he closed the door behind him, he let out a loud burp and exploded into hysterical, sinister laughter. "Woman!" he screamed, "you ready for Big Poppa to run up in ya?"

Dana didn't move, but her paralysis had nothing to do with fear. Fear had long since been replaced by numbness. Tonight Dana was prepared, and she drew comfort from the darkness in the bedroom. Ordinarily, this room was the scene of almost nightly crimes against Dana's mind, body, and soul, but tonight she had the upper hand.

And she had her trinity.

Brian continued to call out to Dana as he stumbled toward the bedroom. The light from the streetlamps guided him to the bedroom door. He kicked it open and bounded into the room. His eyes, clouded by Jim Beam and beer and impaired by the necessary adjustment from darkness to light, did not allow him to focus upon his prey. But Dana saw Brian clearly. In fact, she saw him more clearly than ever before. At six feet, 230 sloppy pounds, drunk, and out of control, no one in their right mind would fault Dana for protecting herself against something like him.

"Bitch, you ain't sleep!" He spat his words through the darkness of the cramped bedroom as he stumbled in the general direction of the bed, where Dana crouched, prepared to do whatever was necessary to kill the enemy that night. "Roll your ass over and gimme some before I take it again." The words *"before I take it again"* echoed in her mind like a clap of thunder between two mountains. Dana shivered at the thought. Brian zeroed in on her location.

The enemy outside lunged toward Dana to take what he thought was his, and as usual, the enemy within retreated to let him have his way. But the new Dana was in control, and business would not be as usual tonight. She slipped from Brian's grasp and pulled open the drawer, vowing to put an end to the madness.

At that moment, Brian noticed the hold Dana had on the drawer, and asked, "What you know about that drawer, woman?"

"I know *this!*" Grabbing the first thing she could, she pulled it out of the drawer. It was the gun. She pointed it in Brian's direction, and he reared back in utter disbelief, his drunken haze now replaced with confusion and fear. Fear because he knew the gun was loaded, and because he suspected Dana might actually pull the trigger. What neither realized was that Dana also had a firm grip on a small piece of paper, the paper that had the power to save both of their lives that night.

In her mind, Dana heard her grandmother's words again: *"If there's no enemy within, the enemy outside can do us no harm."*

"What the hell do you think you're doing, Dana? Have you lost your damned mind? Put that thing down and stop playing."

"I'm not playing, Brian. I'm serious as this gun is. I'm not taking this shit anymore. One of us has to die tonight."

"Girl, if you don't give me that gun, you'll be sorry!" His threats were empty, carrying no weight. He cowered on the floor, too scared to move, too mad to stay still.

"Fool, I'm not afraid of you anymore. I'm not afraid of you!" Dana took another step toward Brian with every word. She found herself standing over him, holding the gun only inches away from his face. She wanted him to feel the pain that she had felt every day. She wanted to hurt him, to see him bleed. Someone had to die that night.

"If there's no enemy within, the enemy outside can do us no harm." Dana heard her grandmother's voice. Looking down at Brian, she no longer saw a powerful man. Instead, the man she saw was pitiful. He was hardly worth the trouble of taking a life. As long as she could walk away with her own life and her sanity, she would be satisfied. Holding the gun steady, she walked backward toward the bedroom door. Dana's eyes were fixed on Brian's. He did not move or utter a sound. He had lost his power over her. *If there's no enemy within, the enemy outside can do us no harm.*

She continued to inch backward, her grandmother's voice growing louder in her mind. Leaving everything she owned but her keys, Dana ran out the door and down the stairs, jumped into her car, and began to drive. She did not know where she was going, but she felt a new sense of power. Tonight she'd killed the enemy. The enemy within.

A Crisis of Faith

Robert Fleming

"We do not struggle in despair but in hope, not from doubt but from faith, not from hate but out of love for ourselves and for humanity." —Black theologian James Cone

It was one of the brightest days of fall. The sky was never bluer, nor were there ever so many birds aloft, or the grass so green and full. No one had alerted the family that he would be coming that afternoon, but the arrival of the reporters with their TV camera trucks and note-pads meant that something was about to happen. They camped out across the street from the small brick house in tiny herds, huddling and talking as they looked up and down the road.

Then it happened. The car containing him—their son, their brother, their uncle—came roaring down the street. The government-issue Ford was led by a single motorcycle cop and followed by another. If someone didn't know, they would assume that it was a motorcade delivering a very important person, a political official or a show business celebrity. But it was only the State bringing him home. After fifteen long years in prison, Danny Poole was finally coming home after being unjustly jailed based solely on the unstable word of a young white woman.

When the car reached the front of the house, Danny remained seated inside while policemen pushed back the horde of reporters who pressed against the vehicle. Slowly he exited the car—no longer thin, no longer young—and limped toward the stairs, steadied by one of the patrolmen. The family burst from the front door, nearly bowling him over with hugs and kisses.

"Hey baby! Welcome home, sweetheart," Alva, his mother, said, wrapping her thick arms so tightly around him that he could barely breathe. "We missed you so much. I knew those prison bars couldn't hold you. I just knew they couldn't."

He tugged at the collar of the cheap black suit given to him as a parting gift by the State—inexpensive fabric that rode up his neck and legs. If anyone noticed that he looked older, his gaunt face more lined and wrinkled, they didn't mention it. Instead, the five close members of his family guided him into the house, mindful of his fragile appearance and apparent bewilderment at his sudden emergence into freedom.

His older sister, Irma, kissed him lightly on the cheek and looked into his ravaged face. The face that was a thinner carbon copy of hers. "Danny, we're so happy that you're home. We all knew you didn't belong there in the first place. We all knew that. Knew it then and know it now. When did they let you go, love?"

"Last night," he finally spoke in a dry rasp, his first words uttered in freedom. "But they kept me there until this morning. For processing or something." He moved to sit on the well-worn couch in the living room, noting that it appeared smaller than he remembered. His hands shook slightly from the nervousness that raced through him, surging and ebbing beyond his control.

He replayed the day of his arrest, the yelling and shoving of the station-house cops, and the young white woman who had pointed at him and said tersely: "Yes, that's the nigger who raped me." A large knot of tension grew in his stomach with the memory.

"Danny, Aunt Cece and Uncle Keith will be coming by later." His mother smiled, brushing a bit of lint from her blue gingham dress. "We're planning a big party for you this weekend. Everybody will be here. Everybody."

He thought about everybody who had attended his trial and who had listened to the white woman talk quietly and earnestly about how he had sneaked up behind her, pinned her arms back, and held a knife to her throat.

"When I tried to shout for help, he told me that one more word and he'd kill me," she'd claimed. She detailed how he'd broken into her house, beaten her up, and forced her to "go down" on him.

Her pink, ruddy face with her thin lips, the tears on her cheeks, were in his mind. What chance did he, a black man, possibly have when going up against the holy word of a violated white woman?

From the kitchen, his younger brother Benny came, tall and proud, bearing a big platter of sandwiches, turkey and ham on wheat. He stood near the doorway, staring at Danny as if he were a ghost. A wide smile emerged by degrees on Benny's dark face, showing his deep joy and wonder at the return of the prodigal son to the fold. The abused, maligned son who had spent half his life behind bars for a crime he hadn't committed. All because he was black and he didn't have an alibi for the night of the sexual assault. Fifteen years, fifteen wasted years. Time that Danny could never get back.

Benny's smile faded and his eyes showed concern. "Did they do anything to you in there?"

"Anything like what?" Danny didn't want to answer any questions about being "inside"—the endless battles between the strong and the weak, the bad food, the dank smells, the horrible feeling of being caged. Like an unruly beast.

"You know like . . . made you into a punk," Benny continued. "You're still all right?"

"Yes, I'm still a virgin if you must know." He grinned harshly. It was the truth, but he could never tell them what it cost him. He had almost killed two men up there. Had almost become a murderer. The brutality, the violence he was forced to commit to keep himself intact, to remain above the level of an amoeba on the prison food chain. His brother and sister laughed uneasily, relieved. His mother looked at him with an expression that said there was something he was not telling her, a truth that was not being spoken. She pointed to the press photographers climbing over the front porch, tramping all over her grass and flowerbeds, aiming their cameras through the picture window, flashbulbs popping with blinding regularity. Where was the right of privacy?

Benny walked to the window and pulled the curtains shut with a dramatic motion, using both hands. Danny clapped, bringing giggles from his sister.

"Lawd, why don't those people leave us alone?" his mother cried, rolling her eyes. "You know they won't have nothing good to say. All looking for new dirt."

He flashed back to the white woman's face during the trial, and the string of lies she told that was certain to send him to jail. "He was so huge, I mean big and tall." Her voice quivered with each syllable. "It was not enough for the nigger, with his animal smell, to take me against my will, but he sat there afterwards and smoked two cigarettes, chatting with me like I was his girlfriend or something. He wouldn't let me wash up, take a shower. I felt so dirty and unclean. Ask any woman who has been raped and she will know what I mean. Add to that, he was a nigger. In the old days, he would have been strung up, without all of this fanfare and expense to the taxpayers." That was what she had said, right on the witness stand.

"Are you bitter, son, for what they did to you?" his mother asked, holding the plate of sandwiches before him.

"How would you feel if someone took all those years from your life?" he replied, his body stiffening. "Took them and you knew all along that you'd done nothing wrong. Knew you were innocent and nobody believed you."

"We believed you, Danny," his sister said quickly.

He couldn't look at them. None of them had believed him. The truth was that his family had believed the white woman, just like everybody else had. How could justice be real for anyone when all a person, especially a white person, had to do was to point a finger and yell that an innocent man was guilty?

Much of the evidence that could have freed him was never introduced at the trial. Even his own court-appointed lawyer had advised him it didn't look good for him, that his only option was to plead guilty to aggravated sexual assault, take the lesser charge, and put himself at the mercy of the court. Which he had done.

The past fifteen years had been a nightmare from start to finish, with the cards stacked against him from the moment he was arrested outside this very house. The cops hadn't believed a word he'd said, even the fact that he lived on this block, until they checked that out. When he saw the composite drawing of the suspect, it looked nothing like him, but to the cops it was a Rembrandt. Perfect. They'd claimed they had evidence linking him to a series of rapes in the swank neighborhood, all petite white women ravished by a big Mandingo buck, who pounded on them afterward. The lead detective, the man who testified, said he never had any doubt of Danny's guilt, not after the woman was able to describe him in full detail.

Danny shook his head to clear the pain of memory.

"You were a Christian before you went in there," his mother said. "I know that's what kept you from becoming like the rest of them. That undying faith in Jesus. I know you must have leaned on Him when it seemed like there was no hope. Right, Danny?"

"God doesn't visit prisons much, Mama," he retorted. Like many men on the inside, his faith was a private thing, a flame he held deep inside, not something he proclaimed to the world. Then—and now—it was nobody's business but his own.

"Don't blaspheme in this house, child," his mother snapped. "I didn't raise you like that. I raised you to have some respect for God and the church. I won't tolerate that under this roof. I don't care what they did to you in there; you won't bring that mess in here." She shook with righteous indignation.

He stood rigidly to signal an end to the conversation, heading stiffly toward the kitchen, where the comforting smells of fried chicken, collards, cornbread, and black-eyed peas wrapped themselves around him like a warm winter coat, taking the chill out of his heart, whispering to him of the times when Daddy had been with them and the word *family* had meant something. Until the moment Daddy had suffered a heart attack and dropped dead right here, near the icebox, family had been a cocoon of safety and protection.

The door sounded and the loud, raucous shouts of Uncle Keith and Aunt Cece echoed throughout the house like a gunshot. Uncle Keith, pale-skinned and rail thin, all dressed in the latest Mack Daddy chic. Aunt Cece, big as a Goodyear blimp, made up like a tart, dressed in colors that glowed in the dark. They were known throughout the entire clan as the most uncouth, uncivilized members of their bloodline, capable of turning out weddings with their antics, skilled at ruining family dinners with their tasteless comments. *Heathens*, his mother called them.

"Where's the jailbird?" Aunt Cece screamed at the top of her lungs. "Come on out and let us take a look at you, boy. Come and give your favorite aunt a hug."

Uncle Keith chortled, his Adam's apple bobbing on the downbeat. "You can run but you can't hide. I won't bite you, son."

Danny eased out of the sanctuary of the kitchen, walking unsteadily toward the intruders, his arms down at his sides. This was the last thing he needed on his first day. Why couldn't they come tomorrow after he was gone? Both of them had spread the worst lies about him during the trial, giving the cops all manner of gossip against him, even leading them to the mother of a girl who'd once accused him of slapping her around. In fact, it was her boyfriend who had done the damage, but Danny had been an easy target, the perfect fall guy. The police had taken him in, but nothing had come of that false accusation because it had happened when he was under eighteen, a juvie. Those records were supposedly sealed. Supposedly. His heart hardened at the remembering, and his arms remained glued to his sides.

"It's a damn circus out there," Uncle Keith said, looking out the window. "The press is all over the place. Cameras, the whole nine yards, even Channel Seven. I talked to the tall, brown-skinned girl from Channel Four, told her I was like a father to you, Danny. That you were pretty much a good kid who got a bad break. 'But you got to keep a close eye on him,' I told her."

"Why did you say something like that?" Danny glared at his uncle. "I'm trying to start a new life and you go and say some stupid shit like that. What are you trying to do to me?"

"Danny, I'm like your father, now that he's gone," his uncle said. "I know you better than anybody. You forget I knew you when you didn't even know how to flush a toilet."

"Keith, nobody knows him better than I do," his mother said, moving between the two men. "I'm his mother. Don't forget that. I know my own boy."

Aunt Cece gently elbowed his mother aside, stretched out her arms, and enveloped him inside them. He was trapped for several minutes, choking on her powerful White Orchid perfume and baby powder.

His uncle peeled Cece away. "Honey, that's enough. I don't want this boy getting any bad ideas. You know, it's been a long time since he's been with a real woman."

Aunt Cece laughed, but no one else did. For once, his family, his close kin, were behind him, with him. That made him feel a little better.

"They had that white girl on the news when they said they was letting you out," Aunt Cece reported. "She said she was happy for you, that the court would not have let you out if you were guilty. Said it still made her nervous and scared to see you outside of prison, said it was just a mistake and that color had nothing to do with it. Said she was saddened by it but she wasn't going to beat herself up over it. Said she was going on with her life."

"Enough, Cee," his mother snapped. "Can't you find something else to talk about? He doesn't need to hear any more about that foolishness, especially about that cracker. She ruined his life."

"Just why did they let you out, anyway, Danny?" Aunt Cece asked, acting as if she hadn't heard one word the older woman said. "I don't get it. They found a hair strand and arrested some other black boy. How does that work?"

"He didn't do it," Benny snarled. "They had the wrong man."

"RNA, right?" his uncle said, proud that he knew the scientific term.

"DNA," Danny snapped, walking away from them. "Are the bedrooms still in the same place? I need to lay down. My head hurts."

The doorbell rang again. It was another reporter and camera crew, asking for a few words from the family for the nightly news. Just something about how it felt to have Danny home, about how the law had finally come through for them, how they felt about the $20,000 check the State had offered for the time he'd spent behind bars. Danny kept walking while Uncle Keith happily filled in the blanks for the reporter.

Wearily, Danny entered his old bedroom, looking at the small bed, the beat-up desk, and the stacks of boxes in one corner. Nothing had been touched since the night of his arrest. He grinned at the familiar sights and smells. He was home. He had survived everything: the beatings by the guards and other cons, the shank attacks, the bad food. Nothing had trampled his spirit. Nothing.

There were times when Danny had to hide his spirit to save it; times when his faith was tested over and over again. He'd had many moments of doubt, even more of despair, but he somehow managed to hold to a spark of belief that God would eventually right the injustice that had destroyed so much of his life.

He hadn't become a fervent religious mouthpiece as many of the men in prison had, spouting their newfound beliefs with an almost desperate passion. For many years, he'd even stopped praying, gave up talking to God altogether. While he thought sometimes that it would be better not to believe in a Higher Power, Danny knew that hidden spark of faith enabled him to survive, so he wrapped it in a cloak of cynicism to keep it burning safely deep within. But no matter how bleak his future looked or how hopeless he felt, even in those moments when Danny feared that perhaps God had given up on him, written him off, and tossed him away, he couldn't bring himself to give up on God.

Feeling the tentative warmth of the spark growing into something greater, Danny sank to his knees on the floor of his childhood room and offered a prayer of sincere thanks. His eyes fluttered, but he kept them shut. That was always the hardest part of praying for him—not the words, but keeping his eyes closed.

"*. . . Yea, though I walk through the valley of the shadow of death, I will fear no evil: for thou art with me,*" he continued, not opening his eyes even when he felt another presence in the room with him. Kneeling beside him. Praying along with him.

He recognized the raw, husky voice as that of his Aunt Cece, saying the words of the familiar psalm right along with him. They finished on the same note. She struggled to her feet with his help, pinched his cheek, and quietly left the room. But before her departure, she put a single finger to her lips. He understood: this was their secret. Their private piece of serenity and joy.

   After she left, Danny was numb. Nothing was as it seemed. She was more than just a loud-mouthed hellion, an uncouth harpy, but a woman who had a devout sense of faith and belief in the Almighty. *Faith*, that word again. In that instant, he realized what had helped him to survive all those years, in the darkest moments of his transformation from being an average hardworking man to a caged animal. He sat on the bed, stunned by his epiphany, and with trembling hands, took out a cigarette. It took him almost five minutes to light it. *Yes, faith, the evidence of things unseen yet believed.* He could now acknowledge it. His divine faith, like that which had sustained all of his kind from the slave ships to the boardroom and beyond. Not just grit, determination, or spunk. But faith. Or something like that.

Senseless

Nancey Flowers

"I freed thousands of slaves. I could have freed thousands more, had they known they were slaves."
—Harriet Tubman, Abolitionist

Isis Baines dragged herself into her son's bedroom, her heart heavy, her footsteps unsure. Crossing the low-shag carpet, she parted the navy-and-white-striped drapes and trailed a finger through a light layer of dust that had settled on the sill. Sunlight spilled into the room, warming her face, but it failed to stir her heart. Lately, she had been consumed with thoughts that rendered her motionless. Straightening the sheets on Shiloh's bed, Isis smoothed out the errant wrinkles as she tried unsuccessfully to conceal the woes and contempt she felt toward her own black people. Bending to pick up Shiloh's basketball jacket, she fingered the sleeve, inhaling traces of her son's scent, and shook her head at the senselessness of it all.

Raising a black man in America was a difficult task. A black man had to will away the multiple odds that assailed him from conception to birth, to manhood. Otherwise he would fall prey to a futile and warped society. These odds didn't seem to exist in the white man's world, and never would, but that wasn't important. Isis wanted to know how, when, and why the black community had become so callous and remote. When did people stop caring for one another? When was the black community going to start taking responsibility for its irresponsibility? Whatever happened to black communities being amalgamated? And why had they let ignorance become their neighbor? Isis knew it took a village to raise a child, but what happened when the villagers became distraught because of their own family situations, nomadic with the hopes of finding a more suitable lifestyle or environment, despondent and willing to settle, or even lost and forlorn?

"Ma," Shiloh said, sneaking up behind Isis, startling her and planting a kiss on her cheek. "You know this game and that trophy are mine this year, right?"

"Boy, you said that last year and the year before," Isis said, using the cloth in her hand to snap him on the behind as he passed her, dribbling his basketball.

"Yeah, and we won the game two years ago. Last year those punks that beat us from uptown just got lucky, but this year the Bombers are gonna take 'em out Brooklyn-style. You sure you can't come?" he asked.

"You know I would if I could, but I promised your uncle Bedford that I would accompany his new wife, Sandy, to some Broadway play. But I'll keep you in my prayers. Good luck!" she said walking over to give him a big hug, which he indulged. "Naima will be there, right?"

"Yup, no question."

"Well, tell her that I said hi. Now remember to breathe, focus, and follow through. Most importantly, bring that trophy home to Mama!" she said, laughing.

"You know I will, Ma. Love ya," he said as he jogged down the steps and exited their three-family brownstone.

"I love you, too."

As Isis continued her chore, she came across a black-and-white composition notebook. On sight she knew that it was Shiloh's book of poetry. Before now she had never invaded upon his privacy, but today was different. She decided to flip through it. The first poem she read was titled "The Hidden."

They stole you from your homeland
They stole your native tongue
And whipped you to build up their land
Not even a thank-you when you were done
They treat you like animals and control your every move
They beat you to death when you do something they don't approve
You have been the obedient Nigger
Nigger, it's time to set yourself free
Unveil the mask you've worn to please them
It's time to please God and thee
Let the truth be known
Let the knowledge flow

Don't hide the truth
Let your children know
The blood that courses through your veins comes from kings
The wonders and crafts that surround you are our doings
These fifty-one states that they call a nation
Have decided to attack, creating an enormous situation
Let's arm ourselves with education and God to avoid being out-
    done
If you allow yourself to fall victim we will never overcome
Look to the east to the rising sun
Keep your third eye open for our day will come.

Tears bathed Isis's face like the falls of Niagara. Shiloh had penned that particular piece in honor of Black History Month when he was ten years old. Isis and her husband, Yarren, were so thrilled about their son's newfound talent and accomplishment that they submitted the poem to a contest held by *The Amsterdam News*. "The Hidden" won second prize—two hundred and fifty dollars—which Isis and Yarren allowed Shiloh to spend any way he chose. Shiloh didn't squander the money on clothes, sneakers, or toys. He consulted his uncle Bedford for financial advice, invested two hundred dollars into a mutual fund, purchased a caboose for his father's train set, and pocketed the remaining change.

Shiloh was the best gift that God had ever bestowed upon Isis. The second gift was her husband, but he wasn't long for this earth. Only three years her senior, Yarren had succumbed to an aneurysm a few years earlier, and Isis and her older brother Bedford continued to raise Shiloh, who had become a man long before he turned twenty-one just a month earlier. Isis and Bedford armed Shiloh with the tools necessary for survival. They taught him how to exist in a world that preferred he become a statistic rather than thrive. Shiloh knew the importance of an education and attended Morgan State University, where he received his bachelor's degree in business management. Understanding the need to apply himself, Shiloh also interned at his uncle Bedford's financial consulting firm.

Shiloh devoted four summers to Jackson & Jackson and earned himself a full-time position at the firm. He was scheduled to begin in his new position on the following Monday, and he wanted to celebrate by taking Isis and his girlfriend, Naima, out to dinner and a Broadway play. It was a very special evening. Shiloh was a complete gentleman, opening doors, pulling out chairs, pouring wine, and ordering their meals. They thoroughly enjoyed themselves. Laughter permeated the air. Isis beamed as her son bestowed affection on Naima and showered *her* with love. Shiloh's ability to express himself emanated from the seeds of confidence planted by his family. Isis replayed that night over again and again in her mind.

Exhausted, she took a seat at the foot of the bed and stared aimlessly at the sapphire blue walls that she and Shiloh had painted together. It seemed like only yesterday, and a slight smile crept across Isis's face as she remembered.

"Boy, you almost finished with your side of the room?" Isis asked, talking to Shiloh's back.

"Why you worried about my side? You handle yours, and I'll work on mine."

"I know you're not giving me lip service over there."

"And if I am, what you gonna do about it?" Shiloh joked, letting out a chuckle.

"This!" Isis flicked her paintbrush in Shiloh's direction. "Oops! You missed a spot!"

By the end of the day, they had managed to paint the walls as well as themselves, and while it took a full can of turpentine to remove the splotches from their skin, all the detergent in the world wouldn't wash the paint out of their overalls.

The walls of Shiloh's room were full of pictures and posters. Isis stared at a photo taken at one of Shiloh's Little League games. He was standing at bat waiting for a pitch, determination and focus—traits garnered from his father—evident. After that photo was snapped, Shiloh had swung and missed once, hit two foul balls, and on the fourth pitch whacked the ball out to left field. Shiloh had been amazed, running his little heart out to second base. Isis didn't quite recall if her son's team had won, but the team spirit had helped Shiloh build strength and good sportsmanship.

Her memories sweet, Isis leaned back onto the palms of her hands and gently rubbed them against the quilted comforter that she had purchased just months ago to give the room additional life. She put away her dusting cloth. Shiloh, also known as "Sloppy Joe," always left his room in disarray—hamper overflowing, clothes and hangers on the floor, shoes thrown about, cups placed on the nightstands, and books stashed under the bed. His room was so filthy you could trip over your own shadow. The only space that Shiloh cleaned and dusted regularly was his glass curio, which held his many awards, plaques, and basketball trophies. Isis had eventually stopped fussing about his room, because after all, he was a good kid and he did have skills on the basketball court.

Shiloh stood at the free-throw line, his yellow-and-blue jersey clinging to his shapely pecs. Sweat trickled along the sides of his face as he steadily dribbled the ball. It was the championship game, and his team needed these two points to win. The score was seventy-seven to seventy-eight in their opponent's favor. The park was almost silent, and the smallest cough or chuckle could be heard. They were playing street ball, and this game was for the victory. With a mere six seconds remaining on the clock, the fate of the game rested in Shiloh's hands as he cradled the ball, aiming it into position. "You can do it, Shy," someone screamed in the crowd. Shiloh knew that it had to be his girl, Naima, and a slight grin came to his face. He kept his elbow in as he prepared to release the ball. He kept his eyes on the spot over the front of the rim. His wrist made a smooth motion, and his finger flipped as he released the ball into the air. *Swoosh.* All net. It was a tie game and the crowd roared. *"Shiloh Baines SCORES,"* the commentator bellowed.

"Yo, Shiloh, good game, man. I was shitting bricks when I saw that second shot rounding the rim before dropping. *Psst . . .* Man, you don't know, but tonight was definitely your night!" Shiloh's best friend, Gary, exclaimed.

"Man, you wasn't the only one scared, I ain't even gonna front. I'm glad it's over, though. I've never felt so much pressure before in my life. It feels good to go out on top. Especially since I probably won't be playing street ball no more on the regular. You know my uncle Bedford hooked me up with the phat job at his firm, right?" he said.

"True dat. So what you got going tonight?" Gary asked as he pulled his triple-X-sized hooded sweatshirt over his head. At six feet, three inches, Gary played point guard and had scored only twelve points in that evening's game.

"Me and Naima just plan to chill and have a private celebration of our own. You know what I'm saying?" Shiloh said, nodding with a sly grin.

"That's cool. I wish I had me a honey to celebrate with tonight, but I'ma chill with the fellas. You checked out Jabar's new ride yet?"

"Nah, man, but I saw him up in the sneaker joint the other day with this chick, and he was telling me about it."

"It's hot kid, word. Anyway, I'ma head out."

"A'ight. I'm sure wherever y'all go tonight there will be plenty of lovelies to quench your thirst. Which way you going?"

"I'm headed to Brooklyn. You and Naima need a ride?"

"Yeah, if you don't mind. She probably got one of her girls with her, though. Maybe y'all can hook up."

"Man, whatever. How she look?" Gary said, trying not to smile, but his lips decided to betray him.

"All of her friends are cute. I don't know who she got with her, though."

"A'ight," Gary said, taking his friend's word for it.

Shiloh went to locate Naima and her friend. They were still hanging around the benches, chatting. Shiloh sneaked up behind Naima and grabbed her by the waist. She was startled and began giggling when she realized that it was Shiloh, and immediately turned around to embrace him and offer a long congratulatory kiss. They were always hugging and kissing, even though they had been together through four years of college.

"Are you ladies ready?" Shiloh asked, his arm draped around Naima's neck.

"We were waiting for you," Naima said, leaning her hip against his long tawny-brown legs. She stood a mere five feet, five inches to his six-foot-two frame.

"Good. Well, Gary is going to give us a lift back to Brooklyn, so let's head home. Trina, are you going straight home? Gary said he'd give you a ride, too."

"That's fine. Are you guys in a rush? I'm a little hungry and was hoping we could stop right quick and get something to eat."

Shiloh and Naima looked at each other to see what the other was thinking, and then they nodded in mutual agreement that it was fine to stop off somewhere.

Trina sat in the front with Gary, and they hit it off right away. They stopped at a little soul food restaurant not far from the park, called Aahirah's Palace. On the ride home, Gary kicked it with Trina while Shiloh and Naima continued their earlier petting session. When they finally arrived at Naima's, Gary parked the car in front of her house. Trina lived only a few brownstones down, so they sat on Naima's stoop, reminiscing about the game, the good food they had shared, and what was in store for the next day.

The ringing chime of a cell phone cut through the air.

"Hey, Ma," Shiloh said.

"Boy, how'd you know it was me?"

"Ma, it's called Caller ID. Anyway, what's up?"

"You tell me. Did you-all win?"

"And you know that!" Shiloh boasted.

"You go, boy!"

"C'mon, Ma. Chill with all that. You still stuck in the nineties."

"So, I'm assuming you and your friends are going out to celebrate, right?"

"Yeah, we just finished picking up something to eat, and I'm about to stop off at Naima's house for a bit."

"Okay, well, call me if you're going to be late. Shiloh . . . I'm really proud of you."

"Thanks, Ma. I will, and don't start crying. Love ya!"

"I love you, too."

Isis had shed many tears on account of Shiloh—his successes and failures, honors and awards, truancy and smoking, broken limbs and fights. Many of the fights weren't his battle to begin with, but Shiloh would defend: "Ma, I had to jump in. How could I let Derek get jumped while I stood there on the sidelines? I'm sorry if you're mad, but he's my boy and I couldn't let him go out like that." Shiloh, the man who would leap to your defense in a single bound! His innocence went beyond the depths of integrity. He was always helping other people.

As he laughed with Naima, a young woman across the street grabbed Shiloh's attention. He recognized her as Yolanda, a girl he'd known from elementary school. Shiloh got up and called her over to the group. Yolanda seemed reluctant but crossed over to join them. After completing the introductions, Shiloh sensed that something was wrong. Yolanda kept fidgeting and anxiously looking down the block. A drop of dry blood on the corner of her lip startled him, and Shiloh expressed his concern, which Yolanda quickly brushed off as nothing.

As the group sat talking and laughing and enjoying the cool night air, a Jeep came barreling down the street, defying the posted speed limit of thirty miles per hour. Yolanda seemed to recognize the vehicle and nervously watched as it speeded closer. The Jeep drove past but then immediately screeched to a halt and then reversed. Yolanda wedged herself between Trina and Naima.

"Yo, Yolanda. Git over here," the driver yelled.

Yolanda tried to pretend that she didn't hear him, and continued with her conversation.

"I know you hear me. Don't make me have to come up outta this Jeep," he snapped.

"Girl, you gonna be okay?" both Naima and Trina questioned.

"Yeah, I'm fine," Yolanda answered. "That *was* my man until tonight, and he's trippin'. I don't know why he won't leave me the hell alone. Raheem . . . please go home. Leave me alone. I can't take this shit no more. I'm tired. Please, just go away."

Raheem got out of the Jeep and, in a rage, slammed the door.

"What? You trying to embarrass me? Yo, come on, let's talk. I said I was sorry."

" 'Sorry' is not gonna help you this time. I'm begging you to leave me be. I'm tired, and I can't go through this no more."

"Raheem, listen, man. Brother to brother, man to man, let this sister calm down. She seems a little upset right now. Maybe—" Shiloh offered, but was cut off.

"Man, do I know you?" Raheem asked, stepping back and sizing Shiloh up.

"Nah, but all I'm saying is, just let the lady chill. Maybe you two can work this out some other time."

"Nigger, please. This is my girl and she's coming with me." Raheem brushed past Shiloh and climbed up the steps toward Yolanda. He grabbed her upper arm, and she yelled out in pain.

"Rah, let go of me damn it," Yolanda screamed, and stood one step higher to be on eye level with him.

"Take her inside, Naima," Shiloh said.

"Yeah, do that," Gary said, agreeing. "Let us vibe with this cat for a minute."

"Yo, I ain't warning y'all no more. Stay the fuck outta my business. Now, Yolanda, bring your ass here now," Raheem said, enunciating every word through the spaces of his teeth.

Raheem's passenger tapped the horn to get his attention.

"One minute, man," Raheem said, waving at his boy and watching Yolanda as she walked to the top of the stairs. Naima took advantage of the moment and quickly pulled Yolanda into the house. Raheem headed down the steps and walked over to his friend while Naima and Trina entered the foyer. Gary lingered, watching Trina take her time sashaying through the doorway, all the while throwing hateful glances at Raheem.

"I'll be there in a minute," Shiloh announced as he walked toward the car. Although he didn't like the way Raheem was treating Yolanda, he wanted to make amends and let him know there were no hard feelings. As Shiloh approached the Jeep, Raheem took something from his friend. Raheem turned toward him with a lethal look, but Shiloh had already decided that he was going to try and set things straight.

"Raheem, man, I just want you to know that everything is cool. I just want Yolanda to hang tight for a minute and for both of y'all to get your heads straight. I don't know what happened earlier, but she seems really upset. We'll make sure she gets home safe and, you know, give her a call tomorrow or sumptin'."

"Oh, yeah, word. Well, I told you to mind ya own bizness, muthafucka!"

Raheem pulled a shiny black object from his waistband, and Shiloh became a statistic.

Five months after her son's death, the shrill of the telephone still startled Isis. That single call informing her of his death had left her jumpy but numb. She ignored the ringing and propped her body up against the wall, hugging her knees to her chest. The task of cleaning out Shiloh's room had left her weak, but she knew she needed to gather the strength to carry on.

Shiloh's composition book beckoned her. The notebook was a collage of sorts, with verses claiming and demanding freedom while other words endorsed love. She flipped through sheets bearing newspaper clippings taped to pages. Stories dating back to the Rodney King case asking, *CAN'T WE ALL JUST GET ALONG?*; Maxine Waters headlines reading, *SHRILL WATERS; MOVE ASIDE;* the accusations and reelection of Mayor Marion Barry, *BITCH SET ME UP*, and *LOYALISTS STAND WITH BARRY;* Abner Louima, *WHEN JUSTICE STICKS YOU;* and Amadou Diallo, *41 SHOTS JUSTIFIED—FEAR TAKES THE FALL.* Isis felt a chill run down her spine at a page that held meaning, more so now than ever before.

During the Christmas break of his sophomore year, Shiloh had come home livid.

"Ma, can you believe that those ignorant bastards had the nerve to come onto our turf and hang these flyers at our university buildings? They must really think that we're stupid!"

At the time Isis told him it was a message intended to scare black people, but in hindsight the sentiments couldn't be more valid. The words hung in the air like a thick fog. The words were so true they'd even paid a visit to her own backyard. Isis clutched the flyer to her chest and wept. She cried for the loss of her only son. She grieved for all parents who had ever lost a child, and she shed tears for the parents who neglected to raise their sons to respect and cherish the value of human life. What did Shiloh do to warrant his demise? She'd done everything she could to ensure that he would not end up this way. How could Shiloh have become just another statistic?

The flyer read:

Black People,

THANK YOU for killing the future lawyers, doctors, politicians, scientists, bankers, and engineers. Our government has done a great job supplying you with the necessary tools. We thought that by freeing your kind it would be disastrous to our nation, but with the drugs, guns, and ignorance, you've managed to take out ten times more of your population. The jails and graveyards have never been fuller. You have made our jobs easier, and for that we will forever be thankful.

Sincerely,
Ku Klux Klan

Queen

Cherryl Floyd-Miller

"Water that has been begged for does not quench the thirst."
—African, Swahili

Karla's yellow perm screamed around her ginger face. She'd checked her watch twice in the last minute and was pacing the sidewalk on the corner of Peachtree and Baker Streets downtown. *This was where Trey had said to meet him at 12:45, right?*

She liked the brisk air goading her nose to flare. Fall chilliness was not the kind that goosed the skin or forced arms to fold while teeth clattered. The air held more cordiality and cleansing than winter's cold frosts with its apparitions dancing from licked-dry lips. Narrowed eyes squinting, Karla waited for each gust of air to reach her from the street. Cars whizzing past dragged their cool breezes across her face, and she closed her eyes, inhaling each gust. Something about the way the wind seduced her into waiting for it was sexy. It was easy to submit to it, give in to the way it charmed her, then pried her tensions free.

Trey was officially late. Karla missed the courtship days, when he always beat her to their spot. Room 317. It had been best (he'd said) to meet in places on the outskirts of town, where they were unlikely to be seen and accused of something dirty.

Back then, Doris would never have left him, and his leaving her would be tricky. He'd had to find a way to make her think it was her idea, that she'd thought of it, wanted it; that she'd be punishing him by losing her. Divorce required complex weaponry, he'd told Karla. You'd have to pretend to be checkmated into defeat. The things you'd concede would be merely the things you didn't care about losing in the first place.

He'd told Karla that the only thing he and Doris shared were bills and a child. It had been only a matter of time before the need for that, too, would fade. Trey had taken the classic route to manipulating Doris into his decision. Leisurely, he had become a stranger, changing the things he liked, altering his favorites: haircuts, cologne, preferences for food, movies, things to do on weekends. His strategy had been to re-place the man Doris had known for twelve years with someone she didn't recognize.

The moment of reckoning had come one Saturday evening, eight months into his separation maneuvers, when he'd rented a Dolemite film and sat alone in the den, bellowing cusses and loud halloos between bursts of laughter. Doris had appeared in the doorway, incredulously moving closer to him but stopping short of the La-Z-Boy, where Trey's body slouched in recline. Trey had seen her there but continued his noise. Arms akimbo and head oscillating in disbelief, Doris had said nothing for two minutes. She had stared at him, waiting for some sign of recognition or an apology. Trey had offered nothing. He had contin-ued his ruckus as if Doris simply didn't exist.

That night he'd come to Karla. Close to midnight, he'd chimed through her door with a duffel bag of toiletries, walking into her life completely.

"It's over. Said she doesn't know who I am. Told me to get the hell out," Trey had said.

This news was the balm she'd needed. No more sneaking, guarding every look and kiss, loving incognito. He could be hers completely, without apology or fear, without her being his inconsequential *second*. For nearly a year, she'd waited for him, hunkered down with her happy ending in mind, on constant deathwatch for Trey's marriage. Now that he'd left the corpse of failed matrimony behind him, Karla just wanted to let him fall into arms that would snare the sorrow for them both. She had listened to the heat of whispers he uttered at her ear:

"BabyI'msoglad we can just betogether. I'm so glad youwaited-forme. You know you're my Queen, don't you? It'sjustsogoodtobe hold-ing you. You'remy Queen, myQueeen."

That night, Karla had scanned his eyes for a moment. Could he read her right now? Queen? As in sovereign first lady of Trey's heart? As in no-wife-before-me Queen? She had blinked long enough to dissolve into his rabid panting.

*   *   *

One o'clock and still no word from Trey. Was he hurt? Was he caught in another of those stuffy financial meetings? Stuck in traffic? Tragically late with no real excuse? She had parked her car in the two-dollar lot because they were going to walk to the new upscale grill three blocks away for lunch. *Ten more minutes, then I'm leaving.*

She stopped pacing long enough to watch a vagrant sax player twenty feet away begin to pack away his gig. The glass Mason jar of coins was only half full, and he emptied it into a worn black leather fanny pack strapped to his waist beneath a bulge of shirts. Unbuttoning the top shirt and sliding out of it, he held the collar and hurled it at the air, allowing it to waft down to the sidewalk like a fresh bed-sheet.

Kneeling on the shirt, he removed his purple tam, unveiling a wilderness of hair burgeoning to various lengths from his matted roots. He flattened the hat against one of his thighs and folded it in half, matching rounded edge against rounded edge and folding it again in quarters. His rugged fingers slid the folded quadrants of the hat down into the open mouth of his saxophone.

A mesmerized man marveling at the bend and inflection of shiny saxophone hips, he massaged the instrument's brass curves, cycling his fingers from the thumb holder to the octave key. He put his mouth close to the reed and mimicked playing her. For minutes he was lost in her silent song, rocking with her in a way that seemed to curl him around her copper-zinc sides. Passersby looked askance at him, clutching their necklines, veering their walking paths closer to the curb, and hastening their strolls into escapist gallops. He did not dare to see them. His sax was the belle of this street ball, and they were the only two dancing. He loved—nearly worshiped—her.

Karla had never seen such honorable craving or respect. It was magical—that a man could breathe life into an object and make it his woman, give it a meticulous purple hat for a crown, create a soundless music—an energy, a life—with it. That a nameless man, not on his way to an office, not late for lunch, not crossing the street against traffic, not sad or promising or begging artifice, could usher an ornament into its majesty astonished her.

It was 1:15. Karla wasn't hungry anymore. She opened her purse, pulled all the bills she had out of her wallet, walked over to the Mason jar sitting empty near the sax player's shirt spread on the ground. She bent over to stuff the bills into the jar and stopped short of swiveling.

"For your queen," Karla said.

The man's glassy eyes were still fixed on his sax. He gave a faint nod to Karla as she turned to walk back to her car. The crossing light at Baker Street was green. She took a long breath and stepped into the intersection, a breeze nipping at her face.

First Thing Monday Morning

Gwynne Forster

"Never declare war unless you mean to do battle."
—African American, C. F. Pope

During the eight years that she had been married to Jeb Harrison, Lettie Harrison had spent practically every Friday and Saturday night with her girlfriends. Jeb had designated Friday night as "boys' night out" and Saturday night as "girls' night out." Naturally, he saw no reason to stay at home on Saturday nights by himself. At first, she had thought it a cute idea, but as the years passed, she saw it as Jeb's way of getting for himself two nights every weekend to do as he pleased.

One Saturday night in late August, Lettie sat on her front porch: fanning the heat, slapping at mosquitoes, and cursing the stench of magnolia blossoms that permeated the air. She'd hated magnolias ever since she first heard Billie Holiday sing "Strange Fruit."

It was hot for June in the small Maryland town of Hedgewood, which embraced the Chesapeake Bay like a hollowed-out orange section and boasted as its chief advantage its nearness to Baltimore, a full eighty miles to the west. The last thing Lettie wanted to do on a Saturday night was play dirty hearts with Ethel and Roxie. After all, she had a husband; her girlfriends passed the time that way because they didn't have a man.

Perspiring from the heat and smoldering with anger at Jeb, she vowed to change her life. When it came to Jeb, though, her mind acted as if it weren't normal. She couldn't count the times she'd sworn to Jeb that she was going to leave him; and just as many times, he'd grinned or winked and said he wouldn't last a day without her. She went inside and drew up a long list of grievances against him so she'd be sure to get them all in before he started feeling all over her breasts and belly and messing up her mind.

Lettie wrote that Jeb could have only one night out a week, and that he had to stay home on her night out. Along with that, she listed his habits of dropping his socks on the floor, tuning her out when she was giving him what-for, not rolling up the tube of toothpaste, insisting on sleeping with the bedroom windows open on cold nights, and leaving the toilet seat up.

"I've got a thousand other complaints against you," she wrote. "Things that love don't cover. And these days, love don't cover much." She pinned the note to his pillow, got in bed, and went to sleep.

Callused fingers skimming up and down her arms awakened her around one o'clock that morning. She slid further over to the edge of her side of the bed, but Jeb slid after her. Annoyance shot through her, and after nearly ripping the cover off him, she drew the blanket to herself and curled up with her back to him.

"Haven't I told you, Jeb Harrison, that thoughts of sex don't enter my head after ten o'clock at night? And wanting it is out of the question. My clock quits ticking." She didn't intend to let him manipulate her.

"Who were you out with?" she asked him.

He curled up to her back. "The boys. You know I hang out with the boys."

"Doing what? Talking about what?"

He kissed the back of her neck. "Honey, you don't expect me to remember all that, do you? Nothing. We just talk about . . . you know . . . nothing."

"Humph. Boys, eh? From what I've been hearing, they must've vacationed in Denmark."

"What? What on earth does that mean?"

"I mean, if they're boys it's because they've had a sex change. You don't expect to have secrets in a town this small, do you? It's been fifteen years since Martha Brixton left her house, but I'll bet she can tell me who called here today. You get your act together, mister. if you don't, I'm hightailing it out of here."

"What're you talking about, woman? I was out with the boys, just like I told you."

She got out of bed, stuck her fists on her hips, and glared at him. "Peaches Johnson ain't no boy, Jeb Harrison! And if you think she is, I've got a bigger problem than I thought."

Jeb rolled over with his back to her. "Honey, for the Lord's sake, come on back to bed and quit all that drama. I'm sleepy."

She wanted to take her shoe to his behind but controlled the urge. "You just wait," she grumbled. "This time, I'm not fooling."

"What you so down about?" Roxie asked as she and Lettie left church the next morning.

"I'm not down, Roxie. I just been making up my mind about things. I'm gonna leave Jeb."

"Oh, hush, girl; you said that before."

Lettie took a tissue out of her purse and wiped the perspiration from her forehead, pushing back the curls of her newly permed hair. "This time, I mean it. First thing Monday morning I'm packing my bags."

"I'll believe that when I see it. You mean tomorrow?"

"I said Monday, didn't I?"

Roxie slanted her head a little and looked toward the sky. "Yeah, you sure did. But tell you the truth, I don't believe a word of it. You're not going to walk out on what you said Jeb's puttin' down."

"He's not the only man who can put it down." She thought for a minute. "Maybe that's Jeb's problem. Maybe I've been making him think he's Hercules in the sack." A smile skipped like waves over her face, painting there an expression of sweet remembrance. "Honey, if he's not the real thing, I sure don't want to traffic with reality." Remembering her vow, she quickly sobered. "Yes, indeed. First thing Monday morning."

"I don't understand you, Lettie. Don't you remember what happened to Effie Strong? Reverend Lucas got engaged to marry her, and the whole town said she was a whore in her miniskirts and spiked-heel shoes, not fit for a minister's wife. So he broke the engagement. She sued him, passed a court-ordered virginity test, and won a bundle of dough for defamation of character. Don't listen to everything that falls off the loose tongues in this town."

"I don't care what you say. He's fooling around with Peaches, and I'm leaving him—"

"Yeah. I heard you. First thing Monday morning."

Jeb spilled himself out of the bed and trudged into the kitchen to get his caffeine fix. He hated waking up Sunday mornings to a quiet, empty house. Worse than that was reaching over for Lettie's soft breasts and getting a handful of rumpled sheets instead. He heated the coffee, let a slug of it slide down his throat, refilled the cup, and walked out on the back porch, the place where he did his best thinking. If Martha Brixton got a good look at him in his bikini shorts, it would serve her right for being such a busybody.

He sat down in the swing, breathed in the fresh morning air, and started swinging back and forth. *Peaches Johnson, indeed!* He wouldn't waste five minutes on that woman. After eight years of marriage, he still didn't understand his wife, and he didn't consider that a shortcoming on his part. After all, he had lived with his mother and three sisters for twenty-three years and couldn't understand them, either. He didn't make a lot of money at the factory, and he was trying to save as much of that as he could, so taking Lettie to restaurants in Cambridge or St. Michaels was out of the question. His idea of their having separate nights out during the weekend was aimed to relieve her of cooking big dinners seven days a week. He sucked his teeth. He didn't enjoy eating pig feet and potato salad all by himself two nights every week in that dump Ed Barns called a restaurant, but anything else you ordered in there was likely to be spoiled. The morning heated up, and he went back into the house.

"If Lettie doesn't straighten out her head," he said to himself, "I'm going to give her a reality check."

Lettie, however, was unaware of Jeb's altruistic reasons for their separate nights out and, in her present frame of mind, wouldn't have accepted that explanation if he'd given it to her. She and Roxie stopped walking and waited for the traffic light at the corner of Bay Bridge and Talbot Streets, and Lettie rolled her eyes when she saw Ethel approaching. Ethel was a member of Wesley AME Church, while Lettie and Roxie attended Mt. Zion Baptist Church, three blocks to the south.

"Jeb didn't go to church with you this morning?" Ethel asked Lettie by way of a greeting.

"You don't see him, do you?"

Ethel pursed her lips. "Well, I didn't expect he would. I hear tell he and Peaches were all over town last night. 'Course, I don't blame you for not going out with them. You never were a rowdy."

Lord, give me strength. "You have a good day, Ethel," she said through clenched teeth.

"Yes," Roxie chipped in. "See you Wednesday night at prayer meeting." The light changed, and they walked on. "Don't pay her one bit of attention, Lettie. She was after Jeb back in high school. She's just jealous."

"Maybe. But what is he doing two nights every week? I tell you, I'm fed up, and I'm going to find myself a place to stay and leave Jeb to his Peaches."

"You seen him with Peaches? First, you were going to leave him because he snores. Then it was the business of the toothpaste. Week before last, you were fed up because he can't cook. Then it was because he reads in bed and you want the light out so you can sleep. Now it's Peaches. Trouble with you, Lettie, is you find fault with everybody. And you could use some guts; if you're gonna leave Jeb, leave. You just talk and talk. My granddaddy always said, 'Talk's easy done; it takes money to buy land.' Quit yakking about it and do something."

Lettie didn't like the way that sounded. "You don't understand, Roxie. I was going to do big things. They said my voice was good enough for the Metropolitan Opera House, and all I'm singing is gospel stuff Sunday mornings while Ruth Ann plays that old out-of-tune piano."

"Then study voice, for heaven's sake. Anyway, what's that got to do with you leaving Jeb?"

They reached Roxie's six-year-old Mercury Sable and got a blast of heat when Roxie opened the door. Lettie slid her ample hips in on the passenger side, took off her hat, and fanned herself. "Roxie, I'll be forty in October, and I haven't done anything or been anywhere further away than Baltimore. When am I going to start living?"

The air conditioner didn't respond to Roxie's prompting, so she rolled down the windows, pulled away from the sidewalk, and headed toward home. "Girl, I've heard of men getting the seven-year itch and going a little crazy when they see forty looming around the corner, but I never knew of a woman getting that kind of angst. Dye your hair or something. At least you can change it back the way it was if you get tired of it. But walking out on Jeb might prove to be something you can't fix. Suppose he found out he liked not being married. Then, what would you do?"

Lettie studied her red fingernails. She hadn't been able to hide them from the pastor when they spoke after church, and he'd wagged his left index finger in her face as he admonished her about the sinfulness of vanity. "The problem is Jeb, Roxie. He came home last night ... no, it was this morning, feeling all over me when I know he's just been doing the same to Peaches. His lousy habits at home don't amount to a thing compared to that."

Roxie hit the brakes harder than she might have if she'd been paying attention to her driving. She'd almost struck a boy on a bicycle and, rigid with fright, slowed to a stop and let out a deep breath. "Whew! That was close." She turned to face Lettie. "Did you ever ask Jeb if he was carrying on with Peaches, or you just taking the word of these gossips?"

Lettie thought back to the night before. "No, I didn't ask him, but when I accused him of it last night, he didn't deny it. Just told me to stop the drama and come to bed. I've got pride, and I refuse to ask him or any other man if he's getting it on with another woman."

"Then let the Ethels of this town run your life. I'm stopping by Freddie's for a can of lump crab meat. It's the best anywhere around here."

"Yeah. I know." She didn't know how to explain it to Roxie. Maybe because she couldn't explain it to herself. "It's not that I don't love Jeb; it's that . . . well, he's doing his thing, and I'm just wasting away. On top of that—"

Roxie interrupted her. "Don't mention Peaches to me again. As long as you stay with Jeb, you must be liking whatever he does."

She parked beneath a shade tree, and they went inside the fish market. "I was afraid you'd be closed, Freddie," Roxie said.

"Now, you know I'd stay here all night waiting for you, Roxie. Sunday or not."

Lettie's eyes widened as she observed the two of them. Crab meat, huh?

"Sorry to hear things not going your way, Miss Lettie," Freddie said. "But the Lord don't like ugly, so you'll come out triumphant in the end."

"What the devil are you talking about, Freddie?"

As if he hadn't heard her, the man began humming "Amazing Grace." "Y'all have a nice day, now."

"See what I mean?" Lettie said to Roxie when they had seated themselves in the car. "Everybody in this town knows about Jeb and Peaches. You just wait. I'm leaving that man. Me, wasting my time teaching music to a bunch of kids who think Baby Face is the greatest singer alive and hip-hop is the world's original and only music. I always had talent, and I'm going to cultivate it and use it."

"What's Jeb got against your studying voice?"

"How would I know? I'm not sure he's ever heard me sing. Anyhow, let's don't get into that. I've made up my mind. You wait till Monday."

*   *   *

Jeb frequently left home for work before Lettie got up, so she thought nothing of his apparent absence when she crawled out of bed and struggled downstairs to the kitchen. She stumbled at the bottom of the steps, gasping as she stared at the three suitcases resting at the edge of the foyer.

"Jeb," she shouted. "Jeb, what's going on here?"

She flipped around as the basement door opened and he emerged with an air of nonchalance, as if she weren't staring at three suitcases. "What's the meaning of this?"

Cold chills swept over her, overriding the effect of the summer heat. "I said, what are these suitcases doing here?" She heard herself yelling but couldn't control her voice. "Jeb," she screamed, "what are these suitcases doing out *here?*"

His shrug, lazy and uncaring, sent a shot of fear through her. Then he said, "You've been threatening to leave almost ever since we got married, and I finally realized you had a point. I figured if I didn't get out of here the first thing this Monday morning, I might not get up the nerve again." He walked closer to the suitcases. "You're sick of me, and you've been saying you want out, so I'm going to be a gentleman and save you the trouble of leaving."

She grabbed his shoulders. "Wh . . . what are you talking about? Where're you going? Man, you put those suitcases back in that closet."

"I'm leaving. That's what you want, isn't it? This way, you'll have the house and you won't have to look for an apartment."

"Who told you I wanted an apartment?"

He leaned against the wall, folded his arms across his chest, and gazed down at her. "I get my information the same place you get yours. Act instead of talking, and nobody but you will know your business."

"What do you mean?" she screamed as panic set in.

Seemingly unmoved, he replied, "I expect you'll be happy now that my snoring can't wake you up. You won't have to pick up after me, either. Of course, if you'd wait until my socks hit the floor before you grab them and throw them in the hamper, I might get a chance to pick them up myself.

"I sweat in that canning factory over in Salisbury fifty hours every week, and except for the little I'm able to save, I dump my money in your lap. You dole it out as if you were the one who earned it. I don't mind that. But after I pay the mortgage on this house, I ought to be able to walk around in it barefooted without you nagging me about it and calling me a slob. I wouldn't even mind *that* if you ever told me something about me that you do like."

A weakness stole over her, but with the floodgates now open, Jeb let it all out, grievances she didn't know he had. Rubbing his fingers across the stubble on his chin, he squinted at her. "When I used to spend the night at your place before we got married, you didn't sleep with those awful pink rollers in your hair. I don't remember seeing you in those Mother Hubbard gowns, either." He glanced at his watch. "If you didn't find so many things wrong with me, I'd probably stay right here. But since that's not the case, I gotta be going."

She yanked the front of his shirt. "You're going to Peaches Johnson. Everybody in this town knows about you and Peaches."

His icy grin would have frightened her if she hadn't known that he would never lay a hand on her or any other woman. "Is that so? I guess you would know whether that was true, wouldn't you?"

He looked at his watch again. "Hayes's taxi ought to be outside about now. You hang in there, you hear? Be seeing you." He opened the door, braced his foot against it, put one suitcase under his arm, picked up the other two, and left.

Lettie stared at the door until her eyes got sore and drummers began a rapid paradiddle in her head. With shock reverberating throughout her body, she flopped down into a kitchen chair. Jeb Harrison was out of his mind! He couldn't leave her; she hadn't given him a reason. Oh, Lord, what on earth was she going to do? She'd die without him. She'd just die.

If He Didn't Go

Sharon Ewell Foster

"Nothing beats a failure but a try." —African American

If he didn't go now, he was never going to go.

There was something about the pimples on her face that made his heart break. They were barely detectable in the dark; there was little light from the bathroom door. He always fingered the tiny bumps with his thumb before he kissed her, before he made love to her. Like somehow his touch, his attention, his compassion would heal her.

It was his touch that made him attractive to her. Her eyes would mist over. It made him attractive to lots of women. He knew it. His frat had voted him least likely to marry. *Don't hate the player; hate the game.* Whatever that meant.

Lying flat on his back, his head turned toward her, he watched Ramona breathing. The sliver of light from the doorway softened when it touched her in the darkness. It shifted each time her chest rose and fell.

He turned on his side and rested his head on his fist. This was a safe time. He could watch her now and not have to explain, commit, dialogue, get in touch with his feelings, or find his inner child. For a moment Ramona snored, and he smiled with anticipation. Her hand flew to her nose as though she were flicking away a fly. Probably no one else would have understood it, but he had to fight to keep from convulsing with laughter. Ramona did it every time, swatting at herself like there had to be a fly . . . as even in her sleep she denied that she snored.

Ramona flicked at her nose two more times—soft brown hands with clipped and unpolished nails—then settled back into her snoreless, peaceful sleep. She was easy to love.

She was not his kind of woman. Everyone said so. Ramona was not high-maintenance; she was almost *no*-maintenance. *Jamal, man, I can't see you with that.* But what did they know? With a light touch, he fingered one of the braids that peeked out from the edge of the blue silk scarf tied around her head. What did they know?

They said he was crazy. *Man, you can pull any woman you want. You have pulled. What's wrong with a brother?* The thing was, he had always liked a woman with a flaw. It made him want to touch her more.

He had caressed lots of too-round bellies, cupped his hand around lots of too-skinny calves, and kissed behind many a too-knocked knee. He always saw the thing women camouflaged—the thing they wanted to hide. He could always find the broken wing. When he found it, he focused his attention there, like a laser. First. It had gotten him through a lot of closed doors and into a lot of tightly made beds.

He was the last man standing. Marriage was not for a man like him, his boys said. *Don't go out like a punk, man. Don't waste your time, man. Why waste your time on oatmeal when you can have steak, or greens and fatback?*

They did not know, could not see that in his arms she was generous and kind. Ramona was gentleness and innocence that rode on a beat of unexpected passion. It served him well to let everyone think she was plain, that she was not exciting. Seeing her this way, in just the pink slip she slept in, her face relaxed and trusting, quieted something inside him. He didn't want to leave her.

And she made him tremble. It didn't make sense. Ramona didn't swing from chandeliers, and he didn't believe that she knew anything about whipped cream, but he always fell into her look of surrender—eyes closed and lips parted, a tiny furrow between her brows—that washed over her face when he touched her. Or maybe it was the way she whispered poetry into his ear from the Bible, from the Song of Solomon, she said.

> *Let him kiss me with the kisses of his mouth— for your love is
>   more delightful than wine.*
> *Pleasing is the fragrance of your perfumes; your name is like
>   perfume poured out.*
> *No wonder the maidens love you! Take me away with you—let
>   us hurry!*

He had been with lots of women, not Wilt-the-Stilt lots, but it was this one who made him weak. "I won't hurt you," she would whisper, and he would lose himself in her.

He sighed without making a sound. There was no point putting it off. He had to go. With almost no effort, he swung his legs from the bed and moved the sheet so that no air would hit her body when he rose. He was good at it. He was expert at it. He had gotten into a lot of beds. And getting in meant getting out.

Jamal stood on his feet and looked back at Ramona. He still couldn't see the pimples. He shook his head, then moved quickly, barely resting any weight on his feet, toward the bathroom. He stopped short, midway, and held his breath. Ramona had turned on her side and then stretched her arm almost into his now vacant spot. He did not want her to awaken.

She cleared her throat and turned onto her stomach. The line of light had moved off her face and now skimmed over her shoulder. When he was sure that she was back under, he continued his journey to the bathroom. He had to go.

Jamal reached in the doorway crack and eased off the bathroom light. In the same way, he eased himself into the bathroom and then, in reverse order, closed the door and turned the light switch on. He stared at himself in the mirror. How did I get here? Jamal shook his head.

Ramona was a good girl. He was not a good boy. This was no stretch, though. It was his pattern. He was attracted to women who sang the very-good-girl blues.

He enjoyed the "no, no" dance. And even though it always ended—most times sooner than later—it was always bittersweet to hear the frightened and unsure "yes." Good girls needed love, too. Jamal looked into the bathroom mirror and shrugged his shoulders as though someone else were watching. Then he thought about Ramona again and closed his eyes.

She had kept it up longer than anyone had. "I can't, Jamal. Really, I can't, okay? It has nothing to do with how I feel or what I want. I want to. I want you. But I can't." He had laughed and used his thumb on her face. He had shifted his eyes from her eyes to her lips and kissed her. "Really, I can't, Jamal. If we do it, we should do it right." Her hand had touched his face. He could hear her breathing turn shallow. "I'm worth a commitment . . . you're worth a commitment. You're a treasure, Jamal; you shouldn't just give yourself away for nothing." That place in the lower part of his stomach had tightened, and at that moment he knew he had to have her.

He was determined. "Nothing beats a failure but a try," his grandfather had always told him. He was patient. "Look, we're friends, okay? No pressure. No demands. It's best this way, anyway. Let's just concentrate on being friends."

Ramona sent him E-mail. She lived on the other side of town, but he willed himself to stay away—the bird needed to stew. The distance worked for both of them, so she sent him E-mail—inspirational E-mail. Like maybe she thought that would throw him off the trail.

"Thanks, baby. That's just what I needed. Keep sending it," he had told her. Jamal opened his eyes, stared at his image in the mirror, then closed them again as he thought about Ramona lying on the bed.

Every day it was E-mail:

> *This one is from John 3:16. "For God so loved the world, that He gave his only begotten Son, that whosoever believeth in Him should not perish, but have everlasting life."*
>
> *It means that God loves you so much, Jamal, that He was willing to sacrifice His son to save you. Can you imagine that thousands of years ago God knew we would be at this point? That we would need Him? And that He had already set the plan in motion, had already sacrificed His son, knowing that you and I would come to this place?*

He remembered how he had smiled when he'd gotten the E-mail. "Keep sending them, baby," he had told her.
Then:

> *Jamal, this one is from 2nd Corinthians, Chapter 5, Verse 21. "For He hath made him to be sin for us, who knew no sin; that we might be made the righteousness of God in him."*
>
> *I sent it to you, Jamal, because sometimes I think you think you've done too much. You know—that God is mad at you and won't forgive you. Or if He does forgive you, once you confess everything, He's going to make you pay—you know, "the wages of sin is death." But you know, the cool thing about God is He knows everything already. He already knows everything and He still welcomes us and rejoices when we come home. The confession is just for us, to take the guilt and shame away from us. But once we confess and believe that Jesus, who never sinned, took on our sins and died in our place, it's over, Jamal. It's forgiven*

*and forgotten. God sees us as though we had never done anything
wrong.*

Ramona was innocent. She believed all that stuff.

After months of e-mailing, they met. Some place safe, she said. So
he had ended up sitting on a pew next to her. Then, in a while . . . he
couldn't explain it to anyone—shoot, he couldn't explain it to himself—
something had happened. It wasn't anything he had thought about,
nothing he had planned to do. No one believed it except Ramona. It
wasn't logical, but something on the inside of him had changed.
Something had changed. Though he still wasn't sure.

One day, in the middle of one of their church dates, he was walking
down the aisle. Maybe it was something about the way *she* believed it
all. Maybe something about the way she *was* that helped him to believe. He got caught up; that was all he could say.

*Did you have to go that far? There are lots of women that want you,
man. What were you thinking?*

What *was* he thinking? He shook his head and opened his eyes. He
had to go. He knew that; that's why he'd gotten out of bed. He couldn't
wait any longer.

He had to *go.*

Jamal walked to the commode and leaned, his left hand propping
him. The relief he felt weakened his knees. He was the last man standing. He *was* the last man standing.

Jamal turned back toward the door, thought about Ramona, then
stopped to wash his hands. He moved quickly from the bathroom back
into the bed and slid between the sheets.

Jamal inched closer to Ramona and hugged her to him. His boys still
weren't having it. *Man, you are slipping. And you are not marriage
material. I give it a month.* Nothing beats a failure but a try.

Finally, she had said yes . . . finally. He stared at the gold band on
his finger. Nothing beats a failure but a try.

A Difficult Lesson

Tierra French

"If you don't stand for something you will fall for anything."
—Malcolm X

I should've seen it coming, but I didn't. I should've stopped it before things got this bad, but I couldn't. Now my baby girl is dead, and there's nothing I can do to change it. I guess I should take this story back about a year, but first, let me explain a few things.

My name is Rosa Lee Sherman. Me and my family have lived in Hopkinsville, Kentucky, since our ancestors planted roots here in the nineteenth century. I have a son, Joseph Lee Sherman, and, well, a daughter, Tonya Lee Sherman, and a crazy-ass husband named Earl Sherman. Things seemed to be going pretty smoothly for my family—that is, until about a year ago.

Joseph Lee was a model student. He made good grades in school, was the captain of the junior debate team, and all in all, a fine son. Joseph even won a trophy for his many debates on the horror women experienced as a result of rape and sexual assault. But Joseph was what most teenagers would call an outsider. He didn't have many friends, and the ones he did have were closer to associates than real pals. He never went out to parties or spent the night over at a friend's house. He never talked on the phone or went to school functions, except for those debates he loved so much.

And then we had my daughter, Tonya Lee. Tonya and Joseph were like oil and vinegar. They hardly ever spoke to each other except to say, "Move," or "Get out of my way." Tonya loved to party; child, that girl could really *party!* There were school nights when she kept me waiting up until four in the morning for her to come home. But through it all, she was my baby, and I loved her.

At this point Joseph was a junior in high school, and he was six feet-six inches at sixteen years old. Child, I tell you that boy was big, and I never thought nothing of it. I guess we had grown used to his size. At the beginning of the first semester, the basketball coach asked him to join the school team. I'll never forget that day Joseph came home grinning from ear to ear. It was the first time I'd seen him that happy in a long while. He said, "Mama, I'm finally gonna be accepted. Finally, I'm gonna be *accepted!*"

The next day, Joseph went to try out for the team, and child, I tell you, he had a ball. The kids was right nice to him. Joseph told me the coach just loved him and guaranteed him a starting spot on the team! So, needless to say, Joseph began playing basketball for the school. It was like he was coming out of his shell. The boys on the team really liked him, or acted like they did, and Joseph began to hang around them more and more.

I noticed that Tonya was still rowdy and unpredictable as usual, but she was learning to like her brother a lot more, and the same with him. I even caught them one night in her room at one in the morning, talking and laughing with each other. That made me so happy, I just went into my room and cried tears of joy. Earl rolled over, looked at me, and went back to sleep. He was a truck driver and he was always on the road, so that is why he's hardly worth mentioning. Anyway, Tonya and Joseph were getting along, and even with Earl gone so much, the family was running smoothly. I was so proud, and the fact that my children were happy was enough for me to be happy. Then Joseph started to hang out with the boys on the basketball team. They just went out for pizza occasionally, or to a movie, but gradually they became really close friends and Joseph started partying and hanging out almost more than Tonya Lee.

What I didn't know at the time was the kind of things this new group of "friends" were encouraging my son to do. Child, I swear to God if I had known I would have beaten every last one of them, then sent them running home to they mamas, but that is besides the point.

Around this time, I found out Earl was cheating on me and we filed for a divorce. We'd just told the kids about it, and they were distraught. Both of them took it the same way—thinking that somehow it was their fault. I started drinking heavily. Sometimes I would come home from work about five P.M. with a twelve-pack of beer, and by seven I was out.

My children and my family were falling apart before my eyes, and I was too drunk and too depressed to see it.

One afternoon, Joseph didn't come home from school, and I knew he was out there hanging out with his "friends." They got really drunk and were roaming the streets all night. From what the police told me, they busted the windows out of someone's car, and too drunk to run, they hid in some bushes and got caught.

Now, I tell y'all, if I'da been in my right mind that boy would've gotten the whipping of his life and I would've made him spend the night in jail, but being as I was drunk and halfway out of my own mind, I picked him up and gave him a screaming about making me come out the house so late at night.

Well, I guess I thought that brush with jail would've been enough to make him not want to get in trouble with the law anymore, but that definitely did not work. It looked like every week the police were either knocking on my door or calling on my phone. Lord, I wish I would've been in my right mind. I could've stopped this before it got so big.

About a week before the prom, Joseph turned seventeen. To celebrate, he and his friends decided that they would throw a party, but they didn't have any money. I don't know whose bright idea it was, but they decided to rob a 7-Eleven. And they did it. No one was caught for that day, but like my mama always told me, "what you do in the dark will eventually come to the light."

I remember Joseph's prom night like it was yesterday. Tonya Lee had been invited by some friends, and she looked so pretty. Joseph even rented a tux even though he hadn't asked any girl to the prom. I took pictures of them and walked them out to the limousine, never imagining that my baby girl would not be coming back home that night.

Tonya and Joseph rode to the prom together, but they split up when they got there. I guess each of them had a good time. Afterwards, Joseph met up with his friends from the basketball team. They drove up to a teen hangout called The Lot, which was really just an old parking lot where kids got drunk.

All night Joseph and his friends had been trying to get girls to sleep with them, but none would. Finally, they did something I thought my son would never do. One of the other boys grabbed a drunken girl who was so far out of it, she was laying across the hood of a car. They put her in the backseat and placed a paper bag over her head so they wouldn't have to look at her. Each one took their turn with her. After Joseph's turn, one of his friends went back for seconds, and while he was on top of her, having his way with her, she woke up and started fighting. The boy tried to hold her down, but the paper bag fell off and she saw his face. He shot her in the head. Joseph heard the gunshot and ran to the car. The boy was already gone, but he found his sister dead in the car. My baby girl was dead in the car.

A week later my baby was buried, and all I could think about was how my son had become the exact same thing that he so forcefully debated against: a rapist. The police had taken him and the other boys to jail, where they were being held until their court date. No bond was set.

At the funeral I cried, begging them not to take my baby away, but she was already gone. No matter how much I cried, it didn't change a thing. My baby girl was gone. Gone.

I cleaned up my drinking habit after Tonya Lee died, and tried to pick my life up, what little I had left. Joseph and the other boys were charged with aggravated rape and were each sentenced to three years in prison.

Like this famous black guy used to say in the sixties, "If you don't stand for something, you will fall for anything." My Joseph just lost sight of everything he stood for. So he fell. But even at my age you still can learn how to stand on your principles, and for us, this has truly been a difficult lesson. Good-bye, Tonya Lee.

Back Then

Michael P. Fuller

"A close friend can become a close enemy." —African, Ethiopia

"**C**ome on," LuJohn whispered. He was kneeling in several feet of tall weeds, his dark face covered in sweat and shining from the reflection of a full moon. Every time I looked his way, I saw Kingfish from the *Amos 'n' Andy Show.*

"Why you whispering? Nobody can hear us," I said, whispering, too. "You know, I heard Wilt scored a hundred points in one game. Did you hear 'bout that?"

"Naw, man," LuJohn said quietly. "I keep tellin' you ain't nobody score a hundred points in one game. I keep tellin' you that's a lie. Can't nobody score one hundred points in a game," he argued. We'd been disagreeing since nursery school.

"Wilt the Stilt did it back in 1962 against the New York Knicks," I whispered.

"Man, I don't care 'bout no basketball no way. Shhh . . . Basketball, who cares? If you wanna talk sports to me, talk 'bout how Cassius Clay knocked out Sonny Liston's ass."

"Clay's a bad dude," I agreed.

"Cain't nobody whip him. He's the baddest in the world. Ain't he callin' hisself Muhammad Ali now?" LuJohn responded.

"I don't know, but James Bond, 007 'll whip him," I boasted.

"Shoooot, Cassius Clay'll kill him wit a haymaker right upside the head." LuJohn loved boxing.

We sat quietly for a few seconds in the balmy night air.

"You hear Malcolm X got shot a little while ago?" I asked.

"Who?"

"Malcolm X . . . you know, the Muslim."

"Man, I ain't hip to no Malcolm X."

Although I had just heard of Malcolm X a day or two before, I peered at LuJohn in disbelief, then turned away, shaking my head.

"What?" LuJohn questioned, hunching his shoulders and challenging my stare. His mouth was all curled and snarled.

"You ain't heard a' Malcolm X?"

"Naw, man, I ain't heard a' no Malcolm X."

"Damn, man, where you been?"

"Ha! I been wit you," he said and turned away like he wasn't going to pay me any more attention.

"Man, you know who he is. The dude that talk all that stuff about freedom and what we need to do to be free."

"Nope, I ain't heard of him."

"Man, chickens comin' home to roost . . . whatever is necessary? Ain't you heard of none of that stuff?"

"Uh-uh."

I didn't know why I was upset at him for not knowing about Malcolm X. I was probably upset at myself for not knowing more about him. I couldn't make out the odd feeling I had.

It had begun the night before, when my uncle Bill and my mother were talking about some things that happened while Uncle Bill was in New York. Evidently, Uncle Bill had had some illegal dealings with Malcolm X back when he was still called Malcolm Little. My uncle couldn't believe "Red" (that's what they used to call him) had turned into this martyr for Black Power and civil rights. My uncle was raving, bragging, and hating Malcolm X all at the same time, saying that the whole Muslim religious thing was a bunch of "who-ew."

Uncle Bill sounded confused about the whole thing, and so was I. I thought once you were a nigga in trouble, you were always a nigga in trouble. It just went hand in hand. So how this nigga named Malcolm Little became this dude named Malcolm X was really a mystery. Uncle Bill just couldn't understand it.

LuJohn cut into my thoughts: "But I did hear 'bout some police attackin' Negroes tryin' to cross some ol' bridge in Alabama. My mom said they was kickin' they asses with tear gas, whips, and nightsticks and shit, man."

"*Damn!* Whips?" I muttered.

"Yeah, man, like they was unruly slaves refusin' to pick cotton."

I shook my head in disgust. "Damn, ain't nothin' change. They still won't leave us alone. Anyway, them Negroes shoulda just stayed home and danced the twist with Chubby Checker." We laughed quietly, caught up in our own lives.

"Yeah, I guess. But they didn't have to hit 'em with whips," LuJohn insisted.

"They lucky they didn't get hung," I mumbled.

We scurried further down the steep hill and rested a few feet from the bottom.

"Where's Dizzy and nem, anyway?" LuJohn asked.

Dizzy, Nate, Duke, and Hap were making their way down the railroad track embankment toward the parking lot. They were barely visible, except for Nate's slicked-back processed hair reflecting the full moon and the dim security light hanging from a nearby telephone pole.

"Let's go," LuJohn snickered.

We spotted Dizzy sneaking between two semi-trailers into the sparsely lit warehouse. Nate and Duke came up behind him and checked the area, first left and then right. Hap was stationed at his usual spot on top of a small storage house that stood about as high as a basketball rim, overlooking the docking area—the same spot that would be the easiest to escape from if things got messy. Hap always fought us for the "owl's perch," as he called it. He claimed that only he could handle the high spot, because just like an owl, he could see in the dark.

Hap swiveled his head, searching for LuJohn and me. He spotted us shuffling slowly towards the others. "Go on, man," he said just loud enough for us to hear.

We scooted farther down the railroad tracks, kicking up loose rocks and dirt off our narrow asses. Prickly weeds and cocka burrs stung our legs and clung to our socks. Cocka burrs always stuck to your ankles.

"Hurry, Langston," LuJohn whispered, pulling farther away from me.

Dizzy was at the foot of the dock, where he leaped onto the floor like a panther after prey. He paused, scanning the dock for security guards. Nate and Duke were right behind him. Duke looked back and spotted us kneeling at the carriage of the trailer. He waved us forward.

LuJohn looked over at me. "Let's go, Langston."

"I'm wit cha," I said.

We sprinted towards the dock, shuffling tiny stones and dust beneath our feet. Then we reached the base of the dock wall, where a crate that Nate had brought earlier was waiting.

"Take this shit, man. Hurry, hurry, man. Here, here—get it, get it;

take it up to the top of them tracks," Nate decreed, like we had never done this before.

LuJohn grabbed the metal crate and hurried along, resting it on his hip and scurrying stiff-legged up the railroad track embankment.

I glanced back to the dock just in time to see Dizzy motioning me toward another crate. I snatched it with all my might and dragged it to the tracks.

My adrenaline was racing and my breathing started to labor, the constant threat of my asthma always a ragweed sniff away. I dropped the crate off about halfway up the tracks and headed back down to the loading dock along with LuJohn, who was gasping for air like he had just run a marathon. He just about toppled down the embankment from exhaustion.

LuJohn had always been heavy. But his heart was much bigger than his girth. Climbing up that embankment was no easy task for him, but his determination to show the others that he was just as strong as they were was his driving force.

We streaked back to the dock as quickly as we could and kneeled against the waist-high wall.

"Let's go in, Langston," LuJohn pleaded with me.

"Naw, man."

He eyeballed me with a challenging stare. "You scared."

"I ain't scared."

"Then let's go."

"We s'pose to stay here," I warned.

"Yeah, yeah, yeah. I know." But LuJohn bounced up and crawled onto the dock floor.

Before I could think, I jumped up and shadowed him. "Man, you gonna get us caught," I cried.

"I'm tired of them always gettin' the good stuff. Let's get some fo' ou'self this time," LuJohn whispered.

He crouched down and walked duck-style along the dimly lit walls. The dock flooring was cool and wet where the refrigeration had seeped through the flimsy plastic strips hanging from the entranceway. "Here, right here! Langston, get the orange juice," LuJohn ordered.

"Yeah, yeah," I grumbled, irritated with myself for actually listening to him. I stepped quickly but grudgingly over to the crate and grabbed it with both hands.

Then like a flash, Dizzy, Nate, and Duke frantically sprinted past me. They pounced over bottles and crates, leaped off the loading dock, and headed straight towards the tracks. LuJohn must have seen them coming, because he was already halfway up the embankment. Shit, he didn't even let me know.

A chubby-ass, doughboy-looking man stumbled out of the darkness of the doorway. I saw the glint of an ice pick in his hand and smelled the beer reeking from him. He was moving as fast as his bloated beer gut could carry his oversized suspenders and jumbo blue jean overall pants. We already knew that this particular night worker was on duty, but all of us, including LuJohn, figured we could outrun him up the railroad tracks. I just never expected him to ambush me with an ice pick.

He turned around fast enough to see me before I could move. His eyes were squinty and hard. He looked like a demon in fat man's clothing.

"Gotcha." The fat man smiled a corrupt, snaggle-toothed grin. He swung the ice pick, and I ducked out of the way as he fell off balance.

I moved to avoid his next swing, while keeping my eyes on his. He still wore a loathsome look that told me he was gonna try to slice me again.

"All—all right. Ya got me." I was defeated, trembling from my toes to my short, nappy hair. Where was 007 when you really needed him? A vision of Negroes being whipped in Mississippi raced through my mind.

The fat white man could barely speak for his heavy breathing, and when he rested his weaponless hand on his hip, I took off again. Although he didn't try to run after me, he swung his ice pick and grazed my left shoulder. I hardly felt the blow as I vaulted off the dock. I seemed to fly weightlessly in the air, farther than I'd ever flown before, almost as if I was flying in one of those Apollo spaceships with John Glenn. I hit the ground without missing a step, then dashed between the two trailers and onto the tracks. On the way up, I snatched a crate full of eight-ounce Melody Dairy Choco chocolate milk and scampered up the tracks to the top of the embankment, where LuJohn, Dizzy, Hap, Nate, and Duke were waiting.

"Damnnnnn, Langston! That fat-ass honky came out a bag on yo' ass," chuckled buck-toothed Dizzy.

"Let's go back down there and kick his pudgy ass," Hap sneered as he picked up a carton of Choco chocolate milk, our favorite. He pinched the opening, brought it to his mouth, and drank the entire thing. "Damn, that was good," he slobbered. To be so skinny, the boy ate like a pig.

"So where's the juice?" I asked, trembling so hard I could barely speak. The adrenaline still raced through my body, and my voice was hardly audible. The night's activity and heavy pollen caused my asthmatic lungs to work overtime. I couldn't believe I was still interested in milk and juice.

I looked behind us, and the jellyroll of a man was still standing where I had left him. He hadn't even looked up the embankment for us. He might have been thinking, what if he had really shoved that ice pick in that little boy's gut and he lay there screaming with his bowels laid out on the wet dock floor? His head was bowed almost like he was ashamed that he'd tried to slice some kid for a few cartons of Choco chocolate milk and orange juice.

I yanked a carton of milk from the crate. The coolness on my throat was refreshing.

"Why ain't you pull mah coat tail when that fat-ass som'bitch come after us, LuJohn?"

"I yelled 'Here comes The Man,' " LuJohn argued.

"None of ya'll said nothin'," I shot back with contempt, staring first at Nate, then Dizzy, then Duke, and finally at Hap. They couldn't look me in the eye. "That fat sucker almost did me. Look, he nicked me in the arm."

They moved in to get a closer look. LuJohn reached for my arm.

"*Damnnn!*" they all yelled out.

"You was fast," Hap said, laughing.

"Man, all of us woulda done what you did. That fat piece of cheese is so slow he ain't gonna catch nobody," Nate chimed in just to take the heat off their asses for not alerting me. He was always placing the blame on somebody else. Nate Armstrong was just too pretty. "Pleasing Nate," the girls would snicker as we grew older. He was a few years older than the rest of us; and already doing the nasty to girls. His chest had more than peach fuzz, and in the sixth grade he showed us the hair around his dick.

"Gimme that crate," I demanded. "I'm taking these home to my moms." I grabbed the crate and slung it across my leg. "Y'all can go get the ones down there." I pointed down the embankment towards the fat man, who was now smoking a square and staring up at us. "Y'all shouldn't have no problems, seeing how he's so slow and all."

"Gimme that milk." Duke rose up like he was about to pound me into the ground. And at almost six feet, two inches tall and weighing about two hundred pounds, he could have too. But Duke was very passive, and playing the dozens was the only thing that would make him fight.

"Fuck you, nigga," I said, and walked away.

"Damn, Langston. That's all of ours," Dizzy pleaded.

But even Dizzy, my mentor, couldn't stop me from taking this milk. "There's plenny mo' down the embankment near the fat man," I shot back. "Since he ain't gonna catch nunna y'all."

Dizzy, Nate, Duke, and Hap peered down at the crates laying on the side of the tracks just a fifty-yard dash away from the fat man. That obese swine fastened his eyes on us.

"He ain't gonna move, Dizzy," huffed Hap.

"Ah-huh," Nate whizzed in.

I headed down the tracks towards home, then turned around and yelled, "Come on, LuJohn." He trotted over to me. "Here, man. Take one." I handed LuJohn a carton of Melody Fresh Choco chocolate milk. There was some OJ at the bottom of the crate, too.

"Thanks," LuJohn said. "Sorry I didn't warn you."

"No problem; you know you my main man." I turned around to watch Hap bolt down the side of the tracks toward the milk crates, pissed off and complaining, "I want that chocolate milk from that fat som'bitch and he ain't gonna stop me." Dizzy, Duke, and Nate followed close behind him.

Hap had just about reached the crate when the fat snowman came to life. He musta been playing possum before, because as soon as Hap reached the crate he hopped up from the dock.

"Here he comes, y'all! Run! Run!" Duke yelled. The others looked up in time to see the little swollen man chugging along as fast as he could towards them.

"Come here, you little nigga boys!" he shouted.

"He's still got that ice pick!" Dizzy yelled.

"Quick! Get the chocolate one, Hap!" Nate shouted, climbing up the railroad embankment. Hap tugged on the crate and began to drag it up through the dirt and weeds.

Hap had slender shoulders and was light in the ass. Although his mind said one thing, his body was telling him a completely different story. This time it was telling him that much more strength was needed to bring that crate of chocolate milk up the embankment.

Nate, Dizzy, and Duke were already up the hill, straining to see through the blackness and down the side of the track, where Hap was pulling, slipping, and kicking the Midwestern dirt as he tried to gather his balance and move quickly uphill.

"Come on, Hap!" Dizzy shouted. "Hurry."

The ice pick-wielding dock-keeper was scuffling up the hill as well, and after losing his balance and rolling backwards a couple of feet, he righted himself and continued in his pursuit of Hap. Pint after pint of the coveted chocolate milk began falling out of the crate. Hap tried to grab a carton here and there but lost his footing and fell into a ditch. The crate flew into the air and crashed into a tree, and chocolate milk splattered all over the fat man, who was wheezing and sweating like a tired work mule.

I ran back to get a good look.

"Get up, Hap! Come on, get up!" Dizzy, Duke, and Nate yelled, encouraging him up the embankment and laughing at the same time.

"Damn!" yelled a weary, frustrated Hap. He gathered himself and tussled with the loose dirt and tall weeds as he scrambled up the tracks.

Sitting nearby, the chocolate milk-covered man smirked and raised his ice pick in the air.

"Damn, we ain't get shit," snapped Hap.

"Here, man." I handed him the crate. You deserve this."

We laughed about how the chocolate-covered cow had just tried to run us down and was now sitting on his side of the tracks, sipping from a carton of spilled milk. We took a seat on the railroad tracks just yards away from him and joined him in sipping on OJ and some of the sweetest chocolate milk under the moon.

Stealing from Borden's Milk Dairy on a balmy summer night was routine. We knew we'd see the fat man again next Friday night, and we knew he'd be waiting.

And back then, those were my friends.

Dancing at Esperanza's

Michael A. Gonzales

For Gil

"The reed that bends will raise its head when wind and rain have gone away." —South African

And so Tito emerged from the heart of darkness, where his blistered fingers held tightly to the silver crucifix dangling from his neck. It had been a gift one of his aunts had placed around his neck the morning of his first communion. Abruptly, he was awakened by the howling of wild dogs. Outside, in the junglelands of Vietnam, it was raining and strange lights flared in the darkness. Through the flimsy bamboo walls of the makeshift hospital, the eternal protest of barking canine creatures later served as a surreal soundtrack of collective madness in each wounded warrior's memory.

"Can I get you anything?" inquired the nurse over the moans of the other suffering soldiers. Even without lipstick or makeup, she reminded Tito of the sassy neighborhood beauties he had once admired from a distance. More than a year had passed since he had last seen New York City, and he missed the hustle of those gritty summertime streets, where pretty girls in tight dresses licked ice-cream cones and flashed flirty smiles to staring strangers.

"How long have I been in here?" Tito asked, his throat sore. His last memory was of being butt-naked inside a rowdy black-market brothel. A simple row of sturdy huts some industrial dudes from Brooklyn had constructed near a swamp, it was where the men went to be serviced. The funky smell in the air—a combination of shit, piss, and decaying animals—was enough to make a brother feel the shadow of death lurking nearby.

"Well," said the nurse, examining his medical chart, "you've been knocked out for three days, Private Tito Hernandez." His skin was the color of coffee with just a drop of milk; his once curly Afro had been shaved. "We thought you were going to lose that leg, but the doctors managed to save it. You'll be hobbling on a cane in no time." Her voice had a melodic quality that reminded Tito of soothing music.

In the distance, there was the deafening cacophony of choppers soaring dangerously low, blasting whining children as they crawled through the thick mud, moaning, crying, and praying until the end. Their sorrowful voices reminded Tito of the whimpered prayers that had tumbled off his tongue the day his own limber legs were forever damaged by piercing debris. Tito listened as the white-shoed nurse walked over to a different bed, offering her comforting words to another.

Although it was impossible to sleep through the apocalypse raging outside, he closed his confused eyes. In his sorrowful state, Tito mentally conjured up the luscious wildflowers of perfumed senoritas and listened to the energetic voices of weekend lovers over the swelling piano solo on Larry Harlow's enchanting "La Catera." As the enchanted couples swooned in his mind, Tito's spirit swayed onto the dance floor of Club Esperanza.

"When your father and I first came to this country from San Antone, we had some good times there," reminisced his moms. She stood over the stove, stirring a simmering pot of tripe soup. Her brown hands were steady as the rich broth brewed. Besides drinking and dancing, cooking had become therapeutic for Carmen. The soulful smells that vapored from the pots were a testament to her healing. "That was our treat to ourselves after slaving away in that damn garment factory," she laughed. "I even went when I was pregnant with you."

His poppi's constant cheating with fast-ass teenaged girls, in addition to losing his paycheck more than once on the bloody floor of a basement cockfight, had gotten him bounced from the house a few years past. Still, Tito's mother never tired of reciting these tales. "We were young and in love, and we thought the dance would last forever." It was obvious that Carmen was in love with the past, which made many of her boyfriends jealous.

On those occasions, when she was beginning to feel melancholy over losing her husband to the slutty seductions of the streets, Carmen would drag Tito into the cluttered living room and teach him the dances from her youth. In the beginning, the ornate steps seemed difficult to Tito. Yet, once the beat of the drums caressed his feet, there was no stopping. "I'm not a rich woman," she whispered, her breath reeking of sweet wine. She always got sentimental when she was in her cups. "So when I go away from this fucked-up world, I'll have nothing to leave you. Teaching you to dance is all I can give you." Afterward, he would help her push back the ratty La-Z-Boy chair so it was closer to the picture of Jesus that hung on the wall.

At night, after taking a steamy bath and being tucked into a bed covered with James Bond sheets, Tito would fantasize about the Club Esperanza's majestic bandstand, where the sons of East Harlem immigrants dressed in stylish suits and conjured memories of an island most had never seen. In Tito's dreams, his mother's slurred voice sounded poetic. "The dancers performed as though gravity barely existed in their universe of pulsating percussion, vicious piano solos, and a wild horn section that sounded more brutal than thunder cracking the sky."

Indeed, it was almost like a dream when his mother inquired what he might want for his fifteenth birthday and he replied simply, "I want to go to Club Esperanza."

With her lips painted the color of ripe cherries, she glanced at Tito and noticed the facial hair that was beginning to sprout from her son's youthful face. Nodding slightly, she smiled. "Fine. On Friday night, me, you, and Gilbert will go." Gilbert was her newest boyfriend, a boisterous black man who was a subway conductor by day and a Budweiser swiller by night. Tito figured he was cooler than a few of the others she had dated. At least he made his moms happy and had so far kept his hands to himself.

"Do you think it's a good idea to take a boy that age to a nightclub?" barked Gilbert. He thought that Carmen spoiled her son. "Whoever heard of taking kids to a nightclub?"

"What could it hurt?" she snapped. "Tito's a good kid, good grades. What could a little dancing hurt?" While others might have considered Tito somewhat geeky because of his aversion to sports, and an unnatural love for the written word and James Bond flicks, his moms was the only one who knew the kid had moves. "It's better than him being cooped up in the room ruining his eyes reading those crazy books about spies."

Built from scratch in the early '50s in El Barrio, the wonderment of Club Esperanza had been considered a rite of passage for young Latinos since the days when their cultural representation was limited to the switchblade cha-cha ballet of West Side Story. Walking through the front door of this brave new world, one was met with a steep staircase that seemingly ascended to heaven, where the walls were painted a splendid shade of blue and the ceiling was covered with twinkling stars constructed from aluminum foil. On the walls were dozens of framed black-and-white photos of musicians from Tito Puente to Celia Cruz to Dizzy Gillespie. Underfoot, the plush carpeting with its gaudy floral design led directly to the door of the club.

Tito was in a state of bliss that could hardly be contained. In his mind, he had finally entered through the divine doors of paradise. "Let's take that table over there," mumbled Gilbert, who guided both mother and child through the crowded club. Each table was draped with a red tablecloth, whose stains were impossible to notice in the semidarkness.

While most of the suited men were gulping Bacardi and Coke, their temptress dates slowly sipped from large glasses of frozen piña colada. Tito's dark-brown eyes, with his thick lashes and bushy brows, were as wide as a child's at Disneyland. "Try not to get away too far," his moms warned before Tito wandered into the haze of warm lights and brand-new affections. "And don't be trying to get any drinks, either."

"I'm just going to take a little walk," he answered, feeling almost grown. Still, it was difficult for him to project the kind of cool persona he recognized in others when this childish fascination of finally being inside Club Esperanza continued to bubble inside him.

Dressed in a white summer linen suit Carmen had bought him especially for this occasion, Tito stood at the bar and admired the voluptuous ladies dressed in luxurious outfits that sparkled and shined, twinkling like shooting stars over the murky Harlem River. "Can I get this dance?" he heard the smooth Romeos moan. With perfect hair flowing like lava down volcanic bodies, the women's personal style was a sort of trampy chic one would never peep in the pages of *Vogue*, but covering their sensual skin it was an art form. If they agreed to dance, the girls would extend their hands like royalty at a ball.

"Can't believe I'm running into you here," said the obnoxiously familiar voice of Carlos García, a jock he knew from gym class at Rice High School. He was one of those crazy militant spics who liked to brag that his brother was in the Young Lords, ". . . ready to bomb the Man if he dares to interfere with life in El Barrio!" Carlos had an amazing Afro, marshmallow shoes, a silk shirt, and pants tighter than a nun's choker hold.

"I didn't think you freedom fighters could hang out at salsa clubs," said Tito snidely. He was often told that it was his sense of humor and lack of glasses that kept him from getting beat up on the regular.

"Shit, that's how much you know, man," snapped Carlos. "Man, don't you know salsa is down with the revolution? Shit, just ask that DJ. If anybody knows, it's that brother right there." Standing in the DJ booth, a young cat named Mercado spun records as though he were a priest serving communion on Sunday morning. While some might think of these island sounds as merely music, for Mercado these were sanctified musings of rhythmic ancient Afro-Rican souls screaming from behind palm trees and garage cans, enchanting oceans and polluted rivers, heavenly skies and midnight police sirens, sandy beaches and streets paved with fool's gold.

On the dance floor, as the patrons wailed loudly with shouts of joy, they were able to transit the misery of the world and return to an imaginary motherland where there was more music than troubles in mind. Hypnotized by the rapture of rhythm, Tito moved closer to the supple-hipped dancers, closer to the heat of their improvised movements under the blinking strobe light and rotating disco ball.

No longer in the living room crashing into the old La-Z-Boy chair or bumping into the newspaper-covered coffee table, Tito was free to explore the ecstasy he felt as the harmonics surged through his body. It was then that Mercado decided it was the perfect moment to spin Eddie Palmieri's salsa symphony, "Vámonos Pal' Monte." Overflowing with countless changes of tone and texture, this cathedral of sound was not constructed for dabblers, but Tito figured he had gone beyond novice status many moons past; perhaps while he was a fetus in his mother's womb he'd felt this desire to soar through walls of sound.

Tito felt her eyes crawling on the back of his neck, and he slowly turned to see the glorious figure of an alluring young girl. Although they had never met, Tito felt a connection. It was as though they had known each other since forever.

In a matter of moments they were on the floor, flittering like African butterflies; there was an aura in their moves that rivaled the most perfect Renoir hanging in a museum, their feet sweeping in movements that resembled complex brush strokes on a vast canvas. Although still strangers, their bodies spoke a passionate language as he guided her in his suddenly masculine arms. Beaming proudly at her son, Carmen was amazed watching Tito shed his protective shell, using a few of the spins and dips she had taught him herself.

"My name is Rosie," said the young girl, her voice nearly drowned out by the din of the clapping crowd.

He almost blurted, "Bond. James Bond," but thought she would take him as some kind of fool. Instead, he simply smiled and dashed away.

For the next three years his mother watched in awe as Tito—whom everyone at Club Esperanza now called Tito Dance—perfected his skills in front of the bathroom mirror as the stereo blasted; in three years he had become a dance elitist and only bothered to swing with the best, always reserving the most difficult dances for Rosie. "Why don't you ever invite your girlfriend over to the house?" asked Carmen one morning, serving eggs and bacon for two. Gilbert had ducked out six months earlier, leaving a pair of battered work shoes by the door that Carmen never bothered to throw away. "Are you embarrassed of me or something?"

"I don't have a girlfriend," answered Tito. "What makes you think I have a girlfriend?" With Rosie, their relationship was never based on anything as conventional as picnics in the park or sexual desire. The only things that mattered were the dance floor and their joy of music. Outside the walls of Esperanza existed another world of dog-eat-dog, and the wages of sin were preached by mothers tired of their babies bringing home babies; while inside the club, lost in the grooves, anything was possible.

"So modest, you," said Carmen, slightly jealous. "You think I don't hear the stories, hear about you and that woman Rosie from the club? Everyone talks of Tito and Rosie dancing at Club Esperanza. I just want you to know I'm too young to be a grandmother."

"All we do is dance, Mother," sighed Tito. "That's all we do, I swear."

"Make sure it's all you do, then," she huffed.

Two weeks after he graduated from high school, Tito felt a sense of doom the moment he walked into the crib. His mother was watching a Spanish soap opera on Channel 47, but she also appeared to be praying. Her eyes were moist; her hands were shaking. "What's going on?" he asked, kissing her on the cheek. She had never been the rosary-beads kind of woman, but her grave expression had him worried.

"I put a letter on your bed," she said; her voice trembled. Without even opening the official-looking government envelope, Tito knew that

Uncle Sam wanted his spic ass to be chased by tigers and machine gun-wielding children. Shit, he had seen those disturbing images on the nightly news programs, and he had witnessed the broken men who returned from those jungles with nothing but deferred dreams and King Kong stomping on their backs. In two months he would be replacing them.

"It's not fair," his moms cried, standing in the doorway of Tito's bedroom. He had planned on taking off a semester before enrolling at City College, but now it had all changed. She hugged him tightly, scared to utter a single sound, afraid of shattering this fragile moment. Carmen decided the following day that her baby's eighteenth birthday party should be a blow-out affair of friends and family, celebrating her only son with a superb feast and a glorious soundtrack that he could carry in his heart while trying to survive overseas. "Of course," she squealed, "it has to be at Club Esperanza."

"August third, huh?" growled the burly manager, chomping on an unlit cigar. "You're in luck. I've already booked Palmieri to play that night. It'll be special, all right."

Tito and Carmen's guest list was extensive, filled with cousins he had never met and aunts he had never liked, basketball jocks from his days at Rice High School and the blond-haired priest, Father Bob, from St. Catherine's. From across the room he saw Carlos García and a few of his defiant Lords trying to rap up some pussy in the name of the revolution. "Tough break, man," said more than a few talking heads, knowing that the madness of war was about to become Tito's reality. Everyone was in a joyful mood, making toasts and rambling speeches about what it means to be a noble man in a world of senselessness.

The audience erupted with intoxicated screams as the bearded keyboard superman Palmieri, a dude from the 'hood, born right on 112th in El Barrio, leaped on the stage followed by his mighty ensemble. Quickly he improvised a minor piece on piano, then stood up to address the crowd. "I heard this next song is a favorite of our boy Tito Dance, so tonight I dedicate this song to him."

It was as though flames were in the hands of the conga guy who opened the song. Tito stood still in the smoky room and smiled as Rosie walked toward him. She wore a seductive dress that her mother had made, highlighting her dangerous curves and slippery slopes. They danced as though possessed by tribal spirits that refused to release their souls until the last note was played. Guided by the master's skillful hands, Palmieri led the musicians through the jungles of Africa, the island of Puerto Rico, and the jitterbug jazz spots that had once populated dark Harlem.

On black wax the track clocked in at over seven minutes, but with his blood-boiling live voodoo, bandleader Palmieri jammed "Vámonos Pal' Monte" for damn near twice as long, swept away in the eternal funky aural fixation that boogied down, baby; this was one motherfucker who could fly a bro to the moon without a rocket ship. In the crowd, the men's suits were sticky with sweat and the women's hair looked wilder than Medusa's. Tito was shocked when the breathless Rosie leaned over and kissed him tenderly on the lips. "Try to make it back," she whispered.

"I'll try my best," he laughed, twirling her in his arms. "Just don't find another partner."

Palmieri soloed with the sensibility of a soulful sorcerer that revealed an undisputed power, his musical wrath conjuring earthquakes, floods, and other supernatural disasters. Perhaps not conscious of the vibrant images being transported through the tinkling ebony and ivory keys, the once-upon-a-time nirvana of the New World slowly became the nightmare of bloody battlefields covered with young boys who had barely ventured from their own neighborhoods before being selected to slay strangers on the other side of the world.

The dogs were still barking. Naked to the world, Tito drifted on the memories of that Nuyorican night. As the bombs rained from the illuminated sky, Tito was lost in mad thoughts. The salty sweat on his face reminded him of the perspiration that rolled down his back the night Eddie Palmieri played until the wee hours of the morning.

The Consequence

Pat G'Orge-Walker

"If it ain't broken, break it." —African American

Wednesday afternoon

I had just climbed up the subway steps after leaving my six-A.M.-to-two-P.M. shift as a token clerk at Brooklyn's Kingston and Throop subway line. It was a relief to surface from what I liked to call "the black hole of death." In three years of eating the A train's dust, I'd endured bouts of painful bladder infections from being locked in the closet-sized token booth. It had taken several trips to the disciplinary board and help from the Transit Workers Union to keep me from giving in to my urge to maim and mutilate passengers and coworkers. It was no secret that I hated my job.

Emerging from the subway, I was shocked to notice that I felt unusually warm. Either the sun was shining brighter, or my self-imposed sexual drought had caught up with me. With the warmth from the sun wrapping me from head to toe, I felt horny. It didn't take a Dr. Ruth to tell me that I needed some good old-fashioned, headboard-banging nookie. For the first time that day, I smiled.

Here I was, standing sexually depleted on a filthy Brooklyn sidewalk, trying to decide what to do with the twenty minutes I had before meeting my cousin Vera at the Red Cross. Why I let her talk me into giving blood, I'll never know. But my younger cousin and roommate had a way of making me want to do the right thing, even though I put up a good front and made her practically beg to get me to agree.

Walking toward the Red Cross office, I feasted my eyes on a gorgeous hunk of African-male DNA all wrapped up in a made-for-him tan shirt that tried but couldn't hide his well-toned shoulders. He was about six feet four of "I'm all that" in pecan tan skin, with the stride of a thoroughbred racehorse.

I slowed my mind to take in every bit of his magnificence, imagining what it would be like to kiss him, touch him, to have him pleading to love me. As my eyes washed over him, I noticed several other women of various colors and ages gawking at him. He reminded me of Denzel in *Mo' Better Blues*—his horn in one hand and every woman's sexual fantasies in the other. Mr. Pecan Tan thrilled his female audience with the confidence of a Serengheti lion on the prowl.

A forty-something white woman took a deep breath as he strode past, straightening the collar on her expensive green silk pantsuit. She was looking at Mr. Pecan Tan so hard I thought she was gonna press her platinum American Express card into his hand and crawl behind him.

I couldn't blame her, though, I thought as he passed me. Looking at that brothah's apple-shaped butt, each cheek fighting for space in his white bicycle shorts, reminded me that I was manless, sexless, and feeling cravings I thought I'd put on hold.

I fell back against the side of the Red Cross building. Almost a whole year. Have mercy! No wonder I was hornier than an Indian Brahma bull. I'd given up sex because of one of my miserable and selfish ex-boyfriends, Levi.

He'd turned out to be the glitch in my "keep two men at a time" plan. Despite my insecurities, I thought the mighty sun set its clock by me and I was too much woman to restrict myself to one man.

Just thinking about Levi made me wanna spit. I'd seen him only twice since he messed things up for me. It had been at a local park, and though I'd never wanted any man who'd done me wrong to do too good without me, I wasn't prepared for how bad Levi appeared to be doing. He looked like he was not just a charter member but also the president of the Slim-Fast Club. His coat looked like it was hanging on a hanger instead of a human frame. His face looked gaunt and sunken-in like he'd spent time in a German concentration camp or been left to starve like the people in Biafra.

I'd overheard Levi telling somebody that he'd just gotten over a bout of pneumonia. It looked like the pneumonia had won that bout! I'd started to walk over and speak, but didn't bother 'cause I was still too pissed. And after all the time that had passed, I still felt I had good reason to be mad.

Whatever Levi's problem was, I felt he'd gotten what he deserved. Our relationship hadn't been broken; it had been working just fine for me. He shouldn't have tried to "fix it" by making his own rules.

The way I saw it, the fact that he hadn't known my rules was no excuse.

I'd met him at my mother's youngest sister, Aunt Dee Dee's, place in Brownsville, Brooklyn.

"Meet Levi. He's here fixing my plumbing," Aunt Dee Dee laughed nervously, handing him a fistful of cash. I didn't believe her. She didn't need to pay a plumber; she was an apartment renter, not an owner.

My fifty-two-year-old Aunt Dee Dee was, by her own admission, a "shameless, asthmatic hussy" with a reputation and appetite for the "not yet legal, but tender" young men. She was also vertically challenged and about forty pounds overweight.

Gray-haired, menopausal Aunt Dee Dee couldn't walk from the kitchen to the front door of her two-room apartment without wheezing. And she loved to wear purple muumuus, which made her look like an Indian teepee with a cloud of smoke on top. Still, young men flocked around her like ants tending their queen. People on the block called her apartment a juvenile day-care center for boys. She wore their comments like a badge of honor. My cousin Vera never saw the humor in the situation and refused to visit.

The first thing I noticed about Levi was his skin. He was shirtless, sporting his six-pack with M'Lisa Morgan's "Do Me, Baby" playing low on the stereo. I wanted to grab and bite into him like a smooth, chocolate brown candy bar. I licked my lips as he leaned against the kitchen counter counting the green blessings that Aunt Dee Dee had just bestowed upon him. I could have swallowed him whole!

He must have felt the same way, because he stuck out his tongue behind Aunt Dee Dee's back as he hugged her, showing me he could use it like a windshield wiper.

Backstabber! That should have been my first clue.

After secretly flirting with each other at Aunt Dee Dee's, I figured she wouldn't miss Levi, so I took him away from her. She'd left to play Monday-night bingo at the local Catholic church. "Come on," I said to Levi, "and see what you've been missing." He didn't take a minute to throw all the new clothes she'd bought him into a grocery bag and follow me out the door.

Even though I did her wrong, Aunt Dee Dee never said an unkind word to me. I guess she knew the rules of the street: *game recognized game.* Before the week was out, she had another boy toy in Levi's place. *C'est la vie.*

Back then I wasn't sorry about a thing, but now I am. And I sure do miss her. Aunt Dee Dee died from AIDS about a year after Levi and I got together. It was messed up because I'd just found out that my dad had been HIV positive for years before his "cancerlike symptoms" were diagnosed as AIDS.

I never knew anything about my father's lifestyle, but I did know about Aunt Dee Dee's. AIDS had struck twice, and they say bad luck always comes in threes.

Levi was younger than me by about two years. Of course, I'd never told him my age, because I knew he was lying when he said he was twenty-one. I'd sneaked a peek in his wallet while he slept soundly from a very exhaustive romp on our first date. I didn't see any reason to tell him my true age when he hadn't told me his.

Two years later, that chocolate niggah went stale on me. He showed his true DNA. From the very first time we got together, I served up Levi the bootylicious twice a week and three times on Sundays.

Levi was from the Pink Houses in East New York. His family had never had much money, so they always fixed things themselves, which is how Levi came to know so much about repairing stuff. Anything I needed done around the house, including me, I called on Levi. Nobody could work a hammer and a *screw* like he could. I saw Levi on Sundays, Wednesdays, and Fridays.

Of course, Levi never knew he had a little help on the side. His assistant was Pablo—fortyish, Colombian-born, with a ponytail at the back of his neck, from a wealthy family who'd made their money in brownstone real estate. At least that's what Pablo told me, but I had my doubts. Because whenever we went out, he had to stop on every sleazy, secluded street corner in central Brooklyn.

Whenever I questioned him, he said he was handling "family business." But all of his people looked like they'd be right comfortable on Rikers Island, or at the very least, in somebody's rehab program.

I overlooked a lot because Pablo was as gorgeous as he was rich, and besides, I never had to leave the car to meet his "clients" or "tenants." He'd return to the car, flash his thirty-two-watt smile, and say, "*Yo tengo cosa por tú.*"

I'd flash him my own twenty-eight-watt smile (not all of my relationships had gone as well as they should have, and I had to donate a few teeth and two short hospital stays before I learned better), and reply, "What do you have for me, baby?"

Pablo would just grin and slide a small gift box up my thigh with his magic fingers leading the way, until it lay just inches from my own silken gift box. It would usually be jewelry, and I'd always be appreciative.

Pablo wore nothing but the latest fashions, and he was cleaner than the Board of Health. He made me feel lucky to be with him. Pablo was shorter than me, but that was okay because he stood on old money. He handled my rent, utilities, and car note. All I had to do was don a pair of kneepads a few times a week.

He wasn't a particularly good lover; in fact, he could have ridden with Paul Revere and the other patriots during the Revolutionary War because he was definitely a one-minute man. He was my undercover, barely-speakin'-English lover.

I saw him on Saturdays, Tuesdays, and Thursdays.

One Saturday, Levi showed up though it wasn't his day, talking about he "was in the neighborhood." Pablo was sitting on my bed in designer briefs, his matted, jet-black chest hair glistening, barely able to breathe since I'd just finished making him holler my name. He was handing me my weekly expense check.

One look at Levi coming through the door with a set of keys dangling from his hand, and Pablo tore up the check, leaped off the bed toward the door, tossed me aside like a soiled towel, and said something foul in Spanish accented with a couple of jabs to Levi's stomach.

He stopped long enough to give the English translation, which was sure to hand him a few Hail Marys, then landed an uppercut to Levi's jaw to make sure he was understood. Yeah, the brothah gave the term "bilingual" a whole new meaning.

"You black mutha—. You like how I taste? How I smell? *Verdad?*" Pablo taunted Levi, spinning around, and jumped into a karate stance. With his boxers falling down on one side, he looked like a broken Pez candy dispenser.

Levi slowly unfolded from the jab to his stomach and growled, "I wouldn't know. Every time I hit it, it felt like unexplored territory, you greasy Italian—"

"Excuse me. I'm Colombian!" Pablo sputtered.

All I could do was run around the room trying to save my expensive stuff, saying "Listen, we just need to act like grown-ups."

They both stopped in their tracks, looking like the outline of the Charlie's Angels symbol with fists clenched and raised and hollered at the same time, "Shuddup, ho!" That little outburst seemed to unite them in their cause.

I stood by the coffee table trying to move a very expensive decorative urn when Pablo quickly pulled his clothes on. They rushed to the door, their palms colliding in upraised high-fives.

Levi turned to Pablo. "Don't sweat it, man. I ain't mad with ya. We both know that girlfriends and wives are to be treasured. But you can't turn no trick into a housewife!"

"*Sí, verdad*," Pablo agreed with a smirk. "Hoes *es por todo el mundo.*"

I couldn't believe those two sorry excuses for Y chromosomes played me like that.

"Get out!" I hollered. "I don't need either one of you. I got your replacements waiting already."

"That's why you a ho!" Levi shot back.

I lost my Levi and my Pablo at the same time, and it was all Levi's stupid fault. He should've stuck to the schedule. I learned how to change locks and vowed never to give any man a set of my keys for any reason.

My bitter memories were cut short by a pigeon whose bodily fluids barely missed my arm. The nasty flashback of Levi and Pablo didn't lessen my sexual appetite, though. I leaned against the Country Kitchen Chinese Restaurant, right next to the Red Cross Clinic, looking at my watch.

I rewound my memory to another old boyfriend. Lucien had been a sailor back in 1987, and whenever his ship docked at the old Brooklyn Navy Yard, he'd give me a call.

Lucien was six-three, with a greasy Jheri curl and a freckled face. He was a thirty-year-old sorry excuse for a male, who left the Navy and moved in with his mama, too ornery even to change his socks. When we were getting down to the real nitty-gritty, he'd take off his shoes. I'd be ready to grab hold to the ceiling fan blades and get my freak on, but I couldn't, because his stinky feet set off the sprinkler system in his mama's basement.

However, Lucien did make me see the stars, the moon, and the invisible man a couple of times. He may have had stinky feet, but Lucien could make me rob a bank full of cops and slap my grandma's face at testimony service with his lovemaking.

I was jerked out of my Lucien recollection by a tap on my shoulder. "Hey, girly, whatchu doing on dis side of town? You lookin' lost."

It was my home girl, Nadine, draped to the nines in several colors of the rainbow. If you asked her why she wore such colorful outfits, she'd reply, "Me tink I look good in all de colors. So me wear dem. 'Tis as simple as dat. Besides, me a brown-skin girly. Me what all de fellas feen fe."

Nadine was not only colorful and confident, she was five-feet-ten, cocoa brown with green eyes, long brown hair, and, as the fellas around the way would say, "built for speed." However, Nadine didn't take no stuff. She'd rather cut you than explain what you did wrong. She said she didn't have time for conversation when she was riled up.

"Hey, Panama Hattie." That was my pet name for her. "What's up?"

"Me come ta give me blood. Ya feget you tell me 'bout it? Tink only you can do it?" She sucked her teeth, knowing I couldn't match the sound.

"I'm glad you're here, girl. I was standing here horny and thinking about going off my no-sex routine and checking out Lucien. He don't live far from here." I stopped and used one finger to circle my head. "I must be crazy and I need you to talk me out of it."

Nadine looked like I had pimp-slapped her. "Ya don't know?"

"Know what?"

"Why ya don't know de boy dead? They just buried he last week, me hear."

"What? I haven't seen Lucien in about a year and a half. What happened to him?"

"AIDS. De boy was infected. Me glad ya stopped ruffling sheets wit' he. I was going to another funeral over dere at the Unity Funeral Home, and who lyin' in de next room but he. Me thinks you was pining fe he and that why ya not call me. Me not call ya, 'cause me wanna give ya grieving space."

Instantly my urges for sex, noncommittal and otherwise, vanished. I saw fleeting glimpses of my father, Aunt Dee, and Lucien, all dead from AIDS. That Lucien had put me at risk.

I also remembered how thin Levi was the last time I saw him. I thought he was on the pipe. No, I *hoped* he was on the pipe.

I hardly remember Nadine opening the door to the Red Cross Clinic, or Vera pulling up at the same time. I don't remember filling out the medical forms or giving permission for them to check my blood for

HIV and other infections. Everything after Nadine's news about Lucien was a blur.

Two Weeks Later

The postman delivered the official-looking, cream-colored envelope with the Red Cross logo in the upper lefthand corner. I slowly opened the letter and read the first line.

> *Dear Ms. Kecia L., As a result of our lab's testing your blood for possible donation, we have discovered the following abnormality . . .*

AIDS. Not even HIV.

I cried nonstop for a week, searching my whole body for telltale signs and running to the library for information. I even went back to be retested a second and third time and still didn't believe the results.

I couldn't stand to look my cousin Vera in the face and tell her that I had AIDS, so I moved out without explaining. I wanted to take care of myself.

I missed Vera more than I'd admit. Because we had shared so much of life's pain, we understood each other. We liked the same type of clothes, sexy yet classy, which made borrowing a pleasure. Our taste in music ran from the sweet, sultry sounds of Marvin Gaye to hip-hop king L. L.Cool J, to the foot-stomping gospel of the Mighty Clouds of Joy that we'd play every Sunday to make us feel less guilty for not going to church.

Our biggest disagreement was why I'd let the sexual abuse from our Uncle LuVaughn turn me into, as Vera put it, "a mat for every man to walk upon."

Our mothers, who were identical twins, left us at early ages in the care of their mother, Grandma Addie, who lived in a small wooden house in Florence, South Carolina. They left Vera and me, their only children, to pursue whatever fantasies Southern girls craved once they saw the bright lights of Harlem. They wanted careers in showbiz; instead, they ended up as prostitutes. After working the streets together, they died mysteriously.

Vera never met her father or even heard anything about him. I learned from Grandma Addie that my father's name was Jaime. He was a Black Cuban who she'd sometimes talk to, calling him "a no-good, sorry piece of worthless human flesh."

One day, a letter arrived with a New York postmark, addressed to me. At first I'd thought it was from my mother; then I remembered that she was dead. And she'd never written me, anyway. I threw the other mail on the dining room table and ran into the bathroom with my letter hidden in my dress pocket. I didn't want Grandma Addie to see it, since it was addressed to *me*.

It was from the man, my father, Jaime. He apologized for not seeing me since I was two months old and sent a picture of himself. I looked at his image and then at my own reflection in the bathroom mirror. We had the same coloring, the same straight hair, and the same permanent, faraway sadness in our eyes.

On the back of the picture was his full name, address, and telephone number, written in a childlike scrawl. Throughout my childhood, I hid the photo, even though I felt no attachment to this mysterious stranger beyond the features we shared.

When Vera was twelve and I was ten, Uncle LuVaughn came to live at Grandma Addie's with us. And he put his nasty forty-year-old hands on us every chance he got.

Somehow, Vera, when in her late teens, had watched enough Oprah, Sally Jesse Raphael, and Phil Donahue and read a few self-help books to send her into months of deep prayer at the Bronx, New York, Garden of Prayer Church of God in Christ's altar, where she learned to forgive Uncle LuVaughn.

I never would—didn't feel I should—forgive that pervert.

When I'd gotten up enough nerve to tell Grandma Addie what her demented son had been doing to Vera and me, she took it all wrong. It was a Monday night; right after the three of us had attended a revival meeting at New Prospect Baptist Church. Grandma Addie was feeling the spirit, so she said, and that made me hope that she'd be receptive to what I needed to tell her.

But she hadn't believed a word I'd said. Instead of calling Vera inside to ask her if what I'd said was true, Grandma Addie beat me with one of several large black leather straps she used to sharpen straight razors. With every stroke she laid on my half-naked body, she'd shout that "None of my sons would do something so nasty. I'm going to beat that lying demon out of you, baby girl!"

Beating me even harder, she prayed, "Lord, banish this lyin' demon to the pits of Hell!"

All I could do was scream and wonder where all the Holy Spirit from the revival meeting had disappeared to.

Grandma Addie continued to testify, pleading, with each blow, "Lord, I done tried to raise this chile as best I know how, but a demon of confusion has taken over her."

Through my tears, I saw that ugly black human snake, Uncle Lu-Vaughn, peeking from behind the bamboo divider that separated the living room from the dining room. He seemed to be enjoying both the sight of my naked young body and the beating I was getting.

For years, I saw Grandma Addie's dark skin glistening from perspiration as the tears ran down her plump cheeks. When I was older, I felt that maybe the tears had been from frustration, the possibility that what I'd told her was true. If she hadn't beaten me, she'd have had to accept the fact that she'd raised a pervert.

After that beating, Grandma Addie put me on punishment for a month to make sure I got her point and would never repeat my accusation. I never said another word. I held it in and it held me captive, powerless to defend myself against any of life's circumstances, good or bad.

With just a few unwanted quick feels and incestuous acts, my uncle had turned Grandma Addie, Vera, and me into his victims. From that moment on, there was always a strain between Grandma Addie and me. I could never trust her again. Yet she was my grandmother, the only real parent I had, and so in spite of everything, I continued to love her until the day she died. In my own way, I will always miss her.

If I hadn't hated Uncle LuVaughn sufficiently before that punishment, I certainly hated him with a passion after. He stopped molesting Vera and me several weeks after my beating, probably because he felt that although his mama acted like she didn't believe me, there was a chance she'd be watching him from then on. If there was a special place in Hell for men like him, I hoped he'd burn there forever.

Vera coped with the abuse by finding a mental hiding place and refusing to see the world as it really was until she was grown. She grew into adulthood pretty much undamaged. She seemed to survive the ordeal or hide it by plunging into her career as one of the premiere Afro American female stockbrokers at Salomon Brothers on Wall Street.

Me, I went to work for the New York City Transit Authority, hiding inside a token booth for more than eight hours a day trying to blend in with the other soot and grime. Most days, I felt as dirty and used as some of the rails and tokens. In a way, Vera was right. I wore my sexual abuse like a banner and used it as an excuse to accept the ill treatment from life and, especially, men, to whom I gave my money, my body, and my soul.

As close as we were, I'd never told Vera when I decided to give up sex. At the time of my diagnosis, I'd been celibate for almost a year. I'd still dated occasionally, but I managed to keep the men from going all the way. If one man wanted more than I was ready to give, I'd just move on to the next. I never let any of them get too close, mentally or physically.

That's why Vera saw so many men in my life. She probably thought I was letting them use and abuse me and that's why they never stayed. I don't know why I didn't tell her the truth.

One Year Later

It rained like all of Heaven's angels had gotten together and decided to hold one big spitfest outside my window. Several jagged streaks of lightning popped across the sky. Were they also giving me the finger?

How much lower could life pound me into the ground? I was already climbing up the back of "ain't never gonna happen" just to reach the curb of "barely makin' it."

My skeletal image with deep, hollow, frightened eyes was reflected in the grimy windowpane. I turned away and crammed more newspaper into the open space to keep the rain out. I was trying to survive in a room where roaches could barely hang on but lived in anyway. A room devoid of everything but a raggedy cot, a sometimey refrigerator, a telephone with no long-distance, and walls painted the color of crap. The doo-doo brown was so appropriate; it reminded me of my childhood in Florence, South Carolina.

I had wonderful thoughts of life with Grandma Addie before Uncle LuVaughn arrived and shattered everything with his groping hands, the hands that had led Grandma Addie to wield that leather strap across my young body for telling the truth.

Reminiscing, I'd see Grandma Addie in my medicated mind as an eighty-year-old, paper-bag brown woman who always wore her hair, the color of a speckled hen, in a bun. She'd be reaching up with a pair of clippers, cutting limbs that looked fine to me, from her walnut tree. Sometimes on the older branches, she'd clip a piece and then put bamboo shoots on both sides to hold it.

"Why you doing that, Grandma Addie? That tree ain't broken, is it?" I'd ask, trying to add to my ten years of knowledge. I was tall for my age but thin as paper, so it always looked like she was looking past me when she spoke.

"Kecia, sometimes things diseased or wrong don't look it, but somehow you just know. You don't wait for it to be broken. You break it first because if you don't, their branches gonna come out all messed up."

"Huh," I'd say, shaking my head so that my mammy-plaited shoulder-length braids stuck out like Pippi Longstocking's.

More rain ricocheted off my grimy window, and the warnings of Grandma Addie's words rode away on the back of a thunderclap. I turned on the radio for a little comfort.

Surfing through several stations, I barely heard the DJ's familiar voice. Then his words came through loud and clear, comforting me like cotton candy. He was speaking like he wanted to put his tongue in my ear, like he knew me. The old me.

"This is WBLS's Voice of Choice, the man who invented the Quiet Storm, Vaughn Harper. I got a call from a young lady in Brooklyn and she sounded like she could use a friend. So to you, Miss Kecia from Bed-Stuy, get yourself together, baby, and break out of that funk you're in, 'cause life is way too short! Check out the Dramatics' 'In the Rain.'"

Despite all of the medicine racing through my body and mind, I was lucid enough to feel his smooth, caressing voice and the Dramatics, singing their song as if only for me. I cried for the way I used to be, turning up the volume and letting the memories take me back as I waddled over to my tiny sink.

I glanced at the calendar hanging over the sink. I lifted the flap with the picture of smiling children playing in the snow. Children I would never have. I marked an X for another day of life.

I'd learned to live each day with both gratitude and dread, knowing each X meant I was one day closer to death. I lifted the faded letter I had sent to Levi telling him that he, too, should be tested for HIV if he hadn't been already. Judging from the way he'd looked when I last saw him, I suspected he might already be infected.

An apology was not enough, but it was all I could give him. I didn't know whether I'd contracted the virus from him, or him from me, but it didn't matter—not now, anyway. I'd heard that Pablo had gone back to Colombia. I could only hope and pray that he didn't take the disease back with him.

Another clap of thunder shook me, making the radio lose its signal. I turned it off and tried to swallow my daily dose of more than fifteen maintenance pills. It was getting harder to swallow since my tongue was usually swollen from a severe case of thrush. I threw my head back and tried to push the pills to the back of my throat with a finger. Finally, they went down. Trying to live when you were supposed to be dying wasn't easy. As I'd done regularly since my diagnosis, I picked up Grandma Addie's picture and talked to her as I wrote in my journal.

> *Well, Grandma Addie, I've checked off another day. And I know that God has all our hairs numbered and it's up to Him when I go. If what the doctors say is true, then I'll be leaving here in about three months.*
>
> *I never took your advice, probably 'cause I never understood it completely. I do now. I should have broken the cycle of whoring around like I figure my daddy probably did and Aunt Dee Dee definitely did.*
>
> *I've already made my own burial plans, and I know you'll be proud of me for at least taking care of that since I didn't want Vera to be burdened with it. I've decided not to have something common like "Rest in Peace" or "In God's Hands" written on my tombstone. Instead, Grandma Addie, I told the funeral home to put "If It Ain't Broken, Break It." Since I know you're always aware of what's going on with me, even in death, you know I've tried to give that same message to as many as I can. I wish I could give it to a few more folks, but I look so scary now that people just don't wanna be bothered with me. Even my homegirl, Panama Hattie, stopped coming around after a couple of months.*
>
> *That's okay, because I was one foine cinnamon-brown sistah. I was a stupid one, but I was still foine.*
>
> *One last thing, Grandma Addie, while you're up there bending God's ear—and I know you are—please ask Him to forgive me. I need your forgiveness and His.*
>
>
>
> *See you sooner than I'd planned,*
> *Your hardheaded granddaughter,*
>
>
>
> *Kecia*

Young Ballers

Tracy Grant

"Don't start none, won't be none." —African American

Tuesday

He ran as fast as his spindly twelve-year-old legs could carry him. Every few seconds he'd tap the bridge of his nose, pushing his glasses back onto his face as he ran. It wasn't the joyous, gleeful run of lunchtime or gym class. Corey Hawkins ran out of fear, the same fear he'd carried since the fifth grade. If he could just make it home, make it up to his apartment, he'd be free. At least for today.

Corey attended I.S. 244, on Kingsbridge Road, one block from the Jerome Avenue subway station that was the heart of his Bronx neighborhood. He had left seventh period ten minutes early, telling his math teacher that he had an emergency. And he did—Jamal Barry was going to beat him up after school.

Ms. King had gotten mad when he ran out of the classroom, but Corey didn't care; he'd rather take on his math teacher than Jamal any day. So he bolted out of math class onto Kingsbridge Road, past the local pizza parlor, and across the street. Corey ignored the crossing guard at the corner and ran into the two-way traffic, oblivious to the screeching cars and buses. He darted past the old ladies and their shopping carts, ran by the younger Catholic-school kids, their burgundy-plaid uniforms a blur as he made his getaway. He passed the A&P, the liquor store, Blockbuster Video, the cellular phone store, the church, and the bodega on the corner of Webb Avenue. By the time he reached Webb, Corey was out of breath and he slowed his pace. Once he got around the corner, he'd be home free. Jamal and his boys were probably outside the school, looking for Corey or some other target. Jogging now, Corey inhaled deeply, and a sense of relief came over him. Then he turned the corner.

Corey bumped into a boy and almost knocked him over. Looking up, his heart sank. He had run straight into Jamal, the boy he wanted most to avoid. Jamal's friends surrounded Corey.

"Whoa, whoa! Where you going, son?"

"Home." Corey looked down to hide the fear in his face.

"Thought you got away, didn't you?"

"Leave me alone, Jamal."

"Leave me alone, Jamal," he mocked. "You ain't get touched today."

"Yesterday was enough. Why you always starting?"

"'Cause I can, bitch!" Corey saw Jamal's open hand and winced as the blow struck his face. His glasses flew off and hit the sidewalk. Corey ignored the stinging pain and reached down for what looked like his glasses. Tony kicked them into the street.

"Why you do that, Tony? I ain't do nothin' to you!"

"Nigga, fuck you. You don't like it, do something!" Tony, Jamal, and the other boys howled with laughter. Corey was more panic-stricken than before. If his glasses got broken, there would be trouble at home. He blocked out the laughter and made his way toward the edge of the sidewalk. He could just barely make out the front of a parked car, and everything else looked foggy. Corey squinted hard into Sedgewick Avenue. He thought he saw his glasses close to the yellow lines that divided the traffic. When he heard cars coming he stepped back, and a seemingly endless line of cars came one after another.

"Ha, ha!" Jamal laughed. "This fool about to get killed over them Coke-bottle glasses. Damn, Tony!"

"You was gonna do the same shit," Tony replied.

Jamal, Tony, and their boys were still laughing. Corey itched with impatience, watching while each car continued to put his glasses, and thus his immediate future, at risk. Finally, the traffic stopped on the near side and Corey ran into the street. He all but ignored the BX 5 bus on the far side of the street, coming toward him.

"Corey! Look out!" a girl shouted. Hearing the warning, Corey ran across the street, but not before scooping up his glasses. He was touched to think that his sister Layla was worried about him, but it was Layla's friend Dee Dee who had warned him. Fitting his glasses back onto his face, he saw the look of utter disgust that Layla was giving him.

It was after three o'clock, and several other kids had arrived. Jamal and his friends threw up their hands at Corey and moved on, having entertained themselves for the day. Layla, Dee Dee, and the other kids followed them.

"Thanks, Dee Dee," Corey called. Dee Dee waved at him and walked along with everyone else. Layla turned her back and ignored him. Corey sighed. His right lens was cracked, rendering him half-blind. He tried to hide his tears; nobody was looking and nobody cared. Corey headed slowly toward home, dreading the punishment that awaited him.

"They fell?" Corey's mother barked. "What do you mean, they *fell?*"

"It was an accident, Ma."

"Always an accident. This is the third pair. I can't afford any more of your goddamn accidents!"

Corey heard Layla trying to contain her laughter.

"Layla, shut up and eat your food," their mother commanded. "Boy, do you know those are three-hundred-dollar lenses?"

"I'll just wear these."

"You know they're prescription! How you gonna wear a broken lens? What are you, retarded?"

Layla couldn't hold it in and fell out laughing.

"Shut up!" Corey shouted.

"You shut up!"

"Both of you shut up and eat! I've had it!" Corey's mother said. When Judy Thomas said "I've had it," Corey and Layla knew they'd better keep quiet. Judy Thomas was not to be played with anytime, and today was a bad day.

The family ate the rest of their red beans and rice without a word. Corey gulped his fruit punch and looked around, trying to keep his mind off his mother's words. The apartment was empty except for some old furniture and a nineteen-inch television, where Regis Philbin introduced the next contestant on *Who Wants to Be a Millionaire?* It was his mother's favorite show; normally there was no cooking, cleaning, or ironing when Regis was on. The fact that she wasn't paying attention to the show this evening meant that she was truly distracted.

"What's the matter, Ma?" Corey asked.

"Nothing." Corey stared at her with his eyebrows raised, unconvinced. His mother sighed.

"I was just thinking that Thanksgiving is in a few weeks. And you know we always have a nice Thanksgiving dinner. We may have to scrap sometimes, but we always eat good on holidays."

"Not this year, right?" Layla predicted.

"Actually, yes, smart-aleck. But Corey . . . Corey needs glasses. So it's going to be tight for a couple of weeks until I get them."

"So it's oatmeal for dinner again?" Layla asked.

"It might not be for long. If I can get some overtime at the hospital . . ."

"Terrific," Layla interrupted. "Thanks, Corey."

Corey couldn't look at his sister. He was frozen with shame.

"Goddamn it, Layla!" Judy shouted. "The boy feels bad enough already. For the last time, shut it up."

"Fine. I'm going to Karen's," Layla announced, getting up from the table.

"Be back upstairs at ten."

"Mommy! Ten o'clock? Come on!"

"It's a school night. I should check your homework right now."

"I did it."

"Just have your butt upstairs at ten."

Layla sucked her teeth and rushed toward the front hallway.

"Don't think I don't know you're with them niggers downstairs." Her words seemed to bounce off the front door as Layla slammed it.

"Karen's house," Judy mocked. "She must think I'm dumb."

"I'm sorry, Ma," Corey said, his voice cracking.

"Don't worry about it," she said, touching his hand. "Just do your best and I'll do my best."

"I'll wash the dishes."

"Sounds good." Corey's mother retired to the television, leaving Corey to the dishes.

At that moment, sitting at the dining room table, Corey felt more alone than ever before. He knew that some of his next-door neighbors, and indeed lots of people on Sedgewick, lived like his family did—in small apartments without lots of money—but they were all in their own world. At least it seemed that way to Corey. He felt like a foreigner in his own neighborhood; kids who had just moved to Sedgewick had more friends than he did. He was always on the outside, looking in.

Corey sprayed the sink with dishwashing liquid and filled it with hot water. He thought about his station in life while he watched the suds build into light, soapy clouds. Seventh grade was shaping up to be the same old thing. He had hoped that this year would be different, that Jamal would move on to another target, but he was wrong. The physical and verbal abuse that the bully had heaped on Corey since fifth grade wasn't going to let up. Corey had tried to defend himself in the past, but he seldom had a clever comeback for Jamal's taunts. The few times he did, it was days too late. And unlike his nemesis, Corey never had a clique to watch his back.

He wasn't good at baseball or basketball, he couldn't rap or dance, and he never had brand-name clothes to wear to school. Jamal was almost three inches taller, and Corey had heard he was even selling weed for Joey over in the Marble Hill Projects. Corey figured Jamal's weed sales financed his hip-hop designer wardrobe. Corey's struggles against Jamal made him a clown among the neighborhood kids. His only refuge was his family's narrow two-bedroom apartment, when Layla wasn't around and his mother relaxed in front of the TV.

Corey finished the dishes and went to his mother's bedroom to do his homework. He hadn't hung around to get the math homework, but he could tackle language arts and social studies. When his mother came in, he would have to return to the living room, where he slept. He looked at his ruined glasses and cursed.

"It's not fair," he whispered. Corey hated Jamal and his boys, but he hated himself for envying their new clothes, their permanent cool status at school, their ability to attract girls. Yet somehow Corey could find tolerance, figuring winter was coming, and Jamal wouldn't be outside as much. Besides, there were only two more years until high school. Then Corey would go to Stuyvesant High or Brooklyn Tech, two of New York City's three specialized high schools. The third, Bronx High School of Science, was too close to home. Corey would get away from Jamal and make his mother proud at the same time. He'd held on for this long; two more years wouldn't kill him. He had a State Regents Exam book for English and math, and he studied whenever he could. Staying after school to study was also a good way to avoid Jamal. Unless he was shooting hoops in the schoolyard with his boys.

That night before going to sleep, Corey's spirits were lifted. Layla had come in after ten, and their mother had yelled at her, to Corey's delight. Corey's laughter had made Layla so angry she refused to speak, which was fine with him. He took his time in the bathroom, brushing his teeth as slowly as he could to extend her wait.

"Corey, hurry up!" she shouted. "Mommy! He won't come out the bathroom!"

When Layla came into the living room to watch television, Judy sent her to her room. Corey got to watch TV in the sofa bed, which rarely happened during the week. Appreciating his mother's small form of justice, he smiled and snuggled into the covers.

Wednesday

The next day began like any other: Corey's mother woke him and Layla up right before going to work at the hospital, Corey argued with Layla, Layla disowned him when they walked out of their building, and Corey walked to school by himself. Layla and her friends wanted no part of him, though Dee Dee looked back at him once in a while. Corey tried to join the other kids talking about singers, rappers, and video games, but he was met with strange looks if they looked at him at all. He consoled himself by remembering that he didn't have cable TV, and a Sega Dreamcast or Sony Playstation was out of the question. That's why nobody wanted to hear what he had to say. Layla, however, didn't have such social challenges. She was aware of the latest trends in everything, but she never bothered to include Corey in her conversations.

Without his glasses, Corey struggled to see what was on the blackboard. Some of his teachers were sympathetic, but Ms. King was still offended by his early exit the day before. He didn't care; it was Wednesday, which was almost Thursday, which was almost Friday. As the day wore on, Corey watched for Jamal. If Tony and the other boys were in class, Jamal was never far away.

Corey didn't see any of them that afternoon, but knew better than to relax. He didn't run home but walked swiftly, trying to look in every direction at once. He decided that the best strategy would be to run as soon as he saw Jamal or Tony, and hopefully he'd be close enough to his building that he could get away.

There was no sign of Jamal or his cronies anywhere on Kingsbridge Road. They weren't near the train station or on Webb Avenue. When Corey reached Sedgewick Avenue without seeing him, he couldn't believe his luck. It was cold outside but not too chilly for kids to play. Besides, Jamal and Tony had Sean John hoodies to keep them warm. Where were they?

Home safe, Corey threw his backpack on the couch. Since nobody was home, he went into his mother's room to look for change. Sometimes she left enough for a bag of chips or a soda, though it was doubt-ful he'd find anything today. While looking on his mother's dresser he heard someone groan. Corey stood still, but then the noise went away. Still hunting for change, he heard another groan. Then he heard a slight thumping sound, like a piece of furniture hitting a wall or the floor.

Realizing that he wasn't alone, Corey came out of his mother's room and followed the thumping sound to Layla's room. *What's she doing?* he wondered. He couldn't figure out what was causing the thumping and the moans, but he knew she wouldn't want him to know about it. So he cracked her bedroom door. His mouth fell open when he saw Jamal, with his pants around his ankles, holding a half-naked Layla from be-hind and thrusting himself into her. Neither of them looked very happy.

"Hurry up and come," he heard Layla say through gritted teeth.

"Uh-uh, fuck that shit," Jamal retorted. Moments later, Jamal picked up speed and the familiar thumping and groans returned. Corey wouldn't let himself blink. Jamal went faster and faster until Corey thought his sister might get hurt. Finally, Jamal let out a wail.

"Aaaaah!"

Just as he stopped, Corey's head hit the door and it swung open. Layla was mortified at the sight of her brother.

"Close the door! Close the door!"

Corey scrambled for the door and pulled it closed. Before long, Jamal emerged, fully clothed. He looked at Corey and laughed.

"S'up, punk?" Jamal laughed himself silly as he walked through the hallway and out the door. Corey was unable to move or speak. He sat at the foot of Layla's door in a heap.

Hours later, what Corey had seen was still on his mind. Their mother had called to say she was working late, leaving Corey alone with Layla. They sat in front of the television, eating huge bowls of oat-meal with raisins.

"You're fourteen and he's thirteen! Why him?" Corey fumed. "Of all people. All the guys you can give it up to and you give it up to him!"

"So what? Jamal got a rep. I wouldn't give it up to a sucker."

"How about not at all? You ever think of that?"

"Knock it off, Corey."

"No, that's what Jamal did."

"Fuck you! He's the main cat on the block and you know it. You're just jealous of him. He bought me a Roca Wear sweatshirt. This winter he's buying me Kenneth Cole boots. Do you even know who Kenneth Cole is?"

"What if you get pregnant?"

"We use rubbers, dumb-ass."

"Don't they break sometimes?"

"Look, mind your business, okay? Damn."

Layla changed the channel, trying to distract him.

Corey stood in front of the television. "He beats me up almost every day. He's been doing it since fifth grade. You know that and you don't care."

"That's between you and him. It ain't got nothing to do with me."

Corey looked down at his sneakers. Hadn't Ma always told him that he and Layla were supposed to look out for each other? Maybe she hadn't told Layla.

"It's not my fault he picks on you, Corey. You gotta stand up for yourself. That's what you should have done in the first place. I can't fight your battles for you. If I did, they would punk you more than they do now."

Corey looked away, determined to hide his hurt. Layla sighed, exasperated.

"I'm not gonna be like Mommy, Corey. She ain't got a dime. I'ma finish school, get a good job, maybe even go to college. But that's years from now. Why should I wait to get money or a car? I gotta do what I gotta do."

"So? I go to school; what's wrong with that?"

"That's your problem right there. You only care about junior high. I been telling you do something else, but no. You can't rap; you don't play no ball; you don't do shit. On the block you ain't shit, Corey."

"I'm your *brother*."

"Don't remind me." Layla got up and prepared to go downstairs, leaving Corey with the TV and most of his oatmeal. His appetite was gone.

Thursday

As usual, Corey walked to school behind the other kids, expecting them to ignore him as they usually did. He thought he saw Layla on the corner of Webb Avenue by herself, but without his glasses he wasn't sure who it was.

"Hey." It sounded like her.

Corey kept walking, not wanting to be bothered.

"Hey! Corey!" Layla caught up to him.

"What?"

"I just wanted to check on you."

"Yeah, right."

"I did. Why don't you believe me?"

"You never talk to me when we're outside. What, your friends ain't come to school today?"

"Don't be like that. I'm sorry, all right?"

The apology stopped Corey in his tracks. He'd never heard Layla apologize for anything, much less to him.

"Excuse me?"

"I said I'm sorry. For yesterday."

"Wasn't nothing."

"When I came home I heard Mommy asking you about me. You could have told, but you didn't."

"I ain't no snitch."

"I noticed. Where did you learn that?"

"Daddy. Right before he went up north he told me there's nothing worse than a snitch."

"He was probably mad because somebody snitched on him."

"You think he'll ever get out?"

"If he does, it won't be anytime soon. Mommy might not let him come back. You'll just have to be the man of the house." Layla put her arm around her brother. Corey was so proud, so thrilled, he felt as if he were walking on air. He and Layla were arm in arm as they crossed Jerome Avenue and headed for the front of the school. Layla looked at him and smiled.

"Don't be blowing up my spot, okay, little brother?"

"I won't."

That day was unlike any other that Corey had ever experienced. He was giddy and animated during every class, as if it were Christmas or the last day of school. He even heard a couple of girls wonder aloud what was wrong with him, but he didn't care. When the last bell rang, Corey bounded out of I.S. 244 on a high. He was optimistic about everything around him—the sport trucks that drove by blasting Jay-Z, the people shopping on Kingsbridge Road, even the flowers at the little grocery store by the subway station. Corey stopped to smell some of the fragrant blossoms, something he'd only seen his mother and old people do. If he had any money he would have bought some flowers for Layla. *Nah,* he thought, *that would be blowing up her spot.*

Corey saw Jamal and Tony standing on the corner of Webb and Sedgewick.

"Corey? Corey! Come here, son!"

Corey approached the corner slowly. Still on guard, he figured that since Jamal was Layla's boyfriend, he might not have any more trouble.

"S'up, man?" Jamal asked with a smile.

"What's up?" Corey replied warily.

"We got something for you, son." Jamal signaled to Tony, who brought over a small brown bag and handed it to Corey. Corey pulled out a twenty-two-ounce bottle of Miller Genuine Draft.

"What's this?"

"That's for you, son," Jamal told him.

"It's a cold one."

"That's how we do. What you want, some hot chocolate?"

"Nah, nah. Thanks."

"Anytime." Tony and the other boys pulled out bottles of Miller. They removed the caps and sipped the cold brew. The group moved away from the corner and walked up the street.

"Drink up, Corey," Jamal advised. Corey had trouble with the top; Jamal handed him a bottle opener. Corey got the top off and took a sip. He grimaced at the bitter taste, then quickly composed himself.

"Tastes funny," he observed. Jamal nodded. Corey took a big gulp this time, but it wouldn't go down. He gagged and spit it out. The other boys burst into laughter.

"Damn right it tastes funny," Jamal yelled, laughing. "You just drank my piss, son!"

The boys fell down, screaming with laughter and pointing at Corey. He stood still. Jamal and his friends laughed so hard that people on the street stopped and looked. Corey breathed heavily, tears trickling down his face. His eyes were fixed on Jamal, who was cracking up and congratulating his friends on the joke.

Corey felt numb. He could still see Jamal, still hear the laughing, but it was faint, in the distance. Jamal was leaning against the wall laughing when Corey ran over and punched him in the midsection. Corey buried his fists into Jamal's chest, one after another, over and over and over again. Jamal hit Corey back a couple of times, but Corey was oblivious and continued to hit Jamal with all the force in his body.

He heard the other boys shouting, but they stayed back. Jamal was now bleeding from his mouth and panting, a loud pant, much louder than what Corey heard in his apartment. Jamal held his hands in front of him to shield himself.

"P-please," Jamal whispered between coughs. "Please . . . I'll die."

"Gimme your money!" Corey shouted. Jamal held his throat, breathing with a strange, mechanical sound.

"Gimme your money!" Jamal quickly tossed Corey a stack of bills wrapped in a rubber band. The action shocked Corey, but he hid his surprise.

"I'm taking this, too!" Corey pulled Jamal's Phat Farm jacket from behind him. The contents of Jamal's pockets fell out, including some change, a set of keys, and a white-and-yellow tube. When Jamal crawled over to get his belongings, Corey kicked the tube as hard as he could down the street. Tony ran to retrieve the tube while Jamal's frantic breathing continued. Tony returned the tube to Jamal, who began sucking on the tube while he pumped it with his hand.

"He's got asthma," Tony said, turning to Corey.

"I don't give a fuck what he's got," Corey retorted.

"We're gonna see you."

"See me now! You can see me right now!" Corey looked directly into Tony's eyes. What he saw was something familiar, except now he saw it in someone else. Fear.

"Tomorrow. We'll get you tomorrow."

"Why not now? Y'all can get me right now! I ain't no punk! Come on!"

None of the other boys took Corey up on his invitation. Instead, they turned their attention to Jamal, who was starting to breathe normally. Corey slowly put on his new jacket, then gave hard looks to the kids who had witnessed the fight, daring them to say something.

Walking home after school, Corey hoped someone would say anything, do anything to provoke him, but no one did. He entered his apartment wrapped in the strange new respect of his peers.

Layla was watching television when Corey came in. He calmly turned off the TV and stood in front of her.

"What do you think you're doing?"

"You don't go with Jamal no more."

"Excuse me?" Layla started to protest, and then she saw what Corey was wearing.

"What are you doing with Jamal's jacket?"

"It's my jacket now."

"Come on Corey, seriously."

"It's my jacket now! What, you think I'm lyin'?"

He reveled in the stunned look on her face. "I'm not going to tell you again. You don't go with Jamal no more."

"What happened?"

"I kicked his ass; that's what happened! Him and his boys had me drinking piss out of a beer bottle."

"Oh. That's messed up."

"No, it's not, 'cause I got a jacket now. And this," he said, tossing her three twenty-dollar bills.

"You took his money?"

"He gave it to me. Go buy some stuff for dinner."

"They'll come after you, Corey. Jamal works for Joey."

"I don't give a damn who he works for! Let 'em come! They'll either kick my ass or put me down, and I'll kick Jamal's ass again. Trust me."

"Corey, you don't understand."

"Will you just go to the store and get some food before Ma gets home?"

Layla reluctantly took the bills and left for the supermarket.

"Take the shopping cart," Corey ordered. "Fill it up."

That night, Corey and his family had a steak dinner with fresh green beans, corn, potatoes, and iced tea. Layla also bought lemon cake and blueberry pie. There was also enough chicken, orange juice, fruit, and canned goods to last well into next week. Corey's mother was incensed when she saw the groceries, certain that Layla had come into some money the wrong way. But Corey said someone on the block had given all the kids money, and Layla backed him up on his story. She also helped him hide his new jacket.

Friday

School was a new sensation for Corey Hawkins. He left his building with Layla by his side, wearing his new Phat Farm jacket. Kids pointed and stared at him while they walked to school; he heard whispers about Jamal and Tony coming for him after school, which he welcomed. The girls who'd always ignored him said hi to him that morning. Corey ignored them all, except for Dee Dee. The boys who laughed at him were saying "what's up" and giving him brotherly handshakes. Corey was a star in homeroom, his morning classes, and at lunch, where the rumors continued and his legend grew. He took it in stride, excited on the inside but acting calmly wherever he went. He made certain to sit up front so he could see what was being written on the blackboard; most kids didn't want to sit in front, and they certainly weren't going to challenge him. When the last bell rang, Corey found himself the focus of every seventh-grader outside and many eighth-graders.

No one had seen Jamal, Tony, or their crew anywhere. With Layla and Dee Dee in tow, Corey walked his usual route home with an army of kids following him. If he had been uncertain that Jamal was waiting for him, he was sure now—kids loved to see a fight, and they wouldn't follow him home unless they knew it was coming.

As Corey suspected, Jamal was waiting on his corner when Corey passed Webb Avenue. Corey was careful not to lose a step, walking even faster when he saw Jamal. Corey saw another boy leaning on a car behind Jamal, probably Tony. The crowd of kids gathered around, on the sidewalk and in the street, surrounding the space that Corey and Jamal occupied. When they saw the crowd of kids, people came out of the Chinese take-out restaurant to see what was going on. People were looking from the bus stop across the street.

Corey saw the resentment on Jamal's face when he saw his old jacket. Corey returned the glare, thinking, *Whatever will be will be.* Jamal stepped forward and Corey met him until they were face to face. Corey saw a cut on Jamal's lip and a scar under his eye. He felt a rush of adrenaline; he didn't care about before, and he didn't care what happened next; it was all about that moment, in front of the whole neighborhood.

Jamal got so close to Corey that their noses were almost touching, but Corey didn't budge. He could stand there all day if he had to. The staring contest didn't last more than five minutes, but it felt longer to Corey. He wasn't moving, and he wasn't going to speak first if at all. Finally, Jamal looked him up and down.

"So you think you hot shit, son? Is that it?"

"Yeah."

"That's my brother's jacket. He's coming home from up north soon."

"You want it, take it."

Jamal was silent. Corey knew they were both remembering the fight.

"You want it, Jamal? You want it? 'Cause if you do, I'll bust your ass again!" The crowd gasped. Corey grew more energized.

"You want it? Huh? Make a move, then! Come on! Come on!" Corey screamed in Jamal's face. Finally, Jamal began to back away. They were slow, tiny steps, but he was backing up.

"That's what I thought!" Corey barked. Jamal retreated until he was leaning against a car.

"That jacket ain't shit, anyway," Jamal said, almost to himself. "That's the old shit." Corey marched up to his face again. In Jamal's eyes Corey saw himself last week, last year: anxious, unsure.

"Don't start none, won't be none," he said. He was speaking directly to Jamal, but he knew Tony, Jamal's other boys, and everyone else there could hear him. He walked past Jamal and glared at his other friends, just as he'd done yesterday. The crowd of kids parted so he could get by. Layla and Dee Dee followed behind him. After Corey left, the corner was quiet.

Sedgewick Avenue would never again be the same.

Panhandling

Kim Green

"The white man lives in the castle; when he dies, he lies in the ground." —African, Ashanti

Last year, Paul Semel was a businessman. He had a corporate card, a car paid for by the company, and a closet full of blue suits. He had a big house in the suburbs, a pretty blond wife, and three small, blonder children. His life was perfect.

Until it all went away. Fell away. Blew away like the winds of Nigeria.

His new secretary had just joined the company. She was on a work-exchange program from Nigeria. Paul had vetoed the proposal when it came to his desk, but in the name of diversity, someone in Human Resources had vetoed *him*. He loved her immediately. She was sexy. The way she moved. The way she Xeroxed those forms. It was amazing to Paul, who was married to a perfect, prudish woman who had no rhythm and whose heart pumped water.

The little Nigerian secretary's skin was deep, dark, and bitter like chocolate. She'd answer the phone like she meant business. But when she'd sway over to the Xerox machine, the coffee machine, or the elevator bank, Paul's heart would stop.

One day he asked her to dinner. Just a friendly dinner between boss and worker. Just to get to know her a little. It wasn't meant to mean anything.

They dined together at an expensive corporate-cards-only restaurant with palm trees and a fish tank. And the little Nigerian secretary demonstrated her hearty appetite. It made Paul Semel wonder where she put it all. After watching her for a while, he decided she stored it in her soul, because that was the biggest part of her. He stared into her dark, deep black eyes and listened to her stories of Nigeria and villages and a fisherman father, and he felt his loins move. He listened intently, wanting to become more to her than just her boss.

He offered her more wine, and she drank it happily and greedily until all of her inhibitions were gone.

"Mr. Paul, you want to love me, don't you?" she said as the waiter left the check.

"Yes. Yes. I do," he said.

She winked and slowly licked her sugar-coated lips.

"Let us go, then," she said. And they did.

The first night was beyond anything Paul Semel could have imagined. It was wild and tender and wet. They promised each other that this was powerful. Powerful as the waterfalls of Zimbabwe, despite the pretty blond wife and the three blonder children.

Paul Semel became reckless. Leaving traces. Coming home late, smelling of rhythm and Nigeria. Ripped clothes, popped-off buttons, and little coils of black hair between his teeth. The little blond wife began to wonder: what was happening to Paul Semel and their perfect little life?

One evening she decided to follow him, his corporate credit card and silk tie, into the city. She waited outside his tall glass office building until 5:00, when she saw him and a dark woman leave the building together. She followed them to a high-rise hotel not far from the office. It was the one that Paul Semel had said was too expensive for them to spend their anniversary in. He had said that seven years wasn't special enough. He'd take her for their tenth anniversary.

The pretty blond wife slipped into the lobby, lost among suits and fancy people doing business. She watched them standing silently, waiting for the elevator. And when they were inside the first, and the tenth floor lit up outside the door, she followed them there in the next elevator.

She turned the corner and saw them fumbling, eager and sinfully trying to get inside. She listened at their door and heard their nervous silence turn into loving, whispering, promising, and kissing. She heard Paul Semel making sounds he hadn't made since they first met at Harvard. She trembled with rage. She trembled with fear. She shook with revenge.

She ran from the hotel into the street, hailing a yellow cab. She took the first one and came directly to their perfect yellow house in the suburbs. The cost was $100 plus the tip. She had the cash, of course, because she was Paul Semel's wife. She called her lawyer, told him the story, and he told her exactly what to do.

She did as the lawyer said. Working quickly, calmly, and without tears. She cleared out their life together meticulously, leaving only a note and furniture pieces in the big, now orphaned living room. She took every last picture of their family vacations, Thanksgiving dinners, and birthday celebrations. She snatched the gold-framed wedding picture off the wall, leaving a gaping hole. She made sure the living room was dead. Her note said simply, *Good-bye Paul.*

She placed the three blonder children into what Paul Semel used to call the "family car" and drove away with revenge warming her heart like a campfire.

Paul Semel returned home that night to something he never expected: a note and nothing else.

Today, Paul Semel resides in Central Park near a pond. The suburbs of Connecticut are now a lifetime away. After he lost his mind, he lost his job, and his beautiful Nigerian secretary was sent back to Nigeria when Paul's replacement decided he didn't like her attitude or the smell of coconut.

Paul Semel spends his days sitting by the pond, panhandling. Asking for quarters by day, and dreaming of Nigeria by night. If you see him, give him a quarter. After all, he lost it all by giving all he had.

And feeling what he felt.

John Q.'s Blissful Journey

Scott D. Haskins

"Equality is difficult, but superiority is painful."
—African, Serere

Stalking, in its purest sense, is an ugly word. *Stalking with great intentions*, however, might be the best way to describe the fashion in which I approached Katrina. I prefer to consider myself the consummate professional who is merely screening his client until he feels comfortable enough to approach her.

I've been coming to East River Drive almost daily from the first time I saw her. Since I almost wrapped my baby blue Volvo around a tree while digging her form, I figured the least she could do was go out on a date with me.

Katrina is the most dedicated runner I've ever seen in my life. Like clockwork, every morning she comes around the one-mile bend at 7:05. Three miles down and two miles back. Seven minutes exactly for each mile. Then she briskly walks the last mile while pumping her arms, doing knee-raises, and power-pounding her abs with both fists to tighten her already fabulous ripple-tum-tum. Her last mile is walked at a quick ten-minute pace. Then she hops into her forest green convertible BMW and drives off without looking back, appearing as though she never breathed hard a day in her life.

Her look of complete concentration while running convinced me that it would be impossible to get her to stop to talk with me. My best friend, Sade, convinced me that the only way I would be able to talk to Katrina was to keep up with her while she ran. So she helped me train for that goal.

The first try didn't go well. I didn't warm up properly and ran too hard, too fast, and too long, which caused me to collapse with charley horses twisting up my legs. Sade changed our training pace, and three weeks later I'd made some visible progress. My body looked more athletic, though not as fit as it was five years ago.

Don't get me wrong—I'm no couch potato. I still play basketball with the fellas on the weekends, bowl from time to time, and have even competed in a 5k run every now and then. However, I needed to get my life and body on one accord with wellness and good health. In looking for love, I was also taking advantage of the opportunity to get myself together.

Just the sight of Katrina inspires me to keep training. She's a slender woman, carrying about 125 pounds on a shapely five-foot-seven-inch frame. Her sun-browned hair with hints of auburn is neatly twisted, accentuating the perfect oval shape of her head. Her face is a work of art. Onyx eyes. Full lips, puffy and perfect. Kissable. Caramel skin that doesn't need the glisten of perspiration in order to glow. And one dimple, on the left side, just below her mouth. I could kiss her dimple and be off in seventh heaven.

She moves as effortlessly as a gazelle on an afternoon trot. Her strides are so graceful that her feet seem to barely graze the ground. It's as if she has wings on her feet. I set the timer on my watch for twenty-one minutes and take off after her, my fake sweat from the spray bottle dripping from my chin, and my muscles not quite warmed up. I am determined to be "the wind beneath her wings."

My weeks of intense training have paid off. Thank God! I was able to catch Katrina in less than a half mile.

"I see you're getting yourself in shape, John Q.," she said, with a hint of an accent that I couldn't quite place. I eased beside her, trying to look and run as smoothly and comfortably as she did.

"Just trying to stay fit," I said in what I hoped was a casual tone. "The older we get, the harder it is to keep our bodies in shape."

This was the longest conversation we'd ever had; until this point, hello and an exchange of names was the most I'd gotten out of her. Today she blessed me with an especially warm smile.

"John, you talk like you fifty years or something, mon," she said, her smile fading to a slightly more serious expression. How old are you, anyway?"

Damn it, she was picking up her pace.

"I'm twenty-six. And you?"

"Now, you know better than to ask a woman her age. I must say, you look great for an old mon of twenty-six."

"Thanks, Katrina. You look great yourself."

We were headed back. I glanced at my watch to see that we had completed the first mile in six minutes and forty-five seconds. Two more miles at this pace or faster, and I would surely die.

"What do you do with yourself when you're not out here running?" she asked, looking so relaxed and pain-free I doubted she was feeling any of the strain that tugged at my muscles, my lungs, and my heart.

"I write freelance articles for various magazines. Mostly African-American," I added, trying not to huff or puff.

"Really?" She seemed surprised. "Is that steady work?"

"Not always, but the pay is great. If I get two stories a month published, I'm okay." The water that Sade had squirted on my head ten or so minutes earlier was long gone. My whole body was as dry as a virgin sponge. As we ran faster, I held my head high, causing the sweat to roll up my forehead. The wind seemed to air dry my face.

Our "getting to know you" conversation was taking its toll on my lungs; each word I spoke was accompanied by a rush of air. Sade always said that if you can talk while you run, you're going at the right pace. As my feet pounded in a tired, rhythmic accompaniment to my now desperate breaths, I knew I was on borrowed time. I asked God to send a special deliverance of mercy to slow Katrina down.

"What-do-you-do?" I blurted out in a quick burst of garbled words.

"Hum?" she asked, the lovely smile returning to her face. It actually contained a tinge of arrogance, but I was blinded by the possibility of our impending night out. As soon as I got it together to ask her . . .

"For-a-living." Shorter sentence. Easier delivery. Ragged breaths.

"I'm training for the Olympics—marathon runner." I noticed that her high cheekbones gave her an Ethiopian look. No wonder she ran so well. Them good genes.

I suddenly realized she had been playin' me the entire time. Now it was personal. I could see our two-mile mark up ahead, maybe a little over a half mile away. I was determined to get there first. Katrina wasn't really fine, anyway, I told myself for motivation, extending my stride and willing my shaking legs into higher gear. Determined like never before to finish first.

Next, I tried quick glances over each shoulder to see how far ahead I was. Katrina was nowhere in sight. I knew she was still behind me. My sudden burst of speed had surprised her enough for me to get in the lead of what was now the most crucial race of my life. I swerved from side to side, glancing to the rear, trying to find my archenemy. Turning completely around would break my stride, costing me precious seconds and a lead that I could not afford to lose.

About two hundred yards away, I saw the overflowing green trashcan that I knew was aligned with the orange painted *one mile* mark on the concrete. I quickly calculated how long it would take me to run two hundred yards: *Carl Lewis runs the hundred in nine seconds. Michael Johnson runs the two hundred in nineteen something seconds. Nineteen plus ten equals twenty-nine seconds, multiplied by the fact that I am not and never will be a world-class runner, equals . . . I've got a lead and I mean to keep it.*

With the finish line just ahead, I risked turning my head to find my more than worthy adversary. Like a synchronized swimmer, she was less than two feet behind me, in perfect step with my rapidly *slowing* stride.

The way I jumped when I saw her, you would have thought Freddie Krueger was back there. She took advantage of my fear and hesitation by moving parallel to me. I changed gears, still determined to win. As sure as the sun rising or setting, the reality of what I wasn't came to me in an instant. My lungs refused to take in air and became vessels for a sandpaperlike substance that was drying my mouth, leaving my lips chapped, my tongue swollen, and my nose hair brittle. With nothing left but the heart of a lion, I pushed onward, head bobbing, arms pumping, and legs . . .

God, NOOO!!! My Legs!!

CRAMPS!! Charley and his horses attacked my left calf and both quads simultaneously. The menacing midget pulled on both hamstrings, refusing to let go.

Any pair of merciful eyes would have been proud of my laborious impersonation of a running paraplegic. But I held on: the pain that had encompassed my entire body could not penetrate my heart.

As I crossed my personal finish line, I raised my arms, fists clinched, chest bulging in a symbolic gesture of victory.

Reluctantly, I opened my tear-drenched eyes, only to see Katrina and Sade standing side by side, enjoying what appeared to be the funniest moment of their lives.

I fell face first into the grass. My neck muscles, the only ones that hadn't been attacked by exhaustion, worked enough for me to raise my head and spit grass out of my mouth. Then I uttered a single, mercy-soaked word of misery: "CRAMPS!!!"

I felt one hand rubbing my left calf. Another, my right thigh. The hands weren't mine or Katrina's. "Where did she go?" I moaned.

"Who?" Sade asked, chuckling. Obviously, she still was enjoying my "gotta meet that girl" running travesty.

"Katrina the blimp!" I said irritated.

"The blimp?"

"She didn't look fat to you? She seemed to be carrying a little too much weight around the hips. Too much curried goat in her diet, I'm guessing." I said, looking for "ugly" clauses in our now defunct "standard contract."

"I thought you said you liked a little "junk in that trunk!" Sade challenged.

"Where'd she go?" I demanded.

"To work."

"Good."

"Are you giving up that easily?" Sade asked.

"Yes." I was no match for Katrina, and my ego didn't like it.

"This is no way to start off the summer, Q. You realize that, don't you?" Sade asked, concerned. She and I had been friends since the third grade, and she genuinely wanted to see me happy.

"I know. She played me from the minute I started running. I should have never tried to compete with her," I said, rolling over so she could massage the backs of my legs as well.

"Male ego!" We said in unison as I contemplated trying to catch Katrina again next week. Next time, I'd be content just to run in her shadow.

Trick Dice

Angela Henry

"Ashes fly back in the face of him who throws them."
—African, Yoruba

It was a beautiful shade of purple, when you got right down to it. Not quite as dark as a Brazilian amethyst, but beautiful nonetheless. It was a shade that Sharita McClain was all too familiar with. Purple used to be her all-time favorite color. Purple was the color of royalty, regality, and let's not forget those purple mountain majesties, whatever they were.

Purple was also the color of bruises, and there was nothing majestic or regal about the vivid purple bruise that spread like a stain across Sharita's left cheek.

He'd lost again.

He being Marky McClain, Sharita's husband. She should have known better than to marry a grown man named Marky, not Marcus or Mark. Marky. A childhood nickname that had stuck, weathering adolescence and adulthood, and at age forty was never coming off. When Sharita first married Marky, she'd made the mistake of calling him Mark in front of his mother.

"Mark? Who Mark? Ain't no Mark here! My boy's name is *Marky*. What's wrong with it? We all call him Marky. Ain't that good enough for you, gal?" Marky and his mother had proceeded to laugh like hyenas as Sharita shifted uncomfortably in her seat, waiting for the earth to open up and swallow her. Or at the very least, send her a reasonable mother-in-law, one without a two-bottles-of-homemade-wine-a-day habit.

When Marky and his mother were together, it was like they were in their own little world, one where Sharita could never win, could never do anything right. She should have known better. It wasn't like she didn't know what she was getting into when she married him. She'd thought things would get better. He'd only hit her once while they were dating, and he was so sorry afterward. He'd even cried. Crocodile tears, but hey, tears were tears.

Well, there was no use thinking about it now. Instead, she pulled makeup and concealer out of the bathroom cabinet and got busy covering up the truth of her existence. He'd lost at craps again last night. Marky never had much luck at craps. Whenever he got in on a game, everyone who'd been losing knew their luck was about to change. But for some reason, Marky fancied himself a gambler extraordinare.

They'd met when he came to her apartment to repair her cable. He was so polite, so handsome in his little work uniform. When he showed up at her door, Sharita's first thought was that it was a joke, and he was going to pull out a tape recorder and start stripping. He was soooo fine! It had been her birthday, and it was just like her friends to pull something like that. She should have just paid her bill and forgotten about him. Instead, she'd accepted his invitation to dinner. Now, twelve years had passed since she'd married the cable guy. He'd been through half a dozen jobs, was forty pounds overweight (smacking her around was his only exercise), and he was unemployed—again. The joke had been on her after all.

She finished getting ready for work and headed for the door. Marky was still asleep on the couch, snoring rhythmically and expelling one-hundred-proof breaths. Unlike his mother, gin was his poison. Sharita tiptoed past him out the door. She headed to the bus stop down the street, not really seeing anyone or anything.

Why had she stayed all these years?

That was a question she asked herself every day. Why? Maybe because everyone she knew would say, "I told you so." Maybe because she was still hoping things would get better. Maybe because she hated failing at anything. If she left, wouldn't that be giving up?

It wasn't like Marky didn't have his moments. He could be so sweet when he was sober, and he could be so funny at times. Yet, his moments of sweetness were growing few and far between. And it seemed as if he enjoyed making her cry a lot more these days. The Marky of old, the one she had fallen in love with, was buried under layer upon layer of self-pity, selfishness, and alcoholism, made worse by a mother who encouraged him to blame Sharita, and the world in general, for all his problems. Maybe things would change if Marky could just start winning.

*   *   *

"Honey, are you sure you're okay?" asked Mrs. Bailey, Sharita's boss at the library. Mrs. Bailey's concerned manner hid her irritation. Her mouth was saying, "Are you okay?" but her eyes were saying, "Fool! Why don't you leave him?"

"I'm fine. I just think I need to go home and lie down." Sharita gathered up her coat and purse and headed for the door and away from the prying eyes of her coworkers. She knew what they were thinking. She knew they knew about Marky. Makeup and concealer couldn't hide everything. She knew they probably thought whatever was wrong with her was the result of a beating. She could feel their eyes burning into her back, and she felt like running. Instead, she headed straight into the women's rest room as a wave of nausea overtook her.

"Oh, please, God. Don't let it be," she whispered as she looked down at the pink plus sign on the test strip. She'd stopped at the drugstore on the way home from work and picked up an early-pregnancy test. She was three weeks late and had been sick every day this week. In the back of her mind, Sharita had known why but couldn't bring herself to acknowledge it. Yes, she was still having sex with him. She could hardly avoid it. It was damn near impossible to reason with a drunk, horny man in the middle of the night. And yes, it was the equivalent of watching paint dry most of the time. Okay, all of the time, but it was better than getting hit.

On the flip side, this pregnancy might be the answer to her problems. A baby! Marky just might straighten out if there was a baby around. Early in their marriage he'd talked about wanting a son. But try as they might, it had never happened. And of course he blamed her for it, as did his mother, who managed to express her opinion louder and louder with every drink. Sometimes calling Sharita at work or in the middle of the night to tell her just what she thought of her. "Little skinny yella heifer. Can't even give my boy a son. What's wrong with you, gal? See, you think you slick. Well you ain't. Think you can do better than Marky? Well, I'm watching you, gal. Sneaky little tramp!"

Sneaky? That was a laugh. The only time Sharita had ever tried to be sneaky was when she was eight years old and fed her unwanted tuna-noodle casserole to Skippy, her peekapoo. Skippy had proceeded to vomit on her new suede clogs while Wild Cherry's "Play That Funky Music, White Boy" blasted from the stereo in the living room, like a soundtrack to a bad dream. Nope, *sneaky* and *Sharita* could never be used in the same sentence . . . and she still hated that damned song!

*   *   *

She cooked all of his favorite foods that night. Pot roast and sweet potato pie. She watched him eat with his face practically scraping the plate.

"Marky, I'm pregnant," she said timidly.

He stopped eating and stared at her like she'd just announced she was an alien and the mother ship was about to land. Then he proceeded to start eating again.

"Marky, did you hear me? I said—"

"I heard you," he grunted between bites of sweet potato pie. When he had finished, he sat back and stared at her while picking his teeth. With the digestion of his food well under way, he could now give thought to Sharita's announcement.

"A baby. Well I'll be damned. After all this time. When?"

"I don't know yet. I have an appointment with the doctor next week. I think maybe I'm about four weeks along."

"Ma will be surprised as hell. She never thought we'd have any kids. Said you must be barren or somethin'." Marky got up from the table and leaned over to give Sharita a sloppy sweet-potato-pie-flavored kiss on the lips. Then he grabbed his jacket from the hall closet.

"Got to go out and earn some money for my son," he said with a big goofy grin. Sharita's heart sank as she saw him retrieve his so-called *lucky dice* from the desk drawer by the front door. If only he could start winning, she knew things would be different.

The next few weeks flew by. Sharita was busy transforming their spare bedroom into a nursery for the baby. Marky was winning a little bit of money here and there. Just enough to keep him happy, his mood decent, and his foot out of Sharita's ass. Things were better than they'd been in years. Even Marky's mother was being nicer to her. Well, as nice as her two bottles of wine a day would allow.

But of course, all good things usually come to an end. It had started out as any other Saturday morning. Sharita had a touch of morning sickness and decided to stay in bed. Marky was snoring beside her, so she got up and moved to the couch. Marky had left his jacket on the floor. As Sharita bent to pick it up, two red dice tumbled out onto the floor. She picked them up and held them in her hand.

"Bitch, are you crazy?" Marky shouted as he rushed into the room, snatching the dice out of her hand and shoving her hard against the wall.

"No one touches my lucky dice! No one! You hear me?"

"I'm sorry. They fell on the floor," Sharita said, ducking from a blow that never came. Marky stood staring at her, panting, with sweat beading his brow. The mad dash across the room had winded him. He huffed back into the bedroom and Sharita stood rooted to the spot, heart pounding, until she heard his rhythmic snoring from the bedroom once more. Then she sank down onto the couch and started to cry.

He lost that night, of course. He came home around midnight, drunk and enraged. He blamed her. She had, after all, touched his *lucky dice*. She'd tried to run and had almost gotten away. She was headed down the steps and toward the front doors of their apartment building, Marky close on her heels. She thought she was home free until she felt Marky's size thirteen in her back. She tumbled down the remaining half-dozen steps into darkness.

She woke up in the hospital. She'd lost the baby. She couldn't even cry. She was empty, numb. Marky seemed remorseful, not quite able to look her in the eye. To him, the baby had been just an idea. If he couldn't touch something, taste it, or see it, then it wasn't real.

Sharita didn't know when the thought came to her. Maybe when she felt Marky's foot in her back. Maybe while she lay in the hospital thinking about having to go home to the same old life. Maybe it was when she walked past Taskey's Joke and Magic Shop on her way to the bus stop when she returned to work a week later.

The sign in the window said *GOING OUT OF BUSINESS SALE*. She must have walked past the store a million times and never really seen it. It was a small shop squeezed between a deli and a dry cleaner. The window held a dusty display. A magician's hat with a stuffed white rabbit in it sat on a small table draped with a red crushed velvet tablecloth. A magic wand was propped against it. Sharita went inside. The bell over the door tinkled, announcing her arrival to no one that she could immediately see. The lighting was dim in the small shop, and it smelled funny, too. An earthy, almost musky scent that Sharita couldn't quite place.

"May I help you, ma'am?" said a voice behind her. Sharita turned and saw a short, plump, elderly white woman, a dumpling in a brown dress. Her eyes were the most intense blue Sharita had ever seen.

"I—I'm just looking. I mean, I saw the sign and just . . ." Sharita didn't know what to say. What was she doing there? "I have to go," she said and turned to leave.

"We have some good bargains," the woman said as Sharita brushed past on her way to the door. "Crystal balls, coin tricks . . . even loaded dice."

Sharita froze. She turned. The woman was smiling at her. Her blue eyes were as hard as marbles. It felt like they were piercing her soul.

"I'm Greta Taskey. Are you sure I can't help you find something? There has to be something here that you can use. My husband Bertram was a magician. He died recently, and I'm going to live with my daughter in Florida. I've got to sell all this stuff. Come on, help an old lady out."

"Um, well, maybe I'll just look around." Sharita just wanted to get away from those eyes. Greta Taskey couldn't possibly know what Sharita had in mind. The bell above the door tinkled, and another woman came in and looked around timidly. "Let me know if I can help you," said Greta as she glided off to help the other customer.

Sharita wandered up and down the aisles looking at whoopee cushions, dribble glasses, tarot cards, magic kits, pens with invisible ink. She stopped in front of a Ouija board. She'd been afraid of them since she was a kid and she and her best friend got a hold of one in her grandmother's attic. Thinking back, she remembered asking it all the wrong questions. She'd asked if she'd meet her Prince Charming. She should have asked if Prince Charming would turn into a monster. She turned around and saw a wall covered with fake spiders, rabbit's foot key chains, and dice—all different colors, shapes, and sizes of dice. There were dice key chains, dice earrings, dice magnets, fuzzy dice, trick dice . . .

Sharita slowly reached out and picked up a set of dice. She read the label. *Amaze your friends and family! Loaded Dice! Roll a Perfect Seven every time!*

A perfect seven. If anyone needed a perfect seven it was Sharita. This could change everything for her and Marky. No more bad luck equaled no more beatings. She carried the dice up to the cash register before she could change her mind. Greta Taskey was ringing up a set of trick cards for the woman who had come in after her.

"I'm sure these will be just what you need, Mrs. Lehman." The customer took her package and almost ran into Sharita as she turned to go. Their eyes met briefly, and Sharita took in the other woman's black eye and defeated expression. They stared at each other a moment, each recognizing the other's plight before the woman hurried out the door.

"I see you found something after all. Let's see what you've got." Sharita handed her the dice.

"Loaded dice. Oh, yes, we've sold lots of these over the years. Who are they for? No, don't answer that. I'm being nosy." She rang up the dice and handed them to Sharita. "I won't give you a bag. No bag, no receipt, no proof." She gave Sharita another piercing gaze.

"What?" said Sharita, nervously looking around.

"Oh, nothing, dear. You enjoy the dice. I'm sure they'll be just what you need." Sharita nearly ran out of the shop.

Sharita stared at Marky across the table during dinner two nights later. The dice were still in her purse. She didn't know what she'd been thinking when she bought them.

"What you lookin' at, Shar?" Marky asked. He only called her Shar when he wanted something and was trying to be nice. Any other time he called her nothing or "bitch."

"Nothing. I was just thinking."

"'Bout what?"

"About the baby." It was the first time she had brought up the baby since she'd been released from the hospital.

"Doctor said we can try again. You wanna try again?" He wouldn't even meet her eyes.

"Do you really want a baby, Marky?"

"Yeah. Don't every man want a son to carry on his name? Hell, I could teach him everything I know. Teach him how to play ball . . ."

Sharita listened to Marky list all the things he would teach their son, and wondered if how to beat and disrespect a woman would be included on the list along with how to drink, lose a job, and be a lazy, lying asshole. Sharita didn't think so, but those were the things you learned by example, anyway.

What had she expected him to say? That he'd straighten up, get a job, and stop hitting her? She knew in that instant that there could never be another baby, not with Marky as the father, and she felt a hatred for him that she'd never felt before. Funny how all the ass-kickings of the past hadn't hardened her heart toward Marky like the loss of a pregnancy that had barely begun.

"Hey, Shar. You listenin'?"

"Yeah, I heard you, Marky."

"Look, baby, you got any money? I'm a little short on funds. A twenty'll do me."

She looked at him for a second and then got up from the table. She went to her purse to get the money and spotted the dice staring up at her like two red eyes from the bottom of her purse. She looked over her shoulder and saw that Marky was on the phone with his back turned. She quickly pulled out the dice and switched them with his *lucky dice*. An hour later, Marky had gone out and Sharita sat in the baby's unfinished nursery, stared at the Mickey Mouse wallpaper, and finally cried for her baby.

Sharita always knew things would change if only Marky could start winning. And change they did. Since she'd switched the dice there'd been no more beatings, no more fear, no more bruises. Hell, there was no more Marky. It didn't take long for the hustlers Marky played craps with to realize that luckless Marky McClain was cheating with loaded dice.

Marky was found beaten and stabbed in an alley. A die placed, rather melodramatically, over each eye as a warning to anyone else stupid enough to cheat. He lingered in a coma for four days before he died. And as he drew his last breath, Sharita felt like someone who'd just been let out of prison. Curiously enough, Marky's obituary ran alongside that of a Ronald Lehman, who'd been shot during a card game for using trick cards. Taskey's Joke and Magic Shop was now a pet store. Greta Taskey was long gone. No bag, no receipt, no store, and no proof.

Sharita was savoring her freedom. It took a while because she still kept expecting Marky to come lumbering through the door. And of course, he didn't. Sharita used the life insurance money to redecorate and buy herself some new clothes. She was admiring a new coat she'd just bought when the phone rang.

"Hello?"

"You sneaky little heifer! I know whatchoo did!" Marky's mother had upped her daily wine consumption to three bottles since he died. Still, her words unnerved Sharita.

"I'm gonna tell everybody whatchoo did! Marky ain't never been a cheat! When he lose, he lose like a man! Always knew you was sneaky!"

Sharita's blood ran cold. She had a new life now, one that no longer included such phone calls.

"Why don't I come over there and we can talk about it?" she said.

"Yeah, git yer bony ass over here. I got things to say to you, gal. Then I'm gonna tell everybody whatchoo did!"

Sharita smiled when she put down the phone. She did need to go check on the poor dear. After all, she was an alcoholic old woman. An alcoholic old woman who'd hauled old photos of her dead son out of the basement to cry over. An alcoholic old woman who lived all alone and could easily fall down those same basement steps and break her neck if she wasn't careful.

Sharita put on her new coat and stopped to admire herself in the mirror on her way out. The coat looked good on her. It was purple.

Rendezvous with Destiny

Donna Hill

"Every good-bye ain't gone. Every shut eye sure ain't sleep."
—African American

The full moon hangs high in the cloudless onyx sky. Its light serves as a beacon for the shadowy figures moving swiftly and silently through a grassy field, following its guiding illumination along the path toward freedom.

The chilling howl of hunting hound dogs raises the hair on the arms and neck of Rufus. His heart beats so loudly it drowns out the slap of his feet against the hard-packed earth. His overtaxed lungs burn from exhaustion. How long had they been running? How long will it be before they are caught?

Rufus glances once at Selena. Sweat glistens on her dark face, making it shine like a new penny. Her breath comes in short, staccato puffs as she struggles to keep pace with the man.

"Won't be long now fo' we reach the river," Rufus huffs. "We be safe then. Dem hounds will lose the scent."

Selena grips Rufus's hand tighter as her long skirt lassos around her legs, tossing her to the ground.

"I cain't go on, Rufus," she cries between gulps of air and dirt-stained tears. "I cain't. You go on an' leave me. Save yo'self."

"Yes, you kin." Rufus bends down, ignoring her plea, and scoops Selena into his arms, taking her weight as his own. "We gon' make it, girl. We gots to. I ain't goin' back. I ain't leavin' you. We be plannin' too long for freedom. Ain't no turnin' back now."

In the distance behind them, the threatening bay of the hounds edges closer, mixed now with the blood-hungry voices of their pursuers—Master Mulberry's voice louder and more chilling than the others. Both of them knew he'd bring them back to the plantation and give them a taste of the snake before the others, the long twisting scars opening on their black skin as a harsh warning to any darkie soul pondering flight from bondage.

"I ain't gonna be made no fool of by some nigrahs! I'm gonna teach them a lesson."

"Let's get 'em," the mob roars in unison. Their torches are now in sight, just a few yards along the edge of the trees bordering the field.

"They gon' kill us, sho nuff, Rufus," Selena whimpers, terror clutching her by the throat. There is a fear in her eyes that he's never seen before, something that acknowledges the terrible fate that awaits them if they give in to the fatigue of their flesh.

"The river be right through these patch o' trees ahead. We almost—"

Suddenly, the impact from a flurry of gun blasts bursts through the thicket, hurling Rufus into the air and Selena into the ditch below.

Darkness swirls around him. Images of black men, women, and children toiling under the brutal Southern sun, strange fruit swinging high from the trees, empty, griping bellies, and the wails of womenfolk as their infants are stripped from them run in a kaleidoscope of shapes and sounds through his head.

Clawing her way up from the muddy ditch, Selena reaches his side, stretching out her callused hand to shake him.

"Rufus! Rufus!"

The hazy shape of Selena's horror-stricken face fades in and out above him. The gentle, comforting touch of her hands cupping his face is like soft pillows that he longs to sleep forever between.

"Go ... run ..."

"Not wit'out you," she sobs.

"Deys gettin' closer, Selena. Dem hounds smell blood. Go ... freedom on the other side ..." His voice strains in a shaky rasp.

Selena's eyes widen with renewed fright as white faces begin to appear like haints between the trees. *Capture means certain death or worse. To run toward possibility ...*

She looks at Rufus one last time, presses her lips to his.

"Every good-bye ain't gone," she murmurs in an urgent whisper.

"Every shut eye ... ain't sleep," he vows.

Selena squeezes Rufus's hand, pulls her skirts high around her hips, and runs toward the river. She jumps into the frigid waters, her limbs numbing with every stroke, every kick. The water rises to her neck, her lips, then her eyes, pulling her down into its inky depths.

Blackness engulfs her, the ebb of the river carrying her toward freedom. With her arms outstretched like a scarecrow, she surrenders to the unseen eddies of the water, allowing it to take her away into the night.

"That's an awful story, Grandma," Maya said, rising from her crouched position on the floor. She bent her stiff limbs. Her grandmother was always good for an afternoon of folklore, and Maya usually found her tales both entertaining and enlightening. But today, this story about Rufus and Selena disturbed her in a way that she couldn't understand. She felt curiously off-center, as if she were suddenly seeing the world through foggy lenses. The muscles of her stomach fluttered as if doves had been let loose inside her.

Grandma Selma chuckled, her old, wise eyes twinkling with mischief. "Sometimes the truth can be awful," she said. "But it don't make it less true." She pulled aside the lace curtain at the living room window and peeked out at the children running down the street, clothed in wool skullcaps and winter jackets. A herd of young souls chasing a red ball along the pavement. Holiday lights twinkled in windows and along porches. Christmas Eve.

"You actually believe all that—about Selena and Rufus?" The young woman took a seat on the old ottoman opposite her grandmother's favorite chair.

"That story's been passed down from one generation to the next, starting with my great-grandmother. It's our duty to pass it along to the next woman, and she is to pass it along to her daughter. With your mama being gone, it was up to me to share it with you."

"Why?" Maya questioned, the doves flapping furiously. She desperately wanted a cigarette.

"Well, as the story goes, yo' ancestors Rufus and Selena made a vow to find their way back to each other. If we keep the story alive, they stay alive. But because Selena left Rufus to die, all the Johnston women been doomed to a life of heartache and loss. Won't ever be set right till Selena goes back for Rufus." Selma looked at her granddaughter as if she knew a secret she was unwilling to share. She remembered the old, timeless tales of ancient Ibo folklore told to her by her own mother, grandmother, and great-grandmother—tales harking back to the hardships of slave ships, the bartering of dark flesh on the auction block, and beyond. Tales that now included this yarn of escape, determination, and freedom.

"Oh, Grandma, that's just some old wives' tales." Maya's urge for a cigarette was overwhelming. Her nerves seemed to vibrate.

"Hmmm," Selma hummed, her ancient, arthritic fingers wrapping themselves around a cup of hot peppermint tea. " 'Bout time for dinner. Almost three o'clock. Why don't you fix the table? I'm gonna set here one more minute."

Maya pulled herself up from her seat and headed to the quaint red-and-white patterned kitchen and gathered the plates and utensils for Sunday dinner. The alluring aromas of roasted chicken, snap peas, fresh collards, wild rice, and homemade apple pie filled the room like a gathering of old friends. She'd grown up in this house, had been here since she was five years old—a relocation made necessary when her mother back-talked a white man and disappeared into the backwoods of Virginia. Her battered body turned up weeks later, floating in the river. Maya had long ago forgotten what her mother looked like, smelled like, or what her smile reminded her of. Most times she didn't even feel her loss. Her grandmother gave her everything she could ever need: love, education, a strong sense of values and history.

According to Grandma Selma, Maya was a descendant of a long line of strong black women that included the slave, Selena. Women who'd endured the unimaginable in order to survive. Who'd loved and lost but beaten the odds. She'd listened to the tales all of her life. Most she believed were mere folklore, stories borne of need and nurtured on myth to larger-than-life proportions. Yet her grandmother, the last griot of the family, insisted that truth was woven within every treasured word of the ancient fables, and that one day she, too, would weave those tales for her own daughter. It was important, Grandma insisted, that Maya learn the art of the telling of tales, the understanding of her history in order to pass their wisdom along to the next generation of enduring women.

That would never happen, she concluded. In order to have a daughter, to pass along the quilted fabric of life, you needed a husband or at least a man. And as far back as the origins of these ancestral stories, all the women in the Johnston family had lost their men in some form or fashion. There were too many graves, too much grieving. She didn't want that kind of pain. The best way to avoid it was never to allow it into your life. Sadly, she would be the last of the Johnston line of women, the first disappointment to them all.

Maya slid on a pair of red-and-white oven mitts and removed the roasting pan filled with a tender golden chicken from the oven and placed it on the table. The wind suddenly tap-tapped against the panes, begging for entrance, causing her to jump. A chill ran through her.

Above her head, she swore she heard the sound of running feet. Standing absolutely still, she strained to listen for the impossible. She knew every nook and cranny, every creak and groan of the floorboards, every squeak of the unoiled hinges. The sounds above her head were none of those.

The wind cried again, a howl almost, while the sound of water flooded her ears. The red-and-white room spun like wool on a spindle, swirling into a cloud of darkness that blotted the remaining rays of the waning sun.

"Dinner served yet, chile? What's taking so long? It's after three," her grandmother chided, silently entering the kitchen and chasing the sounds and darkness away.

Sweat glistened on Maya's face. Her heart pounded against her breastbone as if the fear were chasing it out of its safe haven. Slowly her grandmother's well-lined face came into focus. She took short, measured breaths to slow the racing of her heart.

"What's wrong, chile? Look like you done seen a ghost," Grandma Selma chuckled, shuffling into the warmth of the kitchen.

"Did . . . did you hear noises, Grandma?"

Selma gave her granddaughter a curious look. "What kind of noises?"

"Dogs howling and running feet. Upstairs," she blurted out, knowing how ridiculous she sounded as soon as the words left her mouth.

Grandma Selma stood still as a portrait. Her dark eyes cinched as if she was trying to get Maya into focus. "Hmmm," she murmured. "It's starting." Slowly she nodded her head, sensing the approach of something unearthly.

"What's starting?" A chill rolled through Maya again, and she wrapped her arms around her body, looking around the room as if she expected something unknown to jump out at any minute.

"The prophecy."

"What! What prophecy? I don't want to hear any mumbo-jumbo, Grandma. I need the truth. What are you not telling me?"

Selma leaned on her walking stick and ambled over to the nearest kitchen chair and sat down. "Sit. Sit." Her voice carried a quality akin to dread.

Somewhere on the roof, the screech of the wind could be heard, probing for a weakness. It sounded like a living thing being whipped, being punished. Both women sat still, their eyes heavenward, their hands folded in their laps as if in silent reverence for the divine.

"Have you heard the wind sound like that?" Maya whispered. "I don't like it."

"Hush, chile." That edge in her grandma's voice was still there.

"Are you scared?" She looked at her beloved guardian for assurance.

"No, it was just like that night, that time long ago, Christmas Eve," the older woman said slowly. "It's Selena crying for Rufus, crying 'cause she didn't stay to help him. She been trying to get back to him ever since."

"Grandma! Stop it, just stop it. That's ridiculous. You're talking about ghosts now, spirits walking around upstairs? I don't believe you." She sprung up from her seat as an icy tremor scurried up her spine.

"Chile, chile, you wuz taught to believe." Slowly Selma shook her head. "All these years, all the stories you been told, was to prepare you."

"Prepare me? For what, a heart attack?" The sound of running feet sent Maya right back to her seat next to her grandmother. She clasped Selma's hand. Her eyes burned with terror. "Did you hear that?" she asked in a harsh whisper, her glance straying to the floor above.

"Naw, chile. I didn't hear nothin'. I ain't got it."

"Got what? I know you heard it. You had to have heard it. I'm not crazy. I'm not."

"Got what yo' mama had, and her great-grandmother before her—the gift."

A sudden, long-forgotten memory of her mother appeared like an apparition in front of her. That look of sudden horror that would brighten her mother's eyes, hasten her movements as if she could hear and see things that no one else could. And then the memory was gone. The roar of rushing water raced through Maya's head. She pressed her hand to her ears to shut out the noise.

"What's happening?" she screamed.

"Maya, they need yo' help," her grandmother said gently. "Yo' mama tried, died trying; your great-grandmother did, too."

Tears of fear and confusion rolled down Maya's cheeks. The noise, the footsteps grew louder, closer.

"Died trying. Trying to what?"

"When your mother turned up in the river, it wasn't like they said. She . . . was trying to help them. Help Selena get back to Rufus. That's how she died, Maya. That's the truth. Ever since Selena disappeared in that icy river, the legacy of loss and heartache has been passed down from one generation to the next. All the women in our family lose their men. But only a select few have the gift. Your mother had it and so do you."

"I don't understand, Grandma. I'm scared."

"No need to be scared, chile. What's gon' be will come to pass. I believe you the one who kin take all the heartache away. Make things right again."

"No." Maya shook her head violently. "No. That can't be true. Why me?"

Selma cupped Maya's face between her hands. "The answers will come to you, Maya, and when they do . . . listen," she said urgently. "Listen."

Maya slapped her palms down on the table and stood. "Enough of this. I don't want to hear any more." She wiped the tears from her face. "I'm going to fix us our meal, take a hot bath, and get some sleep. I have a long day tomorrow. And I'm going to put all this foolishness about legacies, gifts, and spirits out of my head." She tugged in a stabilizing breath. "And so are you." She began carving the chicken and serving it up. "Tomorrow I'm calling the roofer and the exterminator. There's probably some loose shingles up on the roof, and maybe mice up there causing all of that noise. I'll take care of it. That will be the end of it."

Selma scooped out a spoonful of collards and plopped them onto her plate. She looked up at her granddaughter, her wise eyes seeing more than Maya could imagine. "If you say so, chile. If you say so."

Maya ran a tub of water, as hot as she could stand it. Maybe it would get rid of the chill that had seeped into her bones and wouldn't let go, she thought. Lighting several candles, she turned off the light, added a splash of almond-scented bubble bath, and stepped into the steaming water, letting it rise inch by inch until it reached her chin. She rested her head against the back of the tub and closed her eyes, willing the bizarre events of the day to the back of her mind.

The winter wind continued to howl outside, begging for admittance. Maya sunk deeper into the water, letting its warmth ease her into a restless sleep, its gentle motion like a lullaby.

The light from the candles dances outside her closed lids, like the flicker of the torch lights so many years ago. The sound of voices, like the roll of thunder, echos in the enclosed room.

Maya tries to open her eyes, tries to pull herself up from the grip of the water, but she can't. Panic seizes her. She tries to scream for help, but no sound comes from her throat. Images emerge from behind the glow of the flame. Dark, looming shapes, their shadowy forms drawing closer. She has to get away.

Suddenly, she is no longer in the safety of the home she shares with her grandmother, the sanctuary of the bathroom. She is running, stumbling through the woods in near pitch darkness. Her heart races with an unnatural fear. The cry of the wind becomes the sound of howling hunting hounds. Their master's voices urge them on, commanding them to capture their prey.

A big, heavy hand grips hers in the darkness, pulling her along. An assuring hand, one she knows will protect her.

"Won't be long now fo' we reach the river," Rufus says. "Come on, Maya, just a little while longer. You kin do it."

Past merges with present. Blackness swirls around Maya as two worlds collide in concert with the blast of shotgun fire.

Maya claws her way out of the muddy ditch where she was thrown and crawls back to Rufus's side.

"Rufus! Rufus!" She tugs at his shoulders.

"Run, Maya. Run fo' the river."

"Not wit'out you."

"Cain't make it, girl. Go . . . run. You knows what they'll do to ya if they catch ya."

The howling of the dogs draws closer. Maya looks once toward the river, then back at Rufus. *Capture is certain death. To run toward possibility* . . .

"Go, 'fo' it's too late."

"Not wit'out you. You my man, my husband, and I ain't gon' nowhere wit'out you."

With all her strength—strength borne from years of labor in the fields, strength borne from watching the horrors of plantation life and finding a way to survive, a strength borne of the desire to be free of folklore and legend—she grabs Rufus beneath his shoulders, and with the baying of the hounds and the hunters on their heels, Maya hauls Rufus to and in the icy river.

Immediately, her limbs begin to numb; her heart nearly stops from the shock; but just as quickly, a soothing warmth flows through her, and the scent of almond fills her nostrils. Her long skirts wrap around her legs, weighing her down, compounded with the almost dead weight of Rufus, and the other side seems an eternity away. She can't stop. She can't go back.

Rufus's weight slowly begins to lessen.

"We gon' make it, Maya," Rufus says between gasps, finding the strength to pull himself along with the ebb and flow of the river. "You kin do it."

His words give her the last bit of strength she needs to get them the last few feet to the other side.

Pulling Rufus onto the riverbank, she helps him to his feet, and bracing his body against hers, they make their way through the woods and to safety. The sounds of the hounds begin to dim; the howling winds cease to blow; the raging voices of the pursuers slowly wane. The sounds of running feet are no more.

Maya bursts above the water, gasping for air, clawing the sides of the tub. Muddy fingerprints dot the white porcelain rim. *Mud?* The dancing lights from the candles dwindle, and the sounds of familiar voices float upward from downstairs. *Her grandmother's voice, her grandfather . . . and her mother and her father.*

God, what was happening? She'd had some horrible dream, nearly drowned, and now it was making her hear things, she reasoned. *But where had the mud come from?* A play of light, she decided, unwilling to believe anything else as she put on her robe and hurried to the top of the stairs. Her grandmother probably had neighbors over. That was the only explanation.

Tentatively she eased down the stairs, and the voices grew clearer and more distinct. When she reached the threshold of the living room, the impossible became reality. There, sitting on the couch, were her mother and father—talking—souls long lost and now found. And tossing logs into the fireplace was her grandfather, while her grandmother rocked in her chair.

Her knees weakened and she gripped the door frame for support.

"Hi, sweetheart," her mother said. "We were wondering how long you were going to be in that tub. You've been up there for hours."

Hours?

"Granddad just fixed some hot toddies. Have one," her dad offered. "Help you to sleep."

"I . . . I . . ." Maya looked in disbelief from one family member to another. "Mama . . . Dad . . . Grandpa . . ."

Selma pushed herself up from her seat and walked to where Maya stood. Gently she touched her tear-streaked face. "You done good, chile," she said gently. "The prophecy's been fulfilled. The years of loss and heartache is done. Everything's just as it should be. Things been made right at last. Everybody's where they 'spose to be."

"I don't understand ... It was just a dream. I was—I was Selena ... and I was pulling Rufus out of the water."

"I know, sugah. Same thing yo' mama tried to do years ago, and yo' great-grandmother. But it was you, sugah. You was the one we been waiting for."

"But how ... she's ... and Dad and Granddad ..."

"See, chile, it's the vow them two made that night in the field: every good-bye ain't gone. Every shut eye sure ain't sleep. A sacred vow. Now, things is the way they would have been if Selena would have saved Rufus that Christmas Eve night; all of us here together, like it never happened." She put her arm around her granddaughter and ushered her into the room. "Come in and get reacquainted with your folks."

Bathed in the glow of the flames from the hearth, stories were told, thanks were given, laughter and hugs were shared, and the spirits of Selena and Rufus looked on, reunited at last. And Maya finally believed.

My Momma Said . . .

Arethia Hornsby

"Never judge a book by its cover." —African American

"Will you please shut up? You tell me your 'crumbs theory' every time I see a man that I like! I get so sick of you saying, 'My momma said if you only eat crumbs, you'll never know what a real meal tastes like.' " Tee mimicked me with a quick toss of her thick, long hair. She has the most beautiful jet-black hair of anybody I know.

I had followed Tee into the ladies' room and I was determined to have my say. I calmly finished applying my lip liner and then carefully ran my raspberry brown lipstick smoothly over my full lips. Looking at my reflection in the ladies' room mirror, I smiled. Damn, I looked good! My short bleached-blond haircut accented my face and made me look younger than my thirty-five years.

"Tee, if you are going to quote my momma, quote her correctly," I said sweetly. *"If all you EVER eat are crumbs, then you'll never know what a real meal tastes like.* The key, my sistah, is *ever* eat. All you *ever* eat are crumbs."

I swirled around in the rattan chair to face my best friend in the world, Tamika Tobbins. "Tee Tee" to me, and only me would she allow to call her that.

"It sounds like you saying pee-pee; it sounds like you calling me pee-pee," she would whine when we were kids.

"I am not. I'm saying your initials," I had explained.

Still, she never liked it. Oh, well. She had been Tee Tee to me for over thirty years, and she would always be Tee Tee. Looking her up and down, I shook my head and sighed.

"What?" she snapped. "What you huffing about now, Linda? What?"

Tamika was a "big girl." She was a size eighteen, but squeezed into clothing that a much smaller woman should wear. Her short red leather skirt was riding up her ample butt, exposing dimpled (she called them dimpled; I called them rolls of fat) thighs. The black lacy top she had on revealed pillows of breasts that prayed for release from the corsetlike blouse. The mesh net showed even more dimples (rolls) around her arms and waist. The red leather high-heel boots she had on, I liked; now they were bad. My girl always wore some bad shoes. The rest of her gear . . . well . . .

Tee Tee had a pretty face, with large brown eyes and what white people called a "pert" nose. Plus, she had all that long, gorgeous hair that I secretly envied. And gold was everywhere on her body. From her ears hung about six pairs of hoop earrings; from her neck, about ten gold chains. Her arms sported bangles galore. There were rings on almost every finger, and an anklet on her right leg. She even had a gold crown on one of her teeth!

"Well, what, Linda?" she asked again. "Why you staring at me like I'm some kind of a freak?" She posed the question like she really wanted me to answer. "I like what I got on, and I couldn't care less if you don't," she announced to me with pride ringing in her voice. "Plus, the brother I was dancing with, you are not going to believe! He said he liked my outfit. Said red was his favorite color."

Tee sounded breathless, I guess from all that dancing. She continued speaking into the mirror, avoiding my eyes. "But Linda, Linda, that's not the best part; that's not the best part!" She was so excited she was glowing. She swung her hair from side to side as she studied her reflection. There was the strangest look on her face, like she was in shock.

Another sistah entered the ladies' room and did a double take at Tee before hurrying into the stall. Tee Tee must not have caught the sistah's look, or she would have definitely called her out.

"Girl, Linda, you not going to believe this! The brother said he likes a sistah with something to hold on to. A woman with some meat on her bones, and not a snack pack."

She threw the last remark in my direction with a smile. If I weighed over 100 pounds it was because I was on my period and bloated. I had been "small" all my life. I got so tired of people telling me, "You're so skinny; I wish I could be skinny like you." I *always* put them in their place. One, I'm not skinny; I'm small. Two, calling me skinny is no compliment! If I call a fat sistah fat, she's ready to fight, so why folks think they can call me skinny? Tee Tee, on the other hand, took pleasure in being a "big girl."

We had the strangest relationship. We were like night and day, left-right-up-down. She was large; I was small. She had long hair; I had short. I was fair; she was a deep, dark brown. She was tall. I was short. She was flashy. I was conservative. But our differences didn't stop on the outside. We were inside-different. Tee Tee would give you the shirt off her back (I wish she'd snatch off that red one tonight, because it was too tight). Me, I tended to be less giving, more cautious. But Tee Tee, she had a heart of gold. She picked up stray animals all the time and tried to nurse them back to health. Her specialty was stray dogs, a.k.a trifling men! That was the problem. Tee Tee was a pushover for a man. Any old piece of a man could win Tee's heart!

Crumbs—that's all she ever settled for. And sometimes the crumbs off another woman's table. Garbage that some sistah had thrown out. Then here comes Tee, picking them out of the trash can, talking about "He *could* be a good man if . . ." You could fill in the blanks with just about anything with Tee Tee's men: *If he could just get a job, get a car, get an apartment, get clean (drug-free), get dry (alcohol-free), or sometimes just get FREE! (Released from prison.)*

Tonight Tee Tee and I were in my favorite Friday-night hot spot, Fargo's, doing some lightweight drinking. Payday was not until next Thursday, so we couldn't really let loose and get our drink on! I had been sipping my Absolute and cranberry with a twist of lime to give it that little kick, when she spotted this tired-looking brother beside the pool table.

"Linda, I think the brother over there in the corner is checking me out," she'd leaned over to tell me, with her breasts almost spilling into my drink.

"Will you watch your damn boobs?" I'd mumbled. I'd only taken one sip from my drink and didn't want her to push it into my lap! I was wearing my brand-new Ann Klein suit that had cost me almost two paychecks. I was looking very sophisticated. Most of the women in the club were designer down, from their clothes to their perfume. They were the cream of the crop of young black professionals, and everybody was at his or her "dress to impress" best.

The place was packed as usual, with all the "Playa's and the Haters." Tee Tee was a "Hater." She hated Fargo's. She said it was phony, and too siddity for her tastes. She preferred the "Chitterling Circuit" when it came to clubs. I called them "dives"; she called them "down." Like I said, we were different. But she's my girl, different or not!

I'd had to drag Tee Tee here from the law firm where we both worked, Frost and Lenders. She worked in the mail room and I was a receptionist. I was in night school for accounting, determined to move "up and out." Tee Tee was satisfied and content. "All I do is deliver mail twice a day for $11.00 an hour, and I'm okay with that," she would brag.

But back to the problem at hand.

"Linda." Tee had nudged me again; I slid my drink around to my other side, just to be safe. "He's looking at me," she squealed, talking loud to be heard over the pumping sounds of DJ Slam." She grabbed my arm and squeezed. "Check him out, Linda!"

"Will you chill?" I hissed. "He looks like he ain't got a dime."

I'd scoped out the brother when we first walked in. He'd looked at me and then zoomed in on Tee Tee, who was busy complaining about the $10.00 cover charge. No doubt he could tell she was in the rescue business, because he sure looked like he needed to be rescued.

He had on some tired-looking jeans—no name brand at all—with some tired-looking gym shoes—again no name brand. Not like the other brothers in the house. They were clean from their fresh fades to their feet, and looked like they couldn't care less about talking to a woman; they just wanted to be seen. The brothers were sure not buying sisters no drinks; that was for sure. As a matter of fact, they wanted you to buy them one! Still, it was my favorite spot. It was classy.

"Linda, Linda!" Tee exclaimed. "He's smiling at me—look, look!" As I turned to look, she screamed over the loud music, "Not now, don't look now!"

"Do you want me to look or not?" I snapped.

Jerking my head around to the left, I saw the tired brother grinning from ear to ear in our direction. He was grinning at Tee Tee!

"If he's all in your grill like that, why don't he come over and say something like, *'Hello, can I buy you ladies a drink?'*" My voice was dripping with sarcasm. The brother looked like he couldn't buy a can of pop, much less two drinks!

"Linda, I can buy my own drinks," Tee Tee snapped back. She took a small sip of her beer.

"That's your problem," I replied before she could finish. "You always supply what's needed. You don't ever get a man who can supply his needs, much less your needs."

"Girl, like I was saying"—Tee Tee did a neck roll that would make any ghetto queen proud—"I don't need a man to buy my drinks. I want a man to love me for me. I can take care of myself."

I stared at her like she had lost her mind. A woman who has a personal relationship with half the check-cashing places in the city had said this. You know the places I'm talking about. *"We will hold your personal check until payday"* loan sharks that keep you in a hole forever. Thank God, I had severed *my* relationship with them!

I turned my attention away from Tee with a shrug of my shoulders that said "whatever." I was admiring a tall, fair-skinned brother in an Armani suit that was fitting his broad shoulders perfectly! He was fine from his wavy light-brown hair to the Ballys on his feet. He had the most beautiful smile, which he was busy displaying to a giddy waitress. I kept trying to subtly make eye contact with him, to no avail.

"Look at you, trying to get that conceited-looking boy-toy to *look at you!* Girl, all he's been looking at all night is his reflection on these mirrored walls. He's not on you! These Negroes are *fake*—like I keep saying, all of them, the men and the women, all of them wannabes. Acting like they all that! They living from paycheck to paycheck just like us!" Tee was on a roll, so I was glad to see the waitress make her way to our table. I *did not* want to hear what she was talking about at all.

I looked at the same waitress who had been smiled upon by "Mr. Gorgeous." I bet he got that drink free, I thought.

"Did you ladies want to freshen up your drinks?" she purred, like she didn't know we'd been sipping the same drink for the last hour.

"No," I replied, "I don't want another one right now, thank you." I shook the ice cubes to let her know I still had something in my glass.

"At these prices, I can't afford another one." Tee Tee rolled her eyes at me. This from Miss I-can-take-care-of-myself!

"Tee Tee," I moaned, "we are not in RED'S, where all the drinks are two dollars."

"I wish we were," she said with an attitude. "Then we could buy more than one drink all night, and the men would talk to us, ask us to dance, and I'd be having fun!"

She leaned forward, and pushed her chair back. "Forget this, I'm going over to that brother and ask him to dance," she announced with a shake of her long hair.

"Don't you dare! Tee Tee, come back here!"

But I was too late. For a "big girl" she moved fast. She was up and across the floor in a blink. I saw her step up to the brother and speak. Whatever she said, he must have liked, 'cause next thing I see, they up on the dance floor, and both of them are grinning from ear to ear at each other! Well, guess what? They stayed on the dance floor for about three jams, while I sat there jamming in my seat.

When they stopped dancing, they moved over to the side of the bar where he had been standing, and started talking like they knew each other from way back! *She attracts them like flies. Negro hasn't bought her a drink yet and she's grinning like she got a prize, when as usual, she got crumbs.*

Tee Tee will never find a real man, I thought sadly. Even with her pretty face, big heart, sweet personality, and beautiful hair, she was always going to get stuck with the "crumbs."

I saw him hand her a business card and smiled. *No, the tired brother isn't carrying a business card.* I laughed! Hey, anybody can get cards free from the Internet, no big deal. I had business cards. Had them designed and printed up real sharp. That was part of the scene here, exchanging business cards. He had his arm around her waist and was brushing her hair out of her eyes with his fingertips. She looked up at him and smiled. Brother was tall; I'll give him that. She said something that made him laugh. He dropped his arm from around her waist and Tee started walking away. She made another comment to him over her shoulder and he laughed again. He was watching her walk like he liked what he saw! Tee Tee glided to the ladies' room as if she were floating on a cloud.

Dear God, I moaned, *what is my girl getting into now?*

I got up and pressed my way through the crowd toward the brother, with a mission. *I had to save her.* Walking up to the brother, my sexiest smile was in place.

"Hello, how are you?" Friendliness was oozing from me. He looked down at me and smiled. He had beautiful, even white teeth. *Well, at least he's familiar with the dentist,* ran through my mind. *That's a positive.*

"Hello to you; I'm good, thank you for asking." His speech was very slow, as if he thought of each word before he spoke. *Oh, my God, Tee Tee got a retard this time!*

"You and my girl were dancing up a storm." I smiled again, my face almost cracking from the effort.

"Yes," he said very slowly, "she is quite a dancer. I haven't enjoyed myself like that in a long time." He had a wistful look on his face. "That felt good. I need to do that more often. Oh, I'm sorry." He slapped his forehead with the open palm of his hand.

"My name is Beauford Laudy the Third." He extended his right hand to me. It was too late; I had spit my drink out with the "Beauford." Forget "the Third"!

He quickly snatched a handkerchief out of his back pocket and offered it to me. "Are you all right?"

His voice was full of concern. He was patting me on the back, as if I were a baby he was trying to burp. I was reeling for real now. A handkerchief? The tired brother—no—Beauford Laudy III, carried a handkerchief in his back pocket! This was too much. I wanted to laugh until I exploded! This was rich! WHO carried a handkerchief in their back pocket? He had stopped patting my back and was leaning over me.

"Did your drink go down the wrong pipe?" He had soft brown eyes and a wide, generous mouth. His skin was smooth, the color of rich, deep chocolate. Beauford's haircut was just plain—no style, with traces of gray around the temples. I'd say about early forties. His body was large, but it looked firm. He was a good two bucks and a quarter, I thought. No wonder he liked Tee Tee. He looked like a big goofy teddy bear. Just Tee's style.

I set my now empty glass down on the side of the pool table. "Could you buy us a drink?" I asked sweetly. "I know with all that dancing you and my girl did, she's thirsty."

I had folded my arms across my chest and leaned back to look him in the eyes as I spoke. My body language said, *I dare you to say no.* Beauford got the funniest look on his face.

"I'm sorry, what's your name?"

"Linda," I replied, extending my hand, "Linda McEnroy. I'm with Frost and Lenders," I supplied.

"Oh, really," he answered, shaking my hand with a firm grip. I grinned to myself, I could tell he didn't have a clue who Frost and Lenders—a law firm—was.

"Well, Linda, umm, I'd love to buy you lovely ladies a drink, but, umm, I really did not mean to come in here tonight."

That I already knew, I thought with a smile still plastered on my face as I stared at him.

"But . . . I left my wallet . . ."

"No problem," I cut him off before he could finish his lame lie. "I'm sure Tee Tee will buy *you* a drink when she comes back." I spoke with as much venom in my voice as I could muster. His eyes opened wide at that remark and he started to reply, but I was already walking away, headed toward the ladies' room.

I pushed the door open with a vengeance and looked for Tee Tee. A woman was standing in line for the next available stall. She stared at me. The ladies' room was nice. There was a small love seat in one corner, and a vanity table that ran the length of the room. There were rattan chairs at the vanity table with pink cushions on them. A full-length mirror stood in the other corner of the room to make sure a sistah was looking good when she walked back out the door. Tee was in the full-length mirror dabbing her face with a wet paper towel. She turned when she saw me, and she was glowing.

"Linda, did you see us jamming? That brother sure can dance. Did you see us?" She was sweating profusely and her chest was heaving, but she looked so happy. Dancing was her thing; she loved to dance.

"How in the hell could I miss you, Tee Tee?" I replied sourly. The two women sitting at the far end of the vanity stopped talking. They looked at Tee, then looked at each other and laughed. Their expression quickly changed when Tee Tee turned to stare at them.

"Did somebody make a joke and I didn't get it?" she spoke to the room in general, staring at the two black Barbies.

"Yeah," I echoed. "Did somebody make a joke?"

I gave Tee a puzzled look. I could diss my girl, but anybody else better not think about it! Plus, like I said, Tee Tee was a "big girl" who was from the hood. She was a pushover for a man, but a sistah she would get with in a heartbeat! The two Barbies fluffed up their hair, glanced at us, got up, and left.

Tee Tee burst out laughing.

"I think you scared them," she said with a big smile on her face.

"Me? You scared them, Tee, not me." I smiled back at my girl.

"Yeah," I said, "I saw you jamming with that brother." I sat down in one of the rattan chairs that had been vacated by the Barbies. I took out my lip-liner, stalling for time to say what I wanted. I could not let her go off on a tangent with another loser. I had to try to talk to her.

"Linda, I really like him. He is soooo nice, He's . . ." She sounded so excited. I had to be blunt.

"Tee," I said calmly, cutting her off. "He's nothing. He's not about anything. I asked him to buy us some drinks, and he couldn't."

I started putting on my lip-liner.

She cut me off, sitting down in the chair beside me. Her eyes were wide with anticipation." Yeah, I know; he left his wallet . . ."

"Tee Tee!" I was losing my calm tone and getting upset." I don't care where he left his wallet; when he has it I bet there's not a damn thing in it."

I was getting pissed. Why did she always fall so soon? Why did she get her hopes up so quick? I wanted to just shake her. Crumbs—here she goes again, getting all excited about some tired brother who has NOTHING to offer her. I felt tears gather in the corners of my eyes. *Dear God*, I silently prayed, *please help me.* I get so tired of seeing her hurt. *Please, God, open her eyes to what she really is, a queen.* Please let her stop being a fool for somebody trying to use her.

My voice was choking up. "Tamika, please, please listen to me, just this one time, please. I love you, girl, and I'm tired of seeing you hurt."

I grabbed her hands in mine. She was giving me a strange look.

"I know you do," she said slowly. "Linda, I know that. You are my best friend in the world. You've been with me throughout everything." She was holding my hands and looking at me, waiting for me to speak.

I swallowed the lump in my throat. "Ain't you tired of tired men, Tee?" I whispered. "Remember Marcus?" How could she forget? She had to have the police remove him from her apartment. She slowly shook her head yes, her eyes never leaving my face. I was holding her hands for dear life. "He lived in your apartment, ate your food, drove your car, and even stole money from you. He beat you, cheated on you, and had you scared to go home after work. I HAD TO MAKE YOU PUT HIM OUT!" My voice was a hoarse whisper.

"He was an artist. I was trying to help him find himself," she muttered, dropping her eyes to the floor. She let go of my hands and leaned back in the chair. I took her hands back in mine.

"God wants the best for you, Tee. You are a fine black queen and you deserve the best. God wants you to have the best and only the best." My voice was getting stronger with each word I spoke. "You should have a man that has something to offer you, that respects you and completes you. You have so much to give; stop throwing away your pearls to swine. All you ever get are crumbs. My momma said if all you ever eat . . ."

Tee Tee shot out the chair like she had a stick of dynamite up her butt!

She went back to the mirror and stared at her reflection. "Will you please shut up? You tell me your *'crumbs theory'* every time I see a man that I like! I get so sick of you saying, 'My momma said if you only eat crumbs, you'll never know what a real meal tastes like.' " Her voice was trembling.

"But it's the truth, Tee." My confidence was returning. I was determined to let her know how dumb she was being. I didn't care how mad she got.

"My momma made me understand that early in life, Tee. 'Don't settle for just any old thing. Don't let life gives you the crumbs' . . . My momma . . .'"

"I'll ask you again, Linda. Please shut up about your momma." Her chest was heaving with each word she spoke, as if she was in pain. "Your momma said, 'don't eat crumbs!'"

There was a meanness in Tee Tee's voice I had never heard before. I stared at her like I was looking at a stranger, somebody I had never seen before. A woman came out of a stall and glanced at Tee, then looked at me through the mirror over the sink as she washed her hands. She took her time drying them, then slowly walked out of the room.

"Tee I'm not trying to bust your bubble about this guy; I'm trying to help you with some good advice from my momma. . . ."

"Shut up about your momma, Linda!"

Tee Tee was screaming! Then she started laughing! She was laughing so hard that tears were running down her face. She was still staring at her reflection in the full-length mirror when she spoke again.

"Your precious *momma* and her crumbs theory!" She turned around slowly and faced me. I heard a toilet flush, and the door to a stall flung open. A thin white girl came out staring at the floor and almost ran out the room. *She didn't wash her hands,* I thought. *How nasty.*

My heart was double-beating in my chest, and I had the feeling that I should get up NOW and leave. Why had I followed her into the bathroom in the first place? Why were we still in here? But I could not move. I sat there staring at this strange woman, glaring down at me with disgust written all on her face.

"Your momma sure didn't buy that theory she was always shoving down your throat, my friend." Tee was looking at me like we were two enemies standing on the street. She was blinking her eyes real fast.

"I choke every *damn* time you tell me that *shit*."

I sat back as if she had slapped me! Tamika *never* cussed! NEVER.

"Your momma didn't mind crumbs, Linda, 'cause she was eating crumbs off *my momma's table!* Your momma was *FUCKING MY DADDY.* So crumbs weren't so bad back then!"

She had big, sloppy tears streaming down her face and converging around her mouth. Tee walked over to the vanity, her legs were wobbing. She grabbed hold of the edge of the table. Me, I had nothing to hold on to. I felt like she had kicked me in the stomach with her high-heeled boots, and I was reeling. I bent over in pain and heard a strange sound escape my lips. The room was spinning.

"Yeah, Linda. Your pretty Miss Educated-high-yellow-prissy momma, I-don't-like-dark-skinned-black-folks Momma, I caught giving my *big, black, Mandingo, gold-toothed, uneducated, ghetto daddy some HEAD!*"

Tee Tee's voice kept getting higher and louder with each word until she was screeching. The look in her eyes was wild and frightening. There was spit running down the side of her mouth, and beads of perspiration stood out on her forehead.

"I caught them." She was panting like she had been running. "I was ten years old and I caught your momma going down on my daddy. They never knew I saw them, and I never told my momma. So what do you think about your momma's theory now, Linda? What you think now?"

I had wrapped my arms around my body to protect myself from another blow. There was a sound coming up from my soul that was like no sound I had ever heard. The room kept spinning, and I could not take my eyes off Tamika. Sometimes it seemed like there were three of her, then four, then five, then one again. She was gripping the edge of the table so hard, I heard one of her nails pop off. I still could not take my eyes off Tee Tee. Her whole body was trembling.

"So what you think, Linda? Huh? Huh? You always got something to say."

She was leaning over me now, her voice lowered. "Oh, before you answer . . ." Her voiced dropped even lower. She was so close I could smell the beer on her breath. Our eyes were locked. I was holding myself for dear life. I felt a tremor in my legs, and the right one started shaking.

"That tired brother I was dancing with, the one *you* said ain't about nothing?"

Tee flopped down in the chair next to me, like her legs could no longer support her weight. I think I heard people enter the room; I was not sure. "The tired brother," she continued, "Beauford—his name is Beauford—he's only in here 'cause his *Porsche* is next door at Good-year, getting new tires. He left his wallet by accident in the glove compartment." Her breathing was no longer ragged, but even, her eyes no longer wild; they looked dreamy. I could not take *my* eyes off her. I was frozen.

"He's taking me out to breakfast when we leave here in about"—she looked at her watch—"in about ten minutes."

"His *Porsche* should be ready then. We're going over to Mannie's, that real expensive restaurant on the east side of town. You know the one we drive by and wish we could afford to go in."

She chuckled as she leaned back in the chair and crossed her legs, making her skirt hike up, exposing more of her plump thighs. "Linda, I read the letters sometimes that come through the mail room. So when he told me his name, I immediately knew who he was." She stood back up. The toilet flushed, and a sistah came out of a stall and slowly walked over to the sink.

Tee fished around in her purse to find her wallet. "Here, Linda." She pulled out a bill, then laid it on the vanity table. "Buy yourself another drink—on me." Reaching into her purse again, she pulled out a small white card, laying it on top of the money. I had not moved or uttered a word the whole time Tee had been talking. I couldn't—my tongue was stuck to the roof of my mouth.

"Linda, I still love you." Her voice was like soft caresses that she was breathing on an open wound. "I'll always love you; you know that. But I guess that had to come out one day; I'm sorry it came out like that." She started to walk out of the room and then stopped with her hand on the doorknob. She spoke without turning around. "My momma thought your mom was her friend, Linda. She thought the sun rose and set in your mother. She thought your mom was such a lady. I never told her, never. She never knew. It would have killed her. I never told her."

Her voice sounded so strong. She straightened her back, squaring her shoulders. Then Tameka turned and faced me with a smile. "Let me share something with you that my momma always told me, Linda." She took a deep breath. "My momma said, 'You should never judge a book by its cover; at least read the jacket.' "

Tameka then tossed her hair, opened the door, and switched out of the room. The sistah that had been in the mirror at the sink finally washed her hands, dried them, then turned to me. "Are you okay?" she asked quietly. I shook my head yes; my arms were still tightly wrapped around my body. The woman walked out of the room, pity all in her face.

I carefully unwrapped my arms and stood up. I stood there a moment, my mind in turmoil, thoughts racing through my head, colliding with each other, then exploding. Tears, which had refused to be released while Tameka was talking, now poured down my face. I wiped my eyes with the sleeve of my suit, streaking makeup all over the creamy white raw silk material.

I never thought she knew about my momma and her daddy. I knew—I had always known. My momma had told me.

She had told me when she started drilling her "crumbs theory" in my head. All these years, Tameka knew. And had still been my best friend. All these years she knew. It was like a song that keeps repeating itself in my head. All these years, she knew.

There was a feeling of weightlessness in my spirit. A feeling of relief. I picked up the twenty and the small white card she had placed facedown. When I turned it over and read it, I sat back down.

The card read: *Judge Beauford Laudy III.* I smiled weakly as I tucked the card and the money into my jacket pocket. A judge—Tameka had caught the eye of a JUDGE! She deserved it.

"Tameka got a JUDGE," I said aloud. "My girl is in for a banquet! That's my girl," I said through my tears. I heard a toilet flush; then somebody said, "My momma always said, 'It ain't over till the fat lady sings.'" The stall door opened and a short, dark-skinned woman waddled out who must have weighed about three hundred pounds! She looked me up and down, then slowly walked to the sink and proceeded to wash her hands, humming some nameless tune and shaking her big butt in time to her own music.

The Cycle

Travis Hunter

"If you want to keep getting what you're getting, keep doing what you're doing." —African American

"*Sticks and stones may break my bones, but words can never hurt me.*" That's an old phrase that my momma used to try and comfort me with when the neighborhood kids called me names. But it's also a lie. I came to this realization on a return trip from prison.

I was sitting in the waiting room at the Jackson State Prison, waiting for the grey-dog to transport me from the living hell that I was sitting in to the one I called home. I felt this old man, who looked to be in his early seventies, staring at me. I mustered as much hate and contempt as I could and returned his stare dead-on, hoping he'd find something else to fix his eyes on.

I had seen this man plenty of times, but we'd never spoken, never as much as exchanged nods. He was a prison guard and, therefore, the enemy. Obviously, he didn't get the memo prohibiting fraternization, because he walked over, sat down beside me, and removed a pack of chewing gum from his shirt pocket. He offered a stick. I twisted my lips and ignored his kind gesture.

"So, how old are you now?" he asked as if he were a family friend.

"I think you have the wrong person," I spat.

"No, I'm talking to you. Your name is Trent and you're Clarrise's boy. So how old are you?"

I ignored him, hoping he'd disappear.

"It's a harmless question, son."

"Look, I don't know you, and you don't know me. So if you don't mind, I'd like to wait in peace."

"Oh, but I do know you, Trent. I've known your family for over forty years. I met your grandfather when he first came here back in sixty-one. I knew your daddy, three of your uncles, a few of your cousins have been through, and now your brother Lance is here. When are you coming?"

"What do you mean, when am I coming?"

"When will you make your journey this way? This seems to be a rite of passage for your family. So I'm just trying to figure out if you're old enough to be charged as an adult."

"Whatever, man."

"You're a very disrespectful young man, do you know that?"

"I don't have to respect you. I don't even know you."

"That's one of the dumbest things I've ever heard. You never know who you're gonna need in this world. I see you up here every week visiting your brother and your uncles, and I think, this young man spends a lot of time behind these bars. He must like it here, or else he's preparing for his arrival."

Truth be told, I've always wondered when it will be my time. It's almost inevitable that I'll spend some time behind bars. My family will use a clean criminal record like some folks use a baby's credit history. There have been plenty of instances where my uncles came to me to do a crime, figuring that if I got caught I'd just get probation since it would be my first offense.

I hid my thoughts behind a scowl. "I'm seventeen, but I don't have any plans to come to your prison."

"Nobody plans to come to prison. You think any of these men made plans to spend years of their lives behind bars? No, son, it was the lack of planning that landed most of 'em here."

I looked in the old man's eyes and saw a look that I'd never seen before. It was a look of compassion. Then it hit me like a ton of bricks. This old dude was not the enemy; he was trying to help me. I wanted to hear more of what he had to say. I sat up and leaned forward so that I could hear him better over the slamming cell doors. I secretly hoped that my bus might be running a little late.

I was seventeen years old, but I had never sat down and talked with a man about life. The only thing that the so-called men I associated with taught me was that life was a hustle and I had to be a hustler. Looking around at the graffiti-covered walls and cold steel, I knew I didn't want to come to prison. But I also knew that, coming up as I had, doing time was a definite possibility.

"Trent, this is a cruel world for young black boys. You have to prepare yourself mentally, physically, and spiritually. With preparation, you'll have more options. Do you know, if you gave most black people in the ghetto a million dollars, within a few months they'd be back on public assistance? And do you know why? Lack of preparation! It's like getting in the ring with Mike Tyson and all you ever trained on was checkers. You gonna get knocked the hell out."

"Life ain't that simple."

"No, it's not. It's a bitch. But you gotta live it to the fullest, and preparation is the key. Most successful people start grooming their children for prosperity as soon as that child leaves the womb. What do we teach our kids? How to recite a stankin' rap song and we think that's cool. Got little boys that ain't old enough to talk good with earrings in their ears. I saw this little boy about a week ago, no more than five years old, with a homemade tattoo. I'm tired of it, Trent. I go home some nights and cry real tears over what's happening to our race."

"Bus number seventeen to Abernathy Commons now boarding at gate five."

"That's my bus!"

He nodded sadly. I hated to leave the old dude. We stood together. After checking to make sure that no one saw us, I shook his hand. He pulled me closer and whispered the words that would change my life.

During the entire trip home I thought about the two sentences that the old man had mouthed. Funny, how he made it all seem so clear. As the driver pulled into the station, I felt different. I walked the few blocks to the projects where my family had lived for the last forty or so years, and felt something that I'd never felt. I wanted out.

As I walked upstairs to our apartment, I heard my little nephew, Gerard, crying. The 100-degree Atlanta heat had me drained, and I really didn't feel like baby-sitting. Judging by his continuous cries, nobody else felt like it, either. I walked into the suffocating heat and picked him up. He was soaked with sweat and urine. I pulled off his diaper and looked for another one, but we were all out.

I walked over to my grandmother, who was sleeping off her liquor. Shaking my head in frustration, I walked into my mother's room, where a strange man was sleeping. I kicked his leg.

"Yo, man, who are you?" I asked. Gerard squirmed in my arms.

"I'm Max," he growled, sitting up and rubbing his face. "I'm your momma's friend, and if you kick me again, I'm going to do something to you. Let's not start off on the wrong foot, boy."

"Man, to hell with you. Where is my momma?"

"The hell with me? The hell with you, too," Max said as he lay back down.

I left the bedroom. I had grown weary of trying to make Momma have some morals. She was who she was, and she wasn't going to change for no one, especially me. She was quick to tell me that I could hit the road, and I knew she meant it.

I looked around the apartment for something to cover Gerard's bottom, but it was a lost cause. I walked back into Momma's room, snatched the pillow from under Max's head, removed the pillowcase, and threw the flat pillow back at him. His smile was a sinister warning. I saw the danger in his eyes. Hell, he wasn't worth a trip to prison or the morgue. Not when my life was just beginning.

I bathed Gerard and wrapped him in the pillowcase, carrying him to the living room sofa. I moved the fan so it could blow a little of the hot air onto Gerard and me, and Grandma woke up fussing.

"Put that got damn fan back on me. You so damn selfish, Trent." Grandma wobbled to her feet and staggered out of the apartment.

Realizing that it was cooler outside, I took Gerard to sit on the front steps. A few minutes later, my little sister Drea walked up.

"Hey, Trent. I thought you went to see Lance."

"I did, but he's in lock-up. No visitors."

"That boy stay in the hole." She reached for her baby boy. "Hey, li'l man. What in the world do you have on?"

"I couldn't find any diapers, so I improvised."

"Give me my baby," Drea laughed, kissing his sweaty forehead.

"Grandma woke?" she asked.

"She went back to her place. Drunk as a skunk."

"What else is new?" Drea said sarcastically.

"I came home and Gerard was losing his mind crying. But Grandma and some dude that's in Momma's room were sleeping like it was quiet."

"Who is that man? He was looking at me all funny this morning."

"Looking at you like what?" I said, figuring that I might have a reason to kill this disrespectful cat after all.

Drea sensed my anger and changed her tone. "Oh, he was just rude to me this morning when I came out of the bathroom."

"Drea, how old is Grandma?"

"I think she's gonna be forty-eight next week. Why, you gonna buy her a six-pack?"

"What about Momma?"

"Thirty-four."

"And you're fourteen. You see a pattern?"

"Trent, don't start. It's hot and I ain't in the mood for no damn sermon."

"Drea, calm down. I spoke with this old prison guard today, and he said something that got me to thinking. Do you remember how Momma acted when you told her you were pregnant?"

"Yeah, but you know how Momma is. She cool like that."

"You think that's cool? Laughing and talking about you knew your thirteen-year-old daughter was giving somebody that coochie. That ain't cool; that's ignorant. But you don't know better, because this is all we know. You see, that's just it. We've been had. There are cats I go to school with that got Benzes and they ain't even selling no dope."

"Some people got it like that, Trent; that's all," Drea reasoned.

"I know, but you don't think you can have it. Neither did I. That's because we weren't taught that we could have anything without doing something illegal. Momma didn't say a thing to you about who Gerard's daddy was, did she? She just took you straight down to the welfare office. That's what Grandma did with her. Look at how Grandma lives right down the hall from us. That should tell you that our family hasn't moved forward in damn near fifty years. If you're not careful, you'll be living down the hall from Momma. I'm getting up outta here."

"Well, where you gonna go?"

I didn't have an answer. The possibility of living a different kind of life was still too new. But I knew I'd be graduating from high school in a few weeks, and I wanted more than sitting around the house doing nothing. Or joining the other men in my family behind bars.

I checked Drea—she was feeling the same spark that the old man had started in me. She was a good person, tried to be a good momma to Gerard. She deserved more than a rat-hole down the hall from the one we'd grown up in.

"I don't know yet, but I'ma figure something out."

"Well, let me know, because you ain't leaving me," Drea said as she stood up with Gerard and walked back up to the apartment.

I sat on the steps for the next hour, thinking about what the old man had said and trying to make plans for my future. I was deep in thought when my lifelong friend Skilz rolled up on a mountain bike.

"What's up, Playa?" Skilz asked, joining me on the step.

"I'm cool. Whazzup with you?"

"Chillin'. Got a pocket full of money and two new chicken heads, so life is grand, my man. Thought you went out to Jackson today."

"I did, but Lance's ass is in the hole."

"Your brother is loco. I got locked up this morning; dumb-ass cops got their big guns and kicked in my momma's door, thinking they had a drug kingpin or something. Ended up with a lame-ass possession charge. I'll beat it with a public defender," Skilz laughed, pulling out a bag of weed and splitting a Philly blunt down the middle.

My watch said it was three in the afternoon. "They must've come for you in the wee hours," I said.

"Man, them fools came at six this morning. I just got out about thirty minutes ago and I went straight to the weed house." Skilz removed a backpack from his shoulder. "But you know why I'm here, baby. I got the package that's gonna stop you from living the broke life."

"Man, I've been thinking. I ain't gonna be able to get down."

"Fool, as long as it took you to come up with your half of the money to load up, you need to sell this. At least until you make your money back. This shit is so good it sells itself. All you do is sit out on these steps all day, anyway. I guarantee you this pound will be gone in less than a week. It'll be the easiest dough you ever made."

"You go ahead. I'll have to take the loss. I gotta do some other things."

"Damn, dog, you sure? I mean, you know I ain't letting you go out with a loss. I gotta get somebody else to move this stuff, but I'll give you your half back. What you got cooking?"

"All I know is I gotta make some moves. I'm tired of living like this."

"Oh, you want some big dough." He grinned. "I told you, I got a connect in Florida."

"Nah, dog, I want to make mine the right way."

"Who the hell you been talking to?"

"I'm just trying to avoid prison. Want to keep livin' free. That's all."

"Prison? Man, that's a piece of cake. They got air-condition, three hots and a cot, cable television. All of the homies up in there. Hell, it ain't as bad as it seems, dog."

"That's just it, man. We living so fucked up that even prison ain't that bad."

"Well, Trent, that's just the hand that God dealt us. I'm dealing from under the deck and playing mine. White man don't want you anywhere but where the hell you at. So I'ma get my grind on," Skilz said, checking his two-way pager. "Look here, my man, I got money to make. I'ma holla at you later 'bout that change. I owe you six hundred, but if he moves it with the quickness, I'll give you seven. You be easy."

"Peace, Skilz."

Skilz straddled the bike frame and stared at me for a moment. "You might make it out, dog. You've always been a square-ass. Maintain."

I stood to go back in the apartment but stopped when I saw Momma walking up with a few bags of groceries.

"Hey, did you get some diapers?" I asked.

"Yeah, now grab these bags. I thought you said you were going to see your brother."

"I did. No visitors."

"That hardhead boy. What'd he do this time?"

"The guards said he got in a fight. Who's that dude in your room?"

"None of your damn business, and you bet' not have said nothing to him. He's the one that bought these groceries. You know your crackhead-ass uncle done came over and stole my WIC card."

She's calling *him* a crackhead? I thought. Ain't that the pot calling the kettle black!

"You know I need money for some shoes."

"Shoes for what?"

"I'm graduating in two weeks."

"Damn, I forgot about that. I just saw Damon riding off. Why didn't you get the money from him? You know he selling all the dope 'round here."

"Never mind." I don't even know why I asked my mom for any money. Maybe that was my way of reminding her that I was graduating. I don't think she's been to the school in the four years I've gone there.

"How you know you graduating, anyway? I don't ever see you wit' no books."

"Trust me, I'm graduating." I didn't tell her that I had a 3.7 grade point average. She probably wouldn't know what that was, anyway. She'd quit school in the ninth grade to have her first baby. Grandma had quit in the eighth grade. I'd wondered if Drea was going to make it all the way.

When Mom and I walked into the apartment, we got the shock of our lives. Max had Drea pinned down on the floor, trying to force her legs apart. I pounced on him like a cat. I pulled him off of my screaming sister and hit him in the stomach with all the force I had. He doubled over and reached in the small of his back and bought out a small silver gun. Before he could get off a shot, Drea threw a glass that hit him in the eye. He dropped the gun and I picked it up.

"You've got five seconds to get the hell out of this house and stay out," I said, aiming straight at his head.

Momma reached over and took the gun from me. She placed it in her purse and told Max to wait. Then she looked at me with hatred in her eyes. "Who in the hell do you think you are?" she spat.

Then she turned her attention to Drea. "You ain't nothin' but fast-ass little heifer, you know that? If you wasn't walking around here with your ass all out then nobody would be trying to stick something in you all the time."

"Momma, I swear I didn't do anything," Drea cried.

"Shut the hell up!" Momma screamed, then turned her wrath back on me. "And Trent, since you think you bad enough to be the man of the house, you get yo shit and leave. Now!"

Gerard's screams matched Momma's.

I walked into the room I shared with Drea and started packing my things. I didn't know where I was going, but I knew I'd never sleep another night in this apartment. My time had come. Drea was right behind me, packing her and Gerard's few pieces of clothes, too. "Drea, you gonna have to stay until I can find a place," I said. "I know it's hard, but you can't have a three-month-old baby out on the streets."

"I can't stay here with her anymore. I'm tired of her men trying to have sex with me. This ain't the first time, Trent."

"You a lying-ass heifer," Momma screamed from the doorway. "I was gonna let you stay, but get your shit and take that knotty-head little boy with you, too."

"Momma, what the hell has somebody mixed up with your crack? Now, you can put me out, but Drea ain't going nowhere. I can't believe you taking sides with some punk-ass man over your own daughter, just cuz he buys you some damn groceries."

"What the hell you ever bought? Huh? Not a got-damn thing. All y'all ever do is take. Now you take your shit and leave. Y'all ain't gonna kill me."

"You died the minute you stuck that crack pipe in your mouth." I said, ducking as she threw a picture frame at my head. "Come on, Drea, I don't want you and Gerard staying here with this shell of a woman."

We packed what we could and walked out into the hot streets. Drea carried Gerard, and I carried the bags. I didn't have a clue which way to go, but I knew we couldn't stay in those damn projects.

"Are we going to a shelter?" Drea asked.

"No. I don't want to ever live off the state again. Come on."

We walked up Abernathy Boulevard and through the West End. I was wondering how much farther we could make it, when something the old prison guard said came to me. "You never know who you'll need," he'd told me. Right now I needed the pastor of this church that I'd attended a few times. We walked up Westview Drive into the church parking lot.

There wasn't a car in sight. All the hope drained from my body. With nothing to lose, I knocked on the doors, and to my surprise, they were open. We walked in. Drea fell into the first chair she saw, exhausted.

"I'm Pastor Streeter. Can I help you?" I didn't recognize him, but I nodded. He brought us cold drinks and offered to hold Gerard while I told him what had happened.

"Could we stay here for the night?" I asked, my heart hammering with nervous hope.

"I can do better than that, son," he said. "Y'all are coming to my house. My wife and I just moved out to Stone Mountain and we have plenty of room for both of you and the little man, too. Y'all can stay as long as you like, until you get on your feet."

Mrs. Streeter was just as nice as the pastor, and welcomed us into their spacious home with open arms.

A few weeks later, I was sitting on the side of the bed in my room, brushing the dust off of the shoes that the pastor let me borrow for graduation, when Mrs. Streeter handed me the telephone.

"Hello?" I said.

"Trent Jordan, this Dr. Wilkins over at Clark Atlanta University. I'm calling to inform you that your application has been accepted. Congratulations. I'll see you in August."

"Thank you. Thank you very much," I said, trying to take it all in. I hung up the phone and called for Drea. She came running. I told her the good news and shared with her what the old prison guard said to me that changed my frame of mind. Before I heard those words, I would've taken Skilz up on his offer to sell drugs, which would've paved my path to prison. But instead, I was going where no other person in my family had ever been: to college.

"Drea, remember when I told you I spoke with this old prison guard out at Jackson?"

"Yeah," she said.

"Well, he summed up our whole family history with an old proverb. He said, *'If you wanna keep getting what you're getting, then keep doing what you're doing.'* Our family has been doing the same thing generation after generation and getting the same results. I wanted something that we've never had, so I had to do something that we've never done. Now, go get my nephew dressed. I'm gonna graduate today!"

"Okay." She smiled through proud tears.

"And Drea?"

"Yeah?" She turned.

"In a few years, you'll be doing this, too!"

And Then She Cried

Edwardo Jackson

"The tears in your eyes do not blind you." —African, Togolese

Divorce is like heart's hangover. The feeling lingers there, a dull, throbbing pain in the back of your spirit, a lead weight of emotion that makes the whole world cloudy and sluggish. If it's possible to have a hangover and be drunk at the same time, I was efficiently working my way there. I didn't know how many Midori sours it would take, but I was on my fifth one and giving it a damn good try.

This was not how I had pictured my life: divorced, single mother of two at twenty-five. How marketable was that? Not that I was going to be in the market for love (or life's bastardization of the concept in practical application) anytime soon, but still . . .

I sat on the bar stool, a world unto myself of sorrow and confusion. It was March 30, 1981. The whole bar was abuzz with news reports of the assassination attempt on the president. TVs all around the bar blazed with well-coiffed, overly articulate anchormen soberly telling us that our actor-president (whom *I* didn't vote for) almost bought the farm today.

I could concentrate only on the divorce papers burning in my hand, branding my palm like a scarlet letter of love's failure and the human mockery of sacrament. What I would pride myself for—*did* pride myself for—was that I would never cry over a man. Any man. Ever.

Finishing off my sixth Midori and gearing up for a seventh, I almost didn't notice him.

"You want my arm to fall off?"

I'm smooth. Classic. Looking and sounding a little like Billy Dee, if I must say so myself.

She looked lonely, like she needed a friend. I had been watching her

for a while. An attractive woman like her—dark, curly natural, busi-
ness pantsuit outfit, eyes that could wash the windows of your soul . . .
Unblemished skin as brown as brushed copper. A dimple in her cheek
that emerged when she frowned or smiled. But I had never seen her
smile.

So I extended the drink to her, holding it out for thirty oblivious sec-
onds.

"You want my arm to fall off?" he repeated.

Maybe I did. Since he was a man, that's not all I wanted to cut—I
mean, to *fall* off. As handsome as he was—in a cookie-cutter, wavy-
haired, professional-black-man sort of way with deep obsidian-dark
eyes that seemed to answer every question you would never dare ask—
I wasn't in the mood today. Not after what I'd been through, freshly divorced at twenty-five.

"Does that still work?" I asked.

"Excuse me?"

"I mean, I love *Lady Sings the Blues* as much as the next black
woman, but I've heard better lines."

He offered a charming smile, a disarming one given my hostile,
drunken state. "Well, I *have* been holding this out to you for almost a
minute now." He slid the glass over to me, brimming with green and
yellow liquid, a cherry adorning the top. "Midori, right?"

She eyed me suspiciously. "Right." She gobbled up the drink, killing
half of it in one elongated sip.

"Care to talk about it?" I offered, sliding onto the bar stool next to
her.

Her face creased like the delicate folds in origami—elegant, com-
plex, and beautiful all at the same time. She considered my proposal.

To be honest, I didn't know where it came from, myself. This was
my day. At twenty-five, I was one of the youngest anchors in the history
of WKOK-TV. Okay. So I wasn't anchor yet. I was going to be, come
Monday. All those years of sacrificing love for career, commitment for
control, and women for work had finally paid off. I had come down to
the bar for a celebratory drink—and to tell everyone I knew. But she
had stopped me. Captivated me with her beauty fighting against itself.
Like her soul was paved beneath a highway of pain. Something about
this woman made me forget myself for once. Something about this
woman made me want to know more, first.

I snorted. "Would it do any good?"

"Surprise yourself," he said.

I examined his eyes carefully. Aw, what the hell. At the rate I was going, I wouldn't remember this conversation in the morning anyway. "What do you call it when the economy slows down?"

"A recession?"

"Oh. You're right. No." I adjusted slowly, ponderously. "I misspoke. What do you call it when a business fails?"

"Oh, no," he gasped. "You're bankrupt?"

"No, *he* is. There was a bankruptcy of emotion, so I filed for Chapter Seven." I waved the papers at him.

"Hmmm. That's kind of deep."

I rolled my eyes. "Not at all. He's shallow. He's a wading pool of a man."

He placed his hand on top of mine reassuringly. Reflexively I drew mine back. "Don't touch me."

"Sorry," I said. I'd always been able to make people feel comfortable, especially after just meeting them. It was what made me work so well in on-camera interviews. It startled me that it didn't work with her. "Do you miss him?"

"Of course I miss him," she said. "I miss him and I hate him."

She finished her drink. "But I hate him more than I miss him."

"Any particular reason?" I inquired. I was determined to find out what could possibly eclipse the brightness of her beauty. I also wanted to know what it was about her that made me act so outside myself.

"He never listened," she muttered. "He never, ever listened."

I grew silent—and listened.

"He would talk about his practice, his patients, his nurses, all this crap that didn't amount to a hill of beans if you took them outside his own little world. He wasn't saving lives; he was a podiatrist. He saved feet. Feet! It was always about him. I was his wife, the mother of his children, and I lived in the margin of his life. His life was all about work, when he needed to work on his life."

I chose my words carefully. "That doesn't mean he didn't love you. It takes a lot of dedication and discipline to be a doctor."

"I'm a writer. I wrote an entire book while we were married and he never once read it."

That shut me up. Momentarily. "How old are your children?"

"Four and three."

"Names?"

I gave him a look. We were getting a little personal, and I wasn't all the way drunk yet. "What's your story?"

"I don't have one," was his answer. "I want to know yours. The man you married never listened to you. The least I can do is listen."

Against my will, my eyes softened. "Thanks. I really could use that."

And then we had it, one of those amazing conversations where you talk about everything and nothing. This was one of those conversations that radiated spectacularly in three dimensions and would forever be wondrously frozen in the fourth. The formula for its success was so simple: I talked, he listened. Even after seven Midoris, I amazed myself with how much I had to say and how clearly I said it. It was as if a five-year dam of personality had been broken. Against the floodgates of my expression, he quietly punctuated my comments with an attentive masculine grunt, acknowledged a statement with a knowing nod, and accentuated a sarcastic quip with a sharp bubble of laughter that ended in an abbreviated snort.

When he did speak—and it was always briefly—our chemistry ranked up there with Hepburn and Tracy, Ross and Williams. So I felt compelled to tell him about it.

"Do you know why Lady Sings the Blues *worked so well?"*

I wondered what made her think of that. I knew why I thought it worked, but I doubted her answer would be, "Because Billy Dee is the smoothest cat alive."

Our conversation had been amazing. I had forgotten all about my promotion and become wrapped up in this slighted woman's tale of marital neglect. How she somehow juggled a blossoming writing career and raising two kids. How she would talk to her daughter's dolls because at least they would listen. How she would wait up for her husband on even his latest nights. How she had wished he had cheated on her instead of simply falling out of love with her.

It was a disservice. This "wading pool of a man" who had married her and done the world a disservice by stopping up all of the love and vitality she had to give. It made me angry that such a wonderful woman could be so woefully overlooked. It made me sad that she would listen all the time but no one would listen to her.

"Why?"

We were in a taxi by now, on the way back to her place. I was not convinced she could make it up the steps to her third floor "transitional apartment" on her own. She had downed ten Midori sours by my count. She was so far above legally drunk, she needed a telescope to see it.

She started to tear a little. "Because he loved her."

I started to have that leaky sound to my voice, so I snipped it with umbilical precision, right at its belly button. Stronger now: "He really loved her. I don't know where acting ended and reality began, but the way Billy Dee treated Diana . . . you could just tell that he really loved her."

"Mmmm." That occasional male grunt that I loved.

"Remember his eyes when he found her strung out in L.A.?"

"Heartbreaking," he said.

"Exactly. Absolutely heartbreaking." I sat in silence for two blocks. "I've never had someone love me like that."

I didn't think he thought about this before he said it, since I have never known a man to be capable of so much depth and unplanned honesty: "Neither have I."

We were at her apartment building now, a brownstone in a respectable part of the city. I helped her out and into her building. She slumped against me, so I carried her. Not too unlike a couple on their wedding night. By the third floor, her floor, she'd regained control and balance. She got on her feet and led the way to her apartment door.

She lingered in the open doorway. I already knew her kids were at her mother's for the week. I already knew she was feeling the heat between us. I already knew she had been celibate by default, the result of a nonresponsive husband and being married with children.

I liked her; I really did. She was so vulnerable and honest. Drunk, too. It didn't seem fair. Definitely wasn't my style. I had respected her enough to listen, and she had respected me enough to tell me. This wasn't the time. Tomorrow, I would start to pack my bags to move to a new city and a new affiliate. Tomorrow, she wouldn't even remember this conversation. Or me.

I drew him in close, inhaled his light masculine scent. Men were good for at least one thing. Tonight, I was determined to see just how good his thing was.

I kissed him. Yes, *I* kissed *him*. It was the first time I had initiated anything with a man since high school. I had never had to; that wasn't my job. But tonight I was drunk, he was hesitant, and I was horny. Thirteen months of marriage without getting any would make anyone horny. It was the softest kiss I had ever had.

Instead of following me inside, he smiled oddly, standing in my doorway. If there had ever been a prelude to sex, that kiss had been it.

I retreated back to him, a question in my eyes that I wanted his all-knowing, question-answering eyes to answer.

"Good night." He said it with all of the gallantry and class of a perfect gentleman. Even in spite of me. His arm did not fall off.

I turned to walk away.

"Brandon and Amira."

I stopped. "Excuse me?"

She smiled. "My kids' names are Brandon and Amira."

I smiled back. Gave a subtle nod. Continued on my way.

I didn't even know her name.

Same script, different cast. For a nondrinker, I was determined to get drunk tonight. Funny, it was this same bar, same story, same stool.

That's right. Divorced. Again. Same two kids, just ten years older. So was I. Ten years older, not ten years wiser.

I didn't know what it was that had made me so optimistic. I didn't know what it was that had made me want to believe in this fable called love. Maybe I was destined to be a writer of love but never to experience it for myself.

Did I love him? No. I didn't even put up a fight. The reason I was with him in the first place was because he was the first one to show a single mother of two genuine affection and commitment instead of angling for a fleeting sexual fling. For some reason, single guys think single moms over thirty are desperate, so afraid we'll never find love again that we fall happily on our backs at the first sign of a man's half-raised eyebrow. I settled for him because I *was* desperate and over thirty. I wanted something, even if it wasn't him. I didn't love him, didn't deserve him, and sure as hell didn't keep him.

At least this one was original enough to be a cliché. This one did cheat on me, and it was all my fault. My second husband, I had determined, was going to listen. I made him listen, and listen, and listen. I had turned into that person I didn't like—my first husband. I had run my second husband into the ground with my drive and determination to be heard. Someone was going to listen to me. I had made him "listen" so much, he couldn't hear me anymore. He had turned to someone else so that he could talk.

The bar was ablaze with activity, just as it was the last time. Divorce papers fresh in hand while everyone else eye-devoured the TVs, I was vaguely aware of what was going on. It was January 16, 1991, and the United States had just invaded Iraq. I couldn't have cared less.

"You want my arm to fall off?"

I didn't know if she was wearing the hell out of that dress or if the dress was wearing her. Her professional elegance only seemed to have gotten better with age. Sumptuous in a long, light-colored, form-fitting but classy dress, she was a testament to a point of mine. Black women aged well, if they ever aged at all. It was that very same woman from this very same bar on that one intriguing, serendipitous night almost ten years ago.

This time I didn't have a drink in my hand. I just had my hand. And that was good enough. Didn't want her to think I existed just to get her drunk. Besides, I wanted her to have a clear head tonight.

"Not before I shake it," she smiled, wobbly. She shook my hand. "How long have you been watching me this time?"

"Long enough to know that I should." I smiled. Slid next to her on the bar stool. "How are Brandon and Amira?"

"What?" That startled her. I suppressed my smile.

"Your kids? How are your kids?"

He remembered. Impressive. So he *had* been listening that night. Either this guy had a memory like an African elephant or he had really been paying attention to me. "They're good," I said, or more like stumbled through words that made a vague attempt at speech. "Growing."

"Fourteen and thirteen, right?"

"Yes," I almost whispered, amazed. "How have you been?"

I wanted to tell her the truth. I had been great. I was great. My career had skyrocketed in the decade since we had met. WKOK had just been the beginning. I had bounced around three other affiliates, each stop being more important than the last. Now I had left the security of an anchor's desk in one of the nation's largest markets for a shot at network. All that was left to cap off my career started tomorrow. This was my last night of national obscurity. But instead of indulging my rampant self-promotion, I could tell, once again, that she needed a friend.

"Okay" was my answer. Again, I noticed a drink in her hand, however lightweight. She had upgraded slightly—Amaretto sour this time. Any drink that came with a cherry wasn't a real drink.

I noticed papers in her hand. "How have you been?"

Her hesitance broadcast her thoughts. By the time the words came out of her mouth, I already knew I shouldn't have asked the question. "Divorced. Again. Today." She waved her drink at the competition on-screen. "Once again, my timing is impeccable."

I started to reach for her hand but halted. She saw me edit myself. Grabbing my hand, she recut the footage.

I laid earnest eyes upon her. "Want to talk about it?"

"No."

"Will you talk about it?"

She sighed. "Yes."

Once again, I opened up my world to this not-so-perfect, all-too-handsome stranger. In ten years, we hadn't missed a step. Our beats overlapped, our lives intertwined, and we fell into a natural rhythm, all in a few hours. Once again, we meshed for success: I talked; he listened. I knew exactly what I was doing: dominating the conversation, unfurling my world to the one man on the earth that I, strangely, felt comfortable with in moments of pain. He did the one thing my husband—*ex*-husband—hadn't. He cared. He listened and he cared. He purposefully put his life on the back burner to console some woman he had met once ten years ago, a woman now working on her *second* divorce. He was a selfless, egoless man.

He was an alien.

"I am *not* an alien!" he laughed.

"I have never met a man like you. I didn't know they *made* men like you."

He put a finger to his lips. "Shh. Don't tell nobody."

I gently shook my dizzy little head. "What is your story?"

"My story?"

"Yes. You know a ton of pertinent details of my life. What is *your* story?"

"Ah, but I don't. I don't even know your name."

I smiled. "True. But don't change the subject. Tell me about you."

I shrugged and then told her, broad strokes only. Typical black-boy upbringing with the middle-class home, single mom, and college scholarship. Atypical rise through the journalistic ranks. Told her some of the stories I had broken. I told her just enough to answer her question but not enough to take the focus off of her. I wouldn't let her. Lord knows when I would see her again.

What in the world was I doing? I had a flight to catch at seven in the morning for London, then to Morocco, then to Riyadh. I would do more talking on camera in the next few months than some people would their entire lives. I didn't even know if I would survive what early pundits were already labeling the "Persian Gulf War." I was more than happy to shut up and let this thirty-five-year-old divorcée with two children talk enough for both of us.

In the cab on the way back to her place, I made an observation.

"You know, I've never seen you cry."

I beamed an inebriated, silly smile at him. "You've only seen me twice."

"I know," he acknowledged. "But still, I've seen you at two of the toughest emotional points in your life. And I have never once seen you cry."

"That's right," I affirmed, sobering up slightly. "I don't cry over men. No man is worth my tears."

I didn't care if I sounded like an *Oprah* devotee—it was true. I truly believed that. And how could I cry over a man I never truly loved? That would be implying an emotion, an effect on me that he never really had the power to give.

"A real man wouldn't make you cry," he observed quietly.

We had been here before. This time, she had made it up the steps to her apartment on her own. True, this was a better apartment building to reflect the fact that she was now a best-selling author, but we were outside her apartment door nonetheless. It was two A.M. Her kids were asleep. I had a plane to catch in the morning.

Did I want her? Yes, I did. I kind of knew where she lived and probably should have asked for her phone number. Problem was, I was back into my self-absorbed careerist mode. I knew it; I admit it. I was back to making the same sacrifices I had made to get me to this point. I was going off to war and I might not make it back. Even if I did make it back, I would be coming back to instant stardom and a network anchor's seat. No way did I want to involve her in that. No way would I push her to the margins of my life as her first husband had. No way would I leave her with anything less than a rose-colored view of this man she had enjoyed meeting, if but for two untarnished evenings. Our evening was over.

She kissed me. I kissed her back. I lost all track of what I was thinking.

"Good-night," I said.

"Good-night," she replied.

I started down the stairs. She looked at me as I descended the steps. It wasn't until I hit the first floor landing that I remembered. I wasn't leaving without her name this time.

"What is your name?" I called up to her.
She told me hers. I told her mine. I left feeling content.

This was the first time I had been in this bar *without* divorce papers in hand. In fact, I had vowed that I would never be divorced again. That's because I didn't think I could fall in love again. What was the point when it would always end in disaster?

I was older now, not necessarily wiser. My kids were grown. All I had these days was my work. With two books on the *New York Times* Bestseller List and a movie in production adapted from another, work was better than a man.

Until I saw that man. Again. My decennial reoccurrence. For a change, he was drinking and I was walking into the bar. I had the advantage of seeing him before he saw me. He seemed to be oblivious to the rest of the bar, which buzzed with hushed awe and fear. TVs flickered with the frightening, chilling footage of yesterday's events. It was September 12, 2001.

Like everyone else, I had watched the horror of the worst day in American history. The nation was in shock, in mourning, and I was no different. Perhaps, like the others in the bar, I came to drown my sorrows as well. What surprised me was that my mysterious male friend was not at work like all of his colleagues were.

With pride, I had watched him grow over the past ten years, as had America. He was a household name, a staple of the network. He was the go-to guy in times of crisis. The Persian Gulf War had been his audition. The '92 presidential election had been his coronation. I never once tried to contact him, because I figured if we were meant to meet again, we would. Either he would track me down or happenstance would "happen" upon us again. This time I took happenstance into my own hands.

"You want my arm to fall off?"

Unbelievable. She had found me. Or rather, we had found each other again.

I looked over my shoulder to see her extending a drink toward me. It was green and yellow and had a cherry in it. I snorted. That figured. It matched the one I was finishing in my hand.

"Hi," I creaked.

"Hi," she said, slipping me the drink. She slid onto the bar stool next to me. "You look like hell."

If only she knew. "That's good. I was working my way down from purgatory."

She acknowledged the TVs for a moment. "Tragic, isn't it? I feel so sad . . . so angry."

I nodded numbly. There was so much to it, I didn't know exactly how I was feeling.

"Why aren't you on the air?" *she asked.*

Good question. I couldn't quite explain it myself. I could, but I couldn't. The explanation didn't satisfy me either. "I quit today."

"You quit?" *she said. This was more a statement than a question.* "Why'd you quit?"

I told her the truth. "I lost my appetite for journalism."

He was one of the most popular anchors in the United States. I was flabbergasted. "What happened? Was it the attack? Why don't you love it anymore?"

Maybe my questions were too on the nose, because he quickly changed the subject. "How are Brandon and Amira?"

"Fine. Grown."

"Are you divorced again?"

Cute. "No, not this time." I modeled my bare, brown left hand for him. "See? No ring tan lines."

He let slip a flash of a smile before dousing it in his drink.

"Since when did you start ordering drinks with cherries in them?" I teased.

"Today. It's a special occasion."

Without his normal inquisitive nature, our conversation sank into a black hole. He was not himself at all, as none of us were at this time of mourning and disaster. Why was it that we never met under normal circumstances? Why was it that we never met on a rain-soaked Friday evening, downtown, trying to catch a train or something? Why did we always end up in this bar every ten years?

"Why is it that we always end up meeting at times of disaster?" *she asked.*

I had no answer for that. At least not immediately. "Maybe it's because at times of disaster, all the artifice of life is stripped away, and all we are left with is ourselves. Our basic, human selves."

"That's the how. I want to know the why," *she clarified.*

"Because when we are left with ourselves, obviously, our energies seem to attract each other in times of crisis."

I didn't even know where the words came from. As much as it was truth, I had to push them out like a wheelbarrow full of bricks. I couldn't even believe I could speak logically at a time like this.

That was a great answer. Our energies attracted each other. It had to be so true. How else to explain these chance meetings every ten years? Fate, karma, God—whatever always pushed us together.

"Where were you when you first saw that movie?" I asked. "You know, *Lady Sings the Blues.*"

His face shut down. It was like his mind went blank, whatever light that had been left in his eyes extinguished. Fearful I had said the wrong thing, I forged ahead.

"I was on a date, at a drive-in. I was only sixteen." The memory made me smile. "He was so awkward and nervous; I was so gawky and unsure of my body. I had braces and I remember the jellybeans getting stuck in them. My teeth looked like a disco ball."

A quick, pained laugh escaped him, instantly relieving me. That is, until he cried. I didn't know what to do. I knew it wasn't because I was just that funny, because I wasn't. I didn't know what to say. I didn't know how deeply yesterday's events had affected him. So I went back to my original question. "Do you remember where you were when you first saw that movie?" I inquired weakly.

"Yes," he choked, fighting back sobs. "I was with my sister."

"You have a sister?" I didn't know he had a sister. I didn't know, because I had never asked. I had always talked but never listened.

"Had. I had a sister. She was murdered. Yesterday. On the hundred-and-fifth floor." It was harder and harder for him to speak, each tortured word being beaten out of his abused and battered core.

"I'm so sorry," I said honestly, in a hushed tone.

"I don't know how I'm going to do this!" I cried. "I'm all alone! I am all alone in the world right now! I have worked so hard, all my life, to live the life I was living. And yet I was so alone. I had no one to share it with except my sister. She was the only woman I loved, the only woman I could trust. She was always, always, *there for me. Our parents are dead, our older brother dead, and now . . . now . . . she's dead! And I don't know why in the hell I am* telling *you this!"*

My head hit the bar. Then again. And again. And again. I didn't even realize I was doing it so hard until she placed her hand on top of mine.

I shouldn't have told her what I had told her. There was no way she could possibly understand. She had a family; she had love; she had loved before. I had experienced none of the above. All of the love I had to give someone, I had given to my baby sister, a thirty-six-year-old stockbroker who had worked on the 105th floor of the World Trade Center. The fires from the 103rd floor had them trapped where they were. Frightened, she had called me on her cell phone and I had tried to talk her through it, despite the network's insistence to get me on the air. I had been on the phone with her up until the very last minute. All the way until the phone went dead. And then I saw the collapse.

I had passed up so many opportunities for love for this career. I had channeled any emotions of love I would have had for a woman over to my sister. Ours was a special bond. I hardly ever talked about her to others, but I was proud as hell. And I always would be. Now that I'd lost her, nothing else in this world mattered.

Her hand was still wrapped around mine. Loving, tender, supportive.

"All the love I had to give to her is gone. There is no more love."

"You're wrong," she said, eyes brimming with tears. "There is always love."

She squeezed my hand. Gave me her caring, sympathetic, loving eyes. They reminded me that my life had been all about work, when I had needed to work on my life. She was right. I rewarded her eyes with a smile.

And then she cried.

Pass It On

Margaret Johnson-Hodge

"A friend is someone who knows the song in your heart and can sing it back to you when you have forgotten the words."
—African American

She was going to have a bonfire.

Shelly Anderson was going to drag the old dented charcoal grill from the tool shed, get briquettes, lighter fluid, a match, and start a fire. She was going to stand in the backyard of her rented bungalow and watch flames reach for the sky.

Shelly was going to accept what she'd suspected long ago when the need to create worlds, real and imagined, had hit her. That it was a silly goal, far from reach, and she was chasing a pipe dream.

She was going to tuck away the need in her soul, ignore the whispers in her head, and say good-bye to her secret life. And she was going do it today.

The bungalows, built at the turn of the twentieth century, were small and efficient. Designed for weekend stays during the sweltering days of July and August, when the Great Depression took hold in 1929, weekend getaways became year-round housing.

A seaside community victim of the times, the tiny, somewhat drafty cottages now housed dozens of families in need of affordable housing, ignoring the original purpose—near backyard access to Far Rockaway Beach.

But for Shelly Anderson, the little house had meant much more.

It had been the proximity of the water that drew her to the twenty-by-thirty structure that would be considered claustrophobic by most. She'd made peace with the tiny kitchen, the minute bathroom, a general area some would call a living room, and a bedroom just big enough to fit a queen bed and a bureau. She'd made peace because the ocean breeze, circulating seagulls, and miles of ochre sand spoke a beauty to her that the peeling clapboard could not.

When she'd first come to inspect it, visions of Earl Klugh on the stereo and the scent of briny ocean was all she pictured, imagining herself crafting her stories in a cacophony of good jazz, lapping waves, and keening seagulls. She had been certain that the Atlantic Ocean, a stone's throw away, would give her creative license. That being close to nature would offer up the opportunity to become a real writer.

That had been three years ago.

The thick manila envelope at her front door when she'd come home from work changed that, and Shelly knew like she knew her middle name that this evening her long-held dream would go up in flames.

"What are you doing?"

She didn't see Brenda standing there, but that's how Brenda had come into her life that first time, suddenly and without warning. Shelly had known the bungalow next to her had been empty. Had heard rumors that someone would be renting it, but she had never spied a moving trunk, a U-Haul, or even a key being slipped into the front door.

She had never seen a light go on, heard music spill from an open window, or spied the blue shadows of a television dancing on the walls. Brenda had just revealed herself one spring day when Shelly had been taking out the garbage, a friendly hello dancing from the other side of the chain-link.

"*I'm Brenda. Brenda Connor-Bey,*" she had offered, a slim caramel hand extended over the fence.

Shelly had hastily wiped hers, extended it, and shook. "*Shelly Anderson. Nice to meet you.*"

"*Nice to meet you, too, Shelly Anderson.*"

That had been a year and a half ago, but unlike that first time, today Brenda's presence on the other side of the chain-link wasn't welcomed. Shelly stood in her backyard, willing Brenda away.

"You barbecuing, this time of year?"

"Something like that."

"Is that what I think it is?" It was like Brenda to notice, even in the dimness, the package nestled in the foot-high weeds. "Don't tell me you're going to burn it."

Born in secret, uncertain of a final destination, Shelly's manuscript had taken on a life of its own, forging a deep, strong bond between the two women. But it was about to go up in flames.

"Yeah, Bren. I am." As Shelly looked at her, all the sorrow, all the disappointment she'd felt over the years moved through her. She'd been riding the merry-go-round forever, arm outstretched, but never able to grasp the elusive brass ring. It was time to get off the ride, a decision that Shelly knew but Brenda was only beginning to sense as she considered her friend across the chain-link fence.

It had been Brenda who had taken a red pen to Shelly's manuscript, slashing and questioning, insisting that it could be better. Begrudgingly Shelly had agreed, and when the time was right, Brenda had taken her to a meet-the-agents affair last fall. Shelly hadn't gotten an agent, but she did gain determination. Taking another six months to fine-tune her story, she had begun the process of sending it out.

Letting Brenda lead her had been easy. After all, Brenda was a *real* writer, with publications, residencies, and workshops under her belt. But that was then. This was now, and the woman coming quickly up her driveway no longer swayed her.

"I'm not going to let you" were Brenda's words as she snatched the still-wrapped manuscript off the ground. "You want to be scared, be scared, but I won't let you burn it." Brenda turned it over in her hand. "You haven't even opened it."

"What's the point?"

"The point is maybe, just maybe, there's a letter inside telling you what you need to fix to make it better. That maybe this"—Brenda shifted the package again, found a name—"this Erin Mercer of Baker Street Press likes your style. Wants to see more, something else."

"They don't send back the manuscript if they like it; isn't that what you said?"

"They don't send back the manuscript if they don't. It's a crapshoot Shelly, just like life. But hiding your head in the sand doesn't get you anywhere, and that's all you're doing. Do you really want to destroy that beautiful paragraph you wrote about your character walking the beach in wintertime with the seagulls painting the sky in somber colors of cinder and ash? Or that other one, where she's on the subway and it's so crowded sweat is running down the side of her face but she can't even lift her hand to wipe it?"

Shelly had forgotten.

She'd forgotten how it had taken eight rewrites to get that subway scene right. How she struggled with the perfect adjective to describe not only the color but the depth of those seagulls.

Silence came, Brenda staring at her hard. She was waiting for Shelly to get it, to accept that this was not the end.

The seconds ticked by, everything about Shelly saying she had stopped believing. Horse to water, Brenda could not make her drink. "You want to burn it, destroy some of the best words I've read in a long time?" She tossed the package on the blackened grill. "Go ahead. Burn it."

"It's the last one," Shelly found herself defending. "Twelve houses and this is rejection number twelve."

"How do you know what it is? You haven't opened it yet."

"It's supposed to be just a letter, a nice little legal-size envelope—that's what I was supposed to have gotten."

"Full of 'we love your work and want to pay you a trillion dollars and get you on *Oprah*'?" Shelly blinked, the secret beneath the secret revealed.

Yes, she wanted to be a writer, but she wanted wealth and fame with it. Shelly wanted to make the *New York Times* Bestseller List, set the literary world on fire.

"What did I tell you?" Brenda asked, face pinched. "Let me re-phrase that. What did *my* mentor tell me?"

John O. Killens, Brenda's mentor. An African-American writer so powerful that the sheer strength of his words caused the Pulitzer Committee to remove the Pulitzer Prize for Fiction category several times during the 1950s and '60s. John O. Killens, author extraordinaire, who had shared his knowledge with the likes of Walter Mosley, Nikki Giovanni, and Maya Angelou. John O. Killens, who had taken Brenda under his wing.

"Long-distance runner, remember that? He said any good writer wants to be one. That you want to get in the race and stay. You don't want to sprint hard and lose steam halfway. You want to pace yourself. Make your success a long journey. Getting a trillion dollars and making the *New York Times* Bestseller List your first time out won't get you there."

Shelly knew the truth of those words, but something in her had been broken. All she wanted was a healing. "I worked so hard," she declared, voice choked. "You know how hard I worked. Getting up at five in the morning, to write. Going to bed at two, three in the morning, to write."

"You think I don't know? Of course I do, and it's all right there in that envelope. But you're too scared to acknowledge that. Would rather destroy it than find out."

Brenda's words were water on a sheet of glass, refusing to stay put, sliding away. Shelly had given her all to that book already. The returned package meant she would have to give more. There simply was no more.

She lit the match. Watched it blaze orange in the gathering darkness. Into the barbecue grill she tossed it, the match making contact with the package. Burning for a split second, it went out.

Brenda reached for the envelope. With a spit-dabbed finger, she rubbed the burn hole. Turning, Brenda headed down the driveway. There was no need to look behind her. No need to see if Shelly was following. She was.

They sat in the front room, honey light spilling from table lamps, the yellowish glow of the old ceiling fixture casting soft shadows. They sat quiet, reflective, without words. Time slipped into slow mode as seconds moved like hours, each measure drawn to an unbearable stillness. Shelly knew why Brenda wasn't speaking, and Brenda had no plans to. She had drawn the horse to water, but it would be up to the mare to drink.

Shelly fidgeted for a seventh time and glanced quickly at the package on the table. She looked away, looked back at it as words trickled up her throat. "Sometimes I think about the words I've written and can see all that it is. Other times, it's like I'm fooling myself."

"That's natural."

"Doesn't feel natural. Just feels like flip-flopping. How come I don't know one way or the other?"

"Because then you'd be settling. You'd be settling by deciding you have talent or you don't. A real writer never settles."

"What do you mean?"

"A real writer will never look at something and say, 'It's the best I can do.' A real writer will say, 'It works, but next time I will make it better.' The moment you start thinking your stuff is perfect, that's the day you stop being a writer."

"I always try to make it better."

"I know."

"But that part you were talking about, where Jackie is walking on the beach and the seagulls are filling the sky, I know I can't make that any more perfect."

"The key thing is, you have to at least try."

Two pairs of eyes dusted the manila envelope. One glanced away, settling on the other. "You ready?"

Shelly took a breath, another, nervous laughter leaving her. "No. I'm so not ready."

"But that doesn't mean you won't . . . you can do this Shelly. I know you can, and somewhere inside of you, you know you can, too. You've been ducking and weaving long enough. It's time."

"For what?"

"To not only accept, but *embrace* the fact that God gave you a talent. To own it, you have to get beyond your fear. The first step is taking this work that you swear on your grandfather's grave is perfect and make it better."

The right hand, second finger had the longest fingernail. This was the one she used to put a small tear into the envelope.

"Just paper—you can open it."

Shelly dragged her finger with force, determination channeling through the digit until it bumped against the opposite edge. Barrier gone; a way in, her whole palm nestled inside. Swallowing, she willed her soul to grab the manuscript, pull it out. Did so.

Her eyes scanned the top sheet, the letterhead embossed, inviting, special. Slowly she let her eyes drift, revealing six paragraphs of words written just for her.

Brenda moved closer. "What does it say?"

Shelly couldn't answer yet, her eyes refusing exact words. She chose the five empty spaces between each segment, conjuring up lost possibility and new hope.

Brenda leaned in closer, trying to read without benefit of her glasses. "What's it saying?"

Brown eyes skimmed to the first paragraph. "Oh. My. God," falling from her lips like shimmery diamond dust.

"What?"

But Shelly couldn't speak, could only read as her mouth gave birth to a smile, the sudden wetness at the corner of her eyes.

"Gotta get my glasses," Brenda decided, vanishing, coming back, glasses fixed on her nose as she nestled next to Shelly, searching out the text, eyes growing wide. "*A Bitter Winter* was one of the most powerful pieces I've read in a long time.' Did you see that, Shelly? Did you see that?"

Shelly was in no position to answer. Words of praises filling her vision, the validation she'd longed for arriving. A thrill ride that left her breathless—Shelly didn't think her heart could bear the joy. She was on the verge of shattering into a thousand pieces when she reached the last paragraph and the joy left so quickly, the muscles of her heart hurt.

She said nothing. Just held the paper stiffly in her hands, allowing Brenda to catch up, get to the bitter destination, too.

"Oh," Brenda uttered a few minutes later.

"Yeah, oh."

"Damn."

"Yeah, damn."

"It happens that way sometimes, Shelly."

"But why now? Why couldn't they have waited to fold? How come when my novel is just what they were looking for, they're closing their doors?"

"But they wanted you; you read it yourself. Baker Street Press wanted *you*."

"What good is that when they are closing their doors?"

"The good is the praise this woman took time and energy to give you. The good is that somebody out there saw you worthy of publishing, and just because they are going out of business certainly doesn't mean this Erin Mercer is. She's going to get with another house, and believe you me, she won't forget about *A Bitter Winter* anytime soon. That's the good. And I bet you my last dollar that when she does, she will be telling anyone who will listen about this fantastic new writer named Shelly Anderson and how she deserves a look."

"You think so?"

"I know so. Five paragraphs of praise? People don't do that. They don't take time from their busy schedule to write to somebody they've never heard of unless they see something potent in their work."

Shelly's eyes left the letter, settled on the woman who had come into her life. She understood all that Brenda had done for her. Realized how she had toted the hope that Shelly herself could never quite manage. A shift came into her, a pressing need to speak arriving.

"Thank you."

"For what?"

"For caring, for believing, for keeping my dreams alive."

"You did the hard work."

"Because you made me. Wouldn't take no for an answer."

"Just passing it on," Brenda said with a careful smile. "John O. passed it down to me, and now I'm passing it down to you. When your turn comes, you'll pass it on, too."

"My turn?"

"Yes, your turn. One day someone will come into *your* life. Some Chicken Little, lacking self-belief and faith. You be there for them. Be there like I am. Like John O. was . . . pass it on."

Shelly's eyes drifted, settling on the darkness pressed against the window. Poised at the gate, ready for the long haul, the faith she had not quite gained glimmered on the unseen horizon nonetheless.

Felicia and the Prodigy

Tayari Jones

"The best advice comes from wisdom and experience."
—African American

When Felicia woke up, she thought that it was nighttime because it was dark and because she was still in the jeans and sweater she had worn the night before. She glanced at her clock and felt the beginnings of a panting panic. Groggy as she was, she knew that it couldn't be six in the evening. She had lain across the bed for a short nap the night before. She hadn't been sleepy but had decided to snooze in order to pass the hours as she waited for the phone to ring. Now, she picked up the phone to make sure that it was still working. The dial tone assured her that the reason that her phone hadn't rung was that Adisa hadn't called. The last time he had called was Thursday night. Friday, Saturday, Sunday made three days.

The situation was fast becoming depressing. Felicia closed her eyes and sank back onto her pillow. Suddenly, she sat up again. Her math test was in just about two hours. Last night, she'd been sure Adisa was going to call before ten o'clock. She'd imagined herself rising from her little snooze, alert, refreshed, and love-inspired. She had planned on using Cupid's little boost to get her through a cramming session for her midsemester exam.

Felicia rested herself on the pillow again. The lilac pouch tucked under the satin pillowcase was supposed to be relaxing. She breathed through her nose, opening herself to the healing potential of aromatherapy. It didn't work. Felicia was miserable. No doubt, Adisa was, too. How long would it be before he put his pride aside and just called her? Whatever she had done to hurt him had been completely accidental. If he would just pick up a phone, she could explain and they could make up and go on.

She let her finger hover over the five numbers on her phone, which would have connected her to his room. But she didn't dial. He would talk to her when he had healed himself enough to communicate. Every man had his own way of mending his heart, or so she had read in *Essence*. A woman could run the risk of accidentally emasculating a man by forcing him to share his vulnerability. Emasculation was serious business, according to the advice column in *Ebony Man*.

She opened her math book in front of her as she tried to eat her breakfast of yogurt, toast, and tea. She swallowed a few creamy spoonfuls of blueberry fruit-on-the-bottom before her stomach threatened to send it all back where it came from. Stress burrowed in her stomach like a family of rats.

At 7:10, Felicia walked to the corner to wait for the campus shuttle. It was cold in the shadow of the huge dormitory in which she lived. Should she dash back inside for a jacket? No, it would warm up by midday. And anyway, her nice coat was in the cleaners. The other one, bulky and boyish, made her look like the Michelin Man. If she ran into Adisa on campus, she wanted to be striking, not cushiony. Felicia shivered in the mauve silk knit and hoped her nose would not run.

The shuttle arrived finally and opened its doors with a sigh. Felicia let out a noisy exhalation of her own as she stepped aboard. The prodigy was sitting on the very back row of the empty bus like it was a stretch limousine. This was just what she needed on a day like this. Prodigies made her nervous. It seemed like they were on campus just to make other people feel stupid. A lot of the time they traveled in little clumps, giggling like a bunch of kids. She hated to see them coming. Adisa felt the same way.

"You know what?" he had told her. "Those prodigies really aren't that prodigious, as far as prodigies go."

"Huh?" Felicia asked through a mouthful of pizza. She wished that she could suck the words back in and come up with something smooth and sweet like the girls who read poetry at Open Mic Night.

"I mean, they're not all that smart."

"Yeah, they are," Felicia protested, feeling like she was giving the obvious answer to a trick question. "You have to be smart to get into college at just ten years old."

"That's what they *want* you to think," Adisa said mysteriously. "Ever wonder why UM got so many prodigies running around? There are more baby geniuses here than at Harvard." He paused for a minute and added, "At least per capita."

"Really?" Felicia had never really thought much about the ratio of prodigies to nonprodigies. But Adisa was the thinker.

"Check this," he said. "The average SAT score for those little guys is only 1350."

"That's good, right?" Felicia had scored 1220, and her guidance counselor had danced around his little office. It had earned her a full scholarship to Howard University. "I mean, 1350 is not bad."

"I got 1340," Adisa said.

"But you were seventeen when you took the test. The prodigies are just little kids."

"And?" Adisa snatched another slice of pizza from the box—one piece over his half, but she didn't bring this to his attention. "Why should they get preferential treatment just because they're young? Every single one of them gets a full ride from the university."

"But Adisa, don't you have a scholarship, too?"

"I don't have a book stipend." Adisa bit savagely at his pizza. "Every time I see one of those little jokers with a bag of books bigger than they are, I get sick to my stomach. Do you know how much those upper-level math books cost?"

Felicia shook her head.

"Well, I do because I have to buy my own. And it's not enough that I have to pay $75 apiece for my books—my tax dollars go to buy theirs, too!" He stuffed the end of the crust into his mouth and finished his thought. "People around here get all worked up about affirmative action, but I haven't heard one peep about all the perks these so-called geniuses get." He slammed his Coke can on the table. It erupted quite dramatically like an aluminum volcano. Felicia had been impressed. Adisa was her dream come true.

As long as she had been old enough to nurture romantic fantasies, Felicia had longed for the opportunity to love an Angry Black Man. Her mother had met her father at Southern University in the spring of 1962. Dad had been expelled for demonstrating with H. Rap Brown. Mama had fallen in love almost instantly, and the two were married the following June. That was the kind of love story that Felicia wanted to star in.

But for the first couple of years there had been nothing. The brothers she met weren't angry at all. There was no segregation to protest, Mandela was free, and L.A. had already burned. The young men's faces were bloated with boredom, and their voices were a generation removed from the rich bass of Felicia's daydreams. More than once, she wondered if she should have accepted that scholarship to Howard.

Three semester hours away from graduation was a little late to contemplate a transfer. She sat at the very front of the bus and tried to stock her short-term memory with the idiosyncrasies of triangles. A pair of eyes tapped her on the back of the head.

She turned to find the prodigy staring at her. He wore a navy blue warmup suit with the university logo on the front. Donated by the basketball team, no doubt. The prodigy stretched his arms across the backs of the seats beside him like he owned the whole bus. In a way, Felicia had to admit, he did. Some rich alumna had donated the entire shuttle system to lend a helping hand to the little tykes who couldn't drive yet. Felicia's parents saw a mention of this gift in the paper and decided that she didn't need that cute little hatchback after all. Felicia fixed her mouth to give the little fellow a dirty look, but he smirked and nodded toward her chest.

Felicia looked down and saw that she had her math book clasped in front of her and he had seen the cover. He, too, had a math book, but it was one of the $75 ones. *DIFFERENTIAL EQUATIONS* was prominently displayed on the cover like the label on a pair of designer jeans. The prodigy turned away to look out the window. His head was large and oddly shaped. His profile approximated a question mark.

Hey hook-head, Felicia wanted to say, *Trig is not all the math I am capable of. It's just all the math I need to graduate.*

The prodigy turned suddenly, as if he had heard her thought words. She was taken aback, even though she knew it was impossible. If prodigies had ESP, they wouldn't waste their time in college; they'd be out buying lottery tickets. The little boy held his hand up like he was waving at her, but only one finger was extended. The middle one.

Felicia gasped like a TV lady saying, "Well, I never!" and turned back to her textbook. The exam was in less than an hour. She didn't have time to worry about some little genius who had probably never had to study for a test in his life. Then, she found herself getting angry at Adisa. If he had called her last night, she would have been able to get some studying done before she went to bed. She took a deep breath and stopped herself. This was her fault. Nobody told her not to study earlier. She had to stop blaming him for all her problems. That's why a lot of brothers didn't like to deal with sisters. *Ebony* had devoted three pages to this subject last February.

The bus passed Adisa's dormitory. She looked up at the building, which looked like a giant honeycomb. His window was the one with a red, black, and green flag in the window. He was up there, she knew. Probably staring at the ceiling, mulling over whatever she had done to offend him. What could it be? She had been overly cautious since their last major fight. She had called him "Murell" at an intimate moment. It was an innocent mistake. He had dumped his slave name only a few weeks earlier. "You don't respect me," he shouted. "Bringing The Man into my bed." He was wrong. She did respect him—admired him, even. And she liked his new name a lot. It sounded angrier than Murell, which had a little bit too much Alabama in it for her liking. It's just that she slipped up every once in a while.

But nothing like that had happened recently. All had been relatively peaceful between them in recent weeks. There was that little thing about the research paper, but she had smoothed that over pretty well. Or at least she thought that she had at the time. But now she revisited the incident. Maybe Adisa was holding some sort of residual grudge. She had only been trying to help. Felicia was typing his research paper when she noticed that he had written *extract* instead of *exact*. She couldn't remember now what he was writing about— justice, vengeance— but whatever it was had to be exacted rather than extracted. She brought it to his attention.

"What are you trying to say?" he had asked.

She said that she wasn't trying to say anything, and let the matter drop. But then she was left to decide if she should type the sentence as written or as she thought that it should be. After a lot of cuticle biting, she typed in what was right. Is that why he hadn't called in three days? Was he exacting vengeance? No, that couldn't be it. They had gotten along quite nicely afterward. She retwisted his locks, gently separating the ones that had fused. He purred contentedly as she rubbed coconut oil into his scalp, and asked her to spend the night. The next day, he drove her to class, sparing her the indignity of riding the prodigy-mobile.

The exam was difficult. Triangles bisected, stretched, and bent into straight lines. Three sides. Three days, not a word from Adisa. Multiple-choice options all looked the same. She chose A most of the time because the letter did have a triangle in it. Could she fail the midterm and still squeak by with a C so she could graduate? Maybe. Would Adisa call her tonight? Maybe. Maybe not.

She excused herself to the bathroom but stopped at a pay phone instead. If she could talk to Adisa, she could apologize for whatever, stop obsessing, and focus on her test. Even though she hadn't studied the night before, there must be some residual knowledge of sines, cosines, and tangents hiding in the crevices of her brain, like mildew in shower grout. If she could just calm down and concentrate, she could extract it.

She slid one quarter of her laundry money in the slot. Carefully dialing with her knuckles to protect her manicure, she played the little song his digits made on the touch-tone phone. It sounded almost like "Twinkle Twinkle Little Star."

Adisa's voice on the answering machine was well-deep and dark. "Leave a message and I'll hit you back when I get back. Peace."

"Hi, this is Feedie." She wanted to sound light and unworried. Unannoyed. Not like she was checking up on him. Not like he had an *obligation* to call her. That was the problem with black women, always wanting to make a man feel obligated. That had been in *Essence*, in "The Men's Issue." Give the man some room, the article instructed, and Felicia memorized that as dutifully as she had the other rules of romance.

"I was just thinking about you since I hadn't heard from you in a while. Call me if you get a chance. Please. Thanks."

She put the phone on the hook and felt not at all better. Hearing Adisa's voice without being able to really talk to him was like sucking a mint that was still in its wrapper. She took a couple of steps away from the phone. But then, with a rush of optimism, she called her own number. "Hello, sorry I missed you. Leave a message and I'll call you back. I promise." At the tone, she pressed the numbers corresponding with Adisa's monogram. A mechanical voice informed her that there were no new messages. Depressing.

Felicia returned to class, slid into her desk, and pondered the tangles of triangles. Her classmates' pencils scratched out equations on scratch paper. Erasers found mistakes, rubbed them out, and replaced them with answers. Felicia filled in the row of A's and handed the sheet to her teacher.

"That was fast," the teacher all but scolded. "Do you want to look it over before you turn it in?"

Felicia shook her head, her hair underscoring the motion with an enviable bounce.

The prodigy was in the hallway, banging on the vending machine. His shirt had come untucked and peeked orange below his jacket. A bag of potato chips dangled from a metal coil inside the machine. With each of his little licks, the bag quavered but didn't drop. Felicia's heart softened. He looked like a regular little boy, mad that his change had been swallowed by the big, bad machine. He brows were lowered with fury and frustration. The prodigy took a couple of steps back from the machine and prepared to kick it with his sumptuous sneakers. Felicia smiled as she imagined the angry young man he might eventually become.

"Let me help." Felicia tilted the heavy machine forward and the chips were freed. The prodigy eagerly retrieved them.

"Thanks," he said. "I'm starving. I'm in the middle of an exam in Diff E.Q. that's killing me."

"Diffyque?"

"You know, Differential Equations."

"Oh," she said. "Diff EQ. I didn't quite understand you at first."

He grinned at her and stuffed his chubby cheeks with chips like a little squirrel. He was cute in a way that only little boys could be. Holding out the open bag of chips, he asked, "Want some?"

Felicia was still much too tense to eat anything, but she was touched by the offer. "No, thank you." She decided that he hadn't given her the finger on the bus this morning. Or, if he had, he didn't know what it meant. She was too sensitive. Adisa was right: she was paranoid. She watched the prodigy munch happily, looking more like he belonged on a playground than on a college campus. Felicia wanted to release him to a world of yo-yos and swing sets like some endangered species she had seen freed on the Nature Channel.

"Tell me something," Felicia said. "Don't you ever feel like you don't belong here? Like you would be better off if you had stayed in grade school?"

The little-boy smile faded into an expression of matter-of-fact genius. "No. That's just propaganda put out by the mediocre people. I fit in here. This is an institution of higher learning, you know." He paused to stuff in another handful of chips. "You, on the other hand, will be lucky if you learn enough math to graduate."

This time Felicia gave *him* the finger, but he had already scampered down the corridor.

By lunchtime, Felicia's appetite had not returned. She sat at a table in the corner of the cafeteria and used the fork to dissect, layer by layer, her vegetable lasagna. She wanted to call Adisa again, but if she left another message she would look like she was stalking him, and that wouldn't be good. Lorena, her roommate from sophomore year, joined her at the table.

"Hey, girl," she said. "What's wrong with you?"

Was it that obvious? "Nothing" she said, hoping Lorena would drop it.

"It's Murell, right?"

"Adisa," she corrected him. "You know he changed his name."

"We got to call him that when he ain't even here?" Lorena laughed and dug into her own meal of roast beef and mashed potatoes. Lorena wasn't exactly *fat*, but Felicia thought that she might want to chill a little bit with the carbs.

"It's not funny," Felicia said.

"Okay, I'm sorry. *Adisa*," Lorena said. "What he do this time?" She had her face in a half smile, like Felicia's life was some kind of sitcom.

"Nothing," Felicia said, not liking the way that Lorena assumed that Adisa was at fault. Women like her, always so quick to jump on a brother's case, are the reason that sisters get no respect. Cut the brothers some slack, cautioned the "Ebony Advisor," or you will be alone.

"Then why you not eating?" Lorena smeared butter on a roll. She looked like she was about to pop right out of her faded blue sweater. *Dress better, feel better; Essence* again. But then again, Lorena probably didn't have a man to dress for. That's why she could sit here and look at Felicia with the same condescending look that the prodigy had. Someone who never had a man didn't know why Felicia would want to keep hers.

Then Lorena smiled. "Come on, Feedie, what's up? I know I give Adisa a hard time, but I don't have nothing against the brother. For real." She slapped Felicia playfully on the forearm. "It's good to see some black-on-black love out here in the Midwest. So you know I'm not going to hate the man."

Felicia appreciated Lorena's use of the word *love*. Adisa never said the *L* word. "How can you just categorize feelings like that?" he wanted to know when Felicia, disregarding *The Sista's Rules*, had asked if he loved her. "You know what's up and I know what's up. Why you need all these specific words?"

"He didn't call me since Friday, and I'm worried about him." Felicia said this like she was concerned that he had been mangled in a car wreck or something like that.

"Don't worry," Lorena said. "I saw him yesterday and he looked pretty healthy." She laughed and pointed at Felicia's plate. "You want that bread stick?"

Felicia didn't want it, but she pinched a little piece off of it and popped it in her mouth to pretend that her digestive system was in good working order in spite of her man situation. The little piece of bread felt like a pebble on her tongue. There was no way she was going to be able to swallow it.

"I saw him this morning, too, come to think of it," Lorena went on, mopping up the gravy from her plate with a roll.

"Where was he?" she asked, even though she meant to project mild indifference. Fat girls always liked to play these kind of games with pretty girls. Not that Felicia thought herself exceptionally pretty. She had a lot of little facial flaws, which she hid with makeup. But she thought that she probably seemed pretty to a girl like Lorena.

"He was right here," Lorena said.

"With who?"

"Nobody," Lorena said.

"He was by himself?" It was too late to pretend that she didn't care. Lorena had a hook through Felicia's bottom lip.

"No," Lorena said. "I thought you meant, was he with a *girl*. He was with some fellas."

"Who?" She tilted her glass of iced tea to her mouth to hide her anxious expression.

"He was with Hanif, Kweku, and them."

"What was he doing?"

"Killing a stack of pancakes, as far as I could tell." She laughed. "I was standing in line behind him. He got so many that I had to wait for them to get some more out from the back. To be so skinny, that brother can really eat."

"He's not skinny," Felicia said reflexively. "He's slim."

"Whatever," Lorena said. "He was all over his breakfast."

It was getting more and more difficult for Felicia to retain the imprint of cool. If Lorena mentioned Adisa's appetite one more time, she was going to scream. How could he stuff himself when they hadn't talked for *three days*? Wasn't his stomach all tied up in knots? Didn't his throat seal itself off at the very thought of her? It had to. They were in (undeclared) *love*. He was probably getting the pancakes for his friends since there was a limit to how many each person could get. They probably just took him out to console him, get him out of the house.

"Did you see him actually *eat* anything, or was he just in here with his friends?"

"What, you think that breakfast is a spectator sport? He was in here grubbin'."

Felicia felt raw, as if she had suddenly broken out in internal hives. This was worse than the time she found a strange hairbrush in his bathroom. The brush had been heavy with crinkled strands. Felicia had held it to her nose. It smelled of sandalwood. All the Open Mic Poetry Night girls wore oils that smelled like incense. And they all had audaciously kinky hair. Felicia stormed out of the bathroom. She stood in the middle of the room, brandishing the brush.

"What is this?" She put one hand on her hip.

He looked up from *The Source*. "A brush, looks like."

"Whose brush?"

"How am I supposed to know? You the one got it in your hand." He turned a page.

"It was in your bathroom."

"No, it wasn't." His eyes didn't leave his magazine.

"You had some other girl in here." She kept her neck rigid. She would not be a chicken-head. A stereotype. She took her hand down from the hip.

"How you know?"

"My hair isn't like this."

"What you mean?" He put his magazine down slowly.

"My hair is not . . ." She searched her mind for the right word, but there was really no synonym. "Nappy like this."

He put his magazine down slowly. The rapper on the cover frowned with disapproval. "You got so many problems that I don't even know where to start schooling you. First off, you got the Eurocentric view of relationships. Monogamy, that ain't African. What's African is polygamy. You got shackles on your brain, Feedie." He walked toward her. "My hair not nappy," he mimicked her with a high-pitched nasal song. "You scared of that hair, ain't you, Feedie?"

She backed up. "I'm not scared. I want to know who has been over here."

"You look scared to me. You think that nappiness is contagious? Worried some of that Africa might rub off on you?" He snatched the brush away from her. "Bourgie girls like you make me sick."

"It's not like that . . ." Felicia hadn't meant to make him *sick*. She was hoping for a dramatic show of affection and contrition. Somehow things had gone terribly wrong and she had to fix them. "I don't have anything against the girls who wear their hair natural. For real. It looks real nice on some of them." She was embarrassed by her scrupulously maintained bob. "I would do mine like that, too, but I don't have the face for it . . ."

She stopped in midsentence because he had turned his attention back to his magazine.

With a tingling scalp, she apologized again, swallowing the betrayal. It expanded in her stomach and kept her too full to eat for three days. Now she was bloated and cramped as if she had eaten the mountains of pancakes that Adisa had scarfed down for breakfast. She tilted her head forward, and her hair, relaxed and limp, covered her moist eyes. She didn't know if she would ever be able to eat again.

"Drama," Lorena said, sucking the foam off a cup of Coke. "Pure drama."

Felicia ignored this last barb and took a long swallow of tea. She knew that the caffeine on an empty stomach was a bad thing, but a caffeine-withdrawal headache was nothing nice, either.

The prodigy entered the cafeteria, struggling with a tray laden with cupcakes. Another prodigy was with him, carrying a tray heaped with french fries. Evidently they worked up quite an appetite in "Diff EQ." The two geniuses paused before the table where Felicia sat with Lorena. The prodigy elbowed his fellow genius and they broke out in giggles. Their tremors of laughter toppled one of the cupcakes. The prodigy stopped laughing and gave Felicia a look that said, *see what you made me do?* and walked away, whispering urgently to his friend.

"I don't know about those prodigies," Felicia said to Lorena.

"What about them? I think they're kind of cute. That chocolate one with the hook head looks just like my nephew."

"Adisa says that they're not really geniuses. Did you know that? He says they get in here on a kind of affirmative action."

"Adisa's just hating," Lorena said with a dismissive wave. Each one of her fingernails had a leftover dab of purple polish in the center.

"Well, anyway, they make me nervous. Especially that one you were talking about." She leaned in closer to Lorena. "He's making fun of me because I'm just in trig. This morning, he gave me the finger."

Lorena laughed so hard that Felicia's breadstick was misted with spittle. "You got man problems all the way around. Brothers got you coming and going. Even the ones in diapers!"

Felicia started to protest, but it was clear that Lorena was enjoying the sound of her own laughter too much to listen to reason. And anyway, there was no reason to argue with a fool. They drag you to their level and then beat you down with experience. Felicia's father liked to say that. He also said "Gulliver doesn't worry about the Lilliputians." And that's all a prodigy was, a miniature college student. She glanced over at the two of them scooting fries across the tops of the cupcakes and then eating the sugary potatoes. Her mind went to Adisa eating pancakes. He liked to drown them in syrup. She imagined him chewing each sticky mouthful, not thinking of her at all.

The cafeteria was a noisy place. There was talking, laughing, heated arguments taking place over plastic trays. But there was also the sound of eating: the crunch of teeth on crusts, the smooth, silvery slide of spoons between lips. Fruit punch rolled noisily down a hundred throats. Everyone was eating except Felicia. Lorena got up to get another macadamia nut cookie. The prodigies feasted on carbohydrates bought with their scholarship money. Her lasagna sat before her, foolishly untouched.

As Felicia took her tray to the conveyor belt, she passed the lunching geniuses.

"You're ridiculous," said the prodigy. The other, eyes wide with sugar-energy, nodded in rapid agreement.

He may have been right, Felicia figured. But she didn't have to take such abuse from a Lilliputian. She fixed her eyes on him and said with woman-authority, "I'm going to tell your mother what you eat for lunch."

He shrugged his shoulders, calling her bluff, but his pal was so taken aback that he spilled his fruit punch, soaking the remaining cupcakes. Felicia smiled as they scrambled for napkins.

Felicia walked to her dormitory in weather that didn't warm up by noon. She passed a half-dozen pay telephones, the quarters in her purse jingling like chimes. She stopped at one, taking the cold handset from the hook and clamping it to her shoulder with her cheek. She slid her hand in her pocket, rooting about for change. A mechanical voice thanked her with each coin she slid into the narrow slot. But a wave of embarrassment washed over her, heating her cheeks despite the cold. She put the receiver back.

She headed back toward the dormitory, thinking of Adisa. She thought of him always, and this would be a difficult habit to break. But she found herself thinking of him differently now. Then, she thought of the prodigy and wondered why she let a little kid unnerve her so. Was it because he was supposed to be smarter than she was? Because he was more special? When she put her hands on her hips, he had responded to her like the woman she was.

What about Adisa? What would happen if she were to speak to him with the same hands-on-hips authority?

Back in her room, she ate a double pepperoni pie while taking the quiz in the current *Cosmo*. She answered the questions honestly, for once, instead of figuring out which answers would give her the best score. The guide at the end of the article advised her that she was "pushy." She should yield and sweeten. After all, you catch more flies with honey than with vinegar.

She reached for another slice, dusting it with parmesan cheese. The phone rang—she'd programmed it to play "Ode to Joy." She hummed along until the caller gave up.

Ultimate Forgiveness

Tanya Marie Lewis

"Devil tempt, but he no force." —Guyananese

February 18, 2001
Sunday night
9:00 P.M.

Jared Duncan reached up from his wheelchair to pull down the last poster hanging on the wall of the rectangular jail cell that had been his home for the past two decades. The image on the poster held his gaze captive as though he were seeing it for the first time: a young NBA point guard seemingly floating in midair, slam-dunking a basketball.

Everything about this poster had changed. The original gloss finish was now yellowed and tattered around the edges, and the vibrant blue and green of the NBA uniform had faded to shades of gray. But it was the muscular athlete on the poster who had undergone the most drastic change of all. The handsome man towered at six feet, seven inches, with a bald head, medium-brown complexion, and piercing green eyes. His looks had been a bonus to his amazing talent for playing ball. Yet, like the poster, the ballplayer had diminished with age. The bald head had been replaced by waist-length locks, the green eyes filled with wisdom, and the long, lean legs now rested upon a vinyl cushion, lifeless for the past twenty-four years. Jared reflected on how a single event could cause a domino effect and change the course of one's life. He took a deep breath and smiled. After twenty-two years of countless appeals in court, justice had finally been served. He was going home.

There were so many people he needed to apologize to, asking their forgiveness for the selfish act he had committed so many years before. His only hope was that they'd be as forgiving as God had been with him. Jared had killed the old selfish child on that poster and become a man of God while in prison. He prayed that Eric, Jason, Michael, Sarah, and Jennifer would accept his plea for forgiveness when the time arrived.

The clanking of keys turning in the rusted lock caused Jared to look up from the poster. He smiled at the sight of Burkes, one of the prison's most feared guards, entering the cell. At six feet-four and 300 pounds, with a face resembling a pit bull's, Burkes intimidated most of the other inmates. But Jared knew Burkes's soul was as meek as a sheep.

When Jared had first arrived at the prison, Burkes had taken a liking to him and encouraged him to follow the word of God.

"Hey, man, what you doing here this late?" Jared asked, wheeling himself toward Burkes.

"I wanted to talk before you leave us tomorrow," he said, glancing down at the harsh concrete floor.

"Awww, come on now, man, don't get all mushy on me. I'll be fine," Jared assured his friend.

Burkes's eyes misted over. "I'm really going to miss you, Brother Jared."

"I'll always be here for you, Burkes; you know that," he said, lowering his head to hide the tears dangling from the corners of his eyes, seeking a place to fall. Jared would never forget how Burkes had helped him obtain his college degree, phoned his attorney on his behalf, and prayed with him when his troubled soul tap-danced on his emotions.

"Well, I can't stay long. I'm pushing it as it is. You know, with Warden Thomas allowing me to pick you up tomorrow morning."

"I know, Burkes. I'll always remember everything you've done for me."

A tear slipped from Burkes's eyes as he moved closer to Jared. "Hey, man, let me help you get ready for bed. You know, one for the road."

Jared hated to rely on anyone's assistance. He prided himself on the self-reliance he had developed over the years, but his heart wouldn't allow him to deny Burkes this opportunity.

"Sure." He steered toward the bed.

Burkes walked over and leaned forward, allowing Jared to grab his shoulder blades for support, then pulled him from the wheelchair. Jared's legs dangled as Burkes eased him onto the bed, pushing him backward until his back rested against the cold, unyielding concrete wall. Burkes wiped his eyes with the back of his hand and backed away from the bed.

"Jared, I'm really going to miss you, man," he repeated. Jared watched as Burkes walked out, locking the cell behind him. Burkes turned to gaze back through the bars. "I'll be here early in the morning, okay?"

"I'll be waiting for you." Jared smiled.

"Try to get some sleep."

"I will," he lied, knowing that no sleep would come that night. "Lights out!" a guard yelled, and then the block went completely dark except for the faint light that glowed from the watchtower. Closing his eyes, Jared recalled the events that had led him to this point.

Jared had been picked up by the NBA at the age of eighteen, married his high school sweetheart, Natalie, that same year, and had become the proud father of Jared Jr. a year later. Everything had been perfect, except for his mother, Selena's, constant manipulations. He and Selena (which is what she had insisted Jared call her) had always been close. In her eyes, he could do no wrong, and so she busied herself trying to be Jared's friend instead of his mother.

She had doted on him, paying little attention to his younger brother, Preston, whom she said wasn't cute enough to be considered one of her kids. Jared had laughed at those words, too young and stupid to realize how cruel Selena really was. He'd made fun of Preston, too, while enjoying all the things he could get away with. As the years rolled by, Jared realized that his biggest mistake had been to allow Selena to interfere in his marriage to sweet Natalie.

He'd fallen in love with Natalie in the fifth grade, and knew even then that there would never be another woman for him. Beautiful Natalie, with the petite frame, dark-brown complexion, and almond-shaped eyes that reflected his love for her. Selena had never liked Natalie, saying she wasn't good enough, even though they both had grown up in the housing projects.

After Jared signed his first multimillion-dollar NBA contract, he'd purchased Selena her first home and a new luxury car and given her every platinum credit card on the market. In just a few months, Selena went from ghetto queen to snobbish, siditty diva, shunning Natalie.

"Baby, why you gon' marry that girl? With your success, you're gonna have women coming at you left and right. You can do *so* much better."

"Selena, don't start."

"Baby, I'm just looking out for you," she said, sipping her third gin and tonic. "I want you to have the very best."

"Natalie is what's best for me. I love her; you know that," he said harshly. Jared took a deep breath, reminding himself that he refused to get upset over his mother's constant dislike of his fiancée.

"Okay, okay," she said, handing him a fresh drink. "You know I don't like to see you upset."

"No, thanks." He pushed the glass back toward her. "I can't drink like that now. You know I need to quit. There's a lot more at stake."

Selena, who had been letting Jared drink with her since he was ten years old, raised a skeptical brow. Most of her friends drifted away because of how she was raising her children. He remembered her kicking out one of her men friends after hearing the man say, "Selena, what you're doing to that boy is plum child abuse."

"You mind your business!" she screamed. "That's my son, and if he wants to drink, he can."

"He don't want to drink, Selena. You're an alcoholic and you make that boy get drunk with you so you won't have to do it by yourself."

The man had said way more than Selena wanted to hear, and she had put him out like she had all the others—family, friends, and lovers—who cared enough to tell her the ugly truth.

"Come on, baby, don't make yo momma drink alone. Besides, we can get drunk and make fun of Preston," she said, giggling in her younger son's direction as he sat in the corner, head buried in a book as usual.

Jared laughed. "Okay, just one." That one had led to another all-nighter, and the next day, he'd arrived at practice late and been scolded by the coach. A few years later, Selena introduced Jared to a new woman, the white girl, cocaine.

Jared was at the top of his game, scoring high, and he was the sole reason his team had gone on to the playoffs two years in a row and garnered the championship title. Neither the coach nor the players ever said anything to him about his addiction, as long as he continued scoring. It seemed like the only people who truly loved him were Natalie and Little J. D. Yet his new loves were gin and cocaine. When one wasn't around, the other was there to shower him with affection.

Natalie pleaded with him several times about getting help. "Jared, I'm worried about you, baby."

"I can handle it," he said tersely.

"This is getting out of hand," she'd press, desperate to reach him. "If you won't do it for me, do it for your son—our son," she'd beg through her tears.

"I don't need no friggin' help. I'm Jared Duncan, DAMN IT!" he'd yell, puffing his chest.

"Jared, I don't even recognize you anymore. Most of the time you're not here, and when you are home, you're either passed out or getting high in the back of the house."

"Look, woman, this *my* house. You wouldn't *have anything* if it weren't for me. Your butt would still be living in that roach-infested apartment I rescued you from."

"Well, that's better than living in this phony home with a coke fiend!" she screamed. "How can you bring this stuff around me, around your son? Don't you care about anything other than your white girl-friend?" she screamed. "I'm leaving."

Fear gripped Jared's heart at the idea of his sweet Natalie leaving him. He ran behind her as she headed toward the bedroom, grabbing her arm. "Baby, please don't ever leave me," he begged, easing his body down to kneel before her.

"Jared, I'm not playing this time," Natalie relented. "You've got to cut Selena's hold on you. She's bringing you down. Baby, you're a grown man and you have a family to think of now."

"I know, I know. I'll get help. I promise," he cried. And with all the love in her heart, Natalie tried her best to believe him.

A few months later, Natalie and Little J. D. returned home from a weekend vacation to find Jared at Selena's house, passed out next to his mother in her living room. White powder littered the glass coffee table, and bottles of gin and vodka were strewn about the living room. Natalie didn't bother trying to wake them. She went home, packed her and J. D.'s belongings, and moved in with her mother. Then she called Jared's coach and told him the truth. Maybe, Natalie prayed, if Jared didn't listen to her, he'd pay attention to the man responsible for having a say in which side his bread was buttered on.

The sound of an inmate singing pulled Jared out of his trip down memory lane. His face and pillow were soaked with tears as he turned the top portion of his body onto his side while lifting the dead weight of his legs. Although his memories remained with him, it had been years since he'd allowed himself to shed any tears. He had hurt so many peo-ple, ruined so many lives.

In the darkness he saw the poster lying on the makeshift table in his cell, the man who had broken so many promises to so many people and lost control of his life. He closed his eyes and remembered the night that had changed everything . . .

Jared's outrage at Natalie's leaving and taking J. D. ignited after his coach confronted him about his problem. Nobody understood, he muttered to himself, speeding to the liquor store. Nobody cared about him and his pain. The pain that had only one cure.

He was drunk and high beyond reason or pain when Selena persuaded him to go get Little J. D. back. When Natalie didn't answer her mother's apartment door, he kicked it in.

"What are you doing here?" she asked fearfully, grabbing Little J. D. and pushing him behind her. Selena tottered behind Jared.

"I'm here to get my son, witch," he said, reaching around her.

Natalie fought him, screaming, "No! No, no, no, you're high Jared; please don't do this," she begged, pushing him away from Little J. D.

Jared grabbed her, pushing her backward into the coffee table. Natalie's hands flailed, grabbing for something—anything—to break her fall, and she screamed at Jared's back as he staggered toward the door with his crying son in his arms. Natalie struggled to stand, then hurled herself onto Jared's back, pounding his head.

He reached back and grabbed a handful of her hair, slamming her body onto the floor like a weightless rag doll. Jared handed Little J. D. to Selena and motioned for her to take him to the car. Jared turned and looked down at Natalie, who was trying desperately to get up again. Jared placed a foot on her chest. "Nobody takes my son away from me, tramp. You got that?" he snarled, turning to leave.

Natalie grabbed his ankles. "No! Pleasssssse, Jared, don't take my baby. Please, stop and think. You're high!" He dragged her down the stairs, the plunkety-plunk of her body going over each step sounding far away.

Jared tried to free his ankles from her hysterical grasp while shielding his eyes from the rain. Grabbing the stairwell railing for support, he took all of his weight and kicked her off, running to the car and driving off, with a gloating Serena in the front passenger seat, and a terrified-looking J. D. in the back.

Natalie slipped through freezing puddles of water, running behind the car, her screams swallowed by the cold night air.

"That'll teach that heffa who to mess with," Selena crowed as they sped off.

Hours later, Jared awoke to the smells of blood and alcohol, and there was no feeling in the lower part of his body. He heard the doctors and nurses talking to him and tried to look up, only to realize that his head was confined by a hard plastic neck brace. Jared tasted the blood on his lips and began cursing at the nurses to let him up when he heard the doctor a few feet away in the next cubicle yelling, "Clear!" The older white doctor extended the electronic paddles toward the victim.

Jared couldn't move his head, and two nurses assisting the doctor blocked his view. His heart beat wildly inside his chest as thoughts of Selena being hurt rushed into his mind.

"'Still no pulse," one of the nurses said.

"Come on, son, come on!" Jared heard the doctor yelling as he continued shocking the victim with the paddles. One of the nurses moved onto the other side of the table, and Jared's heart nearly stopped as he saw his son lying unconscious on the emergency room table. Time stood still as he watched the doctor shock Little J. D.'s body over and over again. A part of Jared died that night as he watched the doctor back away from his son, glance at the clock on the wall, and pull the bloody sheet over Little J. D.'s tiny face. Why couldn't he move? "GOD, NOOOOOOO!" he screamed in agony. "OH GOD! OH GOD! NOT MY SON! PLEAAASSE NOT MY SON!"

Jared had gone into his own comatose hell for seven years after that night. He was numb throughout the trial and had little memory of being sentenced on six counts of vehicular manslaughter. His younger brother, Preston, of all people, was the first person to get through to him, to help dig up the memories of that stormy night. He had lost control of his car, slamming into a school bus on the side of the road, pushing it down into a ravine, killing five kids and injuring ten. On the bus were a group of basketball players and cheerleaders headed home from a game. The bus driver had pulled over because of the bad weather and had never seen Jared's lights until it was too late. Preston told Jared that Natalie had suffered a mental breakdown but was now remarried with kids. Jared had his attorney arrange it so all his money had been given to her after he was incarcerated. It would never compensate for what he had taken from her, but he felt in his heart that it should belong to her.

Jared and Preston had finally bonded and become brothers. Jared had to lose everything, including his mobility and his freedom, before he realized that Preston, like him, had also been a victim. He'd never heard from Selena, who had walked away from the accident without a scratch. She had never so much as written a letter or come to visit Jared in jail. After talking with Jared, Preston finally cut his ties with her, after she stole money from Preston to feed her coke habit. Jared had finally realized that Selena never cared about anyone but herself, and her influence had cost them all. But he had forgiven her, just as he prayed that others would forgive him.

Selena had never been loved herself as a child, and had no idea how to teach her own children. Jared had stayed in her manipulative grasp too long, a day too long to give him a chance to break the cycle. It had taken two dozen yeas behind bars for him to learn what it meant to be a man.

February 19, 2001
Monday morning
8:00 A.M.

Jared had all his belongings packed and ready to go. He was leaving it all behind: the days of no sunlight, the silence of the night, the screams of flowers being plucked for the first time, and the awful smell of confinement. Burkes had kept his promise and come to see him early that morning. They had shared breakfast and prayer for well over an hour. Jared turned to see Burkes standing behind his wheelchair and said, "I'm as ready as I'll ever be."

This was by far the most glorious day in Jared's life. There were so many apologies he had to give, so many hearts he had to help mend, and he couldn't do it here. He prayed to his heavenly Father as Burkes pushed him down the halls of the prison, thanking God for saving him, for forgiving him. He was God's son now, and no one could take that from him. Jared was not the least bit surprised when Burkes rounded the corner to the entrance that would lead him to freedom and saw all the folks who had come out to see him.

There were countless reporters wanting pictures and quotes from the ex-great, Jared Duncan, point guard for the Houston Drillers, and old fans who had never stopped sending him letters of encouragement. There was not a single face in the crowd that he recognized, except Preston, who stood with tears in his eyes. Burkes leaned down and whispered, "Are you okay?"

"I've never felt better, Burkes, never felt better." Burkes opened the door to the vehicle that would drive Jared away to freedom.

Burkes stopped Jared's wheelchair and put it in the locked position. He then lifted Jared from his wheelchair and placed him in the seat, carefully secured his body in place, and made sure the safety belts were fastened properly. Jared looked out the window at the sea of people who had come out to greet him, some with tears, others still filled with scorn.

Jared turned his gaze to Burkes, smiled, and briefly glanced at the other guards who had come to say their good-byes. Jared then nodded to Burkes as if giving him permission to start the ignition. Burkes nodded back at Jared, with his head held high, and turned the switch. The foreign mist coming from the vent immediately blew into Jared's face, burning the lining of his nostrils. Jared smiled and closed his eyes as a cold chill went through his body. A chill reaching beyond his waist and trickling down to his toes, allowing him sensation for the first time in over twenty years. He slowly opened his eyes and gazed out the window again, and thought for a moment that his mind had betrayed him. There, standing among the sea of people, was Natalie, with a single tear sliding down her cheek, and forgiveness written on her face. Jared smiled at her and closed his eyes again, branding her face into his memory forever, along with the images forming in his subconscious mind. In the darkness, images of Eric, Jason, Michael, Sarah, and Jennifer came into focus, the five students killed so many years ago. All of them smiling in forgiveness. They turned and parted the way for the image of Little J. D., who stood with his hand extended toward his father.

Jared opened his eyes once more, found Natalie's face, and smiled. His body felt another chill, and he could feel the white, bubbly foam floating from the corners of his mouth like waterfalls gliding over endless cliffs. His eyes rolled back into his head as he finally reached for his son's hand, just as the lethal gas emanating from the vents cupped the last of his breath in its embrace.

Dead to the World

Brandon Massey

"You can outdistance that which is running after you, but not that which runs inside you." —African, Rwanda

"Where's my check?"

Sitting at my desk in my tiny cubicle, rocking slowly in my chair, I bolted upright and tightened my grip on the telephone handset. Don't let this guy be another one, I prayed. I'd been answering calls for two hours that morning, and I'd taken enough blows from irate policy owners to leave me feeling like a punching bag. I didn't have the endurance to face another angry customer. After all, during my drive to work, I had miraculously avoided what could have been a fatal collision with an eighteen-wheeler. I wanted to spend the day gazing out the window, silently thanking God for sparing my life.

Please, let this guy be a quick transfer to another department.

"Before I can answer your question, sir, I'll need your policy number," I said. "Can you give that number to me, please?"

He rattled off a series of digits. As he spoke, I entered the numbers on my computer. His policy information, visible in green type, filled the black display.

The Chicago-based company I worked for, Lake Shore Insurance, offered medical, disability, group life, and individual life coverage. Separate departments administered each kind of insurance; I worked in the individual life area. Although our toll-free number gave callers a department menu that should have always connected them to the appropriate areas, in the course of a day I often transferred a dozen misdirected calls. But there would be no quick transfer this time. As I studied the screen, I saw that this guy had an individual life policy. Great.

I steeled myself for the oncoming abuse. "And what is your name, sir?"

"Ralph E. Stone, from Peoria, Illinois. Ain't you got that on your screen, boy?"

"Yes, sir, I do, but I needed to confirm your identity," I said. "Okay, Mr. Stone, you were calling about a check?"

"A loan check," he said. "Thousand bucks I need, I'm in a real tight spot. I sent you folks a letter a few weeks ago, but you ain't sent me nothing yet. So now I'm calling about it. Where's my goddamn money?"

"I'll see if I can find out, Mr. Stone. Can you hold for just a moment?"

"Hurry it up."

Oh, shut up, I thought as I put him on hold. I half wished I hadn't been so lucky that morning; a bruise or two that would have justified a brief hospital visit would have been preferable to coming here. On days such as these, I believed that if God ever decided to condemn me to hell, he would put me somewhere exactly like this, to deal with mad customers for all eternity.

I tapped the keyboard, flipping through various screens, searching for information about a loan transaction. I learned two things. One, no loan check had ever been mailed to Stone. Two, Ralph Stone had died on February 12, three weeks ago. The ten-thousand-dollar death benefit had been paid to his beneficiary and sister, Irene Stone.

Obviously, something was screwed up.

I picked up the phone.

"My check on the way?" Stone said.

"Well, sir . . . no. It seems we have some incorrect information on our system. According to our records, you died on the twelfth of February." I chuckled, as if such a thing were funny.

Stone laughed, too. "Then your computer's a piece of shit, boy, cause it's wrong as wrong could be. I wouldn't be calling if I were dead, would I?"

"Of course not," I said. "I apologize for this. I'm not sure how this happened."

"One of you crackbrains up there messed up my policy; that's how it happened."

"We're only human," I said. And some of us are pigs.

"This better not keep me from getting my check, boy."

"No, sir, I promise you it won't. This is a minor error. We'll fix this in no time and get your money out to you."

"You better," he said. "I been paying a lot of cash into this damned thing, and my agent said I could draw some of it out after I'd kept up the payments a few years. He better not've lied to me. Liars don't sit well with me, boy."

"Your agent isn't a liar, sir, and neither am I. We'll fix this and give you your money as soon as possible. In fact, instead of passing this along to someone else, I'll take care of it myself. How about if I order your file, take a look at it, and call you back later today?"

"What's your name, boy?"

"Kevin," I said. "Kevin Jackson."

"I'll call you," Stone said, and hung up.

An hour later, I opened Ralph Stone's thick manila file.

The first thing I saw was the top sheet, a printed document that gives you almost all the information you would ever need on a policy: name of insured, date of issue, face amount, beneficiary, and modal premium, to name a few. When the insured died, the claim adjustor stamped the date of death on the top sheet. And because colleagues thoroughly checked and double-checked the adjustor's work, it was highly unlikely that a top sheet would ever be stamped in error. In my dealings with thousands of files, I had never seen it happen.

Nevertheless, that blood red stamp glared at me from the top sheet: DECEASED 2-12-2000.

Impossible. I had talked to Ralph Stone on the telephone.

Hadn't I?

Searching for some error that would make sense of all this, I dug through the file, spreading papers across my desk.

I found a certified copy of the death certificate, which validated the date of death as February 12. Full name of decedent was Ralph Edward Stone. No wife. Usual occupation was truck driving. Cause of death was a heart attack. Age at death was fifty-three. Place of death was his home in Peoria, Illinois. Informant—the person who had reported his death—was Irene Stone, sister, who also lived in Peoria, though not at Ralph's address. Irene had discovered him dead on the couch at seven o'clock in the evening.

I found a copy of his driver's license. Ralph E. Stone was six-feet-two, 250 pounds. He had a large, square face covered with a wooly gray beard. A pug nose and cold, squinting blue eyes. He was scowling in the photograph, as if angered at the idea of needing a license to drive his vehicle. All of the data on the card matched the data in the file.

Last, I found a letter written in sloppy manuscript on yellow notebook paper: Give me a loan for a thousand dollars. My agent said I could get money after I kept this thing for a few years. I need money now, so send it right away. Thanks, Ralph E. Stone.

The letter was postmarked February 11th. The day before Stone had apparently died of a heart attack.

Looking at these things, I felt as though I might suffer a heart attack myself. What was going on here?

Was the man I had talked to earlier an impostor trying to chisel money out of us? Or was he really . . . ?

No, don't even consider it, because that's crazy.

The man was nothing but a swindler. In my three years at this company, I'd heard about his type. They were doctors who sent in fake claims, insureds who were healthy and working yet trying to get disability benefits, agents who forged applications and got the fat commissions—the insurance industry teemed with treacherous people who'd do anything to grab a dishonest buck. This case was just a little stranger than usual. One call to Irene Stone, the sister (who, incidentally, also had a policy with us that Ralph had been paying for), would clear up everything.

I picked up the phone.

A woman answered on the fourth ring. "Hello?"

"This is Kevin Jackson, from Lake Shore Insurance. May I please speak to Ms. Irene Stone?"

"Speaking." Her voice was frail, whispery. "This isn't about my brother, is it?"

I hesitated. I wished I'd taken the time to plan my conversation. How could you tell a woman that you were getting calls from a man claiming to be her dead brother, without upsetting her? That lesson wasn't taught in any of the customer service classes I'd attended.

"Because if you're calling about Ralph, I'm afraid I can't say much," she said. She sighed heavily. "It still hurts me to talk about him."

"That's perfectly understandable, ma'am. I don't want to upset you, but—"

"He was such a sweetheart, Ralph was," she said. "Took care of me like a father. The man *believed* in family, would do anything for his kin. You don't see that as much these days."

"My deepest sympathies to you, ma'am. But I got a call—"

"I'll never get over his passing. Never." She sniffled, and I feared she was about to break down and weep. "No one ever cared about me as much as Ralph did."

"I'm sure you're right, ma'am. I'm sure Mr. Stone was an honorable man. By the way, do you happen to know anyone who might try to impersonate him so he could con money out of an insurance company?"

"Ralph was so . . . what did you say?" she said, a sudden edge to her voice.

I mentally kicked myself in the butt. Wasn't I just brimming with tact? I ought to open a charm school and educate the less graceful masses.

Determined not to make another gaffe like that, I pressed on. "I hate to discuss this with you, Ms. Stone, but I received a call today from a man who says he's your brother, Ralph E. Stone. He's demanding that we mail him a loan check. He made reference to an actual written loan request from your brother that was postmarked February 11th. And, of course . . . Mr. Stone died on the twelfth, so we never processed the loan. But the man who called me is very convincing. He insists that we mistakenly declared him dead."

"Why're you calling me? I sent you a copy of Ralph's death certificate, didn't I?"

"Yes. But—"

"What else do you need? His poor dead body sent overnight mail?"

"I'm sorry, I didn't mean to upset you. I only wanted to verify—"

"Mister, these past few weeks have been absolute hell for me, and you've just made it worse with your crazy goddamned questions. If this is the kind of compassion I can expect from my insurance company, I don't want anything more to do with you people. Cancel my policy immediately—with a full refund of every cent Ralph ever paid into it!"

Click.

She had hung up on me. I can't say I blamed her; I'd figured my call would piss her off. But I needed to be sure about this guy. And now that I was, I knew what I had to do.

Wait for him to call me back.

I didn't have to wait long. Barely fifteen minutes after I finished speaking to Irene Stone, my telephone rang again.

"Got it all straightened out, boy?" the man claiming to be Ralph Stone said.

"I sure do," I said. I leaned back in my chair, took a sip of coffee. "You're dead, Mr. Stone."

Silence. Then: "Come again?"

"I found your death certificate in the file. You died on February twelfth—a day after your written loan request was postmarked. I'm sure you remember, sir. Dying of a heart attack has to be hard to forget."

Stone chuckled. "I died of a heart attack, eh? I can't say I remember, though I reckon I should." He chuckled again, then cleared his throat. "Now look, boy, I've had enough of these jokes. I need—"

"I need a break from your con act!" I said, speaking louder than I had intended, rising halfway out of my chair. I drew a deep breath, sat down. "Listen, whoever you are, I'm not buying your story. Mr. Stone died, we paid the benefits to his sister, and we've officially closed his file. You aren't getting a dime, so you can quit this tired act of yours. Now, good-bye, sir, and please don't call again."

Without waiting for his response, I hung up. I pressed the button on the telephone that would automatically send any calls for me to my voice mail. It went without saying that if he called again and left me a message, I would not return his call. As far as I was concerned, I'd had my last conversation with Mr. Whatever-his-real-name-was.

Pleased at how I had handled the situation, I finished off my coffee and went to lunch.

When I returned from lunch, I saw the blinking message indicator on my telephone. I frowned, certain of who had called.

I listened to the message. It was him, of course. Mr. Whatever-his-real-name-was.

"You've went and made this personal, boy. I'm in a real tight spot, and *you're* jerking me around with some nutty story about me dying of a heart attack. I wasn't a whiz in school, but I'll be damned if I'm dumb enough to fall for your bullshit. My agent said I could get a loan, and I'm gonna get it. So I'm coming up there, boy. Leaving within the hour, ought to get there by this afternoon. And when I stop in, you better have my check ready. Or else."

He slammed down the phone, a sharp sound that hurt my ear.

My heart was suddenly pounding.

Of all the reactions I had expected from him, I had never expected this.

I opened Stone's file, flipped to the copy of his driver's license. In his early fifties. Square face, wooly gray beard, pug nose. Cold, squinting blue eyes. An angry scowl.

You've made this personal, boy.

This was madness. Sheer insanity.

Ralph Stone was dead. The death certificate said so, and the sister said so. This impostor was blowing smoke. He wasn't getting a thing from me, and he knew it. He probably wasn't actually driving up here. He was only trying to scare me.

And I had to admit that he was doing a good job of it.

Work proceeded as usual until a few minutes after three o'clock that afternoon. Then my phone rang. It was the receptionist.

"A man named Ralph Stone is waiting in the lobby for you," the receptionist said. She coughed a couple of times. "He says you should have a check for him."

I was speechless. I sat there holding the handset to my ear, like a poster boy for AT&T.

"Will you come down here and meet him, please?" the receptionist said. She coughed again.

Tell her no, a voice in me pleaded. *Tell her to get Security to kick the man off company property. Tell her that talking to psycho con men isn't in my job description.*

But I said none of those things. I only said: "I'll be down there in a minute."

Coughing as if she'd caught a terrible cold, the receptionist thanked me and hung up.

I gathered Ralph Stone's file and walked to the elevator.

Ordinarily, I always take the stairs, for the exercise. That time, however, I didn't feel confident about my ability to make it down the stairs without my trembling legs giving way and spilling me on my face.

The elevator doors whooshed open.

About fifteen feet away, a man turned from the reception desk and looked at me as I entered the lobby.

Right away, I knew this man was no impostor. He looked exactly like Ralph Stone.

That is, if Ralph Stone had climbed out of the grave after having been dead for three weeks.

He still appeared to be about six-feet-two, but seemed to weigh not 250 but 350, maybe more; his body was round and swollen, nearly bursting out of the shearling jacket and jeans that he wore. Large blisters marred his bloated face; the skin had a strange green-red tint and seemed to be loose, ready to drip like hot wax from his skull. Half the hairs of his wooly gray beard had fallen out, the remaining hairs were limp and colorless. The cold, squinting blue eyes were now flat, and so clouded up with fluid that they seemed as white as the eyeballs of a voodoo priest caught up in the ecstasy of spirit possession.

And the smell. *Jesus.* No wonder the receptionist had been coughing when she'd spoken to me on the phone. Such a stench filled the air that I felt as though I had stepped into a busy slaughterhouse on a hot August day.

The man—or what had once been a man—shuffled toward me, muddy black boots dragging across the carpet.

The lobby was warm, but a chill gripped me.

To hell with trying to explain his presence. I didn't want to know the inexplicable details. I only wanted to get him out of there.

He stopped a few feet away from me, planted his discolored fists on his soft waist, and scrutinized me from head to toe with his milky pupils.

This close, the stench was too much. I backed up a little, covered my nose with my forearm.

I thought I saw a maggot quivering in his nostril.

"You the boy I talked to?" he said, his voice somehow strong and clear.

"Yes. I'm Kevin Jackson."

He grunted. "Got my check?"

"No, I don't," I said. I clumsily opened the file, riffled through the various documents. Talk about absurd. What was nuttier than explaining a death claim to the decedent?

"See here, Mr. Ralph Stone—or *you*, since I know that's who you are now—died on February twelfth. The death benefits were paid to your sister, Irene. The policy has been terminated. I don't know what else I can tell you, sir. I can't give you anything. Sorry."

Gazing at the file, viewing his own death certificate, he pursed his split lips. "You folks never stop bullshitting, do you?"

"Excuse me?"

He slapped the file out of my hand.

Then he seized me by the front of my shirt.

"No more lies! Give me my goddamn check!"

He shook me hard, in spite of his bloodless muscles that must have gone soft.

His mouth, only inches from my face, spewed forth a fetid breath that struck me like a blow. I wanted to faint, but my body didn't cooperate.

A security guard ran up to us. He clapped a hand on Stone's shoulder. "Hey, mister, let go of—"

With stunning quickness, Stone released me and spun around and punched the guard in the nose, his fist bursting and spilling fluids like a giant pimple.

The guard dropped to the carpet, holding his bleeding nose.

Seemingly unaware of his ruined hand, Stone whirled to face me. "Your turn, boy."

I bolted across the lobby, into the waiting area, where several upholstered sofas and pine end tables sat.

I needed some kind of weapon, and I had a vague idea that something suitable might be over there—though what could hurt a man who was already dead?

Stone pursued me, shambling like something out of a horror flick.

Hadn't he looked in the mirror lately? Didn't he realize that he had died? Or was he so dead to the world that not even seeing the mushy stump that had once been his hand could awaken him to the truth?

Soon, only a sofa separated us. He drummed his fat fingers on top of it, grinning at me with teeth that would've given my dentist nightmares.

"When I get done with you, boy, you're gonna need your own death certificate."

He chuckled, a nasty wet sound.

He slung one leg over the couch, began to clamber over it.

As I moved away, the backs of my legs hit something. I reached behind me. I touched the solid surface of an end table.

Stone was almost across the sofa.

"And after you, I'm gonna take care of that lying sonofabitch agent who sold me that policy."

It was either him or me. And since he was dead already, I figured I had the right to keep on living.

So I snatched up the table, raised it high, and brought it down on his skull with all the force I could muster.

His head exploded like a watermelon hit with a sledgehammer. Rotted flesh and stinking liquids splattering everywhere.

The headless corpse rolled off the couch and thudded to the floor at my feet. It lay there. Motionless. Silent.

I wiped cold sweat off my brow.

The entire bizarre episode seemed to have occurred in some realm of hell, but thankfully, it was over.

In addition to the security guard who'd taken the punch in the nose, a couple of company housekeepers had gathered around, their wheeled garbage cans beside them. They held their noses.

"Why don't we get this mess cleaned up, guys?" I said. "Come on, I'll help you."

Strangely, not one person who had witnessed the incident ventured an opinion about Stone. All of us maintained a weird code of silence, keeping our thoughts to ourselves, preserving our feelings for later reflections—or nightmares.

It took a while, but we managed to clean up the cadaver and remove all signs that it had ever been in the lobby. I believe people deserve a proper burial in a respectable cemetery, but Stone wasn't getting another one of those. One was enough. This time, he was getting shipped to the local trash incinerator.

When we finished, I returned upstairs.

I sat behind my desk. Drew in a few rejuvenating breaths. Took a sip of coffee.

Finally ready to work again, I grabbed the next file from the stack of them on my tray. I opened it.

My full name was written on the top sheet: *KEVIN PAUL JACKSON.*

What?

I looked closer.

And then I saw that familiar blood red stamp on the top sheet: *DECEASED 3-6-2000*

"No," I said, my face flushed with heat.

I tore into the file, found the death certificate, and read the cause of death.

Internal injuries due to auto accident.

Auto accident? That couldn't be. At the last instant, I had avoided the collision with the eighteen-wheeler. It had been close—a miracle, actually, but I had escaped. No, this was a joke, and it wasn't funny at all. I was going to find out who had pulled this prank. I was going to find them and—

My phone rang.

Automatically, I picked it up.

"Good afternoon, this is Kevin Jackson. How may I help you?"

"Where's my check?" It was a woman with a thick Brooklyn accent.

On days such as these, I believed that if God ever decided to condemn me to hell, he would put me somewhere exactly like this, to deal with mad customers for all eternity.

Realizing the truth, I didn't say a word.

I dropped the phone, grabbed fistfuls of my hair, and began to cry—soft, weeping sounds that would stay with me forever.

Death of a Salesperson

Timmothy B. McCann

"Every wise woman buildeth her house: but the foolish plucketh it down with her hands." —Proverbs 14:1

Hot air swung dark and low above the river city. Teasing, taunting, yet never quite touching the earth. It had not rained for weeks, and on the hottest day of the year, toward the middle of July, Ruth Jenkins left the family gathered in her home. She tried to brush away the last vestiges of dust from her skirt as she sat alone in her car. There was no Michael Jackson in the background, only the occasional skip of the engine and the thought of the gravedigger's last shovel tap on her mother's grave.

"In all my life, I've never seen humans eat like that!" Dressed in navy, Ruth stared at the people who laughed and joked as she glanced at her watch and waited for her niece to move the SUV, which blocked her driveway.

"Like a bunch of dogs. Jesus. They ate all the turkey, the roast beef, the ham, the butter—we're even out of ketchup! My God, you'd think they'd have had the decency to run by KFC and pick up a twelve-piece." A volcano on the verge of erupting mounted inside her throat as she watched two kids walk through her flowerbed and then look at her and say, "Sorry, Aunt Ruth."

"And on top of everything else, Jill running up in there with those alligator tears," Ruth continued, with her fingers roaming the edge of the dusty obituary. "I could have slapped her...." She looked once again at her Tudor home, and there was no sign of her niece. "Where in the world is that heifer? I gotta go!" Ruth peered over her shoulder to see if there was a way she could ease her fifteen-year-old BMW around the monster truck, but there wasn't. Her face twitched with frustration. Ruth brought the heel of her palm over the horn, when the front door of her home popped opened and she saw her niece. Instead of running to her truck, she ran toward Ruth.

"I'm sorry Aunt'tee. I couldn't find my keys; Uncle Russell asked me to run to the store for him, and Momma said to ask if you were okay. You all right?"

Ruth stifled her anger with a faux smile. "I'm fine." She then tapped her untrimmed fingernail on the crystal of her watch.

"Oh. Right," her niece said, jingling her keys as she ran to the door of her truck.

Ruth looked at her daughter Annette's spotless car with the Texas plates. She was in Jacksonville for just one day and would soon be on the road returning to Longview. Annette had been the first to leave the nest. She quit'urated on a Thursday, packed that night, and before the sun torched the sky on Friday, she was headed west. After her departure there were three left.

As her niece backed out, Ruth looked at the Georgia plates of Mimi's boyfriend's Cadillac. Red clay dripped from the tires and undercarriage like cave stalactites, and on the dented rear bumper was a sticker that proclaimed, *Wu Tang 4ever*. Mimi was the only Jenkins to obtain a college degree, and when she left, the trio became a duet.

Ruth put the car in reverse, looked over her shoulder, and backed out. In the corner of her eye she saw her youngest daughter, Wendy, walk out of their home. Instead of returning her wave, Ruth drove away. Wendy was leaving for the Air Force in a month, and then there would be one.

"I hope they don't eat the frigging stove and refrigerator." Ruth drove through the intersection with her fingers squeezing the leather wrap of the steering wheel. "Damn people, you'd think they only come to funerals for the food. Who in the *hell* just happens to have Tupperware in the car? Lord help me." She instinctively picked up her cellular phone to make a business call but returned it to her purse. "Half of them didn't even *speak* to Momma when she was living. Now they want to run around telling sob stories—half of which I don't believe—and telling me to be strong. The nerve."

Ruth drove into her designated parking space at West Alliance Mutual and saw the familiar Lexus 400. "Doggone. I can't believe this man is here today. Today of all days, I can't deal with Levi and his nonsense." *Maybe I'll just leave and come in tomorrow.* Looking over her shoulder, she backed out of the parking space but had no idea where to go. She didn't have an appetite, so she couldn't go to a restaurant, nor was home an option. Ruth brought her car to rest and thought about her mother's face. How makeup had given life to her flesh. How the dust formed funnels on the ground and covered everyone who attended the graveside memorial as her body was returned to the earth.

Ruth exhaled the images and parked.

"Mrs. Jenkins? We didn't expect you in today."

Ruth stood before the receptionist with her white purse pinched under her armpit. "Yeah, I decided to come in. Any messages?"

"Yes, ma'am. Unfortunately, they're on your desk, and Mr. Rossini is using your office to do reviews."

"How long has he been in town?" Ruth whispered.

"A couple of hours, I think."

"Jesus Christ. He would come when I had my worst month in years. I knew I shouldn't have come in today." Ruth glanced at her watch. No one but the receptionist had seen her. And then she spied her manager.

Ruth had hired Jeff Roberts out of college, and he was the only other black face in the otherwise all-white-male office. He was "her boy," and she'd watched him blossom into the top salesperson in the state five years in a row. But when the office numbers had fallen, she'd been demoted and "her boy" had assumed her position.

"We didn't expect you in today." Jeff rolled down his sleeves and tucked in his shirt. He looked down at her skirt and said, "You've got a little dirt or dust or something on you."

Ruth's gravelly voice lowered. "How long is *he* going to be in town?"

"I wish I knew. I met him this morning sitting in the parking lot at seven. He was on his third cup of coffee, second donut, and full of piss and vinegar. But I told him about your situation and he—"

In slow motion, Ruth and Jeff watched her office door open as a broken sales rep named Igor walked out. The women in the clerical pool continued to work, but Igor paused momentarily to pinch his nose and gather his composure.

"Man, he just got fired," Jeff whispered. "I tried to get Rossini to give the guy until the end of the month, but he pulled the trigger."

Igor glanced at Ruth and Jeff across the office, straightened his tie as well as his back, and walked into his cubicle.

"Well, go in there and fight for him. That's what I used to do."

"Ruth, with this cracker you have to decide what battlefield you're willing to die on. Every time you talk to him when the sales are down, it's going to be a scrap, and you have to choose your battles carefully.

Igor hasn't had a decent month in the past three quarters. That's a hard one to win."

"Do you think I should leave?"

Jeff paused for a moment and looked at his former mentor as a friend. "Yeah, I think you should leave and take a few days off. He'll never make a move without you here."

Levi Rossini walked out of Ruth's office, and his eyes met hers. "Jenkins? I didn't expect to see you here today. I was told you had a death in the family."

Immediately the receptionist ended her phone call and looked at Ruth.

Ruth lifted her shoulders and squared her chin. "That's me. The team player."

"Well, listen, we're conducting reviews today. But in light of your situation, we can conduct yours by phone when I get back to Tampa."

"No."

Jeff's eyes stretched in surprise.

"You're here. Let's do it now."

"Are you sure?" Levi said, adjusting his belt. "It's going to be comprehensive."

Without moving his lips, Jeff whispered, "Say no, say no, say no."

"I'm sure," Ruth replied. "Let's talk."

"Jenkins—Ruth," Levi began as the lines in his forehead relaxed. "First and foremost, let me say that I'm sorry to hear about your mother. I lost my father a few years ago, and I know that's something you never really get over."

Ruth crossed her arms over her stomach as she sat in her own office on the customer side of the desk. She crossed her legs and looked at the makeshift ashtray by the open window.

"If we'd have heard about this at corporate, we'd have sent some flowers or something. But Jeff told me she died Sunday night and you had the funeral today? Isn't that uncommon? For black families?"

"Most of the family is in the area, so we—I—decided to go ahead and get it over with," Ruth deadpanned.

Levi looked down at her file. "Ruth, you know this process better than me, I'm sure. And I just want you to know that I—I mean, we at corporate are here to assist you in any way we can. Whatever we can do to assist you in sales, be it mailing lists, sales prompts—even lists of renewals—we'll provide because you're important to us."

"Cut to the quick," Ruth whispered.

"Excuse me?"

"Levi, listen. I don't mind having this review today, but let's not waste each other's time. You know me and you know I am a truth woman. Truth me."

Levi closed her sales record. "I don't think this is an appropriate time to talk. Why don't we schedule a teleconference, say, tomorrow or Thursday, and we can—"

"Levi, let's talk now," and again she recalled the company motto. "Truth me."

"No," Levi stood up. He straightened his yellow tie, and his Adams apple slid to the top of his neck and stopped. "I think this is an opportunity to go home and spend some time with your girls. Are they still in town?"

Ruth felt her body throb. "I've been with this company thirty years. Okay?" The words settled like an iron hitting molten steel as she enunciated each syllable. "Thir-tee-years. I've worked my way up from the position of janitor to the job you hold now. There's nothing you can say or do I've not heard before. I don't want to wait all week, with everything happening in my life, trying to guess what's going through *your* head." Ruth's fingers laced together, and her thumbs twirled around each other. "So, if you don't mind sitting down and reviewing the action plan with me, we can get this over and I can *try* to get some work done today."

Levi sat down, reached in the pocket of his suit, and pulled out a Cuban cigar. After he slid it under his nose and appeared to contemplate his next move, he put it between his lips and lit it. Then he blew the gunmetal gray smoke out of the misshapen corner of his mouth. "Ruth, you've given this company thirty-two years, and we appreciate it. But because of that, I just don't want to—"

"Truth me, Levi, Jesus Christ. Why can't you give me—"

"You have thirty days."

"What?"

After a pregnant pause, he repeated, "Thirty days. That's your bottom line." Levi flicked his solid-gold lighter back into his metallic briefcase. "Your numbers over the last six quarters are for shit, and you've been below standards for the last two. We have thirty-eight days in this quarter, Jeff has allowed this office to go to hell in a handbasket, and we're casting off dead weight. There's your truth."

Ruth rubbed her hands together. "How can you give me thirty days to get my numbers up, when you know the entire office is suffering? It's not us, Levi. It's—"

"It's the community. It's the sales program. It's the insurance products," he said, counting off on his fingers. "Which one do you want to pick Ruth? Now, I *did not* want to go through this with you today, but you forced my hand."

"Levi, you've been in this business long enough to know it's the economy. People are out of work."

Levi took another puff from his cigar and looked at Ruth through the smoke. "It was *you* who told me when I was in sales that excuses are just like assholes. Everyone has one and they all stink. That was your mantra. Now, I know your mother was terminally ill for a while, but *you* have been slipping for years, Ruth. For years, and no one had the balls to say it."

"So you think that I am the reason the numbers in this office are low? Not because people can't find work? But because *my* numbers, after thirty-two years, have slipped?"

After he took the cigar our of his mouth and rolled it between his thumb and index finger, Levi looked at the woman who at one time was a legend in the company. "Jeff has the title. But everyone in Tampa knows that you stir the drink in this office. Wanna hear another Ruthism? A fish rots from the head. Remember that one? I still have that sign that used to sit on your desk in my office." Levi slid the cigar between his lips, and they stared at each other without speaking. Ruth had trained her sales people that when they negotiated, the first to speak always lost.

Levi leaned back and gazed at Ruth, refusing to blink. "What if," she whispered, "I just took early retirement in six months?"

"You know the answer as well as I do. I fire Jeff and run the office until I can find a manager to pull this place out of the crapper. And then I give you your gold watch or bracelet or whatever in six months."

"Levi, you and I both know that boy has a child with bone cancer! How could you do that?"

"You can never mix business with emotions. Someone who trained me told me that the first day I took over as DM. And I remember this particular woman firing a woman on Christmas Eve. "

"I never fired *anyone* on Christmas Eve."

"Of course you did. And the fact that *you* don't remember"—a haze of smoke drifted from his lips—"speaks volumes."

"I'm not going to beg you, Levi. You know that's not my style. But I will say that when I inherited this office it was down to a staff of five. I built this place up to twenty people and—"

"And now it's down to fourteen." Levi reached into his briefcase without looking and pulled out the envelope with her name printed on the front of it. He pushed it across the table and said, "If you want to be on the team, if you want to be a player, you're welcome to stay if you want six months. We owe you that much. But you have to make a decision."

"Momma, what are you doing?"

Standing in her office, Ruth answered her youngest daughter without turning to look as she took her fifteen-year plaque from the wall. "What does it look like, Wendy?"

"You're quitting?"

"Can't get a thing past you. What are you doing here? Where are your sisters?"

Wendy collapsed on the armrest of her mother's couch and looked as if she had been blasted with a shotgun shell filled with emotions. "They're coming. I thought you were going to do eight more and retire at sixty-five."

Without responding, Ruth took down her "district manager of the year" award. She remembered the night she received it as she wiped the dust from the beak of the embossed eagle. And then she heard her daughter Mimi walking up the hallway. "Wendy, listen, I need to run Annette by the drugstore. You need anything?" Mimi asked, looking from her sister to her mother. "What's going on?" she whispered. "I saw Jeff packing. You going back into management?"

"No," Ruth answered. "Listen, can you reach that certificate over there?"

Mimi, who was several inches taller than the other women in the family, retrieved the framed document and asked, "Then you're quitting?"

"There you go. Another genius in the family."

"But I thought you—"

Ruth turned to face both of her daughters. She wanted to say words she'd said to her sales staff and to clients on numerous occasions, but for the first time they sounded odd, even to her. "Life is nothing if not a series of changes. You adapt or you die." She swallowed sentiments she refused to grant the honor of showing on her face, "Life is simple. We make it difficult."

Mimi closed the door and asked, "So what happened?"

"They gave me an ultimatum and I had to make a move."

"Did they want you to manage the place again?" Wendy asked.

"No. This time they asked me to—to return to headquarters, and I don't feel like moving."

"But why not?" Mimi asked. "Wendy's leaving home in a few weeks. You don't—well, you don't have the responsibility of taking care of Grandmamma any longer, and you'll be in that big old house all by yourself. It might be a nice change of pace."

"I told them no, I don't want the responsibility. So they wanted me to take over Jeff's job, and I told them I wasn't doing it either, so they fired him and I told them—I told them I was taking my retirement effective immediately."

"Oh, my God," Wendy said as she leaned back against the wall. Her voice quivered. "This all just happened today?"

Ruth paused and sat in her chair. She bit her upper lip and replied, "Yeah. It all—it all just happened a few hours ago."

Mimi ran her fingers over her forehead, glanced at her mother's cluttered desk, and said, "Let me cut to the quick. You took early retirement . . . because of Jeff? Jeff, the guy who campaigned for your job when your numbers dipped? Jeff, the guy who wouldn't nominate you for the Truth Award last year?"

Ruth held her tongue as she heard her eldest daughter walk toward the office singing "The Rhythm of Love." Annette knocked once and entered the office wearing a tie-dyed T-shirt and jeans. "Damn, it's hotter than that stereo Pookie-Poo tried to sell me at the house. Listen, why is everyone so quiet? You'd have thought there was a funeral in here." She took the space on the couch between her sisters and reached into the candy dish on Ruth's desk for a peppermint. "Wussup?"

Mimi replied, "Ruth quit."

"No shit?" Annette said, and her eyebrows rose like the McDonald's arches. "Really?"

"Yeah," Mimi added. "She quit over Jeff."

Ruth looked at her daughters, one by one. Each different in their appearance. Each a distinctive personification of her character. "You know something? Building this office from nothing was a lot like raising you guys. It was tough. I was determined and I took no prisoners. I'm proud of the result, and that's something no one can take from me. But it gets to the point where it's like quicksand. Everything is going fine, and then you find yourself in the midst of it, and the more you fight, the more you're consumed. And the more you're consumed, the more you decide to just give in. To just let go."

Wendy rested her forehead on her knees, as if she didn't want her mother to see her tears. "Momma, what are you talking about?"

"Decent," Ruth answered, and gazed at the top of her daughter's head. "I was a decent mother. A decent churchgoer and a decent city councilperson. A decent daughter. But you know something? I was a great manager. I turned a doggone taxi cab driver into one of the best salespersons this company ever had. And now—and now I'm out of work for the first time since I was—Jesus Christ," she groaned as if she had just realized her current predicament. "Since I was fifteen years old."

"You were a good mother. Tough. Rigid," Annette offered without a smile. "But good."

"When your daughters move out, move on, you can care less about tough or rigid love," Ruth replied. "You think about the times you had to leave them because you had to conduct a sales meeting. Or that appointment that just would not wait until Monday that you took on a Sunday night. You think about uprooting them when they wanted to stay in their school so you could compete with the white boys. The graduation you missed still hurts years later. When your daughters leave . . . when your best friend dies, when your mother goes, these are the things you think of."

Wendy held her head up and the zigzag scar of a tear showed on her face. "Momma, we're here for you. Okay?"

"Mimi," Annette said, "I left Bobby's engine running to keep the car cool. Let me go turn it off."

"No," Ruth interjected. "Why don't you guys go together? I just need to spend a few minutes taking care of things here; then I'll be home."

"You sure, Momma?" Annette asked.

Ruth leaned back and noticed for the first time Levi's cigar ash on the carpet of her office. She tapped it with the dusty toe of her shoe and watched it dissolve. "Yeah," she whispered, looking at the charcoal memory. "I'm sure. I'll see you all later."

Annette took her sister by the hand and headed out the door, but Mimi remained. She read the lines in her mother's face as if they were Egyptian hieroglyphics.

"What?" Ruth asked and returned her daughter's gaze.

"You got fired, didn't you?"

Ruth's first instinct was to deny, but all she could ask was, "How did you know?" She then followed her daughter's eyes down to the yellow, partially covered probation notice on her desk.

"You were always tough. But you were always fair. You were our mother *and* our father. Don't ever beat yourself up for raising us right. Yeah, Annette had a few problems—a while back—but for the most part, we did okay. I tell people all the time that you never dated because if it got serious you didn't want a strange man in the house with your teenaged daughters. You sacrificed love because you loved us so much. How many parents would do that?"

Ruth mumbled words her daughter could not hear.

"Excuse me?" Mimi asked.

"I said, I did not date," Ruth repeated, "because I was too busy trying to be the manager of the year. Too busy trying to be a GM. I sacrificed love for those plaques." Mimi's lips formed a fist as she looked at her mother across the desk. "I used to have a poster on my wall," Ruth continued, "in my very first office, that said, if you destroy the thing you love, the thing you love will destroy you. I used that poster to sell homeowner's insurance and never realized what it meant until this very moment. Everything I've built has crumbled all around me."

"No matter how much you want to beat yourself up, you were a good mother. I know losing Grandmamma, and with Wendy leaving in a few weeks, it's a lot, but in spite of everything you're going through, you were a good mother. Not just decent. But good."

"Listen, Mimi. I need you to catch up with your sisters. We can talk later on when I get home."

"I—Bobby has to be at work at five in the morning, so we're leaving as soon as I take Annette and Wendy back to the house. But if you like, I can—"

"Bobby got a job?"

"Well, he's laying tile for a hot boy. But that's another story in and of itself."

"I'll call you on the cell after you get on the road."

"You sure, Ruth? I don't mind flying back tomorrow. I don't have to be in surgery until Friday."

"I'm positive." And then from nowhere, the first smile she had shown all day appeared on Ruth's wrinkled face. In spite of her circumstances she looked redeemed, as if she was able to rise from the charred ashes of all that had happened to her. Her purple-black skin glowed;

she squared her shoulders, lifted her chin, and winked at her daughter. "Go catch up with your sisters and we'll talk later."

"You gonna be all right?"

"Would I lie to you?"

Mimi returned her mother's confident smile, stood as if she wanted to walk around the opposite side of the desk and hug her, but waved good-bye and walked away.

With her office door cracked, Ruth watched Jeff pass the door with a U-Haul box, stiffly refusing to look in her direction. Then she looked at the wallpaper that showed the faded rectangular blotches where her numerous awards had hung for so long. She looked at the fruits of thirty-two years of service in the cardboard boxes on the floor and tried to decide what she would do with them once she got home. Would they mean as much displayed in a family room where there was no longer a family?

Her back arched with pride, Ruth reached into her purse for a handkerchief but found the obituary she'd held during the funeral. Her body deflated and her heartbeat slowed. Void of enough energy to hold back her feelings, she looked up at the ceiling, opened her mouth, and sobbed into the silence.

Detour

Trevy McDonald

"Hearts do not meet one another like roads."

—African, Ivory Coast

I t was my third cigarette, my second cosmopolitan, and I was still waiting. I looked around at my unfamiliar surroundings. The cubist paintings with muted tones of blue and brown that adorned the walls accompanied the subtle yet inviting bluesy trumpet of Wynton Marsalis, which permeated throughout Vialli's fine Italian restaurant. I took a sip of my drink, savoring the blend of citrus vodka, triple sec, lime, and cranberry juice that had become one of my many favorites. *Drink up*, I told myself. After all, you're supposed to celebrate your birthday, especially a milestone like the thirtieth. But not alone.

I looked around at the couples sharing tantalizing gazes as they laughed, smiled, shared meals and special times in an intimate booth or at a table adorned with candlelight. Other tables held giggling girlfriends keeping abreast of the latest developments in each other's lives. Everyone around me seemed to be enjoying themselves immensely, but somehow I felt all eyes were on me. And my eyes were on the door.

I pulled my engraved chrome case from the designer pony fur bag that went perfectly with my basic black dress—a staple for every woman's closet. I took a slow drag from my cigarette—there were now two left—scanned the room, and glanced down at the sapphire, crystal, and oyster case on my wrist. Only five minutes had passed since I last checked, and still no sign of them.

All dressed up and by myself. This was typical. I had traveled throughout the world on business trips for my firm, often choosing to order room service to spare myself the shame of dining alone. I knew what must have been going through everyone's mind as I sat at the bar; my left leg dangled over the right. I avoided eye contact as I sipped my drink, inhaled my cigarette, and scrutinized the room. What was the problem, and why was I here alone? Was there some mix-up? Were they lost? At the wrong restaurant? Or did they just forget?

Celebrating our birthdays together had been our tradition since freshman year of high school. But here I was, sitting alone on mine. On my thirtieth. I certainly thought by now I'd have my life in order. Husband, maybe a child or two. At least a fiancé by now. Can I get a boyfriend, or just a lover?

My friends always told me I lived the life. A business meeting in Prague, a retreat to Vail, vacationing in Fiji. Constantly zipping off to worldwide venues, yet coming to my River North town home with nothing but my plants and collection of jazz CDs to keep me company. What kind of life was that?

My family told me I had made it. I'd pulled myself up by the boot-straps and transcended my working-class neighborhood by leaps and bounds. My Wharton M.B.A. in finance with an emphasis in foreign markets was my vehicle to success. Yet I found it to be a lonely road, one that was straight, smooth, and much less traveled.

As I extinguished what was nearly the butt of my cigarette, I thought maybe I should have chosen our regular spot rather than venturing out to this new West Loop location, which was more me than our old neighborhood hangout. At least I would have known someone there, but I had evolved. And I was beyond greasy burgers and tacos with fattening french fries. Exotic shellfish dinners, zesty pastas, and the finest cuts of black Angus beef were what tempted my taste buds now.

The decision to order another cosmo or pack it up and call it a night faced me. I was used to drinking alone, but usually at home. I often sat alone on my deck and peered out at the Chicago River. A perfect romantic setting I treated myself to at least once a week. Just as Otis, the bartender with whom I had recently become acquainted, took my order and I lit my next to last cigarette, my handbag shook, indicating I had a call on my vibrating cell phone.

"Reyonna Lawson," I answered. It was Jalicia. We'd been friends since fifth grade, when her family moved to our neighborhood on the South Side. She was a hard worker with a good heart, but she'd made choices that had cost her youth and several opportunities.

"Happy birthday, Rey!"

"Where are you?"

"I got held up at the store." Jalicia managed a discount clothing store in the mall.

"So you're on your way?"

"I know you're having loads of fun without me. But it doesn't look like I'm gonna make it. Damarius's graduation is in the morning, and I have to pick up some last-minute items." Jalicia spoke of her son, who had been born when she was sixteen. While she thought I had it all together because I'd spent my twenties childless, I envied the sacrifices she made for him. She had dropped out of high school and spent many years in dead-end jobs to support him, until a night school G.E.D. program moved her toward greater opportunity. Once Damarius was settled in high school, Jalicia planned to enroll in evening and weekend classes at City College, so she could set a new family trend for her son to follow. I took another drag on my cigarette.

"You aren't sucking on those cancer sticks, are you? I thought you were quitting today."

"Handle your business, girl, and I'll handle mine. See you tomorrow at the graduation." I was Damarius's godmother. He was a good kid and his love for his mother was apparent. He said he wanted to grow up and become a banker so he could help struggling single mothers like his own become homeowners.

"Toodles."

At least Jalicia did have the decency to call me and let me know what was up. While disappointed, I had to respect her for that. Mishon, on the other hand, wasn't as courteous. She might show up, or she might not. She spent her days serving on boards of directors for non-profit organizations and shuttling her little ones off to gymnastics and soccer. She had a successful doctor husband, a North Shore home, and her perfect family. She had achieved the goal she set when she went to college as a nursing major. She and Grant had married right after college graduation, and while their road had been winding while he struggled through medical school, the investment had paid off and Mishon was able to hang up her scrubs for society affairs and humanitarian causes.

Tunisia had a good excuse for not being here. She was out pursuing her dream. Though well rounded and well versed, she had been only an average student in high school. Since her test scores and grades didn't attract college offers or scholarships and she had a host of younger siblings to help support, she'd gone to work for the phone company after high school graduation. Her first day on the job, she'd met Linwood, and the rest was history. Marriage, three children, and now that the youngest was in school, she was able to take advantage of the tuition reimbursement offered by her employer and get her bachelor's. Attending school on a part-time basis while juggling her many balls of family, work, and school left her wondering if there was such a thing as recess.

Life was ironic. I sat at the bar alone, celebrating my transition from the young and perky twenties to the more responsible and settled thirties. I had been successful at attaining my educational and career goals, but failed at my personal goals. Mishon told me I'd missed out when I earned my M.B.A. without gaining an M.R.S. because I hadn't taken her hidden agenda of finding a husband into my pursuit of higher ed with me. Jalicia said she'd love to walk in my designer shoes any day. Tunisia told me not to worry, that love had found her when she wasn't looking.

The likelihood of my spending the rest of the evening at the bar alone was strong. So I took a swig of my cosmo, pulled tab plus tip out of my purse, lifted my jacket from the bar stool beside me, and prepared to plant my feet on the floor for my solo journey to the door. I'd pick up some Chinese carryout and spend my birthday on my deck, watching the river watch me, alone again.

"Leaving without dinner?" I looked around to see who could possibly be talking and who they were talking to. Who had been watching me? Who had noticed my solitude?

"Just stepping away for a moment," I responded to the neatly bearded gentleman with a shaved head and warm, inviting brown eyes. "To the ladies' room," I said discreetly. My plans for the evening had suddenly been modified. What a welcome change. I wasn't accustomed to inviting myself or permitting myself to be invited to dine with strangers. But then, I wasn't about to spend this turning point out on my deck with citronella candles, cold Chinese food, and bitter wine. Not alone, anyway.

"I'm sure I'll have a table before you return," he said.

I held my head high as I floated to my destination. I freshened my makeup, smoothed out my dress, and made certain that every hair was in place. With everything in order, I was ready to revel in fine food and whatever came next.

I scanned the room and immediately located my birthday guest. I hadn't noticed how tall he was, but he stood out, proud and towering. I joined him, extending my hand across the table for a handshake.

"Reyonna Lawson," I said as he gently kissed the back of my hand and shared his name.

"Brandon Shaw."

What an introduction.

"How long had you been sitting there?"

"How long had you been watching me?" We both laughed as the waiter came to take our drink and dinner orders.

"You can't fault a brother for paying special attention to a beautiful woman, can you?" He did have a good point. "Whoever he is should be ashamed of himself, leaving you sitting there all alone. Kick the brother to the curb. He's not worth the time he spends in your thoughts."

"Who said it was a brother?"

He nearly spit out his drink. "In that case, whomever—"

My laughter interrupted Brandon's thought.

"Just breaking the ice." He wiped his mouth with his napkin.

"On a serious note, I was supposed to be celebrating my birthday with my girls. But they have families. Stuff happens. I'm the single one in the bunch."

"Happy birthday."

"Thank you."

"So that makes you the odd man—or woman, rather—out."

"Actually, the one with the most social time on my hands."

"And how do you like to spend that time?"

"Indulging in the finer things in life."

"Aside from fine clothing and fine food, what other fine things do you like?"

I took a sip from my fourth cosmopolitan. "Fine men." I didn't know if it was something about this generational milestone that greeted me this particular day, or the slight inebriation that had taken over, but I found myself comfortable, overconfident, and candid.

When the waiter brought our orders, Brandon reached across the table, took my hand, and blessed the cuisine. "And if I were forward, I'd ask you where I ranked on your scale of fineness."

I took another sip. "Like a vintage Bordeaux." Where was this coming from? I was never this forward. I decided to indulge in my lobster tail and respond only when spoken to.

"So you think I'll just get better with time?"

"There's only one way for me to find out."

"And how might I do that? When you aren't spending your time in-

dulging in fine clothes and fine food, what finer things might you indulge in with a fine man?"

"I'm a patron of the arts—music, dance, theater. You name it, I'm
there. I have quite a collection of original paintings in my home and office."

"What genre?"

"It's pretty eclectic. I find that different paintings set forth different moods in the different rooms of my home. But my collection con-
sists solely of black artists, African and African-American, such as
Bayo, Kelvin W. Henderson, and Everett Spruill."

"Any Shaws, as in Brandon Shaw?"

"Oh, my God! You did the poster for the Chicago Black Arts Fest
last year. I do have some of your work, but no originals."

"Then you'll have to visit my gallery."

"When?"

"How about tonight? After dinner."

"Only if that means we can skip the silly birthday song they always
do in these restaurants." My friends knew I hated those clap-your-
hands, round-the-gang-up-and-bring-the-dessert fests.

"I hate those things, too," Brandon said as he ate the remaining
morsels on his plate. "We can call it a night, if you prefer."

"Night," I said, giggling, knowing I'd had a bit too much to drink,
and I was grateful I'd taxied over from the office. Rather than run the
risk of twisting my Q 45 around someone's tree or light pole, I usually
relied on my girls to see me home safely. But things were changing.

I reached into my purse and whipped out my gold card.

"This one's on me, birthday girl. I can't invite you to dinner and then
expect you to pay."

"Thank you, Brandon."

"Besides, I'm sure you aren't going to leave my gallery empty-
handed."

"If your work is as good as I remember, I'm sure I won't."

We left the restaurant and took the short ride over the river to the
Art District. Brandon's gallery wasn't far from my home. What a coincidence. I wondered why I hadn't noticed it during my Saturday
afternoon gallery walks.

The Shaw Gallery was located on the first floor of a loft building.
Floor-to-ceiling windows allowed the passersby to inspect his oils,
acrylics, and watercolors. Through the moonlight that shone into the

dark gallery, I saw the range of Brandon's talent. On the west wall hung a piece that had to be five by three feet in my estimation. Perfect to go over my new living room sofa..

Brandon turned the key in his lock and flicked the light on. "Surprise!" emanated from the gallery. Jalicia and Demarius, Tunishia and Linwood, Mishon and Grant. And Reese, my business partner, who had obviously arranged this event.

Looking at Brandon, I felt deceived. He was there for one purpose, and it had nothing to do with his finding me alluring. My hopes for what time would tell shattered all around me. Demarius grabbed my arm and pulled me across the room. "Aunt Rey, wait till you see your birthday gift."

Brandon unveiled a portrait of me. It was from a picture I'd taken last Christmas during my vacation to Tahiti. I was speechless. Numb. It was the sweetest thing anyone had ever done for me.

I don't remember much else about my thirtieth birthday party. But each day, as I look at the portrait, and into Brandon's eyes, I recall that fateful evening and all it taught me about life and love. Tunisia had been right. I'd been looking for a good time with girlfriends and had been surprised with an introduction to the rest of my life. I'd learned that love wasn't the straight, smooth, and narrow road that my professional life had been, one where I could clearly see what was ahead and navigate my way to success. I had taken a detour for love. The whole thing was now as clear to me as the compassion that Brandon had seen in my eyes and interpreted so beautifully in his portrait of me. I'd taken a detour onto a winding road and found love, and now I was cruising on the main drag.

The Alcoholist

David McGoy

"Being sober is the best high." —African American

My name doesn't matter. And please don't confuse me with one of those fools who stand up in the middle of a room full of strangers proclaiming the obvious. They claim it's anonymous, but the first thing they ask you to do is say your name. An alcoholist is something totally different.

Unlike my addicted counterparts, I choose not to indulge in alcohol. It is the plight of the alcoholic to live a day-to-day struggle to avoid consumption of beer, wine, and spirits. They consider themselves diseased, victims of some sort of genetic conspiracy. But I am not that. I have a healthy love for alcohol, and it makes me the success that I am.

Long ago I was one of those fools who paid five dollars a sip when I could have had the whole bottle for fifteen from the liquor store on the corner. I was one of those fools who thought drinking alone made me an alcoholic. But I am not that. I extricated myself from the pitfalls of booze, and I am still able to savor the alcohol high.

One afternoon, a few years ago, I arrived at work to find Bob Bales, head of the ISM group, waiting to greet me at my desk with two security officers in tow. I had missed the weekly Global Turnover meeting for the sixth time in the past two months. The Global Turnover meeting was at 11:00 A.M. This week, they had moved it back an hour on my behalf, as I was a critical member of the ISM team. At least I had been.

The whole scene is surreal in my memory now, one of those things that happen in slow motion. I took in all the looks of pity and dismay on my walk to the conference room. Most of my colleagues never said a word to me, and a few would even cross the street if they saw me coming. It should be some consolation, I thought as I marched to my unemployment, that I would never have to see them again. But in a strange sort of way, I felt I would miss them.

The night before was just a blur to me. I woke up facedown on the floor next to my bed, with my pants at my knees and an ugly bruise on my cheek. Apparently, I had stumbled in an attempt to undress myself and go to bed. I had to borrow money from my landlord to get to work. If it weren't for the fact that it was payday and the rent was due, she wouldn't have given me the three dollars I needed.

"Excessive tardiness, failure to fulfill required job functions, making unauthorized long-distance calls . . ." Bob rattled off an entirety of offenses, none of which pointed to the real problem. He was a corporate hotshot who had been handed everything he ever called his own. *Unauthorized long-distance calls!* This was a billion-dollar company with worldwide offices. I just sat there in a drunken daze, the taste of tequila lurking at the top of my throat.

"Your severance compensation will consist of four weeks' pay for each year of service," said the shrill voice of a brown-haired woman who I just noticed was sitting on the opposite side of the conference table. She wore a blue blazer and a white blouse, the corporate uniform for firing day. "You will continue on the payroll for one month. Your health benefits will continue for three months." The HR officer's voice trailed off as I implored myself not to put my head down on the table.

"Here is some information on COBRA, your 401K, settling your stock options," she continued, sliding me an array of folders, papers, and envelopes that looked like a dossier for a covert operation. "Your outplacement counselor is ready to meet with you now." Another figure appeared at the table as if out of nowhere. I made it a point to case the conference room to see if there was anybody else I didn't notice.

"We're here to help you with your transition," said the man with a bad suit and worse toupee. "Our services include workshops, résumé writing, counseling . . ."

As he blathered on about my "transition," his hypnotic, bulging eyes became too much for me to take. I allowed my burning forehead to rest on the cool surface of the conference table. My ear and cheek followed suit. I took a deep breath, inhaling the shocked and confused silence emanating from the members of my firing squad. No one knew what to do. After tennis-watching Bob and me for a moment, the HR officer nodded once and moved briskly from her seat to the door. The guy with the toupee followed suit, leaving behind a business card and yet another folder. "We're here to help you," he assured me on his way to the door.

"Dude, get some help," Bob admonished. "You're in really bad shape. And you *know* what I'm talking about. Take this time to straighten yourself out."

I glared at this hypocrite but said not a word. Bob and I had tossed back more than a few rounds together in our day. Now he was here with his goatee and his corporate jargon, putting on this performance of self-righteous concern. I just took my windfall and ran.

There is another element, a group that is stricken far worse than the nameless, self-pitying sheep that flock to those ghastly AA meetings. Though meek and unempowered, at least they do assert themselves by acknowledging their affliction. This other element, the fools who perpetuate the notion that it is not drinking, but drinking *alone* that is the true indicator of abuse, are the ones with the real problem. I call them *sociaholics*.

These fools frequent bars and clubs every night, night after night, into the night, to commune with other *sociaholics*. A birthday, a resignation, a Tuesday—there's always an excuse. This is the population that I serve. I am a caseworker, specializing in substance abuse research and intervention. I do not work for any government agency or nonprofit organization. I work for myself. The money is good and there's plenty of opportunity, but I do it for the high.

"I work for a law firm. But really what I want to do is be a judge. So what do you do?" Her name was April. Neatly dressed in black slacks and a bright paisley blouse with her hair spun into a hive of braids, she gave the impression of being in constant motion as she swiveled herself atop the bar stool. She had more jewelry than a little bit. She was twirling the straw in her drink as though performing some sensuous maneuver that I was supposed to feel. After the third round of straw twirling I began to feel seasick. But I pressed on.

"I'm a baseball player," I told her, sipping my drink.

"Really?"

I nodded. "I play center field for the Yankees."

I was on a particular high that night. The billion-dollar company I used to work for wasn't about to get involved in some highly publicized legal battle with the likes of me. So they gave me the farm. Between severance pay, unemployment, my 401K, and stock options that I would be promptly liquidating, I was sitting on almost a hundred grand. I wouldn't have to work for a looooong time. They made it possible for me to fulfill a lifelong dream and buy the crowded house a round of drinks, making me the centerpiece of attention at the after-work tavern. It was a position I relished.

Pondering my potential as an athlete, April appeared to be skeptical about my stated vocation. "Not the major league Yankees," I clarified. "The Staten Island Yankees, their minor-league affiliate."

"Oh!" she exclaimed as if she'd just had a great idea. "Wow. Center field. Really? I don't know much about baseball but—"

"I'll never make it to the big leagues," I said matter-of-factly. "I'm too short. And the money's not that great. But I love baseball. And I'm a damn good thief."

"Thief?" she asked.

"I get on first. I steal second." She didn't understand. "Led the league three years in a row in stolen bases."

"No kidding?" she asked eagerly.

As Annie the bartender breezed by, I pointed at our diminishing glasses. "Baseball is an easy life. All you need is good eyes and quick reflexes, and you can play for a looooong time."

She nodded, visibly impressed, trying to contain her excitement over how her evening was unfolding. She knew nothing about baseball, so it was an easy lie to carry out. Confidence and charm are rare talents, precious commodities that really get you far in this world. Unfortunately, I often find myself in short supply.

"Another round?" I asked rhetorically as Annie returned with our drinks.

Nine months was all it took me to go through a hundred grand. I went to bars in almost every baseball city. I bought drinks and told stories, made friends, collected business cards and favors. I didn't know it at the time, but it was the beginnings of my research.

There's nothing like the atmosphere of a good bar. "A clean, well-lighted place" was how Hemingway described it. I have spent much of my time searching for the perfect watering hole, and can gladly say that I have found it again and again.

Sociaholics are gregarious creatures. Even the aloof ones, mulling in the corners, are craving the attention and interest of the room. Long ago, I was one of those fools. Now attention and interest is what I provide.

When it came to drinking, Papa Hemingway knew whereof he spoke. He was the one who said that it wasn't *finishing* bottles that revealed a sickness, but *opening* them. *Sociaholics* pay handsomely to have someone open bottles on their behalf. It is a way of keeping their hands clean. It takes the burden off the drinker and places the responsibility on the shoulders of the ones who pour.

Her timing was always impeccable. Annie returned with another round just as April was just heading off to the ladies' room. This was my chance to make a move. Leaning forward, wearing the silly, knowing grin of a drunkard, I whispered coyly, "Let me buy you a drink."

Annie shook her head with a friendly smile. "You don't have to do that; I can drink for free. Besides, I don't drink." She was a tall, slim Latina from the Bronx, tending this nondescript downtown bar. I had been hitting this spot pretty hard lately because of the one-dollar drafts, the buybacks, and Annie. She was a little older than I was, perhaps late thirties, and her dark features and hair were a faceless man's dream. She didn't drink, but she smoked like a chimney. And she mixed a mean Long Island iced tea. Moving gracefully, she shared a little friendly banter with each customer before moving on to the next order and the next drink. She had a gift for small talk.

"You *don't drink?*" I was incredulous. "Why not?"

"Being sober is the best high," she deadpanned in reply. "I just like to see everyone laughing and talking, dancing and having a good time. I don't have to drink."

"So . . . you actually have fun being surrounded by booze but can't drink?" Annie nodded, tugging at her cigarette. I found both the smoke and the notion of sobriety repulsive. "It's fun to watch. You should try it some time." Grinning knowingly, oblivious to all but my own egotistical thoughts, I blurted out, "So what do you think, watching me?" Anne flicked a few ashes, then rested her cigarette in the ashtray.

"I think you're drunk." She smiled, turned, and briskly moved on to the next order and the next drink.

*   *   *

There are four basic stages of drunkenness: *verbose, bellicose, morose*, and *comatose*. Examining behavior in each of these categories, as I have, would make anyone wonder: exactly what is the appeal of drinking?

Like any mind-altering substance, alcohol is meant to evoke some sort of fantasy in the user, a trancelike state in which perfection is achieved. Unfortunately, alcohol serves very poorly in this capacity. It only can make you *verbose, bellicose, morose,* or *comatose*, not to mention *broke*. *Sociaholics* learn this lesson again and again and again. But they keep coming back.

Why do people drink? The answer remains elusive. No matter what their intent, it is my mission as an alcoholist to give each of my clients their fantasy, but also to take the weaning process a bit further. It is a twofold service.

"What are you drinking, anyway?" the girl in orange giggled as she slid back on top of her bar stool. She was on her fourth Amaretto sour. "Pepsi with a cherry," I replied, offering her a sip. "I made it up, or so I think."

"It's not that strong."

"Oh, yes it is," I assured her. "It sneaks up on you."

"Where's the cherry?"

I pointed to a cocktail napkin holding a cherry stem that was tied into a knot. I had left it there to impress her with my oral prowess. Little did she know I had done it with my fingers. Even on a good day, I couldn't use my tongue to fold a cherry stem in half.

"It's not bad, but too sweet," she thought aloud as she took a sip, then began twirling my straw. "Why is it called Pepsi with a cherry, even though they serve you Coke?"

"Because Pepsi rhymes better." She laughed far longer and harder than the statement warranted. "Would you like one?" I offered.

"I better not. I should go."

"Let me see you to a cab."

"You don't have to do that. I was gonna take the train."

I shook my head profusely. "No way. You have a long way to go and I've been sitting here getting you tipsy and I want to make sure I don't read about you in tomorrow's paper. Please. Let me do this for you." She laughed a little, visibly charmed. We exchanged a few more pleasantries while we finished our drinks and I paid the bill. I tipped

Annie handsomely. We walked out into the January cold and hailed a cab.

"I like you," she said flatly as I opened the cab door. "You're a gentleman. There aren't too many of you."

"There are more of me than you think. Besides, I'm not really a gentleman. A gentleman would see you all the way home."

Our eyes lingered for just a moment before she pulled me into the cab and we were off.

"I'm a dealer," I told the gentleman with the sweater vest and Movado watch. His name was Calvin. He was just finishing the last of a pitcher with his bureaucrat coworkers. There was Trudy, the birthday girl, and her sidekicks Simone and Rudi. Marco from Belize and Dan from Queens were like a comedy team. All of them showed the classic symptoms of *sociaholism*, but I had my sights set on Calvin.

"Art dealer, drug dealer?" He asked playfully.

I giggled. "No, a card dealer. Croupier. In Harrah's Casino, Atlantic City."

"Oh, wow!" he laughed. The group was impressed by the novelty. "I didn't think you looked like a drug dealer."

"Well what *do* I look like?" I asked surreptitiously, fixing my eye on his. His dark, cratered face reminded me of a sandwich cookie. With his pink lips and large white teeth, he bore a strong resemblance to a certain British pop singer from the 1980s whom I despised. After my subtle flirtation, we suffered through a few moments of stilted silence until Trudy broke in.

"So what's it like, working in a casino?" she asked.

"Actually, it's really not too different than what you all do—push papers." The statement had built upon earlier humor, so we all laughed heartily, starting and stopping almost simultaneously. "It's a living," I said somberly. "A good one if you like smoky rooms and being surrounded by booze but can't drink." The group was slightly troubled by the idea, as I once was.

"How do you become a dealer?" she asked. "Do they have schools?"

I nodded. "The hard part is mastering the rules and getting a good gig. It's a good job, but it's not for everyone. As long as you have good eyes and keep your hands in shape, you can do it for a loooong time."

I told them stories of cities, casinos, and places I'd been. Places they would never go. Some of it I made up as I went along. The bureaucrats

nodded pensively, listening with heartfelt interest, comparing my life
to the workaday existence they all shared. But I wouldn't let them remain somber.

"Another round?" I offered as Annie appeared.

If you ever want to get on the good side of someone in a bar, just
buy them a drink. Redneck, Republican, radical, whatever. Buy them a
drink. And all your differences, all your hostilities, can be set aside for
a little while. Buy a drink, and you will love your enemy. Buy a drink,
and you will find common ground, the willingness to spend time. I use
this lure to engage *sociaholics* in a familiar, comfortable setting. It is
then that I administer the most tender of treatments.

Long ago, it was enough for me to navigate a simple conquest like
the mind, body, and interest of a woman like April. But I have no use
for matters of the heart. These days my charm and confidence lead me
to endless treasures.

"I'm taking him home. You guys want to come party?"

Calvin was slumped over at the bar, and I was right next to him.
Trudy and the other ladies had gone home to get ready for another day
of pushing papers. Dan and Marco were debating some enormous so-
ciopolitical issue, impassioned beyond recognition of the world around
them, disturbing the karaoke singers with their heated exchange. They
were asked on two occasions to keep quiet by a huge bouncer who was
all too willing to pick a fight with any drunken fool who gave him just
cause. Lucky for them, I was there to save them by stunning them into
shocked silence as I shamelessly flirted with their colleague. I had been
making subtle advances and innuendos throughout the evening. It was
easy to tolerate while I was buying them drinks, but now at the end of
the night, the inevitable began to pose a problem for them. Annie appeared.

"Last call."

There was an enormous pause, then a low gurgle about having to
get up early for work tomorrow, but I persisted. "One for the road, on
me!" I said festively, then put my arm around Calvin and kissed his
cheek. "But no more for him." Paralyzed, stuck in alcohol inertia, Dan
and Marco weighed the implications of what was transpiring. I could
see the questions in their eyes. Was it possible? Was he . . . ?

"Here's to new friends," I offered as a toast, and looked upon the object of my desire. Remaining cautiously polite, Dan and Marco were rapidly becoming *morose*, lacking the coherence to intervene. We touched glasses. Finishing my drink quickly, I paid the tab (tipping Annie handsomely, of course), and gave both of my new friends a warm embrace. Then I guided Calvin along in his drunken stupor, leaving his work buddies behind to speculate. His driver's license said he lived in Jersey City. With a little good fortune and directions from the gas station off the exit ramp, I made it in thirty-five minutes.

"Calvin." I shook his shoulder, first gently, then harder. He didn't budge. I moved closer "Cal. Wake up." I said it directly in his ear, resting one arm on his thigh and the other on his shoulder. He was *comatose*. I left his apartment with $120 in cash, a jug of silver ($87 when counted), a guitar, and a thirty-inch television. I lament that I forgot the watch. I consider the fee a symbol of lost values, something that can never be replaced. It is a calling card that says, *you were at the mercy of a total stranger. . . . What could have happened?*

Not all nights are like this. Some nights I come home with nothing, and have even lost a few dollars on occasion. I even have a few bruises and a dog bite to show for my troubles. The risks are great, but the reward is greater. And like I told you, I do it for the high.

Calvin would get his wallet in the mail, along with a credit card bill from a certain nondescript after-work tavern. But he wouldn't care much about that, nor would the loss of possessions really matter. What would haunt him most of all would be the strange blurs of remembrance to which he would not commit belief. The thing that would haunt him most of all, the memory that would make him reconsider ever letting another drop of spirits touch his lips, would be his horror at waking up facedown on his bed, with his pants at his knees.

Being sober is the best high. That bit of knowledge changed my life. It made me realize that becoming an alcoholist was the best solution. After that, giving up drinking was easy. Now I have a lucrative career providing a valuable service to people in need. I'll be doing this for a loooong time.

You might consider me just a hustler, a pickpocket, or a petty thief. But I am not that. I do not lurk in subways or cause collisions on rush hour sidewalks. I reach out to people and give them what they want and what they need. I try to help them. In the long run, I think I do.

Annie gave up smoking, and now we're engaged. I don't know how it'll work out, but we've been partners in this business for some time, and we're a good team. We're going to leave New York and hit Vegas, where the big money is. There are plenty of gigs out there for slender Latina bartenders from the Bronx who love small talk. And of course, there are plenty of *sociaholics* in need of intervention. She'll pour and I'll provide the treatment. When things heat up or slow down, we'll just move on to the next city, the next order, and the next drink.

Handwriting's on the Wall

Gregory K. Morris

"When you believe in things you don't understand, you suffer." —Stevie Wonder

Mabel had to pee. Crouched low and straining, she gazed at the front door thirty feet away. Her head was twisted back, almost to the point of breaking her neck. Her legs were crossed at the knees, her thighs jammed together. As quickly as she could, she shuffled her feet backward, one step at a time over the paved walkway, toward the bathroom in the house that her children had just rushed her from.

"Never thought I'd see the old woman do the moonwalk," Junior cracked to his sister, Bernice. The two stood on the front lawn watching Mabel back her way to the toilet. "Mama, you ain't Michael Jackson," he bellowed at the seventy-four-year-old. "Now, turn around and go on to the bathroom, so we can go!"

Mabel stopped to take a breath. The large black pocketbook dangling from her right hand weighed a ton. It made her arm ache, as did her feet, nestled inside the tight but stylish high-heeled, black patent leather, pointed-toed shoes she'd gotten herself for her seventieth birthday. "It's bad luck to go back, once you get started," she managed, inching her way again toward the door.

"This is stupid!" Bernice chided. "Mama, we're going to be late for church. If you care about us at all, then don't make us late."

"I'm the one's got to pee!" Mabel said, having reached the front step. With her left hand she reached back for the handrail, but stopped short, feeling her grip on her bladder slip. A tear formed in her eye as she struggled to grab hold of her water and the handrail at the same time.

"Junior," Bernice directed, "go help that crazy woman before she messes herself and we have to be here for another hour!"

"Makes no sense being so superstitious," Junior mumbled. He grabbed Mabel and muscled the small but sturdy woman to the top of the steps, opened the front door, and helped her into the house. Once there, Mabel continued her backward journey across the front room, down the hall, and into the bathroom.

Moments later, she emerged through the front door again with a slight smile on her face. "We can go now. I'm all right."

"Well, get in the car, then," Bernice said as she walked around and got into the passenger seat. Junior headed for the driver's door and climbed in. Mabel stepped gingerly around to the rear door. Though her bladder was relieved, her feet still ached from the tight shoes.

Junior watched her tiptoe to the car. "Why don't you wear some decent shoes?" he preached as Mabel got in. "Ain't nobody lookin' at you. They don't care what you wear."

"I . . . am lookin' at me, and I care," Mabel responded indignantly. "These shoes are nice and go so well with this outfit. Ain't nobody in that church going to say that Mabel Jacobs didn't know how to dress herself."

"Mabel Jacobs could be buck naked in that church for all they care," Junior replied as he pulled out onto the main road. "And I don't see how you can be religious and superstitious at the same time, anyway."

"The Bible says, 'It'd do well for a child to respect his parents.' "

"Well, what it say about respectin' a fool?"

Mabel bit her lip and cast her eyes on the passing trees by the roadside.

"Crazy old woman," Junior mumbled, and fished a cigarette out of his shirt pocket.

"Mama," Bernice said as Junior raised a lighter to his face, "Junior's right. You can't be religious and superstitious at the same time. It's not natural."

"Says who?" Mabel asked.

"I mean, what sense does it make to back your way to the bathroom? You're still going back."

"Makes sense to me," Mabel answered. "And I've never been late for anythin' a day in my life." Suddenly, Mabel gazed around the car's interior. Spotting the wood-grain panel trim running along the dash, she lunged over the front seat.

"What in the hell are you doin'?" Junior blurted, and swerved in the road as Mabel's elbow struck his shoulder. Determined, Mabel reached for the dash and struck it three times with her knuckles before Junior and Bernice could shove her back into the rear seat.

"Knock on wood," she whispered, and fell back breathless. "Thank the Lord."

"You are out of your mind," Junior said, half turning to face her. The car veered again.

"Best keep your eyes on the road," Mabel suggested as she straightened the pillbox hat and netting on her head. "And ain't that callin' the kettle black, you sittin' up there puffin' away on that death stick but I'm the one's crazy. That smoke is gonna kill us all." She waved her hand in front of her face, coughed twice, then cranked down her window.

"Woman, it's cold outside!" Junior yelled. "Put that window back up!"

"Your father, he didn't smoke, God rest his soul, and he wasn't sick a day in his life!"

"And he still dead!" Junior sniped. "Guess if he'd smoked like me, he'd still be alive, huh?"

"Boy! You better respect the dead!"

"More stupid-stition, huh, Mama?"

"It ain't stupid. Sometimes the dead is all we got. Can't get to heaven if you don't die for your sins! That's not just respect; it's hope!"

"Hope, smope, Mama. That's all a bunch of bull and you know it."

"No, no," Mabel replied with a sassy shake of her head. "What's bull is you livin' with that woman."

"Don't go there, Mama."

"Why don't you marry her like decent folk? Her poor kids don't know whether to call you 'Daddy' or 'Uncle Junior.' You know you bringin' God's wrath down on you *and* her. God said, 'The two shall marry, the two flesh shall become one,' and . . . and, 'Thou shalt not shack.' "

Junior grinned.

"Our flesh becomes one every chance we get. You ain't got to worry 'bout that."

"Good! Cause I remember havin' to tell a certain eighteen-year-old, 'better in a whore than on the ground.' "

"Mama, please!" Bernice exclaimed.

"It's true. If your brother had spent as much time poundin' the pavement lookin' for a job as he did poundin' his fist, he'd be rich by now."

"Mama, shut up!" Junior grimaced.

"Junior!" Bernice yelled. "Watch your mouth!"

"But she tellin' a damn lie, Bernice. She ain't never told me no such thing."

"Regardless, she is still our mother," Bernice chided. Junior rolled his eyes back to the road.

Mabel slid back in her seat and started counting the tiny ventilation holes that were punched in the car's roof. "But he's got himself a woman now," she said absentmindedly.

"We been together for over seven years, so it don't matter," Junior huffed. We're common-law married."

"What's common is you refusin' to take that woman before God and askin' His blessings. How you think her mama and daddy feel? Or her children? And what do you call them little hardheads of hers? Jacob's daddy's babies? Thugs? What?"

"Those my kids, Mama. I'll call them whatever the hell I want."

"And why'd you stopped bringin' them to see me? I ain't seen that littlest one since last Christmas. I know you just bringin' them over to collect their gifts, but still, I'd like to see them. And that woman of yours, I want to see the two of you in my house . . ."

Bernice stared at Junior as he drove and puffed away, as Mabel sat raving out the open back window. The cool wind stung her nose and made her eyes water. "Why you have to get her started on that?" Bernice whispered to Junior.

"Now, don't you start," Junior warned. "Mama's craziness is enough without your help."

"I know that. But you *know* she's crazy. Why can't you just humor her like we agreed?"

"Cause she ain't bustin' your chops; she bustin' mine."

"And you ain't all squeaky clean yourself," Mabel said, rolling her eyes at Bernice. "I told you, Miss College Education, to keep readin' your Bible. But seems like you read everythin' else but. The Bible says clear as a bell to 'be fruitful and multiply.' But you marry a fine man and only have one child and I bet that one wasn't your idea. I had seven and would have had more if I could."

"One is enough," Bernice defended.

"Yeah, enough to raise a hellhound. That boy of yours is spoiled rotten. He was spoiled the day he fell from your wound."

"It's womb, Mama."

"And now he's a strung-out sixteen-year-old, out there doin' God knows what. When was the last time you seen him—Christmas? Must be somethin' about Christmas and kids. Don't they ever just think of home, some time?"

Bernice shook her head slowly but kept staring at her mother.

"More kids would have forced you to raise that boy," Mabel continued. "You wouldn't have had a choice. Each one would have pushed the last one out' the nest till they all were gone. It would have trained you on how to parent."

"One was enough, Mama."

"Couldn't trust the Lord, no. Couldn't trust your mama, either. Put your trust in your job and birth control. And your son, he trusts the welfare. But ain't none of you readin' the Bible. Did you ever think what all that does to our family? Somebody done already made all them mistakes and done wrote it down for you to learn. But you too educated to learn and too stupid to listen. So you got to repeat every one of them mistakes over, for yourself."

"Look, Mama," Bernice snapped, and pointed a finger at her mother. Catching herself, she pulled her arm down slowly. Junior smirked. "Mama," Bernice continued, "why don't we all just sit back and relax. We are on our way to church, for God's sake. Let's start acting like it. Now I suggest that we all just sit back and be quiet." Bernice eased back into her seat. "Let's all just pray . . . silently, meditate, or just ponder life—anything but talk for a while." She closed her eyes and took a deep breath. Junior started laughing. Rolling down his window, he tossed the cigarette butt out. The wind grabbed it and blew it back through the rear window, where it landed atop Mabel's pillbox hat.

"Shouldn't have spent all that time workin'," Mabel resumed, talking more out the window than at her two children. "Could have raised that child better if you'd been there for him. Probably would have had more children, too, if you'd been there cookin' and cleanin' for that man, keepin' his bed warm . . . instead of him warmin' it with somebody else."

"Mama!" Bernice yelled but didn't turn around. Incensed, she grabbed her pocketbook, fished out a pair of fingernail clippers, and then started popping nails about the car. The top of Mabel's hat began to smoke. Junior caught sight of the smoldering cigarette and smirked.

"Your job ain't your life; it's a paycheck!" Mabel continued.

"That's enough, Mama."

"And when was the last time you seen your husband?"

"Look!" Bernice snapped. "You're the one who taught me to stand on my own two feet, so don't go getting so 'holier than thou' now!"

"I taught you to stand up, not stand alone! Look at you. Where's your man, Bernice? Where's your son?" Mabel turned to Bernice as a liberated nail flew over the seat and popped her on the lips. Sputtering, she swiped a hand across her mouth. Bernice stared angrily out the front windshield.

"Bad luck to cut your fingernails on Sunday," Mabel admonished. Bernice glared. Without thinking, she locked the jaws of the clipper down on the quick of her thumbnail.

"Awwh!" she yelled.

"I told you," Mabel smirked. "And you shouldn't swear on Sunday, either." Bernice screeched, then threw the nail clipper just beyond the tip of Junior's nose and out his window. Her thumb started to bleed. Rising smoke from Mabel's hat began rushing out her window. Melting fishnet filled the car with a burning-polyester aroma.

"Bad luck to fish on Sunday, ain't it, Mama?" Junior cracked.

"Yep," Mama replied. The car bounced off the main road and into the church parking lot.

"Bad luck to work, bad luck to fish, bad luck to iron, bad luck to cut your nails? I guess everythin' is bad luck on Sunday, huh, Mama?"

"Not everythin', Junior," Mama replied. "Go to church. Give the day to the Lord."

"Well, is it okay to put out fires on Sunday?" he asked as he parked the car.

"The Bible says, 'ox in ditch on Sunday, get him out,'" Mabel replied.

"Good," Junior answered. Reaching under the seat, he retrieved an old newspaper and rolled it up before getting out and opening the door for his mother. Bernice jumped from the car as it stopped, and wrapped a glove around her wounded thumb. She rounded the back fender just as Mabel emerged from the car, her hat billowing smoke.

"Somethin' burnin'?" Mabel asked as she stood and sniffed the air. "Junior, your common-in-law mama-in-law must be cookin' for the pastor again."

"Mama, you on fire!" Junior yelled. Then he grabbed her by the arm and began beating her over the head with the rolled-up newspaper.

"Stop, fool!" Mabel yelled.

"Get that hat off her, Junior!" Bernice cried, "before her Jheri-Curl lights up!" With a clean smack to the back of the head, Bernice slapped her mother's hat to the ground, then jumped on it with both feet, stomping it violently into the powdery dust.

"My hat!" Mabel yelled, and reached for it, but Junior's strong grip prevented her. The two watched as Bernice jumped gleefully up and down, smashing the hat to bits. After a minute, Bernice stopped and looked about. The parking lot was devoid of people, except the three of them. "Thank you, God, for making us late," she whispered.

"That wood-grain panelin' was plastic!" Mabel answered. "That's why we late. You two see what you do when you mess with things you don't understand?" Junior and Bernice looked at each other incredulously. Mabel jerked her arm free of Junior's grip and marched off toward the church. "You make wood panelin' out of plastic . . ." she ranted as she walked, ". . . destroy the sanctity of marriage, put work life before home and family, turn this world upside down . . ."

Bernice and Junior watched until she disappeared inside. "I ain't doin' this no more," Junior protested.

"If everybody takes a turn, then it's only seven times a year," Bernice replied.

"I say we put her in a home and throw away the key," Junior said.

Bernice nodded her head in agreement.

"Mama!" Bernice yelled as she searched the parking lot. Church service had been over for thirty minutes. Most of the cars had gone, leaving only bustling dust clouds in the unpaved lot. "Junior, where's Mama?"

Junior stood with his foot propped against a large root protruding from the ground underneath an oak tree in the churchyard. He flicked cigarette ashes from the lit Marlboro lodged between his fingers. Several other men stood with him. "I ain't seen her," he answered. "Bet she done made it across the street to the graveyard." Junior motioned with his cigarette hand toward the rumpled two-lane road fifty feet away from the front of the red-brick church. Worry creased Bernice's face as she stared across the road and toward the Jacobs family plot on the other side. Thick maple, hickory, and oak foliage, dazzling in full autumn colors, blocked her long-distance search for her mother. Infuriated, she headed toward the road.

Large, brilliant, fire orange maple leaves danced in the cool October breeze. Sunbeams from the afternoon sky trickled through the leaves onto the large Jacobs family plot. Mabel Jacobs lay sprawled across a bed of fallen leaves, next to a large mound of dry, red North Carolina clay marking the plot of "Papa" Jasper Jacobs, her late husband. She spread her arms wide, raked the leaves over her body, and peered dreamily up into the autumn color burst. Red dust coated her deep-gray wool suit. Dry clay slowly mingled with the glistening Jheri-Curl juice on the back of her head. "I see, Papa," she said with a smile, "peace in the valley." She reached out and lovingly stroked the mound of dirt beside her. "Won't be long, Papa. It'll be you and me, together in the Lord's hands . . . forever. What the Lord hath put together, let no man put asunder."

"Mama!" Bernice yelled after making it across the road, dodging between speeding cars.

"Better make that, 'or woman put asunder,' Lord," Mabel sighed as she caught sight of her distraught daughter.

Bernice hustled to her mother's side. "Get up off that ground! I can't let you out of my sight for a minute! Look at you, all dirty. And look at the back of your head!" Grabbing her arm, Bernice muscled her mother up from the ground, spun her about, and smacked her backside, knocking away the leaves, grass, and dust. "Beats anything I've ever seen!" Deep, gritty red juice began easing off Mabel's dyed curls and onto her wool suit.

"Crazy ol' woman," Junior recited as he walked up. "Mama, I know you ain't this crazy. Why you doin' this?"

Mabel looked up at her son as she straightened her glasses. "Woman ain't got to have a reason to visit her folk. I was just payin' respects, that's all."

"You should try paying attention, Mama," Bernice yelled. "Didn't I tell you that that road was too dangerous for you to cross? What if you'd been hurt?"

"Y'all don't come out here no more, do you?" Mabel quizzed.

"What for?" Junior replied. "The past is gone, Mama. Let it go."

"If you don't know your past, then you're destined to repeat it," Mabel answered.

"Look, don't start that preachy stuff again, Mama, okay?" Junior stared hard at his mother.

Mabel looked up at her forty-two-year-old, balding son. He had his father's eyes. "Y'all sold this land, my place, Papa's place in eternity," she said.

"We did no such thing!" Bernice snapped, still pounding away at Mabel's suit. "This land is church burial ground. The church sold it."

"It was ours before it was theirs," Mabel replied. "This has been our family plot for a hundred years. My mama, she's over there; my daddy, he's right beside her; and Papa Jasper, your own daddy, he's lyin' peaceably right behind you." She smiled down at Papa's grave. "And my place is right here, under this tree, right beside him. This is our eternal restin' place, Papa's and mine. It's sacred."

"It's done, Mama," Bernice said. "It's too late for that."

"You were on the committee, Bernice. Why didn't you stop this? You know I didn't want to sell."

"I said, it's done, Mama. The land is sold and the graves will all be moved."

"Over my dead body!" Mabel shouted.

"That can be arranged," Junior snickered.

"This ain't funny, Junior," Mabel chided. "Look at Papa Jasper lyin' there. That man is at peace."

"That man is dead, Mama," Junior replied. "And I seen him at peace, plenty of times . . . when he was into his liquor bottle."

"Where is your respect, boy?" Mabel hollered. "That man is your daddy and he is dead! And all you can do is crack jokes."

"*Was* my daddy, Mama. Papa been dead for fifteen years. And he can't hear me." Junior kicked a rock at Papa's grave marker. "Besides, respect is earned. Papa never earned my respect."

"Junior!" Mabel exclaimed.

"Well, he didn't. All he did was beat me and stop me from doin' things I wanted to!"

"He fed you," Mabel said. "He clothed you; he raised you."

"Well, he was supposed to. I can't help that. I didn't ask him to."

"Junior," Mabel pleaded, and looked deep into her son's eyes, "your father loved you."

"Well, he was supposed to do that, too. He had me; I didn't have him. He fed me, but he only respected himself, not us; didn't he, Bernice?" Junior looked at his baby sister. Bernice's mouth fell open, but no words came.

"Bernice?" Mabel asked, turning to her thirty-seven-year-old daughter.

"Mama . . ." Bernice began, "Mama, well, Papa, he . . . It's time to go! Come on." Bernice grabbed Mabel by the hand and began pulling her along. Junior grabbed Mabel's arm to help.

"No! Wait!" Mabel bellowed as tears welled inside her. "I can't believe I'm hearin' this from my own children! Let go of me!" She stiffened her knees and planted both heels into the soft red clay. But Junior grabbed her under her arms, and together, he and Bernice wrestled her back to the car. Once there, Junior used the seat belt to strap her in the backseat. Then he slammed her door shut.

"She got to *go*," he said to Bernice before opening his door.

"I know," Bernice replied. They climbed into the car and headed toward Mabel's house, the old Jacobs place. The three rode in silence for a few miles. Salty tears streamed down Mabel's face.

"It . . . it's not that we didn't appreciate Papa," Bernice broke the silence.

"Yeah," Junior agreed. "He did feed us and all. And that was good." They paused and half smiled over the seat for Mabel to see. She peered at them both but continued to cry.

"All this time," Mabel whimpered, "I thought you loved him. But you had no love, no respect for him at all. You got no respect for him now." She turned and stared out the window. "And that means that you got no respect for me, either. For the life of me, I don't understand. All my life, I've lived for you. I gave you everythin' I had. And so did Papa, God rest his soul. We suffered many times just so you could have a good life. And all we ever asked in return was a little love, a little respect. All we needed to know, all we could ever hope for, was that you felt the same way toward us that we felt toward you. That's love. That's respect. I don't understand you." Mabel sniffed hard.

"Now, don't worry, Mama," Bernice said softly. "You're just tired; that's all."

"All the preachin', prayin', and superstition, I understand," Mabel sobbed to the listening window glass. "'You don't go back once you've started'; that way you're never late. 'Knock on wood' when you talk about somethin' good you want to keep happenin' to you. That reminds you to be humble. 'No workin' and no playin' on Sunday make you go to church and keep the Sabbath holy. Even findin' a whore gets you out of the house to meet people." Mabel dried her tears. "All that," she sighed, "I understand. But you, you disrespect me, Papa, the dead, the church, your marriage, and your family. Is nothin' sacred to you?"

"Just relax, Mama," Bernice coaxed. "Don't get yourself all worked up again."

"You don't get it, do you?" Mabel asked, and tried to stare into Bernice's eyes, but Bernice quickly turned away. "You think this is about me."

"Mama, I told you to relax," Bernice insisted. Junior pulled into

Mabel's driveway and parked. Quickly, he jumped out, opened her door, and loosed the seat belt about her.

He reached for her hand, but she slapped at him. "I don't need your help," she said, and scooted out the door around him.

"Mama, don't be like that," Junior said. "Me and Bernice, we gonna take good care of you. But you are gonna have to work with us."

"You and Bernice, " Mabel said as she watched Junior climb back into the car, "got your heads stuck deep up your own rear ends. That way you can keep right on doin' whatever you want to do whenever you want to do it." Junior cranked up the car as he stared out the window at his mother. "If you can't see around you," Mabel continued, "then you don't see no rules. If you don't respect nobody but yourself, then you don't need no rules. You just make them up as you go."

"Mama, you're just making things worse for yourself," Bernice warned.

"But you forgot somethin'," Mabel continued with a slight grin. "The only way you can live by your own rules is to be by your own self." She smiled.

"You're the one that's alone, Mama," Junior countered.

"Think again, fool," Mabel replied. "I got five other decent children. I got my church and my neighbors. I even got friends and family waitin' for me on the other side. You two think I'm just a crazy old lady waitin' on you to come take everythin' away from me?"

"Now, look here, Mama!" Junior shouted.

"No! *You* look, Junior," Mabel said as she charged up the driveway. "I bought the car you sittin' in! And I been talkin' to that woman of yours for weeks, tryin' to convince her not to put you out! She's fed up with you and your unemployed self. Why you think I been tryin' to convince you to marry the girl? It wasn't for her sake, or your kids. It was for yours. Well, you can count that gone. You'll be out by Friday."

"She won't put me out! Mama, you makin' this stuff up."

"And don't even think of comin' back here!" Mabel continued. "I'll have you arrested for trespassin'."

Junior jumped from the car. "You'd do that to your own son, Mama?"

"Nah, but I'd do it to you. Now get out of my face." She shoved Junior aside and stuck her head through the driver's-side window. "And as for you, Miss Thang, your son's been stayin' with me the past few months." Bernice's eyes bulged at the mention of her long-lost child. "I been tryin' to get him off those drugs and back into school."

"My boy is here?" Bernice asked with sudden concern.

"I guess he wanted to be close to his father. Yeah, that's right! Your husband has been livin' with Janetta, your best friend from high school, right across the street." Mabel pointed to a tall blue house. Bernice's head spun around to stare.

"Janetta Foster? Mama, why didn't you tell me?" Bernice screeched.

"I didn't want to hurt you, Bernice. I kept tellin' you that your family needed you. But I'm just a crazy old woman, ain't I? Well, this crazy old woman gonna send your son back to you tomorrow. You can deal with his drugs and his babies' mommas. I'm tired. And when your husband comes over to cry on my shoulder next week, like he's been doin', I'm not defendin' you anymore. I'm gonna tell him to do what I'm doin', kickin' the both of you to the curb."

Mabel withdrew from the window and strode off toward her house.

"And you best make room for your homeless brother. He's gonna need a place to stay." Mabel kept walking until she reached her front porch, where she turned and looked back. Bernice stood outside the car, staring across the road at the blue house. Junior rubbed his bald spot with one hand while fishing for cigarettes with the other.

"I saw through you two ingrates years ago," Mabel chided. "You can't get to my land, my house, or my money. And after I make a few phone calls, you gonna be out of my will, too. You were my children, my own flesh and blood, and I loved you. So I tried to help you. But you get used when you love somethin' that can't love you back. Well, you two have gotten all you're gonna get out of me. Handwritin's on the wall," she called, unlocking her door. "And if you don't understand, then you suffer."

Mabel strolled into her house, then closed and locked the door behind her.

The Sunday Smile

Marilynn Ngozi Griffith

"If you know the beginning, the end will not trouble you."
—African, Wolof

A brown tornado of braids and books tumbled into the screen door. The fan whirred on low, churning stale September air. An Afroed Jesus peered down from a canvas of black velvet at an old woman nodding with sleep on a high-backed bench below.

The girl tugged at her elbow. "Wake up, Grandma! Wake up!"

"Robert?" she said, lifting one creased eyelid and dropping it again.

"No, Grandma. It' s me. Sara Louise."

"Wha—what is it, chile?"

Goldie Bond pushed a wayward hairpin into place beside the others, restraining a tidal wave of steel-gray hair from escaping and washing over her shoulders. She wiped her eyes of the dead friends she had visited in her dreams and reached for the newspaper, now resting against her ankle. Sara picked up the paper and offered it with anguished eyes.

The absence of Sara's gap-toothed smile wasn't lost on her grandmother. Goldie forced a smile and took the *Hopefield Testimony* from Sara's trembling fingers. The old woman's nose crinkled as Sara's hair, fluffing like a cloud of brown cotton, brushed against her nose. She sighed at the thought of another battle at the stove with that head. A glance at Sara's wrinkled clothes and the long scratch on her neck told the rest of the story. A fight.

"You've been sweating, girl. I told you not to run home from school. We've got midweek service tomorrow and I'm not pressing that head again . . ."

Sara plopped onto the deacon's bench, her hands waving. "I had to run, Grandma, before I killed that girl. Oooh, she made me so mad!"

Goldie squinted over the top of her glasses at Sara, her eyes narrow and her skin nestled into the dimples beneath her high cheekbones. Her "Cherokee look" as her children called it. "Nobody can make you mad, baby. That's a choice you have to make for yourself. And as for killing folks . . . I think you know what I think of that."

Sara's elbows jutted at her sides as she twisted her waist, scooting back until her back touched the oak couch, a relic of a church burned down long ago. "You don't understand. She said—she said black folks don't go to heaven. She said God is white and He won't let us in. I know that isn't true, but she still made me mad."

A laugh, deep like thunder, flowed from Goldie and filled the room. Sara blinked and scrunched up her face at her grandmother. Goldie laughed even harder. Finally, she calmed down enough to speak.

"Baby, that little white gal was just messing with you 'cause she don't know no better. See, now, God is any color you want him to be. Jesus had hair like lamb's wool, and I ain't seen but one woolly-haired white man in my life."

Sara looked confused. "But wasn't Jesus a Jew?"

Goldie nodded. "Yes, baby, he was, and it's good of you to remember it. He was King of the Jews, but even then he didn't have no blond hair or blue eyes. Now, He's spirit and truth and He loves everyone—even little white gals who tell tales and little black gals who get mad at 'em." Her gaze locked with Sara's.

Sara broke the connection and averted her eyes to her lap. "I know you don't want me to apologize to that girl, Grandma. I hope not, because I don't think I can. It's like you say, 'Ignorance is one thing, but stupidity is too much to swallow standing up.' "

Goldie giggled again, her chest heaving in rhythm through her cotton shift. "Baby, you listen to everything I say, don't you? I would rather you apologize. You just as wrong for hitting her—"

Sara's braids swung from side to side as she shook her head. "I didn't mean to. Really, I didn't. She told that lie and the next thing I knew I was all over her. She got in some good licks, too, though," she said, fingering the scratch on her neck.

Goldie reached behind her for a needle and thread from the curtain and lifted Sarah's shirt over her head. "I'm not going to say any more. You know what I think. Just remember that sometimes ignorance and stupidity are the same, and folks ain't always what they will be or what they once was."

Sara sighed and shook her head, her naked shoulders slumped at her sides. "Now, Grandma, I know you say I'm smart, but that's just plain over my head."

Goldie pinched her eyes together and dug another hairpin into her scalp to keep from laughing. Her granddaughter's wounded look sobered her enough to clear her throat. "What I'm saying is, that gal won't be ten forever. One day, maybe tomorrow, she's going to meet somebody with love under their brown skin, something her momma and daddy forgot to warn her about. When she does, she's going to feel mighty bad about what she said today. I'm trying to make sure you won't look back on today and feel bad, too."

"But I will feel bad. Even if I apologize. Oh, why do I have to let people get to me?" Sara wailed, her face buried in her hands.

Goldie stared at the black-and-white picture a few feet away in the living room. Her ten children, thirty-two grandchildren, ten great-grands, and two folks she still couldn't identify smiled back at her. Sara's mother, Cynthia, now dead, frowned in the third row. *She's just like you. She takes things too hard.*

Goldie turned back to Sara and took her hands in her own. "Baby, look outside," she said, motioning to the picture window purchased by her children two Christmases before. "What do you see?"

"People."

"What kind of people? What do they look like?"

"Like—like me. Black people."

"And?"

Well, and Chinese. And Puerto Rican. And . . ."

"Uh-huh. What colors are they?"

Sara shifted back again and sat erect like a princess on her throne. "I see caramel, toffee, honey, fudge, ebony, sweet cream, butterscotch . . ." She turned to her grandmother, wide-eyed, beaming.

"Go on."

"Tan, brown sugar, milk chocolate, cocoa—I could go on for days. And they're pretty folks, too. Some of them been beat down, like Miss Eva, or treated bad, like Big Red, but they all keep going with rain-bows in their eyes." Her voice was rising now, her words piling on top of each other.

Goldie clapped her hands together. "Yes, baby. That's it. Now, do you honestly think God would say no to such beautiful folks for looking the way He made them?"

Sara's eyes widened again. "No, Grandma! When you put it that way, I think God might let a few of us in early so he can look at us a while. The ones who act right, of course," she said in a serious tone.

"Of course," Goldie said, nodding and restraining another smile. "Now, you go get them skates and a fresh shirt and go on outside. And worry more about how you act than how you look, hear? Miss London is watching on her porch."

Sara rolled her eyes. "Don't I know it? I still don't think that woman is blind. She just tells us that so we'll let our guard down. She's probably got X-ray vision sitting on that porch acting like she can't see."

Goldie bowled over with laughter, her newspaper sliding to the floor a second time. Sara tried to offer it on the way out the door, but her grandmother waved her on, her false teeth in her palm.

Sara's thrilling skate spanned only a half-block in each direction, but to her it seemed an endless adventure. She smiled at each passerby, drinking in their vibrant colors and smells. Even the crackheads looked marvelous today. Well, almost.

She pivoted at Miss London's porch and exchanged greetings. The wide smile under her dark glasses told Sara that her grandmother's phone call had beat her down the street. Her cheeks burned as she pushed off with one skate and rolled down the hill, her hands out to her sides.

All too soon, the stubborn streetlight clicked on, and Sara speeded up the driveway and dived onto the porch. Her grandmother stood in the door, watching her eagerness.

"You going to make sure you got a story tonight, huh?"

Sara nodded, out of breath. "Yep."

"All right. Come on."

As usual, the story was hilarious. Goldie's voice flowed in and out, changing speed and volume, allowing time for each phrase to sink in. Sara tried to stretch each word as well, knowing that when the story ended it would be time for her bath.

"What did you do then, Grandma?" she asked, shaking her head in disbelief at the tale. It was hard to believe that old people had so much fun back then. They looked so . . . old.

"Chile, I hit him! I hit him with an ice pail in the mouth," she said with a wry smile.

Sara covered her mouth. "You did what? Did you hurt him? What happened?"

Goldie frowned. "Girl, no, I didn't hurt that fool boy. He lost a tooth, is all. He never got fresh with me again. Not until he married me, anyway." She batted her eyelashes.

"What? That was Granddaddy?"

"Yes."

Sara's head cocked to the left. "I don't understand one thing, though. If you liked him then, why did you hit him? Why didn't you just let him kiss you or whatever? You married him anyway."

Goldie took a deep breath. "Girl, if I had let him kiss me or whatever, he never would have married me. He knew I was going to hit him. He just wanted to let me know he liked me and to make sure I was what he thought I was—a good girl."

"That doesn't make any sense."

"Not much in life does, baby. 'Bout as much sense as what that girl said to you today. Folks say and do one thing when they mean another. That's why you have to follow God and not people. He never changes."

Sara hugged her grandmother and planted a kiss on her forehead. "And neither do you."

Goldie pretended to wipe the kiss away and looked at the clock. Eight-thirty. "I sure don't. Now put those skates away and get in the tub. You know what to do."

Sara lay awake watching her grandmother sleep in the next bed. Goldie took shallow breaths, her right arm dangling from the edge of the bed. Sara's fingers crossed the divide between them and latched onto Goldie's wrinkled hand.

"Baby, what's wrong?" Goldie asked from somewhere in her sleep.

Sara sobbed between her words. "I-I dreamed that you died. Promise you won't leave me. Promise?"

Goldie laughed, still half-asleep. "Sweetheart, I hope the Lord sees fit to let me see you grow up. You the last grandbaby I raised. But I'm an old woman, and if somethin' happens to me, you got to go on livin'. Remember what you said this evening. He might want to look at me a while."

Sara stayed awake a long time that night, planning how she'd keep Goldie from the arms of death for years to come.

Yet sometime after three A.M., sleep claimed her again and she floated into a vivid dream. Through a cloud she saw a line of people in every shade. Brown, white, tan, yellow, and everything in between.

Some held banners of flags Sara recognized from social studies. Ghana. Australia. Nigeria. China. Kenya. Italy.

The cloud moved closer, and Sara could see now how wide and long the line was. It went on forever. A group of giant men with red wigs and stonehead spears stood above the crowd in one place, their faces smooth like black glass. Bare-breasted women with brown velvet skin danced throughout the crowd

Sara recognized a few faces. Big Red's little brother was there. Sara even saw a woman who resembled her own mother in the crowd.

They were singing. The song started as a low rumble and echoed, shaking Sara's body and the cloud of fog that engulfed her. Then one voice sifted to the top, crisp and full. The cloud followed the voice, higher and higher until Sara passed into another cloud at the front of the crowd.

Goldie.

In a purple-and-gold African gown and head wrap, Goldie stood at the head of the choir belting out "Amazing Grace." A man was with her. He was missing one tooth. He winked at Sara and drew his hand to his mouth. He blew her a kiss.

The kiss turned into a gale first, and then a zephyr wind, and finally a freezing, biting tornado pushing Sara away from the people and back into her bed in Hopefield, Ohio.

Sara jolted awake, her grandmother's hand cold in hers.

She pried her fingers away and looked at Goldie's face. A wide smile wreathed her mouth. A smile Sara saw only on Sunday mornings when Goldie sang solos with her eyes closed.

Her Sunday smile.

Colours

Kambon Obayani

"When a man is educated, a family is educated. When a woman is educated, a nation grows and is educated."

—African American

October 2, 1837

Today is the first day; we have set sail for the dark continent. I pray that God will be gracious, just, and kind in blessing us with a safe trip and protection. I have been coughing up my insides for the past hour and have been humiliated already by this peasant captain and his crew of ruffians. They had me drink this foul-tasting substance:

"All men drink this, Mr. Baylor," they said.

In one gulp they poured the drink down their throats. I did the same. First my throat caught fire, and then my stomach felt like a cannon had exploded in it. My eyes blurred; I know I turned red; then I coughed and heaved all right on the deck. They laughed at me. I felt smaller than a sewing needle. So now I've retreated to my cabin. The motion of the ship and the alcohol has my head and stomach turning inside out. Whenever I try and stand, the floor rises up and slaps me in the face. I swear by the grace of the Almighty, who made it possible for me to come into this world, that I shall never touch another drop of this wicked brew. The captain's mate has come to my door three times and, smothering his laughter, has asked how I'm doing. The young peasant has even volunteered to empty my waste bowl. I want to be left alone, to read my Bible and think of my loved ones left behind. This separation undoubtedly will be helpful to my/our situation. My wife, oh, fair Clarissa, if you only knew how much I love you. If you only knew that I cherish every moment we are together. How I long for the day when your fears will be washed away, like the smudges on a mirror, and we shall hold each other again. The children drive you batty, you say, with their constant badgering and their endless questions. They look to you for direction and for the warmth they need while I am away. But you sit in your drawing room with Mrs. Cabot and Mrs. Adams, sipping sherry while they run like wild horses throughout the fields, being cruel to our servants. And you sleep with your body closed in a tight ball at night. And I lie awake late at night, my heart and my body throbbing.... You are a woman, Clarissa, and I am a man. God has placed us together, a Christian bond to bring forth little ones and to keep our line going.... The nanny will have arrived at home, in Abbeyville by now. I'm sure the red dirt and the sweet blossoms of Carolina will have soothed her dark, damp English soul by now. I'm sure that the love and the operatic nights we spent in England, laughing, dancing, and being gay, will sustain her until I return once again. But I wonder what I shall do with you, Clarissa. What shall I do when my bosom longs for a sweet embrace and you lie there, curled in your ball, and the memory of our nanny's perfume and the soft wave of her flesh dances in my memory? What shall I do, Clarissa? If I extend my hand to you, will you let my longing fall to the floor, to be stepped over like a piece of cloth, ruined . . .

October 14, 1837

I have just witnessed a scene more sinister than Lucifer himself could have ever created: the captain and his men taking turns on an indentured servant. She lay on the deck, her legs spread open, while each man, drunk and vulgar, exorcised his evil on her flesh. They asked me to go first and, when I declined, laughed and asked if it was a man I wanted. They have a young boy who, when they tire of this woman, they take and rub cooking grease on his buttocks and use as if he is a woman. This young boy dresses in women's clothes and serves us our meals. He is no more than seventeen and wears lip rouge and silk chokers around his neck. I have said my prayers daily so I may not become weak with lust.

I have watched while the clouds, like little puffs of smoke, float in a wedge across the sky. I have watched how the birds, diving for food, have preyed on the fish in the ocean, and wondered about this treatment of God's creation, man on this earth. And I have looked in my mirror at myself to see if my very presence on this voyage, my very involvement in this expedition, is turning me into one of the descendants of Lucifer, who are above me. For we are all in quest of riches. My land needs more workers. My business needs a large amount of currency. The land alone cannot give us all we want. Like anything, when used continuously, it will eventually give way. So, with the convincing of my brother and my partner, I have set upon this voyage with the blessings of our minister, to get gold. Black gold. But like the woman and the young boy, God has undoubtedly carved out their destiny. For as Ham looked upon the naked body of his father, Noah, he was cursed—all his children shall be the slaves of slaves, cursed black, hewers of wood, carriers of water, and tillers of the soil. I know that God is good and kind, a just and fair God. His blessings are indeed upon me.

November 11, 1837

We have just returned from going ashore on the dark continent. This is indeed Satan's land. I was first in awe at the sounds and colours. I saw purple, green, and yellow birds with an abundance of shrubbery. Only Lucifer could exist in such a hot place. We were met by a savage named Booto, who must have been seven feet tall. He uttered the sound "Boo-to," which I took as boot and to. This savage, Booto, spoke through the captain's bastard son, a mulatto, his cargo. The captain's black wench kissed his feet when she saw him. We were told that, God willing, Booto would arrange for us to get men and women. The men would be very difficult. We must arm ourselves.

I was frightened by this savage. He wore gold earrings, a gold necklace, multicoloured beads, gold bracelets, a cloth around his waist outlined with jewels, anklets, and a large headpiece made of some kind of animal hair, feathers, silver, gold, and plaster. And black as the pits of hell. He smelled sweet, almost like raspberries, and picked at his privates whenever the urge came. Such muscles I have never seen. He was terrifying . . .

We left the shore after exchanging twenty kegs of rum, a few broken flintlocks, English pounds, the young boy, and the woman, who by this time had sores under their clothing. I watched them being inspected yesterday by the captain. He made the woman pull down her undergarments and lie on her back. There were sores and yellow pus running down her privates. I tried to look away, but my eyes kept returning. The young boy bent over, and the same horrible disease existed. The captain stood back, then made one of the mates cover the sores with a white paste. I went to my cabin and read my Bible.

This evening, night is falling. I went to sleep but woke up with a dreadful nightmare. Beset, in the corner of my room was a small female elf. Whenever I came near her I was stabbed with daggers and my eyes pulled out. I went on the deck of the ship, looked up into the sky, and I swore I saw a blood halo around the moon. The moon is full. Drums, I hear. Tomorrow we shall pick up our cargo. I shall pray all night tonight.

November 12, 1837

Night is falling and I am back in my room. But I dare not turn my back, for in the corner sits a young woman that I captured when we went ashore. Oh, what a struggle she put up. The bruises are very deep on my body. Never have I witnessed such a holocaust. I can still hear the screaming of those poor devils being killed. Old men with their heads chopped off and their insides spread all over the ground, men with spears stuck in their throats. I thank God that I am alive. This was completely contrary to what I'd been told. The whole affair was to be peaceful, "an easy deal," the captain said, just a few children, a lot of women, and young men. Violence would only be necessary if the people resisted. But the captain started the whole affair by laughing while he shot the savage Booto right between the eyes. There was a rush of violence. I found myself caught up in their pace. I knew I had to have that woman.

Earlier in the day, while we were waiting for their ceremony to begin, I had seen her bathing in the river. My flesh, against my will, had risen up. I was struck by her beauty. A long neck, very smooth blue-black skin, slanted eyes, and her breasts looked like two ripe pieces of fruit. I was almost discovered when I stepped on a branch. She looked around, but I ducked down and made my way back to our hiding place. The captain was furious. But as I told him, I'm a man too. The swine laughed. . . .

I watched as a primitive ceremony took place. This struck me as odd. How could these soul-less animals have a ceremony? A wedding ceremony, with old men standing in front and children carrying some smoking sacrifice to their heathen gods. I thought that these animals would merely grab a woman and take her off. But the procession was very orderly. As soon as I spotted this young woman again, I realized that I must have her. The rest of my cargo I no longer cared about. I had to have this woman. So when we leaped upon them I went right after her. She was lying face first on the ground next to an old man. I grabbed her by the hair and tried to drag her, but the old man struck me, so I shot him through the stomach. He bent over and fell headfirst onto the woman's body. This must have winded her, for she started gasping for breath, but when I tried to drag her away, she clung to the man's body. I took the butt of my revolver and hit her on the head. My blow didn't seem to affect her. She jumped up and began kicking, clawing, and scratching me, so I struck her until she fell to the ground. As I was carrying her over my shoulder, I saw out of the corner of my eye this tall savage coming toward me. The captain shot him in the back of his neck, and blood spurted from his mouth. But he kept coming toward me, vomiting blood. I couldn't move. I just stood and watched while this dead man staggered toward me with his arms outstretched. He pitched forward and grabbed my boot. I tried to pull away, but he kept hold, so I pulled out my machete and started hacking at him.

He pulled himself up and bit into my boot. I chopped his head off at the neck, but his teeth were still in my boot, so I continued cutting into his skull. His pink, sticky brains and flesh got all over my boot. Finally, he let go. I vomited all the way to the boat, which brought us back to the ship safely. I smelled the man's blood all over me, so I pulled off my boots and threw them into the water. The savage's teeth prints were on the side of my boot. He barely touched my skin, thank God. . . . I carried the woman to my room and laid her in a corner. She immediately came to. She hissed, ground her teeth like a mad dog, and glared at me. Then she pulled out this bag around her waist and spread a semicircle of white powder around her and started shaking bells and rattles. Whenever I go near her, the rattles start shaking, and her hissing noise starts. Her eyes have an evil burning light in them, and though black, she is very beautiful. I must get some air. . . .

I just returned from the deck of the ship. The captain and his crew are having a celebration. They are drinking rum and torturing the savages by sticking hot irons in their mouths, in their stomachs, and up their bottoms. The savages don't make a sound. They merely stare straight ahead. The captain has advised me to cut the throat of this woman. He says that she is a devil and will only bring me hell. . . . I can see her arms. My mind continually flashes back to her body bathing in the sun. My flesh rises. I have noticed that my letter opener is missing. She used the pot when I was out of the room. Also a piece of my shirt has been torn off. There is a strange smell in my cabin.

I can see the smoke, but I can't find out where it is. I've found little clumps of dirt in places around the room. Some spread under my pillow, some under my desk, and even dirt inside one of my boots. I have tried to go near this woman but when I approach her, the bells start to shake, the rattles start, and this hissing like a snake begins. When she does this, I can't move. I try, but my body is frozen. Time seems to move around me in a continuous way. I have lost track of what day it is. Whenever I close my eyes, the dream returns. I wake up screaming, holding my eyes. When I go on deck the captain asks me has the demon in my cabin turned my penis into a snake. I have nothing to say. Last night I broke out into a ferocious sweat. I had another dream. The whole room was a blood red, and snakes were hanging from the ceiling, reaching down, trying to bite me. I struck out at them wildly and knocked over my lamp, almost causing a fire. When I looked at the woman, she was moving her hands in all kinds of motions. Some of her movements seemed like birds, some like flowers blooming, others were clouds moving across the sky. Then she was nursing a baby, rocking the child in her arms and then stroking the child in her lap. I'm confused. I can't remember when last I slept or ate. . . .

I went on deck again recently. One of the native women was tied with her legs and arms spread open. Whenever the captain felt like fornicating, he would climb on the woman. She never moves. The captain and his mates take the water from the sea and throw it on her. She will not eat. The captain and his men offer her to me. I want the woman. I have found out her name. But still I cannot go near her. My room is so hot, I walk around naked. I have been coughing up my insides constantly. When I sit down to write, the paper rises up and tries to strangle me. I must rest. . . .

Today or whatever this day is, I walked on the deck and witnessed the captain and his men throwing bodies over the side of the ship. After doing this and laughing, they turned to me and asked when would I bring my wench on deck. I looked at them and with my eyes told them that I would kill if anyone even came near my cabin. When I returned to my cabin, I loaded my guns. I smell; my room is hell. I just heard the captain and his men outside my door. I went to my bed and began jumping up and down to make the bed squeak. I heard them laugh and move away. . . . A strange thing just happened. I believe another day has passed. . . . For the first time, I have no fever. But I have just passed, surely, through the gates of hell. . . . My room suddenly began to shake; the smoke became so thick that I could not see. My body felt as if it were chained to the bed. I could only move my head. When I opened my mouth to scream, nothing happened. Suddenly, I saw the woman standing over me with my letter opener raised. Her eyes were two snakes, and long pointed fangs came from the sides of her mouth. Just as her hand was raised and ready to strike, the captain and his men were at my door, trying to get in. She looked down at me with her hand raised, looked at the door, then disappeared. The smoke cleared, the smell was gone, and I could move my body. I took my revolver and shot at the bottom of the floor. The captain and his men went away. . . . I stared at the woman and started to cry. I couldn't help myself. Tonight I shall read my Bible. . . .

December 1, 1837

Communication was made today. I held up one finger, one object, and said one. She said the number in her language, then repeated, one. We did this up to three. . . . I have given her one of the dresses, which I bought in England for my wife. I laid the dress outside her circle. She moved her hands over the top of the dress, mumbled some words, then lifted the dress into her circle. From her bag she has pulled out berries and is using them to make designs on the dress. Someone has just shouted land. . . . I feel confused and afraid.

December 2, 1837

Darkness has descended upon my life. I returned home to find that the woman, the nanny for my children, has returned to England. There was an immediate disapproval of her by my wife. The nanny was too young and pretty. Clarissa, my wife, has crawled into her ball. After so many months on board a ship, I can think only of the woman. . . . My heart moves between fear and longing. . . .

She came off the boat willingly, carrying the dress I gave her and her bag of spirits. My wife and the people in town were immediately afraid of her. People stopped and stared. A slave like this, with flowers in her hair and mud on her face, is rare to see. Moreover, she does not hold her head down like the other slaves. . . . I have sent for my lawyer in Charleston; she and all her children and grandchildren shall be free. She spared and saved my life. . . . There is a place not far from our house, but in the woods, where I've decided that she will live. My wife wants her to work in the house. I can see that she wants to break her. But in all honesty she would die first . . . or my wife. I am happy to see my children. Until they fell to sleep, I could not keep them off of me . . .

December 9, 1837

I know this is her name. I pointed at myself, said my name, and she pointed at herself and said "Ayanna." A week has gone by and I have only once been out to see Ayanna. My life has been a continuous stream of my wife's parties and business. All my slaves are accounted for now, and the papers assuring Ayanna's freedom have been safely stored away. I have truly tired of these social affairs. How many of these men have seen the trade? How many of these women have endured what Ayanna has endured? Who of these people have been to the pits of hell and returned? When I try to tell them about my trip, they grow red and give glances to each other. I have heard my wife telling these visitors that I have been suffering from prolonged seasickness. I find myself sitting naked in the darkness. I dream nightly of Ayanna. At times I feel more comfortable walking in the slave quarters than at these gatherings. And I have stopped reading my Bible. . . . My business is flourishing. . . . and Ayanna is out back all alone. . . . When I visited her, the same half circle of dirt was spread in front of her door. She still paints herself and has gathered the red dirt of Carolina and mixed it with the dirt from her pouch. Nine mounds of dirt sit in front of her cabin. . . . The clothes I have sent to her are painted with the berries and flowers from around my plantation. . . . The other day Ayanna frightened my wife.

Clarissa was strolling through the woods when she saw Ayanna walking around naked. Her body was painted with red all over, pink spots on both sides of her buttocks, breasts, and a long line going from her neck to her stomach. When my wife, Clarissa, reached out to touch her, Ayanna hissed. Clarissa said her hand felt as if it had been stung

by a bee. Clarissa wants me to either kill Ayanna or sell her. She has
given me an ultimatum. Either Ayanna goes or she will leave with the
children. I love my children.... Ayanna has a halo around her head.
Her dress is blue, with flowers and trees. Her hair is braided. She holds
up one finger, says my name, John ... I must go to England tomorrow.
I must find the nanny. Her name was Lorraine. When I return, a decision must be made.

January 15, 1838

Eight months have passed. I have had to return from my heaven's
paradise with Lorraine still in England. There I sat among the journey-
men and scholars, the people of culture, those who have traveled the
seas and experienced the interior. I told them of my experiences, and
everyone understood. And Lorraine has my heart glowing and dancing. She is a light that never flickers. But I have had to return, for
Clarissa is dead. I am sad but I am not crying. Instead of thinking of
Clarissa, I only see my children's faces.... They hug me, and their little bodies shake.... I shall have Lorraine come here as soon as possible.... There is so much mystery around Clarissa's death. It seems
that a war was continuously being waged upon Ayanna by Clarissa.
She had sent one of my strongest slaves out to Ayanna's cabin to live
with her. The slave had walked out of Ayanna's cabin, mumbling inco-
herently, then finally fell dead with his eyes popping out. The other
slaves would not touch the body. Our slave doctor said it was an unknown disease, which only slaves get. This infuriated Clarissa. When
last seen, she was walking toward Ayanna's cabin with my rifle in her
arms. The next morning, one of the house slaves found her dead in our
flower patch. Instead of a rifle, she held flowers.... Clarissa had swallowed her tongue, and her eyes had popped out of her head. Both eyes
rested on her cheeks.... After the burial, I found myself at Ayanna's
door. I stood outside the circle and called her name. When she came
out, I held up three fingers. Ayanna held up six fingers and said six. She
opened her door, and six was written on the inside. Her house is a mixture of flowers and live birds. The colours and pictures drawn on the
walls are the same as what I saw on the dark continent....

Three weeks have passed. I have observed Ayanna walking through
the woods naked; her body is painted; the sun glistens off her back.
Every day I go to her cabin and leave gifts outside. Yesterday I watched

Ayanna sitting in an open clearing. There were hundreds of birds all around. Some sat on her head, legs, arms; others ate out of Ayanna's mouth. The other slaves stay clear of her. But when there is an illness, they go to her. . . . Like myself, they fear her. . . . Ayanna can now read and can count up into the hundreds. Tonight I shall go to her very late, and hope to see the sunrise. . . .

The Day Chano Died

Nancy Padron

"There is the love of power, and the power of love. When one enters, the other leaves." —Afro-Cuban

"Yoruba spirits didn't stop the bullets this time."

I spun around on the bar stool to see who was talking. It was Charlie Loco, staring down at the brown splotch in front of the jukebox. He was slowly sliding a toothpick into a space he'd found in his back teeth. I jumped off the stool, straightened my skirt, and, taking my Scotch double, joined him. Dropping a nickel in the jukebox, I selected Chano's favorite tune, "Cubano Be, Cubano Bop." I remembered the first time they played it, Chano's unmistakable conga rhythm with Loco blowing serious on his horn, but inside the box the seventy-eight vinyl remained unmoving on its turntable, silent, refusing to play.

"He never should have left Cuba," I said, shaking my head, looking at the brown patch that was Chano's dried blood.

"He had to leave, Chelo," was all Loco said, now chewing on the wet, jagged piece of wood.

"I remember one night last summer, we were at an after-hours basement party on the lower East Side. He was clowning and joking about his first gig in Monte del Sol, a small club in the hills of Oriente that played music for the *guajiros*. His only transportation was a mule. *Pero*, it was the only club, even after his fame, where he could come in the front door. That's where he met me and Ramón; that's when he came to New York."

"He was the Son of Shango. Man, he was the Cu-Bop King." I recognized Ramón's gravel-filled voice right away, coming from the back of the club. He walked up to me, rubbing his horn for luck.

"He had the drum-spirit," Loco joined in, spitting the wet wad of wood at a sawdust pile on the floor. "When he jammed, especially solo, m-a-a-a-n. He'd throw his head back and shake like he was under the power of a spell." Loco shook his shoulders, pushed his fat, wet lips into a smile, squinting his eyes.

"Never should have left Cuba?" his shoulders pulsed back and forth, faster, to a rhythm only he could hear. Loco suddenly stopped shaking. "It was the mob, man. Mafioso. La Cosa Nostra." He turned to Ramón and rubbed the toe of his Stacys on the dried bloodstain.

"Careless. Got too full of himself." Loco spoke low, in a clipped monotone. He wiped his eyes, found a fraction of sleep on his handkerchief.

"Play 'Manteca' for me," I said. "Ramón, would you play 'Manteca'?"

It was Chano's tune, Loco's first hit. He wiped his brow and slowly lifted his horn. The music was sharp, cutting, like slicing winds in sugar cane fields. Loco thumped the palms of his hands against the Wurlitzer in a two-four beat, the same way Chano beat the conga, throwing his head back, biting his lip.

Their matched rhythm was forest chants and river calls. Chano was the music. Chano, the beat that made mambo love chants, that made rhumba more than an ankle-chained slave dance, all hips and trance. I closed my eyes and saw Chano, with the power to call the spirits for all the *santeras* on 116th Street. I sang the chants like he taught me, sang them in his voice, caught up in the spell of his spirit. The chants to *Shango* and *Yemanja*. The chants to fire and water.

"Well, for my money, he was a damn fool. All that spirit talk is what got his dumb ass killed. Mafioso, Cosa Nostra, Casa Nuestra—it wasn't the mob and it wasn't the spirits; it was Chano."

Loco's words shattered my Chano-trance. Tears fell from his eyes like muted notes and harmonized with the splotch on the floor, turning it purple, Chano's favorite color.

"*Seguro que sí*, it was Chano," Loco whispered. "When he left the band last summer, I knew something was coming. 'Me no come to America to live like Cuba.' He kept saying it over and over and over. Going in the back door in the South, and playing segregated clubs downtown. He didn't dig it—at all. I told him it was only temporary, but you know how Chano was."

"Black as tar and twice as hard," Ramón said, trying hard to see the reflection of Chano's tar face in his patent leather shoes.

"When I came back to New York, he was on 106th Street, doin' the samba in the middle of traffic. I ran up and bear-hugged him and that's when I felt it. A big long shank hidden in the pit of his back."

"That's a damn shame. Chano was too big to need a knife." Loco spit on the blotch.

"He started carrying it *after* he left the band," Ramón reminded him.

I agreed, then added, "I remember when I was singing at La Habanita, before it burned down. One evening after my first show, Chano showed up wearing a blood red silk shirt, open at the neck, that red-and-black pin-striped zoot suit, and his pointy-toed two-toned shoes. We had a couple of drinks, a *danson* or two, but he didn't stay for the second set.

"Where you going, Chanito?" I asked. "He started talking real fast in Spanish, mostly with his hands. Then he shoved his tongue down my throat, slapped me on my ass, and pimp-walked out the back door. I figured he had another woman."

I took a drag off my Camel and blew out a smoke ring.

"It wasn't until later I found out he was strong-arming the reefer man," I added, staring at the still-silent jukebox.

"The spirits don't like ugly," was Ramón's guttural response while still looking down.

"When I found out what he was doing, I pulled him close to me. 'Chano, *querido*, you'll anger the spirits if you keep this up; they'll leave you,' I begged. 'You can't keep bullying people and pushing them around. And please, get rid of that goddamn knife.

"He laughed at me, waving me away like a pesky fly. '*¡Yo no soy un huerfanito! Recuerdes y no olvidas, yo soy un hijo de Shango.* I'm not an orphan! Remember and don't forget I am the son of Shango. In-vin-ci-ble. The spirits protect me, no? *Coño*, Chelo, shit, you worry too much.' "

"His eyes stayed red," Loco said, "always high on that jive. I believe that's why he didn't see the midget who shot him in the back." Loco blew his nose on the blood. It was green now.

Ramon raised his eyebrows. "What midget?"

"The Puerto Rican midget," Loco answered.

"Ramón, you remember the reefer man who used to sell peanuts on 106th Street? He's the one who shot him. Man, Chano took a whole bag of peanuts from him and wouldn't pay. And you know what else was in those bags."

"You mean *el manicero* was the snowman, too?" Ramón stuttered.

"That's right. And Chano, fire on the right and water on the left, thought the spirits of Shango and Yemanja would protect him. That even bullets couldn't kill him. He didn't even turn around when the door opened," Loco said, pointing to the swinging doors behind him.

Just at that moment, a warm wind wound its way inside, wrapping itself around the silent jukebox. Ramón quickly crossed himself and kissed his crucifix.

"Look." I pointed to the Black Madonna above the entrance to the Río Café. Suddenly, the lights from the jukebox came on and *"Cubano Be, Cubano Bop"* started to spin the seventy-eight magically. The red, yellow, blue, and green colors of the Wurlitzer flickered rhythmically against the Madonna's eyes, and purple teardrops formed on her cheeks. Ramón gazed up at the Madonna, cradling his horn, falling to one knee.

"The spirits, Chelo," he whispered. "They abandoned him?"

I kept my eyes on the Madonna, watching her tears fall while the jukebox played.

"No, Ramon. *He* left *them*—when he became too human."

Lessons

Roy L. Pickering, Jr.

"You learn how to cut down trees by cutting them down."
—African, Bateke

I can do this; I know I can do this.

So what if she's the prettiest girl in the whole wide world, while I'm just . . . I'm just a guy who's terrified. I don't want to be rejected. More than that, I don't want to be rejected by her. If only I were more experienced at this sort of thing. If I could look back at a time when I had been successful, I'd be more confident this time around. But since it's my first time, how can I know if I'm doing it right? My grandpa says that some things can't be taught. Certain things you just do, and when you're done, then you'll see how they went.

The problem is, I can't afford to do this wrong. I'm pretty sure I'll get just one shot. Screw it up and somebody else will be quick to take their turn, probably a smooth-talking senior who'll know exactly what to say and how to say it. I couldn't take it if she shot me down. Not after I've spent so much time daydreaming about us being together. Night dreaming, too.

Perhaps I shouldn't give her the chance to rewrite my dreams. After all, if I don't ask, then she can't say no. But then, she wouldn't have a chance to say yes, either. And maybe she will say yes. It wouldn't be the craziest thing ever to happen. I've seen her smile a few times in a way that seemed custom-made just for me. It could have been my imagination. That's what my best friend says. But I don't think so. I think I have a shot at winning her over. If I do this just right. If I do it perfect. Like my grandpa says, loving is a much braver act than simply loving back, and sweeter, too.

There she goes, taking books for her first classes from her locker.

I'm lucky enough to have a locker only a few feet away from hers. As Grandpa says, never underestimate the value of location.

Other students walk by laughing, talking loud, horsing around, completely unaware that I'm about to do this extraordinary thing, that my knees feel as wobbly as a newborn colt.

Her hair is prettily separated into dozens of spaghetti-thin braids. Her hair clip is shaped like a butterfly perched on a flower in full bloom. Last year she wore braces, which did not keep her smile from speeding up the beat of my heart. But after they were taken out, the impossible happened. She became even more beautiful.

I had thought these last steps would be the hardest to take. Never would I have expected to grow so calm, so bold. I suppose I feel that this is beyond my control now. I'm like my grandpa's great big Cadillac, moving forward on cruise control.

But once I'm next to her, I realize the calm was a mirage. My mouth refuses to open. I feel dizzy. I think I might puke.

Time to regroup. I walk past her and stop in front of my own locker. Why am I freaking out? I've spoken to her several times before. But never about anything important, just the small talk that I've managed to sneak in whenever she wasn't occupied by the attention of others. She has never made me feel that my clumsy attempts at conversation were unwelcome. But I've never been convinced that she was inviting me to say more, to speak what I really think, what I truly feel, how I truly feel—about her. I know that once I do, everything will change. It may change into bitter disappointment and heartbreak, or else transform into something absolutely amazing. There is only one way to find out which.

I was hoping to take command of the situation today like an action movie hero. I was planning to follow my grandpa's advice, to tell her that I like her and, more important, what I like: her big hazel eyes, the pitch of her laugh, the magical scent of her hair, her ability to expertly mimic the nasal voice of our school librarian, and the way she purses her lips in concentration when we're taking a test and she doesn't realize I'm paying more attention to her than to the exam.

Instead of saying these things, I just stand here, peeking helplessly from the corner of my eye, afraid to be caught staring, afraid that if I let her out of my sight, the opportunity to act on my runaway feelings will be gone forever. Resolve is much tougher to locate once it's already been had and lost. So my grandpa says.

Some might say I'm biting off more than I can chew. My best friend,

Kurt, says she is one of the hottest sophomores in school, as if I had not figured this out for myself. She's very popular, usually surrounded by friends from the school journal or the tennis team she's on, not to mention muscle-bound admirers from the football team who think they can effortlessly charm her because they wear jockstraps and jerseys, never mind that they won only four games last year. But Kurt doesn't see, or can't see, that her main priorities are not about being beautiful and in demand. She's not like the extra fine, extra shallow girls that he lusts after, girls who would pass on a guy like me with scarcely a glance.

If she were like that, she wouldn't need to reject me, because I wouldn't be interested in her to begin with. It so happens that she is an honor student, just as I am. And like me, she can often be found in the library checking out not only assigned books, but also those chosen for pleasure. Yes, she is pretty, athletic, and popular. But she is also smart, ambitious, creative, funny, and sweet. In short, she's perfect. Perfect for me.

Oh, there is one other thing. She has the finest-looking butt you ever did see, sweet as a chocolate-covered cherry, especially in the jeans she wears every other Wednesday. They hug her hips just right, outlining her curves with expert precision. In anticipation of seeing her in those jeans, I wake up extra alert on those days. Or at least a certain part of my anatomy does.

What does Kurt know about what girls want? Not a whole lot, no matter how much junk he talks. He's had exactly one more girlfriend in his life, and that lasted only a month. He says I'm chasing after a girl who is out of my league, but there's nothing wrong with the league I'm in, whatever that is. I may not be a jock or one of those guys who walks around in phat gear and blinging jewelry like a rapper, but I don't think I'm someone a girl would be embarrassed to be around, either. I've been called cute plenty of times—well, at least a few times, the message usually delivered secondhand. But the girls who have lazily pursued me in the past weren't the ones I was interested in, and the ones who have sparked my interest did not pay me much mind.

I'm not sure what the problem is. I often see much dopier-looking guys than me with pretty girls on their arms while I stand by alone and envious. Maybe those guys are simply luckier than I am. Or braver. Probably a combination of the two. Lady Luck won't just fall in my lap. I'll need to test whether she'll work for me. As for bravery, I'll have to fake it. Maybe brave people are sometimes nothing more than cowards who do a good job of acting.

My grandpa told me recently that my dad was quite awkward and shy in high school. I think he was saving the story until I reached puberty. Dad was tall, usually a plus, but he was gangly and scrawny. Apparently, he tripped over his feet and his tongue when trying to impress girls. But his frame and his confidence filled out as he grew older, and by the time he graduated from college he had successfully managed to win over the most beautiful girl he'd ever met—my mom. So maybe there was hope for me, too.

I've met the girl of my dreams at a younger age than he did, so I'll need to grow into my own at a faster pace. I'll need to get off the sidelines and into the game, as Kurt would put it.

I wonder what my grandpa would say if he were here beside me, an invisible guide coaching me to action. How would he motivate me to push away this gigantic boulder that my fears and insecurities have merged into? I'm surprised to draw a blank. The boulder seems too heavy for even Grandpa's endless wisdom to budge. He told me that if you can't push something out of your way, you need to find a way around it. But this boulder is not only impossibly heavy, it's also much too wide to circle.

While I stand idly considering my options, the bell rings and she goes to her homeroom. Everything speeds up: lockers clang shut; conversations are cut short to be resumed later in the day; sneakers squeal as their inhabitants rush by in a blur of colors. Not wanting a detention for late arrival, I have no choice but to join the stream.

I don't hear a single word all day. The teachers' words won't stick in my head. In history, they talk of wars fought long ago. Geometry presents a bunch of fancy names for simple shapes. My French teacher communicates in a strange, curvaceous tongue. In chemistry class, I absently create colorful potions that sizzle in beakers. And if all of this isn't thrilling enough, I am forced to grunt, groan, and sweat for the entertainment of Mr. Bellamy, who apparently was unable to decide between becoming a gym teacher and a drill sergeant and decided to split the difference. But not a single lesson taught from bell to bell explains how to find the courage to speak to a beautiful girl.

When my final class ends, I rush outside and head home, desperate to avoid an encounter that would only deepen my ocean of shame. I don't want to risk seeing her again today. I don't want to be reminded of what I let slip away before I was ever able to grab hold. But I realize that my flight is senseless. I can hide from her today, but there are still three years of high school to go. And even if I were able to keep our paths from crossing for all that time, it wouldn't stop me from remembering how crazy I am about her. And worse, remembering that I'm a coward.

I arrive home to the sight of Grandpa nestled in his easy chair, spectacles hanging precariously at the very tip of his nose as he reads a thick, leather-bound book. I've seen him in this pose a thousand times, watched him run his large, veined hands over his neatly trimmed salt-and-pepper beard when he's about to turn a page, observed his bushy eyebrows rising every day to acknowledge my return from school.

It comforts me to know that some things can be relied upon no matter what is happening in the world.

Instead of waiting for him to greet me and ask how my day went, I break our ritual to ask the question I came up with on my lonely walk home.

"Grandpa, what's the hardest thing you've ever had to do?"

He answers every question of mine as if he was expecting it and had rehearsed the perfect response. "I tried to make myself be to you the father I never was to your dad. I'm still trying."

"I don't understand."

He removes a bookmark from his shirt pocket to hold the page he's on, places the book on the table beside him, and takes up his pipe. He makes no move to light it. My grandpa gave up smoking years ago, transferring from daily packs of cigarettes to a few cigars after dinner, to one smoke of his pipe late in the evening, until arriving at his goal of total abstinence. He still holds the pipe in his mouth sometimes, usually when he's worried or in deep concentration over some important matter. This tips me off to pay especially close attention.

"You see, when your dad was growing up I wasn't around for him very much. I used the excuse of trying to build a career, providing amply for my family. But even when I was home, I wasn't involved like I should have been. I left the day-to-day details to your grandma, not realizing that those details are what make up our lives. She's the one who went to the PTA meetings, bandaged your dad's bruises, attended his school plays, protected him as a growing boy, and showed him how to be a good man. The most I did was watch the occasional ball game with him."

I am stunned. Grandpa's words don't match the deeds of the man I know him to be. Recognizing the disbelief in my eyes, he explains himself further.

"I was amazed by the kind of father he turned out to be, especially under the circumstances of having to do it mostly by himself. I used to make excuses for the way I'd been, saying I'd had the worst possible role model in my old man. But what he passed down to me, I failed to pass along. Maybe the fact that your dad had to become both father and mother to you had something to do with it. He needed to somehow fill the void left by your mother's passing, and he did one hell of a job. I watched him raise you with enormous pride, and in the process, I got my first lessons on how to be a real father, not just the man who pays the bills."

I manage to hold my tears in check. Okay, most of them. Can you blame me for letting a few slip out?

"When you moved in with me after the accident, I was given the opportunity to put into practice what I had learned. And I must be doing an okay job the second time around, because you've grown up to be a wonderful young man, even if you do wear your pants too baggy for my taste. I'm guessing you'll grow out of that eventually. In life you grow in and out of all sorts of things."

"You're doing a great job, Grandpa." I would have hugged him if he were more of the touchy-feely type, but knowing better, I just return his contagious smile. He puts his pipe down and takes his book up, pushing his glasses closer to the oval auburn eyes that I inherited. I cross the living room of our bachelor pad, as he jokingly calls our house, and head upstairs to my room.

Grandpa's words have relieved my apprehension. I find myself able to get to the business at hand. Knowing her last name and the street her family lives on, locating her phone number in the white pages is a breeze. My fingers do not tremble as I dial. There is no quaver to my voice when I ask if she is at home. And when she appears on the other end of the line, I simply speak to her as if it's the most natural thing in the world, rather than the near-miracle I know it to be.

Our first real conversation lasts nearly two hours. It goes more easily than I could have ever imagined, like a baby squirrel figuring out how to climb a tree. She seems to have expected my call—to have been waiting for it, even. I learn countless new things about her. We have a lot in common, sharing the same favorite flavor of ice cream and favorite song currently in the Top Ten countdown, and favorite book read in literature class last year, and mutual annoyance at the frantic hand-waving done by a certain pigtailed know-it-all in every class. I quickly grow fond of the phrase "me, too."

As the phone call draws to a close, my nervousness returns. To calm myself, I close my eyes and recall the first time I ever rode a bicycle without training wheels. I remember the shock of looking back and learning that my father had stopped running alongside to keep me balanced, that I had been riding for a while all by myself. I remember how unstable the bike became after that, how I lost control, the skinned knee earned for the effort. I remember getting back up, brushing myself off, hopping on the bike again, and riding toward my dad like I had been doing so all my life.

The details of life when my dad was still around grow fuzzier as time passes. I don't want to forget anything about him, but little by little my memory fades. Once I ran home in a panic after school because I suddenly realized that I couldn't picture what he looked like. I flew into my house and straight to the nearest photograph with him in it. That picture is of my parents, the father taken from me by a drunk driver, and the mother I never got to know at all, because she died while giving birth to me. Neither of them died as heroes, such as what they're calling the firemen and police officers who rushed into the World Trade Center back at the beginning of the semester. If you have to die, I guess it would be nice to be called a hero by those you leave behind. My father and mother were just ordinary people with worse-than-ordinary luck, I suppose. Then again, Grandpa says heroes come in all shapes and sizes, some of which we don't always recognize.

With all of this in mind, I ask her out on a date. It is the first time I have ever done such a brave and wonderful thing. I probably didn't do it perfectly. But I did it.

As my grandpa says, sometimes it is the journey that matters, not the destination. She answers that this weekend isn't good for her. My heart drops. Then she says that the following weekend would be much better. So my destination is the movies next Saturday night.

I don't know how I'm going to wait so long without bursting. I sure do wish it were sooner, although I'll probably need all the time I can get to prepare myself. It will take at least a few days for me to learn how to be charming and clever and whatever else girls like a guy to be.

Fortunately, my grandpa is a great teacher.

Charitable Roy

Kharel Price

"Richness of spirit and heart begets richness of cloth and coin." —African, Cameroon

The tangerine sun was just emerging on the horizon when a ragged peasant set out for a long day of begging. His ailing eyesight and arthritic back caused him to stoop over and peer into the vast divide of nothingness that stretched out before him on the road leading to town.

Nearby, Roy Snyder was heading to work. Roy worked as a field hand for the wild and corrupt James Cole, whom Roy thought of as an eccentric and bizarre man. Mr. Cole was notorious amongst the towns-folk because of his abundance of money and his obsession with alcohol. Rumor had it that Mr. Cole had once shot a man's hand clean off for trying to steal his beer, and hacked off the arm of another man who had stolen a few pennies. After working with Mr. Cole for five years, Roy was convinced the stories were absolutely true.

Roy whistled as he made his way toward Mr. Cole's fields and another day of backbreaking, skin-scorching work. As he neared the end of his street, he heard a commotion coming from around the corner. He rounded the corner and found an elegantly dressed gentleman of apparent wealth, arguing loudly with a poor, twisted-backed beggar. The rich man seemed to be scolding the beggar for some unknown offense. Roy moved in closer in order to hear their conversation better.

"Get away from me, you dirty rat!" shouted the wealthy man as he pushed the beggar against a wall. Immediately, he frowned and wiped his hands on his trousers as if he regretted touching the beggar.

"Please!" cried the starving beggar. "All I'm asking for is a little money, or even some food!"

"That's not my problem, now, is it? Go away, street scum!"

Roy felt an instant dislike for the well-dressed man, who he now realized was no gentleman, and an abundance of sympathy for the beggar. As he neared the two men, Roy saw the awful state of the beggar—his painfully bent back and runny eyes—and he quickly offered the strange man food and money from his satchel.

"Thank you very much, sir," said the beggar, quickly swallowing down the food.

Roy then turned toward the wealthy man. He stared into the man's crafty, evil eyes and was utterly disgusted by the greed he saw within them.

"How could you mistreat a man who asks you for help? Do you not have enough money to help him and still provide for yourself?"

The wealthy man sneered. "So what if I have money? I'm not giving it away! If I did, then I'd be poor, just like him."

"Oh, so that's it." Roy shook his head. You don't help the poor because you're afraid of becoming poor. You must live a sad life."

The wealthy man became angry and left, cursing at Roy for standing up for the "street scum." Roy proceeded on his way through town to Mr. Cole's farm. It was beginning to get very hot as the sun inched higher into the sky. Roy walked happily through the streets, loving the sights of the small town, the smell of the fertile earth, and the caress of the warm weather. When he arrived at Mr. Cole's farm, he found his boss looking dejected and very unhappy.

"Hello, boss," Roy called out in greeting. "What's wrong?"

"Hi, Roy," Mr. Cole answered with anguish in his voice. "I hate to tell you this, but I'm nearly bankrupt. It seems that my drinking and fast living has finally gotten the best of me. I'm sorry, but I can't pay you anymore. I have no money to give you for your work."

"That's okay, Mr. Cole. I'll just help you out for free today."

Mr. Cole stared. "Thank you, Roy. That's mighty charitable of you."

The two men worked side by side, sweating profusely under the hot sun until they were both exhausted. Mr. Cole invited Roy inside, and they enjoyed the shade of the house while they shared the remnants of Roy's meager lunch. Finally, Roy got up to leave.

"It's time for me to go, Mr. Cole. I'll see you around."

"I don't know how to repay you, but thanks for your help, Roy."

"Good-bye, Mr. Cole. I have to go into town and look for work."

Roy looked for work in many of the town's small shops. He looked for work in the bakery and the butchery and in the blacksmith's barn.

He walked through the town with high hopes that it would be easy to find a job, but after five hours of fruitless searching, he was almost ready to give up and admit otherwise.

Roy trudged sadly homeward, crushed in his spirit. He'd walked all day and into the evening without finding a new job. As Roy walked, he caught the attention of the old man who, a few hours earlier, had been a starving peasant. Although stooped in the back, this man was now clad in fine fabrics and adorned in large jewels.

"Hello," said the man, whom Roy had just fed earlier in the morning. "You'll never believe what happened to me!"

"Well, hurry up and tell me!"

"I just won a million dollars at a horse race!"

"Wow," said Roy, "that's great for you!"

"And I just bought a thousand acres of land."

"That's a lot of land. What will you do with it all?"

"Well, I'm going to put a mansion on the land. Would you like to be my assistant?"

Roy was ecstatic. Finally, a job! "Sure!" He grinned broadly. "Let's meet tomorrow morning on the corner where I first saw you. Good day, friend!"

"Good day to you, too!"

On his way home, Roy met up with Mr. Cole. He, too, was dressed in fine clothing, and he held a large bottle of whiskey in his hand.

"Hello, Roy!" said Mr. Cole, "I've got some good news to share with you."

"What is it, Mr. Cole?"

"Well, after you left my house to go looking for work, I discovered an oil field on my farmland!"

Roy laughed loudly and clapped his hands in glee. "Wow, that's great, Mr. Cole!"

"I now own all the land in every direction for twenty acres around my house, and for your charitable assistance today, I've deposited a fifth of my wealth into an account in your name."

Roy was almost speechless. "Thank you very much, Mr. Cole!"

"It's my pleasure, Roy."

Roy went back to his small house to eat. After a simple supper, he got into bed, but he could not sleep. He lay there just thinking of all the great things that had happened to him that day, and how while helping others he'd found a new job and earned enough money to continue helping others. What wonderful things Roy received for his kind charity!

Miss Mary Mack

Tracy Price-Thompson

"The compassion of a People is cultivated at a grandmother's knee." —African, Zimbabwe

When folks get to talkin bout the Sanders wimmins, more'n likely theys referring to Big Euleatha and Genessa, cause it's the two of them what did the most livin before the freedom come, but me and Genera got our rightful share of Sanders blood too, and I for one, has my own little story to tell.

Genevieve Marie Sanders Black is my name, but folks been calling me Miss Mary Mack for so long till now I just *answer*. I came to live in these projects back in 19 and 36, a year after they's built as part of the Marcus Garvey renovation effort. That's what they named em, too— Marcus Garvey Houses, after that big ole black man what tried to get all us black folks a free ticket back to Afry-ca. Hear tell he took shiploads a coloreds to some place by the name of Liberia, and if you believes what they tell you, they peoples is still livin there to this day.

Me, I lives in Brooklyn. Brooklyn, New York. Come up here from Norse Carolina by way of Weeziana more years ago than I like to remember. I'm nigh bout one hundred and six years old from what I can count, and while my bosoms done went flat, thank God my waist ain't half as thick as my chest, and I'm real proud a the fact that I still gots all my own teets. Uh-huh, all thirty-two of em, cause there ain't too many things uglier'n an old woman wit'out a toot in her head! Grinning and carrying on with all a' them gums. No, siree. You won't catch me yankin my teets outta my mouth and settin them in no cup!

I don't get around much these days. Just go from this here chair by the windah to the bathroom, and then back to this here chair. I even sleeps here. Haven't stretched out proper in a bed in going on five years. Can't breathe right if'n I'm on my back. Got something to do with the floo-id in my lungs. My doctor say if'n I lay down flat again it'll kill me—and he didn't have to say it twice!

One of them Bookers done built this here chair up to where it's soft where I like it and firm where I need it. I kin lay it back like a bed if'n I mash this here red button, but of course I keeps it in the high position. I don't mind sleeping upright, either. Don't even miss stretching out, cause one day soon I'll be laid out flat on my back in a hard-hard box, and honey-chile, I'll stay that'a way for a long, long, time!

So I spends my days and my nights setting here at this second-floor windah, sucking on my peppermints, poppin boiled peanuts in my mouth, and keepin watch over things.

I gots no choice, cause Lawd, what would these poor project folks do without me?

"Get out from under this windah!" I yell at the little gals playing down there, the warm spring air whippin round they greasy brown legs, they short dresses billowing out like sheets that done just been shook. They don't pay me no never-mind. Just stay put and keep right on going like they don't even hear me. These days chirren is so mannish and grown you can't tell em much. Sometimes when I'm setting here sleeping with one eye open, I hear em down there skipping ropes and singing bout how bad they backs ache.

My back is aching, my belts too tight . . .
My hips are shaking from left to right!

Don't look at me—I didn't make it up! That's zactly what they say! Now what on earth could these chirren know about a hurtin back when alls they had time to grow is a leet-lil gristle?

"Move your mannish tails way from here!" I holler, and then make like I'ma stand up. Most times they just laugh up at me, tossing they little braids wit all a them colorful bo-rettes hanging from the ends, and call out, "Hey, there, Miss Mary Mack!"

And then they get to singing that durn song!

I balls up my lips and shakes my fist down at them, but all the while I'm tapping my feets where they can't see me, and sometimes I even hum along with them as they sing.

Miss Mary Mack-Mack-Mack
All dressed in black-black-black

With silver buttons-buttons-buttons,
All down her back-back-back . . .

Yesss, sometimes I gets all wrapped up in them chants and those sweet, tender little voices, and I wish them babies would just go on singing bout me forever. When they done they look up at me and laugh, and I smile and toss em down a few peppermints and watch them scatter like bugs, digging round in that deep grass trying to find those sweets.

Yes, I sets in this here windah and keeps watch over this here building. I feels I got a right to. I'm the oldest tenant livin here, and every one of my chirren was born right here in this same room. It weren't always like this, though. Back in my day, I was what they call a sweet young thang.

Honey-chile, I was a dish!

I was the youngest of Big Euleatha's three gals left for Aunt Mattie and Uncledaddy to raise, and my sisters, Charming—that's Genera—and Ma'Dear—that be Genessa—always said I was too grown and too fast. All the menfolk loved my peaches and would cut each other up for a chance to shake my tree. Ma'Dear predicted the first man what patted me on the knee would get me to part with my treasure, but she was wrong.

I may have been fast, but I was nobody's fool. I knew how to keep my pocketbook closed, latched, zipped, *and* locked! The way I figured, if what was tween my legs was good enough to make a grown man act a fool, it had to be wurf something. Weren't no way I was jes gonna hand it over to the first passing stranger! Honey-chile, the man what finally claimed me had sense enough to pat my head and my hand and leave my knee be!

Buck Brown was the lucky man's name, and he was a good bit older'n me. Back in the Souse, Buck's daddy was an important man in town, and Buck managed to get some training and whatnot in e-lectwicity. In them days it was a rare thing to see a black man who could figure wires and stuff, but Buck knew that 'twicity better'n he knew hisself.

The first time I laid eyes on him, I knew he was the one for me. Tall and black like country coal, Buck came to run some lights in Uncledaddy's house, and Lawd ha mercy, that man looked better'n a big ole bowl of grits and gravy!

And believe me when I tell you I was hongry!

By and by, us got married and Buck came norse to find work. After saving up enough money, he sent me fifty dollars and a train ticket to New Yawk Ciddy! Honey-chile, I left Norse Cacky-Lacky on the first thang smoking, and I have yet to look back!

Over the years many of my kinfolk visited up here, too, and it made me happy to be near my family again. Buck made good money and was real gen'rous, so I was always able to send a few dollars down souse to help Ma'Dear and Charming. Buck gave me two boys and six girls, and us was happy.

Just plain happy.

Well, the years passed like they been known to do, and Aunt Mattie and Uncledaddy went to glory in the same week. Uncledaddy first, and then Aunt Mattie a few days later. That didn't surprise me none, cause us Sanders wimmens love real hard. We stays with our men thru thick and thin. Just weren't no real reason for Aunt Mattie to keep on livin wit'out Uncledaddy, so she upped and follahed him, just like she'd been doing for near bout seventy-nine years.

But me? Follah a man to the grave? Now, that's a horse of a whole nother color! When my Buck left me twenty-six years ago come this Ju-ly, I almost broke my poor arm off waving good-bye! I stayed put *right-chere* cause I didn't see no sense in having them chirren throw moist dirt down on top the both of us! Buck had done lived a longer life! He'd been born first, and rightly so, I had some catching up to do. So I kissed my man gone and told him I'd see him tirectly in the by and by, and then I turned him loose an let him *go!* I ain't had even half a mind to follah him!

Well, after they buried they Daddy, them chirren was round here watching me like a hawk. All the time waking me outta my sleep. Taking my pulse and fanning my cheeks!

"Git way from here!" I told them. "Ain't nobody round here pinin to die! I'ma outlast a few a y'all yet!" Sadly, I done lived to see my words come true. Three of my daughters have gone on to Jesus, and another one look like she ready to go any minute. And the two that are left here, healthy? Ain't got ten teets between them!

Jennie, that's my great-grand, she takes care a me. After her husband died—I forget his name, but I called him Booker—she and her two boys moved in here for a small spell, and they been here ever since. She a good ole gal, that Jennie. Take real good care of me—except she don't eat no pork. She call a pig a nasty swine.

I call him a meal!

Now you know back in the Souse, long as the food was clean, us weren't hardly particular, an us sholy ain't had a drop to waste! Us ate everything on a hog from his rooter to his tooter! Us boiled it, fried it, baked it, steamed it, roasted it, salted it, pickled it—Lawd, us just ate it!

Yesss, I sure do miss a big ole plate of grits and scrapple, or crackling bread topped with liver pudding, but I don't fuss. Honey-chile, even wit'out the pork I knows I is *loved*. Besides, each of my chirren had a bunch of chirren themselves, and most every day three or four of my grandchirren and great-grandchirren come through here to see bout me and ask me what I need.

Aside from sneaking a bag or two of barbecue skins, some red-and-white peppermints, and my boiled peanuts, I don't ask for much. The funny thing is, I don't even know which granchile or great-granchile belongs to which of my own chirren. Since our blood runs so strong and we look so much alike, I don't know one chile from the next. All of they faces blend together and gets me confused. To solve that problem, I calls all the boys Booker and all the gals Betty, and you know what? That might not be they name, but they *answer!*

But somehow, while I probably couldn't tell my great-grandbaby from yours, I can sho nuff tell you the name of every chile outside of my windah! Yes, siree. I knows 'em all.

See that boy down yonder there? You see him! The one what head look like a turnip! That's Sammy Beals. Myrtle's boy. I helped him come into this world. And that'n over there, too. That be Pryor. Jane's son. Pryor was a twin, but that other baby was stubborn as a mule and wouldn't come outta there wit a wrench and a shoehorn, no matter how much I poked, prodded, and begged. We nearly lost Jane that night, but I used one of Ma'Dear's secret herbs to stop her flow, and she is still here today.

And take a looky at LuCeal's Sanderella. Waving up here at me wit' her pretty black self. Smart but dumb. Gal done broke her leg and had a baby for every Jim, John, and Joe in town, but she doin' good now, though. Miss Sandie done finally shut her pocketbook and got her act together! That there is one gal who can stand on her own two feets! Done joined up wit the army and been marchin round the world ever since!

And that chile over there wearing them hot pants and no brassiere? That be Becca. Marty's Rebecca. She gits herself in a whole heap a trouble, so I'm told, but none of it under this here windah where I can see it!

"Git some clothes on!" I tell her. "Act like a young lady what got some decency, fore I come down there and lam you with this here walking stick!"

Becca just smiles and says, "Yes'm, Miss Mary Mack," and keeps on gittin' up. But I know she respects me, cause I know she loves me. She betta love me, see's how I'm the one who reached inside her mama and pulled her scrawny tail out into daylight! And to this day I still ain't got my full payment yet! But sweet Becca knows I got bout much chance of walking down those steps as her mama got a coming home to the family she left behind. It weren't long after Becca's birth that Marty up and runned off with Mister Holmes on the ninth floor, leaving her husband with six head of chirren to feed, and Missus Holmes with seven.

Yes, it was always Miss Mary Mack that the wimmens in this community called for when they was laboring. I was known to be the best. Course, I was always clean; I gived them a little something from Ma'Dear to help ease some of the pain, and most of all, I treated them with dignity and respect.

The babies that came nice and easy was good, but the ones that fought getting born could be pretty bad. There was a few times when I just reached in and grabbed hold of an ankle, a foots, or any other soft little baby-part I could find, and yanked at it for all I was wurf.

Near bout every chile in this building got here with a little help from ole Miss Mary Mack. In this here concrete tower what stretches twelve floors up to heaven, there ain't many I missed. All in all, if my memory serves me like it should, I done helped more'n a thousand souls enter this world. And I loved every one of them.

See, us wimmens is closest to death when we is giving birth, and that's when a strong hand, a soothing voice, and a midwife what loves you makes all the difference in the world. All my mothers knowed I delivered they babies with *love*, and that's why Miss Mary Mack can sit here in this windah till God comes for her, and not a soul walking these streets would ever wish me a lick a harm.

But like all the city projects, Marcus Garvey done went down. Way down. They done yanked the setting benches right out from the ground to keep the bad boys from using them as cots or meeting spots to sell drugs. Broken glass shines like diamonds in the moonlight cross what useta be the playground. The spot where I planted my garden every year for over fifty years is now littered with dirty diapers, beer bottles, and anything else what's likely to come flying out some of these here windahs. I hear tell folks allow they chirren t'use the restroom right outdoors like animals! They say the elevators never run, and most of the streetlights been broke out for months, but I still see as much as I need to.

Many nights I set here with the stars and watch young teenagers come in and out at all times a the night, doing things I probably never heard the likes of and know I don't ever want to, but never once do they fail to look up here and give a smile or a wave at ole Miss Mary Mack. Like I say, I knows I am loved, and by way more than just my blood kin, and that's why I knows my job is now done.

I useta think I wanted to live forever. Just had too much work to do to ever lie down. But these days I knows better. These old bones are ready for a good long rest, and any day now they gonna get it. Sides, I miss my Buck. Miss the way my man useta wrap me up in them big ole strong arms and make me feel like couldn't nothing ever hurt me. Don't get me wrong. I ain't had half as much sorrow and misery as some folks I know. I'm bout near a hundred and six, but I still got joy in my heart, hope on my mind, and all my own teets!

Yes, God has been good to me, and I've been his good and faithful servant, but still . . . some days as I set here and listen to the voices of them chirren down below, I know them sweet voices will be the last thing I ever hear. I'll never leave this here project building alive. Feets first is how I'm gone outta here, and that's all right with me. My bones is tired, I'm telling you. Just tired. Won't be no whole lotta fuss, neither. Jenny won't let em take a drop of blood from my body. And they'll lay me out and bury me all in the same day, the way it was decreed by my ancestors from way cross the waters. And I can't hardly wait, either. Can't hardly wait to see my old family: Big Euleatha and Joy, Sugar Baby, Ike, and Zeke, Aunt Mattie and Uncledaddy, Charming, Ma'Dear, my babies, and Buck Black, my man.

So one of these days when my sweet Jennie come in here to kiss me good night, I'ma kiss her extry hard and hug her extry tight. She a good ole gal, my Jennie is, and I'm gon tell her zactly where to find that little stash me and Buck managed to hide away all them years ago. I'ma tell my Jennie just how much I love her, and how much God is gonna bless her for putting up wit a musty old lady like me. I'ma tell Jennie to be sure an let all of them Bookers and Bettys know how much I loves them, too.

Then I'ma tell my Jennie bout that dress I been meaning to get out and buy. The one I wants her to go to McCrory's and pick up for me. I seen one there years ago, and I'm sure they still got it, or one near bout like it. The dress with the silver buttons what run all the way down the back. The one my chirren been singing bout for all of these here years.

I sure hopes they be out there singing when the time come. Wouldn't that be fitting? That my chirren be right underneath my windah singing bout Miss Mary Mack when she finally close her eyes and mash that lil red button that'll turn her comfy high-backed chair into her low, flat deathbed and stretches out to wait for her Buck?

Miss Mary Mack-Mack-Mack
All dressed in black-black-black
With silver buttons-buttons-buttons
All down her back-back-back . . .

20/20 Foresight

Deirdre Savoy

"When you set out to dig a grave, dig two" —African, Congo

Sandra Trent always woke before her husband, but on this morning, she feigned sleep, tossing from side to side, apparently in the grip of a dream. Justin shook her shoulder, and in a voice full of annoyance and interrupted sleep, said, "Wake up. You're dreaming."

She let out a great gush of air and turned on her back with a hand pressed to her forehead. "Thank goodness," she whispered, in awe and relief. "I was having a terrible nightmare."

"No shit," he said in the tone of the disinterested, as he turned on his side, facing away from her and attempted to go back to sleep. Sandy was always dreaming something, none of it good. If a human tragedy existed that hadn't visited her dreams, it had yet to be invented. And afterward, she would hear some news report or speak to some neighbor or read some article somewhere that chronicled the fate of someone whose fate she'd predicted. "See?" she would say, letting her words hang there. Vindicated once again.

At one time, Justin had considered her "prophetic visions" charming, especially the one in which she predicted he'd propose. Back then, her visions hadn't slipped into the macabre and borderline bizarre. Back then, she hadn't used her supposed psychic flashes as a tool to draw attention to herself or to keep him in line. He'd considered them as exotic and mysterious as her bone-straight black hair, lent to her by an Indian interloper in her Jamaican family tree, or her fawnlike hazel eyes.

Justin ground his teeth together and let his lips form a few words the brothers at Mount St. Michael's Academy had actively discouraged. He leaned back and looked over his shoulder. "I have fifteen minutes before I have to get up for work. You know *work*? That thing you used to do? Talk to me when my time is up."

"You can't stand it, can you? I was given a gift and you refuse to appreciate it."

"It can't be a gift. A gift is something that makes people happy."

"A curse, then. Call it whatever you want, but I see things and then they happen."

"Yeah, you and Miss Cleo."

Sandra glared at her husband's back, wishing she had the ancient powers to damn with a glance. Justin had always viewed her predictions with an American-grown skepticism and sardonic wit that annoyed her. She expected that. Even her own mother thought she'd fallen off the wrong end of the turnip truck when it came to her nighttime visions.

But to lump her in with a woman who couldn't even fake a convincing Jamaican accent, let alone predict the rise of the sun each morning, pushed the limit of what she could stand. To mock her gift in this way was to malign something fundamental and precious in her character.

"I am telling you that I saw someone falling, landing, broken." She hoped the sob that escaped her lips sounded authentic. "What if it's you I'm seeing?"

"Please, Lord, let it be me," he muttered. "Maybe I can get a few minutes' peace and quiet in the hospital."

With a growl of frustration, Sandra threw off the covers, went to the kitchen, and brewed coffee. She leaned her elbows on the counter, her gaze fixed on the dark-brown liquid slowly drizzling into the pot. The plop, plop, plop of the leaking faucet provided a staccato counterpoint to the hissing melody of the coffeepot. As little as a week ago, she might have tried to wrench the tap to silence. A week ago, she might have done a lot of things.

She fixed two mugs of coffee, one with cream and sugar for herself, one black for Justin, and padded back to their bedroom. She'd hoped to smooth the way to further discussion with her steaming peace offering. Standing in the doorway of their room, she realized Justin had already risen, and from the whooshing sound coming from the adjoining bathroom, she knew he'd already started his shower.

On impulse she left his coffee on the bedside table and followed him into the bathroom. Cradling her own mug in her hands, she sat on the commode lid and watched Justin rinse, then lather his body, visible to her through the clear shower curtain.

Physically, he hadn't changed much since the day they'd married five years ago, except for the inky mustache that shaded his lip and the small pot belly he'd been working on lately. If anything, the years he'd spent working construction had given more depth and definition to the swimmer's physique he'd earned his first two years at NYU. For a moment, the heat of desire fired her belly. She tamped it down. So much time had passed since she'd put in more than a token performance in bed that he would swear she'd lost her mind if she tried to initiate anything now. But tonight, he would expect her overture. A butterfly frisson of anticipation added to the confusion in her stomach.

He saw her sitting on the commode, waiting for him, like a vulture sensing that its prey was about to die. Abruptly he shut off the water and flung the curtain open. "I'm not discussing it any more, Sandra. Forget it."

Without bothering to dry himself, he stalked out of the bathroom, trailing a path of water behind him. He dressed quickly in a T-shirt and black jeans. When he sat on the bed to put on his boots, his gaze snagged on her form standing in the open doorway. She leaned one shoulder against the jamb, her arms crossed in front of her, the toes of one foot resting on the ankle of the other. The frown on her lips mirrored the sullen expression in her eyes.

Justin held the long breath he inhaled and let it out slowly. He hated to see her like this. Having spent the first twenty-one years of her life smothered by her mother's ample and imposing shadow, Sandy had never been a confident woman. He'd met her at a party given by mutual friends. He'd spotted her standing off to the side, holding an untouched glass of wine in her hand, in typical wallflower fashion. Something in her doe-eyed, vulnerable expression had reached out to him. He'd asked her out, hoping to make her smile.

He walked to where she stood, and took her fingers in his, swinging his arm slightly, like a pendulum. "Walk me to the door?"

She nodded, not trusting herself to speak. She stopped at the threshold, tilting her head up for his kiss. His lips touched hers fleetingly, such a brief caress that she wanted to hold him to her for just a second more. It didn't feel solid, that kiss, and she wondered at her own need for reassurance.

He took a step back and winked at her. "See you tonight."

She managed a smile, as false as the dream she'd had the night before, watching avidly as he turned toward the steps. The second step from the top wobbled as he ambled down to the pavement, but he didn't seem to notice. Without looking back, he got into his ancient brown Chevy and drove away.

Sandra looked up at the old monstrosity of a house that was their home. A big white nightmare with peeling pale-blue shutters and trim. Justin had inherited the house from a distant uncle. Any sane man would have sold the property or razed the ancient white elephant and built something suitable for human habitation. Not Justin. He'd wanted to fix it up with his own hands, and she, wanting to please him, had agreed.

She'd still had newlywed stars in her eyes then.

Now, three years later, she'd tired of the mess, the noise, the expense of repairing this old behemoth of a house. She resented the time and dedication and care he devoted to something she considered foolhardy. A lifetime ago, while she'd still worked and before she'd lost the baby, she'd been content to help him, content to anticipate what beauty their ministrations would create.

But after the accident that had robbed her of her growing child, the emptiness in her womb spread to her whole body, to her mind, and she'd become restless. No longer patient, she'd stopped helping and had at times sabotaged Justin's efforts. Supplies he ordered would never show up; tools would mysteriously disappear; any appeal for help from her was met with claims of being busy, when in reality she had nothing to do. Secretly, in a small, petty place in her heart, she wished that life would take away Justin's dream, the way it had taken away hers.

Three days ago, an idea had seized her. She'd returned from the supermarket, her arms loaded with bags, and her mind weighted with its usual pervasive ennui. She'd paused at the base of the twelve steep and decaying steps that led to their front door. The same black cat—no more than a kitten, really—had nestled itself in the corner of the next to the last step and fallen asleep. That cat frightened her on a primitive, superstitious level, and on a more pragmatic one as well. Every time she'd reach that step, the cat would bolt awake and dart between her legs in its haste to escape. She'd be lucky if she didn't break her neck one of these days.

Gooseflesh pricked up on her arms as she started her ascent up the stairs. The cat didn't awaken, but her foot wobbled on the step, from a source other than her screaming nerves. She put down her bags and examined the step. The mortar holding the stone in place had started to crumble. If left alone, it wouldn't take long for the entire step to come undone.

And then she'd known what she would do. Maybe she would finally prove to Justin that the house was not only a money pit, a drain on their pocketbooks and their psyches, but that it would never, ever be the dream house he'd envisioned.

So, she'd spent the night before, crowbar in hand, prying the mortar from beneath the stairs—not much, only enough to make the stair less stable. With Justin's athletic reflexes and the balance he'd acquired working on narrow steel beams, she knew he'd never fall. Besides, he'd still have her prediction of doom ringing in his ears. He'd catch himself and swear under his breath about one more thing that needed to be repaired. One more piece of evidence that the house was coming down faster than he could fix it up. In the bargain she might also convince Justin of the value of her gift, even if this was the one time she hadn't seen anything. She'd promised herself that when that moment came, she wouldn't gloat too much.

Well, she wasn't gloating now. Nothing she'd envisioned had gone as planned. She went back inside the house, sank down on the kitchen stool, and clasped her hands between her knees. What to do now? Lifting her head, her gaze fell on a poster of Ocho Rios she'd hung on the wall across from her. Her lips tilted upward as she reached for the phone.

Arriving home that night, Justin locked the car and stared up at the house. His house. His alone, since Sandy had no interest in it. The only baby he would ever have, since fate had chosen to rob them both of that option.

He'd accepted that reality with his usual Protestant stoicism. But part of Sandy had shut down, refused to go on living. Having grown up fatherless and poor, deep in the South Bronx, she'd dreamed of giving their children everything her background had denied her. Her career as a nurse had been undertaken only as a diversion until she could retire to the suburban bliss of carpooling and changing diapers.

Having come from a similar deprived background, only in Newark instead of New York, her dreams of domestic tranquility had appealed to him. When Sandy had told him she was pregnant, he'd been elated. When she lost the baby, he'd sunk into the same deep pool of depression that Sandy had toppled into. But unlike her, he'd climbed back out, determined to build a new future on the bones of the old. If Sandy wanted to wallow in regret for what might have been, she'd have to do it alone.

He started up the stairs, stepped over a kitten sleeping on the next to last step, and went inside the house to find his wife.

At dinner Sandra broached the dreaded subject. "Mama wants to come for a visit." The peas and rice in his mouth slipped down the wrong way and had to be coughed up. Justin wiped his mouth on his napkin, wondering if she'd gauged the precise moment to bring the subject up to get that reaction from him. Having her mother, a woman with the physique and demeanor of a battleship pushing out to sea, come to stay with them was untenable to him, the one thing she could ask of him that he wouldn't at least try to give her.

He looked down at his plate: peas and rice, curried chicken, and a salad of julienne vegetables, just like mom used to make—her mom, not his. An assertion of her heritage, one she considered superior to his Southern "descendent-of-slaves" background, as she called it. For all either of them knew, their families could have left the homeland on the same ship; her family got off on the first stop, his on the second.

"Absolutely not."

Sandra chafed at his belligerent tone. "Mama is getting older; she's getting frail." Justin put down his fork and stared at his wife in disbelief. "Your mother is about as frail as Mount Rushmore," he said. To himself he added, *and almost as large.* Plus, the only reason she sought to have her mother anywhere near was to bring him to heel. Sandy had failed to "train" him properly, as her mother called it. Now Sandy sought to bring in the big guns. A louder voice to lend to her chorus of abandoning the old house. He'd have to be brain-dead, drool-rolling-down-chin insane to allow Hortense Shaw to step one foot over the threshold.

Sandy glared at him but said nothing, allowing him to finish his meal in silence.

There was one thing he could always count on when Sandy wanted something from him: sex. She'd trot out something from her neglected lingerie drawer and offer herself to him. He wanted her—he always had—but a roll in the sack wasn't going to make him stupid. Not when the affection she gave would be rescinded the minute he gave in. The moment she got what she wanted, she withdrew.

When she sat beside him and touched her fingertips to his cheek, he closed his eyes, craving intimacy on both physical and emotional levels, but knowing she'd given up on either a long time ago. He grasped her wrist and pulled her hand away. "Not tonight."

She blinked and swallowed. For an instant, Justin thought he saw real disappointment in her eyes, not merely dissatisfaction that he'd thwarted her plans. He went down to the den, where translucent sheeting separated the part that was finished from the part that was not. He settled onto the sofa, the lone piece of furniture in the room, closed his eyes, and after a while he slept.

The next morning, the slam of a car door jolted Sandra from sleep. She brushed her hair from her face, rubbed at her tear-swollen eyes, and peered at the bedside clock. Nearly nine-fifteen. She'd overslept. Justin must have left for work without waking her. She rolled onto her back, staring up at the stark white ceiling. He'd be back that night, and then she would talk to him, make him see her side of things, without trickery or dire predictions or pretense.

At the edge of her consciousness, she heard a woman's voice below on the street—her mother's voice, arguing with a taxi driver over the price of the fare. Yesterday morning she'd called her mother to find out if she was free to come for a visit. She must have decided to come without hearing from Sandra whether she really needed her or not.

An image flashed in her mind: the faulty step, her mother's heavy tread, a foot teetering on the stair. Sandra burst from her room and down the stairs, fumbling with her robe as she ran. "Mama, mama," she called, but couldn't seem to get out the words to tell her to stay put.

Hortense Shaw heard her daughter calling out to her. With a determined stride, she stepped over the cat, intent on getting to Sandra. But before she could draw her bulk upward to the higher step, the cat bolted, startling her. The step above crumbled, and she teetered backward. Eyes wide, arms flailing, a cry of alarm trapped in her throat, Hortense lost her footing and tumbled to the concrete sidewalk below.

"Mama!" Sandra cried, running toward the stairs. "Mama!" She made it past the broken stair, but two steps below the cat darted out, tripping her. A cry ripped from her throat as she fell to the sidewalk to land beside her mother.

Justin arrived at the hospital to find that the hardheaded old bat who was his mother-in-law had suffered a severe concussion but was already making a nuisance of herself on the ward where she was being kept under observation. Sandy rested on another floor. He sat in the chair beside her and took her hand. She looked so pale and fragile that for a moment his heart lurched.

Slowly she opened her eyes and focused on his face. "Hi." He stroked her hair back from her face, revealing a bandaged bruise at her hairline. He wanted to be sure she was all right, but more than that, he wondered how she could have kept this secret from him. She must have known how much revealing it would have changed things between them.

Finally, he said, "Why didn't you tell me you were pregnant?"

She blinked and tried to sit up, then, with a wince of pain, settled back down. "What are you talking about?"

"The doctor told me you lost the baby."

"The baby," she echoed vacantly.

And he knew that she'd known nothing about it.

"We can try again."

The words rushed out of him, sounding hollow to his own ears. They'd had their miracle; there wouldn't be another. He bent and rested his forehead against their entwined fingers as silent tears slowly trickled from beneath her lashes.

The Bag Lady

Kim Stanley

"You need not have it together to hold it together"

—African American

Whew, I'm tired. It seems like the blocks keep growing longer and longer with each step. And boy, is it cold. I can't even feel my fingertips through these paper-thin gloves that I found in front of City Hall last week. I hate the city in winter. I mean, after the Christmas decorations are taken down from the front of the downtown department stores, this time of year is ugly. The sky is always a hazy gray, and the bare trees move eerily in the wind. Even people are ugly. No one wants to take off their thick, fur-lined gloves to hand me money, even after I clean their dirty, snow-smudged windows. I feel like pelting their cars with snowballs as they drive off without paying me for cleaning their windshields. But I'm too old for that sort of nonsense, and I can't move fast enough, anyway. If it weren't for the shelter, I don't know how I would eat.

God, I don't think I'll ever make it there. Did I mention that it seems the blocks are growing longer? I'm sorry if I did. I hate repeating myself, even if it's only to myself. Well, you know what they say about people who talk to themselves—they're either crazy or have money in the bank. And since I don't have any money in my pocket, let alone in the bank, I must be crazy.

I've got to stop and take a breath. I must be older than I think. I haven't celebrated my birthday in several years, but I can't be older than fifty. I just can't understand why I'm so tired. I'll tell you, life on the streets is hard. I'll get myself a nice hot meal at the shelter if the lines ain't so long. That's all I need, something in the old belly. You know what I'll do? I'll sneak the food out and eat in the park. That way,

I can hear the noisy traffic and try not to notice the people scowling at me as they pass by.

You know, I love loud noises. That's mainly why I live on the streets. No need to feel sorry for me. I'm living the type of life I want to live. I'd go crazy living in a quiet house. Well, I guess I should say I'd go crazier. There's no shame to my game. I know I'm crazy. Say it loud: I'm crazy and I'm proud! But I'm happy. Happier than I was about ten years ago.

See, back then I craved peace and quiet. I lived in this nice Cape Cod house with my husband and son. We had a Caddie in the garage and were living the suburban life. I was a teacher, and the first thing my fourth-graders learned was to be quiet in my classroom. No talking out of turn, and no talking without permission. At home, my eleven-year-old son knew to be as quiet as possible, but my husband just had to watch his ball games all loud on the TV. So I bought him one of those little portable televisions. You know, the kind that runs on batteries. That way he could watch the game outside. I know you may think that's kind of mean, but the man loved being outside—really, he did.

We had the best lawn in the neighborhood. He would trim shrubs and pull weeds for hours. We had flowers blooming all year 'round. Even in the wintertime he would find something to do out back.

As for me, I really didn't have any hobbies. I just enjoyed being alone and quiet. My husband found that strange, so he bought a puppy to keep me company. Now, what he was thinking, I don't know.

Well, he bought a little white terrier who annoyed the hell out of me. All that dog did all day was whine. And when I say whine, I mean whiiiiiiine. It was a high-pitched, irritating sound. I would walk him, feed him, scratch behind his ears—anything to shut him up. But that damn mutt always found something to whine about. So one night, after listening to him whine and whine and whine, I decided to do something. I found some weed-killer in the garage, mixed it with Alpo, and fed it to that dog. I know, I know. But I couldn't take it anymore. So like I was saying. I fed it to him.

Well, stupid me, I thought he would die instantly. But he didn't. He started to make this horrible noise. A deep, gurgling cry. I felt sorry for the little thing, so I tried to get him to eat some more. You know, to put him out of his misery. But he couldn't. He couldn't even hold his head up. All he did was make that terrible noise.

To this day, I still hear that sound.

When he finally died, I took him out back and buried him in the yard, thinking my husband and son would believe the dog ran away. Mistake number two. Remember, I said my husband loved working in the yard? Well, one day he was cultivating that remote part of our yard and he found the remains of that puppy. Of course he asked me what happened. And so I told him.

Boy, he looked at me like I had two heads.

After that, he treated me differently. But I didn't care, because I had my quiet house back. Or so I thought. Because there were times when I was really enjoying the quietness when I could hear the horrible sounds that dog made before dying. Whenever things got quiet, I heard that terrible, moaning cry—while I was cooking, or in the shower, or trying to sleep. Finally, it drove me out of my house.

So for ten years now I've been running from that sound. See, I can't entirely erase it from my head, but I can sometimes drown it out with big noises. Noises I hear out here on the streets. So you see, living on the streets is best for me.

And it's best for my son, too.

See, I knew my mind was deflating like a leaking balloon. And I knew that, in order to save myself and my family, I had to leave. But I had to put things in order first. You know, like when you go on vacation, you put a hold on your mail, tell the newspaper boy not to deliver the paper, have a neighbor check on your place—you prepare to leave. So before my mind completely collapsed, I started making plans for my son.

Being a black male is hard enough, and being one with a crazy mama is downright pitiful. I had to hold it together for a little while. I couldn't leave him with memories of me screaming at some long-dead dog. So I gathered women around him. I joined two churches, attending eight-o'clock service at one, and eleven-o'clock service at the other. I had him baptized in both and practically shoved him on the youth ministers. I brought him every book I thought he would need, and posted his walls with pictures of Martin Luther King Jr., Malcolm X, and even a picture of Bill Gates. For hours, he sat up with me listening to Nina Simone, Louis Armstrong, Miles, Bird, Vaughn.

When the police pounded on the doors because of the noise, I pounded into him everything I thought he would need to survive without me. I loved him long, hard, and strong. I pushed as much love as I could into him, hoping it would carry him through the empty years. I knew I wasn't coming back. I tried to do the same with his father, but his heart was too chilled with fright to be reheated. He knew my eccentricities bordered on hysteria, and it frightened him.

But my son loved the attention. And he lapped up everything I poured into him.

He was wearing his Boy Scout uniform the day I left. He was going on and on about some camping trip, but I couldn't hear a word he said. I just smiled as my ears reacted to the piercing sounds ricocheting through my head. I poured my son a glass of lemonade and watched him drink as I backed out of the kitchen. The last I saw of him was his sleek brown throat as he sipped the sweetness, and I remember wondering if he would have a large Adam's apple like his father.

But I don't miss my son too much, because I see him all the time now.

Like yesterday, I saw this policeman, and he could be my son—same coloring and everything. Sure enough, he even had a gap in his front teeth. I marveled over the sharp crease in his pants, imagining that I'd pressed them myself. And this morning, I saw a young man with a widow's peak holding hands with a white girl, and I just grinned at him. Hoping he'd grin back and I could see his teeth. But he just pulled her closer like I was the boogieman. He could have been my son, too, confident enough because of the love I lavished on him to hold hands with a white girl, yet ashamed of me enough to ignore Black women.

I look forward to the day when I really do run into my son. And I pray that the howling ain't too bad, because I want to be able to tell him how I squeezed everything I held in my heart into the little time I had with him. I want him to know I managed to hold it together, although briefly, just for him.

The Fire This Time

TaRessa Stovall

"The world is a mirror: show yourself in it and it will reflect your image." —African, Ashanti

Just trying to think is sheer torture. But I've got to solve the puzzle somehow.

A doctor examines me, pops another painkiller into my mouth. I fight the medicine's rush of brain fog to identify myself. Who: Kyla D. Sampson. What: newspaper columnist. Where: some hospital in Los Angeles, 3,000 miles from home in Brooklyn. When: April something, 1992, right? Been in L.A. a day or two, in this greenish hospital room for a day, maybe two. Why: had to get that story. The one my gut led me on. How I got here: something happened—something bad, something painful, something my mind won't let me recall. And I'm fighting to name the madness that's turning my soul inside out.

Somewhere in the void between sleeping and waking, memories unfold. It started about a year ago with the video of Rodney King's beating shown nonstop on every TV station. Facts had dueled with emotional imprints till it felt like a dream. I strained to retain some "journalistic objectivity" as I wrote columns and news stories about one man's savage assault by a circle of cops, Black and White. Made me remember why we called them "pigs" back in the sixties, in the day when we were going to have a revolution, Power to the People, right on.

To this day, I can still see every second of that tape, still feel the sickening impact of each blow. It was all anyone could talk about in the newsroom. The consensus was that they would put those cops *under* the jail. Anyone could see they'd gone too far!

After the video, the trial. Cops indicted for what? Doing what they were trained to do? Stomping the "bad guy," kicking the "villain"? The one wearing the black hat, the black clothing, the black skin. Rodney King, a regular brothah whose beat-down had made him today's black Everyman, Everywoman, Everychild. Each blow conjured memories of fire hoses and barking dogs, the weight of chains, and the agony of whip lashings.

Hungry to be closer to the action, I boarded a plane from LaGuardia to the City of Angels. Couldn't quite explain, didn't necessarily understand, but I had to be in L.A. for the verdicts in the trials of the cop-pigs. Years in the newspaper biz had taught me that the gut is never wrong. And mine was telling me that the cops would be found "not guilty" and Black folks would riot in the streets. All my friends and fellow reporters said I was off base. "There's no way those cops will walk," they assured me. "Not after that videotape."

My editor, Ron, a toe-the-line guy who wears his white maleness like a monogrammed badge of superiority, said my hunch was "interesting, but pretty far-fetched." That's why I didn't even bother asking the paper to send me. Just took some vacation time, prayed I wasn't over the limit on my one credit card, and hopped that bird from NYC to L.A. I knew deep in my bones that an explosion was on the way.

My premonitions started when the trial was moved to conservative, almost lily-white Simi Valley. They intensified when the cops were charged with attempted murder—much harder to prove than "excessive force." I would have loved to have been wrong. I would have been the happiest person in the world if those cops had been put away. But I felt the weight of four-hundred-plus years of waiting, yearning, praying, and believing bearing down on those verdicts. I felt black and white hearts intertwined in a collective wish that our country's nagging racial bloodstains would be washed clean by due process. And the swirl of blood mingled within my own body boiled at what it sensed was coming.

So I booked and paid for that ticket without a second thought. Got off the plane, rented a car, and headed for South Central, the 'hood, straight into the heart of the volcano. Drove past the requisite liquor stores, hair salons, and Korean-owned markets. Listened to the news on the car radio, pulling over as the verdicts were announced.

A crowd formed on the sidewalk. I grabbed my bag, fished out my tape recorder, made sure everything was working. And wondered why I didn't feel better about having the first part of my prediction come true. Those cops had walked—no, *strutted*—out of that courtroom in the land of the free and the home of the brave.

The spring air crackled with warning. The group on the sidewalk chattered restlessly. I smiled, introducing myself as a reporter, looking for their reactions. A Chicano man answered me in Spanish. I shook my head impatiently. *"No hablo Español. Habla Ingles?"*

He looked at me incredulously, and I knew he thought I was one of his people, fronting like I didn't speak the mother tongue, trying to "pass" for something other than Mexican. I excused myself and hunted for someone else to interview. Walked toward some people up the block, mumbling my impressions into the recorder. "Young people, lots of them male, some of them wearing gang "colors," red, blue, bandannas on their heads. Folks are starting to throw things, breaking windows, lots of glass flying, sirens screeching, alarms blaring . . ."

A police car raced around the corner only to have its windshield shattered by flying rocks. There was a roar; then a horde of bodies covered the blinded vehicle like vultures on fresh kill.

I felt the spirits of long-dead slaves rising up for retribution. Tasted the metallic flavor of all the blood spilled, skin tattooed with scars from whippings, hearts shredded when family and friends were sold away. Breathed in the terrifying funk of pure, unadulterated rage, the tragic stench of a fragile hope betrayed. I just needed a local citizen to put it into their own words. It was hard to find anyone who wanted to chat. Everyone was either walking like zombies, running and cursing, or scurrying toward safety.

A group of youngbloods sauntered toward me, piercing the air with vulgarities, eyes searching wildly for prey. "Perfect," I thought. "If I can just get them to put that into words, answer a few questions . . ." I started the recorder, approaching them with a smile.

"Excuse me, I'm a reporter and I'd like to—"

"Ain't you in the wrong 'hood?" the biggest one sneered, his eyes crawling up and down my body. He was handsome, muscular, face too hard to be so young. If I could just get inside his soul for one minute . . .

"Well, I'm a reporter and—"

"Then report this," a shorter, thinner one said, knocking the recorder from my hand.

Their laughter spurted harshly from their throats without moving their lips upward. I shook my head as they moved closer. I fought to steady my breath, trying not to feel like captive prey. "No, I'm a sistah . . . I'm not . . . can't you see . . .?" I had a wallet full of ID, but none could confirm my racial identity.

"Shut the fuck up!" a third one said, looking me dead in the eye as he pushed me to the ground. I saw that his skin was as light, his hair as straight, as mine. His eyes told me that he knew I wasn't white. Or Mexican, either. He knew we were the same. And had to attack me to prove himself.

They punched and kicked as I tried to shield my head, thinking this would be a hell of a way to die: from an ass-whuppin' by Black folks who knew I was one of them but needed to strike out so badly that they made me a stand-in for the folks they couldn't get this close to, the ones they were afraid to confront eyeball to eyeball.

My hand closed on a rock. I aimed and threw it in the light-skinned one's face. He reeled slightly, blood spurting from his nose. He roared, and they kicked harder. I kept one arm over my face, and used the other hand to grope for another rock. Felt myself wishing I had a gun, though I'd never even touched one before. Heard myself calling for help, begging them to stop, sickened at the whine of fear in my voice.

Somehow, through the space between their legs, I saw a cop car and aimed myself at it in a desperate stumble. Rammed the door with my shoulder while the cop inside appraised me warily.

I banged on the window. "They're gonna kill me!" A second cop leaned across the backseat and pulled me in. "Get down, lady." Now I know they think I'm white, I thought, ashamed at my relief in escaping the young attackers. No white man would call a Black woman "lady."

I tasted blood in my mouth. The cop next to me watched and moved away, a reflex in the wake of HIV and AIDS. He had no idea that my blood was disease-free, but a complicated cocktail of Black daddy, White mama, and the requisite Native American on Daddy's side. Mixed high-yella half-breed redbone interracial biracial zebra blood. Disguised as a thick, salty crimson to make me seem like everyone else.

The car swerved wildly as shouts, rocks, fists, and bottles pelted the windows. I waited for a brick to fly through the glass. Or a bullet to pierce my aching flesh. I closed my throbbing eyes, leaned my tortured head back onto the seat, and prepared to die.

After a few minutes, the cop next to me said, "Okay, lady, this is your stop. Daniel Freeman Hospital. Good luck." His hand on my shoulder encouraged me out the car door.

I croaked out a "thanks," and they speeded away. I dragged my bruised, bloodied self to the emergency room, which, to my one half-open eye, looked like a war zone, packed with the newly injured. I signed in and prepared to wait my turn, hoping those booted kicks hadn't caused serious damage.

It was a relief to close my eyes. I flashed back twenty-four years to April 1968, when I was a shy, awkward bookworm teetering on the precipice of adolescence. Even my hometown of Seattle, Washington, was peppered with race riots in the aftermath of Dr. King's assassination. Our normally placid black folks poured their mourning into outrage. "Burn, baby, burn!" seared my junior high school and the blocks around my house, just as they had inner-city neighborhoods across the nation. Cars driven by white folks were pelted with rocks as they rolled through the Central Area, past our front door. I feared for my mother, but despite the fact that my skin was barely darker than hers, I never worried about my own safety. A few of the angry black folks took extra time to scrutinize me, but that was nothing new. And my gut told me I was safe.

But this time, in 1992 Los Angeles, my gut had been too preoccupied with getting the story to warn of my attack. Or I'd been too hardheaded to listen. Maybe it was that I'd made my sense of individual self one with black folks for so long that I couldn't believe I'd be seen as anything other than kin.

I opened my one working eye and studied the skin on my arm. If I was fruit, I guess I'd be an apricot, darkening to near-peach with enough summer sun. Hair dark, wavy-straight, with nary a kink to be found. The hair people stroked and pulled and worshiped as if it possessed magical powers. The hair they swooned over sometimes, imagining how easy it was to care for. The hair that had taught me, at a young age, about an obsession that obliterated all reason.

Guess over the years I'd learned to forget all the "What are you?" looks and words, the "You don't look like you're . . ." comments, the doubt expressed when I said "I'm Black. Mixed-Black. Light-Black." Some wanted to argue; others claimed they knew it all along. Made some Black folks a little too fond of me, and others hate me more than if I'd been White. Made lots of White folks choose to disregard my Blackness, disrespect the complexity of my truths.

Moans filled the emergency waiting room, and since the adrenaline had stopped racing through my body, I felt the full misery of my injuries. But that wasn't what made me want to cry. It was being attacked by Black folks, knowing they'd tried to kill me, and not because of "mistaken identity," which is what I might have expected if I'd been thinking straight in the first place. It hurt me even more to know that I'd have gladly tried to kill them if I could have. Shocked me to know I could feel such hatred toward folks I considered "my own." Worst of all was the shame I felt knowing how I'd played my trump card: running to the cop car, knowing they'd help me because they'd think I was White. What kind of hypocrite was I? What kind of traitor? How could I call myself a proud Black sistah, one with the people, down with the cause? It wasn't racial or individual pride that had fueled my actions. It was the raw, unadulterated instinct for sheer survival.

I shuddered, remembering how much I'd wanted to kill my attackers. I'd lusted for a gun, longing to spray them with a hail of deadly gunfire and walk away, triumphant.

After the ER doctors examined me and checked me into the hospital for further observation, I called Mom in Seattle to tell her where I was. She fussed, worried, and asked whether she should come to L.A.

"No," I said. "I'll tell you everything the doctors say. And I'll come home as soon as they discharge me, I promise." She didn't like my answer, but she at least pretended to accept it for the time being.

Nurses fed me painkillers, and I drifted in and out of jagged dreams. I awoke to see an Asian doctor writing on my chart. "It will take a few days for you to begin healing properly," she said, her smooth face creased with concern. None of my bones were broken, she reported, and there were no signs—yet—of a concussion, but I was badly bruised all over. "You're lucky," she said softly. "We've got wall-to-wall injuries, some of them fatal. It's as if there was a war."

When I was awake, I watched the endless television news coverage of the riots. My mind fixed on the fact that twenty-four years ago this month, black America exploded after Dr. Martin Luther King Jr.'s assassination. Now it had exploded again in response to an attack on another man named King. Same madness, different details. The atrocities of injustice hadn't changed at all. And when our frustration turned to blind fury and became too much to contain, we unleashed it on each other, then listened as outsiders judged what they could not possibly understand.

It didn't take long for the newscasters to declare the riots "the worst in the history of America." One said it was "a virtual inferno, an orgy of hatred, raw and unrestrained." My bruised bones and torn, battered flesh throbbed in agreement beneath the thick haze of painkillers.

The ache in my soul reminded me of wounds that were less obvious and would take much longer to heal: knowing I'd been attacked by the people I considered kinfolk, and saved by those I'd felt were a threat to my safety. Waves of shame washed over me. No drug or bandage could quell the agony of knowing that I'd betrayed, and been betrayed by, my deepest beliefs.

For the eternal minutes of my beating, nothing I'd ever felt, done, or believed in had made any difference. Those youngbloods didn't know or care who I was, didn't know my struggles or my triumphs, didn't give a damn where I'd laid my soul. Worst of all was the light-skinned one, the one who could have been my younger brother, who'd made me the punching bag for his own inner demons.

I was still disgusted at my inability to fight back or defend myself. Words had always been my weapon, and they'd never failed me before. I cringed, recalling the relief I'd felt at the sight of that LAPD car, knowing I'd banked on the white cops' ignorance to make my escape. I couldn't confess my shame to anyone; surely it would cause them to hate me as much as I was suddenly hating myself.

The next day, I was released from the hospital with strict orders for lots of rest and prescriptions for more painkillers and salves. I thought briefly of my abandoned rental car as a nurse wheeled me from the hospital to a waiting taxi.

"Let's go through South Central," I told the cabbie, a dark-chocolate brothah with close-cropped hair, a thick neck, and wary eyes.

"You sure?" he asked incredulously.

"I'm sure," I sighed. "I have to do it. And I'll need you to wait. It won't take long."

He shrugged and steered the aging yellow chariot toward the street where the rioting had been the worst. Two blocks over, I found the rental car—filthy, dented, but otherwise apparently unharmed. *Hmph,* I thought, that hunk of metal fared better than I had. I eased out of the taxi, welcoming the pain that accompanied each movement. I hobbled slowly to the spot where I'd been beaten, looking desperately for anyone who looked familiar. I scanned each young male face, half wanting to find my attackers. I stopped on a bloodstained patch of concrete. Saw people of all colors walking, dazed through the aftermath of what James Baldwin had called *The Fire Next Time.* Watched them sift through ash and debris, hunting for clues to the mysteries that live within our souls.

I wanted to howl my own conflict to the moody spring skies, beg forgiveness from someone, and remember what it felt like to be so confident of who and what I was that no questioning glance or querying remark could faze me. Opening my eyes to the river of broken concrete, glass, and trash around me, I wasn't sure that person existed anymore. Perhaps she never had.

I remembered the sixties philosophy that "Blackness is a state of mind." I recalled the thousands of appraising looks, all the interrogations about my pedigree, my identity, which side of the fence I was on. For the first time in my life, my confidence was shaken. What had happened in those terrifying moments? Whom had I betrayed?

I scanned the rainbow of people trying to piece a community back together from the ground up. "Hey!" the taxi driver yelled, "how long are we gonna be here?"

"Keep the meter running," I shouted, grabbing a broom and sweeping the glass around my feet into a pile. Some of the people around me lived here; others obviously did not. I was startled to see the taxi driver sweeping next to me. "Meter's off," he said brusquely. Were we all striving for the same thing—the realization of a hope, a dream, that the vision one man named King had died for would prevent others from being beaten down? Or was each of us frantically trying to resurrect our own truths and identities in the wake of this hate-filled storm?

With each movement my nerves screamed anew. I ignored the tablets the discharging doctor had pressed into my hand, and welcomed the brief escape the pain provided from the far more troubling meditations of my soul.

A soul ablaze with questions too excruciating to ignore, and no easy answers in sight.

Sink or Swim

ReShonda Tate Billingsley

"Only a fool tests the depth of the water with both feet."
—African, Senegal

G reg turned up his nose in disgust. *Look at her. It's like she doesn't even care anymore.* Greg hated the way he was feeling. But he couldn't help it. The sight of her was starting to repulse him.

His wife of nine years turned to him and smiled. "So, baby, which dress should I wear?" She held up two different dresses. A green silk sarong knee-length dress and a long, black rayon flared dress. Greg stared blankly. Both of them were ugly. Just like his wife. Well, actually, Greg didn't think Tangela was ugly. She just wasn't the same vibrant, superfine woman he'd said, "I do" to.

What I wouldn't give to have her go back to when we first met. When she was the first runner-up in the Miss Black America pageant. When her long wavy hair, hazel eyes, and perfect shape were the envy of men. But now, all she had left were the eyes. She had chopped off all her hair (he still hadn't gotten over that), and her shape was far from perfect. In fact, it was downright disgusting. She had to have gained forty to fifty pounds since they'd been married. Granted, she wasn't what some people would call fat—she wore a size eighteen (he knew because he had checked the tag in her clothes). But she wasn't the same thin woman he had married. And she knew how he felt about that. Everyone knew how he felt about that. He preferred thinner women. Always had, always would. But it was like Tangela didn't even care about that anymore.

"Hel-lo! Are you listening to me?" Tangela waved her hands in front of Greg's face.

"What?"

"I said, which of these dresses should I wear?"

They were getting ready to go to his best friend's birthday party. Greg had been excited about it all day, but the mere sight of his wife standing there in her bra and panties had spoiled his mood.

"Ummm . . ." Greg hesitated, then turned and walked into her huge closet. He scanned the rack, then reached way in the back and pulled out a red halter dress. He held it up. "Why don't you wear this?"

Tangela laughed. "Don't be silly. You know I haven't been able to wear that since the twins were born. I'll just wear the green." She hung the other dress up and headed to the bathroom. "I'll be ready in a few minutes."

Greg wanted so desperately to say something. That's why he had pulled out the halter dress. He knew she couldn't wear it, but he was hoping she'd get the hint and do something about losing weight. She blamed it on having three kids. But Greg thought that was just a cop-out. He didn't know much about having babies, but he knew she could get that weight off if she really wanted to. She was just too comfortable with him. That's what the problem was. She obviously believed it didn't matter if she looked like a slob, because she assumed he wasn't going anywhere. "Keep putting on the weight and we'll see about that," he muttered.

"Did you say something?" Tangela yelled from the rest room.

"Nah, just hurry up."

Greg was still in a sour mood, and they'd been at Jordan's party for over an hour. He was upset because he used to be so proud of his wife, and he didn't like the way he felt now. It had started after the birth of the twins, three years ago. That's when Tangela started putting on even more weight. She'd gained some after Gavin was born, but the majority of it had come after the birth of the twins. Greg knew Tangela was a good woman, but it wasn't good for a marriage when the attraction was gone. And it was definitely gone. He knew marriage was supposed to be for better or for worse, but to him, this was the "worse" part, and he didn't know how much more he could take.

"Yo, man, you don't look like you're having too much fun." Jordan came up behind Greg and patted him on the back.

Greg turned and managed a slight smile. "I'm aw'ight."

"Come on. I've known you long enough to know when you're all right. And you're not all right. What's up?" Jordan was a psychiatrist and always trying to get people to talk about their problems.

Greg didn't respond. He just stared across the room at Tangela, talking with some other women. She was the fattest one in the group.

Jordan noticed what Greg was staring at. "Don't tell me you still trippin' on that weight stuff?"

Greg nodded. "I'm not trippin'. Fat women turn me off."

"I've told you a thousand times, your wife is not fat."

"She's not the same size as when we met."

"*And?* You shouldn't have knocked her up."

"There you go, sounding like her."

"I'm just telling it like it is."

"Whatever." Greg took a sip of his drink. "Plenty of women have babies and they don't blow up."

"Yeah, Tangie has put on a little weight. But it's not that big of a deal. She still looks beautiful. Besides, you're supposed to love your wife for what's inside, not outside."

"Save that shit for one of your patients. I'm being real. I fell in love with a thin woman, I married a thin woman, and I wanted to grow old with a thin woman. Call me shallow or whatever. But that's what I like. That"—he pointed to his wife—"is not what I like."

"You're crazy, man," Jordan laughed.

"Say what you want. You know we don't even make love like we used to. She used to be a stone-cold freak. Could turn me *out* in the bedroom. Now, we just go through the motions. We have to do it with the lights off because she's all self-conscious. If she's that damn self-conscious, why doesn't she lose that blubber?"

Jordan laughed again and shook his head. "You're wrong. But that's between you and your wife. I do know you need to shake that mess off and have a good time at my birthday party."

Greg finished off the rest of his drink. "Yeah, I'll try. I don't . . ." He paused and stared straight at the entrance door. Jordan turned to see what he was looking at. Both of their mouths dropped at the sight of the beautiful woman who had just strutted in. She had flawless caramel-colored skin, long brown hair, and almond-shaped eyes. She wore a short black skirt and a burgundy see-through blouse. Sexy and classy.

"Like that!" Greg said almost in a daze. "That's how I want my woman to look. DAMN! She's bad!"

"I'm with you on that," Jordan said. "If I wasn't happily married . . ."

Greg cut him off. "But you are. I'm not." They both watched the woman run her fingers through her hair. She exuded confidence. "See, that's what I'm talking about," Greg said. "That's how a woman should look!"

Jordan just laughed and shook his head. "Remember, you came here with your wife."

Greg glanced around the room, looking for Tangela. He spotted her over in a corner talking with some friends. "Go talk to T and keep her distracted. I'm going to make a little conversation."

Greg knew he should show Tangela a little more respect, but he was getting to the point where he didn't even care anymore. Plus, he didn't make a habit of cheating on his wife. He'd only done it four times in their entire marriage, but he'd thought about it a lot. Especially over the past few months.

Greg walked over to the bar, where the woman was getting ready to pay for a drink. "Let me get that." He pulled out a ten-dollar bill and handed it to the bartender. "Keep the change." He turned back toward the woman.

She smiled. "Thank you. But I can buy my own drink."

Greg leaned against the bar. "I'm sure you can. I just wanted to do something nice for a beautiful woman. By the way, I didn't catch your name."

"I didn't throw it."

"Dang. Well Miss 'I didn't throw it,' I'm Greg."

The woman looked like she was contemplating whether she should give her name. Her eyes made their way up and down his body and stopped on his hands. "I'm Veronica," she finally said. "Thank you for the drink, Greg. Your wife would be happy to know that she has such a thoughtful husband." Veronica smiled again and walked off before Greg could say anything. He watched her glide across the room, a smile plastered across his face. Just when he was about to follow her, he felt hands wrap around his waist.

"Hi, honey. You having a good time?" Tangela had eased up behind him. He froze, wondering if she had seen him. But he guessed she hadn't, since she was hugging him lovingly.

Greg turned toward his wife, and his high immediately faded. Tangela didn't seem to notice. "Let's go to the buffet table. I'm hungry."

So what else is new?

Tangela noticed the exasperated look across Greg's face. "What's wrong?"

"Nothing." He turned his back.

Tangela pulled his arm, swinging him back around. "I can see that something's wrong. Talk to me. You never talk to me anymore."

Suddenly, Greg couldn't hold it in anymore. He'd spent months keeping his feelings bottled inside. He was absolutely miserable in this marriage, could barely stand looking at her. He had thrown hints, but she had never caught on—or at least didn't acknowledge that she had. Now he felt like he was about to explode. "Maybe you should try staying away from the buffet table," he finally said.

Tangela stared at her husband. "What is that supposed to mean?"

"What do you think it means, T?" Greg was about to let it all out. He knew it would hurt her feelings, but he was tired of caring.

A shocked look crossed Tangela's face. She shook her head like she couldn't believe what she was hearing. "Are you trying to say something about my weight?"

"I'm sorry, but I've been feeling like this for a while. I want to know, what happened? You used to be so beautiful."

Tangela's eyes started to water. "So you don't think I'm beautiful anymore?"

"Do you?"

She stood speechless, with a pained look across her face. "Why are you doing this to me?"

"I'm just tired of pretending like . . ." he waved his hand up and down her body. "Like you, and the way you look, doesn't bother me. You used to be so sexy." Greg knew he was going overboard, but it was as if the truth had taken him over. Maybe this harsh approach would shock her into doing something about her weight. However, at this point, he didn't even know if it would make a difference.

"But you know I gained weight after I had Gavin; then the twins . . ." Tangela took deep breaths, trying to ward off the tears.

"Stop blaming the weight on the kids. Look at Patrice," he said, pointing across the room to Jordan's wife. "She's had two kids and she's still thin. So stop using that as an excuse. You're fat because you don't give a damn about being fat!"

This had to be the meanest he had ever been, but Tangela was pretty passive when it came to him, so Greg knew she wouldn't cause a scene. She took another deep breath, unable to hold the tears back any longer. "I'm leaving. I'll get Tricia to take me home." She glared at her husband with tear-filled eyes, then turned and left.

Greg contemplated going after her. But he decided against it, grateful that his wife finally knew how he felt. Besides, with Tangela gone he'd get a chance to hold a conversation with Veronica.

He spent the next hour looking for Veronica, with no luck. About midnight, he decided to head home and deal with Tangela.

It was a slow ride home. Greg took his time, trying to delay having to face his wife. He had just pulled onto the 635 Expressway when he noticed a car with its hazard lights blinking and parked on the shoulder. He almost didn't stop, but when he noticed it was a woman who was stranded, he decided to check things out.

The woman was leaning over the trunk, studying the Lexus GS300 manual. Greg stopped, got out of his car, and made his way over to the woman. She looked up and they both broke into big smiles.

"Veronica?" Greg couldn't believe his luck.

Veronica breathed a sigh of relief. "Am I happy to see you! It's Greg, right?"

"You remembered. What seems to be the problem?" he asked, eyeing her car.

"I had a blow-out, my cell phone is dead, and I don't know the first thing about changing a tire."

Greg hadn't changed a tire in years. He always called AAA and let them do it, but he wasn't about to let Veronica know that. He gently put his hands on her waist and eased her to the side. "Relax your pretty little self. I'll take care of this."

Veronica grinned and let him get to work. After a brief struggle, he managed to get the tire off and the spare on.

"You're all set," he told her once he was done.

"Thank you so much." Veronica handed Greg a tissue to wipe his hands. He accepted it, never taking his eyes off her.

"You know, maybe I should follow you home to make sure you don't have any more problems with that tire," Greg said with a sly grin.

Veronica licked her lips seductively. "I would really like that, but I don't do married men," she said, pointing to his wedding ring.

Greg eased the ring off and held it up. "What if I told you that this doesn't mean anything?"

"I'd ask why you're still wearing it. Are you or are you not married?"

Greg didn't want to start off lying to Veronica. He had a good feeling about her.

"Unhappily," he responded.

"Yeah, right. I've heard that before."

"Seriously. And I've been wanting to leave for over a year now." He leaned into her. The smell of her perfume was tantalizing. "I just think I needed something, or someone, to help me muster up the strength to do what I know I need to do."

Veronica opened her car door, reached inside, and pulled out a pen and a piece of paper. She wrote her number on the paper then handed it to Greg. "I hope you're being honest about your relationship with your wife. I can't stand a lying man."

Greg folded the paper and put it in his jacket pocket. "I believe in being honest. Besides, you look like you don't take any mess from the men in your life."

"I don't."

"Is there a man in your life?" Greg asked as Veronica slid into her car. She started her engine.

"If you play your cards right, there just might be." She blew Greg a seductive kiss, then speeded off.

He smiled, pulled the number out of his pocket, and stared at it. "Oh, yes. Veronica, you may be just the catalyst I need to leave my wife."

"Well, I did it," Greg said. "I told T I was leaving."

"Get out of here," Jordan responded. "I can't believe you did that."

Jordan and Greg were sitting at the bar of a Cajun restaurant. They had stopped by after work to enjoy a drink. Greg had also wanted to break the news to his best friend about his doomed marriage.

"Yeah, I broke it to her last night. I told her I'd be staying with you."

"Oh, really?"

"I'm not really going to be staying with you. I'm staying with Veronica."

"The girl you met at my party?"

"Yep."

"You have got to be shitting me! You just met this babe. It's been what, six weeks? And you're leaving your wife over her?" Jordan was dumbfounded.

"I know, man, it's crazy. But we're vibing. We like doing the same things."

"Have you lost your mind?" Jordan tried his best not to raise his voice. "You throw away your marriage over some chick you just met! And for what? Because she's skinny?"

"Jordan, you know how I feel about being attracted to my woman. And I'm just not attracted to T anymore. I can't even stand the sight of her. But Veronica, she's everything I want."

"What if she gains weight five years from now? Are you going to dump her, too?"

"That's not going to happen. She said she would die before she ever let herself get fat. We work out together every day before I go to work."

"You see her every day?"

"Every single day. You know me and T hadn't really been talking since your party, so she doesn't say anything about me being gone all the time. She just sits in the house and sulks."

"What did Tangela have to say about you leaving?"

"She just cried and got all hysterical and shit. She begged me to stay, even going as far as saying she'd go on Jenny Craig. But my mind was made up. I'm just glad the kids were at my mom's. They're still there. I'm going to swing by when I leave and explain things to them."

"Why didn't you at least try that counselor I recommended?"

"We're beyond counseling. The only thing that can help us is my leaving. And being with Veronica." Greg smiled.

Jordan shook his head in amazement. "So, have you had sex with Veronica?"

Greg's smile grew at the thought. "The best sex I've ever had. We did it all over her house, even on the balcony. Unlike T, she has no inhibitions about her body, and it's exhilarating."

"Man, maybe it's just lust. You love Tangela."

"It's not lust. I think this is the woman I was meant to be with."

Jordan knew it would be useless to argue any further. "I just hope you know what you're doing, man."

"Don't worry about me. Veronica's the one. I'm sure of it."

Almost two months had passed since Greg moved out. And they were the best two months of his life. Veronica was a dream come true. He loved the pure looks of envy and jealousy he got when he and Veronica were out together. She was that beautiful. She could be a little possessive at times, but he thought it was cute. He was officially separated and had filed for a divorce. Tangela had stopped tripping and was even letting him spend time with the kids. Greg was happier than he'd been in a long, long time.

He was leaning back in his chair at work, thinking about the wonderful love he and Veronica had made that morning, when his secretary came on the speakerphone. "Mr. Jones, your son's school is on line one."

Greg sat up. "Thank you, Cecily." He wondered why they were calling him. Tangela usually handled all the stuff with the kids. He picked up the phone. "This is Greg Jones."

"Mr. Jones, this is the principal at Gavin's school. We're having problems with your son. He got into a fight with a student, then kicked and bit a teacher when they tried to break it up. He has been suspended. We tried to get in touch with your wife but were unable to. We were wondering if you could come to the school immediately."

"I'm on my way." Greg placed the phone back on the receiver, pressed the intercom to let Cecily know he was leaving, then headed out to the parking garage.

An hour later, he pulled into his former home with Gavin sitting in the passenger seat. Gavin wouldn't talk to him. He just sat there with his arms crossed, pouting. Jordan had warned Greg that Gavin might react to his parents' separation by getting into trouble.

"So, you don't have anything to say?"

"Nope." Gavin opened the door and climbed out of the car. Greg followed him. Tangela met them at the door. Greg had caught her on her cell phone, and she had agreed to meet them at the house.

"You have a lot of explaining to do, young man," she said as Gavin stomped past her. "Go sit in the living room!"

Gavin grumbled something before plopping on the sofa.

"Do you want to handle this yourself?" Greg was standing in the doorway, not sure if he should go in.

"No," Tangela responded. "He's your son, too. You come in here and talk to him."

Greg made his way inside. He and Tangela spent the next hour trying to get to the root of Gavin's problems. He blamed the fight on the other kid and accepted no responsibility.

Both of them were highly frustrated when there was a pounding on the front door. Tangela marched over and swung open the door. "Can I help you?"

"Where's Greg?" the woman standing there demanded.

"Excuse me?"

"Tell him to get his ass out here!"

Tangela looked at the woman like she was crazy. "Who are you?"

"I'm Greg's *woman!*" Veronica pushed her way past Tangela and into the house. "Greg!" she called out. She stormed into the living room. Gavin and Greg looked up at the same time. A shocked look crossed Greg's face. "What the hell . . . ?"

"I want to know what the hell you been doing up in here for an hour!" Veronica screamed. She looked like a wild woman. Her mascara was running, and her usually perfect hair was disheveled.

Greg stood up, a look of disbelief still across his face. "I don't believe you stormed into my house with this bull."

Veronica got in Greg's face, waving her index finger. "This ain't your house no more. You live with *me!*"

"You live *where?*" Tangela was standing off to the side trying to figure out what was going on.

"Daddy, who is this?" Gavin asked.

"I'm your daddy's girlfriend," Veronica replied without looking away from Greg.

Tangela was fuming now. "Greg, I think you and your *girlfriend* need to leave."

Greg didn't respond. He was still in shock over the whole scene. He never would've imagined Veronica acting like this. He grabbed her by her arm and pulled her toward the front door. "You need to leave."

Veronica snatched her arm away. "I AIN'T GOING NOWHERE! How you going to play me? You said you and that bitch were *through!*"

"Veronica, I'm not going to do this with you. I'm here trying to deal with my son."

"FOR OVER AN HOUR? YOU'RE A LIE!"

Greg's mouth dropped open. He had never seen this side of her. "How do you know how long I've been here? Were you following me?"

Veronica crossed her arms, a look of defiance on her face. "I came to meet you at work and saw you leaving. So I followed you. I'm not stupid like your wife. I'm not going to let you make a fool of me!"

Greg caught Tangela just as she lunged toward Veronica. "Get out of my house!" Tangela yelled.

"Mama!" Gavin screamed. He jumped up and raced toward his mother. Before anyone could blink, Veronica reached in her purse and pulled out a switchblade. She popped it, then jumped at Greg, just missing his chest. "Motherfucker, I told you I'd cut your ass if you messed over me!"

Greg was in absolute disbelief. She actually had said that, but he'd thought she was joking. Never in a million years did he think she'd actually try it. He grabbed her arm just as she was coming at him again.

He wrestled her to the floor. Gavin was screaming. Tangela had raced to the phone to call the police.

"Veronica! Calm down!" Greg screamed. Veronica broke free and scooted against the wall, the knife still pointed at him. She saw Tangela on the phone and glared at Greg. "This ain't over." Then she stood up and threw her hair back, closed the knife, picked up her purse, and strutted out like the classy woman Greg had first thought she was.

Greg stood at the front door of his home, feeling like a stranger. It had been a month since Veronica had gone ballistic. After that, he'd broken things off and she'd become even more psychotic, following him around and even harassing Tangela. Veronica had even showed up at the twins' school and tried to convince the teacher that she was their stepmother. Greg regretted the day he'd met her.

But surprisingly, the separation had seemed to empower Tangela. She had actually gone and lost weight. Not much—maybe ten, fifteen pounds. But she was looking better and better each time he saw her. It was last weekend, when he dropped the kids off, that he realized what a mistake he'd made. He spent the entire week trying to clear his mind and figure out his next move.

Now here he was, making that move.

Greg glanced at the bouquet of flowers clutched tightly in his hands. They were a small token, but he knew how much Tangela loved flowers. He also knew how much she loved him, so he was counting on her taking him back.

He rang the bell once before Tangela opened and stood aside to let him in.

"Hi."

Tangela closed the door. "You came to talk. So talk." She seemed so confident, not at all like the passive woman she had been during their marriage.

Greg decided not to sugarcoat things. "Tangela, I'm sorry."

"I know that." She sat down on the sofa.

Greg rubbed his temples. "You're not going to make this easy, are you?"

"Should I?" She picked up an *Essence* magazine and started flipping through the pages.

He handed Tangela the flowers. She just looked at them and kept reading her magazine. He laid them down on the table. "I messed up big-time."

"That you did."

"I need you."

"Oh, really? What happened to your girlfriend?"

"That was a mistake."

"Was it, now?" Tangela snickered.

"T, please, can we try and work this out?"

"You know, I really can't think about that now. All this fat is squeezing my brain." She still didn't look up from her magazine.

"T, I was wrong for that. I don't care about your weight."

Tangela slammed the magazine down and stood up. "No. You obviously care about it a lot. Yes, I have gained weight. But I'm still beautiful."

Greg stared into her eyes. They seemed so hard. "I know that."

"Shut up and let me finish. It's not like I sit around eating Ding-Dongs all day. I put on weight after giving you three children. I probably could've worked it off. But honestly, that wasn't a priority for me. Being a good wife and mother was my priority. I have a clean bill of health, so I don't see what the problem is. I've only lost weight now worrying behind your ass!" She paused, waiting for Greg to say something. When he didn't, she kept on talking. "I thought you were married to me, not my appearance."

"T, I messed up. That's all I can say."

"Yeah, you messed up, and you think you can just waltz back in here and I'll forget what you did to me?" Tangela paced back and forth. "You didn't even bother to get to know this woman before throwing away our family, our marriage. If you had known her more than five minutes, you might have known she was a psycho. Get to know her; that's the least you could've done!"

Greg didn't know what to say. For some reason, he had thought this would be easy, but it was like he was dealing with a different woman. "So would you have rather I had a long affair with her?"

"Damn it, I would rather you had honored your vows and been faithful. But if you had to cheat, if you had to leave me, at least it could've been over someone you knew, without a doubt, was worth it!"

Greg couldn't say anything. Tangela had never talked to him like that. He didn't even know she had it in her.

"You know, you're a fool," Tangela continued. "You didn't even bother to test the waters. You just jumped straight in with both feet. And you know what happens to people who do that? They sink."

Tangela composed herself, wiped away the few tears trickling down her face, then walked toward the door. "You made your choice. Now live with it. I don't want you. I don't need you. Good-bye."

"Tangela, please . . ."

"Good-bye, Greg!"

Greg felt himself about to cry—something he hadn't done in years. She was right. He'd been a fool. And now it was too late. He wanted to beg, plead, anything, but he could see the determination in his soon-to-be ex-wife's eyes. It was a determination he had never seen before.

Greg slowly walked through the door. He looked back at Tangela, hoping he could see some hint of her wavering. There was none. Just as he stepped outside the door, he turned to her.

"T, no matter what you think, I love—"

Tangela slammed the door on the sound of Greg's voice. It was a hard, forceful slam, one that let him know his marriage was indeed over, and there was nothing he could do to change it.

The Willow Tree

Mel Taylor

"All things must change." —African American

More than anything, Joe Humphrey was a singer. More than a handyman, a cook—even more than the great lover he had convinced himself that he was. Joe Humphrey could sing the blues—not the drugstore kind watered down by imposters to capture a crossover audience, but the gut-wrenching, low-down, dirty blues as sung by Gate Mouth Brown and the great Jimmie Reed.

Even as a boy, Joe had drawn his strength and gained recognition from his singing. Under the hot Mississippi sun, in the cotton fields where his entire family—except his mother and his older brother, Willie B.—toiled. Joe, dripping sweat from his brow into his mouth, sang the blues. He sang from his heart, sang songs that lightened the load and helped to pass the time.

His fellow workers encouraged Joe to "Sing dat song, boy; sing it!" And if the overseer wasn't around, the women would sometimes snap their fingers and work their hips into a slow, sensuous grind. This made Joe feel good, like he was somebody, and he imagined himself in another place with another audience, spotlight, and applause. He was sportin' a big diamond ring and the finest threads. Joe dreamed of nothing except becoming a star.

Tonight, these boyhood memories brought a smile to Joe's face. The warm Southern nights, the scent of magnolias, and the flight of a hundred racing fireflies stirred his soul. He recalled the old rickety porch of the four-room wooden shack that his father had built from the ground up, and the guitar that his oldest brother, Willie B., had given him. He remembered the delight in the eyes of his brothers, sisters, and their friends when he sang.

Sometimes Joe's parents, staunch Southern Baptists, had stood in the doorway listening to Joe's songs with mixed feelings. While they disapproved of what they called "the devil's music," they were unable to conceal their pride in Joe's God-given gift.

Growing up, Joe had been forbidden to sing the blues on Sunday ("Dat's de Lawd's day, son") so on that day he sang the gospel in the small, overcrowded church with the leaning cross a mile up the road. When Joe's rich, raspy voice rose to a crescendo, his father, the head deacon at Pleasant Green Baptist Church, and the whole congregation shouted, "Amen!" and drummed their feet on the hardwood floor like a herd of cattle. And Joe felt like the star he knew he was bound to become.

I was born Joseph Elijah Humphrey in 1942 in a small Mississippi town, to impoverished parents who sharecropped the land we lived on. I was the youngest of four boys; two girls would soon follow.

Life was not easy in Mississippi for Negroes (we hadn't become "black" yet.) Racism was so pervasive that we were always at risk, always in a state of fear for our well-being. The first thing my mother, Sadie Humphrey, taught me was to be submissive to white people. "Don't be lookin' white folks in they eyes when they talks to you, else they think you tryin' ta be smart, you hea'? And don't play with white chilun', especially little white gals," she warned.

As I grew older there were other rules to follow, mostly when going into town. Don't drink from the white fountain; don't use the white bathroom; step aside to let white folks pass when walking down the streets. And never, ever, stare at a white woman!

But Momma Sadie taught me even more by example. Even in her submissiveness there was pride and a kind of strength that both Negroes and white folks respected. She was a large woman, close to two hundred pounds, with a pretty face and a close-lipped smile that could make any child feel like the most special person in the world. Her big brown eyes sparkled when she laughed, or grew dark and pointed when she was angry. She carried the wonderful aroma of the kitchen where she performed her labors of love.

Momma Sadie was governed by four uncompromising principles: devotion to God, love of family, complete honesty, and obedience to her husband. She considered obeying Daddy God's will, but she didn't take no mess off her children. She knew the rules where white folks were concerned, but she didn't take no mess off them, either. That is to say, she always walked a thin line, performing a delicate balancing act made possible by her total faith in God.

My father, Rufus Humphrey, now he was different—quiet and slow to react to things. Not that he was unintelligent. Had he had the opportunity for book learning, he could have surely been more than a sharecropper. He may even have excelled the way his oldest son, Willie B., had. Daddy's lackluster personality was mostly a result of his extreme caution and the deliberate way he went about life's business. Very simply, Rufus Humphrey rarely made mistakes. Errors were not a luxury that Negroes could afford, he told us. Negroes had to be on their toes at all times, ready to seize the few opportunities that were available to them. But most of all, Negroes had to know how to read white folks. This knowledge had been given him by his father, which he in turn had passed on to Willie B. "You handle white folks by makin' 'um think you think they's better 'an you, an' smarter 'an you, but showin' them they ain't at the same time," he'd told Willie B., who had mastered that strategy.

Rufus Humphrey was as God-fearing as Momma Sadie, but rather than using force where his family was concerned, he preferred to use his considerable insight and homespun philosophy to address any issue. But when he got angry, look out. He glared with a power that told you he was a man to be reckoned with. At these times, everyone knew who the head of the family really was. The few times he shut my mother up with a simple "That's all, Sadie!" the house grew suddenly quiet, us children frozen in place, as Momma bowed her head and tended to her housework.

My father believed there were only three things in this world even worth talking about: The good Lord, family, and the land. "Everything else in the worl' got to do wit' dem," he said. So he had devoted his entire life to church, his family, and working the land he lived on, which had been a parting gift from the landowner when he died. That old redneck had set aside twenty acres for Rufus Humphrey, whom he regarded as "The best damn nigger in the whole world." That's exactly the way the will read.

This was the stock I had come from: two parents committed to their faith and their children, without contradiction, pure in thought and deed, strong in their resolve. But it was Willie B., the senior brother, who I worshiped. I didn't much care for BayBay and John L., the two younger brothers.

Tawana and Clara, my two sisters—well, they were just girls.

Tawana was okay, actually smart in school and all, even cute, but Clara, the baby, was a spoiled-rotten pest. I wasn't much bothered by them, though; everybody knew girls were not as important as men, except for maybe Momma Sadie. But then, as even she was quick to admit, it was her manchild, Willie B., who was the gifted one. "It is true, Baby Brother" (that's what I had been dubbed by Willie B.) "can sing up a storm. But singing ain't near as important as being smart," Momma Sadie said. "Not out in the worl', it ain't."

Willie B. was smart, maybe the brightest young man in the whole town, maintaining a straight-A average before graduating from the run-down schoolhouse the colored kids attended. Even Mr. Stein, the white man who owned the all-around store in town, secretly had Willie B. help with the books and inventory. This was not something commonly done in Mississippi, and it was surely the first time it had happened in our small town. Negroes were not permitted to work for white folks in positions that suggested they might have a brain. But Mr. Stein was a Jew, and a survivor of Auschwitz, where he had lost his entire family. He hated tyranny and racism of any kind. To him, the stand he took, even though it was secret, somehow honored the memory of his family.

Strangely enough, Mr. Stein wasn't the only white man impressed by Willie B.'s abilities, which included repairing anything with a movement or a current. But he was the only one willing to admit that a Negro was mentally superior to most people, white or black. Where Mr. Stein formed an intellectual bond with Willie B., the others simply availed themselves of Willie B.'s talents, then turned their heads in denial when overwhelmed by his brains.

Such was their denial that in Willie B.'s preteen years, the whites saw his abilities as a form of entertainment. Their inability to accept a Negro boy's genius, combined with the insights that our father had given him, afforded Willie B. an opportunity to serve as an apprentice in several trades, all of which he quickly mastered. As a result, Willie B. never spent one day in the cotton fields.

Not only was my brother a near-genius, he was handsome as well— tall and lean like Daddy, but strong of limb, with bold, chiseled features that leaped out at you like a statue cast in ebony. His smile was toothy and quick, and the girls went wild over him, as I witnessed with an envy that cheered rather than despised his popularity. But Willie B. was no womanizer. He enjoyed a few indiscreet nights in the backseat of some car he had taken in to repair, and the occasional romp in the hayloft of the barn he had helped Daddy enlarge. However, he spent most of his quality social time with Cindy Lou Robinson, a plain, dark-complexioned young virgin who wore bifocals and was impishly cute.

In my eyes, Willie B.'s only flaw was his choice of women. He could have had any pretty girl in town, even a white one if he had dared. In fact, I'd seen Judge Stevenson's daughter smile at Willie B. in the too-friendly way that revealed her crush on him. She made up excuses to ask his assistance: something in her convertible didn't sound right; she needed him to retrieve some item from the garage, or her bicycle needed repairing. On one occasion her father had called her inside from the back porch, warning her to "leave them boys alone!" Willie B. had given me a knowing smile. I couldn't have been prouder if she'd had the hots for me.

I lived vicariously through my brother, coveting his every success, making them my own, gloating because he and I were of the same blood. Even my singing talent took a backseat, in my mind, to Willie B.'s achievements.

But Willie B. was proud of me, too, almost like a father is proud of a favorite son. Maybe in many ways he did function as a parent to me. It was Willie B., not Momma Sadie, who taught me to cook, to make biscuits from scratch, cook hot-water cornbread, and prepare mustard greens the right way. And Daddy had Willie B. teach me the necessary survival trades.

My bond with Willie B. had been cemented just weeks after I had entered this world, instantly mimicking his smile and clasping my tiny hand to his. Momma Sadie sometimes joked to her church friends that her oldest son had stolen her baby boy. He taught me to catfish, swim, and hunt rabbits. And his best lessons at the old willow tree that stood guard over the river, the tree we had claimed as our own. That's where Willie B. taught me what he knew about life and being colored. "Why white people hate us?" I had asked.

"Because they done us so wrong, baby brother," he said. "Because the way they do us lets 'um see how evil they can be."

"We ain't slaves no mo'," I pointed out.

"We know that, and they know that. But the hardest thing in the world for some people is to say when they wrong. So they just keep on acting like they ain't."

"Sometime I'm scared, Willie B. Sometime I think they gonna hang me like they done Tim Tidmore."

Anger flashed in Willie B.'s eyes. "Ain't nobody gonna hang you; they got ta kill me first," he said. And I believed him. Whatever my brother said, I knew he meant.

Willie B. told me about girls, too. Told me to judge them from the inside out rather than only from the outside. A good girl won't drink or smoke, run around with a lot of boys, and she will always respect her mother and father, he said. That's what Daddy had taught him. Momma Sadie had been just that kind of girl when they'd met, and she was the standard by which all women were to be judged.

The willow tree was my friend. It was strong and ever-present, unchanging, silently listening to our lessons. In its bosom were secrets a hundred years old. Stories of riverboats passing in the night, of gamblers, murderers, and scarlet women entertaining wealthy men.

It was there that I ran on the worst day of my life. Tears streamed down my face and I tasted their bitterness as I walked slowly along the riverbank with my guitar strapped to my back. There was no mystery in the river's calm, muddy waters that day. Its distant gray face held no promise to fire the imagination or cause my heart to pound. The damp, musty smell was stronger than ever.

I felt empty as I neared the tree. My brother wasn't by my side. Removing the guitar from my back, I sat propped against the trunk. It had been bound to happen, but I'd held out hope that something—anything—would change Willie B.'s mind or even her mind, which I had been sure was impossible.

I screamed my anger at the river, a high, piercing screech like a man gone crazy. At that moment, I hated Willie B. He'd had no business goin' ta marry no Cindy Lou Robinson no-how. Just last week, things had been so different, been so fine. Willie B. had talked to me like I was a man, right here in this same spot. He'd said things to me that had made me a little unhappy, but proud at the same time. I'd been playing the guitar and playing a song I'd made up. When I finished, Willie B. looked at me with what I thought was a new respect, as if he was seeing his little brother for the first time.

"Baby brother," he began, looking me softly in the eyes. "You listen real good to what I'm gonna say. You're not like BayBay and John L. You're not like Daddy; you're not even like me."

Tears welled up in my eyes.

"No, baby brother, that's a good thing. Just look at BayBay and John L. Ain't never gonna think about nothin' but funky-buttin' with some funky-butt gals. It's good you ain't like Daddy, cause he learned a long time ago to accept things the way they are, put 'um in God's hands. Even me, baby brother. I ain't like you, 'cause I ain't got your heart."

"You got plenty heart, Willie B—"

"Oh, I'm gonna be a success, all right, but just in an ordinary way. Now you, you're gonna be great!"

My face lit up. "You think so?"

"I know so, baby brother. You the only one with heart enough to live out your dreams, and that's what it takes to be great."

Remembering his words just a week before, I felt emptier than ever before. But I still had my music. I began to play, and a slew of words just welled up from the floor of my soul and flew out of my mouth.

> *"Ye-es, I'm gonna leave this worl',*
> *'cause Love won't set me free.*
> *Gonna leave this ol' worl',*
> *'cause Love won't set me free.*
> *Think I'm gonna drown myself*
> *in some big ol' muddy sea."*

As I sang, my voice lost its adolescent waver and grew deeper. I moaned and cried with the guitar, fueled by the misery of a hundred broken hearts.

> *"Love can thrill you,*
> *it can cause you so much pain;*
> *Love can bless your life,*
> *or make you go insaaaaaaaane."*

I'd wallowed in musical self-pity for about an hour when I felt some-one watching. I slowly turned to see a large pair of brogan shoes on the other side of the tree. Daddy sat nonchalantly carving a wooden doll for my baby sister, Clara. After a long silence, he spoke.

"Sometime a person give another person all the love they got to give." He paused and looked me hard in the eye. "Sometime, boy, dat other person make a fool of hisself askin' fo' mo'."

I started to speak, but his expression cut me off. "You love Willie B. so much you think you in him and he in you, don't cha? He can't have no life lessen he live the life you want him to. Ain't that right? That ain't love, boy; that's just selfish. Maybe you just love yo'self and not Willie B. atall."

He rose up, brushed off his overalls, and began the three-mile walk back home. I pondered his words, respecting them as I always had, but torn between his wisdom and my anger. What right did Cindy Lou and Willie B. have to be so happy? I'd felt betrayed when they'd told everyone at the church they were getting married and moving to California. What about me? They never thought nothin' 'bout me.

I'd done everything Willie B. had ever told me. Learned everything he had taught me, almost. I'd even made up some songs for him and Cindy Lou. But they didn't care one little thing about me!

I stomped my feet, talked to myself, and then cried. But my tears made me angrier because real men weren't supposed to cry. I put on a brave mask to camouflage my hurt feelings.

I walked slowly, holding my guitar as if it were my only friend. Told myself I didn't care *what* they did, or if I did care, I wouldn't let it show. I reached the house and stood on the porch, listening to the cheerful jokes and laughter, which hurt me still more. I told myself I could run away, far away where no one could find me. Maybe I would catch a freight train and hobo it to California or go to New Orleans to play in a blues band. But Willie B. wouldn't be in California then, and I didn't know any bands to join in New Orleans. Fighting back the urge to cry, I went inside, avoiding the eyes that followed me to the room I shared with Willie B., BayBay, and John L.

The room was as musty as the river-bottom land, dominated by the pungent odor young boys in a hurry to go nowhere leave behind. John L. and BayBay's side was a mess of smelly socks piled in a corner and dirty clothes strewn over the double-deck cots they slept on. I crossed the small room to the bunk beds where Willie B. and I slept. Our side was neat and orderly.

I didn't want to stay in this room, not alone with those two messy spooks who always picked on me when Willie B. wasn't around. At that moment, they rushed in, roughhousing loudly the way they always did. BayBay chased John L., who carried an imaginary football, falling on me and striking my guitar. I went wild, kicking him off me with both feet and pulling my guitar close. Before John L. could react, Momma Sadie's voice boomed loud and clear from the front of the house. "I know y'all don't want me to come back there."

John L. and BayBay stopped in their tracks. It had never occurred to them to defy Momma Sadie. And if they were ever foolish enough to entertain such a thought, they'd still have Daddy to deal with.

"I oughta break that ol' guitar," John L. whispered.

"I bet you won't," I challenged boldly. I hated John L. He couldn't even fight.

"You been crying' like a little old' punk," he snarled.

BayBay stepped in and stood wide-legged in front of me. He was sixteen and the second eldest, a menacing bulk of solid muscle who struck fear in the hearts of those unfortunate enough to incur his disfavor. His unpleasant face was redeemed only by an electric smile that appeared as if by divine error. "And Willie B. ain't sendin' fo' you ta come to no California, either," BayBay sneered.

I almost punched his ugly face, but the certainty of the whuppin' I'd get for bloodying his nose stilled my fist. I just mustered up all the hate I felt. "Well, I won't sing for the girls you tryin' to get anymore, then!" I threatened.

They laughed, knowing it was a bluff. I could threaten, but they and everyone else knew that I *had* to sing.

Tawana rushed in with Clara close behind. "Momma say come here Joe. It ain't right fo' you not to be at yo' brother's wedding announcement."

"Yeah, Momma said," Clara echoed, poking out her tongue and following Tawana out of the room.

All right. I'd go, had no choice, but I found a way to get my revenge. I rose from my cot, leaving my guitar behind and walking past John L. and BayBay as if they weren't there. They dashed past me into the living room, which had been converted into a dining area for the Sunday dinner.

The large, wooden table, as solid and dependable as my family, was filled with food. I sat with my head bowed before Daddy began to say grace, which, as usual, turned into a long prayer. While the others dug into the mashed potatoes and fried chicken, I ignored the food. John L. and BayBay crammed their mouths and taunted me with big eyes. Tawana was unconcerned, but Clara had to signify. "Momma, Joe ain't eatin' his food!"

"You just mine yo' business, little woman," Momma warned. "Clean yo' plate. And eat them peas."

Daddy ate in silence, looking from time to time at Cindy Lou, who sat stiffly, taking bird bites from her plate. Willie B.'s concern for my discomfort was visible. He ate slowly, his eyes never leaving my face.

Although no words were spoken, the two of us communicated. I knew before he rose that he was going to walk to where I was sitting. "Let's take a walk," he said with a loving gaze, as if there had been no tension between us.

I rose awkwardly, stumbling over my feet and bowing my head, to follow him out the door. Dust had settled in on that warm Southern night, dominated by an early moon, which followed our silent walk to the willow tree. Willie B.'s arm felt good around my shoulder, which made me feel guilty for having hated him. His words made me feel even worse.

"Baby brother, you gonna break my heart."

I looked up and saw his tears. I began to cry, too.

"I ain't tryin' to break yo' heart, Willie B." He put his strong arms around my shoulders and held me tight.

"I know you ain't." I know you just don't want me to go. But I got to. I got to follow *my* life and *my* dreams. Just like you gonna have to follow yours."

My heart began to soften and my tears to dry. And my feelings soon mended. Maybe that night was the beginning of my coming into my maturity, standing beneath that willow tree in the presence of the incandescent moon, with my beloved brother wiping the tears from my face. A soft, sweet song echoed in my mind, and finally I began to understand.

Valley of the Shadow

Maxine E. Thompson

"The blacker the berry, the sweeter the juice."

—African American

"Is her plane here yet?"

Lord, you would think it was the second coming of Jesus! Willa looked on in amazement at her father's fawn-colored irises leaping like a baby's at the sight of its mother. In an attempt to keep down the lava bubbling up in her breast, she held her breath.

If she had not seen it happen so many times over the years, Willa would not have believed it herself. But slowly, almost imperceptibly, she was fading . . . disappearing . . . In a moment, she would be invisible . . . no ears . . . no eyes . . . no face . . . nobody. Voices boomeranging overhead confirmed these phenomena.

"She at the airport now."

"Oh, yeah?"

"Say she gon' rent a car, but if someone can pick her up from the airport, she'll do it later."

"That girl always was something. Tell her she bet'not insult me by rentin' no car. Sister here. She can go get her."

How gracious, she thinks. So like her father to volunteer her services freely, and so like her sister, Gazelle, to pretend that she did not want to impose on anyone, but . . .

Briefly, several pairs of family eyeballs flickered in the direction of the chair that Willa, the invisible one, was glued to. Then they turned away.

"That's all it took." She felt her mouth twist into a smirk. One phone call, and there went all her years of hard-won respect. She, the one who had sacrificed and stayed home to care for her ailing mother, M'Deah, was obliterated to nothing.

From the time that Uncle Lucious, M'Deah's brother, had answered the pay phone in the corridor outside the hospital waiting room, everything had changed. Up until this point, she had been called Willa by Aunt Hattie, Uncle Lucious, Cousin Opal, and the others. Now, she was Sister again.

She was no longer seen as vital to M'Deah's three-year battle against cancer. (Willa had not realized how, in spite of her anguish, she had relished being seen as an individual in her own right, and not as her sister's shadow.) With her father calling her by her childhood nickname, she felt as small and insecure as the girl in her had.

Peering out of glazed eyes at her father, Willie Fred, she was startled by the transformation. If possible, Willie Fred suddenly looked younger than his sixty-eight years. Fluorescent lights from above reflected on the broad expanse of his face. They did not reveal the webbed wrinkles and deep furrows of his life. Instead, they highlighted the polished patina of his hickory-colored skin.

The strain on his face from long hours of keeping a vigil at the hospital seemed to vanish as he beamed, not for Willa, the daughter at his side, who devotedly nursed, fed, and bathed her dying mother, but at the prospect of seeing Gazelle, who had come all the way from the big city to Muskogee, Oklahoma. M'Deah, his wife of forty-nine years, was dying. But Gazelle, the light of their lives, had come. Maybe her presence could hold back the dark horse of death.

From her invisible space, Willa saw all of her relatives in the waiting room's cubicle mentally dismissing her, their eyes brimming in anticipation of "the light-skinned one." In 1988, after forty years of living, things hadn't truly changed for Willa at all.

Suddenly, Willa felt really tired. Now she knew how a worn-out rag doll, cast aside by its youthful owner and staring dumbly at its replacement, must feel.

If you're yellow, you're mellow.
If you're brown, stick around.
If you're black, STAND BACK—
Way back!

As Willa drove toward the airport, a slow drizzle of rain began to fall. Her windshield wipers struck a painful rejoinder to the pulse of her emotions. Inquietude was new to her.

Fields of hazy buttercups, black-eyed Susans, gladiolus, and daffodils danced across the screen of her mind. The flower of girlhood, the bloom of which, for her, had never been consummated.

Willa thought of Gazelle as a buttercup: always tawny of limb, honey-kissed as its pistil, and lemony-round of face. As girls, self-assurance had come as naturally to Gazelle as diffidence had come to Willa. They were as different as day and night, so much so that the other children nicknamed them Salt and Pepper. Willa was so like Willie Fred, for whom she was named. In her opinion, she had always been too broad of nose, too full of lips, too short of hair.

But why shouldn't they be different? She sighed. After all, as she had learned at the age of eight, they had different fathers. On an especially tearful Saturday, she had been having a tantrum in front of the kitchen stove, where she underwent a bimonthly form of torture. On this particular day, though, she wanted to know why she had to have her crinkly locks straightened with a pressing comb while Gazelle's cinnamon-colored locks escaped the ordeal. M'Deah explained brusquely that Gazelle had a different father. Period.

M'Deah never mentioned the subject again, and Willa was too afraid of her to bring it up. Over the years, Willa managed to piece together the story like a patchwork quilt. It was said that Willie Fred and M'Deah had married while they were still in high school, back in the late 1930s. During World War II, when Willie Fred enlisted in the army and was shipped overseas, M'Deah met and fell in love with a Creole man from out of New Orleans. Called "Black Jacques," he was a professional gambler and—gathering from what the relatives whispered—also quite a ladies' man.

Apparently, after the affair, M'Deah wrote Willie Fred a "Dear John" letter, asking for a divorce. However, before the divorce ever had a chance to take place, Black Jacques had skipped town, leaving M'Deah in a family way.

No one ever knew what M'Deah and Willie Fred had said, or how they reconciled behind M'Deah's cheating, but after the war they resumed living as man and wife. No mention of Black Jacques was ever heard in their house. As far back as Willa remembered, Gazelle had never been treated as though she was anything but Willie Fred's natural daughter. On the contrary, she had been pampered and, as an adult, catered to when she came home to visit.

One story in the annals of family folklore had it that when Gazelle was about four years old, she had developed scarlet fever. The family lived way back in the country part of Muskogee, and the closest doctor was miles into town. Willie Fred and M'Deah hadn't owned a car back then. They say that Willie Fred carried Gazelle bundled in his arms until he found a white doctor who would save his baby's life.

Two years later, the appearance of Willie Fred's own biological daughter, Willa, did little to change his attitude toward Gazelle. Willa had her father's meek temperament. Gazelle, though she had Black Jacques's hazel-green, sometimes murky-gray eyes, had definitely inherited M'Deah's bossiness.

Gazelle's willfulness seemed to even intimidate grown folks even when she was a child. All anyone seemed to notice were the two sandy ropes hanging to her waist and the dusky melon complexion. Even when grownups scolded Gazelle, there was a beam of pride in their voices. No one seemed to notice Willa, the timid, dark sister. Only M'Deah was ever stern with Gazelle, calling her "Miss Prissy." Everything Willa had ever done was eclipsed by Gazelle's accomplishments. Of the two sisters, Gazelle was the only one to go to college.

When Willa graduated from high school, M'Deah had to have a leg amputated due to complications stemming from her sugar diabetes. Needless to say, Willa would not hear of going off to school and leaving M'Deah. She worked graveyard shift at the post office for years and spent her days caring for M'Deah and cooking for Willie Fred.

Gazelle, on the other hand, married what the family considered a successful businessman and had two honey-colored children who were attending college.

At forty, Willa had no husband, no children, and no prospects of getting a family, either. She felt bereft, naked, and exposed. She remembered how, when M'Deah's leg was amputated twenty years before, Willie Fred and the others kept saying, "We don't know what we would do without Sister." Over the years she had gained a certain long-sought-after peace. Gazelle's return felt to Willa like the epicenter of an earthquake.

Willa had never questioned the way things were. This day, she did. *I am reclaiming lost saffron shores of the River Nile of my soul.*

"Girl, aren't you going to hug me back?"

Icy fire seared Willa's brain at the sound of Gazelle's citified voice. She willed herself to embrace her sister. Impeccably dressed in a tailored white linen suit accented with a dash of magenta, Gazelle was as self-possessed as ever. Her perfume rode daintily upon the air behind her as she switched her hips in a provocative swivel. From habit, she walked ahead of Willa, with the younger sister on her heels. Glancing down at her own drab brown tweed outfit, Willa felt like the dowdy country mouse, like a drab winter blast next to the springlike whirlwind that was Gazelle.

As usual, when around Gazelle, Willa became aware of her plumpness. Unconsciously she bridled herself, sucking in her stomach and throwing back her shoulders. This time, though, she noticed with satisfaction that Gazelle's sylphlike figure had become fuller, lusher. She was no longer as svelte as she had been only two years before. Willa couldn't get over her sister's new fleshiness, especially as Gazelle had always prided herself on being petite. "My husband, George," she would pout with her rosebud mouth, "is such a fuddy-duddy about my weight."

Willa noticed Gazelle's skin turning darker, subtly, like an autumn leaf that browns first around the edges. *She's getting older*, Willa thought incredulously. Then she remembered, *And I am, too.*

As they waited for Gazelle's luggage in the baggage area, Willa asked, "How's Detroit?"

"The same."

Detroit, where Gazelle had lived in a large brick house on Outer Drive Street for the past twenty years, was forever the "Big City" to people from Muskogee. Willa winced, recalling the many years when Gazelle returned home like a babbling river through a desolate valley, washing them with the news from the "Outside World."

This day was different, though. As Gazelle clasped Willa's hands between her own, Willa felt her sister's fear pulsing through her blood. "How's M'Deah? Don't lie to me. Give it to me straight," Gazelle begged.

"M'Deah. You woke?"

"Yes, Daddy." The voice was so faint it was barely audible.

"Your baby home. Gazelle be here, soon as Sister git her here."

The little mound under the hospital covers was scarcely larger than a child's grave. M'Deah, once a big-bosomed, velvety black woman, had always been a citadel of strength. She had never apologized or offered an explanation for her life to anyone.

She was no different in the face of death. Under the ravages of the disease, her hands, which had become birdlike claws, clutched at the covers. She beckoned weakly for Willie Fred to lean closer.

"Sister . . ." M'Deah whispered.

"I can't hear you, M'Deah."

"Sister . . ."

"What about her?"

"Tell her—Tell her—"

With that M'Deah drew her last breath, too soon for her firstborn to set foot in her room and too late for her lastborn to say her good-byes.

"Why are you packing? I thought I was the only one leaving."

Willa studied her sister, standing arms akimbo in the doorway of the bedroom they had shared. She stared so long and hard that Gazelle became uneasy and looked away. Willa returned to her packing.

"Well, you're not the only one leaving. Not today." Her voice shook with rage.

Gazelle gave her that searching look that Willa had seen throughout the week of the funeral. "What's wrong, Sister? Things seem fair to me. I'm glad M'Deah left you her half of the house and the biggest part of the insurance money. I know we're all sad, but you seem angry. I just don't understand why you're acting like this. I don't even know you anymore."

"I guess you don't understand," Willa snapped. M'Deah's death seemed to bring her out of her shell. "It's not the money."

The house was quiet for the first time all week. Most of the guests had left. This had always been home for Willa, at least until now. She didn't worry about Willie Fred. Will, he was inconsolable in his grief, but the presence of full-hipped church sisters, swarming in and out of the house with warmed dishes for the wake meant that he wouldn't be lonely for long.

"You have no idea what it's like to be dark-skinned," she said coldly. "Especially for a woman. Overlooked by your own kind. Told you're ugly till you begin to believe it yourself. But I don't blame M'Deah and Willie Fred or even you. It's just the way things were. M'Deah and Willie Fred did they best for us. This ain't about y'all.

"This about me. I fault myself for what I've accepted as my lot in life. I've lived in the shadows so long, I don't even know if there's anything I can do on my own. Now, I've got to find out who I am."

After a moment of silence, Willa continued. "I feel like I've lived a lie. I don't even know where I fit into this world."

"You're crazy, Sister," Gazelle cried. "You're the one who fit in! I was 'the outsider,' M'Deah's mistake. I'm the one who has had to prove that I wasn't bad blood. True enough, Willie Fred has been good to me—he's the only father I've known. And over the years, when I hear the horror stories of my friends who grew up with stepfathers, then I know I've been blessed. Willie Fred is a good man. But he was good to me because he loved M'Deah so."

"That's not true, Gazelle, and you know it," Willa countered. "Willie Fred couldn't have loved you more if he had been your real father. If anything, he loved you more because of your color. I guess he knew that with it, life would offer you more, and it has."

"Poor black people. I guess we can't help being so color-struck. Still, I'm the one who has accepted being limited by my color." Willa shrugged sadly. "That's what I'm going to change. I guess it's not your fault the way things are."

Biting her lower lip until it turned red, Gazelle was silent. When she found her voice, her words were heavy with resignation. "Since we're being honest with one another, let me tell you something about living a lie."

Willa stared at Gazelle quizzically.

"Did you know that George and I have been divorced for two years? Yes. I've been lying to my family, but most of all, I've been lying to myself. Hah! Convincing myself that I couldn't tell M'Deah since she was so sick. Truth is, I didn't want to give up the image we had as the perfect couple."

It was Willa's turn to be stunned. "What happened?"

Gazelle's laughter held the bittersweetness of crushed amber leaves underfoot in the fall. "The usual. Another woman. Plus, after the kids went off to college, we looked up and found out we were strangers. Well! Now. I've said it. That wasn't so bad."

"I'm sorry to hear that." Willa was dumbfounded. So many changes. What next?

"Don't be sorry. Best thing ever happened to me was George's leaving." Gazelle paused. "Willa, where will you go? How will you make it?"

"I have money saved," Willa replied. "Plus my part of M'Deah's insurance money; I'll make it. Anyhow, I'm going someplace, anyplace but here." Willa's tone was even, resolute.

"Why don't you come and stay with me? I still have that big empty house," Gazelle offered.

"No, thanks."

The two sisters looked at each other with new insight and quiet understanding. Finally, Gazelle reached over to hug Willa. "If you ever need anything, don't hesitate." Her voice was muffled. Slowly, Willa hugged her in return. Gazelle pulled away and left the room, shaking her head.

Willa snapped her suitcase with a resounding click. She marched out of her father's house, intent on leaving for the first time, eyes set on horizons unknown. A vermilion sunset splashed across the sky to announce twilight's nearing. In the front yard the medley of crickets and whippoorwills and the redolent fragrance of jasmine and juniper jumbled together to become one and the same.

Willa paused. Her eyes settled on the tiny row of espaliered cypress trees, which queued up the driveway. She gazed at them longingly. Though she had planted them with her own hands, she understood that she would not see the trees mature. Bracing herself, she tore away from it all. She climbed into her car and drove away, never looking back.

She Planted Faith in Her Dream

Denise Turney

"If ye have faith, and doubt not ... if ye shall say unto this mountain, be thou removed, and be thou cast into the sea; it shall be done." —Matthew 21:21

Way my mother told it, I've been born forever. Born in a small town too far from anywhere important. It was the way my mother's people wanted it. My father, he didn't care. He dropped a seed like a farmer who knew he wouldn't be around to till the land. Slept with my mother long enough to get her pregnant; then he up and moved on. To this day I call my father "the traveling seedsman."

It was hot something awful the day I was born. Old Man Baxter was sitting on his front stoop just like always. Hat pulled down over his brow. Them horn-rimmed glasses pushed back on his face like they was a part of his skin. I swore it then, and I swear it now: Old Man Baxter saw everything that went on over in the black side of Knoxville, and all because he had those thick horn-rimmed glasses.

I used to stare at them when I was a little girl. They was like magic to me. Gosh, how I wanted to get a hold of them glasses. Snatch them right off Old Man Baxter's face and push them right up against my own brown skin. I wanted to push those glasses up on my nose until they was like a cowboy riding a lone horse. Then I wanted to stretch my neck, squint, and look way out into the future. See everything that was going to happen to me and my mother long before it came up on us. That way we wouldn't have no more surprises to knock the wind out of our spirits, knock us down flat, hit us and break us hard.

But I'm going too fast.

Mama had been out back laughing with her girlfriend, Rose, when she said she felt something move in her stomach real hard. She never called me her baby, not even before I was born, not even before I started getting into trouble, not even before I started to worry her nerves real bad-like. "Something ain't right," she leaned over and told Rose while she held her stomach with her hand.

Can't tell you how warm I felt each time my mother touched me. I wasn't ready to be born; even the doctor said that. It was too early, but I always been ahead of my time. I ain't never been like other kids around me. I always been different, from even before when I was born.

"Girl, you ain't looking good," Rose said. "You fixing to have that child. Let me get you indoors so I can lay you down. I'll run and call Miss Fletcher."

Miss Fletcher lived four houses down from where my mother was staying with Rose. Still, it took forever for Rose to come running back up the front walk with Miss Fletcher at her side. They were just a-huffing. They moved so fast that the fat on their legs and arms was rolling and bumping together.

All on account of me coming into the world.

Miss Fletcher went to calling out orders. "Mattie, lay down. What you doing up walking around? You gonna hurt that child. A woman's got to lay down when she's ready to give birth, help life move along. If you ain't flat on your back when that baby starts moving down, something's gonna be wrong with that child. It ain't never gonna be normal. You gonna mark that child, sure 'nuff." Then she pushed at my mother's shoulders. "So lay down." She raised her voice. "Lay down right now."

Then Miss Fletcher turned to Rose. "Boil me a pot of water," she bossed loudly. "Hurry up them back steps and bring me down some towels, sheets, and washrags. It's gonna be a bloody mess in here real soon. This child is a-coming. This child is steady coming."

Rose raced all over that house, lookin' like she'd go crazy just trying to get everything Miss Fletcher called for together in her arms. The more she came back with, the more Miss Fletcher sent her running into another room to get. If not for the wailing and cursing from my mother, I would have laughed.

By the time I was ten years old, I was a big girl. Had me the prettiest brown eyes anybody in all the world ever did see. Eyes shaped almost like almonds, except they too round for that. High cheekbones, with dimples right smack-dab in the center of them. My forehead was smooth and flat and soft to run your hand across. Whether it was hot or cold out, whether I was sweating or not, I liked to raise my hand and run it back and forth across my forehead. It felt so good to do that. For so long it seemed like it was all the fun I had in the world.

Old Man Baxter was a big reason I felt so beat down. He told me I was gonna kill my mother. Had them thick glasses on. I was standing on his porch drinking the lemonade he always gave me after we played horsie. No other kids never did come play with us, and I asked more than twice. Old Man Baxter just looked at me and told me, "Now, you know you's different. You know you ain't like no other child. Rest of these kids out here don't want to play with you. You ain't their kind. Why, you ain't really like a child at all."

Did I think my mother knew Old Man Baxter was giving me lemonade as a prize for playing horsie with him so good? He'd moan and rock and squeeze on me while I slid up and down his lap, my dress going higher and higher up my back while we played. When I told Mama that playing horsie didn't feel right and that I wanted her to come see the game so she could tell me if everything was okay, she looked at me real hard and said, "At least you getting something to drink and eat. Old Man Baxter's taking care of you. You getting a sandwich and some of that sweet lemonade every time you play horsie, so close your mouth. You ain't got nothing to complain about."

And so I played horsie with Old Man Baxter until all that rocking started to make me sick. "You gonna get big now," Old Man Baxter leaned over on his pretty, shiny cane and told me while he watched me get sick in his bathroom toilet. He had them glasses on. I swear he could see into the future. It wasn't long before my stomach just started going straight out. I got sicker and sicker. Soon my mother and Rose started looking at me real funny. They'd give me these long, down-the-nose, back-up-straight-again stares. Made me pull down on my shirts and try to cover up my stomach.

I didn't want to be fat, but didn't no other kids around where we lived want to play with me. I didn't know no exercises on my own to get rid of the fat. I even asked the other kids if they'd play with me. "I'll skip rope with you. We can play hopscotch. We can even run in races. I run real fast," I told them with a big grin until I finally gave up and walked away. They shook they heads, stuck out their tongues at me, laughed real hard, and ran. Ran away from me, but not before they kicked dirt and sent it flying right into my face. My eyes would burn. Dirt ain't good for your eyes. Maybe that's why Old Man Baxter wore them thick, see-into-the-future glasses. Maybe somebody kicked dirt in his eyes a long time ago.

We didn't play horsie no more, because I kept getting sicker. I don't know why Old Man Baxter stopped calling me up into his yard and onto his porch as I walked by his front gate. I never got another sandwich, and the lemonade juice must have dried up, because I didn't get no more of that sweet water, either.

Everything around me just kinda fell down after my stomach started getting big. Mama told me that, "You evil and I don't want you in my house no more. You done brought evil into my home. You more messed up than your daddy. No wonder he didn't hang around after you started growing inside me. He knew you was gonna be no good. I ain't claiming you no more. Don't you go telling nobody you's my child." Then she spit in my face, as if by doing so she could wash the evil off of me.

That was the only thing my mother ever gave me. I took that spit and rubbed it all over my face. I licked it and let it slide down the cracks of my mouth. If she wasn't so mad at me, so balled up and tight, I would have ran into her arms and hugged her like never before. Oh, my mother was a beautiful, special woman. Ain't another woman in all the world just like her. It makes me sad to think I ain't seen her since that day. She gave me all she had; then she turned on her heels and left. Didn't say good-bye. Just threw some few things in a big brown paper bag, the kind they give you when you give them money at the store, and walked out the door.

"But, Lady, where you going?," I cried, running after her. She never would let me call her "Mama" or nothing like that, so when I say it, it's just between you and me.

My mother was gone out of there like a jet on a long, lonely runway. And I was all alone. Rose let me stay with her until after my stomach opened up like a ripe melon. Out came a boy and a girl. I never knew I could do something like that. Make babies all by myself. I felt so special, it took the hurting from pushing them babies out away. I held and rocked them babies and kissed them and talked to them and loved them real good. I told them to call me "Mama, Mama, Mama, Mama, Mama," all they wanted. They just cooed and laid their heads down on my chest, which was starting to look like them two big things Miss Fletcher had at the front of her dress.

I didn't have long to rest, sleep, or nothing. Rose put me out as soon as my babies was a week old. Told me to "get out and take all that trouble with you. You always was a troubling child. I knowed you was gonna be trouble even before you was born. Told Mattie not to keep you. Tried to talk her into going to Doctor Shug down by the creek, but she wouldn't hear me. Betchu she would now, though." She tossed her hand in the air. "Look at you. Big all over and got two kids already. You ain't even grown yourself. Go on. Go on, now."

I went out of her house and out of her yard like a cat nobody wanted no more. But I had my babies. We slept some of everywhere for the first months they was born. Then I found this house nobody was living in. Just climbed right on through the window and made myself a home. It was big in that house. Big and wide and open. Everything was shiny and brown or shiny and almost clear-looking. It was food in the house almost like being in a grocery store. The food just never did end. My babies got warmed up and we slept under good-good covers that was thick and soft and just fell down right on your skin.

Moving pictures started coming to me at night then. Just out of the blue. I saw my kids walking, and holding my hand and smiling at me. I saw myself sewing and selling my own clothes so I could feed my babies after the food finally did end in the big kitchen. I saw people smiling at me and telling me I was special that I had been special ever since I was a child.

I saw this man. He didn't have no name. He was tall and dark like night, just like me. He laughed so loud, he could drown out the sound of a mad thunder. He had hands like forever. They was soft and strong both at the same time and they had my whole life in them. That man's hands knew about my mother. They knew who my father was. They knew about Old Man Baxter and Rose and Miss Fletcher and all the kids in the old neighborhood who never would play with me no matter how much I asked. They knew about my babies. They knew about my hurts and about all the times I was scared. Oh, them hands . . .

That man had eyes that could see way out. Eyes that didn't need no big, thick glasses to know what was coming way up from out of the future. Eyes that could see things and make them hands get ready even before it happened. He was like magic. He just knew when to do things to make things come or go. Just make things happen. I dreamed about the magic man every night.

One day I was sitting on the porch watching my babies crawl around on the porch floor when I heard this noise coming from way out back. I got up off the porch and stood on my toes, but I didn't see nothing. When I sat back down the noise started up again. Soon I got up off that porch. Took my babies with me and went out into the yard. I followed that noise until I got to what was making it.

They was beautiful. Two big, shiny animals with hair all over they necks. They feet was like hard shoes that never came off. They tails was made all of hair, stringy and easy to run your fingers clean through. They looked down at me and my babies and just made all kinds of noise. We touched them and put our faces up against theirs. It was the softest thing. We laughed and smiled and liked each other real good.

Every day me and my babies went out to the backyard. We talked to them animals and made them our friends. Then one day while we was out back, a car come making dust all the way up the little stretch of road at the side of me and my babies' house. People in the neighborhood, women with the prettiest clothes and little white balls running on string going clean around their neck, and tall men in pants and shiny, short coats with the prettiest rope coming around their neck, just stared at me and my babies each time they saw us going in and out of that house. I know they knew we was special.

Out of that car came a black man the color of tar. He stopped all that dirt from flying, got out of that car, and looked right at me and my babies. When he looked at his hands, he went to shaking. Stopped looking at me and my babies. I knew he knew we was special.

Then he talked. His voice was loud and rocky, mad like a bad storm. "What are you doing here? Who are you? Who told you that you could come here? How did you get in? Where are the horses? What did you do to the horses? Where are your parents? Are you a runaway?"

The questions came so fast I couldn't catch them. I didn't want to say "Hunh?" or "Come again?" so I just kept quiet.

Then he turned and looked at the house next to me and my babies' house. "Where is Mr. Stewart? He was taking care of my horses while I was away on a business trip. I'll find out from him why you are here." His eyes went almost closed, like lines that could see. "You shouldn't be here."

He stomped his way to the house next to me and my babies' house just like he said he would. Banged on that front door until it opened. The man on the other side looked like he was about my age except his skin didn't have no color.

"I paid you decent money to watch after my house and my horses while I was away." He turned and pushed his hand out toward me and my babies. "How did they get here?"

The man's mouth went open. "I thought you knew this woman. She's been here since two days after you left."

"She's been here this entire time?"

The man on the other side of the door shook his head up and down. "Yes, she has. I thought she was your sister or a cousin or something."

The man from the car turned and went down the walk.

"I did feed your horses, though," the man called out from his porch. "I fed them early every morning."

"Thank you," the man said. Then he walked me and my babies back to our house. "You cannot remain here," he said, looking at me real hard. "I hate to put your children into the street, but you simply cannot stay here."

"But this is me and my babies' house," I said.

His eyes went almost closed again. He shook his head real fast. "You're mistaken. You're confused."

"I know you know," I said while he grabbed me hard by my arm and dragged me to the phone.

"Call your mother and tell her to come get you. She's bound to be worried sick about you and her grandchildren by now."

"No, she ain't. She don't care. She left before I did."

His eyes went big. Then he put his head into his hands. "You cannot stay here." When he looked up, he said, "I have to find a shelter for you."

And he did. For one, two, three, four months . . . years. It was a lot of other mothers and their babies there. No men was allowed; at least I never did see none come by. We was the special women in the world, women who made babies all by ourselves. We held and rocked our babies together. We laughed and cried together. We ate together and slept in one big room together. We was each other's friend.

"Sister-Girl," one of the mothers called me.

I turned and looked at Bettye. Then I smiled. She always was nice to me.

"Come here."

I followed her pointed, moving finger over by the window.

She pulled out a big book. "Know them dreams you always telling me about?"

"Yeah."

"They can come true if you keep seeing them, see?" She went from page to page to page. Finally, she stopped. She was at page 1706 in that big book, where it said, *The righteous will live by faith.* She looked up at me. "Mattie showed me this book two weeks ago. She told me to start dreaming and seeing things." She smiled at me. "Guess what?"

"What?"

"I'm leaving here today. I met a man downtown months ago who said he loved me. He wants me and Little John to come live with him."

"That quick?"

"He loves me, Sister-Girl. I can see it in his eyes."

I was scared for her.

"You have to see it first," she told me before she closed the big book.

"But so fast."

"I believed it that hard."

"You mean anything you see, you can have—is yours?"

She looked at me, shook her head up and down, and said, "Yes. Just like that."

I went to dreaming so hard at night, I almost started calling out to strange men on the street, saying, "Hey, Mister. If you a nice man, I'll go home with you." But my dreaming must not have been hard enough, because nobody ever did love me back.

"Sister-Girl."

"What 'chu doing here, Mattie?"

"I came back to see how you were doing." We hugged and smiled and laughed at each other. Then she said, "I got a job for you if you feel like working."

I almost jumped. "I'll take it."

She took me to her house and gave me food and lemonade. I looked at it and told her, "I'm not thirsty for nothing except water." My babies played on the floor down around by my feet.

"My husband has an opening for a seamstress at his job. When he said it last night, I thought about you. I went over to the shelter first thing this morning looking for you, but they told me you had gone downtown, so I waited for you. I'm glad I did. It's good to see you and your babies again, Sister-Girl. I think you're really going to love this job."

I left the shelter the next day before the sun came up in the sky. It was so early, my eyes hurt from still being tired. I kept rubbing my eyes and picking crust out of the edges. Even though I left my babies with Wilma, a mother who had two babies like I did, a hard feeling went through me like a cold-cold knife when I walked out the door. I had never left my babies, not for a day, not even for an hour. I felt naked while I walked down the street to the bus stop, naked without my babies.

The first day was hard, but it got easier. My babies were three years old when I left the shelter for good. I had saved enough money to rent my own apartment. All the mothers waved and clapped and hugged us when we left. We climbed on the next bus and went to the place we called home for the next two years.

One day Mattie came out to the job and asked, "You still dreaming?"

I wiped sweat from my face and told her, "No."

"I can tell."

"How?"

"You look tired. Promise me," she said, resting her hand against my shoulder, "Promise me that you'll start dreaming again tonight. Dream at night. Dream while you're sitting here sewing. See what you want until it's real. It'll come to you if you see it first."

I never saw Mattie again after that. Her husband sold his business and moved Mattie and their children to Atlanta. Mattie writes me a lot. She said they have a bigger house than they had in Knoxville and that her husband's business is doing better than ever before.

I'm happy for Mattie, but I want something of my own. I dream so hard at night, I wake up with headaches. Got me another sewing job in a building that's so hot I always feel like there's a fire going just a few inches away from my back. I sweat so hard in that building, regardless of what I eat I stay skinny.

"Mrs. Brown," my supervisor called to me one day a month into the job. (Don't ask me why, but when I took the job I told everybody my name was Mrs. Brown.)

I followed my supervisor into his office.

"There's a man coming by the store today. We sold him a few pieces last week. They made such an impression on him, he wanted to know who the seamstress was."

"The winter coat and the pants?"

"Yes." He narrowed his gaze and stared at me. "You didn't follow our pattern to specification. This could cost you your job. Do you understand?"

The door opened.

My supervisor stood from his desk. "I've been expecting you, Leonard. Please have a seat." He looked at me and said with his eyes, "We don't need you anymore. You can leave."

I did.

I could hear the man talking loud on the other side of the door. He was in the clothing business and had ordered the coat and pants for a special client. "I want to meet whoever sewed the coat and pants. Obviously, they did not stick to a pattern. Never before have I seen a coat or a pair of pants like these. Is the seamstress out on the floor? If so, I'd like to meet her now."

I hurried out to the floor. I nearly sprinted from that door to the sewing floor. After that man met me, he said he wasn't leaving the building without me by his side. He took me out to lunch and told me he wanted me to be his head designer.

That night I went home and dreamed so hard, I didn't get more than two hours of sleep. Me and the man had a lot of meetings, several times a week. Production, design ideas, fashion shows—we talked about so much when we met. I made and invested so much money, I telephoned a real estate agent and started looking for my own house. When I told Leonard about it, he said to be careful because taxes were high. Then before I went home for the day, he called me into his plush office and asked if he could fix dinner for me at his house that night. I laughed into my hand. Then I thought about it and told him, "Yes, but I have to bring my children. Even though they're nearly teenagers, I'm not leaving them home by themselves, and I feel guilty about hiring a sitter as much as I do already so I can work late nights here creating more designs."

He smiled and said, "Okay."

It was dark outside when we pulled up to Leonard's house. As soon as Leonard opened the door and ushered us inside, the color on the walls, the cathedral ceilings, the winding staircase, and the fireplace made me feel like I was home. I was quiet most of the night. It was long past dinner when Leonard looked at me and asked, "Something wrong? You don't seem like yourself."

"I've been here before."

"Really?"

"I'm certain. How long have you lived here?"

"Almost four years now."

"Really?"

"Really. Why?"

I sat back on the sofa. "Oh, nothing."

After a few moments I asked, "Who did you bu—"

"I bought it from my brother four years ago, when he packed up his family and moved to Atlanta to start a clothing store there. This house has been in our family for three generations. No way was I going to let anyone else buy it."

"I'd love to live in a house like this."

"It's funny that you should say that. I've been meaning to talk with you about buying a house." He swallowed hard and played with his hands. "Carmen, I'd really like to get to know you better."

I took in a deep breath. "How did you know my name was Carmen?"

He chuckled. "I asked around about you. You seemed so secretive and kept to yourself so much, almost like you had something to hide. So I asked around about you. People pointed me to East Knoxville and a Mrs. Fletcher, a Rose, and a man named Baxter. He wasn't there—Mr. Baxter—he died of a stroke a year ago. Rose and Mrs. Fletcher told me about your mother, Mattie, and that your name was Carmen, not Mrs. Brown." He chuckled; then he sat up straight. "Carmen. . . ." He took my hand inside his. "There's something very special about you. You're different in a real good kind of way."

"Can I go out back?"

He looked at me quizzically, then said, "Sure."

I walked slowly. The closer we got to the barn, the louder the sound became. I saw their shiny eyes before I saw them. I stared at the horses for a long time, and then I wept.

That Nigga's Crazy!

The Urban Griot (Omar Tyree)

"To know wisdom and instruction; to perceive the words of understanding." —Proverbs 1:2

Ants

Antonio looked down and studied the massive business of tiny ants as they combined forces to build a miniature mountain of light-brown sand between the cracks of the sidewalk. He nodded and said, "It's gonna rain today."

His boyhood friends, Chuck and William, looked at him and frowned. Chuck said, "Man, there's not a cloud in the sky. What are you talkin' about?"

William looked up and searched the wide, blue skyline hovering above the earth but couldn't find any clouds, either. He seconded Chuck's response. "Yeah, man, it ain't gon' rain. Tony don't know what he talkin' about. He must think he a Indian."

And they laughed. But Antonio wasn't bothered by it. He knew what he knew.

As the three friends continued to play on the sidewalk with their plastic green army men and toy tanks, they forgot all about the lack of clouds in the clear blue sky. But it eventually grew dark with gray clouds that snuffed out the bright blue. The rain started with one drop, and then a few more before it began to pour. The boys grabbed their toys and scattered for cover on Chuck's patio.

Chuck looked around, bewildered.

He said, "That rain came out of nowhere."

William said, "I know, man."

And Antonio smiled at them and held his tongue.

Chuck grinned back and said, "I know what you thinking already, Tony. You told us."

"But how did you *know* that, though?" William asked him.

Antonio said, "I just watched the ants, man."

Chuck said, "Ants? What do *ants* have to do with the rain?"

Antonio said, "Every time they get together and build those little mountains like they do, it just rains."

Chuck and William laughed again.

Chuck said, "So, you're telling us that the ants know when it's gonna rain?"

Antonio answered, "They must do. And that's why they all organize like that. I guess they use that mountain thing to collect the rain or something."

Chuck looked at William, and they began to laugh harder.

Chuck said, "Aw, man, that's crazy. Ants don't know nothin' about no *rain*. They ain't nothin' but insects."

Antonio just shrugged his shoulders and said, "Aw'ight," because he *knew* what he knew.

Steady Ballin'

By the time the three friends had matured into teenagers, they were spending most of their days at the neighborhood playground, playing basketball.

William, who was the tallest by then, continued to shoot the round, orange ball on a straight line, and would hit the rim of the hoop nearly every time.

Antonio said, "Man, you need to arc the ball more when you shoot it."

Chuck nodded. "Yeah, you do, man. Just because you're taller than us don't mean the ball is gonna go in like that."

William began to shoot the ball higher, so it could fall through the net without banging on the rim.

"You see how that feels?" Antonio asked.

William nodded and smiled. "Yeah."

When they teamed up with the other boys at the playground, the three friends found that they were not as good as some of the other ball players.

When they were all played out for the day and headed back home, Antonio said, "We all need to practice some more, man."

Chuck asked, "For what?"

"So we can be as good as some of those guys," Antonio answered. William said, "Yeah."

But Chuck didn't believe that practicing would make much of a difference. He argued, "*They* ain't out there practicin'. I mean, some people can just ball better than others, that's all."

Antonio and William met up at the playground the next morning to practice anyway. Antonio decided they should do jumping and cutting drills to make themselves quicker on the court and more explosive when they jumped for the ball.

"Where'd you get these practicing ideas?" William asked.

Antonio told him, "I was watching this college special on ESPN." "Do you think it'll work for us?"

Antonio smiled and said, "I guess we'll see when we play."

When they played later that day with the other boys, the practicing didn't seem to make much of a difference. Chuck found that realization comical.

He laughed, "I told y'all practicin' ain't gon' work. You either got it or you don't. We're just average players. That's all there is to it."

Nevertheless, Antonio and William continued to practice each morning before the afternoon pick-up games, and over time they began to see a difference in their level of play.

Antonio told William forcefully during a game, "You can jump higher than that boy, man. Out-jump him next time, William."

Chuck laughed and said, "No, he can't. William ain't got no hops like that." Antonio passed William the ball anyway.

"Jump over him, William! Jump over him!" he yelled as his pass hit William's hands. But William hesitated. He failed to jump as high as he could, and the defender smacked the ball away.

Chuck burst out laughing again. He said, "How many times I gotta tell y'all, man? We just average players out here."

Still, Antonio ignored him and continued to pass William the basketball until the rest of his teammates became angry.

"Hey, man, what are you doin'? We in this game, too! Don't keep passing him the ball." Antonio ignored them all until William began to outplay his defender.

"Aw'ight, now dunk it next time, William. Dunk it!" Antonio coached his friend. *Everyone* laughed at that.

Chuck said, "You crazy. William can't dunk, man."

Antonio said, "Yes you can, William. You jump high enough. So just *dunk it* next time."

Antonio even switched off of his man on defense to set William up for another pass.

"Yo, let me guard him with the ball. I'm quicker than him," Antonio told his teammates.

Chuck grinned and said, "Aw'ight. Watch that boy break your ankles."

But as the more skilled player approached Antonio with the basketball, Antonio realized the boy liked to take off to his right after a slight hesitation move to his left. So Antonio waited for him to show his move before he countered it and stole the basketball.

"GO, WILLIAM!" he yelled as he dribbled the ball rapidly up the court.

William took off in front of him and caught Antonio's pass in perfect stride before he exploded from the ground like a powerful deer and jammed the basketball through the hoop.

The guys began to holler. "OOOHHH! WILLIAM GOT HOPS! HOPPIN' WILLIE! HOPPIN' WIL-LAAAAY!"

William had earned new respect at the playground.

Chuck said, "I didn't know you could jump like that, man."

William smiled and said, "I ain't know, either."

But Antonio knew.

He said, "You're the best player out here, man. You just have to believe in yourself more. I mean, I've been watching how you move to the basket sometimes, and your steps are all right on, man, but you gotta believe that you're gonna *score*. Every time. That's why I kept giving you the ball like that. You're better than everybody at the playground."

Chuck frowned at Antonio's ego-boosting.

He said, "Man, you just pumpin' his head up now. He ain't all *that* just 'cause he got one dunk."

Antonio said, "Aw'ight, watch him. And I'm just gonna keep giving him the ball. Sometimes it's better to start from behind. Because you have to work harder for it, and then you *keep* working hard at everything you do."

William agreed. "Yeah, man, you play that point guard pretty good. You always put the ball right on the money when you pass it."

"Yeah, because everybody else wants to show off with the ball,"

Antonio responded, "They sit there and take the ball through their legs and around their backs before they finally decide to pass it to you, and by that time the defense is ready. So I just pass the ball as soon as somebody is open."

Chuck asked, "Y'all thinking about going out for the summer league? They start tryouts next week."

Antonio smiled and answered, "Yeah, we know. We're going out."

By the time the tryouts for the summer basketball league approached them, William and Antonio were such a tandem that they became immediate stars on the team and took their momentum straight into the high school level.

Computer Games

As their senior year of high school approached, William and Antonio had some serious decisions to make about what colleges they would accept scholarships from. They had become a standout tandem in high school basketball at the small forward and point guard positions. Meanwhile, Chuck became a popular DJ and party thrower. He was as popular with his parties as they were with basketball.

Chuck smiled and said, "I'm proud of y'all, man. Y'all both 'bout to go to Division-One colleges for ball, and I gotta figure out where *I* wanna go now."

But Antonio was hesitant about jumping on the Division 1 bandwagon too soon. He said, "Actually, I'm thinking about taking a scholarship to a small school that has, like, a good computer science program."

William looked at him and asked, "For what?"

Chuck said, "Yeah. Why would you do that?"

Antonio leveled with them.

He said, "Man, I'm all right in basketball, but I'm not *special* in it. I mean, William is a star, and he's been making me look good all these years. But I can't fool myself into believing that I can take it to the next level like he can."

William protested, "Aw, man, what was all that you were telling me about *believing* in yourself? You got *me* to believe. Now I'm the man. And you're gonna sit here and tell me that you don't believe in yourself. I couldn't have gotten this far without you, man."

Chuck nodded his head and said, "Dig it. You knew back in the day that William was good." Then he added with a laugh, "That's why they started callin' him 'Hoppin Willie.'"

Antonio grinned and said, "Yeah, but I never said that *I* was that good. I just knew when to pass the ball."

Chuck said, "But that's what all good point guards are supposed to do."

"I know," Antonio responded. "So I'm passing the ball on this, and deciding to take this opportunity to do something else with my life."

William frowned at him and said, "Like what?"

Antonio paused. He knew that his friends would laugh at him again. But they had always laughed at his far-reaching ideas. So he went ahead and told them.

He said, "I've been thinking about . . . designing computer games."

Chuck looked at William and broke out laughing as usual.

Chuck said, "Computer games? Nigga, is you *crazy*? I mean, you gon' give up a scholarship to play Division One basketball to fuck around wit' some computer game shit?"

Antonio said, "I'm saying, man, a lot of people are into computer games. You got updated sports games coming out every year with Sega Genesis. Every time they get new football and basketball players in the leagues, they have to update the system."

"So what?" William snapped. "That don't mean they gon' let *you* in it."

Antonio said, "It's all about new ideas, man. I've always had ideas. I'm just trying to use 'em." He looked at William and said, "Besides, man, I don't like playing basketball every day like that. I just kept doing it for you. But it's time for you to do it on your own now, man. That's the only way you gon' make it to the pros. You *got* the talent, but you gotta have the *drive*. And there's nothing I can do to help you with that at this point." He smiled and continued, "Like Chuck used to say, 'you either got it or you don't.'"

Chuck grinned and said, "Yeah, and I was wrong, too. You proved me wrong."

Antonio said, "No, I didn't. You were right. I just knew that William had it in him to play basketball. Like I said back then, I watched his movements. And he already had the height to play, he just needed the confidence and practice drills."

He looked at Chuck and said, "Just like you have the ear for music in you. I mean, you have *all* the parties rockin'. You just know what people like in music. So if I was you, I wouldn't waste time going to a regular four-year college. I'd take, like, a few classes in general studies at a community college or something, you know, just to stay sharp on general information and whatnot, and then I'd enroll in some kind of music production school. I mean, they have trade schools, man, to teach you to do just that. Engineer good music."

Chuck smirked and said, "Oh, so y'all get to go to regular college, and I end up in some community college and trade school. Get the fuck outta here," he snapped. He felt slighted.

Antonio said, "You have to find your gift in life and do it, man. That's the only thing that will make us *happy* in this world. Going to college won't make you happy if that's not what you need to do. So if I can go to a computer school without going to a four-year college to get what I need, I'll do it."

Chuck looked at William and decided to challenge Antonio on that.

He said, "Aw'ight. You let me see you do that, then. Turn down your scholarship to play basketball for some damn computer school, and I'll do the same and go to a music school."

Antonio thought about it and nodded.

He said, "Aw'ight. I'll show you, then."

But when Chuck and William were alone together, William doubted their friend.

He said, "That nigga's crazy! Tony better *not* turn down no scholarship for some computer game."

Chuck laughed hard and agreed. "I know, man. That nigga always got some weird ideas."

After graduating from high school, Antonio enrolled in a computer technology program to learn all that he could about creating hi-tech games for the millions of young people who were enthusiastic about computers and action games all around the world. He also took courses in the fields of humanities at a local community college to develop a fuller understanding of human nature.

But Chuck ignored his promise to follow suit, when he enrolled in a four-year college to study business instead of enrolling in a music production school. And William accepted a Division One basketball scholarship, as was expected.

And in five years, Antonio was well on his way to becoming a multimillionaire in the field of computer games, where there were no limitations on his creativity. William had signed a four-year rookie contract as the number one draft pick of a new franchise basketball team, and Chuck had spent *five* years receiving mediocre grades in a *four-year* college, while he continued to throw the most talked-about parties on campus.

It pained Chuck to say it, but it was better late than never. So he told Antonio, "You were right again, man. I wasted all these years fuckin' around with that college shit, knowing damn well that I should have been somewhere learning how to make my own music."

Antonio smiled at him and said, "Don't even worry about it, man. I mean, you still got it. I'll give you a loan to get you started with the music school."

Chuck studied his friend's face to see if he was only pulling his leg. He asked, "You would do that for me for real, man?"

Antonio told him, "Yeah," with no hesitation. He said, "Because I know it'll be a good investment."

And that's what he did. He invested in Chuck's gifted ear for music.

Love and Marriage

William easily had the most women chasing after him, with his high visibility and known income as a professional basketball player. And Chuck was second because of the community's love for parties and swinging music. But outside of computer game geeks and the executives who ran the billion-dollar game companies, few people realized that Antonio had a higher income than both of his friends combined. However, Antonio liked it that way. He said, "That gives me a chance to choose a woman who's really into *me*."

William didn't have that opportunity, and he was constantly asking Chuck and Antonio what they thought of his dates when he brought them around for meets and greets, until he had finally found "the one."

Chuck said, "She looks *good*, man. I'd make her my one, too. You wanna trade her for three of mine?" he joked.

But as William and Chuck shared a laugh, Antonio was hesitant.

"So what do you think about her, Tony?" William asked him.

Antonio answered, "Well, anyone with eyes can see that she looks good, man, but . . ."

"But what?" William pressed him.

Antonio shook his head and said, "She just seems too . . . *snappy* to me. She's not at peace with herself. And I don't think that's a good thing, especially with the profession that you're in. I mean, she's gonna have a whole lot to snap at when you're out on the road during the season every year."

Chuck started laughing because he knew it was true.

Antonio continued. He said, "Any woman who marries you or any one of us is going to have to have a lot of patience and tolerance, because we're not men who are going to be home and available all the time. It's not like we have straight nine-to-five jobs. And we damn sure don't have nine-to-five *incomes*. So you might just have to look a little longer for that "one," William. Because I'm not feeling good vibes from her."

William took in Antonio's comments and nodded. Then he said, "Well, you know what? You don't have to feel her, Tony. *I* do. And this is *my* decision. So are you gonna be in my wedding or what, man?"

Antonio said, "Of course I'll be in your wedding. But I just want you to know that you're probably making a mistake here, that's all."

William responded, "Yeah, well, everybody makes some mistakes in life."

Antonio shrugged his shoulders and said, "Aw'ight."

When Antonio was alone with Chuck, Chuck admitted, "I don't think she's right for Will either, man. She don't even sound like she *likes* basketball. I can't imagine settling down with a girl who don't like music."

Antonio smiled and said, "There's not that many women out there who don't like some form of music, man. So you're probably gonna have to use a different criterion from that."

Chuck asked, "Well, what kind of woman are *you* looking for, Tony?"

Antonio answered, "Well, that's easy for me. All I have to do is talk about my many ideas, and the women who can't hang usually don't have much to say. So I'll just marry the woman who can hold the longest conversation with me."

Chuck looked at Antonio and broke out laughing like he had always done. He said, "Man, you just . . . you just a crazy motherfucka, man. But I'm used to that by now."

And five years later, Antonio was happily married, with kids, to a woman who was as idealistic as he was. Chuck was happily married, with kids, to a woman who had a sharp eye for business. And William was miserably *divorced*, and paying astronomical child support fees to an ex-wife who seemed illogical.

William complained, "What the hell is *wrong* with this woman, man? I mean, nothing I ever did seemed to satisfy her. She just seems . . . *insatiable*, man. And *selfish*! Everything's all about *her*. She's not even thinking about the kids in none of this shit. And she never cares how ridiculous we look with our business always being printed up in the newspapers."

And Antonio didn't say a word. He had said his piece years ago.

Family Fortunes

While on the last leg of his basketball career, and at age thirty-seven, with his third wife, who was pregnant with his seventh child, William called to ask Antonio what he should invest his money in to buffer his wealth for retirement.

Antonio answered, "Gold."

William shook his head and grinned over the telephone.

He said, "Man, Chuck told me you told him that shit. And I didn't believe him. But here you are telling me that same *shit*."

Antonio explained, "The value of gold has always outlasted everything. And if the economy crashes, it's gonna start back over with what? Not *paper*, I can assure you of that."

William said, "So you're telling me that with all of the money you've made by now, that you have it all riding on nothing but gold?"

"No, I didn't say that," Antonio answered him. "But like you just said, I've made a lot more money, and I kept more money, so I can afford to lose some in other investments. But I've bought a hell of a lot of gold, too, to make sure that I'm protected in case any atrocities happen with the economy as we approach the new millennium."

William called Chuck as soon as he hung up the phone with Antonio.

"Hey, man, I just talked to Tony about that investing in gold shit that you told me about, and he seems to be taking it for real," William commented.

Chuck said, "Oh, yeah."

William said, "I thought you were joking when you told me that shit, man."

Chuck said, "Naw, man, you know how Antonio is. He's always been on some off-the-wall shit."

"So did *you* invest in any gold?" William asked him.

Chuck answered, "Well . . . yeah. I mean, Antonio always been right before. So I figure it's time for my ass to finally start *listening* to him."

William snapped, "Well, how come you didn't tell me that shit in the first place, man? You try'na hold out on me?"

Chuck said, "Naw, man, but you know, I didn't know if you wanted to get involved in it or not; that's all. So I just brought it up to you in a jokin' manner."

William said, "Damn right I wanna get involved in it, man. What do you think I was asking for? These greedy-ass women been eatin' up my cake for *years*. So hook me up with this gold shit. I'm ready to retire in another year."

Chuck said, "Aw'ight, let me go get the phone numbers."

And William invested a chunk of his money in gold as well, before his retirement from basketball in 1999.

On September 11, 2001, two hijacked airplanes crashed into the twin towers of the World Trade Center in the financial district of New York, and an already weakening American economy came crashing down with the buildings.

"SHIT! Did y'all see that shit on the news, today?" William asked Chuck and Antonio. They were on a three-way phone conversation.

Chuck said, "Every motherfucka alive is watching this, man."

William asked, "So what do we do now, Tony?"

Antonio said, "We just sit back, let Bush take us to war, and when the dust all settles, we ask our price for the gold. Then we wait for the economy to get back on track, and we all buy our gold *back* again."

William said, "Well, got'damn, Tony! You're a motherfuckin' *genius*, man! You're a crazy-ass *genius*!"

Chuck laughed out loud over the phone, just like old times.

And Antonio just smiled, because he knew what he knew.

Fate

The three friends ended up as highly wealthy men who had plenty of gray hair and baldness between them by the time their grand-children began to arrive. They took a cruise on Antonio's yacht down the Atlantic coastline from Boston to Florida, while reminiscing on their many years of friendship.

Chuck shook his head and asked, "Now, Tony . . . for once and for all, man, how did you ever know all the things you knew before we ever did?"

Antonio laughed while lying back in his sun chair on the large deck of his yacht.

He answered, "I just paid attention to what the world was telling me; that's all. I've never been a *rocket* scientist," he joked.

William said, "Yeah, but you *could* have been. You was just a born genius, Tony; that's how I read it. I was a genius in basketball for a few years. Chuck was a genius in music production. And you, Tony . . . you was just a damn genius, *period*! And you still are."

Chuck laughed and couldn't deny it anymore. He nodded and said, "Yeah, William is right, man. And it's about time we had a genius of our own instead talking about them goddamned *white boys* all the time. I'm just happy that you grew up around us."

But then Antonio went and dropped a nuclear bomb on his long-time friends as he sat with a cigarette in his hand.

He said, "Well, I just wanted to make sure that we all got together for this last great cruise before I finally tap out on you guys."

Chuck and William both looked at Antonio with steady eyes.

"What are you talking about, Tony?" Chuck asked him first.

"Yeah, man, what are you talking about?" William seconded him.

Antonio looked into the beauty of the Atlantic Ocean and said, "These damn cigarettes I've been smoking are finally putting an end to me."

William said, "Well, stop smoking the damn things, then. I've been telling you guys that for *years*."

Chuck said, "Aw, nigga, that's easy for you to say. You ain't never smoked no cigarettes."

"And I'm glad I didn't," William responded tartly.

Chuck said, "Yeah, but you smoked through some got'damned *women*, I'll tell you that."

And Antonio had a laugh while William shook his head, embarrassed at the truth. He was on his fourth wife by then.

Chuck looked over at Antonio and said, "Man, you aw'ight. I ain't been diagnosed with nothin', and you started smoking *long* after me."

Antonio said, "Yeah, but my system is weaker than yours. Everybody don't have the same tolerance in their body. With all that late-night partying you've done in the music business, you've built up a whole lot of tolerance in your body for stress. And with William being a professional athlete, he's just in great shape altogether. But *my* clock is about run out on this world. I've done about all that I can do."

Chuck and William refused to believe that. They didn't *want* to believe it.

William said, "Cut that shit out, man. You ain't leaving us no time soon. At least let Chuck die on us first."

Antonio laughed again, while Chuck frowned at William.

He said, "You gon' be the one who goes *first*. And they're gonna find you tangled up with one of the young *women* of yours, while she's screaming to get your *dead ass* off of her."

Antonio continued to laugh and said, "I love you guys, man. I just want y'all to know that."

And when he passed away from lung cancer a few weeks after the completion of their Atlantic Coast cruise, Antonio left instructions to have his body frozen in ice with a smile on his face, while wearing only a pair of Hawaiian swim trunks.

When his friends and family members all showed up to view his body frozen inside a block of ice at the funeral, to be locked away inside a temperature-controlled mausoleum, everyone found it difficult to mourn for him properly.

Chuck looked over at William as they viewed the ridiculous frozen smile on Antonio's face and wearing a pair of oversized Hawaiian swim trunks, and he couldn't help himself. He smiled and told William, "That nigga's crazy!"

But William *knew* better by then.

William said, "I read in that *Scientific* magazine that Tony started reading, that medical doctors are working on different serums to see if they can bring humans back to life after death."

Then he looked back at Chuck and smiled.

He said, "So Tony's about to fool us again. But this time I'm hip to him. So I'm gon' call my lawyer up tomorrow morning to have *me* done up the same way when I die."

Chuck laughed out loud.

And when he calmed down, he admitted to William, "I was thinking the *same* damn thing. But I'm not even gon' wait until tomorrow. I'm calling my lawyer *today*. That nigga Tony was crazy like a fox."

William paused for a long minute and thought about it before commenting. Then he told his friend Chuck, "That's because Antonio wasn't no *nigga*. So I ain't gon' be one no more, either."

Chuck looked at him with seriousness and seconded William's conclusion.

He said, "Amen to that, brother. *Ay-men*."

And that's all they needed to say, because they *knew* what they
knew.

Playin' the Role

Franklin White

"Wood may remain ten years in the water, but it will never become a crocodile." —African, Bambera

Hollywood

Glamorous Aja Ives lounged inside her trailer—every inch the star in her white linen robe, on a white leather Natuzi couch—looking as if she were modeling for a photo shoot while on the set of her latest film project. Though cheers for the wrap of the film could be heard outside the trailer on the lot where they'd been shooting for the past three months, she was not in a particularly festive mood. In fact, she was bordering on a serious funk.

Aja sat still as an assistant placed a tray of alcohol swabs in front of her. She never liked to stay in makeup any longer than necessary. As she began the process of stripping down to her striking natural beauty, her best friend and manager, Mack, set a drink in front of her.

"Hey," he said with a look of sudden concern, "you okay?"

She put down the makeup-covered swab, picked up the drink, and nodded.

"If I were you, I'd be ecstatic right about now, with film thirteen in the can," he announced. "Shit, let's drink to that." Raising his glass, Mack took a big gulp of his drink, then stuck his head outside the trailer door to observe the crew, celebrating about fifty meters away.

"Could you shut the door, Mack?" Aja asked in a tight voice.

"Why? It's party time!" he sang. "C'mon, put on some clothes and let's go out and enjoy this!"

"I don't feel like hearing all that noise tonight," she grumbled.

"Maybe that assistant director can cheer you up. He couldn't keep his eyes off you," Mack teased.

"No, I'll pass," Aja said, still removing what seemed like layers of makeup. "I think you want him, anyway."

"Is it that obvious?" Mack laughed. "He's so quiet, though . . . you think he swings that way?"

"Mack, please," Aja sighed, deep in thought. For months, she'd obsessed about where her career was going—and where it was not. In her mind's eye, she rewound and played back her climb to stardom. She'd broken into the movies in 1989 at twenty-three years old, playing a teenage heroine crazed on crack, willing to sell her body for a hit of the pipe. It was a shallow role, but from there she was offered a steady stream of supporting roles. The makers of Black films began to see her marketability, and she became the darling of Black cinema, making no less than three million dollars per film for lead roles. She had it better than most of her competition. She was thirty-six, still playing women in their twenties, and her audiences loved her. So why was she dissatisfied?

"Girl, what's your problem tonight?" Mack asked, exasperated.

"It's this business."

"What about it?" he inquired. "You're doing fine. Better than fine, if you ask me."

"I'm doing all right," Aja said. "Let's leave it at that."

"Aja, you just made three million. Shit, if that's *all right*, that's what I want to be, too."

"I want *in*, though, Mack."

"In where?"

"In the mainstream. I'm tired of doing just Black movies. Don't you think I can hold my own in a cast of white actors?"

"Yes, *I* think you can, but the industry isn't hiring many Black females in mainstream pictures. You know that. They have their 'quota' and the door has slammed shut. As your manager, it's my job to give you these little reality checks. Besides, wouldn't you rather be a big fish in a small, Black pond?"

Aja sipped her drink thoughtfully, then picked up her cell phone, hit a key to speed-dial, and waited for the connection. "Andrew? What's happening with my request? Do we have an answer yet? How long do I have to wait until you get me something in the mainstream, Andrew? It's been nearly eight months.

"What do you *mean*, 'it can't be done'?" Aja's rising voice revealed her anger. "If it can't be done, then I guess you'll have to go. As of this minute you're no longer my agent. Yes, you heard me. You're *fired*, Andrew. That's right. You'll receive official notice by fax in a few minutes."

Aja slammed down the phone and turned toward Mack. "You still think there's no room for me in the mainstream, Mr. Manager? Because I need a new agent, one who believes in me two hundred percent. The job is yours if you want it. But I won't settle for less than total success."

Mack sat down, no longer in the mood to party. He knew the odds and the battles they'd have to fight to get Aja past the Hollywood quota system. But the chance to be manager and agent of a top star was irresistible. "Miss Aja, I'm your man. All we need is a plan. Let's get to work."

They toasted each other with fresh drinks in their plastic glasses and settled in for an all-night strategy session.

Phase One of their plan began when Ike, the king of Black cinema, called to offer Aja a leading role.

"Sorry, Ike, but I'm not feelin' the part," Aja said, putting the call on the speakerphone so Mack could hear both sides of the conversation.

"What do you mean?" Ike asked, irate. "You've been in six of my last ten movies, and each one has made you a bigger star than you were before. I get you the press, the talk shows. Damn, if I recall correctly, you even got three magazine covers!"

"It's just the thought of playing *another* mother trying to keep her teenage son off the streets," Aja sighed. "Can't you write something with more substance or more variety, Ike? You're a creative genius. Can't you write something deep that isn't totally black?"

"Is five million dollars enough substance for you?" he offered.

"Actually, it's not," Aja said casually as Mack broke out in a sweat, as he always did at the mention of more money. "I'm only doing mainstream movies now, Ike. When you write something that appeals to all kinds of people, then I'm there. But until then, I'm sorry. Can't do it."

"Aja," Ike sang, "You're gonna be sorry you missed out on this one. And by the way, in case you haven't heard, they're only giving mainstream parts to two Black chicks, and you ain't one of them. Trust me, I know."

"Thanks, Ike, but no thanks. Best of luck, though." Aja hung up on the director's protests. She knew he'd obtained financing by guaranteeing her in a starring role; her name, image, and talent were enough to take to the bank. She was counting on that to launch her to the next level—true superstardom. And she wouldn't settle for anything less.

"It's time to go to Phase Two, Mack," Aja said, pacing the luxuriously padded carpeting in her penthouse apartment. "Out with the old Aja, in with the new."

First, they hired a new cook, who cut all the sugar and fat from her diet, and a new personal trainer, who tripled her gym time and pushed her till she thought she'd die.

She dropped pounds and inches and sculpted a body that drew open-mouthed stares and double-takes in the land of dazzling physiques. A few discreet visits to a top plastic surgeon guaranteed her lusher, firm breasts for life, and she moved with even more grace and confidence than before.

She traded in her trademark braids for a honey-gold waist-length weave that made Asian women's hair look kinky. And, for the first time, she hired a white makeup artist who gave her a slinkier, more seductive image than before.

Mack glowed with pride. Everything was on schedule to unveil Aja's transformation before the best audience of all: the cameramen and television viewers of the Academy Awards, which were only a week away. The final touch was a visit to a new designer who whipped up old-school glamour gowns worthy of Dorothy Dandridge. The allure of covered flesh hinted at by subtle draping of sensual fabrics would attract attention among the scantily clad actresses who competed to see who could wear the least and show the most without getting arrested.

Accompanied by Mack in a custom-designed tux, Aja worked the red carpet like a true queen diva. She strode slowly, as elegantly as royalty being presented to her court, and the paparazzi went crazy. Blinded by flashbulbs and deafened by the crowd chanting "Aja! Aja! in adoring tones, she and Mack felt as if they'd died and gone to heaven.

Exchanging a look of triumph that their strategy was unfolding as planned, they preened, smiled, and played to the cameras. Aja tossed her honeyed mane every chance she got, and Mack learned to get out of the way when her tresses came flying toward his face.

Mack and Aja celebrated the next morning over champagne mimosas and croissants. They sat surrounded by the dozens of newspaper photos and interviews featuring Aja—who, as a presenter, attracted more attention for her bold makeover than some of the nominees and winners had with their performances, awards, and acceptance speeches.

"Look at this, Mack!" I told you it was gonna work," Aja squealed with delight. "It won't be long before the phone rings with an invitation to the big house!"

Mack tried to hide his concern. He didn't want Aja to get hurt. He knew that beneath her strong, independent image was a soft, compassionate woman who was more sensitive than she let anyone know. He only hoped that her hunger to make this change wouldn't cause her to lose the status she'd achieved with her Black fans. It had happened to many others before her, he thought. It'll take more than her determination. Kissing her cheek good-bye, Mack whipped out his cell phone and began making the endless calls that would hopefully yield the white gold his longtime friend and client was craving.

Less than a week later, Mack waited excitedly for Aja in a quaint sushi joint on Melrose Avenue. He rose to greet her, kissing her bronze cheek and subtly assessing how many eyes were upon her as she slid gracefully into her seat.

"Jacques Schafer wants you to come in and read for a role," he said quickly.

"Oh, Mack, you're amazing! I *know* you could do it. How'd you manage?"

"Trade secret, Cinderella."

"Where'd you see him?"

"Private party," he sighed with a glazed smile. "And what a party it was!"

"And Jacques was there?"

"Yes," Mack answered, defensively.

"I didn't know he was—"

"And you still don't, honey," Mack teased. "You know we boys don't kiss and tell."

"What's the role?"

"The lead in a spec he's very excited about. It's called *Money for Good*, a legal thriller. Scott Nathanson is already attached."

"I've always wanted to work with him. Damn, Mack, this is really good news!"

"Your appointment is at noon Friday."

Aja nodded, sipping her designer water. Studying Mack's face, she noticed lines of tension and deep shadows under his eyes. And his smile seemed tight around the edges. "What's the matter," she asked. "You having problems with *him* again?"

"Stop trying to read me, Aja."

"I told you to leave him alone, Mack." Aja's heart hurt for her friend.

"This has nothing to do with Tommy. He's history, anyway," Mack sniffed delicately.

"Since when?"

"Since last night, if you must know. He couldn't handle some things that went down at the party. But I'm not stressing that boy. I'm more worried about you."

"Well, there's no need to worry, because I'm fine, thank-you-very-much."

"That's what I've been telling everybody, but I don't know, Aja. Seems like you're—"

"Who's 'everybody,' and what have you been telling them about me?"

"The gang. They want to know why you've changed so much."

She tossed her golden mane as if she were deliberately trying to annoy him. "Oh, they do?"

"Yes, they do, and I'm getting tired of telling them it's because you're 'moving in another direction.' It's almost like saying you're too good for them now."

"Well, when I get this part in Jacques's film opposite Scott Nathanson, they'll know why I've been keeping my distance. I can't keep doing the same thing I've been doing for years and expect this town to take me seriously. Success, true success, requires sacrifice. And show business is all about the image, Mack. You of all people know that."

"Everyone knows that, Aja. Just like they know that there's a double standard for 'us,' and Black actors are still expected to be grateful just for working."

"Yeah, like we're supposed to jump up and down for the same old shitty roles," Aja grumbled.

"But they do have a legitimate beef with you, Aja."

"Like what, Mack? What the hell have I done to any of *them*?"

"For instance, the last seven parties you've had in the last five months. Girl, you haven't had seven parties in ten years, and now all you do is invite big-name white actors who make millions of dollars, without even giving a whisper to the crew."

"Negro, hello?" I'm—no, *we're*—going through an image change here, remember? I suppose the 'gang' expects me to invite the same tired Negroes I've been partying with forever so I can get my black ass in a mainstream movie?

"I think not," she said, attracting more stares with her rising voice. "It doesn't happen that way, Mack. Not now, not ever. Big-time producers party with big-name actors, and that's how you get the big-time roles. This isn't a cure for anthrax, Mack. I'm just doing what I have to do to get to the top. You'd think the gang would be happy for me, wouldn't you? But instead they want to play Black folks' crab-in-a-barrel and try to keep me squashed down at the bottom with them."

"Well, what about your new friend, Sharon? You've been hanging with that white girl for months and neglecting your other friends. Nobody knows whether you're trying to get into the mainstream, Aja, or just totally forget your roots."

"Mack, we're friends, okay? To get the big roles, the roles I deserve, I have to learn to speak as white people speak, think as they think, and do as they do. Damn it, it's called playing a part, remember? I'm an actress, and knowledge is power, baby."

"I know where you're coming from, Aja. Just remember, those 'Negroes,' as you call them, have had your back ever since you were playing hooker roles and eating tuna straight out the can every night. Never get so high and mighty that you forget there was many a time they fed your ass, too."

"But they don't anymore, Mack, now do they? I feed you, and I need you to be on my side, two hundred percent. Halfway won't do. It's time to move on, and I don't intend to miss the boat."

Sometimes my people can be so small-minded, Aja fumed. True, her friendship with Sharon DiOrio had rubbed off, but that was the whole point, wasn't it? Sharon was a longtime fan of Aja's and one of the best supporting actresses in the business, with at least a dozen films to her credit. Aja studied Sharon and copied her movements. In the process, a true friendship had evolved.

Sharon was cool, loved R&B and hip-hop, and always wanted to know about the brothers that Aja had worked with. Aja didn't mind. As Aja prepared for her meeting with Jacques, Sharon advised her to be alluring, daring, over the top. "Those are the guidelines for Schafer," Sharon confided. "Trust me, I know."

Jacques Schafer was much younger-looking that Aja expected. She couldn't tell how tall he was, because he didn't stand up when she walked into his office. He was lean and wore a white T-shirt. His full head of brown hair was cut into asymmetrical European style, and he wore a ring that matched his platinum wristwatch.

When he finally stood to refill his coffee cup, Jacques rose a few inches over six feet.

Aja commented on each of his films, even detailing some of the scenes. Jacques asked about her family; when she told him she was an only child, he teased her about never having to work hard for anything in her privileged life. He was moved when she told him she'd lost both parents at a young age.

"I was up all night reviewing your films." Jacques smiled. "You're an excellent actress, Aja, for that type of movie. But I feel you deserve more. You can certainly handle it. The parties you've been giving are a great way to let people know you're a player."

"Thanks, Jacques. I'm ready for new challenges, and your new film would be perfect. I've always wanted to work with you."

"Good." He returned her smile and handed her a script. "Let's read."

Aja fought to maintain her composure, glad for the mock rehearsals Sharon had made her endure. Unlike her roles in black films, where she defined the character for the director and audience, this one required her to mold herself to Jacques's vision. She threw herself into the brief audition.

"I like your interpretation, Aja, very much. You've got the role. It's a great beginning. And if you do as well as I expect you to, you'll be in line for many other opportunities."

"Thank you, Jacques," she said sincerely. "You won't be sorry for giving me this chance."

Torchlight Pictures decided to fast-track the film. Prominent investors came on board late, and shooting was scheduled to begin right away. Aja threw herself into rehearsals, working all day and late into the night.

"Careful," Mack warned. "We don't want you to have to get plastic surgery for those bags under your eyes."

"I just want everything to be perfect," Aja confided.

"It will be; don't stress," Mack reassured her. "This is just the beginning."

"That's what Jacques says." Aja smiled dreamily.

"Really, now?" Mack's eyebrow shot up.

"Um-hmmm. He thinks this is just the tip of the iceberg for me, and I believe him."

"Oh, you didn't know that until he said it?"

"I did. But it just sounds so *good* when Jacques says it."

"Is there somethin' you ain't tellin' me, Aja? 'Cause if there is, I need to know. Not only as your manager and your agent, but as your friend. Spill the damn beans, girl, and spill 'em quick!"

Aja simply smiled mysteriously.

"Give it up, Aja," Mack prodded.

"Jacques wants me to go to Europe with him next week."

"'Scuse me . . . Europe? He wants to *parlez vous* your *Francais?*"

"He asked me three days ago. Wants to go unwind before shooting starts. He says it would be good for me to accompany him to get into my character, since she was born there."

"And you fell for that shit?"

"He's genuine, Mack. You don't know him like I do. We've become very good friends."

"Friends, my ass. He's just tryin' to get you over to the other side of the world so he can fuck your brains out. That is," Mack said, staring deeply into her eyes, "if he hasn't already."

Aja laughed nervously.

"I ain't jokin' and you know it, Aja," Mack fussed. "You know how these motherfuckers are in this business. Shit, you've been tried by niggas who haven't got nearly as much money or power as this asshole. He's lettin' you know up front that he just wants to taste your chocolate goodies."

"That's what Sharon says."

"Shit, at least she's got some sense. 'Cause you're actin' a complete fool."

"She told me to get on that plane and suck his dick all the way across the ocean."

"I guess that's how she gets her roles. But Aja, you haven't made it this far by suckin' and fuckin' your directors, and I know that isn't why you wanted to swim in the mainstream with the big fishes. Or is it?"

"Sharon says I should pussy-whip him quick, fast, and in a hurry."

"Fuck her. I don't like you hanging around her, anyway. Never have. Bitch ain't nothin' but trouble. That's why she can't get a lead role in this town."

"Leave her alone, Mack. I've made up my mind. I'm going with Jacques."

"You're *what*?" he screeched.

"You heard me. If that's the price I have to pay to play in the big leagues, I'm ready."

Despite Mack's mounting protests, Aja packed her bags and left just as she'd said she would. She relaxed on the private jet while Jacques called to assure the film's investors of its certain success.

"Are they getting jittery?" Aja asked, placing a grape in her mouth and following it with a swallow of expensive champagne.

"Yeah, but they'll get over it." Jacques smiled confidently.

"Are *you* getting jittery, Jacques?" she asked, noting the worry lines creasing his brow.

Jacques looked so deeply into her eyes that Aja thought he was about to stick his tongue into her mouth. She took another sip of champagne and smiled. "Is everything okay?"

"You trust me, don't you?" Jacques asked intently.

Aja's mind whirled as she tried to figure out where his question was leading. She'd never opened her legs at thirty-thousand feet above ground, but the champagne buzz was pleasant. Yeah, she was willing, even though Mack had confided that Jacques Schafer was bisexual.

"Yes, I trust you," she said softly. I wouldn't be here with you if I didn't. You're really down-to-earth, and I like that."

"Good, good. Because I want to talk to you about something."

Aja's eyes widened with curiosity as he spoke.

Aja didn't mind the extra attention of the media who were present on the first day of filming. After all, it was exactly what she'd worked so hard for. She'd slept in her trailer on the film lot the night before and awakened in character, ready for her shot at the big time.

Mack was unusually quiet as he watched Sharon stand next to Aja's Swedish makeup artist and remind Aja about some of the things they'd worked on about her character. Then Sharon gave Aja a quick kiss on the cheek and left.

Mack sighed, still getting used to the quickie nose job Aja had had in Europe. He'd already spoken his piece when he first laid eyes on her. He was even more shocked to learn that Aja had been bleaching her naturally bronze skin for several weeks. *She's sellin' her soul to some kind of devil*, he thought. *I just wonder when the bill is gonna come due.*

There was a quick knock on the door, and Jacques strode in. He nodded at Mack and walked over to Aja. "Hey, how are you?" he asked, kissing her on the cheek.

"Fine, thanks for stopping by. Have you seen all the media out there? This is something, Jacques. I don't know how to thank you."

Jacques didn't respond. He looked over at Mack, then intently at Aja.

"What's wrong?" Mack asked, his instincts sensing trouble.

"Aja, there's been a change," Jacques said to the star as if Mack hadn't spoken.

"What kind of change?" Mack asked, moving directly into Jacques's view.

"It's the investors. They don't think this color-blind casting will work out."

"What do you mean?" Aja cried. "I did what they wanted, didn't I?" She touched her still-tender nose.

"Yes, yes you did, Aja, and you're the only one I wanted for the role. But they still think you're 'too black' for the part. No matter what I say, they keep insisting that your features are just too ethnic."

"What the hell is this bullshit?" Mack demanded. She's perfect, Jacques. More than perfect. You know that and so do they. What's really going on?"

"Mack, you know Aja's my first choice, but this time around, I'm not top dog. This is a big-budget film, and these investors have a lot to say.

"Not to worry, though." Jacques turned to reassure Aja. "You'll be paid every dime you signed for. I made sure of that."

"Forget the money!" Aja growled, waving the makeup person out of her face. "I want the role. That role is mine. I worked hard for it, I deserve it and I'm not walking away."

Jacques sighed and looked to Mack for support. Mack gave him a cold stare. "There is nothing I can do, Aja. Believe me, I tried everything."

"Jacques, look at me!"

"You're gorgeous; you're perfect, no question."

"Bullshit! Do you know I looked in the mirror this morning and almost didn't recognize myself? I changed for this role, and damn it, I want it."

Jacques looked squarely at Aja, then Mack, and said, "Sorry. It's not my decision. Out of my hands completely, I'm afraid." He shrugged.

"Who's getting the part?" Mack asked.

"Yeah, who's taking over for me?" Aja demanded angrily.

"Sharon DiOrio. We met with her last night and she's unbelievable. Knew the lines right off . . ."

"Sharon? Of course she knows the lines—I taught them to her!" Aja struggled not to hit someone or something as righteous fury rose within her.

Jacques moved to the trailer door. "I'm sorry, Aja, Mack. I truly am. I wish it had turned out differently. Maybe Hollywood isn't as progressive as it should be. But hang in there."

Mack and Aja stared at one another, dumbfounded.

"This is too fucked up," he fumed. "Just raw."

"Yeah, Mack, it is," Aja said, suddenly calm. "But you know what?"

"What?"

"I'm not going to sweat it. Shit, I should have known better. You tried to tell me and I wouldn't listen. It's like my grandmother told me a long time ago."

"What's that?"

"She told me that 'no matter how long a log sits in a river, it will never turn into a crocodile. A log it was, and a log it will remain.'"

"Meaning?"

"Right now it means, 'a nigga is, a nigga was, and a nigga shall always be.'"

They laughed, and Mack pulled out the phone, praying that Ike hadn't yet cast the female lead for his upcoming black film.

Miss Amy's Last Ride

Christine Young-Robinson

"Death is only sleep's older brother." —Africa, Ivory Coast

In Fairfield County, in Winnsboro, South Carolina, folks sat out on their porches drinking cold iced tea, chatting, and fanning themselves with recycled heat. The children of the community, filled with energy, gathered in an open field to challenge one another in a game of softball, cheered on by barking dogs.

An elegant ranch-style brick house sat quietly apart from the rest of the homes, lonely and devoid of signs of life. In front of the house was a bed of flowers carved in the letter *C*, which stood for the owner's name, Campbell. At the far right side of the house, a few ducks swam in a small man-made lake. Folks who drove through Fairfield County often stopped and admired this picturesque home with its lush carpet of green grass.

Behind the double-paneled bronze doors, down a long corridor with marble floors and rich deep-burgundy walls, was a door that led to the bedroom of the last member of the Campbell family.

It was none other than Miss Amy Campbell, who gasped for breath as she struggled to cough, lying under a lightweight quilt that had been sewn stitch by stitch with her own bare hands. The quilt was made up of pieces of fabric from clothing that had once been worn by her family members who had left this earthly world.

Miss Amy's cough calmed, and she delicately lifted her head to follow the beam of sunlight that sparkled through the drawn curtains and into the bedroom. Her gaze landed on a crystal lantern sitting on top of a carved mahogany eighteenth-century hutch, and mesmerized by the sparkling glass, she didn't notice the figure entering the room.

"Mornin', Miss Amy," Holly, her long-term companion, said with a

German accent. She entered the room with a towel folded across her left shoulder, a wet washcloth in one hand, and a bottle of Listerine in the other.

"Mornin'," Miss Amy mumbled with toothless gums.

Holly, stricken by the sight of Miss Amy's age-thin skin, relieved her hands of the washcloth and bottle of Listerine, placing them on the nightstand next to the bed. She reached in the pocket of her nurse's uniform and pulled out a worn hundred-dollar bill, which she knew was worthless compared to the one hundred years of life Miss Amy had endured.

Miss Amy began to fret as she fought to free her feather-light body from beneath the heavy quilt. Holly immediately shoved the hundred-dollar bill back into her pocket and slid her hand under the back of Miss Amy's head and neck and gently eased her back on the pillow.

"You not comfortable, Miss Amy?"

"I need to get up," Miss Amy replied. "It's Sunday."

"No, ma'am, today is Monday." Holly smiled. "And it's your birthday, too."

Miss Amy kept right on chatting, ignoring Holly. "The sun mighty bright, and it's a good day to take a drive." Miss Amy dangled her legs out of the bed, her shins and calves covered with bruises that shone through her bronze skin.

"No, ma'am, Miss Amy." Holly smiled as she gently tucked Miss Amy's legs back beneath the cover. "You haven't driven a car in more than twenty years."

Miss Amy grabbed the end of the quilt and covered her mouth, trying to hide the smirk on her face. "That's what you think. I drove last Sunday to the Lord's house."

"If you say so, Miss Amy," Holly giggled, paying her no mind. "You hungry, ma'am?"

Miss Amy didn't utter a word as Holly began her daily care regime for the woman who hired her when she had come to America from Germany.

She'd never forget responding to the ad in the paper for house-keeper/home-care person wanted by Mr. Butch Campbell, owner of Campbell's Commercial Construction. She'd walked up to the huge double doors with only five dollars left in her pocket and rang the bell. A petite, well-dressed black woman had greeted her at the door. Holly's first impression was that the woman must be Mrs. Campbell's personal assistant. But she soon found out that the black woman was the lady of the house, and by the grace in Miss Amy's soft voice and her ample kindness, Holly knew right then that she would love to have an opportunity to work in the Campbell home.

Holly took the white towel off her shoulder, wiped the drool from Miss Amy's mouth, and removed the soiled cloth nestled under Miss Amy's neck from the night before, then washed the inside of Miss Amy's toothless mouth with Listerine.

After wiping Miss Amy's face with the wet cloth, Holly spoke, "Now, there, Miss Amy, I'll go get your breakfast. I'll make you a bowl of grits and—"

"Sausage and a piece of buttered toast."

Miss Amy's mind had been wandering lately. She'd recently begun mistaking Holly for her deceased daddy.

"Daddy, you know I can drive. I always drive to the Lord's house. I'll make it to the Lord's house if I don't make it anywhere else," Miss Amy said, with a sparkle in her eyes.

When Miss Amy spoke of the Lord, her voice would become deep and strong. The atmosphere would be filled with peace and nothing but peace.

Holly let her speak. She no longer corrected Miss Amy when she started talking about her family or the Lord. She just let her be, and after a while Miss Amy would return to the present and recall her proper surroundings.

Miss Amy called out, "Holly!"

"I'm right here, Miss Amy." Holly leaned over the bed and made eye contact with her.

"I see you, Holly," Miss Amy grinned. "Holly, where's my breakfast?"

"I am going to get it right now, ma'am." Holly laughed as she left the room to tend to Miss Amy's breakfast.

Alone in the room, Miss Amy chuckled, then mumbled, "Time for my Sunday drive. The Lord's house is waiting on me."

She took her childlike hands and pushed the covers off her. She took a deep, long breath and lifted her fragile body into a sitting position, pulling her flannel knee-length gown down to cover her wrinkled thighs. She slid one leg at a time off the bed and eyed her walker, which sat about a foot away from the bed. Miss Amy stood with her back slightly hunched, and held on to the nightstand as she slid her foot into one slipper, leaving the other slipper on the floor near her bedside. Her bare foot was cooled from the hardwood floor.

"Ain't nothing like a Sunday drive. The Lord's house is waiting on me," Miss Amy said in a melodious tune as her trembling lips formed a smile.

Miss Amy's hands fumbled on the nightstand as she picked up her glasses. She placed them crookedly upon her face and held on to the nightstand as long as she could, until she had no choice but to take a few toddling steps to grab onto the walker. She took another deep, long breath and inched her walker along step by step toward the bedroom closet.

Miss Amy admired the suits, dresses, and all the rows of clothes she hadn't worn for several years. Her shoes were lined up against one side of the wall like marching soldiers. She smiled at the sight of a favorite floral dress as she searched the closet for her pink sweater, thinking, *Oh, Butch, my honey, loves to take me for strolls in the garden in that floral dress. Butch says I look like a ray of flowers in that dress. I wonder if he be a-calling to come take me for a stroll in the garden on Saturday.*

Thinking of her deceased husband of more than forty years, she spotted the pink sweater that she had crocheted with her own hands during her younger years. She wiggled the sweater until it fell off the coat hanger. One arm at a time, she eased it on, putting it on backwards. She reached in the pocket of the sweater to fumble for keys, but only pulled out a white sheer scarf, which she placed on her head and tied loosely under her chin. On the dresser she picked up a tube of red lipstick. She smoothed the lipstick on her upper lip only. She rubbed the lower lip with her upper one, not realizing that she had let go of the tube, and the contents had clattered to the floor.

Where are my keys? I can't get to the Lord's house without any keys.

She again took one step at a time with her walker and browsed on the other side of the crowded dresser filled with pictures and perfume bottles to search for the car keys. She had no luck finding them there. She placed both hands on the drawer knobs and opened the top drawer just enough to scramble things around.

Holly was busy in the kitchen, preparing breakfast. Miss Amy could hear her singing in German at the top of her lungs. She'd never understood Holly's German language, but most of the time she could recognize the tune if it was a spiritual hymn. Today, Holly was serenading her with an unfamiliar tune.

"What in the devil is Holly singing today? That's not a Lord's tune.

I know a Lord's tune." Miss Amy became agitated. "I tell that German lady don't sing nothing in this house 'less it's a Lord's tune. The Campbells sing praise to the Lord."

Miss Amy finally put her hands on a cutoff tan mesh stocking and noticed the silver car key in it.

"Thank you, Lord." Miss Amy smiled, taking the key out, leaving a run in the stocking. "Now I better hurry. I don't won't to be the last one walking in the Lord's house." She began to mumble a tune. "Ain't nothing like a Sunday drive. The Lord's house is waiting on me."

Miss Amy placed the key in her sweater pocket and made her way out the bedroom with the help of her walker. She headed down the dark hallway in the opposite direction of the kitchen, stopping in front of a portrait on the wall, of her beloved daughter, Gwendolyn.

"Hey, Gwen, Mama going for a Sunday drive. Don't you want to come along?" Miss Amy smiled. She paused for a few seconds as if to wait for an answer from her daughter.

"Okay, Gwen, you stay home. Mama be back soon."

Miss Amy moved on, finally making it to the garage, wheezing and coughing every step of the way.

She cried out, "Lord, please don't fail me now. If I just get to the car I will make that Sunday drive to Your house."

Miss Amy closed her eyes and rested for a quick second, praying for strength. She opened her eyes and reached out to open the garage door. There in front of her was the sight of the shining, radiant blue 1960 Chevrolet.

Her voice lifted with joy and praise. "Hallelujah!"

She held on to the door, leaving her walker behind. Her knees buckled slightly as she stepped gingerly down off the two concrete steps. She hugged the wall and the car's fender for support.

Miss Amy eased her way to the driver's door and reached in her pocket for the key. She struggled for a second or two with the lock, until it gave. It took all her strength to swing open the heavy door, but she was determined. She slid into the car, leaving the door ajar, and started the engine. The car made a choking sound as if it were gasping for breath, then cut off. Miss Amy pressed her foot on the gas pedal and turned the key in the ignition again. This time the car fired right up. She twisted the rearview mirror to take a final look at herself.

Back in the house, Holly entered the bedroom carrying a tray of grits, sausage, buttered toast, and a small glass of fresh-squeezed orange juice.

"Here's your breakfast, Miss Amy."

Holly looked over at the empty bed. Miss Amy was nowhere in sight. She dropped the tray and screamed, "Miss Amy, Miss Amy! Where are you, Miss Amy?"

Recalling Miss Amy's mention of a Sunday drive, Holly ran down the hall toward the garage and saw the silver-tone walker. She just knew Miss Amy was somewhere lying on the cold concrete floor in the garage, but as she got closer she could heard the engine sputtering on the old Chevrolet. She looked in the garage, and to her amazement, she saw Miss Amy sitting in the driver's seat with her hands on the steering wheel, with the car door open. Holly let out a sigh of relief.

"Miss Amy, you know better than to get out of the bed. You about to send me back to Germany in a box."

Holly carried the walker over to the driver's side of the car to help Miss Amy out.

"Come on, Miss Amy, let's take you back to bed. Your breakfast is getting cold."

Holly went to reach for Miss Amy but saw the peaceful look on her face.

"Oh, Miss Amy!" Holly cried out.

Miss Amy had a giant smile on her face as she sat in the driver's seat. Her fragile hands rested on the steering wheel, and she stared straight ahead. The frosted strands of her hair peeped through the white sheer scarf.

Holly hurried to the passenger side of the car. She opened the door and slid in next to her employer and friend. Holly stared out the windshield at the closed garage door. Then she reached over to the driver's side sun visor and hit a button, and the door slowly rose and the warm air circulated in the garage. The sunlight penetrated the gloomy darkness.

Untying the scarf from around Miss Amy's hair, Holly placed it on her own head. She removed the pink sweater from Miss Amy's body and pushed her own arms through its sleeves, enjoying the fading scent of Estée Lauder left in the sweater.

"Now, Miss Amy, let's enjoy that Sunday drive together."

Miss Amy had no doubt taken her last breath and her last earthly Sunday drive, but she'd made it to the Lord's house on time. Holly closed her eyes and imagined the ride. She clutched the sweater tightly across her chest, speaking aloud to Miss Amy with tears flowing down her chin.

"Ma'am, I want to thank you for all you done for me. You gave me a job and a home when I came to America. What will I do without you, Miss Amy? You a good black woman with a heart of gold." Holly grinned. "But you stubborn, ma'am, determined to do what you want to do. You taught me a valuable lesson today, Miss Amy."

Holly's grin left her face and turned into tears. She brushed the water from her cheeks, rested her head on the car seat, and continued to speak as if Miss Amy could hear her.

"You were determined to take your Sunday drive, no matter what the cost. You taught me a valuable thing; that as long as the Lord gives me life and strength, it's not over until it's over."

Holly said no more. She reached over and turned off the ignition. She took the car key out and placed it on Miss Amy's lap and placed her fingers over Miss Amy's eyes, shutting them.

Holly got out of the car and went back over to the driver's seat. She picked up the walker and threw it across the entrance of the garage. She lifted Miss Amy's petite body and carried her back into the house, down the long hallway, pausing before the photo of Miss Amy's daughter.

"Gwen, take good care of your mother in heaven."

Holly moved on and placed Miss Amy's body in bed beneath the quilt, then dialed the funeral home that would put the last member of the prominent Campbell family to rest.

CONTRIBUTORS

Amanda Ngozi Adichie was born in Nigeria and lives in Connecticut. Her stories have appeared in *In Posse Review*, the *Allegheny Review of Undergraduate Literature*, *Conspire*, and *Zoetrope All-Story Extra*. She has published a play in her homeland about the Nigerian civil war, *For Love of Biafra*.

Vicki L. Andrews is the author of *Midnight Peril* and *Lighter Shade of Brown*, and was also nominated for Best Contemporary Romance Novel at the African-American On-Line Writers Guild in Atlanta. Ms. Andrews has been featured in the *Voice and Viewpoint*, the *San Diego Monitor*, and *San Diego Reader*.

Elizabeth Atkins is the author of the best-selling novels *White Chocolate* and *Dark Secret*. She has written for *The New York Times*, *Essence*, *Ms.*, *BET.com*, *Black Issues Book Review*, *HOUR Detroit*, *The San Diego Tribune*, and contributed to a national tribute program for Rosa Parks. Her most recent novel is *Twilight*, an epic love story with acting legend Billy Dee Williams.

Nicole Bailey-Williams is the author of *A Little Piece of Sky* and has recently been commissioned by the secretary of the Pennsylvania Department of Labor and Industry to write a biography of William P. Young, Pennsylvania's first African-American secretary of Labor and Industry.

Venise Berry is an associate professor of journalism and mass communication at the University of Iowa, in Iowa City. She is the author of two *Essence* magazine and *Blackboard* best-selling novels, *So Good, An African American Love Story*, and *All of Me, A Voluptuous Tale*. Her third novel, *Colored Sugar Water* was released in January 2002.

Parry "EbonySatin" Brown is the author of the novel, *The Shirt Off His Back*, which launched the new Strivers Row imprint for Random House, as well as a self-help book, *Sexy Doesn't Have a Dress Size*. Her third release, *Sittin' on the Front Pew*, was published in 2002.

Zaron W. Burnett, Jr., is the Atlanta-based author of *The Carthaginian Honor Society*. His work appeared regularly in *Catalyst* magazine for nine years. The recipient of grants and commissions from the Rockefeller Foundation, Just Us Theater Company, and The Fulton County Arts Council, Burnett is married to author Pearl Cleage.

Pearl Cleage is an Atlanta-based playwright, essayist, and novelist whose works include *What Looks Like Crazy on an Ordinary Day*, an Oprah Book Club selection and *New York Times* best-seller, *I Wish I Had a Red Dress, Deals with the Devil, Other Reasons to Riot*, and *Mad at Miles: A Blackwoman's Guide to Truth*. She is a contributing writer to *Essence* magazine and the former artistic director of Just Us Theater Company.

Evelyn Coleman, an Atlanta-based author, has written several books for adults and young readers including *Mystery of the Dark Tower*, *What a Woman's Gotta Do, White Socks Only, To Be a Drum, The Riches of Oseola McCarty, The Glass Bottle Tree*, and *The Foot Warmer and the Crow*.

Tracy Scott DesVignes is a native of Brooklyn, New York. A technical writer, she is currently completing her first murder mystery novel and has been published in *The Oklahoma Eagle*.

Frank E. Dobson, Jr. is a 1994 winner of the Zora Neale Hurston/ Bessie Head Fiction Writers Award and the author of the novel, *The Race Is Not Given*. The recipient of an artist's fellowship from Montgomery County, Ohio, Dobson is associate professor of English at Wright State and the director of its Bolinga Black Cultural Resources Center. He is currently at work on his second novel, *Barbershop Testimonies and Dreams*.

Crystal Irene Drake works for CNN News Group in Atlanta as publicist, CNN Public Relations. The winner of the Hurston/Wright Award and the Andrew Purdy Award, she is a graduate of Spelman College and holds an M.A. in English literature and creative writing.

Phill Duck is the author of *Sugar Ain't Sweet,* a novel about the pathways of marital love. He currently is at work on his next novel, *The Goodness.*

Jamellah Ellis is the author of the previously self-published title *That Faith, That Trust, That Love,* which will be re-released by Strivers Row in 2003. A graduate of Spelman College and Northwestern University School of Law, Ellis is working on her second novel.

Tonya Marie Evans is the self-published author of *Seasons of Her* and *SHINE!* Her forthcoming releases include *Desire True* (poetry) and *The Blues* (fiction). A practicing attorney, she has been published in the *Caribbean Writer, Health Quest Magazine,* and *AIM.* She and her mother, Susan Borden Evans are the founders of Find Your Own Shine, Inc.

Robert Fleming's writings have appeared in *UpSouth, Brotherman, Sacred Fire, Dark Matter, Brown Sugar, Black Issues Book Review, Quarterly Black Review of Books, Omni, U.S. News & World Report* and *The New York Times.* His recent releases are *The Wisdom of The Elders* and *The African American Writer's Handbook.* Fleming is the editor of *After Hours: A Collection of Erotic Writing by Black Men.*

Nancey Flowers is the self-published author of *A Fool's Paradise.* A resident and native of Brooklyn, New York, where she hosts the new National XM Radio program "Black Scribes" and works as a freelance editor, Nancey is also the editor and publisher of the erotic collection, *Twilight Moods.*

Cherryl Floyd-Miller is a Cave Canem alumna fellow and Indiana Arts Commission associate fellow for literature (1994–95). She has appeared on *The Oprah Winfrey Show* with Dr. Maya Angelou and is an active member of ASCAP. Floyd-Miller lives in Atlanta, where she is a directing intern with Actor's Express Theatre Company and is writing a novel entitled *Color Never Returns.*

Gwynne Forster is an award-winning, best-selling author of twelve romance novels and five novellas. Her first mainstream novel, *When Twilight Comes,* was released in February 2002.

Sharon Ewell Foster is the author of the Christy Award-winning *Passing by Samaria.* Her second novel, *Ain't No River,* won the Black

Writers Alliance Award for best work of Christian fiction in 2001. Both books have been the subject of NAACP national essay scholarship contests. Foster's latest release is *Riding Through Shadows*.

Tierra French is a fifteen-year-old high school student in Clarksville, Tennessee, who aspires to become a published novelist.

Michael P. Fuller is a graduate of Southern Illinois University and completed his postgraduate work at Keller Graduate School of Business Management. An account executive for a security services company, Fuller is an avid writer.

Michael A. Gonzales is the co-author of *Bring the Noise: A Guide to Rap Music and Hip-Hop Culture*. His column "Black Metropolis" appeared in *New York Press*. Gonzales has published fiction in *Brown Sugar, Brown Sugar 2: One Night Stands, Trace, Untold* and *Black-Film.com*. His collection *Babies & Fools* will be published in 2003. He currently resides in Brooklyn and has dedicated this story to Gil.

Pat G'Orge-Walker is the recipient of the Gold Pen 2000 Innovative Writer Award who writes stories for the *Ain't Nobody Else Right But Us—All Others Goin' To Hell* collection. The author of *Sister Betty! God's Calling You, Again,* Walker is also writing a political thriller and Christian-based mystery novel.

Tracy Grant is the self-published author of *Hellified,* and has worked as a freelance writer for *Generation Next, YSB,* and *Today's Black Woman.* The Brooklyn, New York, native continues to write for *Today's Black Woman, Black Men, Mosaic, Black Issues Book Review* and *Africana.com.* Grant's next novel, the political thriller *Chocolate Thai,* is coming soon.

Kim Green is the owner of Veritas Communications, a full-service marketing and communications firm based in Tucson, Arizona. The New York native authored and edited *On a Mission* and co-authored *The Truth of the Matter,* a guidebook for aspiring artists. Green's most recent project, *When Butterflies Kiss,* was released in September of 2001.

Scott D. Haskins, the author of the Blackboard bestselling novel *Sasha's Way,* lives in the Baltimore area where he is working on his next novel.

Angela Henry is the author of *The Pleasure of His Company: A Kendra Clayton Mystery*, and received an Honorable Mention in *Ebony* magazine's 10th Annual Gertrude Johnson William's Writing Contest. She is also the founder of the MystNoir Website, which promotes African American mystery writers.

Donna Hill is the author of fifteen published novels and six novellas. Three of her novels have been adapted for television. She has been featured in *Essence*, the *New York Daily News*, *USA Today*, *Today's Black Woman*, *Black Enterprise*, and others. Hill's mainstream debut, *If I Could*, was followed by her latest release, *Rhythms*.

Arethia Hornsby is an aspiring novelist with several plays to her credit.

Travis Hunter is a songwriter, motivational speaker, and the author of the novels *The Hearts of Men* and *Married but Still Looking*. Hunter is the founder of the Hearts of Men Foundation, through which he mentors underprivileged children.

Edwardo Jackson is a graduate of Morehouse College and the author of the novels *Ever After* and *Neva Hafta*. Edwardo resides in Los Angeles and is an actor, screenwriter, novelist, and co-president of JCM Enterprise, LLC.

Margaret Johnson-Hodge is the author of *Essence* and Blackboard Bestsellers *Warm Hands, Butterscotch Blues*, and *Some Sunday*. Her latest work, *True Lies*, was released in 2002.

Tayari Jones is the author of the acclaimed novel *Leaving Atlanta*. A graduate of Spelman College, she is the winner of the Hurston/Wright Award, Arizona Commission on the Arts Fellowship, and LEF Foundation Prize.

Tanya Marie Lewis is the author of the self-published novel, *Bittersweet Chocolates*. She has written for *Prolific Writers Network, Gulf Coast Woman's Magazine, Litline Newsletter*, and *Good News Magazine*.

Brandon Massey is the author of *Thunderland* and the winner of the 2000 Gold Pen Award for Best Thriller from the Black Writers

Alliance. His work has appeared in such publications as *Tomorrow's Speculative Fiction, Frightnet On-line Magazine*, the *Atlanta Tribune*, and *Elan Magazine*. Brandon has been featured in *Black Issues Book Review, Time Digital Magazine*, and *Black Enterprise*.

Timmothy B. McCann teaches the Art of Commercial Fiction at Santa Fe Community College in Gainesville, Florida. Best known for three highly acclaimed novels, *Until . . .*, *Always*, and *Forever*, McCann's latest Kensington release is entitled *Emotions*.

Trevy McDonald is the self-published author of *Time Will Tell*, co-editor of *Nature of a Sistuh: Black Women's Lived Experiences in Contemporary Culture* and *Building Diverse Communities: Applications of Communication Research*, and a contributor to *Sisterfriend Soul Journeys: The Spirit and Expression of African American Women on Tour*. A college professor and radio personality with a Ph.D. in Mass Communication Research, she is the President of Reyomi Enterprises, Inc., a publishing and production company.

David McGoy is a freelance writer and editor from Staten Island, NY, who holds editorships at two community newspapers: *Black Reign News* and *Spring Creek Sun*. He is also the editor and webmaster of NEB Publishing.com, a literary website, and writes book reviews for various websites, including *Mosaic* literary magazine and *The Book Reporter*.

Gregory K. Morris, a chemical engineer who lives in Charlotte, North Carolina, is the author of *Zon*.

Marilynn Ngozi Griffith is the assistant editor for *The Black Women's Breastfeeding Alliance Newsletter* and has been published in *Honey for the Homeschooler's Heart, Crumbs in the Keyboard: Women Juggling Life and Writing, Christian Families Online*, and more. She also moderates the Christian writers group for the Black Writers Alliance.

Kambon Obayani is the author of the novel *Colours*. A professor, musicologist, and radio talk show host, Obayani teaches at Pierce College and California State University Northridge. He has written four novels, had fifteen plays produced, and has taught and traveled in Africa, South America, the Middle East, and Asia. His work has been translated into ten different languages.

Nancy Padron is a Los Angeles–based Afro-Cuban fiction writer, poet, and visual artist whose work has appeared in *Drumming Between Us: Black Love & Erotic Poetry, Familiar Breath: What the Body Remembers*, and *Flash-Bopp Journal,* "Nedra and the Ghost." Nancy is currently completing her first novel.

Roy L. Pickering, Jr. is a freelance writer who has recently completed his debut novel, *Patches of Grey*, and is working on his second novel. Pickering writes a monthly column entitled *Sports Issues* for Suite101.com.

Kharel Price is a fourteen-year old gentleman and scholar who aspires to earn a full academic scholarship to a prestigious university where he plans to study law. An honor student at Pemberton High School in New Jersey, Kharel is the youngest son of author Tracy Price-Thompson.

Tracy Price-Thompson is a highly decorated Desert Storm veteran and the author of the national best-seller, *Black Coffee.* A Brooklyn, New York, native, Hurston/Wright award winner, and Ralph Bunche Graduate Fellow, Price-Thompson's second novel, *Chocolate Sangria*, was released in February 2003.

Deirdre Savoy is a New York native and the author of the novels *Always, Once and Again*, and *Midnight Magic*. Deirdre lectures on such topics as marketing your masterpiece and getting your writing career started.

Kim Stanley is a journalist-turned-novelist who holds a graduate degree in African American studies.

TaRessa Stovall is the co-author of *A LOVE SUPREME: Real-Life Stories of Black Love, Catching Good Health: An Introduction to Homeopathic Medicine*, and *The Buffalo Soldiers.* TaRessa has written articles for *USA Weekend, BET.com, Emerge*, and *HealthQuest* magazines and is a contributing author for the *New York Public Library African-American Desk Reference* and *Staying Strong: Reclaiming the Wisdom of African-American Healing.* Stovall was featured in *Black Silk* and is currently writing a novel.

ReShonda Tate Billingsley is a reporter for an NBC affiliate in Oklahoma City, and an adjunct professor at Langston University. Her first novel, *My Brother's Keeper*, was the winner of the Greater Dallas Writing Association Nova Lee Nation award.

Mel Taylor is the author of *The Mitt Man*, a novel praised by Nikki Giovanni as "frightening, yet comforting." He lives in Los Angeles, where he is at work on his second novel.

Maxine E. Thompson is the author of *The Ebony Tree, No Pockets in a Shroud, A Place Called Home, and How to Promote, Market and Sell Your Book Via eBook Publishing.* She is a columnist for two online publications, Black Women in Publishing, and The Black Market. She has been featured in *LA Times, Our Times, Black Issues Book Review, Dialogue Magazine, Inland Valley News*, and *Black Enterprise*.

Denise Turney is the self-published author of the novels *Portia* and *Love Has Many Faces*. Her works have appeared in magazines and newspapers including *Today's Black Woman, Essence, Sisters in Style, KaNupepa, The Trenton Times, The Bucks County Courier Times, The Pittsburgh Quarterly, Obsidian II*, and *Your Church* magazine.

The Urban Griot (Omar Tyree) is the non-compromising alter-ego of *New York Times* best-selling author, journalist, lecturer, and poet Omar Tyree, who won the 2001 NAACP Image Award for Outstanding Literary Work in Fiction. His *Urban Griot* series of hard-core male novels to combat what he calls the "feminization" of African American fiction, premiered in February 2003 with the title, *One Crazy-ass Night.*

Franklin White is the author of three best-selling works. *Fed Up with the Fanny, Cup of Love*, and the Gold Pen Nominated collection of stories *Til Death Do Us Part*. His next book, *No Matter What*, is the story of Bridgett Stewart, who has appeared on the Rosie O'Donnell show. Franklin is the Features Editor at *UPSCALE* magazine.

Christine Young-Robinson is the author of *Isra the Butterfly Gets Caught for Show and Tell*, a children's book that received "Honorable Mention" in the Carrie McCray Award Contest, bestowed by the South Carolina Workshop, 2000 Conference. Christine is currently working on a young adult book entitled, *Hip-Hop & Punk Rock* while putting the finishing touches on her novel, *Mama, Why?*